Praxis's atmosphere had become superheated and unbreathable. From the high ground above the caverns, Rick glanced back at the wrinkled terrain. Volcanic light blasted through a dense shroud that stretched from the hills all the way to the base of a distant escarpment. And out of this storm two lone Veritechs flew, returning from a final reconnaissance patrol. Rick's worst fears were soon confirmed: not a safe region on the planet.

Beneath a swirling, agitated pall of cloud cover, Praxis was fractured beyond recognition. Great, furious rivers of molten stuff coursed across its surface, burying forests and villages in liquid fire. Praxis bellowed and roared like a tortured animal, rattling the GMU with its clamorous cries; the planet seemed to be expanding, bursting its geological seams, while Rick watched.

Published by Ballantine Books:

THE ROBOTECH™ SERIES:

THE SENTINELS™ SERIES:

Also by Jack McKinney
Published by Ballantine Books:

KADUNA MEMORIES

THE SENTINELS:

THE DEVIL'S HAND # 1
DARK POWERS #2
DEATH DANCE #3

Jack McKinney

A Del Rey® Book
BALLANTINE BOOKS • NEW YORK

A Del Rey® Book
Published by Ballantine Books

Library of Congress Catalog Card Number: 95-92017

ISBN 0-345-38901-8

Manufactured in the United States of America

First Edition: August 1995

10 9 8 7 6 5 4 3 2 1

ROBOTECH CHRONOLOGY

1999	Alien spacecraft known as SDF-1 crashlands on Earth through an opening in hyperspace, effectively ending almost a decade of Global Civil War.
	In another part of the Galaxy, Zor is killed during a Flower of Life seeding attempt.
2002	Destruction of Mars Base Sara.
2009	On the SDF-1's launch day, the Zentraedi (after a ten-year search for the fortress) appear and lay waste to Macross Island. The SDF-1 makes an accidental jump to Pluto.
2009-11	The SDF-1 battles its way back to Earth.
2011-12	The SDF-1 spends almost half a year on Earth, is ordered to leave, and defeats Dolza's armada, which has laid waste to much of the planet.
2012-14	A two-year period of reconstruction beings.
2012	The Robotech Masters lose confidence in the ability of their giant warriors to recapture the SDF-1, and begin a mass pilgrimage through interstellar space to Earth.
2013	Dana Sterling is born.
2014	Destruction of the SDFs 1 and 2 and Khyron's battlecruiser.
2014-20	The SDF-3 is built and launched. Rick Hunter turns 29 in 2020; Dana turns 7.

Subsequent events covering the Tiresian campaign are recounted in the Sentinels series. A complete Robochronology will appear in the fifth and final volume.

THE DEVIL'S HAND

FOR NICHOLAS, JEREMY AND MATTHEW
WHOSE ENTHUSIASM HAS BEEN A CONTINUING
SOURCE OF INSPIRATION.

CHAPTER
ONE

I leave it up to the historians and the moralists to judge whether our decision (the Expeditionary mission) is right or wrong. I know only that it is prudent and necessary—necessary for our very survival both as a planet and as a life-form. If the Protoculture has taught me anything, it is that one must simply act! When all is said and done the inevitabilities and reshapings will have their way, but to remain either complacent or inert in the face of those fatalities is to invite catastrophe of a higher order than any of us dare imagine.

From the personal journal of Dr. Emil Lang

IN THE MIDDLE OF THE NIGHT ON AN ALIEN WORLD, AN ARMY OF insentient warriors dropped from the sky. Tirol, as this small moon was known, represented a prize of sorts—the end of a long campaign that had taken the invaders through a dozen local star systems and across the varied faces of twice that number of worlds—the remote realms of the once great empire of the Robotech Masters, forged and secured by their giant soldier clones, the Zentraedi. But Tirol itself was all but deserted, abandoned almost a generation earlier by those same Masters. So in effect this conquest was something of a disappointment for the horde who had raised savagery to new heights, something of a nonevent.

But just as a rock tossed into a pond will make its presence known to distant shores, the Invid's arrival on Tirol would send powerful waves through the continuum; and nowhere would the effects of their invasion be more greatly felt than on the world already inundated by previous tides from this same quarter—a blue-white gem of a planet that had seen better days, but was struggling still to regain control of its own fragile destiny . . .

Earth had captured its second satellite in the year 2013, when a joint Terran and XT force had wrested it from the control of the

Zentraedi commander, Reno, faithful to the Imperative even after Dolza's fiery demise. The factory satellite was an enormous monstrosity, well in keeping with the grotesque design of the Zentraedi fleet, that had been folded instantaneously through space-time by Protoculture-fueled Reflex drives. It was radish-shaped and rose-colored in starlight, with fissures and convolutions suggestive of cerebral matter. Attached along its median section by rigid stalklike transport tubes were half a dozen secondary sacs and appendages, smaller by far, but equally vegetal in aspect, veined and incomprehensible.

There were some 15,000 Humans and Zentraedi living onboard, a sizable portion of Earth's post-apocalyptic population. The majority of these men and women had labored for six years inside the factory's weightless belly to construct a starship, a dimensional fortress soon to be Tirol-bound—there to confront the Robotech Masters, and with luck curtail any threat of continued warfare.

Among those onboard were Vice Admiral Rick Hunter and his close friend and trusted commander, Max Sterling. From a viewport in the admiral's quarters, the two men were watching null-gee construction crews put the finishing touches on the massive ship's deliberately misleading superstructure.

"I just don't know whether we're ready for this," Rick was saying. He had turned from the viewport and was three strides toward the center of the room. "There are so many *variables*, so many things that could go wrong now."

Max followed him, a grin beneath a sympathetic look he had adopted. "Come on, what could go wrong?"

Rick whirled on him. "Maybe I'm just not *ready*, Max!"

Rick's voice cracked on the word and Max couldn't suppress a short laugh. "Ready? It's been six years, Rick. How much more ready can you expect to be?"

"Guess I'm not as good up against the unknowns anymore." Rick shrugged, lowering his gaze. "I mean, we've got something good going already. So why jeopardize it, why tamper with it?"

Max took his friend by the shoulders and gave him an affectionate shake. "Look, you and Lisa love each other, so quit worrying. Everything's going to turn out fine. Besides, everybody's excited about the wedding. And what are you going to do, walk out on ten thousand guests?"

Rick felt the wisdom of it sink in, and smiled, self-mockingly.

They had both aged well, the rigors of life on- and off-world notwithstanding; both had turned twenty-nine in March and had at least a few good years left in them. Rick stood taller and straighter now than he had during the war, and that combined with some added weight gave him a stronger, more capable look. This was enhanced by the cut of the Expeditionary Force's high-collared uniform and torso harness, a crisscross, tailed, and flare-shouldered affair of black leather worn over tight-fitting trousers. He still wore his black hair stylishly long, though—a fashion the Veritech flyboys of the Robotech Defense Force had been largely responsible for. Max, too, had left behind the innocent look that had been something of a trademark. While Rick, Dr. Lang, and Lisa Hayes had devoted themselves to the SDF-3 project, Max had been busy distinguishing himself in the Southlands, especially during the Malcontent Uprisings of 2015–18. He still favored the blue hair tint he had affected during the war, likewise oversize aviator glasses to contacts or corrective microsurgery. Less than perfect vision had never handicapped his flying skills, in any case.

Rick was glancing back at the SDF-3 now. "And everybody gets to ride in the limo." He smirked.

Fabricated from the hull and power drives of Breetai's dreadnought and the salvaged remains from the SDFs 1 and 2, the ship was itself a wedding of sorts. Pursuant to Lang and Exedore's requests, it was more Zentraedi than Terran in design: a nontransformable deepspace leviathan, bristling with antennae and blistered across its crimson surface with scanner ports and laser-array gun turrets.

"We'll make sure you two get the backseat," Max said. "For at least a couple of hours, anyway."

Rick laughed from across the room; Max joined him at the external viewport, Earth's incomparable beauty filling the view. Sunlight glinted off the alloyed hulls and fins of dozens of in-transit shuttles. Rick was staring down at the planet wistfully.

"When's Lisa due back?" Max asked him.

"Tomorrow. But I'm thinking of shuttling down to meet her."

Max made an approving sound. "I'll ride with you."

"When haven't you," Rick said, after a moment.

With the destruction of the SDFs 1 and 2 on that fateful winter night in 2014, Macross's sister city, Monument, had risen to the fore as Earth's unofficial capital. The irradiated remains of Macross had been bulldozed flat and pushed into what hadn't been boiled away from Lake Gloval. Three enormous manmade buttes marked the resting place of the superdimensional fortresses, along with that of the Zentraedi cruiser that had destroyed them. But those mounds had not been completed before volunteer teams of valiant Robotechnicians had braved slow death to salvage what they could from the devastation.

Thrice-born Macross, however, was not resurrected, as much by choice as anything else; but the name lived on in a kind of mythic way, and Monument City, to the southwest over a rugged ridge, was doing its best to carry the tradition forward. This would change after the SDF-3 departed, but in 2020 things were much as they were in the Macross of 2014. That is not to say that there weren't sinister currents in the air for one and all to perceive; but the Expeditionary mission to Tirol was foremost on the minds of those who could have prevented the subsequent slide.

Monument was the seat of the United Earth Government, but the most important building in that burgeoning city was the headquarters of the newly-formed Army of the Southern Cross, a politico-military party that had its origins in the Southlands during the Malcontent Uprisings, and had all but superseded the authority formerly enjoyed by RDF, most of which was slated for the Expeditionary mission. The headquarters was a soaring megacomplex whose central tower cluster had been built to suggest the white gonfalons, or ensigns, of a holy crusade hanging from high crosspieces. The high-tech needles were crowned with crenels and merlons, like some medieval battlement, announcing to all the world the ideals and *esprit* of the Army of the Southern Cross.

Just now the building was host to a final press conference held jointly by members of the Expeditionary Mission Plenipotentiary Council, the RDF, and the Southern Cross. Dr. Emil Lang and the Zentraedi Ambassador, Exedore, spoke on behalf of the twelve-person council, while the military factions were represented respectively by Brigadier General Gunther Reinhardt and Field Marshal Anatole Leonard. The press was there in force, crowding the hall, jostling one another for position, snapping off shot after stroboscopic shot, and grilling the four-member panel with an overwhelming array of questions from special-interest groups and insulated power bases as distant as Cavern City and Brasilia in the Southlands.

Lang was doing his best to respond to one of these; for the third time, someone in the press corps had returned to the issue of Earth's potential vulnerability in the wake of the SDF-3's departure. As the high priest of Robotechnology, Lang had little interest in such mundane concerns, but he was doing his best to restate the importance of the mission and repeat launch details that had already been covered in the press releases.

"Final selections for the crew are proceeding and we should

have no trouble meeting our launch schedule. If we are to avoid a second Robotech War, we must make peaceful contact with the Robotech Masters and establish a relationship of mutual cooperation. That is the mission of the SDF-3."

Murmurs of discontent spread through the crowd, and several reporters hurled insults of one sort or another. But then, could anyone expect anything in the way of a concrete response from someone like Lang? When the man chose to be profound, there were perhaps only a handful of scientists on Earth who could follow him. The rest of the time he came across as alien as any Zentraedi. Rumors and speculations about Lang went as far back as the early days on Macross Island, when he and Gloval, Fokker, Edwards, and a few others had first reconned the SDF-1, known then as "the Visitor." He had taken a Zentraedi mind-boost, some claimed, a megadose of Protoculture that had somehow integrated his internal circuitry with that of the ship itself. Certainly his marblelike eyes lent credence to the tale. Although he had been more visible, more accessible these past few years, he was still the same ethereal man who had been the driving force behind Robotechnology since the turn of the century.

"I want to take this opportunity to reemphasize that the Robotech Expeditionary Force is intended as a diplomatic mission," Exedore added without being asked. "The SDF-3 will be traveling to the homeworld of the Robotech Masters, the third moon of the planet Fantoma, known as Tirol." The Zentraedi motioned to the huge projection screen behind the speakers' platform, which showed a color schematic of the ringed giant's extensive system.

"The Masters themselves have not engaged in actual combat for nearly six generations. However, it is impossible to predict with certainty how they will react to our mission. For that reason the SDF-3 has been outfitted with a considerable arsenal of Robotech weaponry. In the event that we are met with force, we shall be ready and able to defend ourselves. But I must press the point that the departure of the fortress will not leave the Earth undefended. Commander Leonard and his staff have all the capabilities for defense necessary to repel any invasion force. And as the planet is not presently threatened by any enemy, we feel confident that the Earth is in no jeopard—"

"If I may interrupt for a moment," Leonard said angrily, getting to his feet. He had been biting back his words for half the press conference, but had reached his breaking point when Exedore— the *alien*!—began to imply that the SDF-3 would be facing greater potential danger than abandoned Earth. Reporters throughout the hall—certainly those who had been planted there by the Southern Cross command to steer the conference toward this very confrontation—took advantage of the moment to get shots of the bearish, shaved-skulled field marshal confronting and towering over the XT ambassador. Leonard's hatred of the Zentraedi was no secret among the general staff. He had never met Exedore full-size, as it were, but perhaps detested him even more in his Micronized state, especially since Terran cosmologists had gone to work on him, styling his hair with a widow's peak, and concealing the clone's dwarfish anatomy beneath specially-tailored uniforms. Leonard often wished that Exedore had been among the Zentraedi Malcontents he had hunted down in the Southlands. . . .

"I'm not as optimistic as the *ambassador* about the lack of an enemy threat," Leonard continued, his face red with rage. "Mark my words, the departure of the SDF-3 and its weapons systems will leave the Earth hopelessly vulnerable to attack! Even that factory satellite's going to be nothing but a useless shell when the Expeditionary Force leaves. They've stripped it clean—and you've stripped us clean!"

"Gentlemen, please," Lang tried to interject, stretching his arms out between the two of them. Reinhardt, with his bald pate, beard, and fringe of premature gray hair, leaned back in his chair, overshadowed by Leonard's bulk.

"It's all very easy for him to say we'll be safe," the field marshal ranted. "When the attack comes, *he'll* be on the other side of the galaxy!"

"Frankly, I think you're a bit paranoid, Commander," Exedore announced evenly, almost clinically. "What attack do you mean—by whom, from where?"

Leonard's great jowls quivered; his eyes flashed a hatred even Exedore couldn't help but feel. "For all we know, there could be a fleet of your fellow Zentraedi out there just waiting for us to drop our guard!"

"That will be enough, Commander Leonard," Reinhardt said at last. "Alarmist talk is of no use to anyone at this point."

Leonard swallowed the rebuke as flashes strobed without pause. He was aware that his position with the general staff was still somewhat tenuous; and besides, he had made his point.

"Gentlemen, you're cutting our defenses to almost nothing," he concluded, as shouts filled the hall. "Once the SDF leaves orbit I won't be able to defend the Earth against a flock of pigeons."

The press conference was being carried live around the world, and to Luna Base, Space Station Liberty, and the factory satellite.

But where many were finding cause for concern in Leonard's contentions, there was one viewer aboard the satellite who merely laughed it off. He had a drink in hand, his feet crossed on the top of the monitor in his spacious quarters.

Leonard was overplaying the role, Major General T. R. Edwards told himself as he set the drink aside. But his performance would have the desired effect nonetheless.

Edwards knew even then that the Southern Cross would eventually gain the upper hand. If necessary, Professor Lazlo Zand would see to that. And Senator Moran, whom they had spent years grooming for high office, would ascend to the seat reserved for him.

Edwards fingered the ugly raised scars that coursed across the right side of his forehead and face—diagonally, from his hairline to the bridge of his nose, and from there in a reverse angle to the heel of his jawbone. The eye at the apex of this triangular disfiguration was dead, sewn shut to a dark slash. He would not be around to reap the immediate rewards of these complex conspiracies and manipulations, but all that could wait until his return from Tirol. First, there were scores to settle with older adversaries, scores that went back more than twenty years.

Not far from the Southern Cross headquarters in one of Monument City's more upscale shopping districts, Admiral Lisa Hayes was being fitted for her wedding gown. She had chosen one her late father would have approved of; it had a traditional, almost antebellum look, lots of satin, lace, and tulle, with a full, two-petticoat tiered skirt, long sleeves, and a simple round neck. The veil was rather short in contrast, with baby's breath and two silk roses affixed to the headband. Lisa gave an appreciative nod as the two fitters fell back smiling, allowing her center place in the shop's mirrored wall. She ran her fingers under the flip of her shoulder-length auburn hair—still unaccustomed to the cut—and said, "Perfect."

In the front room, Dr. Jean Grant and Captain Miriya Sterling wondered aloud what was taking Lisa so long, not out of concern but anticipation. The day was something of a shopping spree for Jean and Miriya as well; in less than a week they would be on their way to Tirol, and on this trip out the SDF wouldn't be traveling with a full city in its belly. *And who knows what to expect in the way of shops on Tirol,* Max had quipped when the two women left the factory satellite. They had brought the kids along, Dana and Bowie, both nearing eight years old, presently bored and antagonistic.

Bowie had Jean's petiteness and dark honey complexion; his health had never been robust, but that didn't prevent blond and lanky Dana from teasing him whenever she could. He was standing sullen-faced in the shop's doorway when she snuck up behind him to yank his SDF cap down over his face.

"Hey, cut it out!" Bowie yelled. "Why'd you do that, Dana?"

She returned a wide-eyed look of innocence, elaborate concern in her voice. "I didn't do anything. I think your brain must be getting smaller."

"Ahhh, *whose* brain's getting smaller?" Bowie said, working the visored cap up to where it belonged.

"Okay, I admit it, I'm guilty," Dana answered him, sincere all of a sudden. "I guess I can't pull the wool over *your* eyes."

Jean and Miriya had both turned at the sound of Bowie's initial howl, but they had long ago decided on a policy of nonintervention when it came to the kids. Though children were included in the Expeditionary mission, Bowie and Dana would not be among them. In Bowie's case it was a matter of health—a fact that had since steered Jean into research medicine. But Dana was exempt for reasons less clear-cut; as the only child of a Human-Zentraedi union, she had been studied, tested, and evaluated since birth, and was judged too precious a commodity to risk on such an enterprise. This, in any case, was the thinking of Professor Zand, who had headed up the medical teams, and Max and Miriya had reluctantly accepted the logic of it. The decision was unalterable now, no matter what, and it was guaranteed that Bowie and Dana would grow up as near siblings under the care of the Sterlings' close friends, Rolf and Laura Emerson.

Miriya was thinking these things through while she watched the children's bickering escalate, then dissolve into playful banter. "Look at them, Jean," she said the way only a mother can. "Do you think we're doing the right thing?"

Jean gave one of the clothes racks a casual spin. "Of course we are, sweetie. You know that."

The two women showed strained smiles to one another. How often they had talked about the irony of their friendship; how often they had remembered Jean's sister-in-law, Claudia Grant, who died in Khyron's suicide run against the SDF-1. And perhaps the conversation would have taken a turn in this direction even then, had not Lisa chosen just that moment to present herself as bride-to-be.

"Well, what do you think?" she asked them, turning around for their inspection.

Miriya, who had worn her hair emerald green for years, was

too surprised by the gown's conservative cut to say much; but Jean said, "I think you picked a beauty, Admiral. That gown is shipshape from stem to stern."

"Yeah, but how will it travel in hyperspace?" Miriya thought to ask.

"You two . . ." Lisa laughed, while her friends began to finger the gown here and there. None of them were aware that a newcomer had entered the ship until a female voice said, "Excuse me."

Lisa looked up and uttered a surprised gasp. Lynn-Minmei was standing in the doorway. Lisa had been thinking of her not five minutes before, standing in front of the mirror seeing new age lines in her thirty-five-year-old face and comparing herself to the seemingly ageless star of song and screen.

"I—I hope I'm not interrupting, Lisa, but I heard you were in town, and well, I just wanted to congratulate you before the wedding. I mean, it's going to be such a madhouse up there." They had hardly been strangers these past six years, but hadn't seen each other since the wedding date had been officially announced some five months ago. "I'd love to help out any way I can—that is, if you'd allow me to, Lisa."

"Minmei," Lisa said with a note of disbelief. "This is so unexpected. But don't be silly, of course you can help," she added, laughing. "Come here."

They embraced, and held hands as they stepped back to regard one another. Lisa couldn't help but marvel at Minmei's youth and radiance. She really was the one constant in everyone's lives.

"Oh, Lisa, I want so much to let bygones be bygones. That dress is lovely—I always knew you'd make a beautiful bride."

"Ms. Minmei's right, Admiral," enthused the shop owner, who had appeared out of nowhere. It was obvious that the man was thrilled to have a celebrity of Minmei's stature in his boutique; he risked a glance at the street, hoping some passersby had noticed her enter.

"I still think she should get married in her EVA suit," Bowie said from across the room, only to have Dana pull the cap down on his forehead again.

"Children!" Jean scolded as the bickering recommenced.

Minmei asked to see the engagement ring, and Lisa held out her hand.

"I can't tell you what it means to see you again, Minmei," Lisa said softly.

* * *

"That devious little Zentraedi's got the whole Supreme Council eating out of his hand!" Commander Leonard complained to Rolf Emerson after the press conference.

Emerson, soon to inherit two eight-year-olds, was every bit the commander's opposite, in appearance as well as ideology; but the two of them had nevertheless managed to maintain a working relationship. Major Emerson, handsome, clean-cut, and fine-featured, was, strictly speaking, RDF; but he had become something of a liaison officer between the general staffs of the military factions. Well aware of Leonard's xenophobia—and of the infamous "thigh wound" the field marshal had sustained during the Malcontent Uprisings—Emerson was willing to let the racial slur slide, even though he numbered several Zentraedi among his closest and dearest friends.

"It's unbelievable," Leonard was railing, the huge brass buckle of his uniform dazzling even in the dim light of Emerson's headquarters office. "A diplomatic mission . . . If it's a *diplomatic* mission, then why are they arming that ship with every Robotech weapons system we've ever developed?"

"It's called 'gunboat diplomacy,' Commander," Emerson replied, willing to concede the point. Lord Exedore and Breetai claimed that they had no real knowledge of what the Robotech Masters might possess in the way of a war machine now that their race of warrior giants had been all but erased from the galaxy.

"Well, stupidity's what I call it. It jeopardizes the very survival of this planet." Leonard paced in front of Emerson's desk. "Something stinks here, Major, and it's not in the ventilation system."

CHAPTER TWO

> *In the midst of all the ironies and reversals, the struggles, treachery, conquests, and betrayals, the mad scramble for mutated Flowers and irradiated worlds, it was easy to lose sight of the war's central concern—which was not, as many have claimed, the Flowers of Life, but their deified stepchild, Protoculture. Even the Regis seemed to forget for a time; but it could hardly be said that the Regent's Invid, the Masters, or the Expeditionary mission, had anything other than Protoculture as their goal and grail. Protoculture was needed to fuel their mecha, to drive their war machines to greater and greater heights. And it was all but disappeared from the galaxy. What a trick it played on all of us!*
>
> Selig Kahler, *The Tirolian Campaign*

As IT WOULD HAPPEN, COMMANDER LEONARD'S FEARS were justified, but eleven years would pass before the spade fortresses of the Robotech Masters appeared in Earthspace. And perhaps history would have vindicated Leonard if the man's misdeeds had not stayed one step ahead of his contributions. Fate offered him one consolation, though: he would be dead two years before the Invid arrival. Earth would fall, just as he had predicted; just as Tirol fell after the Masters had begun *their* long journey through space and left their homeworld defenseless.

The Invid, however, were less confident in those days. Optera—their native planet—and Tirol had been at war for generations, and the Invid especially were at a disadvantage in terms of firepower. They had, after all, been deprived of the one thing that had cemented the social structure of their race—the Flower of Life; and more importantly, they were novices in this game called warfare. On the other hand, the Masters were adepts, addicted to Protoculture, obsessed with control, and driven to transform themselves—not through any measure of spiritual evolution, but through sheer conquest of the material realm. Profligate, they

13

lived for excess; cloned a race of warrior giants to police their empire, then, still not content, cloned an entire society they could rule at whim. They took the best specimens with them when they abandoned Tirol; all that remained were the three Elders of their race, several hundred imperfect clones—lost without their clonemasters—and Tirol's preclone population of humanoids, who were of no use to the ascended Masters.

Tirol, the third of Fantoma's twelve moons, was not the Masters' original homeworld; but they had successfully transplanted themselves on that utterly barren planetoid from one of the outer satellites. Tiresia, the capital, a blend of Tirol's analogue of Greco-Roman architecture and ultratech design, was the only occupied city; and as such was aware of the Invid's coming ahead of time.

Aware . . . but hardly prepared.

Early-warning sirens and howlers had the humanoid population scurrying for shelters beneath the city well in advance of the midnight attack. The clones wandered the streets in a kind of daze, while the Elders who were responsible for their reaction made certain to hide themselves away in specially-designed chambers the Masters had seen fit to construct before their mass exodus. But there were two who remained at their work while the alert sounded through the city: the scientist Cabell, and his young assistant, Rem.

"Whoever they are," Cabell was saying, while his fingers rushed a series of commands into one of the lab's data networks, "they've put down near the outpost at Rylac."

"Is their identity in any doubt, Cabell?" Rem asked from behind the old man's chair. Video monitors showed a dozen burnt-orange oysterlike troop carriers hovering over a jagged ridgeline of mountains west of the city. The network spit out a data card, which Cabell immediately transferred to an adjacent on-line device.

"I don't suppose there is, my boy," the scientist said without turning around. Several of the ships had put down now, and were disgorging mecha from their forward ramps.

"Will the city's defenses save us?"

Cabell left the question unanswered; instead, he turned his attention to activation switches for the remote cameras positioned at the outpost's perimeter, his long snow-white beard grazing the control studs while he reached across the console. He was every bit a wizard of a man, portly under his tasseled robes and laurel-collared capes, with a hairless knobbed skull and thick white eyebrows, mustache, and beard. He was indeed old enough to be the young man's father, although that wasn't precisely the case. Rem was tall and slender, with an ageless, almost elfin face and a thick shock of slate-blue hair. He wore a tight-fitting uniform with a long cape of royal blue.

"We're defenseless," Rem said a moment later, reacting to Cabell's silence. "Only the old and the sick remain on Tirol."

"Quiet!" the scientist told him. The central viewscreen showed the transports lifting off. Energy-flux schematics scrolled across half-a-dozen lesser screens. "Now what could they have in mind?"

Rem gestured to a secondary video monitor. "Frankly, Cabell, I'm more concerned about these monsters they've left behind." Waves of armored, felinelike creatures could be seen advancing up and out of the drop zone.

Cabell leaned back from the console to contemplate the images, right hand stroking his beard. "They resemble drones, not monsters." One of the creatures had stopped in its tracks and seemed to be staring at the camera. Cabell brought the lens to bear on the thing, focusing in on the four-legged creature's razor-sharp claws, fangs, and shoulder horns.

"It spotted the remote!" Rem said, as the cat's eyes began to glow. An instant later a metal-shod claw swiped at the camera; the image de-rezzed, and the screen crackled with static.

The Invid were a long way from home—if Optera could still be thought of in those terms. That their strikes against the Masters' empire were fueled by revenge was true enough; but the conquest of worlds like Karbarra, Praxis, and Spheris had had a more consequential purpose, for all these planets had been seeded by Zor with the Flowers of Life—the renegade scientist's final attempt at recompense for the horrors his discoveries had inadvertently unleashed. But the resultant Flowers had proved a sterile crop, mutated at best; and so the search was under way for the one key that could unlock the mysteries of Zor's science: the Protoculture matrix he himself had hidden aboard the Superdimensional Fortress.

The legendary device had never been uncovered by Lang's teams of Robotechnicians, and now that ship lay buried under tons of earth, rock, and Macross debris far from where the Invid were directing their quest. But at the time they had no way of knowing these things.

The Flowers had been their primary concern—their nutrient grail—but that purpose had undergone a slight perversion since Zor's death at the hands of Invid troopers. For not only had he transgressed by seducing the Flowers' secret from the Invid Regis; he had also spread a kind of contagion among that race—a pathology of emulation. And within a generation the Invid had refashioned themselves, and, with a form of self-generated Protoculture, created their own galactic war machine—a fleet of disc-shaped starships, a strike force of bipedal crablike mecha, and an army of mindless battle drones—the so-called Inorganics. But this was chiefly the work of the Invid Regent, not their Queen, and a schism had resulted—one that would ultimately affect Earth's fragile hold on its future.

The Invid fleet was anchored in space above Tirol when word spread through the ranks that the Regent himself had decided to take charge of the invasion. Companies of Inorganics had already been deployed on the moon's surface to counter ground-force resistance. Now, aboard the fleet flagship, one thousand Invid troops stood at attention in the docking bay, backed by more than two hundred Pincer assault mecha.

The unarmored individual Invid was primate in shape. Bilaterally symmetrical, they stood anywhere from six to eight feet tall, and walked upright on two powerfully-muscled legs. Equally massive were the forearms, shoulders, and three-fingered hands, with their opposable thumbs. The bulbous head and huge neck—often held parallel to the ground—approximated that of a snail, with an eye on either side, and two sensory antennae at the snout. The skin was green, almost reptilian, and there was at this stage no sexual differentiation. The Regent himself was by and large a grander, nearly twenty-foot-high version of the same design, save for his purple hue and the organic cowl that rested upon his back like some sort of manta ray. This hood, which could puff like a cobra's at times, was ridged front to back with tubercle-like sensors that resembled eyeballs.

The commander of the flagship troops genuflected as the hatchway to the Regent's ship hissed up, spilling brilliant light against the soldier's crimson body armor. Helmet snout lowered to the floor, the trooper brought its right hand to its breast in salute.

"My lord, the Inorganics have met only token resistance on Tirol," the commander reported, its voice distorted by the helmet filters. "So far there is no sign of the Robotech Masters."

The Regent remained on the shuttle's rampway, his bulk and flowing blue robe filling the hatch.

"Cowering beneath their beds, no doubt," the Regent said in a voice so deep it seemed to emanate from the ship itself.

The commander raised its head some, with a whirring of mechanical adjusters. "Our beloved Regis has expressed some displeasure with your strategy, my lord." It offered up a cassettelike device in its left hand. "She wanted this to be given to you."

"A voice imprint?" the Regent said dubiously. "How thoughtful of my *wife*." He snatched the cassette in his hand. "I can hardly wait to hear it."

He activated the device as he moved from the docking bay into one of the flagship's corridors. The commander and a ten-trooper squad marched in formation behind him, their armored footfalls echoing in the massive space.

"Do you truly believe that you'll find what you seek on this wretched planet?" the synthesized female voice began. *"If so you are even a greater fool than I ever suspected. This idiotic invasion of yours is the most—"*

"I've heard about enough of that," the Regent said, deactivating the voice. "Tell me, where is our *beloved* Regis?" he asked the commander after a moment.

"She has returned to her fleet flagship, my lord." When the Regent had reached his quarters, the commander thought to ask, "Shall I tell her you wish to see her, my lord?"

"Negative," the Regent said sternly. "The farther she is, the better I like it. See to it that my pets are brought aboard, and let the invasion proceed without her."

The Invid squad snapped to as the door hissed closed.

The humanoid soldiers at the Rylac outpost were easily overrun. Given the few weapons at their disposal, they made a valiant stand, but the Inorganics proved too much for them. The forward assault wave was comprised solely of Invid feline mecha; but behind these Hellcats marched companies of Scrim and Crann and Odeon—Invid robot analogues, which in some ways resembled skeletal versions of their own Shock Troopers and Pincer Ships, a demonic, bipedal infantry.

A schematic representation of a Scrim came to life on one of Cabell's monitor screens, rotating and shifting through a series of perspectives, as intact remotes from the Rylac sector continued to bring the action home to the lab.

"There is only one species capable of producing such a device," Cabell commented flatly.

"The Invid," said Rem. "It was only a matter of time."

"The strategy is typical of them: they won't descend until their fighting drones have cleared away the resistance. And after they've devastated Tirol, they'll leave these things behind to police us." Hellcat schematics were taking shape on the monitors. "These machines are puzzling, though. It's almost as if . . ."

Rem looked back and forth between the screens and the old man's face, trying to discern Cabell's meaning. "It's hopeless, isn't it?"

"I'm not saying that, my boy," the scientist replied, leaning in to study the data flows. "This feline drone is like its two-legged counterparts: computer-driven and incapable of independent action. Its functions, therefore, must be controlled by an external centralized power source of some kind." He swiveled around in his chair to gaze at his assistant. "That is its weakness, the one flaw in the system, and we must take advantage of it."

"Cabell—"

"Is it not easier to attack one target than a thousand? If we can locate that power source and disable it, then all these dreaded machines will be deactivated."

Alert lamps flashed in another part of the room and Cabell swung around to them. "The Inorganics are closing on the city. Now we'll see how they fare against real firepower."

"The Bioroids!" Rem said excitedly.

"They're our only hope."

Rick and Max had shuttled down to the surface simply to ride back up with Lisa, Miriya, Lang, and other members of the mission command team. Both men were aware that the short trip constituted their last visit to Earth for an indeterminate period of time, but neither of them made much of this. Max was still nursing some concerns about leaving Dana behind, but was otherwise fully committed to the mission. Rick, on the other hand, was so preoccupied with the wedding that he had begun to think of the mission as a simpler and more certain voyage. So it was during the return trip that he was paying almost no attention to the discussion taking place in the command shuttle conference chambers.

"I only hope this plan works," Jonathan Wolff was saying. "Coming in disguised as a Zentraedi ship . . . It could backfire on us."

"Oh, you're forgetting your own Earth history, Colonel," the Zentraedi ambassador told him. "The Greeks and their Trojan horse."

"I think you're confusing history and mythology, Lord Exedore. Wouldn't you agree, Admiral? Admiral?" Wolff repeated.

Rick surfaced from his own thoughts to find everyone at the table staring at him. "Huh? Sorry, I was, um, thinking about something else."

Wolff recapped the exchange: justification for the disguise had been something of an issue from the start. Exedore and Lang were of the opinion that Tirol's defenses would annihilate any ship that registered an alien signature. According to the Zentraedis, the Robotech Masters had been at war for generations with a race called the Invid, and any unannounced entry into the Valivarre system would be tantamount to an act of aggression. Wolff, however, along with several other members of the general staff, advanced the view that the Zentraedi themselves might no longer be considered welcome guests. After all, they had not only failed in their mission to reclaim the SDF-1, but had allied themselves with the very "Micronians" their armada had been ordered to destroy.

Wolff was a persuasive speaker, and while Rick listened he couldn't help but be impressed by the scope of the man's learning. Handsome, articulate, an inspired commander and deadly hand-to-hand combatant, the full bird colonel was considered something of a glamour boy; he favored wraparound sunglasses, wore his dark hair slicked back, and his mustache well-trimmed. But the leader of the notorious "Wolff Pack" was anything but glamorous in the field. Wolff had made a name for himself and his ground unit during the Southland's Malcontent Uprisings, where he had first come to the attention of Max Sterling. When the Zentraedis who survived those days spoke of Wolff, one couldn't help but hear the mixture of reverence and dread in their voices; and anyone who had read the declassified documents covering the Control Zone mop-up ops had no trouble understanding why Wolff and Breetai were often mentioned in the same breath.

"I'm just saying that disguising the ship and loading it down with mecha only serves to undermine the so-called diplomatic thrust of the mission." Wolff snorted. "No wonder Leonard and the Southern Cross brass tried to make mincemeat out of you down there."

"What do they expect us to do?" Max wanted to know. "Go in there flying a white flag? At least we've got some bargaining power this way."

"Let's just hope we won't need to use any of it," Rick said at last, straining against his seat harness. "Without the Zentraedi, the Masters could be defenseless for all we know."

Exedore shook his head. "Oh, I wouldn't count on that, Admiral." Breetai had already briefed everyone on the mecha the Masters had been developing before Zor's death—Hoverships and Bioroids.

"Gentlemen, the time is long past for arguments about strategy," Lang cut in before Rick could speak. "We've all supported this plan, and it seems rather late in the day to be changing our mind."

"I agree," Max said.

"Look, *I* agree," Wolff wanted the table to know. "I'd just like us to agree on an approach. Are we going in with fists raised or hands up? The Masters aren't going to be fooled by our outward appearance—not for long, at any rate."

"Possibly not," Exedore answered him. "But if we allow *possibilities* to influence us, we'll never leave orbit."

"I've got as many doubts as anybody," Rick said from the head of the table. "But the time's come to put them behind us. We've made our bed, as the saying goes ..."

Brave talk, Hunter, he thought, listening to his own words. *And I'll keep telling myself that when I'm walking down the aisle.*

Two RDF officers were watching the approach of the command shuttle from a rectangular bay in one of the factory satellite's peripheral pods. One was a slim and eager-eyed young major who had recently been appointed adjutant to General T. R. Edwards; and the other was the general himself, his disfiguration concealed beneath an irregularly-shaped black-alloy plate that covered most of the right side of his face and more than half his skull. On the uncovered left side of his head, long blond hair fell in waves to the collar of his tight-fitting uniform. He was high-cheekboned and square-jawed, and might have been considered handsome even with the plate, were it not for the cruelty in his eye and downward-turning mouth.

"So tell me, Benson," Edwards said, while his one eye continued to track the shuttle's course, "what do you know about the illustrious vice admiral?"

"I know that Hunter's one of our most decorated heroes, sir," Benson reported to the general's broad back. "Leader of the Skull during the Robotech War, commander of the RDF after the destruction of the superdimensional fortresses, about to marry the admiral ... That's about it, sir."

Edwards clasped his hands behind his back. "That's right. The high command likes to award medals to people who end up in the right place at the right time."

"Sir?" Benson asked.

"Anything in your academy history books about Roy Fokker?" Edwards said nastily over his shoulder. "Now there was a real VT ace for you. I remember turning those blue skies red trying to nail his ass ... But you're too young to remember the Global War, aren't you, Benson? The real heroes." Edwards leaned forward and pressed his fingertips against the bay's permaplas viewport. "Fokker taught Hunter everything he knew, did you know that? You might even say that Hunter is what Fokker would've been, Major—that Hunter *is* Fokker."

Benson swallowed hard, unsure how to respond, uncertain if he even should.

Edwards touched his skullplate, remembering, forcing himself back over tormented terrain—to what was left of Alaska Base after Zentraedi annihilation bolts had destroyed the Grand Cannon and made a hell of that icebound site. And how one man and one woman had survived. The woman was unharmed, protected where she cowered while her father had fried alive; but the man, *how he had suffered*! What agony he had endured, down on his knees shamelessly trying to push the ruins of an eye back where it belonged, fingers pinched in an effort to knit together flesh that had been opened on his face and forehead. Then the rapture he had known when a solitary Veritech had appeared out of those unnatural clouds. But it was the *woman* that VT pilot had come for, and no other. It was the *woman* who had been flown to safety, the *woman* who had risen through the ranks, while the man had been left behind to die, to rot in that alien-made inferno . . .

"Ah, what a wedding this will be, Benson," Edwards continued after a moment of angry silence. "Admirals Rick Hunter and Lisa Hayes. Star-crossed lovers, if ever there were. Born and reborn for each other."

"Till death do them part," Benson returned with an uncomfortable laugh.

Edwards spun on his heels, face contorted, then erupting in laughter. "Yes, Major, *how right you are!*"

Most of the Zentraedi had been off scouring the galaxy for Zor's ship and its hidden Protoculture matrix when the Robotech Masters first perfected the Bioroids. Sixty-foot-tall nontransformable goliath knights piloted by low-level clones, they were meant to act as the Masters' police force on the remote worlds that comprised Tirol's empire, freeing the Zentraedi for further acts of conquest and continued warfare against the Invid. The Masters had never considered that Protoculture would one day be in limited supply, nor that their army of giant warriors would be defeated in a distant corner of the Fourth Quadrant by so simple a weapon as love. So it fell on the Bioroids by chance and Protoculture's own dark designs, to defend the Masters' empire against Optera's ravenous horde. But try as they might, they were no match for the Invid Shock Troopers and Pincer Ships, with their plasma weapons and energy discs. And as Protoculture grew more and more scarce, they could barely defend against the mindless Inorganics.

"It is sheer numbers," Cabell explained to Rem as they watched Tiresia's first line of defense fall. The clonemasters left behind to rule the Bioroid pilots were an inferior lot, so the fight was not all it should have been. *The Masters have thrown them our world,* Cabell left unsaid. Those massive space fortresses with their clone populations were the Masters' new homes; they had no plans to return to Tirol.

Command-detonated mines took out wave after wave of Hellcats, but this did little more than delay the inevitable. The Bioroids dug in, finding cover behind hastily-erected barricades, and fired until their cannons and assault rifles went red-hot and depleted. And when the Inorganics began to overrun their lines, they went hand-to-claw with the marauders, employing last-stand tactics worthy of history's finest. Cabell could feel no sympathy for them as such; but staring at the lab's central viewscreen he was overcome by a greater sense of pathos and loss. External mikes picked up the clones' anguished cries, their desperate utterances to one another in that raspy, almost synthesized voice the Masters so loved.

"There's too many of them!" the pilot of a blue Bioroid told his teammates along the front, before two Hellcats leaped and crashed through the mecha's visorlike faceshield. A second blue blasted the intruders with the last of his weapon's charge, only to fall an instant later, Inorganics ripping at the machine's armor in a mad effort to get to the pilot within.

Disgusted, Cabell stood up and reached across the console to shut down the audio transmissions. "The Flower of Life, that's what they've come for," he told his apprentice in a tired voice.

"But that plant hasn't been present in this sector for generations," Rem said, slipping into the padded con chair.

"Then they'll want the matrix. Or failing that, vengeance for what the Masters ordered done to their world."

Rem turned his attention to the screen. Scrim devils and Hellcats were tearing through the Bioroid base, eyes aglow like hot coals, fangs slick with the clone pilots' blood. "They'll rip the planet apart looking for something they'll never find."

"No one ever accused the Invid of being logical, my boy, only thorough."

"Then the city will fall next. Those drones are unstoppable."

"Nonsense," Cabell exclaimed, anger in his voice. "They may be intimidating, but they're not unstoppable."

Rem shot to his feet. "Then let's find their weak spot, Cabell." He drew a handgun from beneath his cape and armed it. "And for that, we're going to require a specimen."

CHAPTER THREE

Try as he might to offset the suffering his discoveries had unleashed, Zor's mistakes kept piling up, compounding themselves. He'd sent his ship to Earth only to have the Zentraedi follow it there; he'd hidden the matrix so well that the Masters had ample time to wage their war; his seeded worlds had drawn the Invid . . . What remained but the final injustice?—that by trying to replicate his very form and drives, the Regent and Regis should become prisoners of appetites they had never before experienced. Is it any mystery why even the Masters banished his image throughout their empire?

Bloom Nesterfig, *The Social Organization of the Invid*

B RIGADIER GENERAL REINHARDT, HAVING SHUTTLED UP TO the factory earlier that day, was on hand to meet the mission command team. He informed Lang, Lord Exedore, Lisa, and Rick that things were still running on schedule; the last shiploads of supplies and stores were on their way up from Earth even now, and most of the 3,500 who would make up the crew were already aboard the satellite, many aboard the SDF-3 itself. Max and Miriya joined the others by an enormous hexagonal viewport that overlooked the null-gee central construction hold. They were joined after a moment by Colonel Wolff and Jean Grant, who had Bowie and Dana by the hand.

The view from here was fore to aft along the underside of the fortress. Lisa often wished that the bow wasn't quite so, well, *phallic*—the euphemism she employed in mixed company. But the twin booms of the main gun were just that: like two horned, tumescent appendages that took up nearly a third of the crimson ship's length. If the weapon had none of the awesome firepower of the SDF-1's main gun, at least it had the *look* of power to it. Autowelders and supply shuttles were moving through the hold's captured sunlight, and a crew of full-size Zentraedi were at work on one of the sky-blue sensor blisters along the fortress's port side.

"How many kilometers out will we have to be before we can fold?" Wolff wanted to know. Everyone remembered all too plainly what had happened when the SDF-1 attempted to fold while still in the vicinity of Macross Island.

"Lunar orbit will suffice," Exedore told him. "Doctor Lang and Breetai concur on this."

"Speak of the devil," Lisa said, looking around the hold, "I thought he was supposed to meet us here."

Miriya laughed shortly. "He probably forgot."

"He's been pretty busy," Rick offered.

"Well, we can't wait," Reinhardt said, running a hand over his smooth pate. "We've got a lot of last-minute details to attend to and—"

Everyone reacted to Dana's gasp at the same moment, turning first to the child's startled face, then to the hatchway she had her eyes fixed on.

There was a giant standing there.

Half the gathered group knew him as a sixty-footer, of course, but even micronized Breetai was an impressive sight: almost eight feet of power dressed in a uniform more befitting a comic book hero than a Zentraedi commander, and wearing a masklike helmet that left only his mouth and lantern jaw exposed.

Before anyone could speak, he had moved in and one-hand heaved Lisa and Miriya atop each of his shoulders. His voice boomed. "So I'm not important enough to wait for, huh? You Micronians are an impatient lot."

He let the women protest a moment before setting them back down on the floor.

"I never thought I'd see you like this again," Lisa said, tugging her uniform back into shape. The only other time Breetai had permitted himself to undergo the reduction process was during the search of the SDF-1 for the Protoculture matrix.

"It takes a man to give away a bride," Breetai said in all seriousness, "not a giant."

Dawn marked Tiresia's doom. The troop carriers returned, yawning catastrophe; but this time it wasn't Inorganics they set loose, but the crablike Shock Troopers and Pincer Ships. They attacked without mercy, skimming discs of white annihilation into the streets, dwellings, and abandoned temples. The humanoid populace huddled together in shelters, while those masterless clones who had become the city's walking dead surrendered and burned.

Left to fend for themselves, the old and infirm tried to hide from the invaders, but it was hardly a day to play games with the Reaper: his minions were everywhere, and within hours the city was laid to waste.

Cannon muzzles and missile racks sprang from hidden emplacements, spewing return fire into the void, and once again the Bioroids faced the storm and met their end in heroic bursts of orange flame and blinding light. From the depths of the pyramidal Royal Hall rode an elite unit on saucer-shaped Hovercraft outfitted with powerful disc guns and particle-beam weapon systems. They joined the Invid in an airborne dance of devastation, coupling obscenely in the city skies, exchanging thundering volleys of quantum death.

Morning was filled with the corkscrewing trails of angry projectiles and crisscrossed with hyphens and pulses of colored light. Spherical explosions strobed overhead, rivaling the brightness of Fantoma's own primary, low in the east behind clouds of debris. Mecha fell like a storm of blazing hail, cutting fiery swaths across the cityscape.

Here a Pincer Ship put down to give chase to an old man its discs had thrown clear from a Hoverchair. Frustrated, the Invid trained its weapons on Tiresia's architectural wonders and commenced a deadly pirouette. Statues and ornaments slagged in the heat, and five of the antigrav columns that marked the Royal Hall's sacred perimeter were toppled.

Ultimately the Invid's blue command ships moved in, forming an unbreachable line as they marched through the city, their top-mounted cannons ablaze. Inside the shelters the citizens of Tiresia cowered and clung to one another as the footfalls of the giants' war strides shook Tirol's ravaged surface, echoing in the superheated subterranean confinement.

Cabell and Rem had chosen a deserted, now devastated sector for their Hellcat hunt. With most of Tiresia's defenses in ruin, the fierce fighting that typified the early hours of the invasion had subsided to distant hollow blasts from the few remaining contested areas. A patrol of bipedal Inorganics moved past the alley where the scientist and his assistant waited. Rem raised the muzzle of the assault rifle he had slung over one shoulder, but Cabell waved him back.

"But it doesn't sense our presence," Rem insisted, peering over Cabell's shoulder. "Now's our chance."

"No," Cabell said firmly. "I want one of the feline droids."

They began to move into the street after the Inorganic had

passed. Cabell kept them to the shadows at first, then grew more brazen. Rem understood that the old man was trying to lure one of the creatures out but he had some misgivings about Cabell's method.

"I hope we snare one of them and not the other way around," he said wearily, swinging the rifle in a gentle arc.

Cabell stopped short in the center of the street as a kind of mechanical growl reached them from somewhere nearby. "I have the distinct impression our progress is being observed."

"I was about to say the same thing."

"Perhaps our behavior is puzzling to them," Cabell mused, back in motion now. "They probably expect us to run in terror."

"And I forget, why *aren't* we?" Rem started to say when another growl sounded. "Guess they're not puzzled anymore ... Show yourself, fiend," he growled back, arming the rifle.

"There!" Cabell said all at once.

The Hellcat was glaring down at them from a low roof not twenty yards up the street, midday light caught in the beast's shoulder horns, fangs, and razor-sharp tail. Then it pounced.

"On stun!" Cabell cried, and Rem fired.

The short burst glanced off the cat's torso, confusing it momentarily, but not long enough to make a difference. It leaped straight for the two men before Rem could loose a second shot, but he did manage to shove Cabell clear of the Inorganic's path. The cat turned sharply as it landed; Rem hit it twice more to no avail.

"Get away from it, boy!" Rem heard Cabell shout. He looked around, amazed that the old man had covered so much ground in so little time—although the Inorganic was certainly incentive enough: it was hot on Cabell's trail.

Rem chased the two of them, firing wildly, and rounded a corner in time to see his mentor barrel-ass down a rubble slide and throw himself into the cockpit of an overturned Bioroid transport ship. Fixed on its prey, the Hellcat seemed unaware of Rem, and was busy trying to claw through the ship's bubble shield. Rem reached down to up the rifle's charge, only to find the thing depleted. He was busy cursing himself when he spied a fallen Invid command ship nearby, one of its cannontips still aglow with priming charge.

Cautiously, he approached the ship, the useless weapon raised. The command plastron was partially ajar, a four-fingered hand lodged in the opening. Rem clambered up and over one of the mecha's arms and gave the hatch a violent tug, forcing the rifle down into the invader's face as he did so. But the Invid was already dead, its bulbous head and stalklike neck split wide open.

Rem ignored the stench and took a quick look at the cockpit's be-wildering gadgetry. The alien's right hand was hooked around what Rem decided was the trigger mechanism, and from the looks of things the Hellcat was almost perfectly centered in the cannon's reticle. Rem grunted a kind of desperate curse, slid down into the cockpit—his legs going knee-deep into a viscous green bath of nutrient fluid—and hit the trigger.

A pulsed beam of crimson light threw the Hellcat clear from the transport and left it on its side thirty feet away, stunned and enveloped by a kind of St. Elmo's fire. Cabell threw open the can-opy and glanced back at the crippled command ship with a bewil-dered expression.

"Why did you save me?" the old man yelled in Zentraedi, *lingua franca* of the Masters' empire.

Rem heard the call and was tempted to stay put for a moment, but thought better of it. He showed himself and said, "Hello, Cabell. All safe and sound? You didn't really think I'd abandon you, did you?"

The scientist scowled. "You could have killed me, you young—" He bit off his own words and laughed, resignedly. "My boy, you amaze me."

Rem jumped to the ground and approached the transport. "Frankly, I amaze myself." He looked away from the alien ship he had fired, and gestured to the Hellcat. "Now all we've got to do is figure out how to get this thing back to the lab."

"My lord, we've found no trace of the Flower of Life any-where," the voice of an Invid lieutenant reported to the Regent.

"But that's impossible, you *idiot*!" the Regent shouted at his monitor. "This is their homeworld. They must be here! Scan the entire planet."

The flagship throne room, like the Invid castle and hives on Optera, was an organic chamber, so given over to the urgings of Protoculture that its very bulkheads and sensor devices resembled living systems of neural-tissue circuitry. Visceral greens and pur-ples, they pulsed to rhythms dictated deep within the ship's ani-mate drives. So, too, the contoured control couch itself, with its graceful curves, the slender arcing neck of its overhead sensor lamp, its proboscislike forward communicator tube. The Regent did not so much sit as reshape his being to the seat's demands.

On either side of him sat a Hellcat larger and more polished than any of the standard versions, with collars encrusted with gems handpicked from the spoils of a score of conquered worlds.

Elsewhere, in cages, were living samples from those same worlds: sentient prisoners from Karbarra, Spheris, and the rest.

"We have searched, my lord," the trooper continued. "The Sensor Nebula registers no presence of the Flowers. None whatsoever."

"Fools!" muttered the Regent, canceling the transmission. He could hear his wife's laughter behind him.

"Congratulations, husband," the Regis mocked him from across the room. "Once again you have impressed us all with your supreme stupidity."

"I don't like your tone," the Regent said, turning to her.

One might have almost mistaken her for a humanoid life-form; certainly she was more that than the ursoid and vulpine beings that populated the Regent's personal zoo. But at the same time there was something ethereal and insubstantial about her, an inhumanness that lurked in the depths of her cobalt eyes. Twenty feet tall and slender, she clothed her completely hairless form in a red full-length robe and curious, five-fingered tasseled gloves. Four emerald-green sensor scarabs that might have been facelike adornments decorated the robe's bracelike collar and neck closure.

"I told you the Robotech Masters were too clever to hide the matrix in their own back yard."

"Silence, *woman*!" the Regent demanded, rising from the throne.

But the Regis stood her ground. "If you hadn't been so desperate to prove yourself a great warrior, we might have sent spies to learn where they've taken it."

The Regent looked at his wife in disbelief. "Are you forgetting who got us into this predicament in the first place? *I'm* not the one who fell under the spell of Zor and allowed him to steal our Flower of Life."

"Must you keep *harping* on that!" the Regis screamed, shutting her eyes and waving her fists in the air. "It happened a long time ago. And since then *I* have evolved, while you've remained the spoiled child you always were. You took his life; now you won't rest content until you've conquered his empire." She gestured offhandedly to the Regent's "pets" and caged life-forms. "You and your dreams of empire . . . Mark my words, husband, some day these beings will rise up to strike you down."

The Regent laughed. "Yes, you've *evolved*—into a pathetic imitation of the females of Zor's race."

"Perhaps so," she countered, arms akimbo. "But that's preferable to imitating the Masters' toys and bloodlust." She turned on her heel and headed for the door. "I'm returning to Optera."

"Stop! I forbid you to go!" the Regent told her, furious.

"Don't provoke me," she shouted from the doorway, "you spineless anachronism!"

"Wait!" the Regent demanded, cursing her. He whirled around as the door hissed closed, Tirol huge in the room's starboard viewports. "I'll show you," he muttered under his breath. "Tirol will feel my potency . . . and I'll win back your love."

"Toys," Dr. Harry Penn told Lang, an undisguised note of disapproval in his voice. "War toys, when we could be fashioning wonders." He was a large man with a gruff-looking exterior that masked the gentlest of spirits. The thick mustache and beard he had grown to mask the pockmarked, hooked-nose cragginess of his face had only ended up adding to the effect he had hoped to minimize. It was a scholarly, academic image he was after, and as the oldest member of the Plenipotentiary Council and one of Lang's top men he felt he deserved no less.

"There'll be time for that when this mission returns," Lang said evenly. "Until then we have to be sure of our strengths."

Penn made a disgruntled sound. "A peaceful mission, a diplomatic mission . . . Am I the only one who remembers the meaning of those words?"

The two men were standing by one of the factory's observation bays; in the blackness of space beyond, two Veritechs were being put through their paces.

These were not the first generation VTs the Skull and other teams had flown against the Zentraedi, but Alpha fighters, the latest prototypes from Lang's research department laboratories. The SDF-3's arsenal wasn't limited to these reconfigurable one-pilot craft—the last six years had seen the development of Hovertanks, Logans, and an array of new and improved Destroids—but the Veritech remained something of Robotechnology's favored child, weapon *extraordinaire* and near-symbol of the war. The Alpha VT had more armor than its older sibling; it packed almost twice the firepower and was equipped with ablative shields and detachable augmentation pods for deepspace flight. Moreover, it had the capability to link up with the so-called Beta VT—a bulkier, thinwinged variant that appeared to lack an appropriate radome—and thereby more than double its range and occupancy capabilities.

Lang indicated the blue fighter as it twisted through space, reconfiguring to Guardian, then Battloid mode. "I just wanted you to see for yourself the progress we've made, Harry."

"Sterling, here," said a voice over the ob deck's speakers. "The Alpha handled the last sequence beautifully. No sign of stress."

"Fine, Max," said Lang, directing his words to a microphone. "The prototype looks good so far. Now comes the real test," he added for Penn's benefit. "Max, Karen, move yourselves into position for trans-docking maneuver."

Max rogered the transmission; Karen Penn, Harry's only daughter, said, "We're on our way."

Lang risked a quarter turn and found Penn regarding him with a mixture of surprise and rage. "You're awfully quiet, Harry, is something wrong?"

"Have you gone mad, Lang! You know I didn't want Karen participating in this test."

"What was I supposed to do, Harry, refuse her permission? Don't forget, she volunteered, and she's one of our most able young pilots."

"But I don't want her to get mixed up in this, Emil. Can't you understand that? *Science* is her future, not warfare."

"Control," Max's voice squawked over the speakers, "we are in position at T-niner-delta. Standing by to reconfigure and align for docking sequence."

The maneuver called for each of the Veritechs to jettison and exchange their unmanned Beta modules, blue to red, red to blue. Max carried out his part without a hitch, imaging over to fighter mode and engaging the VT's retros for a solid linkup with its sister module. But Karen slipped up. Max couldn't tell at first whether she had been too heavy-minded, or had simply misread the VT's telemetry displays. In either case she was in trouble, the blue Beta off on a ride to eternity, and Karen in what looked like a planet-bound freefall.

Max tried to reach her on the net, through a cacophony of questions and exclamations from command—most of them from Dr. Penn himself. Karen wasn't responding, but there wasn't real cause for concern—yet. Assuming she wasn't unconscious or worse—something unseen, an embolism, perhaps—Karen had ample time to get herself into the Veritech's EVA suit; and failing that, the factory could bring its tractor beam to bear. But Max wanted to see Karen pull out of this one without an assist; she was bright and full of potential, and he wanted her for the Skull.

"Stabilizers are gone," Karen said suddenly. ". . . Power surge must have fried the circuitry."

Then Dr. Penn's panicked voice bellowed in Max's ears. "Sterling, do something! You've got to help her!"

"Karen," Max said calmly. "Go to Guardian and bring your thrusters into play. I'm right behind you if they fail."

"Roger, Skull leader," Karen returned.

On the factory ob deck, Penn muscled his way through a crowd of techs to get close to the monitor screen. He sucked in his breath seeing his daughter's red Alpha in a slow-motion end-over-end fall; but the next instant found the VT reconfigured, its bird-of-prey foot thrusters burning bright in the night. And in another moment she was out of danger and there were hoots and hollers ringing in his ears, tears of release in his eyes.

Lang and Penn were waiting in the docking bay when the VTs came in. Max missed the days of flattop touchdowns, the cat officers and their impromptu launch dances; but the *Daedalus* and *Prometheus* supercarriers were part of the SDF-1 burial mound now, and unnecessary in any case.

"Karen, thank God you're all right!" Max heard Dr. Penn call out as the blue's canopy slid open. "That little escapade nearly gave me a heart attack."

Guilt's his game, Max thought as he climbed out of Skull One.

"Well, if you were scared, imagine how I felt," Karen was telling her father. "I'm still shaking."

Penn waved a forefinger at her. "This proves once and for all you've no business being a test pilot."

"Don't overdo it, Dad." Karen removed her thinking cap, spilling honey-blond hair to her shoulders. She had small delicate features, eyes the color of pre-Columbian jade. "I'm a professional. This stuff comes with the territory."

"I'll say she is," Max chimed in before Penn could get in another word. "That linkup wasn't her fault. Dollars to donuts you'll find some glitch in the guidance computers."

Penn glared at him. "I'm sure you mean well, Commander, but all this is—"

"Meaning well has nothing to do with it. I just don't want to see Ensign Penn's talents go to waste. She impressed me, Dr. Penn—and I'm not easily impressed."

Penn blanched some; he wasn't about to debate Sterling's words. But Karen was still his daughter. "Well, I'm not impressed," he told Karen after Max had walked off. "I have other plans for you."

She flashed him a look he remembered from way back and started to move off, but Dr. Lang put out his hand to stop her.

"Karen, a moment please."

"You gonna chew me out now?"

"Calm down," said Lang. "I'm going to recommend you for assignment to a Veritech team."

"Just a minute, Emil," Penn said, one hand clasped around Karen's upper arm. "Don't you think you're overstepping your authority?" He had already lost his wife, and Karen's joining the RDF had threatened to destroy what had once been a close relationship. Now Lang seemed bent on trying to scuttle what small joy he had left.

Lang pried his friend's fingers open and motioned Karen along. "I'm sorry, Harry, but she's old enough to make up her own mind. You can't hold on to her forever. Besides, if this mission *should* encounter resistance, we're going to need experienced pilots."

"Resistance," Penn snorted, and began to storm off. But half-a-dozen steps away he swung around. "All the more reason to hold on to her for as long as I can."

CHAPTER FOUR

Evidence points to the existence of a plethora of mystery cults in the years immediately preceding Tirol's so-called Great Transition (i.e., that period in which most of the moon's humanoid population were put to death and the Robotech Masters began their extensive cloning experiments). In fact, some of these cults survived well into the First Period ... The labyrinth, apparently, was constructed for ritual use, and the Pyramidal Royal Hall added later as that subterranean cult gave way to one of stellar orientation. Several commentators have felt compelled to bring Minoans, Egyptians, and the Maya into the discussions but aside from certain structural similarities, there was little in common between Tirol and Earth's religions.

History of the Second Robotech War
Volume CCXVI, "Tirol"

WITH THE WEDDING ONLY A DAY OFF NOW, RICK SAT IN his soon-to-be-vacated quarters aboard the factory satellite contemplating the future. Earth hung in the blackness of the viewport behind the desk. Around him were stacked boxes of personal items he had accumulated over the course of the last four years: photographs, citations—memorabilia dating back to his late father's air circus, the SDF-1 and New Macross before the storm. He came across a snapshot taken by a robocam unit of Minmei standing by the Macross park's fountain; poking out from the top of a shopping bag were two posters of the singing star from those early days: one an RDF enlistment ad, and the second a Miss Macross pinup. On the recent side, Lisa was equally well represented. But the more Rick pored through these things the more depressed he became. He had no doubts about his love for Lisa, but what would it mean to abandon all this space and free time he had grown accustomed to? Not that there had been much of either, given mission priorities and such, but the *idea* of personal time, the options. Rick's hand was actually trembling while he packed. He had begun to wonder whether a drink might help, and was reaching for the bottle he kept around for special occasions, when Vince Grant announced himself at the door and stepped in.

At just a shade under seven feet, Grant was the only man aboard who could come close to filling Breetai's shoes. He had brown skin and close-cropped tight curls, and a long face lent a certain nobility by his broad forehead and chiseled features. His dark eyes were bright and full of expression, and he was a man known to speak his mind, consequence be damned. Technically, he was Rick's adjutant, a commander, but he was also attached to rapid deployment's new all-terrain mobile base, the Ground Military Unit, or GMU. Grant had headed up a crackerjack Excaliber unit in New Macross, but Rick hadn't really gotten to know him until after the death of his sister, Claudia.

"Just wanted to see if you needed help with anything, sir," Vince said, offering a casual salute.

Rick turned a sullen face to the assortment of bags and boxes piled about. "Not unless you're good at juggling."

"What, these?" Vince said uncertainly.

"No, Vince, the past and future."

"Sir?"

Rick waved dismissively. "Forget it. What's on your mind, Vince?"

Vince took a breath. "Edwards, sir."

"General Edwards?" Suspicion rose in Rick's eyes. "What about him?"

"Would the general have any reason for acting against our best interests, sir? I mean, is there something I'm not privy to that might explain certain . . . *proclivities*?"

" 'Proclivities'?" said Rick. "Say what's on your mind."

In a rush, Vince said, "It just seems to me that the man has some designs of his own. I'm not saying that it's anything I can put my finger on, but for starters there's his friendship with Leonard and that character Zand. You've been busy, sir, and preoccupied. You're insulated from the scuttlebutt—"

"If you have allegations," Rick broke in, "you'd better be prepared to back them up with some hard facts. Now, do you have any—yes or no?"

Tight-lipped all at once, Vince shook his head. "Only hearsay, sir."

Rick mulled it over after he dismissed Vince. The idea of going halfway across the galaxy with a divided crew was hardly a comforting thought. And in fact there was an underlying feeling of disunity that continued to plague the mission. Lang and Exedore on one side, Edwards and the political machine on the other, with the Southern Cross somewhere in between ... Rick tried to put together what he knew of Edwards. Roy Fokker had often spoken of Edwards's self-serving allegiances during the Global Civil War, his later alignment with Admiral Hayes, Lisa's father, and the Grand Cannon project; but then, that was years ago, and a lot of good men had been lured over to the UEDC's side. In the decade since, Edwards had become a force to be reckoned with in Monument City, and a high-ranking intelligence Officer in the UEG. Presently, as leader of the infamous Ghost Squadron, he had what amounted to an unassailable power base.

It was with all this on his mind that Rick went in search of Max and some objective input.

But it was Lisa he found in the Sterlings' quarters.

She was standing behind the dummied gown he wasn't meant to see until tomorrow.

"Isn't this supposed to be bad luck or something?" Rick asked, looking back and forth between Miriya and Lisa.

"Don't go getting superstitious on me, mister." Lisa laughed. "Besides, I'm not *in* the dress." She stepped out from behind the dressmaker's dummy and saluted stiffly. "Now show some respect."

Rick played along, snapping to and apologizing.

"Impending marriage is no excuse for relaxing discipline."

I'll have to remember that, Rick thought as he approached Lisa and took her by the waist. "Hi," he said softly.

"I beg your pardon, Admiral, but aren't you exceeding your authority?"

Rick pulled her close. "I can't help myself, ma'am. So take away my star, throw me in the brig. But please, not until the honeymoon's over ..."

Miriya made a sour face and turned to Max, who had entered unobserved. "Sounds more like a court-martial than a marriage."

Max allowed the lovers a brief kiss before announcing himself, and five minutes later he and Rick were on their way to the factory's combat-simulation staging area, where Max had a young ensign he wanted Rick to meet. En route they discussed Edwards, but Max didn't have much to offer in the way of facts or advice. Lang was the one Rick needed to speak with, Sterling suggested, and until then the less said the better.

Cadets underwent actual mecha and weapons training in the factory's null-gee core, and out on Moon Base; but it was during sim-time that a cadet faced combat scenarios, and psychological profiles were established and evaluated. Robotechnicians took a good deal of pride in what they had created in the staging area, with projecbeam and holographic effects of such intensity that even veterans were sometimes overwhelmed. The object was not, however, to score bull's-eyes or dazzle the audience with space combat maneuvers, but to demonstrate that one could keep cool under fire and make prudent, often split-second decisions.

Jack Baker was the ensign Max had in mind. Rick watched him being run through one of the advanced scenarios, designed to place the trainee in a position where he or she would have to decide between adherence to command dictates or altruistic heroics. Rick had little fondness for the scenario, because it happened to feature him—a holo-likeness of Rick, at any rate—as the downed pilot, awash in a 3-D sea. For want of an actual enemy, cadets found themselves up against stylized ersatz Zentraedi Battlepods.

Baker's scores were well above average throughout the first portion of the scenario, but ultimately they dropped to standard after the ensign opted to go after his downed wingman, instead of following orders to reengage.

"Not the smoothest performance," Max commented, "but you have to admit he's got something."

"Yeah," Rick nodded. "But I'm not sure it's something I like."

Baker was ordered up to the control booth, and joined Rick and Max there a few minutes later. He was a slight but energetic youth, with thick, unruly carrot-colored hair and bushy eyebrows. Blue-eyed, pale, and freckled, he impressed Rick as something of a discipline problem. At the same time, though, Baker was forceful and determined; a seat-of-the-pants pilot, a natural.

"Sir, I know my performance wasn't perfect," Baker started right in. "But that test wasn't a fair demonstration of my abilities."

Rick wagged a gloved finger in the ensign's face. "In the first place, you went off auto-pilot, contrary to orders. Second, by doing so you endangered the rest of the team. And *third*, you didn't even manage to *rescue* me."

"Yes, but—"

"Dismissed, Ensign."

"But, sir, I—"

"You heard the admiral," Max chimed in.

Baker closed his mouth and saluted. "I appreciate the admiral's input, sir," he managed before he left.

"Funny, but he reminds me of someone," Max said, watching Baker walk away. "Flyboy by the name of Hunter, if memory serves."

"I guess he does have a certain reckless sense of style about him."

"And I suppose that's why you were so hard on him, huh?"

"Just trying to improve him as a team player, Max. Besides," Rick added with a laugh, "the look on his face was priceless."

Max accompanied Rick back to his quarters after they had watched a few more cadets and officers run through the simulator. Rick was in a reminiscent mood, so they talked about the first time they had set foot in the factory after *liberating* it from Commander Reno, and about baby Dana's part in that op. Max wanted to talk about leaving Dana behind now, but Rick didn't seem to want to surrender his train of thought.

The factory was buzzing with activity; shuttles were arriving every few hours with supplies and personnel, and boarding of the SDF-3 was under way, with techs lined up for last minute briefings, assignments, and med-scans from Jean Grant's extensive med staff. In another area of the satellite, maintenance crews, carpenters, and caterers were setting up for the wedding.

"And it's not just the wedding," Rick was saying when they entered his quarters. "I keep thinking about the enormity and importance of this mission. Maybe ... maybe we've taken on too much this time."

"I hope you're not going to start in about how you're the youngest admiral in the force, and how undeserving you are."

"The best and the brightest," Rick said to his reflection in the viewport. "That's me."

Just then the door tone sounded and T. R. Edwards strode in on Rick's welcome.

"Hope I'm not disturbing you, Admiral."

"What's on your mind, General?"

"Why, I just wanted to wish you good luck, Hunter."

Rick noted that Edwards's faceplate made it difficult to tell whether he was sincere. And it was just as difficult for Rick to put Vince Grant's suspicions from his mind.

"What d'you mean by that, Edwards?" Rick said defensively.

Edwards showed a surprised look and turned an uncertain glance to Max. "Well, the wedding, of course. What else would I mean?"

"Oh, oh of course," Rick said, getting to his feet. He extended his hand. "Thanks, Edwards."

"Admiral Hayes's daughter," Edwards mused while they shook hands. "Imagine that ... The irony of it, I mean. No love lost between you and him back then, was there?"

Rick stared into Edwards's eye.

"Oh, I'm sorry, Admiral. I guess you don't like to remember those days." Edwards relaxed his grip and walked to the door. "Just wanted to say good luck. To you, too, Sterling."

Rick and Max exchanged baffled looks as the door hissed shut.

Cabell and Rem had managed to get the Hellcat back to the lab undetected; it was no easy task, but a little muscle power and an abandoned Hovercar did the trick. Cabell had the Inorganic on one of the scanner tables now. He had rendered it harmless by removing a transponder from the machine's flank. Having witnessed Bioroids blowing Hellcats to bits—literally—it came as no surprise to find that the thing was hollow, its entire circuitry contained in its thick skin. But if Cabell had discovered *how* it worked, the source of its power remained a mystery—one he hoped to solve by analyzing the transponder.

On the other side of the room, Rem was up to his ears in Pollinators. Explosions had loosed them from their cage and they were all over him, now, screeching up a storm, attaching themselves to his arms, leg, and neck, and trying desperately to bury themselves in the folds of his long cloak. They might have passed for small white, mop-head dogs, except for their muffinlike paws and knob-ended horns. For a long while Zor had kept their secret from the Tirolian elite, but eventually the Masters had discovered the crucial part they played in spreading the Flower of Life. So Zor went a step further and hid most of the creatures, naming Cabell as their guardian.

"What's happening to these things!" Rem shouted in a muffled voice, pulling one from his face. "They're going crazy!"

"They have a biogentic link to the Flower," the old man answered calmly, hefting the Hellcat's transponder. "The presence of the Invid is disturbing to them."

"And to me," Rem started to say, when something truly monstrous appeared on one of the viewscreens. It was an enormous ship, he decided at once—because nothing so ghastly green and hideous could live in the real world. Its central head and torso resembled a kind of armored, hump-backed slug with two mandibularly-horned lizard heads on segmented necks arising Siamese-like from where arms might have been. There were three tails, two of which were tapered with stinger ends, and eight legs protruding from a suckered belly more appropriate for a sea creature than a terrestrial behemoth.

Cabell narrowed his eyes at the screen and grunted. "Their Enforcer transport. It's meant to frighten us into submission. It's captives they want now, my boy."

His thoughts turned briefly to the three Elders, who had secreted themselves somewhere in Tiresia's labyrinthine underground. *What the Invid Regent would give for their few hides,* Cabell thought. He began to consider using them as a bargaining chip for the release of Tirol's surviving populace if it came to that, but judged it best to let that decision rest until the moment came. Safety for himself and the boy was all that concerned him just now.

"Cabell, we've got to abandon the lab," Rem said, as renewed fighting shook the city. "We can't allow your research to fall into their hands."

"I've got what I need," Cabell told him, indicating the transponder. He began to gather up data cards and chips; then, as he activated a bank of switches above the main console, two floor panels slid open, revealing a stairway that lead to the labyrinth beneath the Royal Hall. In times prior to the Great Transitions, the labyrinth had been used for religious rituals.

"What about the Pollinators?"

"Take them. We'll need them if we're ever to duplicate Zor's experiments."

Rem suppressed a curse as the Pollinators he had pried from his uniform reattached themselves, screeching their mad songs all the while. He hesitated at the top of the dark staircase.

"Do we stay down here until the Invid leave?"

Cabell laughed from the blackness deeper in. "Till they leave? You're an optimist, my boy."

From his quarters on the Invid flagship, the Regent watched the descent of the Menace with obvious delight. In a moment the hydra-ship was bellowing its arrival, three sets of jaws opening to belch forth squadrons of Enforcer troops, the invasion group's mop-up crew and police force. They rode one-pilot strike ships, golden-colored tubular-shaped crafts with hooded, open-air cockpits and globular propulsion systems. They picked up where the command ships left off, dispatching what remained of Tiresia's pitiful defenses. As scenes of death and destruction played across the viewscreen, the Regent urged his troops on, mouth approximating a smile, sensor antennae suffused with color. But follow-up transmissions from the moon's surface were enough to erase that momentary blush.

"Scanners continue to register negative on all fronts, my lord."

The ground troops had completed their sweep of Tiresia, but

the Regent still wasn't convinced. "You're certain there's nowhere else the Robotech Masters might have concealed the Flowers?"

"Yes, my lord. We would have detected even the slightest trace."

The Regent leaned back in the control couch. "Very well," he said after a brief silence. "I wash my hands of this wretched world. Do what you will, my legions."

He had expected an immediate response, an affirmation of his command, but instead the lieutenant risked a suggestion. "Pardon me, my lord, but shouldn't we delay the extermination until they've told us everything they know?"

"Good point," the Regent replied after he had gotten over the soldier's audacity. "Have your units round up any survivors at once, and prepare them for questioning. We shall see if we can't persuade them to tell us where their Masters have taken the Flowers of Life. I shall conduct the inquisition myself. Inform me when you have secured the city."

"It is done, my lord." The soldier signed off.

The city's temples became prisons. Those Tiresians who survived the enforcers' roundup, who survived the plasma hell they poured into the breached shelters, were packed shoulder to shoulder in improvised holding zones. They were a sorry lot, these bruised and battered sackcloth-clad humanoids; but even greater indignities awaited them. Some knew this and envied the clones, all dead now. For the first time in generations no clones walked Fantoma's moon. Save one, that is . . .

"Are they bringing more in?" a man asked his fellow prisoners as the temple's massive door was opened, admitting light into their midst. "These monsters mean to smother us alive."

"Quiet, they'll hear you," someone nearby said.

But the man saw no reason to remain still. "Invader, what do you want from us?" he shouted when the Regent's huge form appeared in the doorway.

The Invid looked down at them, his antennae throbbing and hood puffed up. "You know very well what I want—the Flower of Life." He reached out and plucked the man from the crowd, his four-fingered hand fully encompassing the man's head. "Tell me where it is."

"Never—"

"You fool," the Regent rasped as he lifted the man to shoulder height, applying pressure as he dangled him over the screaming prisoners. The man's hands flailed wildly against the Regent's grip. "Where are the Flowers?"

The Tiresian's responses were muffled, panicked. "We don't know—"

"Tell me, you insignificant little worm!" the Regent said, and crushed the man's skull.

"We know nothing," someone in the crowd shouted. "The Masters never told us of such things!"

"My friend, I believe you," the Regent said after a moment. He released the now lifeless body. "Enforcer," he added, turning aside, "reward these creatures for their honesty."

The lieutenant stiffened. "At once, my lord." While the Regent exited the hall, the enforcer armed a spherical device and tossed it over his shoulder before the doors shut, sealing the prisoners inside.

An old man caught the device and sadly regarded its flashing lights. "What does it mean?" someone asked in a horror-stricken voice.

The old man forced himself to swallow. "It means our doom," he said softly.

The explosion took most of the temple with it.

Returned to his flagship, the Regent met with his scientists. They were barefoot beings much like himself, although no taller than the soldiers, dressed in unadorned white trousers and sashed jackets suggestive of oriental robes. In the presence of their king, they kept their arms folded across their chests, hands tucked inside jacket cuffs.

"Tell me what you know," the Regent asked them, despondent after this brief visit to Tirol's surface. "Is this moon as worthless as it seems?"

"We have yet to find any trace of the Flower," their spokesman said in a modulated voice. "And most of the population is too old and sickly to serve as slave labor. I'm afraid there is very little of use to us here."

"Perhaps it will simply take more digging to find what we seek. Come," the Regent instructed their overseer, Obsim, "there is something I wish to discuss with you."

As they walked—through an enormous hold lined top to bottom with Shock Troopers, Pincer and Command ships, and inward toward the very heart of the flagship—the Regent explained his position.

"Just because the Regis is somewhat more *evolved* than I am, she treats me like I just crawled from the swamp. I fear she'll try to undermine my authority; that's why this mission *must* succeed."

"I understand," Obsim said.

"I'm placing you in charge of the search on Tirol. The Inorganics will be your eyes and ears. Use them to uncover the secrets of this place."

Obsim inclined his head in a bow. "If this world holds any clue to the matrix's whereabouts, I will find it."

"See that you do," the Regent added ominously.

A transparent transport tube conveyed them weightlessly to the upper levels of the ship, where the Invid brain was temporarily housed. The brain was just that, a towering fissured and convoluted organ of Protoculture instrumentality enclosed in a hundred-foot-high bubble chamber filled with clear liquid.

The Regent's attempt to emulate the Masters' Protoculture Caps: his living computer.

King and scientist stood at the chamber's pulsating, bubbled base.

"The invasion is complete," the Regent directed up to the brain. "I have brought Tirol to its knees."

A synaptic dazzle spread across the underside of the instrument brain, tickling what might have been the pituitary body, the pons varolii, and corpora albicantia. The brain spoke. "And yet your search for the matrix continues."

"For a while longer, yes," the Regent confirmed in defense of his actions, the chamber effervescence reflected in his glossy black eyes.

"Find Zor's ship and you will have what you seek. Not until then." The brain seemed to aspirate its words, sucking them in so that its speech resembled a tape played in reverse.

"You've been talking to the Regis again!" the Regent growled. "You expect me to search for a ship that could be halfway across the galaxy."

"Calculations suggest that such a journey would constitute a minor drain on existing Protoculture reserves when compared to these continued assaults against the Masters' realms."

"That may very well be," the Regent was willing to concede, "but conquest is growth. *Conquest* is evolvement!" He turned to Obsim. "My orders stand: section the brain. Transport the cutting to the surface to guide the Inorganics. Bring me what I seek and I will make you master of your own world. Fail, and I will leave you to rot on this ball of dust for an eternity."

CHAPTER FIVE

> *What with all the major players from the RDF and the Southern
> Cross in attendance [at the Hunters' wedding], one would have ex-
> pected at least one newsworthy incident; but in fact the only negative
> scene was one touched off by Lynn-Minmei's song, which provoked ex-
> clamations of disapproval from a few members of the Sisterhood Soci-
> ety. "We'll be together," the chorus went, "as married man and wife."
> Here was Lisa Hayes, first officer of the SDFs 1 and 2, admiral of the
> fleet, and commander of the entire SDF-3, suddenly reduced by
> Minmei's lyric to Rick Hunter's wife!*
>
> Footnote in *Fulcrum: Commentaries on the Second
> Robotech War* by Major Alice Harper Argus (ret.)

RICK WATCHED THE EARTH AS IT SWUNG INTO VIEW FEELING
a little like he imagined the starchild did in that old science fiction
classic. He knew it was stretching things a bit to feel that way, but
in a very real sense the future of the planet was in the hands of
a council of ordinary men and women. *Human* beings, not
superheroes or protectors, or starchildren who had already crossed
over.

Earth looked unchanged from up here, its recent scars and still-
open wounds concealed by a mantle of white swirls and dense
fronts. But Rick had walked Earth's scorched surface for six years
and knew the truth: his world would never be the same. And it
took a new kind of strength to accept this fact, to overcome the
inertia of age and surrender a host of childhood dreams.

"Penny for your thoughts," Lisa said from behind him.

He hadn't heard her enter, and swung around from the viewport
with a guilty look on his face.

"Am I interrupting something?"

He smiled at her and shook his head. "A penny, huh . . . Is that
all they're worth?"

"A nickel, then."

She came over to kiss him, and immediately sensed his remoteness. He turned back to the view as she released him. Sunlight touched the wingtips of dozens of shuttles ferrying guests up to the satellite for the wedding.

" 'The stars my destination,' " he mused. "I can't help wondering if we've made the right choice. It's like a crazy dream."

Lisa pursed her lips and nodded; Max had prepared her for Rick's mood, and she wanted him to understand that her shoulder was the softest around. Still, she didn't like his waffling and sudden indecisiveness. "It's not a crazy dream," she told him. "If we succeed, we'll be insuring a future for ourselves."

"I know, I know," he said dismissively. "I'm not as mixed up as I sound. It's just coming down so fast all of a sudden. The mission, our wedding . . ."

"We've had six years to think about this, Rick."

Rick took her in his arms; she linked her hands behind his neck. "I'm an idiot."

"Only if you're having doubts about us, Rick."

"Not now," he said, collecting on the kiss Max had interrupted earlier.

In his small cabinspace aboard the SDF-3, Jack Baker was softly thumping his head against a computer console. There was just *too much to learn*. Not only did you have to prove yourself in air combat maneuvers, you had to know all this extra *stuff*! Ordnance specifications, drill procedures, TO&E nonsense, *Zentraedi*! for crying out loud . . . If he'd known that mecha piloting was going to involve all this, he would have just gone to college or something!

The computer sounded a tone, urging him to enter his response to the question it had flashed on the screen.

"Plot a course from A to B," Jack read, "taking into consideration vector variants listed above . . ." Jack scanned the tables hopelessly and bellowed a curse at the ceiling.

At the same moment, the cabin door hissed open and a VT lieutenant walked in. He took a long analytical look at Jack, then glanced at the monitor screen.

"Troubles, Baker?" he said, barely suppressing a grin.

Jack reached over and switched off the monitor. "No, no troubles."

The pilot sniggered. "Here, this oughta cheer you up."

Jack took the envelope and opened it: inside was a handwritten note from Admiral Hunter inviting him to the wedding reception.

" 'I hope you can make it,' " Jack read aloud three times, trying to convince himself that the note was on the level.

"From Richard A. Hunter," Jack said to the pilot, gloating. "My buddy, the admiral."

The hold chosen for the wedding was on the factory's upper level, where a massive overhead viewport had recently been installed expressly for the event. The space could accommodate several thousand, but by three o'clock on the afternoon of the big day every seat was filled. Rick and Lisa had demanded a simple ceremony nonetheless, and in keeping with their wishes the hold was minimally outfitted. Two tiered banks of chairs had been set up to face a raised platform, behind which rose a screen adorned with a large stylized cross. The stage was carpeted and matched by a five-hundred-foot-long red runner that covered the center aisle. Large floral arrangements had been placed along the aisle and perimeter of the stage, and in the hold beyond sat two rows of gleaming Alpha Veritechs, red on the right, blue on the left.

The front rows had been reserved for close friends and VIPs, who sat there now in their finest gowns, pleated uniforms, service ribbons, and golden-epauletted dress blues. The hold was humming with hundreds of individual conversations, and organ music was wafting from a dozen theater speakers. Bowie and Dana, who were supposed to be waiting with the wedding party, were playing a game of tag among the rows, and Jean Grant was chasing both of them, asking her son if it was too much to request that he behave himself just this once.

"Can't you act like a grown-up!" she screamed, at the end of her rope.

"But I can't, Mom," the youngster returned to the amusement of everyone within earshot, "I've got the mind of a seven-year-old!"

Seating hadn't been prearranged along any "familial" lines, but a curious breakdown had begun from the start. On one side sat Field Marshal Anatole Leonard and most of the Southern Cross apparat—T. R. Edwards, Dr. Lazlo Zand, Senator Wyatt Moran, and dozens of lesser officers and dignitaries—and on the other, the RDF contingent: Vince and Jean Grant, Miriya Sterling, Drs. Lang and Penn and the rest of the Plenipotentiary Council, Jonathan Wolff, the Emersons, and others. In a tight-knit group behind the council members sat Exedore, and Dana Sterling's three Zentraedi godfathers, Rico, Konda, and Bron. Breetai's micronized troops were farther back, along with some of the Wolff Pack, the Skull and Ghost Squadrons.

Up front, on the sunny side, were Lynn-Minmei and her singing partner, Janice Em. Lisa's response to Minmei's offer that day in the gown shop had been straightforward: she had asked her to sing at the wedding.

Janice Em was something of an enigma to the media. Word had it that she was Dr. Lang's niece, but rumor linked her to the wizard of Robotechnology in more intimate terms. In any case, she seemed to have appeared on the scene out of nowhere two years earlier, only to become Lynn-Minmei's much needed tenor and constant companion. She was a few inches taller than Minmei, with large blue eyes set in a somewhat pale but attractive face. Her hair color changed every few months, but today it was a delicate lavender, pulled back in a rose clasp behind one ear. She had chosen a yellow spaghetti-strapped gown to complement Minmei's blue halter and offset it with a necklace of ancient Egyptian turquoise.

"Did I ever tell you about the time Rick and I got married?" Minmei was saying just now.

Janice heard the sadness in Minmei's voice, but chose to react to the statement. "Maybe you should be telling Lisa," she suggested. "Or are you saving it for when the chaplain asks if anyone can show 'just cause'?"

Minmei reacted as though she had been slapped; then she let out her breath and laughed. It was so typically *Janice* to say something like that. When the press grilled her for the scoop on Janice and Dr. Lang, Minmei would often reply, "Well, if she's not related to him, she's certainly got his sense of humor."

"It was a fantasy wedding, Janice," Minmei explained. "When we were trapped together in a hold in the SDF-1."

"And here you are trapped with him in another hold."

Minmei ignored it. "I just can't stop myself from thinking about what might have been."

" 'The saddest are: it might have been,' " Janice quoted. "But forget it, Lynn. The past is only an arrangement of photons receding at lightspeed."

"That's very romantic, Janice."

"Romance is for storytellers."

"And what about our songs—you don't call them romantic?"

Janice turned to her straight-faced. "Our songs are weapons."

Above the would-be chapel, on an observation balcony Max had christened the "ready-reaction room," Rick stood in front of a mirror trying to tie a knot. His tux was white with sky-blue lapels.

"The balloon's about to go up," Max enthused, bursting in on him.

"I can't do it, Max. You're going to have to do it for me."

It took Max a moment to understand that Rick was referring to the tie; he breathed a sigh of relief and went over to his friend. "Here, I'm an expert with these things."

Rick inclined his head to the view below while Max went to work on the tie. He felt as though his stomach had reconfigured itself to some entirely new mode.

"There," Max said. "It's a matter of finesse."

Rick thanked him. "A man couldn't have a finer best man or best friend. I mean that."

Max blushed. "Hey, I was saving that for the toast."

"Okay," Rick said in a determined voice. "Let's move." He reached up to give a final adjustment to the tie only to have it slip and loosen up.

Max looked at it and shrugged. "Well, maybe you'll start a trend."

In the end you go it alone, Rick was saying to himself ten minutes later as he turned to watch Lisa come down the aisle. Breetai, in his helmet-mask and Ironman getup walked beside her, and Rick couldn't help seeing them as some kind of whacko father-and-daughter tag-team couple. Max's daughter was one step behind them. But as Lisa drew nearer the image left him, and so did the nervousness. She had roses and baby's breath in her hair, a choker of real pearls, and she looked radiant. Behind Lisa's back, Dana made a face at ringbearer Bowie and curled her fingers at her mom.

Max and Breetai left the platform soon after, and the chaplain began to read the short service Lisa had written. A few minutes later Rick and Lisa were joining hands, exchanging rings and vows, and suddenly it was over.

Or just beginning.

They kissed and a thousand strobe lights flashed. Cheers and applause rose from the crowd above a flourish of strings and horns; and outside the viewport, teams of Veritechs completed a series of slow-mo formation flybys. A fanfare sounded as local space came to life with starbursts, roostertails, and fountains of brilliant color.

Rick and Lisa shook a thousand hands and kissed a thousand cheeks; then they danced together to Minmei and Janice's song. Spotlights found them in a hold as they moved through gentle arcs and twirls across the floor. Rick held her lovingly and caught the glint of teardrops in the corner of her eyes. He squeezed her hand and felt a wave of sadness wash through him. It was the song perhaps, a love song to be sure, but one sung with a sense of implied loss, an awareness of the ephemeral nature of all things.

> *A world turns to the edge of night,*
> *the moon and stars so very bright;*
> *your face glows in the candlelight,*
> *it's all because tonight's the night . . .*
> *Now hold my hand and take this ring*
> *as we unite in harmony.*
> *We can begin to live the dream,*
> *the dream that's meant for you and me.*
>
> *To be together,*
> *For the first time in our lives,*
> *it's us together.*
> *As married man and wife, we'll be together*
> *from now on, until death do us part;*
> *and even then, I hope our love lasts forever.*

"Oh, Rick," Lisa whispered in his ear, moved to tears by the Voice that had conquered an army. "How I wish Claudia and Roy could be here."

Rick led her through a turn that kept her back to the guests. *And Ben,* he thought. *And Gloval and Sammie and Vanessa and Kim and the countless millions sacrificed to war's insatiable thirst . . .*

> *I promise to be always true*
> *until the very end's in view.*
> *In good times and the bad times, too,*
> *I know that we can make it through.*
> *As one united we'll be strong;*
> *because together we belong.*
> *If I could sing to you a song,*
> *I'd sing of love that won't go wrong.*
>
> *If we're together,*
> *we'll make a brand new life for us together,*
> *as married man and wife, we'll stay together . . .*

Couples began to join them on the dance floor, and when the song finished, the party began in earnest. Happily, Rick found himself with some free moments while Lisa was off circulating table to table. Oddly enough, members of the Southern Cross and RDF were mingling without incident, and everywhere Rick looked he saw people having a good time. Except perhaps for Jean Grant, who was looking a little frazzled after having spent most of the ceremony chasing Bowie and Dana around.

A photographer brought Rick and Lisa back together for the cake cutting, but Rick drew the line at that, and refused to take part in any of the archaic dances the band insisted on playing. Instead, he wandered around with a smile frozen in place that misrepresented his true inner state. He had realized, as though waking from a dream, that there was only the mission now. No wedding to absorb his concerns, no higher priority than the SDF-3 and his command.

It was a frightening realization.

Elsewhere, Jonathan Wolff was zeroing in on Minmei.

"This has got to be the biggest reception I've ever played," Minmei was exclaiming to Janice as Wolff came over.

"You sang beautifully," he began on a confident note.

Minmei recognized a certain look in his eye and began to glance around for an escape route. "Uh, thank you," she said in a distracted way.

"The name's Wolff. And do you know how long I've wanted to meet you?"

Wolff! Oh, terrific, Minmei was saying to herself, when Janice suddenly blurted out, "Try humming a few bars."

Wolff's smile collapsed and he began to look back and forth between the two women uncertainly. "I, uh—"

"Oh, right, you were talking to Minmei, not me," Janice said. "Look, I'll relocate and you can give it a second try."

Minmei and Wolff watched her walk off.

"Don't mind Janice, she's got a very peculiar sense of humor."

Wolff cleared his throat meaningfully and was about to say something, but Minmei excused herself and wandered away.

"There's someone over there I want to talk to," she said over her shoulder.

Undaunted, Wolff straightened his torso harness—in case anyone was watching. He saw Minmei talking to Exedore and three other Zentraedi men. But then Wolff noticed something else: a man about his own age standing nearby was also watching Minmei. Watching her with an almost palpable intensity. Wolff repositioned himself for a better view of the stranger, a maintenance tech by the look of his uniform. But there was something disturbingly familiar about him. Wolff was sure he had never met the man, but was equally certain he had seen him somewhere. As he studied the man's tall, lean figure and bearded face, an image began to form. The beard would have to go, Wolff decided, and the hair would have to be a lot longer and darker ... But *where* had he seen him—in the Control Zone, maybe—and why did martial arts and old movies come to mind?

Karen Penn, her father, and Dr. Lang were eating slices of wedding cake when a slovenly-dressed civilian joined them at the table. Lang introduced Karen to Dr. Lazlo Zand, a cold-handed man with eyes as pupilless as Lang's own.

"Good to meet you," Karen said, forcing a smile and wondering if Zand ran on ice water.

"Charmed," he returned. "That blond hair. You remind me of little Dana."

Karen felt a chill run through her, and something seemed to make her fork leap from the plate. She bent to retrieve it, but someone had beat her to it.

"Allow me," a red-haired ensign told her. "I'm pretty handy with hardware."

"Karen, Ensign ... Baker, if I'm not mistaken," offered Lang.

She and Baker were both still holding on to the fork and locked in on each other's eyes.

"The pleasure's at least fifty percent mine." Baker smiled. He let go of the fork. "Consider me at your service, ma'am."

Karen's eyebrows went up. "I'll keep it in mind."

"And I'll keep *you* in mind," Baker said, excusing himself and moving off.

"Bit of a hotshot," commented Lang.

"That's the sort of person you'll be wasting your time with from now on," Harry Penn added gruffly.

Karen smiled. "I'm not so sure about that, Dad."

"But your father's right," Zand interjected, narrowing his eyes. "Scientists are more fun."

Karen couldn't hold the man's gaze. Absently, she tried to raise a forkful of cake to her mouth. The utensil was twisted beyond recognition.

The party was still cooking eight hours later, but Rick and Lisa were ready to call it a day. They said their farewells from the balcony overlooking the hold; and Lisa got ready to give the bridal bouquet a healthy send-off.

At the last minute, Janice had thrust Minmei into the midst of the crowd of eligible women, but had herself taken off for parts unknown. Now Minmei was pressed tight in the center of that mass of supercharged youth, surrounded by officers, enlisted-rating techs, and cadets, most of whom were younger than she was. One honey-blond-haired ensign to her left couldn't have been more than seventeen.

On the balcony, Lisa was warning that anyone who hoped to remain single should stay out of the line of fire. Then she gave the thing a windup underhanded toss, and Minmei saw it coming.

She barely had to stretch out her hands, and what was stranger still, the women around her seemed *to give it to her.*

"See you all after the honeymoon," Lisa shouted, perhaps unaware of the bouquet's landing zone.

"Yeah, in about eight hours from now!" Rick added, tugging his bride away.

Minmei lowered her face into the flowers, then gave her head a quick shake when she looked up. *It's over,* she thought, recalling a sad song she used to sing. *Now I've got to get on with my life.*

"Good-bye, Rick," she said softly. *It is you I still see . . .*

On Optera, the Invid Regis learned of her husband's imminent return and made immediate plans to leave the planet. She didn't delude herself with thoughts that this might be some trial separation. Of course, it meant abandoning all the Genesis Pit experiments in evolution she had begun here, her progress in the Great Work of transmutation and freedom from the *base condition*; but what strides could she hope to make in his presence, what chance did she have to fulfill herself? No, he had held her back long enough. Further, it meant that she would have to decide what constituted a just division of their resources. He already had the living computer; but there were other Protoculture instrumentalities that would serve her as well as the brain once had. And she would take along half her active children, but leave him that sleeping brood she had not yet seen fit to awaken.

Their home on Optera, their *castle,* was an enormous hemispherical hive, once the sacred inverted chalice of the Great Work, but now a profane *dwelling* filled with his *things*—his servants and ridiculous possessions. He had claimed to be doing all this for her sake, and for a time she could almost believe him, pitiful as his attempts were. But she soon realized that he was merely nurturing himself with these conquests and acquisitive drives.

The Regent's ignorance and stubbornness had been enough to drive her mad. He was in every way her intellectual and spiritual inferior; and yet his will was powerful, and in his presence she could feel his sick mind reaching out for her, trying to smother her. She was certain that unless she left Optera, he would one day succeed in dragging her down to his barbaric level.

But she was free of him now, her mind clear on the path she had to take. No longer subservient to his dark demands, she would strike out on her own. If the matrix was to be found, it was she who would find it. Not by sanitizing the Masters' insignificant worlds, but by sending out her sensor nebulae to the far reaches of the galaxy to locate Zor's dimensional fortress. Then she would take the Flowers back from the thieves who had stolen them; she would liberate them from their matrix prison and find a new Optera for her experiments!

In the meantime the planet Praxis would suffice.

And woe to any who would stand in her way!

CHAPTER SIX

Actually, I've been thinking about it for months now, but I just didn't know how to ask, and I wasn't sure if you would understand my decision. Could you see me walking up to Lang or one of those council stiffs and saying, "Uh, do you think I might be able to go along on the ride?" And then have to tell you that I was going to be doing a tour by myself this time. Taking my act to Tirol—you would have brained me. I hope you'll forgive me, and I want you to know that we'll pick up right where we left off when the Expeditionary mission returns. I mean, who knows, maybe I'll have added a bunch of new stuff to our repetoire. Anyway, I'm certain the experience will be good for me.

Lynn-Minmei's good-bye note to her manager,
Samson "Sharkey" O'Toole

THE ALARM WENT OFF AT 5:15 A.M. "RISE AND SHINE," SAID A synthesized, possibly female voice from the room's control deck.

Rick pulled the sheet over his head and buried his face in the pillow. He could sense Lisa stirring beside him, sitting up and stretching. In a moment he felt her warm hand on his bare back.

"Morning."

"What good is it being an admiral if you can't sleep late?" he asked without lifting his head.

She laughed and kissed the nape of his neck. "Not today, Rick."

"Then tell me why five-fifteen never seemed this early before."

"Maybe because bed never felt this good before," she purred, snuggling against his back.

Rick rolled over and put his arms around her. "That's a fact, ma'am."

The door tone sounded, ending their embrace. Rick muttered something and climbed out of bed, stepping into trousers before answering the door.

"Good morning, Mr. and Mrs. Hunter," a robo-butler announced. The thing was squat and silly-looking, with a rubber skirt that concealed its wheels; it was holding a full breakfast tray in its plasticized grips. "Dr. Lang wanted you to have breakfast in bed," the butler continued in the same monotone. "Please enter the appropriate commands."

Rick allowed the piece of Robowizardry to enter, but shut it down soon afterward, taking over the butler's program and conveying the tray to bed himself.

He bowed theatrically as Lisa sat up. "Service with a genuine smile."

They ate hurriedly and said little, famished all of a sudden. Then they showered together and began to dress. Rick watched Lisa in front of the mirror, smoothing her uniform and adjusting the collar of her jacket.

"Off to work," he said, looking himself over. "Do you realize that the next time we're in this room together, I'll be asking you what you did today, and you'll tell me that you commanded a starship across the galaxy. Does that sound a little *odd* to you?"

"Odd how?" she said, with a crooked smile.

"Odd like not something we do every day."

Lisa came over to tug his black torso harness into place. "Just think of it as a honeymoon."

Rick made a face. "I'll be sure and tell that to the Masters."

Jean Grant had cried at the wedding; those, however, had been tears of joy and remembrance, while the ones streaming down her cheeks today were anything but. Bowie was on the verge of tears himself, but was trying hard to be a *man about it*. Not that mom and son stood out any, though; the shuttle hold was filled with like scenes: tears, embraces, heartfelt exchanges. Wedding guests and family members would be shuttled home over the course of the next few days, but with the SDF-3 launch window less than four hours off, this was the crew's last chance for good-byes. Within a month, Human factory personnel would be transferred to new assignments on-planet, or at Moon Base or Liberty Space Station. No decision had been made concerning the satellite itself, but speculation was that the Zentraedi crew would remove the installation from Earth orbit—to where, no one knew.

Vince Grant bent down and put a hand on his son's head, giving it an affectionate rub. "It's going to be all right, Bowie. We'll be back before you know it."

"But why can't I come with you?" he wanted to know. "Other kids are going—kids not too much older than us," he added, including Dana. Bowie was thinking of one kid in particular he had met at the wedding, Dr. Lang's godson, Scott Bernard.

"That's true, sweetie," Jean said, smiling through her tears. "But you know you can't go." She touched Bowie's chest with her fingertips. "Your heart won't let you go."

Dana, who was bored and practicing spin kicks against a bulkhead, frowned and said, "Come on, Bowie. We don't want to go with them anyway. Space is no fun, anybody knows that."

Max and Miriya regarded each other and shook their heads as if to say, *where* did that one come from?

"Dana's right, Bowie," Jean smiled, tugging in a sob. "It isn't going to be any fun."

"Yeah, Dana, but you were in space already," Bowie pointed out. "*I've* never been there."

Rolf Emerson took advantage of a momentary silence to step forward and put his arm around the boy. "We're going to have a good time, Bowie. You wait and see."

Vince and Jean embraced Rolf. "Take good care of him for us, Rolf," Vince said with a serious look.

"You know I will."

Just then Lazlo Zand walked by headed for the shuttle ramp. Instinctively, Emerson hugged Dana and Bowie to his legs, a look in his dark eyes like he wanted to put a stake through Zand's heart.

Elsewhere in the shuttle boarding area, Janice and Minmei had received their seat assignments and were walking off in the direction of the VIP lounge. They were ordinary folk this morning, dressed in slacks and simple blouses. There was plenty of time to kill until the prep call, and Minmei wanted to get a drink.

"What's with you today?" Janice asked while they moved through the crowd. "The clouds are below us, so I don't see how you can have your head in them." When Minmei didn't respond, Janice took her by the arm. "Earth calling Lynn-Minmei. Please relay your hyperspace coordinates."

"Huh?" Minmei said, turning to her.

Janice made an exasperated sound. "What is it—Rick?"

Minmei looked away. "He always looked out for me. I just don't know if I can leave him like this."

"Look, Lynn," Janice began in a worried voice, "I don't think Lisa is going to appreciate your cutting into their—"

"If I could just see him once more. *Both* of them. Only to wish them good luck."

"You already did that—about two dozen times!"

Janice could see that she wasn't listening; Minmei's eyes were searching the bay for something. "There!" she said after a moment, pointing to a small EVA vehicle near a secondary launch port reserved for maintenance craft.

"I'm afraid to ask," Janice said warily. But Minmei was already on her way.

"Admiral on the bridge!" a young enlisted-rating tech announced, snapping to as Lisa stepped through the hatch. She couldn't help remembering Captain Gloval constantly smacking his head on a hatch very similar to this one. And indeed he would have felt right at home on the SDF-3 bridge, which for all intents and purposes was identical to that on the SDF-1. Lisa had insisted it be so, even though Lang had tried to convince her of the giant strides his teams had made since reconstructing that doomed fortress. There were redundancies and severe limitations to the design, he had argued; but in the end Lisa had her way. It was her command, and this bridge was as much a tribute as anything else. To Gloval, to Claudia and the others ... Of course, there were *some* changes that had to be allowed. The crew, for example: they were all men.

"At ease, gentlemen," Lisa told them.

She led herself through a tour of the now completed room, running her hands across the consoles and acceleration seats. Along the rear bulkhead were two four-by-four monitor screens linked to internal systemry and astrogation. Starboard was a complex laser communication and scanner console, crowned by a tall multiscreened threat board. And forward, below a wraparound forward viewport, were twin duty stations like the ones she and Claudia had manned for almost three years.

Lisa shook hands with her exec and crew—Forsythe, Blake, Colton, and the rest. It was a formality, given the fact they all knew one another, but a necessary one. She wished each man good luck, then moved toward the raised command chair that was hers alone. She took a long time settling into its padded seat, but why not: the moment was six years in the making.

A terrible memory of her last short-lived command flashed through her mind, but she willed it away. She took a lingering glance around the room and declared in a determined voice, "Mister Blake, I want systems status."

If Lisa's new space was compact, tidy, and familiar, Rick's was large and impersonal. Constructed concurrently with its Earthside counterpart, the command, control, and communications center was an enormous room more than two hundred feet square and almost half as high. A fifty-by-fifty-foot screen dominated the bulkhead opposite Rick's command balcony with its half-dozen consoles and monitors. Below, a horizontal position board was surrounded by more than twenty individual duty stations, and adjacent to this forward, a bank of as many stations tied to the central display screen. Along the port bulkhead were peripheral screens, tech stations, and banks of sophisticated instrumentality, with a great Medusa's head of cables, feeders, and power relays running floor to ceiling.

"Quite a sight, isn't it, Admiral?" said someone off to Rick's right.

Rick turned, aware that he had been staring open-mouthed at the room, and found T. R. Edwards regarding him analytically from the command balcony railing. "Uh, impressive," Rick returned, underplaying his amazement. He had of course been here often enough, but still struggled in unguarded moments with the enormity of his responsibility.

" 'Impressive.' " Edwards laughed, approaching Rick now. "Interesting choice. I think I would have said 'awesome,' or 'incredible,' or even 'magnificent.' But then, I didn't spend three years in space on the SDF-1, did I? Did you think the Grand Cannon *impressive*, Admiral? You did get to see it, didn't you?"

"Actually, I didn't, General," Rick said, wondering what Edwards was getting at. "I only saw it in ruins ... where it belonged in the first place."

Edwards grinned. "Oh, of course. I forgot. *You* were the one who rescued the Hayes woman, uh, the admiral."

Rick caught a reflection of himself in Edwards's faceplate, then looked directly into Edwards's good eye. "Something bothering you, Edwards?"

Edwards took a step back, motioning to himself with elaborate innocence. "Me? Why, no, not at all. I suppose I'm just a bit overcome by this room of ours." Edwards folded his arms and stood at the rail, a prince on a battlement. He turned to Rick and grinned. "Has anyone ever had a finer War Room, Admiral?"

Rick's lips were a thin line. "I prefer Situation Room. I thought I made that clear at the briefings."

"Forgive me," Edwards said, throwing his hands out apologetically. "*Situation* Room." He swung round to the view again. "What an impressive Situation Room."

Belowdecks, Jack Baker cursed—the RDF, his commanders, his luck, himself ultimately. *It was because of that oversight in the simulater,* he decided. *That* was what had done it, that was what had turned off Hunter and Sterling. A—and that handwritten invitation to the reception—*ha!* Richard A. Hunter indeed. Richard Anti-Baker Hunter was more like it. Or why else wouldn't he have pulled the assignment he wanted? Skull Squadron ... that was where the fun was. Even Ghost would've done the trick, although he did have some reservations about that General Edwards. But, *hell!* to be stuck with Commander Grant! Grant was all right, of course, but his unit was ground-based, for cry'nout loud. And what kind of action could a guy expect to see on land on a mission like this! And what was an *ensign* doing there? Temporary duty or not, it just didn't make any sense, no sense at all.

"I shoulda gone to college," Baker muttered as he shouldered his way through a group of enlisted ratings to report in.

Most of his Expeditionary Force mates in the mecha hangar were marveling at the two transports that were central to the battalion's strength—the GMU, and the dropship that conveyed it planetside—but to Jack the devices were just modular nightmares: overworked, underpowered, and unimportant. Veritechs were what made it happen. One pilot, one mecha. Plenty of speed, range, and firepower, and nothing to drag you down. *Nothing extraneous in mind or body,* as Jack was fond of quoting, often fantasizing about what those early Macross days must have been like, pushing the envelope and *azending! Yeah!*

These ... *monstrosities,* on the other hand, were about as sleek as an old-fashioned tank. Course there were plenty of good things inside—Hovertanks, Logans, and such—but he would have to get himself transferred to the Wolff Pack if he ever hoped to ride one of those.

Jack decided to circle the GMU and see if he couldn't find something, *something* he could get excited about. The thing was huge, maybe five hundred feet long, with eight one-hundred-foot-high globular wheels affixed to massive transaxles, banks of superspot running lights, hidden particle-projection cannon turrets, and multiple-missile launch racks. Up front were two retractable off-loading ramps, and up top, behind blast deflectors, two external command stations positioned on either side of the unit's real prize: an enormous pulse-cannon, which, like a fire engine's tower ladder, could be raised and rotated.

Jack was still appraising the unit five minutes later when Karen Penn suddenly appeared on one of the ramp walkways. The body-hugging RDF jumpsuit did things for her figure that the dress hadn't, and Jack's scowl gave way to a wide-eyed look of enchantment.

Karen saw him, smiled, and waved. When she was within earshot she called brightly, "Hey, Baker, what are you doing here?"

Jack smiled back and cupped his hands to his mouth. "Luck of the draw!"

"I am beside myself," Dr. Lang confided to Exedore as the two men completed their prelaunch inspection of the fortress's spacefold generators and Reflex drives. They were the same ones that had once powered Breetai's flagship, but Lang's Robotechnicians had spiffed them up a bit. It had long been the professor's wish to cannibalize one of the spacefold generators just to take a peek at its Protoculture core, but he knew this would have to wait till a time when fold systemry could be spared. Presently, however, Protoculture remained the most precious substance in the universe, and Lang's teams had yet to discover the philosophers' stone that would enable them to create it. So chips and sealed generators were transferred intact from ship to ship or mecha to mecha. But even with all the energy cells the RDF had managed to salvage from the Zentraedi warships that had crashed on Earth, the supply was hardly inexhaustible.

How had Zor created the stuff? Lang was forever asking himself. He understood that it had something to do with the Flowers Exedore spoke of—the Flowers of Life. But Lang had never seen one, and how in any case had Zor gone from Flower to Protoculture? It was one of the many questions he hoped the Masters would answer once peace negotiations were out of the way. And then there were all the unresolved puzzles centering around Zor himself. But for the time being Lang was content with his own minor triumphs.

"It's more than I ever hoped for."

Exedore might have recognized the look on Lang's face as one often observed on the faces of children on Christmas mornings. The Zentraedi ambassador picked up on Lang's tone of anticipation as well.

"Well, can you imagine how I must feel, Doctor, to be going home after so many years?"

Lang looked at Exedore as though noticing something for the first time. "Yes, yes, I see what you mean, my friend. And in a strange way I, too, feel as if I'm returning home."

Exedore thought he grasped Lang's meaning, and shook his head. "No, Doctor. You will see that Tirol is not for you. Earth is your home, and ever shall be."

"Perhaps," Lang said with a glint in his eye. "But we have seen more radical reshapings in the past few years, have we not?"

Exedore was about to reply when a tech interrupted the conversation to inform Lang that all systems were go and the bridge was awaiting confirmation.

"Well, give the admiral what she wants, Mr. Price," Lang declared. "The moment has arrived."

A murmur of excitement swept through the crowds waiting in the shuttle boarding area. Suddenly people were moving in haste toward the viewports and breaking into spontaneous applause.

"Now's our chance!" Minmei said over her shoulder to Janice.

From the forward seat of the EVA craft where she and Janice had been hiding for the past few hours, Minmei could just discern the rounded, main-gun booms of the SDF-3 nosing into view from the satellite's null-gee construction hold.

"Now, Janice, now!" Minmei urged.

Janice bit her lower lip and began to activate a series of switches across the craft's instrument panel. Displays came to life one by one, suffusing the small cockpit with whirring sounds and comforting amber light. Abruptly, the small ship lurched forward as a conveyor carried it toward the launch bay.

Minmei searched for some indication that they had been spotted, but it appeared that even the techs' attention had been diverted by the unannounced emergence of the fortress. And before she could complete the silent prayer she had begun, the craft was launched.

Minmei had nothing but confidence in her partner's ability to pilot the craft and position it in close proximity to the SDF-3; she had seen Janice do far more amazing things during their two-year friendship.

She frequently recalled the first time Dr. Lang had introduced her to Janice. He talked about Janice as though she were God's gift to the world; and later on Minmei understood that Lang's hyperboles were not so far off the mark. Minmei felt that Janice was somewhat cool and remote—the only man in her life was that Senator Moran, and it seemed a strange sort of relationship—but Janice could fly, fight, absorb and retain incredible amounts of information, and speak a dozen languages, including Zentraedi. Her considerable talents notwithstanding, however, it was Janice's *voice* that Lang had raved about; about how she and Minmei could complement each other in the most perfect way imaginable. And not solely for purposes of entertainment. What Minmei's voice had achieved with the Zentraedi, Minmei and Janice's combined voice could replicate tenfold. And should the Robotech Masters decide to send a new wave of bio-engineered warriors to

Earth in the SDF-3's absence, that *defensive harmony* might very well prove the planet's saving grace.

Our songs are weapons, Minmei heard Janice saying.

Minmei was no stranger to grandiose dreams or grandiose purpose, and she had readily agreed to keep Lang's secret. Janice, too, agreed, and the two women had become close friends as well as partners. But after two years of that, dreams were suddenly a new priority, and Lang's concerns seemed paranoid now. So as the EVA craft began to approach the slow-moving fortress, Minmei told Janice to hold to a parallel course.

"But we can't remain here, Lynn. The ship is going to fold in a matter of minutes."

"Just do it for me, please, Janice."

Janice was quiet for a moment; then she said, "You have no plans of returning to the satellite, do you?"

Minmei swung around in her seat and reached for her friend's hand. "Are you with me?"

Janice saw the commingling of fear and desperation in Minmei's blue eyes, and smiled. "Do I have a choice?"

Minmei looked down on Earth's oceans and clouds, and completed her prayer.

"Engineering confirms attainment lunar orbit," Blake updated. "We are go for launch, Admiral."

Lisa turned in her chair to study a peripheral monitor screen. There was a steady bass rumbling through the entire ship that made it difficult to hear statements voiced on the bridge. But at the same time Lisa was aware of the background blare of klaxons and alert sirens ordering all hands to their launch stations.

"Mr. Colton, start your count," Lisa ordered, hands tight on the command chair's armrests.

"T-minus-ten and counting," Colton shouted above the roar and shudder.

"Nine . . ."

"Admiral!" Blake said suddenly. "I'm showing an unidentified radar blip well inside the fold zone!"

"Five, four . . ."

Lisa craned her neck around. "What is it?!"

"Ship, sir—EVA craft!"

"Two, one . . ."

"Too late!"

"Zero!"

"Execute!" Lisa shouted.

And the mile-long ship jumped.

CHAPTER
SEVEN

*While the life expectancy of a standard Zentraedi mecha pilot has
been determined by the Robotech Masters at three years, the life expectancy of a comparable Invid pilot was never even addressed. In effect, all Invid troops (save the sexually-differentiated scientists) could
be activated and deactivated at a moment's notice—initially by the
Regis only, and later by the living computers the Queen Mother helped
create to satisfy her husband's wounded pride (after the "affair" with
Zor)... A self-generated variety of Protoculture was essential to mecha
operation, in the form of a viscous green fluid that filled the cockpit
space. It was through this nutrient bath (liquified fruits from the ma-
ture Optera plants) that the living computers, or "brains," communicated with the ranks.*

Selig Kahler, *The Tirolian Campaign*

"**Y**ES, MY BOY, I'VE BEEN MEANING TO SHOW YOU THIS
place for quite a long time," Cabell confessed, gesturing to the
wonders of the subterranean chamber. The scientist and his apprentice were deep in the labyrinth beneath Tiresia's pyramidal
Royal Hall. "A pity it has to be under these circumstances."

It was a laboratory and monitoring facility the likes of which
Rem had never seen. There were wall-to-wall consoles and
screens, networktops piled high with data cards and ancient print
documents, and dozens of unidentifiable tools and devices. In the
glow of the room's archaic illumination panels, the place had a
dusty, unused look.

"And this was really *his* study?" Rem said in disbelief.

Cabell nodded absently, his thoughts on the Pollinators and
what could be done with them now. The shaggy creatures had become quiet and docile all of a sudden, huddling together in a tight
group in one corner of the room. It was as if they had instinctively
located some sort of power spot. Cabell heard Rem gasp; the
youth was staring transfixed at a holo-image of Zor he had man-

aged to conjure up from one of the networks, the only such image left on Tirol.

"But ... but this is *impossible*," Rem exclaimed. "We're identical!"

Cabell swallowed and found his voice. "Well, there's some resemblance, perhaps," he said, downplaying the likeness. "Something about the eyes and mouth ... But switch that thing off, boy, we've got work to do."

Mystified, Rem did so, and began to clear a workspace on one of the countertops, while Cabell went around the room activating terminals and bringing some of the screens to life. The old man knew that he could communicate directly with the Elders from here, but there was no need for that yet. Instead, he set about busying himself with the transponder, and within an hour he had the data he needed to pinpoint the source of its power.

"As I thought," Cabell mused, as schematics scrolled across a screen. "They are almost directly above us in the Royal Hall. Apparently they've brought some sort of command center down from the fleet ships. Strange, though ... the emanations are closer to organic than computer-generated."

"What does it mean?" Rem asked over Cabell's shoulder.

"That we now know where we must direct our strike." He had more to add, but autoactivation sounds had suddenly begun to fill the lab, drawing his attention to a screen off to his left, linked, Cabell realized, to one of Tirol's few remaining orbital scanners. And shortly, as a deepspace image formed on the screen, it was Cabell's turn to gasp.

"Oh, my boy, tell me I'm not seeing things!"

"It's a starship," Rem said, peering at the screen. "But it's not Invid, is it?"

Cabell had his palms pressed to his face in amazement. "Far from it, Rem, far from it ... Don't you see?—it's *his* ship, Zor's!"

"But how, Cabell?"

Cabell shot to his feet. "The Zentraedi! They've recaptured it and returned." He put his hands on Rem's shoulders. "We're saved, my boy. Tirol is saved!"

But the moon's orbital watchdogs weren't the only scanners to have picked up on the ship. Inside the Royal Hall—converted by Enforcer units to an Invid headquarters—the slice of brain Obsim had transported to Tirol's surface began to speak.

"Intruder alert," the synthesized voice announced matter-of-factly. "An unidentified ship has just entered the Valivarre system on a course heading for Tirol. Estimated arrival time: one period."

The cerebral scion approximated the appearance of the Regent's living computer, and floated in a tall, clear fluid bubble chamber that was set into an hourglass-shaped base.

"Identify and advise," Obsim ordered.

"Searching . . ."

The Invid scientist turned his attention to a spherical, geodesiclike communicator, waiting for an image to form.

"Insufficient data for unequivocal identification."

"Compare and approximate."

"*Quiltra Quelamitzs,*" the computer responded a moment later. A deepspace view of the approaching ship appeared in the sphere, and alongside it the various memory profiles the brain had employed in its search.

"Identify."

"Zentraedi battlecruiser."

Obsim's snout sensors twitched and blanched. *The Zentraedi,* he thought, *after all these generations, returned to their home system.* He could only hope they were an advance group for the Masters themselves, for that would mean a return of the Flower, the return of hope . . .

He instructed the computer to alert all troopship commanders immediately. "Stand by to assault."

Much as spacefold was a warping of the continuum, it was a mind-bending experience as well. The world was filled with a thousand voices speaking at once, and dreamtime images of externalized selves loosed to live out an array of parallel moments, each as real and tangible as the next, each receding as swiftly as it was given birth. The stars would shimmer, fade, and emerge reassembled. Light and shadow reversed. Space was an argent sea or sky shot through with an infinite number of black holes, smeared with smoky nebulae.

This marked Lisa's sixth jump, but familiarity did nothing to lessen the impact of hyperspace travel, the SDF-3's tunnel in the sky. It felt as though she had awakened not on the other side of the galaxy but on the other side of a dream, somehow exchanged places with her nighttime self, so that it was her *doppelgänger* who sat in the command chair now. Voices from the bridge crew surfaced slowly, muffled and unreal, as if from a great depth.

". . . reports entry to Valivarre system."

"Systems status," she said weakly and by rote. "Secure from launch stations."

Some of the techs came to even more slowly than she did, bending to their tasks as though exhausted.

"All systems check out, Admiral. Dr. Lang is on-screen."

Lisa glanced up at the monitor just as the doctor was offering his congratulations. "I've taken the liberty of ordering course and velocity corrections. Hope you don't mind, Lisa."

Lang seemed unfazed by their transit through hyperspace; it was one of the strange things about a jump: like altitude sickness, there was no way to predict who would and would not suffer side effects. She was certain that a number of the crew were already being removed to sick bay. Surprised at her own state of well-being, Lisa shook her head and smiled. "We've made it, then, we've actually made it?"

"See for yourself," Lang said.

Lisa swung to study a screen, and there it was: a magnified crescent of the ringed and marbled jadelike giant, with its distant primary peeking into view—a magnesium-white jewel set on the planet's rim. A schematic of the system began to take shape, graphics highlighting one of Fantoma's dozen moons and enlarging it, as analytical readouts scrolled across an ancillary screen.

"Tirol," said Lisa. The moon was closing on Fantoma's darkside. Then, with a sinking feeling, she recalled the EVA blip.

"Still with us," a tech reported in an anxious tone. "But we're leaving it farther behind every second."

"Dr. Lang," Lisa started to say. But all at once alert signals were flashing all over the bridge.

"Picking up multiple radar signals, sir. Approach vectors coming in . . ."

Lisa's eyes went wide. "Sound general quarters. Go to high alert and open up the com net. And get me Admiral Hunter—*immediately*."

"We've got them," Rick was saying a moment later from a screen.

"Do we have a signature?" Lisa asked the threat-board tech. Her throat was dry, her voice a rasp.

"Negative, sir. An unknown quantity."

Lisa stood up and moved to the visor viewport. "I want visuals as soon as possible, and get Exedore and Breetai up here on the double!"

"Well?" Lisa said from the command chair, tapping her foot impatiently. Klaxons squawked as the ship went on alert. She had not forgotten about the EVA craft, but there were new priorities now.

Exedore turned to look at her. "These are not Tirolian ships, Admiral, I can assure you."

Breetai and Rick were with him, all three men grouped behind the tech seated at the threat board. "Enhancements coming in now, Lisa," Rick said without turning around.

The computer drew several clamlike shapes on the screen, pinpointing hot areas.

Breetai straightened up and grunted; all eyes on the bridge swung to fix on him. "Invid troop carriers," he announced angrily.

"Invid? But what—"

"Could they have formed some sort of alliance with the Masters?" Lisa thought to ask.

"That is very unlikely, Admiral," Exedore answered her.

Rick spoke to Lang, who was still on-screen. "We've got company, Doctor."

"The ship must be protected."

"Sir!" a tech shouted. "I'm showing multiple paint throughout the field!"

Rick and the others saw that the clam-ships had opened, yawned, spilling forth an enormous number of small strike mecha. Pincer Ships, Breetai called them.

"I want the Skull scrambled."

"Ghost Squadron is already out, sir," Blake reported from his duty station.

"What!"

The threat board showed two clusters of blips moving toward each other. Rick slapped his hand down on the Situation Room com stud, demanding to know who ordered the Veritechs out.

"General Edwards," came the reply.

"Edwards!" Rick seethed.

Blake tapped in a rapid sequence of requests. "Sir. Ghost Squadron reports they're moving in to engage."

Cabell was puzzled. It was not Zor's ship after all, but some sort of facsimile. Worse, the Invid had sent its small fleet of troop carriers against it, and their Pincer Ships were already engaging mecha from the Zentraedi ship out near Fantoma's rings. Initially, Cabell wanted to convince himself that the Zentraedi had for some reason returned in Micronized form; but he now dismissed this as wishful thinking. It was more likely that the starship had been taken by force, and he was willing to guess just who these new invaders were. Presently, data from one of the network computers confirmed his guess.

He had pulled up trans-signals received by the Masters shortly after the destruction of Reno's fleet and the capture of the factory satellite. Among the debris that littered a vast area of space some eighty light-years out from Tirol were mecha almost identical to those the would-be Zentraedi had sent against the Invid. The invaders, then, would have to be the "Micronians" whose world the Masters had gone off to conquer, the same humanoids who had been the recipients of Zor's fortress, and with it the Protoculture matrix.

And while Invid and Terrans formed up to annihilate each other, a small ship was leaving Tirolspace unobserved. Watching the ship's trail disappear on his monitor screen, Cabell smiled to himself. It was the Elders, fooled like himself perhaps, into believing that the Zentraedi had returned. *For their skins!* Cabell laughed to himself.

So Tirol was suddenly Masterless. Cabell considered the battle raging out by the giant's ring-plane, and wondered aloud if Tirol was about to change hands yet again.

In the Royal Hall Invid headquarters, Obsim was thinking along similar lines. These starship troopers were not Zentraedi, but some life-form similar in makeup and physiology to the population of Tirol or Praxis. And yet they were not Tirolians either. By monitoring the transmissions the invaders were radioing to their mecha pilots, the brain had discovered that the language was not that of the Masters.

"Sample and analyze," Obsim commanded.

It was a primitive, strictly vocal tongue; and the computer easily mastered it in a matter of minutes, along with the simple combat code the invaders were using.

Obsim studied the communications sphere with interest. The battle was not going well for his Pincer units; whatever the invaders lacked in the way of intellect and sophistication, they possessed powerful weapons and mecha more maneuverable than any Obsim had ever seen. A world of such beings would not have been conquered as readily as Spheris, Praxis, and Karbarra had. But firepower wasn't war's only prerequisite; there had to be a guiding intelligence. And of this the invaders were in short supply.

"Computer," said Obsim. "Send the mecha commanders new dictates in their own code. Order them to pursue our troops no matter what."

The starship itself was hiding inside Fantoma's ringplane; but if it could be lured out for only a moment, the troop carriers might have a clear shot at it.

Obsim turned to face the brain. "Computer. Locate the starship's drives and relay relevant data to troopship commanders." He contemplated this strategy for a moment, hands deep within the sleeves of his robe. "And prepare to advise the Regent of our situation."

The tac net was a symphony of voices, shrill and panicked, punctuated by bursts of sibilant static and the short-lived sound of muffled roars.

"Talk to me, Ghost Leader," a pilot said.

"Contact, fifty right, medium range . . ."

"Roger, got 'im."

"Ghost Three, Ghost Three, bogie inbound, heading zero-seven-niner . . ."

"Ghost Six, you've got half-a-dozen on your tail. Go to Battloid, Moonlighter!"

"Can't get—"

". . ."

Rick cursed and went on the com net. "Ghost Leader, do you require backup? Repeat, do you require backup? Over."

"Sir," the pilot replied an instant later. "We're holding our own out here, but it's a world of shi—er, pain, sir!"

"Can you ascertain enemy's weapons systems? Over."

Static erased the pilot's first few words. ". . . and some sort of plasma cannons, sir. It's like they're throwing . . . -ing energy *Frisbees* or something! But the mecha are slow—ugly as sin, but slow."

Rick raised his eyes to the ceiling of the bridge. *I should be out there with them!* Breetai and Exedore had returned to their stations elsewhere in the ship; and by all rights Rick should have been back in the Tactical Information Center already, but everything was happening so damned fast he didn't dare risk pulling himself away from a screen even for a minute. Lisa had ordered the SDF-3 to Fantoma's brightside, where it was holding now.

"Has anyone located General Edwards yet?" Rick shouted into a mike.

"He's on his way up to the Sit Room, sir," someone replied.

Rick shook his head, feeling a rage mount within him. Lisa turned to watch him. "Admiral, you better get going. We can manage up here."

Rick looked over at her, his lips tight, and nodded.

"Sirs, enemy are in retreat."

Rick watched the board. "Thank God—"

"Ghost is in pursuit."

Rick blanched.

"Contact them! Who ordered pursuit—Edwards?!"

Blake busied himself at the console. "Negative, sir. We, we don't know who gave the order, sir."

"Direct the Skull to go—*now*!" Rick raced from the bridge.

Lisa regarded Fantoma's ring-plane and remembered a similar situation in Saturn's rings. "Activate ECM," she ordered a moment later. "We're bringing the ship up. And, dammit, send someone out to rescue that EVA craft!"

Jonathan Wolff left the SDF-3 launch bay right behind the last of Max Sterling's Skull Squadron fighters. He was in a Logan Veritech, a reconfigurable mecha that would one day become the mainstay of the Southern Cross's Tactical Armored Space Corps. The Logan was often jokingly referred to as a "rowboat with wings" because of the bow-shaped design of its radome and the mecha's overall squatness. But if it was somewhat less orthodox-looking than the Alpha, the Logan was certainly as mean and maneuverable—and much more versatile—than the VT. In addition, the mecha's upscaled cockpit could seat two, three in a pinch.

Scanners had indicated there were two people aboard the hapless EVA craft that had been caught up in the SDF-3's fold. And they were alive, though more than likely unconscious or worse. There had been no response to the fortress's attempts to communicate with the craft.

Empowering the fortress's shields had made use of the tractor somewhat iffy, so Wolff had volunteered for the assignment, itching to get out there anyway, even if it meant on a rescue op. Now suddenly in the midst of it, he wasn't so sure. Local space was lit up with spherical orange bursts and crisscrossed with blue laserfire and plasma discs of blinding light. Zentraedi Battlepods were one thing, but the ships the VTs found themselves up against looked like they had walked out of some ancient horror movie, and it was easy to believe that the crablike mecha actually *were* the XTs themselves. But Breetai and Exedore had said otherwise in their prelaunch briefings; inside each ship was a being that could prove swift and deadly in combat.

And that was indeed the case, as evidenced by the slowmo dogfights in progress all around Wolff. Skull's VTs were battling their way through the remnants of the Invid's original strike force in an effort to catch up with the Ghost Squadron, who'd been ordered off in pursuit of the main group. Wolff watched amazed as Battloids and Pincer Ships swapped volleys, blew one another to fiery bits, and sometimes wrestled hand-to-pincers, battering each other with depleted cannons. Wolff watched Captain Miriya Sterling's red Veritech engage and destroy three Invid ships with perfectly placed Hammerhead missiles. Max, too, seemed to be having a field day; but the numbers were tipped in the enemy's favor, and Wolff wondered how long Skull would be able to hold out.

He was closing fast on the EVA craft now, and thought he could discern movement in the rear seat of the cockpit. But as the Logan drew nearer, he could see that both pilots were either unconscious or dead. Reconfiguring now, he imaged the Battloid to take hold of the small ship and propel it back toward Fantoma's brightside and the SDF-3. But just then he received a command over the net to steer clear, and a moment later the fortress emerged from the ring-plane and loomed into view. Inexplicably, the Skull Squadron was falling away toward Fantoma's opaline surface, leaving the ship open to frontal assaults by the Pincer units, but in a moment those ships were a mere memory, disintegrated in a cone of fire spewed from the SDF-3's main gun.

Harsh static crackled through Wolff's helmet pickups as he turned his face from the brilliance of the blast. But when he looked again, two clam-shaped transports had materialized out of nowhere in the fortress's wake.

Reflexively, Wolff went on the com net to shout a warning to the bridge. Secondary batteries commenced firing while the fortress struggled to bring itself around, but by then it was too late. Wolff saw the SDF-3 sustain half-a-dozen solid hits, before return fire sanitized the field.

A score of lifeless men and women lay sprawled across the floor of the fortress's engineering hold. Damage-control crews were rushing about, slipping in puddles of blood and cooling fluids, trying to bring dozens of electrical fires under control. A portion of the ruptured hull had already self-sealed, but other areas ruined beyond repair had to be evacuated and closed off by pocket bulkheads.

Lang and Exedore ran through smoke and chaos toward the fold-generator chamber, arriving in time to see one of the ruptured mechanisms vanish into thin air.

Lang tried to shout something to his team members above the roar of exhaust fans, but everyone had been nearly deafened by the initial blasts.

Just then a second explosion threw Lang and Exedore to the floor, as some sort of black, wraithlike images formed from smoke and fire and took shape in the hold, only to disappear from view an instant later.

Lang's nostrils stung from the smoke of insulation fires and molten metals. He got to his feet and raced back into the chamber, throwing switches and crossovers at each station. By the time Exedore got to him, Lang was a quivering, burned, and bloodied mess.

"They knew j-just where to h-hit us," he stammered, pupilless irises aflame. "We're stranded, we're *stranded* here!"

CHAPTER EIGHT

I'm of the opinion that in this instance Lang (with regard to Janice) was emulating the Masters—or more accurately perhaps, serving Protoculture's darker side. Zand, and anyone else who conspired to control, was serving this purpose as well. Protoculture's bright side had yet to reveal itself, for what had it wrought so far but conquest, war, and death? Indeed, it could be argued that Protoculture's only bright moment came at the end, when the Regis wed herself to it and was transformed.

Mingtao, *Protoculture: Journey Beyond Mecha*

O BSIM WAS PENSIVE AS HE REGARDED THE COMMUNICATOR sphere; four troop carriers and countless Pincer Ships had been lost, but he had achieved a good portion of his purpose: the invaders' starship was crippled if not destroyed. It had come into full view now from Fantoma's brightside, and was holding in orbit near the giant's outer rings. ECM had foiled Obsim's attempt to reach the Regent, but a messenger ship had since been dispatched and reinforcements were assured.

But what now? the Invid scientist asked himself. Surely the outsiders recognized that Tirol would soon be entering Fantoma's shadow. Would they then move the ship into orbit, risk some sort of landing perhaps?

Well, no matter, Obsim decided. The command ships would be there to greet them.

On the fortress, meanwhile, a mood of apprehension prevailed while the RDF licked its wounds and counted the dead. Unprovoked attack was one of many scenarios the crew had prepared for, but the Invid hadn't been seriously considered. Lang, for one, had thought that the Zentraedi had all but eliminated the race; and while he remembered the image of an Invid ship included in Zor's SDF-1 "greetings message," neither Exedore nor Breetai had been forthcoming in supplying him with any additional information. Moreover, the arrival of the "Visitor," and the subsequent Robotech War, had left the Earth Forces with the mistaken notion that *humankind* dominated the galaxy. Although the Zentraedi were giant, biogenetic clones, they were still in some way under-standable and *acceptable*. But not so this new enemy wave. There had of course been prelaunch briefings that addressed the alien is-sue, but the Zentraedi's descriptions of the Invid, the Karbarrans, the Spherisians, might as well have been campfire ghost stories or horror-movie tribute—*War With the Newts*! So as rumors began to spread through the ship, everyone was left asking themselves why the mission had once seemed a sensible idea. And Lang had yet to tell everyone the really bad news.

In an effort to curtail some of the loose talk, Rick called for a immediate debriefing following the return of Ghost and Skull squadrons. Everything would have to be kept secret until all the facts were known.

He was pacing back and forth in one of the ship's conference rooms now, while the general staff and squadron commanders seated themselves at the U-shaped arrangement of tables. Livid, he turned to Edwards first, calling for an explanation of the man's motives in superseding command's orders regarding engagement. Edwards listened attentively while Rick laid it out, allowing a pregnant silence to fill the room before responding.

"The SDF-3 was under attack, Admiral. It was simply a matter of protecting the ship."

Rick narrowed his eyes. "And suppose those ships had come in peace, General—what then?"

Edwards snorted, in no mood to be censured. "They didn't come in peace."

"You risked the lives of your men. We had no idea what we were going to face out there."

Edwards looked across the table to the Ghost Squadron com-manders. "My men did their job. The enemy was destroyed."

Rick made a gesture of annoyance, and turned to the VT pilots. "I want to know why your teams gave pursuit. Who gave those orders?"

Max stood up. "Admiral, we received orders to pursue."

"With the proper authentication codes?"

"Affirmative, sir," half-a-dozen voices murmured at once.

Rick knew that he could do little more than demand a report, because Edwards could only be censured by the Council itself. Where Rick and Lisa would ordinarily have had complete run of the ship, the dictates of the Plenipotentiary Council had forced them to share their command with Edwards and other representatives of the Army of the Southern Cross apparat. This was the arrangement that had been made to satisfy the demands of Field Marshal Anatole Leonard's burgeoning power base in Monument City. Edwards's presence, in fact, was an accommodation of sorts, an appeasement undertaken to keep the RDF and Southern Cross from further rivalries—the Expeditionary Mission's peace treaty with itself. The last thing anyone wanted was to have the SDF-3 return to a factioned and feudal Earth. Moreover, Edwards was the xenophobic voice of those Council members (Senators Longchamps and Stinson, chiefly, the old guard of the UEG) who still felt that Captain Gloval and the SDF-1 command had been too soft with the Zentraedi during the Robotech war—granting asylum for the enemy's Micronized spies and suing for peace with Commander Breetai. And as long as Edwards continued to enjoy support with the Council, Rick's hands were tied. It had been like this between generals and governments throughout history, he reminded himself, and it remained one of the key factors that contributed to his growing discontent.

Rick glanced at Edwards. "I want full reports on my desk by fourteen-hundred hours. Is that understood?"

Again, Rick received eager nods, and talk switched to the issue of secrecy. Rick was listening to descriptions of the mecha the VTs had confronted, when a lieutenant jg entered with a personal message. It was from Lang: the EVA craft had been taken aboard and its passengers moved to sick bay.

Rick went pale as he read the names.

It was a terrible dream: there she was on stage all set to perform, and the lyrics just wouldn't come. And it seemed the hall was in space with moons and planets visible in the darkness where an audience should have been sitting. Then Rick was, what?—God! he was coming down the aisle with Lisa on his arm . . .

Minmei's eyes focused on Rick's face as she came around. She was in bed and he was leaning over her with a concerned look. She gave him a weak smile and hooked her arms around his neck.

"Oh, Rick, what a dream I had—"

"Minmei, are you all right?" He had unfastened her embrace and was holding her hands.

"Well, yeah," she began. "Except for that . . ." Then it hit her like a brilliant flash.

Rick saw the shock of recognition in her eyes and tried to calm her. "You're aboard the SDF-3. You're safe, now, and the doctors say you'll be fine."

"Where's Janice, Rick!"

"She's right next door." Rick motioned. "And she's okay. Dr. Lang is with her."

Minmei buried her face in her hands and cried, Rick's hand caressing her back. "Why did you do it, Minmei?" he asked after a moment.

She looked up and wiped the tears away. "Rick, I just couldn't let everyone leave. You're all so important to me. Do you understand?"

"You could have been killed, do you understand that?"

She nodded. "Thank you for saving me."

Rick cleared his throat. "Well, actually you'll have to thank Colonel Wolff for that. But listen, you better get some rest now. There's a lot I have to tell you, but it'll keep."

"Thank you, Rick."

"Go to sleep now," he said, standing up and tucking her in.

She was out even before Rick left the room, so she didn't see the orderly who entered, or the astonished look Rick gave the bearded man. It was a look of recognition but one tinged with enough disbelief to render the first impression false. But as the orderly studied Minmei's sleeping form, he recalled how *he* had once protected her from giants and worse.

In the room adjacent to Minmei's, Dr. Lang was staring into Janice's blue eyes. Her skills had certainly saved Minmei's life, but why had Janice listened to Minmei in the first place? Their little stunt had destroyed all the plans he had taken such pains to set in motion; and coming as it did on the heels of the damage done to the fold generators and what that meant for the Expeditionary mission, it was almost more than he could bear.

"Janice," he said evenly. "Retinal scan."

Janice's eyes took on an inner glow as she returned Lang's all but forehead-to-forehead stare. But in a moment the glow was gone; her eyes and face were lifeless, and her skin seemed to lose color and tautness.

"Yes, Dr. Lang. Your request."

"I want you to replay the events prior to SDF-3's departure, Janice. I want to understand the logic of your decisions. Is that clear?"

"Yes, Dr. Lang," Janice repeated in the same dull monotone.

Lang laughed to himself as he listened. He had foreseen the *possibility* of such an occurrence, but to be faced with the reality of that now ... That part of the android that was its artificial intelligence had actually developed an attachment, a *fondness* for Lynn-Minmei! The specter of this had been raised and discussed repeatedly by the Tokyo Center's team, but in the end Lang had rejected the safeguards they had urged him to install, and suddenly he was face-to-face with the results of that uninformed decision.

The android had taken more than a decade of intensive work; but when Janice took her first steps, all those hours and all that secrecy seemed justified. It was shortly after the destruction of New Macross that Lang had begun to think about teaming the android with Lynn-Minmei, and the singer had easily been convinced of just how important such a partnership might prove to Earth's safety. But defensive harmonies aside, Lang had chosen Minmei because of her undenied access to political sanctuaries Lang himself could not enter, the Southern Cross apparat especially. So Lang was understandably thrilled to learn that Senator Moran had taken an interest in Janice, the young sensation some people were calling his niece, some his mistress. But what good was his spy to him now, stranded as she was along with the rest of them light-years from Earth.

Lang uttered a resigned sigh as he reached behind Janice's neck to remove the dermal plug concealed by her fall of thick hair. The plug covered an access port Lang could tap for high-speed information transference. He had the portable transfer tube prepared, and was ready to jack in. But just then Rick Hunter came through the door.

Undetected, Lang dropped the tube behind the bed and voiced a hushed command to Janice. Hunter was staring at him when he turned from his patient.

"Uh, sorry, Doc, guess I should've knocked first," Rick said uneasily.

"Nonsense," Lang told him, getting to his feet.

Rick looked back and forth between Lang and Janice; he didn't know Minmei's partner all that well, but he was aware of the scuttlebutt that linked her to Lang. Janice was offering him a pale smile now.

"How are you feeling?" he asked.

"Homesick," Janice said. "And less than shipshape."

"Well I don't know what we're going to do about your homesickness, but I'm sure some rest will help the way you're feeling."

"That's good advice," Lang seconded. He switched off the lights as he and Rick left the room.

"She's ... sweet," Rick said, uncomfortable with the silence the two men fell into.

At the elevator, Jonathan Wolff stepped out from the car, managing a salute despite the two bouquets of flowers he carried. "Thought I'd try and cheer up our new passengers," he said by way of explanation.

Rick and Lang traded knowing looks.

"Guess every SDF's meant to carry civilians, huh, Admiral."

"Does seem that way, Colonel," Rick said. "Minmei's in room eleven," he added, motioning with his chin.

Wolff moved off down the hall, and Rick and Lang entered the elevator. "I think our dapper young colonel has more than good cheer on his mind," Lang opined.

Rick felt his jaw. "Doesn't he have a wife and coupla kids back home?"

"Ask him."

Rick shrugged. "It's none of my business."

A second debriefing was held later that afternoon. In addition to those who had attended the earlier session were Commander Vince Grant, Brigadier General Reinhardt, Wolff, Lang, Breetai, and Exedore, along with various squadron and company commanders. Photo images and schematics filled the room's numerous screens this time; the crew was still on standby alert, and the ship would shortly reposition itself for an orbital shift.

Lang at last revealed that two of the spacefold generators had been destroyed during the assault. He explained that a fold might still be possible, but there was no guarantee the fortress would emerge in Earthspace, and anything short of that was unacceptable. The twelve-member Plenipotentiary Council had voted to withhold this information from the crew. But it was therefore imperative that the Masters be contacted as soon as possible.

"The Invid presence might prove a blessing in disguise for us," Lang continued. "Because if the Masters are indeed being held captive on Tirol, the Expeditionary mission could well be their salvation."

Lang called up an image of the Fantoma system on the main screen. Like Uranus, the planet had been tipped on its side eons ago. It had an extensive ring system held in check by shepherd satellites, and numerous moons of varied size and surface and atmosphere. Tirol was the third moon, somewhat smaller than Earth, and the only one with an hospitable atmosphere. It was, however, a somewhat desolate world, barren, with much of its topography muted by volcanic flows. Just why the Masters had chosen to remain there with half the galaxy at their disposal was a question Lang had recently added to his long list. In a matter of days the moon would enter Fantoma's shadow, which could complicate things considerably.

"Surface scans and intensity traces have given us the picture of an almost deserted world," Lang added as a closeup of Tirol came up on the screen, "except for this one city located close to Tirol's equator. I have proposed to the general staff that we begin here."

Rick stood up to address the table. "There's evidence the city's seen a lot of nasty action lately, so we've got to assume the Invid have a strong presence down there. I think our best move is to drop the GMU to recon this entire sector and ascertain the Invid's strengths. The SDF will be holding at a Lagrange point, so you'll have all the backup you need in case we've underestimated their defensive capabilities. Any questions so far?"

The men shook their heads and grumbled nos.

"Has everyone received the new authentication codes?" Rick directed to Grant and Wolff.

"We have, sir."

"I've asked Lord Exedore—" Lang started to say when Breetai interrupted him.

"Exedore and I have decided that my troops should accompany Commander Grant's ground forces."

Rick regarded the Zentraedi with an appraising look. "You're not required to become involved with this, Commander Breetai. You're not under our command . . ."

"That has nothing to do with it, Admiral. You seem to forget that I have walked this world."

Rick smiled. "I haven't forgotten . . . Grant, Wolff, do you have any problems with this?"

Vince shook his head and extended his hand to Breetai. "Welcome aboard, Commander."

"Well, that's settled," Lang said, getting to his feet again. "I have one thing to add. It concerns the Invid ships." Perspective schematics of a Pincer Ship took shape while he spoke. "Their central weakness seems to be this scanner that looks like some sort of mouth. So direct your shots there if it comes to that."

"And I hope it won't," Rick interjected. "It's possible that our initial confrontation was a misunderstanding, and I don't want us going down there like liberators. This is still a *diplomatic* mission, and you are only to engage if provoked." Rick shot Edwards a look. "Is that understood?"

"Affirmative," Wolff and Grant answered him.

"All right, then," Rick said after a moment. "Good luck." *And I wish I could be down there with you,* he said to himself.

The dropship hangar bay was the scene of mounting tension, tempers, and liveliness when the word came down to scramble. Men and women ran for gear and ordnance while the massive GMU rumbled aboard the ship that would take it planetside. Jack Baker was among the crowd, Wolverine assault rifle in hand as he lined up with his teammates for a last-minute briefing. Like the rest of them he had missed yesterday's EV action, but stories had spread among the ranks of an engagement with some new breed of XTs, who flew ships that resembled giant one-eyed land crabs. And now the GMU had been chosen to spearhead a ground assault on the Robotech Masters' homeworld. Jack would still have preferred piloting an Alpha Fighter with the Skull, but under the circumstances this op was probably the next best thing to that.

He looked down the long line of mecha pilots waiting to board the dropship and spied Karen Penn just as she was donning her helmet, blond hair like fire in the red illumination of the hangar.

"Karen!" he yelled, waving and hoping to get her attention above the sound of alert klaxons and high-volume commands. He was tempted to give it one last try, but her helmet was on now and he knew he wouldn't be heard. He did, however, lean out of line to watch her rush up the ramp.

At the same time, he peripherally caught sight of a captain taking angry strides toward him. Hurriedly, Jack tucked his chin in, steeled himself, and muttered a prayer that the line would get moving.

"Just what the hell was that all about, Ensign!" the captain was yelling into his face an instant later. "You think this is some kind of goddamned *picnic,* bright boy! You've got time to wave to your friends like you're off on some cruise! Well, let me tell you something, you deluded piece of space trash: it's no picnic and it's no cruise! You got that, you worthless little sublife protein! Because if I see you stepping out of line again, you're going to be sucking vacuum before we even hit!"

Jack could feel the woman's spittle raining against his face, but told himself it was just a cooling sea spray washing over the bow. The captain continued ranting for a while longer, then gave him a powerful shove as the line suddenly jerked into motion.

Oh well, he reminded himself, *the worst she could do was chew him out, which didn't amount to much considering there were things down there waiting to kill him.*

* * *

In another part of the hangar, Minmei was saying thank-you to Jonathan Wolff. A personal note from Admiral Hunter had gotten her past security, and now she and Wolff were standing by the broad and flattened armored bow of the dropship. Several Micronized Zentraedi were gaping at the singer from a respectable distance, but Breetai soon appeared on the scene and hurried them to the ship with some harsh grunts and curses.

"I just had to thank you before you left," Minmei was saying. "Janice wanted me to tell you the same. You saved our lives, Colonel." She vaguely remembered him from the wedding; but then she had met so many men during those few hours . . . Still, there was something about Wolff that caught her attention now. Maybe it was the mustache, Minmei told herself, the man's swashbuckler's good looks and tall, broad-shouldered figure. She wished she had chosen some other outfit to wear. The RDF uniform just wasn't cut right for her shape.

Wolff didn't seem to mind it, however. "Actually the honor could have gone to anyone," he said, showing a roguish grin. "But I was lucky enough to volunteer."

Minmei liked that. "Janice and I were just trying to get a better look at the fortress, and all of a sudden . . . well, you know."

Wolff's eyebrows arched. "Really? That's strange, because I had your flight recorder checked, and it seems you two actually flew directly into the vortex of the ship's spacefold flash point."

Minmei's face reddened. "Well, whatever happened, I'm glad about it now."

"Me, too," Wolff said, holding her gaze.

Suddenly Minmei went up on tiptoes and kissed him lightly on the corner of the mouth. "Be careful down there, Colonel."

Wolff reached for her hand and kissed it. "Can I see you when I get back?"

"I'd like that, Colonel—"

"Jonathan."

"Jonathan." She smiled. "Take care, Jonathan."

Wolff turned and was gone.

"That little fool," Lisa said after Rick told her about Minmei. They were alone in a small lounge not far from the bridge. "What was she trying to do, get herself killed?"

"You have to see it from her side," Rick argued. "She felt like everyone she cared about was leaving her."

Lisa regarded him suspiciously. "No, I don't *have* to see things from her side. But I'm sure you were understanding with her, weren't you? Did she cry on your shoulder, Rick?"

"Well, what was I supposed to do? You know I'd send her back if we could."

"I wonder," Lisa said, folding her arms.

Rick made a conciliatory gesture. "Whoa . . . Look, I don't like where this one's going. She's here and there's nothing we can do about it, okay?"

Lisa looked at him for a moment, then stepped in to lean her head on his shoulder. They hadn't had a chance to say two words to each other for more than twenty-four hours, and their comfortable bed was beginning to feel miles away. They were both exhausted and still a little stunned by the events that had transpired since they'd *gone off to work*!

"Is it the honeymoon you hoped for?" Rick asked, holding her.

She let out her breath in a rush. "It's the nightmare I wished we'd never have to live through." She pulled back to gaze at him. "We came here to sue for peace. And now . . ."

"Maybe that doesn't exist anymore," Rick said, turning to the viewport as Tirol loomed into view.

In the nave of Tiresia's transformed Royal Hall, Obsim listened patiently to the computer's announcement. A flash of synaptic sparks danced across the brain section's fissured surface, strobing orange light down at the scientist and a group of soldiers who were gathered nearby. For the past several periods the starship had been trying to communicate with Tirol, but Obsim had elected to remain silent. If indeed they had come in "peace," why were they equipped with such a mighty arsenal of weapons? More confusing still, their ship and mecha were Protoculture-driven, a fact that linked them beyond a shadow of a doubt to the Masters' empire.

And now they were sending one of their transport dropships to the moon's surface, just as he had guessed they would.

"Tell the Command ships to prepare," Obsim instructed his lieutenant. "And have your units stand by for a strikeship assault."

"And the Inorganics, Obsim?" the lieutenant asked. "Will the brain reactivate them now?"

Obsim came as close to smiling as his physiognomy allowed. "In due time, Enforcer, in due time."

CHAPTER
NINE

I suppose I should have been surprised that it didn't happen a lot sooner. Rick never believed that he was cut out to command, and I can remember him already trying to talk himself into resigning his commission when work first began on the SDF-3. I wanted to get to the bottom of it, but he didn't want my help. Basically he didn't want to hear his fears contradicted. So I was left to puzzle it out like a mystery, and I was convinced that both Roy Fokker's death and Rick's continuing "little brother" attitude had a lot to do with his behavior.

Lisa Hayes, *Recollections*

IT WAS AN HISTORIC MOMENT: THE DROPSHIP'S ARRIVAL ON TIROL marked the first occasion humankind had set foot on a world outside the Solar system. But it was business as usual, and that business was *war*.

The GMU rumbled down out of the dropship's portside ramp onto the moon's barren surface, and within minutes Wolff was shouting "Go! Go! Go!" into the Hovertank cockpit mike as his Pack left the mobile base. Their landing zone was at the foot of a towering black ridge of impossibly steep crags; but soon the Pack was moving across a barren stretch of seemingly irradiated terrain. The massive GMU dwindled behind the twenty-unit squadron as they formed up on Wolff's lead and sped toward Tirol's principal city—Tiresia, according to Breetai. It was late afternoon on Tirol.

The Hovertanks were ground-effect vehicles; reconfigurable assemblages of heavy-gauge armor in angular flattened shapes and acute edges, with rounded downsloping defection prows. In standard mode, they rode on a cushion of self-generated lift, but mechamorphosed, they were either Battloid or guardian—squat, two-legged waddling mecha the size of a house, with a single, top-mounted particle-projection cannon.

Wolff called up the GMU on the comlink for a situation report, and Vince Grant's handsome brown face surfaced on the mecha's cockpit commo screen. A defensive perimeter had been established around the base, and so far there was no sign of activity, enemy or otherwise. "You've got an open channel home," Vince told him. "We want to know everything you're seeing out there."

Wolff rogered and signed off. There were no maps of Tiresia, but bird's-eye scans from the SDF-3 scopes had furnished the Pack with a fairly complete overview. The city was laid out like a spoked wheel, the hub of which appeared to be an enormous Cheops-like pyramid. Eight streets lined with secondary buildings radiated out from the center at regular intervals, from magnetic north right around the compass. Nothing came close to rivaling the pyramid in size; in fact, most of the structures were the rough equivalent of three stories or less, a mere fraction of the central temple.

Exedore had described Tiresia's architecture as approximating Earth's Greco-Roman styles, with some ultratech innovations that were Tirol's alone. This is precisely what Wolff found as his Pack entered the city; although hardly a learned man, Wolff had seen enough pictures and renderings of Earth's ancient world to corroborate the Zentraedi ambassador's claims.

"Um, fluted columns, entablatures, peaked pediments," he radioed back to the GMU. "Arches, vaults ... buildings that look like the Parthenon, or that thing in Rome—the Colosseum. But I'm not talking about marble or anything like that. Everything seems to be faced with some nonporous alloy or ceramic—even the streets and courtyards."

But this was only half the story, the facade, as it were. Because elsewhere were rectilinear and curved structures of modernistic design, often surrounded by curious antennalike towers and assemblages of huge clear conduits.

And much of it had been reduced to smoldering rubble.

"I'm splitting the squadron," Wolff updated a few minutes later. Straight ahead was the central pyramid, still a good distance off but as massive as a small mountain in Tirol's fading light. He switched over to the mecha's tactical net. "A team will follow me up the middle. Winston, Barisky, take your team over to the next avenue and parallel us. But stay on-line with me. One block at a time, and easy does it."

"Roger, Wolff Leader," Winston returned.

"Switching over to IR scanners and moving out."

There was still no sign of the Invid, or anything else for that matter, but Wolff was experiencing an itchy feeling he had come to rely on, a combat sense he had developed during the Malcontent Uprisings, hunting down renegade Zentraedi in the jungled Southlands. He checked his cockpit displays and boosted the intensity of the forward scanners. At the end of the broad street where it met the hub were a pair of stacked free-floating columns with some sort of polished sphere separating them. He was close enough to the pyramid base now to make out a stairway that ascended one face; the pillared shrine at the summit was no longer visible.

Just then Winston's voiced cracked over the net, loud in Wolff's ears.

"We've got movement, Wolff Leader! Multiple signals all over the place!"

"What's your position, Boomer?" Winston gave the readings in a rush. "Can you identify signatures? Boomer, do you copy?"

"Nothing we've seen," the B-team leader said over a burst of angry static. "Bigger than either ship those flyboys registered. *Much* bigger."

"On our way," Wolff was saying when something thirty feet tall suddenly broke through a domed building off to his left. It was an inky black bipedal ship, with cloven feet and arms like armored pincers. The head, equally armored, was helmet-shaped but elongated in the rear, and sandwiched between two nasty-looking shoulder cannons. Wolff watched spellbound as orange priming charges formed at the tips of the cigar-shaped weapons. An instant later two radiant beams converged on one of the Hovertanks and blew it to smithereens.

Wolff gave the order to return fire as four more enemy ships emerged from the buildings and a fifth surfaced in front of him, *right out of the damned street*!

The Hovertanks reconfigured to Gladiator mode and singled off against the Invid, the streets a battle zone all at once, filled with heavy metal thunder and blinding flashes of explosive light. Wolff saw another of his number go down. On the tac net, Wilson reported that his team was faring no better.

"Go to Battloid mode. Pull back and regroup," he ordered. Then he tried to raise the GMU.

In the GMU's command center, Vince Grant received word of the recon group's situation: four, possibly five, Hovertanks were down and Wolff was calling for reinforcements or extraction. His Pack had been chased to the outskirts of the city, where they were dug in near the remains of what the colonel described as "a kind of Roman basilica."

"Tell him to hold on, help's on the way," Grant told the radio man. Then he swung around to the command center's tactical board. At about the time Wolff's Pack had been ambushed, Invid troops had begun a move against the mobile base itself. Deafening volleys were rolling in from the line, echoing in the sawtooth ridge at the GMU's back. Night had fallen, but it was as if someone had forgotten to inform Tirol's skies.

"Ground forces are sustaining heavy casualties in all perimeter zones," a com tech updated without having to be asked. "The enemy are employing mecha that fit yesterday's profiles, along with teams of one-pilot strike ships."

The commander studied a computer schematic as it turned and upended itself on the screen. Vince tried to make some sense of the thing. *A deadly kazoo,* he thought, *with forward guns like withered arms and an undercarriage cluster of propulsion globes.* Whatever they were, they were decimating the forward lines. He had already lost count of the wounded and dead.

"Wolff on the horn, Commander," a tech said. "He's requesting backup."

"Get his present location," Vince told the woman.

The tech bent to her task, but got no response. She tapped her phones and repeated Wolff's call sign and code into the net.

Vince leaned over the console and hit the com stud. "Go ahead, Colonel. We're reading you. Colonel."

"God, I don't believe it!" Wolff said at last.

"Colonel," Vince said more loudly, "Respond."

"They're ... they're going after my men, pulling them out of the tanks ..."

Several command-center techs turned to watch Vince at the com station. "Who is, Colonel?"

The net was silent for a moment; then Wolff added, "Cats, Commander. Some kind of goddamned *cats!*"

Grant lifted an ashen face to the room. "Notify Breetai that his Battlepod team has a green light."

"Bah," Cabell muttered, switching off the remote sensor's audio signal. "Our Bioroids were a better match for the Invid than these Earthers. It's a mystery how they defeated our Zentraedi."

Rem kept his eyes on the monitor screen while the old man swiveled to busy himself with other matters. Almost two dozen Human mecha had entered the city, but there was scarcely half that number now. They had successfully turned the tide against the Command ships that had surprised them, but Invid reinforcements had since appeared on the scene. The remains of countless

Hellcats littered the streets the Humans had chosen for their last stand.

"But Cabell, isn't there some way we can help them?"

The scientist showed him his palms. "With what, my boy? We are effectively trapped down here." He motioned to the Pollinators who were peacefully huddled in a corner. "Would you drive these ferocious creatures against them?"

Rem made an impatient gesture. "We can tell the Humans about the Royal Hall."

"Break radio silence?" Cabell asked. "And draw the Invid right to us?"

"Would you rather the Invid inherit our world?"

Cabell stroked his beard and regarded the youth. "How like him you are . . ."

Rem beetled his brows. "Who?"

"Uh, why, your father of course," Cabell said, turning away. "He, too, would have thought nothing of such a sacrifice. But listen, my boy, how can we be certain these Humans are any better than the Invid? After all, we know the Invid's capabilities. But the Humans' ways are unknown to us."

Rem gestured to the screen. "Perhaps this will change your mind, Cabell."

Skeptical, Cabell faced the screen: a score of Battlepods had arrived to back up the Terran tanks.

"Zentraedi mecha," the brain announced. "Regult and Glaug."

"Yes," Obsim said, registering some surprise. "So there is a connection between these invaders and our old foes." He looked back and forth from the communicator sphere to the living computer. "Perhaps we are in some jeopardy, after all. Computer: evaluate and advise."

"Extrapolating from previously displayed battle tactics . . ." the brain began. "Defeat for our ground forces in seven point four periods unless reinforcements arrive from Optera. Substantial damage to aliens' mecha and casualties in excess of six hundred; but not enough to threaten their victory."

"Advise, then."

A bundle of raw energy ascended the floating organ's stem and diffused in the region of the midbrain. "Conserve our strength. Take the battle to the invaders' base. Sacrifice the troopers to keep the invaders from the city. And await the arrival of reinforcements."

Obsim mulled it over. "Is there more?"

"Yes," the brain added a moment later. "Protect the brain at all costs."

"Headless ostriches" was the term VT pilots had given Battlepods during the Robotech War. Bipedal, with reverse-articulated legs and a laser-bristled spherical command module, the pods had been designed for full-size warriors. There was just enough room for a single, fully expendable pilot, and little in the way of cockpit padding or defensive shielding. But Lang's teams had reworked the mecha, so that they could now be operated by two Micronized pilots with plenty of room to spare. RDF mechamorphs were trained in pod operation, but there existed an unspoken taboo that kept Humans to their own mecha and Zentraedi to theirs.

But there were no such lines drawn when Breetai's team leaped in to lend the Wolff Pack a much-needed assist. Battlepods and Hovertanks fought side-by-side hammering away at the Invid Command ships. Pulsed-laser fire and conventional armor-piercing projectiles split Tirol's night. An entire quadrant of the city burned while the battle raged, and friend and foe added their own fire and smoke to the already superheated air.

The Hellcat Inorganics had abandoned the scene, as though frightened off by the pods, and now the Command ships were suddenly turning tail.

Wolff sat in the mecha's seat, convulsively triggering the Hovertank's weapon as the enemy ships disengaged and began to lift off. The colonnade of a building collapsed behind him, sending gobs of molten metal airborne. He raised the GMU on the net to update his situation.

"We're being overrun," a panicked voice informed him in response. "Commander Grant says to pick yourselves up and get back here ASAP!"

Wolff ordered his few remaining tankers to reconfigure, and addressed Breetai. "We're moving out. The base is ass deep in pincers."

"At your command, Colonel," the Zentraedi responded, pleased to be taking orders once again, to have an imperative to follow.

Every bed and table in the GMU's med-surg unit was filled, and still the wounded kept coming. The mess hall was a triage area and battle dressing station now, and Jack Baker had found himself in the midst of it, pulled there from supply to lend a hand. All around him men and women were stretched out on the floor and tabletops in postures of distress and agony. A young woman with

third-degree burns across half her body flailed her arms against the
restraints the medic was attempting to fasten, while a nurse struggled to get an IV drip running. Elsewhere a man drugged beyond
pain stared almost fascinated at the bloody stump that had been a
leg less than an hour before. Some of the wounded groaned and
called on God and relatives for help; but Jack saw others expire
with no more than a whimper, or a final curse.

Jean Grant, the front of her surgical gown red-brown from
blood and antiseptic washes, was moving from table to table
checking wounds and shouting orders to her staff.

"Move it, soldier!" Jack heard someone behind him yell. He
felt the edge of a stretcher smack against his hip, and turned as
two women medics rushed past him bearing a lieutenant he recognized to surgery.

A warrant officer called to him next, waving him over to a
bloodied expanse of wall, three bodies slumped lifelessly against
it. "These men are dead," the officer announced, getting to his
feet and wiping his hands on his trousers. "Get them out of here,
and get yourself back up here on the double." The officer looked
around. "You!" he said, finding another aide in the crowds. "Get
over here and give this man a hand!"

Jack bent down to regard the dead, unsure where to begin.

"You take his arms," a female voice said over his shoulder. Karen Penn was beside him when he turned. She gave him a wan
smile and wiped a damp strand of hair from her face with the
back of her hand, leaving a smear of someone's blood on her
cheek.

"I want to get out there," Jack grunted as he lifted the body.
"Some paybacks are in order."

"Maybe that's what this guy said," Karen bit out. "Let's just do
our job and forget the heroics."

"We'll see."

When they had eased the body down onto the floor in the next
room, Karen said, "If I see your sorry face show up in here, I'm
going to remind you of that remark."

"You do that," Jack told her, breathing hard.

The SDF-3 was still at its orbital holding point above Tirol.
The general staff was kept informed of the situation below by
continuous updates from the GMU. One such report was coming
into the fortress now, and T. R. Edwards left the TIC's balcony
rail to listen more closely. A tech loyal to the cause was making
adjustments for reception, and punching decoding commands into
the console.

"It's from Grant, sir," the tech reported, seeing Edwards peering over his shoulder. "The situation has deteriorated and is growing untenable."

Edwards glanced around the balcony area. Hunter and Reinhardt had gone off to meet with Lang and some of the council members. "Speak plainly, Lieutenant," he said, narrowing his eye.

"They're getting their butts kicked, sir. Grant is requesting air support from the ship."

Edwards straightened up and felt the stubble on his chin. "How do we know this isn't some enemy trick, Lieutenant? Did the GMU use the proper authentication codes?"

"Affirmative, sir."

Edwards was silent while the planetside transmission repeated itself. "But then they broke our code once already."

The tech risked a grin. "I think I understand, sir."

"You'll go far," Edwards told him, leaning in to dial the gain knob down to zero.

At the same time Edwards was gloating over having eliminated Vince Grant from his life, Minmei was fantasizing about how to get Jonathan Wolff into hers. It was the flower arrangement the colonel had had delivered to her cabinspace that kicked off the fantasy; obviously he had called in the order before he left, perhaps right after they said good-bye in the dropship hangar. She was toying with the flowers now, lost in a daydream, while Janice studied her from across the room.

"Keep fooling with those things and they're going to wilt before they have a chance to bloom," Janice said from the couch.

Minmei showed Janice a startled look, then gave the arrangement one last turn before she stepped back to regard it.

"You're thinking about catching that bridal bouquet, aren't you?"

Minmei smiled. "How could you tell?"

"Because sometimes I can read you like a screen," Janice sighed. She patted the cushion next to her. "Come over here, you."

Minmei fixed two drinks and sat down, kicking off her shoes and curling her legs beneath her. Janice sipped at her glass and said, "Now tell your partner all about it."

"Do you believe in omens?"

"Omens?" Janice shook her head. "First I'd have to believe that the future has already been written, and that's simply not the case. Reality is shaped and reshaped by our words and deeds."

"I'm not asking you *philosophically*, Janice."

Janice took another sip and glanced at the flowers. "You think destiny has thrown you and Jonathan Wolff together."

Minmei nodded. "Don't you?"

"No. Not any more than I think destiny brought you and me together. We have a tendency to highlight moments we wish to think preordained."

"I promised myself I'd never get involved with a military man," Minmei continued, as though she hadn't heard Janice. "Not after Rick. And now here I am worrying about Jonathan, just the way I used to worry about Rick." She met Janice's eye. "I don't want to lose him, Janice."

"Worrying doesn't change anything, Lynn."

"Then what does it matter if I worry? Maybe I just didn't worry *enough* about Rick."

" 'They also serve . . .' " Janice mused.

"Huh?"

"Just something I heard once." She took Minmei's hand. "Go ahead and worry. We all have our appointed tasks."

"I'm sick of having to listen to everyone," Rick complained bitterly, sitting down on the edge of the bed. He and Lisa had taken advantage of a short break to rendezvous in their quarters. "The council has decided we should recall the GMU and leave Tirolspace. Suddenly they're all convinced this bloodshed has been a misunderstanding. They want to remove our 'threatening presence'—those are their words—and try to open lines of communication. Station a small unarmed party out here or something . . ." Rick exhaled forcibly. "War of the worlds . . . Even Lang has reversed himself. Ever since his teams started picking apart those Invid mecha we salvaged. All at once he's fascinated with these butchers."

Lisa rested her hand on his shoulder. "Don't do this to yourself, Rick."

He looked up at her, eyes flashing. "Yeah, well, I'm tired of being the one who has to walk around with his guts tied up."

"Rick, nobody's asking you—"

"My place is with the VTs. I just wasn't cut out for command."

Lisa kneeled down to show him the anger in her own eyes. "Maybe you weren't, if you're going to talk like that. But first tell me who we should have in command. And tell me what good you think you can do in combat?"

"Are you saying I'm rusty?"

Lisa's eyes went wide. "Stand down, mister, I'm not saying that at all. I'm asking you what good it's going to do to add another *combatant* to the field, when what we need is some enlightened decision making." She relaxed her gaze. "You're not thinking clearly, Rick. You need some rest, we're all frazzled."

"Maybe you're right," he allowed.

The door tone sounded just then, and Max entered.

"Rick, Lisa. Sorry to barge in."

"It's all right, Max," Rick said, getting to his feet. "What's up?"

Max hesitated for a moment. "Rick, why are we ignoring the GMU's request for backup?"

Rick stared at Max blankly. "What are you talking about?"

"They've been sustaining heavy losses down there."

"Why wasn't I informed of this? Who's in the Situation Room now?"

"Edwards."

Rick cursed under his breath. He give Lisa a brief kiss and grabbed hold of Max's arm, tugging him from the room.

The two men burst into the Tactical Information Center a few minutes later. Rick glanced once at Edwards and demanded an update from a tech.

"Colonel Wolff and Commander Breetai have pulled out of Tiresia with scarcely half their command, sir. Latest reports shows them in sector November Romeo—"

"Admiral!" a second tech shouted from further along the threat-board console. "Priority transmission from the GMU."

"Go ahead," Rick told him.

The tech listened for a moment, then swiveled to face Rick again. "They say they're receiving transmissions. From Tirol, sir—from somewhere in the city. The message is in Zentraedi, sir."

"Have they identified themselves?"

"Negative, sir, other than to say they are Tiresians, and that they have important intelligence for our forces."

"A trick," Edwards spat. "An Invid trick. They've been sending in false messages all morning."

Rick regarded him a moment, then turned to Max. "Scramble the Skull, Commander. Get down there and lend support."

"Aye, aye, sir." Max saluted, leaving the room in a rush.

"Tell Commander Grant to continue monitoring transmission," Rick instructed the tech. "I want them to patch us in so we can hear it for ourselves." Rick slapped his hand down on a mike switch. "Notify Exedore and Dr. Lang to meet me in the briefing room. I'm on my way now!"

Rick ran for the door, already considering the decision he would have to make.

CHAPTER TEN

Cabell's age was incalculable, as had been the case with Exedore, Breetai, and several other Zentraedis who'd permitted Zand's team to study them. But whereas the warrior clones had been "birthed" full-size and ageless, Cabell had enjoyed an actual childhood, adolescence, and adulthood. His decision to undergo the Protoculture treatments that fixed his age was a conscious one. It has yet to be demonstrated how DNA and Protoculture combine to allow this miracle to occur. Like the Micronization process, it remains a complete mystery.

Louie Nichols, *BeeZee: The Galaxy Before Zor*

"**M**Y NAME IS CABELL. I AM A TIROLIAN SCIENTIST. Our people are being held prisoner by the Invid in structures throughout the city. The Invid ships and Inorganics are receiving their orders from a computer that has been placed in Tiresia's Royal Hall. To defeat them, you must destroy the computer. And you must do this quickly. The Invid are many and merciless. Reinforcements will arrive if you do not take immediate action. My life is now forfeit; but I place the future of this world in your hands. Act swiftly, Humans, and be equally as merciless. For there is much more at stake than this tiny moon."

Cabell repeated the message twice more, then shut down the com device and turned to Rem. "Well, that does it, my boy. We have compromised our location."

Rem answered him in a determined voice. "But we may have saved Tirol, Cabell."

The old man began to look around the room, his face a mixture of rapture and longing. He ran his long fingers over the console. "Such a waste ... What wonders we had at our disposal, what miracles we could have worked in the Quadrant."

Rem raised his eyes to the ceiling, as a sound like distant thunder shook the lab. This was followed by the sibilant burst of far-away energy beams. "It's too late for dreams, Cabell."

"I fear you're right. Their search has commenced."

Rem reactivated the communicator and gestured to the console audio pickups. "Repeat your message. We have nothing more to lose."

"The transmission is being repeated," the Invid brain informed Obsim.

"Pinpoint the source, computer."

A wiggling current coursed over folds of computer cortex. "Below this very chamber. There are vaults and corridors, a mazelike complex."

Obsim swung to an Enforcer lieutenant. "I want the Inorganics to flush them out. Tell your troops to stand by."

The soldier saluted and left the nave for an adjacent room where several Invid were watching an armored Shock Trooper bring its annihilation discs to bear on a stretch of ceramiclike floor. Already a wide wound several yards deep and as many wide had been opened.

"Continue," the Enforcer's synthesized voice commanded. "Locate and destroy."

"What does he mean by 'Inorganics'?" Rick wanted to know.

Lang leaned back from the briefing-room table and steepled his fingers. "I think he must be referring to the fiendish drones Colonel Wolff faced in the city. Certainly the ships we salvaged are anything but *inorganic*."

Lang tried to keep the excitement from his voice, but he was sure Rick and the others caught it. He had passed the better part of twenty-four hours in the laboratory dissecting those ships and the remains of one of the alien pilots. And what he'd uncovered about the Invid had been enough to send him into a veritable delirium. Thinking back even now to those hours of experimentation and discovery was like some wild roller-coaster ride. The very shape and form of those beings! As though they existed outside any *rules* of evolution. And the incredible similarity their brain patterns had to the emanations of Protoculture itself! The green nutrient the pilots bathed in inside their crab-ships, the myriad mysteries of the ships' propulsion, communication, and weapons systems, the integrity of pilot and ship that rendered Robotechnology's advances primitive and childlike by comparison . . . It had all sent him running—literally *running*!—to the Council to sue for a course other than the warlike one they had embarked on . . .

"Dr. Lang," Rick was saying. "I asked you if this message will be enough to change the Council's mind about leaving Tirolspace."

Lang started to reply, but Exedore's late entry interrupted him. The Zentraedi ambassador apologized and seated himself at the table between Lang and General Edwards, who was plainly disturbed by Exedore's arrival. Rick had the transmission replayed for Exedore's benefit and waited for his evaluation.

Exedore was silent for a long moment. "I . . . hardly know what to say," he began. Rick had never seen the Zentraedi so, well, *moved*.

"Cabell," Exedore uttered. "He was a contemporary of Zor, a *mentor*, I think you would say. And to me, as well. He . . . he *made* me."

Lang and Rick exchanged astonished looks while they listened to Exedore's explanation. This Cabell had apparently been instrumental in the creation of the first biogenetically engineered clones. "Then this message is on the level, Exedore?"

"No one would use the name Cabell to evil purpose, Admiral. Of this much I am certain."

"Bullshit," barked Edwards. "This is another Invid trick. They're trying to lure us to this . . . 'Royal Hall.' Why? Because they have some sort of weapon there. They're playing with us."

"What about it?" Rick asked the table.

One of Lang's techs spoke to that. "Scanners indicate the source of the transmission is subterranean—perhaps beneath the very structure we've identified as the Royal Hall. Colonel Wolff described it as . . ." the tech checked his notes, " 'a flat-topped pyramid as big as a small mountain, crowned with some kind of columned shrine.' We've picked up intense energy readings emanating from the structure."

"A weapon," Edwards interjected.

Rick tried to puzzle it out. "Suppose it is legit. Would Cabell knowingly call a strike down on his own head, Exedore?"

"Without question, if Tirol could be saved by his actions."

"Then the Robotech Masters may still be alive. Is it enough to convince the Council, Doctor, yes or no?"

"I think they'll listen to reason. But if we can possibly achieve these ends without destroying—"

"Raise the GMU," Rick instructed one of his aides. "Inform Commander Sterling that I want a recon flyby of that pyramid. I don't want anybody trying anything stupid. Tell Grant to keep the GMU dug in and wait for my word to move in."

"And Cabell?" said Exedore.

"Yes," Lang seconded. "Surely a rescue team—"

"I'm sorry, Doctor," Rick broke in. "You, too, Exedore. But I want to know what we're dealing with before we send anyone in."

Edwards snorted. "We'll say some kind words over his grave," he said loud enough for Exedore to hear.

In the tradition of that apocryphal cavalry who were always arriving in the nick of time, the Skull Squadron tore into Tirol's skies from the shuttles that had transported them to the edge of the envelope, and fell like wrathful birds of prey on the enemy's Pincer Ships and Shock Troopers. Cheers from Hovertankers and mecha commanders filled the tac and com nets as the Guardian-mode VTs dove in for missile releases and strafing runs.

Captain Miriya Parino Sterling led her team of red fighters against a group of blue-giant Command ships that were going gun-to-gun with Breetai's Zentraedi cadre. The smoking remains of Battlepods and strike ships littered a barren, now cratered expanse of high plateau where the Invid had successfully breached the GMU's forward defense lines. Miriya's Alphas hit the massive twin-cannoned mecha where they lived, chattering undercarriage guns stitching molten welts across cockpit shields and torso armor, and red-tipped heat-seekers finding the ships' vulnerable sensor mouths. Explosions geysered fountains of white-hot alloy into the waning light as ship after ship fell, leaking viscous green fluids into the dry ground. Renewed, the Battlepods leaped to regain their lost ground, trading energy salvos with the larger ships, their orange and blue bolts cutting swaths of angry ionization through the moon's thin atmosphere.

Elsewhere, Max's blue team backed up the Wolff Pack's devastated Hovertank ranks, reconfigured to Battloid mode for close-in combat, while overhead, solitary Veritechs went to guns with the less maneuverable Shock Troopers. Ships boostered and fell, executing rolls and reversals as they engaged.

Even the GMU's main gun was speaking now, adding its own thunderous punctuation to the battle's murderous dialogue. A second and third wave of mecha burst from the base's forward ramps—Mac II cannons, Excalibers, and drum-armed Spartans—but the Invid would neither fall back nor surrender.

It was all or nothing, Max realized as he bracketed two of the alien ships in his sights. Missiles tore from the Battloid's shoulder racks and found their mark; the ships came apart in a dumbbell-shaped cloud of flame and thick smoke. In the end, once the RDF's debris was carted from the field, it would look like a slaughter had taken place; but in the meantime men and women continued to die.

Max ordered the Battloid into a giant-stride run, pulled back on the selector lever, and imaged the VT through to fighter mode. He went ballistic, instructing his wingmen to follow suit, and was about to rejoin Miriya when Vince Grant's face appeared on one of the cockpit commo screens.

"You've got new orders, Commander, straight from the top."

"Uh, roger, Home. Shoot."

"Your team's to recon the Triangle. Just a flyby with a minimum of sound-and-light. Do you copy, Skull One?"

"Can do, Home. Waiting for your directions."

"We're punching them in now," Vince said.

Max's onboard computer came alive, stammering vectors and coordinates across the display screen.

"And Max," Vince added. "Be sure to keep in touch."

Evening's shadow was once again moving across Tirol's face; a crescent of Fantoma loomed huge in the southern skies, its ring-plane a shaft of evanescent color. The battle was over—for the time being, forever, no one could be sure, any more than they could be sure who had won. If it went by the numbers, then the RDF had been victorious; but there was no known way of conveying that to the five hundred who had died that day.

Jack had been returned to his outfit and was out at the perimeter now, finally out on Tirol's surface, where he felt he should have been all along. There was a good deal of activity going on around him—mecha tows and transports and APCs barreling by, VTs flying recon sweeps—but he still wasn't content. He had been assigned to take part in a mine-emplacement op, which meant little more than observing while Gladiators planted and armed AM-2 Watchdogs across the field. (These anti-mecha mines of high-velocity plastique had been developed by one Dr. R. Burke—who was also responsible for the Wolverine assault rifles—and came complete with an Identification Friend or Foe targeting microchip housing a library of enemy ground signatures, even those recently cooked up by the GMU's computers to indicate Invid Scouts and Shock Troopers.) So instead of giving the Gladiator his undivided attention, Jack had slipped away to eavesdrop on a conversation that was in progress at one of the forward command posts. Jack understood that the enemy had been soundly defeated, but things were still a bit sketchy with regard to follow-up plans. He sensed that something important was up, and in a short time he had the astounding details.

A message had been received from Tirol's occupied city—sent by some sort of rebel group, from the sound of it—giving the lo-

cation of the Invid's central command. The Skull had been ordered to recon the site, but nothing was in the works to save the
rebels themselves, who were apparently holed up in the very same
neighborhood. Having seen a crude map of Tiresia, Jack knew the
place would be easy enough to suss out. And if a small team—
even *one man*—could infiltrate, the rebels would be as good as
free. All it took was the *right* man.

But chief among the things Jack *didn't* know was that his actions over the past hour had been observed at rather close range
by Karen Penn. And she stuck with Jack now as he began to angle his way behind the command post and into the forward supply
area. He waited until the sentries were preoccupied, then moved
in and grabbed hold of a Wolverine and an energy-pack bandolier.
Karen drew her hand weapon and decided it was time to confront
him.

Taken by surprise, Jack swung around with his hands raised,
prepared to assume the position. But realizing it was Karen, he
simply shook his head and shouldered past her. Karen armed the
handgun, with came to life with a short-lived but unmistakable
priming tone. It stopped Jack in his tracks.

"Now, you want to talk to me, Jack, or the unit commander?"

"Look," he said, turning around carefully, "there's something
I've got to do." He explained what he knew about the communiqué and the rebel group, and how a small group could get in
and out unnoticed.

Karen listened without comment, then laughed shortly and deactivated her weapon. "You're certifiable, you know that?"

Jack made a face. "I'm going in alone, Karen."

"Oh no you're not," she said, grabbing a Wolverine from the
rack. " 'Cause I'm coming with you."

Jack showed her a grin. "I know where there's a coupla
Hovercycles."

Karen pulled the bandolier's straps taut. "Lead on, hero," she
told him.

Obsim peered into the trench the enforcers had opened in the
floor of the Royal Hall. Fifty feet down they had broken through
the roof of a narrow corridor, a stretch of the mazelike subterranean works the brain had discerned.

"The Inorganics will locate the Tiresians within the period," the
brain informed Obsim when he reentered the Hall's central nave.

"I am pleased," Obsim said, trying on a regal tone.

"There are other concerns . . ."

"Prioritize."

"A group of airborne mecha are closing on our position."

Obsim glanced at the communicator sphere, where a holo-image of six blue Veritechs was taking shape.

"Advise, computer."

"Protect the brain. Activate the shield."

Obsim tried to calculate the resultant energy drain. "You are so instructed," he said after a moment of reflection.

Bubbles formed, percolating in the brain's tank.

"It is done."

Max had his team complete two high-altitude passes over the city before dropping in for a closer look. Schematics of Skull's topographical scans had revealed that Tiresia's Royal Hall was an enormous structure indeed, a truncated pyramid almost a thousand feet tall capped by a classical Roman-like shrine. It dominated the city, which was itself a kind of circular mandala set into Tirol's bleak surface. Scanners had also picked up dusk activity in the city's street; but whatever was moving around down there was smaller than the Invid ships the Skull had thus far gone up against.

"All right, let's stay alert," Max said over the net as the team followed him down. "Keep an eye on each other. Blue Velvet, you've got the number-one spot."

"Roger, Skull Leader, I'm on my way," the mechamorph responded.

Max watched him peel away from the group, roll over, and drop in for the run. They were all closing on the Hall, scarcely five hundred feet above it, when a translucent envelope of scintillating energy suddenly mushroomed up in front of them. The envelope expanded to encompass the entire Hall, and with it, Blue Velvet's lone Veritech. The rest of the team broke hard and climbed.

"It's a force field of some kind," Max said. "Blue Velvet, get yourself out of there!"

"No can do, Skull One, my systems are down! Reconfiguring and going for touchdown . . ."

Max was heading back toward the Hall again, and could see the Guardian-mode VT falling. But all at once there were three bizarre shapes on the shrine steps—headless, demonic-looking bipedal mecha, with dangling arms and orifice-dimpled weapon spheres.

"You've got company, Blue Velvet!" Max shouted the pilot's call sign twice more, but got no response. The Alpha was preparing to land when the creatures opened fire and blew it off course.

Max watched helplessly as the Veritech grazed the edge of the pyramid and exploded, raining fiery debris down the Hall's steep side.

"Hit them!" Max ordered.

Missiles dropped from the Veritechs' undercarriage pylons and ripped in twisting tracks toward the Inorganics, only to detonate harmlessly against the Hall's repellent dome. But the enemy could fire through the shield and did, catching a second VT before Max could order the team away. He was trying to decide what to do next, when one of his wingmen came on the net. "Skull Leader, I'm picking up two friendly blips down below."

Max listened for the coordinates, tipped his Alpha, and leaned over to take a look. "You sure they're friendly?"

"Affirmative. The IFF says they're Hovercycles. They're approaching the Hall."

Hovercycles, now what the . . . Max said to himself. "All right," he said, "let's go down and see what's cooking."

"Wha-*hoo!*" Jack shouted, throttling the Hovercycle down a slope of arid ground and onto one of Tiresia's central spokes. "Life in the fast lane!"

"Idiot," Karen muttered to herself, goosing the handbar grip in an attempt to catch up with him. "He's going to get us both killed."

The cycles were face-effect vehicles, with conventional grips, right-angled bars rising up and back from a single shaft, and a front Hover-foot that resembled an old-fashioned carpet sweeper. The seat and backrest was a sweeping, padded affair, and although the cycles were built for one, the rear storage deck could accommodate a second rider if need be. They were fast, silent, and maneuverable, but essentially weaponless.

"What are you trying to prove?" Karen said, coming up alongside Jack's cycle. "Is this a rescue op or a joyride?"

Jack glanced over at her and began to lay out his philosophy about how self-confidence was what mattered most; but instead of listening she was just looking at him wide-eyed, and the next thing he knew, she had her handgun raised and aimed in his general direction—

"Duck!" she yelled, firing off two quick bursts that nearly parted Jack's carrot-colored hair.

"Jeez!" he said, when they'd brought the cycles to a halt. "Whaddaya think—"

"Take a look at that."

Jack twisted around in the seat and spied the Inorganic Karen's shot had neatly holed. Still on his feet and slumped against a wall, the thing reminded him of a character from an old cartoon. "Tasmanian devil," Jack recalled, snapping his finger, as the Crann slid to the smooth street.

"Is it alive?" Karen asked, looking around warily.

"Not any more."

"But what is it?"

"I don't know," Jack said, bringing the Wolverine off his shoulder, "but there's three more of them coming our way."

Karen reholstered her sidearm and followed Jack's lead. Suddenly, half-a-dozen blue energy bolts were zipping past her, impacting against a wall and sending up a shower of white-hot gunk. A blast of superheated air washed over her, stinging her eyes and nose while she brought the assault rifle to bear on the drones.

Jack was already firing; his rounds had managed to connect with one of the Inorganics, and Karen watched as the thing flashed out and crumbled, as though hollow. An instant later the other two went down, breaking open like ceramic figurines.

"Let's get out of here!" Jack yelled, as bolts began to rain down on them from the surrounding rooftops.

Karen kept up with him, piloting the cycle one-handed while she loosed an arc of rear fire, dropping two more Cranns with well-placed sensor shots. "What now?" she said, her voice raspy from the heat, smoke, and all the shouting.

Jack motioned up the street, toward a small mountain of a structure. "Straight ahead. That's the Hall. The message originated from somewhere underground. I figure there's gotta be a way down."

"You figure," Karen said in disbelief. "I'm for turning back."

"Uh-uh. But I am for *turning*!"

Karen looked up: ten or more Inorganics were blocking the street. Their weapons were raised.

Perplexed, Cabell regarded the weapon Rem had given him; he fumbled with the rifle's selector lever. "Like this?"

"No, no, Cabell," Rem said, close to losing his patience. "Like this," he demonstrated, activating his own weapon.

Cabel mimicked Rem's movements. "Ah, I see . . . and you hold it like, er, you put your right hand, um, let's see, you—"

"Give me that thing!" Rem snapped, snatching the rifle from the old man's hands. Cabell was offering him an imbecilic shrug. "You'll probably vaporize your own foot."

"I wouldn't doubt it for a moment," Cabell agreed. "I'm sorry,

I've never had any talent for the fine art of combat. Why, back when the Masters were first—"

"Save it, Cabell. Are we going or not?"

Cabell took one long last look around the room. Still-functioning remotes had permitted them to view the Humans' recon attempt, and later, their failure to breach the barrier shield the Invid computer had deployed. But with Inorganics closing on the subterranean lab now, there was no time for further monitoring of the situation. Cabell had insisted that they not be caught in the lab. The Pollinators would be his gift to the Invid; with them and some seedling Flowers, perhaps they could refoliate ravaged Optera, end this incessant killing . . .

"Well, what have we here?" Cabell said suddenly.

Rem came back into the lab, cursing, and found the scientist pointing to one of the screens. Here were two Humans just outside the force field, a male and a female, straddling strange-looking Hovercrafts.

"Could they be searching for us, Rem?"

"Don't flatter yourself," Rem answered him, tugging Cabell into the corridor. They could hear the Inorganics nearby, blasting through corridor walls and breaking into rooms.

"But they *could* be looking for us."

Rem continued to drag Cabell down the corridor. "Fine, fine . . ."

Cabell reached for one of Rem's weapons. "Then let's just go out and meet them."

CHAPTER ELEVEN

Finally all the principal players had been introduced to one another: Masters and Invid, Zentraedi and Humans, Humans and Invid, Humans and Masters. Surely this was Protoculture's doing; but what would make the contest especially bizarre was the fact that not one of those players had all the puzzle pieces. It was a mad, mad, mad, mad world.

Dr. Emil Lang, *The New Testament*

THE REGENT WAS RELAXING IN HIS BATH WHEN OBSIM'S MESsage finally reached him. The sunken tub in his private chambers was as large as a backyard swimming pool, surrounded by ornate fixtures the Regis had detested. *You have too many things,* she used to scream. *Things!*—when the very goal had always been to move away from such material trappings. Her goal, at any rate. *Freedom from this base condition* . . . her words to describe their world after the affair with Zor. After Optera, an Eden if ever there was one, had been defoliated by the Masters' warrior clones, robbed of the Flower that was infinitely precious to the Invid, so *essential.* They were like starving creatures now, feeding off what nutrients had been stored up in their flesh, but hungry, ravenous for sustenance only the Flower could provide.

The Regent sighed as he climbed from the tub, regarding the sterile green bath fluids with a mixture of sorrow and disdain. To be sure, the bath had been drawn from Flowers and fruits, but a mutated variety from Peryton that had to pass for the real thing, for absent, too, were the Pollinators, those shaggy little beasts critical to the Flowers' reproductive cycle. As a result, the Regent no longer bathed to empower himself, but simply to sustain a memory of brighter times.

Brighter times indeed, he told himself as a servant moved in to drape a robe over him. *You have taken a wrong turn,* the Regis had warned him. *A turn toward deevolution and evil purpose.* She

103

was already in Tiresioid form then, desperate in her attempts to emulate Zor's race. She had begged the Regent to join her in that novel guise, but he would hear nothing of it. His queen, his *wife*, had been defiled, his world contaminated, and still she would ask for such a thing. When his very heart was burning with a rage never before known to him. Was it any wonder then that he had chosen his own course? The goal—the goal, my *dear*—is conquest and consumption; and *things*—warriors and weapons and battle mecha—are pivotal to that end.

To hell with her if she couldn't understand his purpose!

And yet . . . and yet how lonely this place seemed without her. Surrounded by nothing but servants and soldiers now, he could almost miss the arguments of those final days. The passion. She had fled with half her brood to carry on with her mad experiments in transmutation, her quest for the perfect physical vehicle to inhabit while she completed her Great Work, a form more suitable for her wisdom and dreams, more supportive than his embrace.

"Curse her!" he seethed, taking quick steps toward the antechamber.

A messenger genuflected as he entered, lowering its head and bringing an arm to its breast. The Regent's Hellcats were restless, pacing the room, sniffing and snarling. He put them at ease with a motion of his hand and bade the messenger rise and state its purpose.

The messenger handed over a voice-imprint and withdrew. The Regent activated the device and listened, running it through again and again until satisfied that he had memorized Obsim's every word, every nuance.

Tirol under attack—by what Obsim had initially believed were Micronized Zentraedi, but were now thought to be a coalition of Zentraedi and some unknown Tiresioid race. A race of beings with Protoculture-driven starships and mecha! *This* was the astonishing thing. Protoculture could only be derived from the Flowers, and the potent Flowers were indigenous to Optera, and Optera *only*. Look what had become of those seedlings Zor himself had tried to implant on Karbarra, Spheris, and the rest.

"What could it mean?" the Regent asked himself. An undiscovered world, perhaps, rich in the Flower that was life itself, ripe and waiting to be plucked.

He summoned the messenger to return. "Make haste to inform Obsim that reinforcements are on their way." He turned to his lieutenants next, his stingraylike hood puffed up, betraying his agitation.

"The Regis is not to learn about these matters. This new world will be our . . . our *present* to her."

But only if she agrees to listen to reason, he kept to himself. *Only if she accepts the path of conquest!*

The Regent's huge hand closed on the voice device, splintering it to bits.

Jack and Karen stood transfixed at the edge of the Royal Hall's shimmering shield, unsure of what they were up against. They had given the enemy drones the slip for the moment, but there was no time to dally.

"I say we try to go in," Jack was saying.

Karen gazed into the field's evil translucency. "And I say you ought to have your head examined."

"Maybe if I just touch—"

Jack reached his hand out before she could stop him, and in a flash was flat on his back unconscious.

Karen screamed and ran to him, kneeling by his side, wondering if there was anything she could do, her hands fluttering helplessly. "You stupid idiot!"

Jack came to and looked up at her stupidly, then shrieked as the pain caught up to him. His left hand flew to his right wrist, clutching it as though aware of the torment above. Karen pried Jack's fingers loose and pulled his hand to her. It was blanker than a newborn's, void of prints and lines. She told him to lie still, ran to the idling Hovercycle, and returned with a first-aid kit. She hit him with a preloaded syringe of painkiller and waited till it took effect.

Jack's face was still beaded with sweat a moment later, but the drugs had done their job; he offered her a weak smile and forced his breath out in a rush. "Now, what was that you were saying?"

"About you needing to have your head examined? Forget it." She showed him his effaced palm. "You're going to need a whole new personality."

"No big deal," Jack muttered. "The old one was about used up anyway."

"I'm glad you said it." Karen laughed, helping him to his feet. "Now let's get back to base."

They started for the cycles, only to swing back around to the sound of metal-shod feet. Five Hellcats came tearing around the corner, for some reason slithering to a halt instead of leaping. The drones fanned out and began to stalk the two Humans as they backed themselves slowly toward one of the Hovercycles. Karen had her blaster drawn.

"Nice kitties," Jack said in a calming voice. "On three we leap for the cycle," he told Karen out of the corner of his mouth.

"But—"

"Don't worry, I can drive. You keep those things away from us."

Karen thumbed the handgun's selector to full auto. "Ready when you are."

"One, two . . . three!" he yelled, and they both bolted. Two of the Hellcats jumped at the same time; Karen blasted them out of the air, pieces raining down on the Hovercycle as Jack toed it into gear and took off.

A third Hellcat tried to keep pace with them, but Karen holed that one, too, right through the thing's flashing eyes. She had one arm around Jack's waist, loosing rear fire as he threw the cycle into a turn and raced down a side street.

"Where to?" she yelled.

"Left!" he answered, just as two more 'Cats leaped to the streets from the peak of a pediment.

Karen twisted on the cargo seat and laid down an arc that seared one of the beast's legs off. But others were joining in the pursuit; she stopped counting at eleven.

"How's our fuel?" she thought to ask.

"Going fast," he said, his bad hand up by his shoulder, comically mouthing the words. "Any suggestions?"

"Yeah. Remind me to let you go it alone next time something like this comes up!"

"I've got them, Skull Leader," one of the VT team confirmed. "They're both on the same cyc now, west of the Hall on a connecting street between two of the main spokes. 'Bout a dozen drones behind them."

"Have they spotted you, Blue Lady?"

"Uh, negative. They've got their hands full. Some rough terrain up ahead—craters, devastated buildings . . ."

"Can you exfiltrate?" Max asked her.

Blue Lady fell silent, then said, "Think I see a way."

"Coming around to cover you."

"I'm going in," the woman announced to her Beta copilot. "Breaking hard and right . . ."

"Heads up, you two!" a female voice shouted from the Hovercycle's control pad speaker.

Jack thought he was hearing things and wondered if his brush with the force field hadn't damaged more than just his hand. Karen was discharging bursts from the cargo seat, but for every drone she killed another two would appear; it was as if some controlling intelligence was directing the chase.

Jack had been forced to take some bad turns back toward the Royal Hall, and was trying to puzzle out a way through the wreckage in front of them when that disembodied voice repeated itself.

"Heads up!"

Even Karen heard it this time, so Jack new he wasn't imagining it. "An Alpha," she said, waving her free hand in front of his face. He looked up and saw the VT dropping in to match the Hovercycle's pace and course.

"Looks like you two are a long way from home," the pilot said. "I'm coming in for a pickup. Acknowledge."

"Fine with us," Jack said. "Hope she's not changing her mind?" he added when the VT didn't respond.

Karen interrupted her fire to peer over Jack's shoulder. She smacked him on the shoulder. "You idiot, use the net!"

Jack winced and opened the net, acknowledging the VT.

The Alpha dropped and let loose with two missiles that took out half the Hellcat pack; then the mecha split, its Beta hindquarters lowering a stiff ladder.

"Grab it," Jack told Karen.

They were near the central plaza again in an area of the city that had seen a lot of action, skirting the rim of a huge blast crater.

Karen holstered her weapon, got into a kneeling position on the seat using Jack's shoulders for balance, and took hold of the ladder, heat from the VT blasting her face all the while.

"Come on, Jack!" she was shouting into the wind a moment later.

Jack stretched out his bad hand, thought better of it, and took his good hand from the front grip. Karen curled herself on the ladder and leaned down to help him. But all at once, two Hellcats came tearing out of an alleyway making straight for the cycle. Jack caught sight of them in time, but forgot about his injured hand as he reflexively reached for the handlebars.

Pain like liquid fire shot up his arm. Out of control, the Hovercycle veered to the right and ramped up the rim.

Jack felt himself leave the cyc's contoured seat and go airborne. In an instant's passing, he was once again questioning his sanity, because floating out in front of him he saw some kind of unanchored column—two of them, actually, separated by an equally free-floating featureless sphere. Jack impacted the uppermost column at the same moment he heard the Hovercraft crash in the smoky crater below him. His hands, knees, and feet tried to find purchase, but he soon found himself sliding . . .

He hit the sphere and clung there a moment, wishing he had suction cups instead of hands, then recommenced his slow slide, flesh squealing along the thing's smooth surface.

"*Whaaaaa . . .*" he sent into Tirol's evening chill.

Jack's fingertips somehow managed to catch the edge of the lower column. Breathless, he hung there, nose buried in one of the flutes as the Beta circled him. And all at once his hand began to remember something . . .

He screamed and let go, recalling the hotfoot he had given a cadet back in academy days, and hit the ground with enough force to instantly numb both his legs.

On his butt now, dazed and hurting, Jack directed some choice words against himself.

Muttering, he tried to stand up.

Six pairs of glowing eyes were approaching him out of the crater's groundsmoke.

"Can you see him?" Karen asked the Beta's pilot, as she threw herself from the ladder into the mecha's passenger space.

"Not yet," the pilot answered her with a hint of anger. "I've got a biosensor reading, but there's just too much smoke down there."

Karen tried to peer out the canopy. "We've got to go back."

"Suddenly you're not suicidal."

"Hey, look," Karen said, "we just went—"

"Tell it to the judge," the pilot cut her off. "I've got one of them, Skull Leader," she said over the net. "Number two's on his own. The cyc's a memory."

Karen heard Commander Max Sterling reply, "Reconfigure and go in. But keep it simple. First sign of big stuff and I want you out of there."

"Understood, Commander. Reconfiguring . . ."

Jack slapped his hip holster and gulped. He was weaponless, and the cat drones had effectively cut him off from whatever remained of the Hovercycle. Not that Jack was even sure he could find it in all the smoke. He turned through a three-sixty looking for some way out, and spotted the partially-ruined archway of an ancient-looking building. He ran for it without hesitation, ignoring the shock waves each ankle sent up his quivering legs.

Presently, he could discern broad steps in front of him, a short flight that led to a pillared platform, and beyond that the arch.

Galloping, clanking sounds told him that the Inorganics weren't far behind.

But there was another sound in the midst of all that eye-smarting smoke: the sound of a Beta's VTOL flares. Jack realized that the mecha had changed modes and was descending. Trouble was, it was putting down on the wrong side of things. Six drones were standing between him and rescue.

Jack decided to try and wait it out; let the VT handle the drones, then show himself when the coast was clear. He limped his way up the stairs and hastened toward the building.

All at once a Hellcat landed in front of him. Jack dug his heels in and threw himself behind one of the columns as the creature leaped. He felt the closeness of its passage, and began to scramble around the column base, while the Hellcat turned and leaped again. It hit the opposite side of the pillar with a resounding crash, its clawed paws embracing the base and almost tearing into Jack where he stood. Jack jumped for the next column and the next, slaloming his way down the platform one step ahead of the infuriated drone.

He reached the end of the row and tumbled down a flight of steps. The Hellcat was above him snarling and preparing to pounce when he rolled over. Suddenly Jack heard a weapon discharge behind him; at almost the same moment the drone came apart in a shower of fiery particles. He tucked and rolled as heat and a concussive wave battered him.

Then someone's hand touched his shoulder.

It was an old man with a bald, knob-topped head and two-foot-long snow-white beard. Jack was certain he was dreaming now.

"Good work, my boy, good work!" the man was congratulating him in Zentraedi.

Jack shook his head to clear it. Behind the man was a youth his own age, a handsome lad with tinted hair and a long cloak. He was cradling an assault rifle.

"Are you the rebels?" Jack stammered, unsure if he had chosen the correct words.

Cabell stepped back, surprised that the Human knew the old empire's *lingua franca*. "Rebels? No. But we are the ones who sent the message. I am Cabell, and this is Rem."

Rem nodded and said something in a language Jack had never heard.

Cabell nodded and pulled Jack to his feet. "Your ship," he said quickly. "We must get to your ship."

"But—"

"Hurry! There's no time!"

Cabell and Rem put Jack between them and ran in the direction of the Beta's landing zone. Jack wanted to warn them about the drones, but pain was intercepting his words. Besides, the two Tiresians seemed to be aware of the things already.

Angry flashes of orange and white brilliance were piercing the groundsmoke up ahead of them. Jack heard the characteristic chatter of the Beta's in-close weapons, and follow-up explosions he hoped accounted for the last of the enemy drones. The old man, Cabell, had most of Jack's weight now; Rem was moving out front through a hair of white-phosphoruslike debris.

Then all at once the firing was over as quickly as it had begun, and Karen's voice echoed out of an eerie silence.

She called Jack's name, but he was too weak to respond. Rem and Cabell exchanged a few unintelligible sentences, got Jack between them once again, and hastened toward the call. They were close enough to hear the Veritech's whistling hum and feel the heat its thrusters were spreading across the bottom of the crater.

The glow of running lights brought out a low moan of relief from Jack. Cabell voiced a Zentraedi greeting; Karen picked up on it after a moment and instructed them to come out with their hands raised.

She was waiting in a combat crouch by one of the VT's back-swept wings when the Tiresians appeared out of the smoke. Jack thought he saw a look of astonishment on her face before Cabell and Rem set him down on the ground. She uttered something he couldn't catch and directed a question toward the Beta's open canopy.

Cabell stepped forward and addressed her.

Jack heard her nervous laugh. She had lowered the muzzle of her Wolverine, and was repeating Cabell's words for the pilot.

"You've got to be kidding."

"No, I swear it," Karen confirmed. "He said, 'Take me to your leader!' "

CHAPTER
TWELVE

Cabell impressed all of us as a kind, peace-loving man. And I knew he was one of us when he suggested that we might be able to rendezvous with the Masters in deepspace and give them what they were after (the Protoculture matrix). He'd just finished describing the horrors the Masters had spread through the Fourth Quadrant, and now he was telling us that we still had a chance to make our peace with them. Only a Human could think like that.

The Collected Journals of Admiral Rick Hunter

"I DON'T GIVE A DAMN ABOUT WHAT YOUR LITTLE ESCApade turned up!" Vince Grant was saying two hours later. "The only thing keeping me from throwing both of you in the brig is Admiral Hunter's request for leniency on your behalf. And when all the details of this are known, I'm sure he's going to change his mind as well. Do you read me?"

Karen and Jack swallowed hard and managed to find a collective voice. "Yes, sir; perfectly, sir."

Grant glared at them. He had his large hands pressed flat against the desk, but straightened up now and advanced to where the two former ensigns were standing at stiff attention. They had returned to the GMU scarcely an hour ago, just enough time for a pit stop at sick bay before being dragged off to Grant's office. Jack's right arm was in a sling, his head shaved and bandaged along his forehead. Karen had fared somewhat better, but perhaps because of that the commander was directing most of the flak her way.

"I would have expected as much from *him*," Grant continued, gesturing to Jack, "but I'd been led to expect better things from you, *Cadet* Penn. *Much* better things! Are you aware of the several *other* ways your self-appointed rescue mission could have turned out? Are you aware that *your* rescue endangered lives? Well?"

Karen gulped. "I am, sir. I apologize, sir."

Grant stared at her in surprise. " 'Apologize,' Penn—*apologize!* That is the *least* of what you're going to be doing, believe me. Now I want to know which one of you came up with this bright idea."

"The cadet doesn't recall, sir," Karen said, eyes straight ahead.

"Really," Grant sneered, looking back and forth between Karen and Jack. "A conspiracy, huh?" Arms akimbo, he sidestepped, dark eyes flashing as he regarded Jack from his towering height. "And you, Baker . . . Born-to-be-a-hero, Baker." Grant motioned behind him. "I read you were looking for a VT assignment, is that true?"

Jack raised his eyes. "Yes, sir," he said weakly.

"You'll be lucky if you end up piloting a fanjet for the sanitation squad, mister!"

Jack blanched. "The cadet would consider it an honor to fly for the s-sanitation squad, Commander, sir."

"You bet you will, Baker."

Grant returned to his desk. "Where are the prisoners?" he asked one of his aides.

"In the holding area, sir. The shuttle and Skull Squadron are awaiting the commander's word."

Grant ran his eyes over Penn and Baker a final time. It was incredible that they had stumbled on the two Tiresians, that their joyride could possibly have resulted in just the break the RDF needed right now. But breaches of discipline couldn't be treated lightly, even when the results were more than anyone could have hoped for.

Vince knew Karen's father, and was aware of the friction between the two of them. Busted now, she would have little recourse but to follow Harry Penn's lead into research. Max, however, had appealed to Vince to go as lightly as possible; seemed that he and Rick had a special interest in Karen's fight for independence. And Baker's cause as well, although Vince couldn't quite figure it. Baker was too independent already.

"Get the prisoners aboard the shuttle, Captain. And as for these two," he said, twisting in his chair, "confine them to quarters. I don't want to see their faces. Understood?" Karen saluted, and Jack did the best he could.

"Sir!"

"Now get them out of here."

Jack followed Karen out of the office. "How about dinner in, say, six months, if we're out of this by then?" he asked under his breath.

Karen bit off a laugh. "Try me in about six years, Baker. Just maybe I'll be ready to talk to you."

Jack made a face. This wasn't supposed to be the way it worked out. But, then again, at least he had some great stories to tell over at the garbage dump.

Rick was hoping to have first crack at the prisoners, but the Council wouldn't hear of it. He had presented his case directly to Lang: the Tiresians were essentially military property; and if indeed they were the same group that had made contact with the GMU, their knowledge of the Invid's command and control was of vital importance. "We will be certain to address that," Lang had told him. The Council had even found unexpected support from General Edwards, who still considered the Tiresian message suspect. Rick, however, had succeeded in limiting the interrogation committee to four members of the Plenipotentiary—Dr. Lang, Lord Exedore, Justine Huxley, and Niles Obstat—and four members of the RDF—himself, Lisa, Edwards, and Reinhardt.

The eight, along with security personnel, secretaries, and translators, were assembled in one of the Council's briefing chambers now, a long, narrow room with a single table and two rectangular viewports that dominated the starboard bulkhead. Tirol would be fully visible for the session, while the SDF-3's position had reduced Fantoma itself to little more than a slender background crescent. Presently, Cabell and Rem were escorted in and seated at one end of the table opposite Justine Huxley, a UEG Superior Court judge, and Niles Obstat, former senator and head of Monument City's regional legislature.

Rick heard someone gasp; when he leaned in to look to his left, he saw Lang half out of his chair.

"Is it you?" Lang was asking of the young Tiresian.

Lang's mind was racing, recalling a day more than twenty years before when he had stood in front of a data screen on the recently arrived SDF-1, and a face with elfin features and almond eyes had greeted Gloval's recon team. Then a robot with reconfigured wiring had walked into their midst, and while everyone was preoccupied, Lang had tried to activate that mainframe, had inadvertently taken the mind-boost and altered his very life . . .

"Is it you?"

The caped Tiresian wore a puzzled look; he turned in his seat, certain that Lang was speaking to someone behind him.

"Zor," Lang said, more shaken than Rick could ever remember seeing him. "You, you were the one . . ."

Cabell cleared his throat meaningfully and smiled, one hand on the youth's shoulder. "No." He laughed. "No, there is some resemblance––around the eyes and mouth, perhaps—but this is not Zor. Zor has been dead a long time."

Lang seemed to come to his senses. "Of course . . . I knew that."

Cabell followed Lang's gaze down the table, where it came to rest on an uncommon-looking man with dwarfish features, cropped red hair, and a thick brow ridge. The Tiresian's mouth dropped open.

"Welcome, Cabell," Exedore said evenly. "No, your eyes have not deceived you, as Dr. Lang's have."

"But, Exedore, how is this possible?" Cabell glanced from face to face, searching for other surprises, then returned to Exedore's. *The first of the Masters' biogenetically engineered clones!* The one whose very history Cabell had been forced to reshape and re-create after the Masters had turned their giant miners to warriors . . .

Little by little the story unfolded: how the SDF-1—identified by Cabell as Zor's ship—had crash-landed on Earth, and how some ten years later the Zentraedi had followed. And how a war for the repossession of that ship had commenced.

Cabell was on the edge of his seat, attentive to each added fact, and silent except when he interrupted to provide a date or refine a point.

"And the armada was actually defeated?" he said, as if in shock. "Almost five million ships . . ." Suddenly a maniacal expression surfaced. "Then, you have the *matrix*! You do have it, don't you!"

"It didn't exist," Lang answered him. "We searched—"

"No, no, no, no," Cabell ranted, shaking his head, white beard like a banner. "It does exist! You searched the fold generators, of course."

Rick, Lisa, Lang, and Exedore exchanged looks.

"Well, no," Lang said, almost apologetically. "We didn't want to tamper with the fold mechanism."

Cabell slammed his hand on the table. "It's there! It's hidden in the fold generators!"

Lang was shaking his head.

"What happened?" Cabell said, disheartened.

Exedore answered him. "The ship was destroyed by Khyron, Cabell. Its remains are buried on Earth."

Cabell grew strangely silent. He put a hand to his forehead, as though stricken. Rick recognized what he took to be a look of concern and abject terror.

"But . . . don't you see," he began. "No mere collision could destroy that device. It exists—the one source of Protoculture in the Quadrant—and the Masters have left Tirol to find it!"

"Left for *where*?" Rick demanded.

"Earth, Commander," Rem answered him.

"Oh my God," Lisa said.

Edwards and Rick looked at each other. The same names were on both men's minds, but for different reasons—Zand, Moran, Leonard. The field marshal's prelaunch warnings about Earth's vulnerability assumed a sickening immediacy. Rick suppressed a panicked scream that had seemed to lodge itself somewhere beneath his diaphragm.

"But you can overtake them," Cabell was saying. "The Masters' fortresses have superluminal drives, but there wasn't sufficient Protoculture reserves to permit a fold. They have been gone for ten years in your reckoning. You could meet them and arrange an exchange for the device. Surely they do not want war with your world—not when there are so many worlds available to them." Cabell let his words trail off when he realized that no one was listening to him. It was at this moment that he decided to say nothing of the Elders who had left Tirolspace only a short while ago. *Let them be marooned in that cruel void,* he said to himself.

Brigadier General Reinhardt grunted sardonically. "This mission was undertaken to avoid just such a war. We came to tell the Masters that Earth didn't have what they were looking for."

"Unfortunately, we knew nothing of the situation here," Lang added. "The Invid's attack against us damaged our fold mechanism. We reasoned that by allying ourselves with Tirol . . ."

"You would have what you needed to return to your world."

"Precisely."

Cabell stared at his hands and said nothing.

"What about the message you sent our troops?" Rick cut in, anxious to return the interrogation to its central issue. "What's the situation down there?"

Briefly, Cabell explained the circumstances of the Invid's recent conquest of Tirol. He described and named the battle mecha the RDF had found itself up against: the Shock Troopers, Pincer Ships, Command ships, and the Inorganic drones—the Scrim, Crann, Odeon, and Hellcats.

"Their troops are known as Enforcers," he told the committee. "Essentially they have no independent will, save for certain evolved ones, who are thought of as 'scientists.' But the brain controls all of them."

"Brain?" said Edwards. "What is this idiocy?"

Cabell stroked his beard. "It is a computer of sorts—but much different than anything either of our races would fashion. We believe it is linked to a larger unit the Invid keep on Optera. But if you can get to the one they've placed in the Royal Hall, you will defeat them here."

"They've deployed some kind of force field," Rick said as all eyes turned to him. "So far we haven't been able to penetrate it."

"What about a surgical strike, Admiral?" Niles Obstat suggested.

Cabell stood up. "Please, Earthers, I know I have no right to ask, but our people are being held prisoner . . ."

Rick made a calming gesture to reassure the old man. "We're not going to do anything rash. But we do need a way in, Cabell."

"You can go in the way we came out," Rem said suddenly. "Cabell will map it out for you."

Cabell flashed his assistant an angry look. He had hoped to keep Zor's laboratory secret a while longer, but he supposed there was no hope of that now. "Of course I will," he told Rick.

Edwards was already in touch with GMU control. "Grant apparently had the same idea," Edwards reported. "He's sent the Wolff Pack in."

"The computer is invaluable," Cabell urged. "You must inform your troops that there are ways to deactivate the brain without destroying it. It could be of great use to all of us."

Edwards felt his faceplate and stared at Cabell obliquely.

It is invaluable, it controls all of them . . . It could be of great use to us. The words rolled around in his mind, settling down to a dark inner purpose.

"I want command and control," he said into the com while everyone's attention was diverted. "Get the Ghost Squadron ready for departure. I'll be down to lead them in personally."

Exedore and Lang met separately with Cabell and Rem after the committee session was dissolved. While the military faction was off deciding how best to deal with Cabell's revelations concerning the Invid brain, Lang, fully aware of the regulations he was violating, took the two Tiresians to the SDF-3's engineering section and eventually into the hold that housed the spacefold generators. On the way Cabell talked about the history of Tirol and the sociopolitical upheavals that had paved the way for the Great Transition and the emergence of Robotech Masters.

Lang and Exedore were as rapt as Cabell had been only an hour before. At last someone knowledgeable was filling in all the gaps of the saga they had tried to patch together from records

Exedore was standing alongside him now. "But will we have enough time, sir?"

Lang said, "We have nothing but time."

The lights in the sky are stars, Jonathan Wolff told himself short of the tunnel entrance. He had dismounted the Hovertank and was gazing up into Tirol's incomparable night. But there was at least one light up there that wasn't a star, and he made a wish on it.

Minmei was somewhere on that unblinking presence he identified as the SDF-3, and the wish was meant to ascend to her heart. Wolff had hardly been able to keep her from his thoughts these past two days; even in the midst of that first day's battle he would recall her face or the fragrance of her hair when she had come to the dropship hold to wish him luck, to embrace him. He wondered how he had allowed her to take hold of him like this, and considered for a moment that she might have *witched* herself into his mind. Because it was out of control all of a sudden, a flirtation he had played on the off-chance, never figuring she would respond. And what of Catherine? he asked himself. Was she, too, staring up into evening's light, her arm around the thin shoulder of their only son, and sending him a wish across the galaxy? While he had already forgotten, broken the pledge he had promised to stick to this time, so they could have the second chance their marriage so desperately needed.

Odd thoughts to be thinking on such a night, Wolff mused.

"All set, sir," the lieutenant's voice reported from behind him.

Wolff took a quick breath and swung around. "I want it to go by the numbers, Lieutenant," he warned. "Two teams, no surprises. Now, where's our voice?"

The lieutenant shouted, "Quist!" and a short, solid-looking ranger approached and snapped to.

"You stick to me like glue, Corporal," Wolff told him. "Every time I put my hand out I expect to find you on the end of it, got that?"

"Yes, sir."

Wolff gave Quist the once-over. "All right, let's hit it."

The lieutenant got the teams moving through the smoke toward the subterranean corridors. It hadn't taken a genius to locate the entry once they had gotten a clear fix on where the Beta from Skull had touched down. And that crazy kid, Baker, had a good memory if nothing else, Wolff had to concede; his recall of the ruined buildings in the area bordered on the uncanny.

Wolff signaled for everyone to hold up at the entrance. He

peered down into the darkness, then took a look behind him, where four Hovertanks were guarding the rear. The corridor was tall and wide, but not big enough to accommodate a mecha. Stairways, secondary corridors, and some kind of huge lenslike medallions could be discerned from up here.

Wolff found himself thinking back to the journals his grandfather had kept during a minor Indo-Chinese war few people remembered. Back then, Jack Wolff and a handful of tunnel rats used to go into these things with flashlights and gunpowder handguns. Wolff checked the safety on his blaster and had to laugh: his grandfather wrote about the booby traps, the spiders and rats. Today it would be mindless feline robot drones and a host of other stuff they probably hadn't seen yet. But all in all it was the same old thing: a sucker's tour of the unknown.

"Bring those Amblers in," Wolff ordered.

Two squat, bipedal Robosearchlights moved up to throw intense light into the hole.

Wolff and his Pack began to follow them down.

CHAPTER
THIRTEEN

If Exedore had an Invid counterpart, it would have to be the scientist [sic], Tesla, for no other of the Regis's children was possessed of such a wide-ranging intellect and personality. It is interesting to note, however, that although fashioned by the Regis, Tesla had much more of the Regent in his makeup. One has to wonder if the Regis, taking Zor as her only model, mistakenly assigned certain characteristics to males, and others to females. Marlene, Sera, and Corg—her human child—immediately come to mind. Was she, then, in some sense culpable for fostering the Regent's devolved behavior?

Bloom Nesterfig, *The Social Organization of the Invid*

IT WAS TESLA WHO TOLD THE REGIS ABOUT THE TROUBLE ON Tirol. He was one of the Regent's "scientists"—how she laughed at this notion!—and currently the commander of the Karbarran starship that was transporting life-forms back to the Regent's zoo on Optera. Tesla had been something of a favorite child, but the Regis had become suspicious of his ostensibly metaphysical strivings, and had nothing but distrust for him now that he had allied himself with her estranged husband. Tesla reminded her of the Regent; there was the same burning intensity in his black eyes, the same distention and blush to his feelers. He had no details about the situation on Tirol, other than to note that the Regent had dispatched two additional warships from Optera to see to some new emergency.

"So he's gotten himself into another fix," the Regis sneered.

"A possible entanglement, Your Highness," Tesla replied, offering her a somewhat obligatory and half-hearted salute. "A complication, perhaps. But hardly a 'fix.' "

The two were on Praxis, where a shuttle from the Karbarran ship had put down to take on supplies and specimens. The starship itself, a medley of modular drives and transport units from a dozen worlds, was in orbit near the Praxian moon; it was crewed by slaves, ursine creatures native to Karbarra, a world rich in the Protoculture Peat that fueled the ship.

A sentry announced that one of Tesla's lieutenants wished to speak with him. The Regis granted permission, and the lieutenant entered a moment later. Two Praxians, cuffed at wrist and ankle, followed. They were ravishing creatures, the Regis thought, appraising the duo Tesla had handpicked for the Regent's zoo. Tall, Tiresioid females with thick, lustrous pelts and strategic swaths of primitive costume to offset their smooth nakedness. The Regis confessed to a special fondness for the Praxians and their forested, fertile planet; but Praxis held even greater charms in its volcanic depths. Tesla, however, was unaware of the Genesis Pits she had fashioned here—her underground experiments in creative evolution.

"Shall I take these two to the ship?" Tesla's lieutenant asked.

As Tesla approached the females to look them over more closely, the taller of the two began to spit and curse at him, straining wildly against the cuffs that bound her. The Enforcer turned to silence her and took a bite on the hand.

Ravishing, the Regis told herself, *but warriors to the last.*

Ultimately the lieutenant brought a weapon to bear on the pair; stunned, they collapsed to their knees and whimpered.

Tesla nodded and adopted the folded-arm posture characteristic of his group. "Yes, they'll do fine," he told his soldier. "And see that they're well caged."

The Regis made a scoffing sound when the females had been led out. "My husband's need for *pets.* Instead of furthering his own evolution, he chooses to surround himself with captives—to bask in his self-deluded superiority." She glared at Tesla, finding his form repugnant, in so many ways inferior to the very beings his ship carried like so much stock. "So what are you bringing him this time, *servant?*"

Tesla ignored the slur. "Feel free to inspect our cargo, Your Highness. We have choice samples from Karbarra, Spheris, Garuda, Peryton, and now Praxis. A brief stopover on Haydon IV, and our cages will be full."

The Regis whirled on the scientist. "Haydon IV?" There was a sudden note of concern in her voice. "Have you given clear thought to the possible consequences of such an action?"

Tesla shrugged his massive shoulders. "What could go wrong, Your Highness? Haydon IV is our world now, is it not?"

Haydon IV belongs to no one, the Regis kept to herself. Captives aside, Tesla would be lucky to leave that world alive.

Her husband was about to make a serious mistake, but she could not bring herself to intervene.

The raucous sound of a static-spiced squawkbox woke Janice from dreams of electric sheep. One eye opened, she spied Minmei on her knees across the room trying to adjust the radio's volume.

"Too late," Janice called out.

Minmei swung around, surprised, fingertips to her lips. "I didn't mean to wake you."

Janice sat up and yawned. "I'm sure." She'd fallen off an hour ago, just after Lynn had left their new quarters for parts unknown. "What is that—a transceiver?"

"No one will tell me anything about Jonathan. This is a kind of, uh, unscrambler. I thought I could pick up some combat reports."

Janice stood up to get a better look at the radio and its decoder feed. "Where'd you get this, Lynn?"

"Promise not to tell?"

Janice looked around the room, calling attention to their confinement. "Who am I going to tell?"

"A woman who works for Dr. Lang got it for me. I explained the situation."

"Stardom does have its advantages, doesn't it?" Janice kneeled down next to Minmei and reached a finger out to readjust the radio's tuner. In a minute she located the com net's frequency.

"—neral Edwards and the Ghost Squadron are already on their way, over," someone was updating. After several seconds of static a second voice said, "That's good news, com two. We've lost Wolff—"

Minmei's gasp erased the next few words; then Janice succeeded in quieting her. "Listen, Lynn, just listen."

". . . had him for a while, but we're getting nothing now. Probably that force field. Everything was roses up till then. No sign of enemy activity."

"You see," Janice said. Minmei was still upset, but hopeful again. "It'll be all right, I promise."

Trembling, Minmei shut off the receiver and got to her feet. "I can't listen to it," she said, wringing her hands. "I just can't think about the horrible things he must be facing." She collapsed, crying, into Janice's open arms.

In the nave of the Royal Hall, the Invid brain looked as though it might succumb to a stroke at any moment. Cells were flashing out one after another as power continued to be shunted to the force shield and energy reserves were depleted. A dozen or so soldiers stood motionless, awaiting the brain's command.

Obsim, too, was on the verge of panic, convinced now that the Regent meant to abandon him there. Looking frightened and desperate, he paced back and forth in front of the brain's bubble chamber under the expressionless gaze of his Enforcer unit.

"Don't watch me like that!" he shouted, suddenly aware of their eyes on him. "Who let the Tiresians escape? It wasn't me, I can tell you that much. Don't I have enough to do already? Do I have to do *everything* myself?" He waved a four-fingered fist at them. "Heads are going to roll, I promise you!"

Obsim tried to avoid thinking about the punishment the Regent would have in store for him. A one-way trip to the Genesis Pits, perhaps, for quick devolvement. Nothing like a little reverse ontogeny to bring someone around. Obsim had seen others go through it; he recalled the sight of them crawling from the pits like land crabs—obscene representations of an evolutionary past the Invid had never lived through, a form that existed only in the shape and design of the Pincer Ships and Shock Troopers.

Obsim stopped pacing to confront the brain.

"Situation," he demanded.

The living computer struggled to revive itself; it floated listlessly in the middle depths of the tank, dull and discolored. Obsim repeated his command.

"Intruders have entered the subterranean vaults and corridors," the brain managed at last.

"Show me!" Obsim barked, fighting to keep his fear in check. "Let the Inorganics be my eyes."

An image began to take shape in the interior of the communicator sphere; gradually it resolved, albeit distorted, as if through a fish-eye lens. Obsim saw a small group of armed invaders moving through the corridors on foot. There were males and females among them, outfitted in helmets, body armor, visual and audio scanners. The Inorganic remained in its place of concealment and allowed them to pass by unharmed.

"There is a second group," the computer announced. "Closer than the first. In the area where the Tiresians' transmissions originated."

That place had not been found; the Inorganics had instead given chase to the Tiresians themselves.

"They entered the way the others left," Obsim speculated. "Could they be in league?"

The brain assessed the probability and flashed the results in the communicator sphere.

Obsim made a disgusted sound. "As I feared. They must be stopped."

"Activating the Inorganics will substantially weaken the shield," the brain said, second-guessing Obsim's command.

"Do it anyway." The scientist straightened his thick neck, allowing him to regard the room's distant ceiling. "Let them waste their firepower battering us from above, while we destroy their forces below."

"Puppies?" Wolff repeated, exchanging puzzled glances with the radioman. "Ask him to clarify."

Quist listened for a moment. "She says they look like little sheepdogs, sir, except there's something funny about their eyes and they've got some kind of horns. Sounds like there's a whole bunch of 'em."

"You can hear them?"

"Yes, sir."

Wolff pressed the headset to his ear and heard a chorus of shrill barks. "Sounds like they're crying," he commented. "Verify their position. Tell them to sit tight."

Aware that the external links were down, Wolff sent a runner back to the entrance, then gave the signal for the team to move out. His group had encountered nothing but mile after mile of corridor and serviceway, with the occasional cavernous room to break the monotony. By all accounts they were well beneath the Royal Hall, but they had yet to locate a way up. The B team, however, had wandered into a tight maze of even smaller tunnels, and were now in what their lieutenant described as a database lab. That's where they found the puppies.

Half an hour later the two teams reunited.

It was indeed a computer room, consoles and screens galore, but the lieutenant's "puppies" were anything but. The creatures remained huddled together in one corner of the lab, screaming their sad song, loath, it appeared, to leave their spot.

"Sir, I tried to pick one of them up and it just seemed to disappear right out of my arms," the lieutenant told Wolff.

He gave her a dubious look and was about to try for himself when the voice of one of the corridor sentries rang out.

"We've got movement, people! From all directions!"

Wolff studied the motion-detector display briefly. There was a wider corridor two hundred yards left of the lab that led almost straight to the entrance, with two or three jags thrown in. He dispatched a second runner with instructions for the tankers, and began to hurry everyone along toward the corridor.

"The . . . *things*, sir, do we leave them?"

Wolff glanced into the room at the Pollinators' white-shag pile. "They're probably just Tirol's way of saying 'rat.' Now let's move!"

Delivered into the upper reaches of Tirol's envelope only moments before, the Ghost Squadron dropped out of Tiresia's dawn like brilliant tongues of flame, half to batter away at the Royal Hall's evaporating shield, while Edwards's elite rushed in to follow the Wolff Pack's trail. Edwards had Cabell's map of that subterranean maze in hand now, and was determined to get to the Invid brain before anyone else.

The commander of the Hovertanks waiting by the crater entrance to the corridors didn't know what to think as he watched General Edwards leap from the VT's cockpit and commence what looked like angry strides in his direction. He jumped down from his own turret cockpit and ordered everyone to attention. But it was obvious in an instant that Edwards wasn't interested in formalities or honorifics.

"What's Wolff's position?" Edwards demanded, pulling off his helmet and gloves.

A lieutenant ran forward and produced the sketchy map Wolff had sent back with one of the runners. Edwards snatched the thing away before the officer could lay it out.

"They're about half a mile in, General," the lieutenant said, while Edwards began comparing Wolff's map to the one Cabell had drawn.

"Who was the last man in there?" Edwards asked, preoccupied.

A young corporal presented herself and articulated a summary of the present situation. "The colonel has pulled back to a position . . . here," she said, indicating a corridor junction on the cruder map. "The colonel hopes to lure the enemy along this corridor—"

"It's plain what the colonel proposes to do, Corporal," the squadron commander said before Edwards could turn on the woman.

Edwards studied the maps a moment longer, then grunted in a satisfied way, and began to suit up in the gear one of his number brought over. "I want you to see to it that no one follows us in there, Captain—*no one*, is that understood." Menacingly, Edwards flicked his rifle's selector to full auto and all but brandished the weapon.

"Understood, General, we'll hold them here," the captain responded, trying his best not to have it come out sounding confused.

Edwards tapped the man roughly on the shoulder as he stepped past him. "Good for you." He waved his twelve forward and they disappeared into the floodlit entrance.

Five minutes along, Edwards pulled Colonel Adams aside to give him special instructions. Again they consulted the Tiresian's map, and Edwards pointed out the tunnels that would lead directly to the heart of the Royal Hall.

"Wolff is closer to the Invid brain than he probably realizes," Edwards began. "And if he can break through whatever it is they're throwing against him, he's going to find the way in. Detail three men and make certain that doesn't happen. Give him rear fire if you have to, anything that'll pin him down." Edwards showed Adams the route he would be taking. "I'm going around him, but I need some extra time."

Adams glanced at the corridor's smooth walls and ceiling. "Maybe we can arrange a cave-in for him."

"Do whatever it takes," Edwards said harshly, repocketing the map. "It'll be no one's loss if he doesn't make it out of here."

Elsewhere in the corridors, Wolff had ordered his Pack to open fire. They couldn't see what they were shooting at, but the energy hyphens the enemy was returning were similar to the drone bursts they had faced on the surface. There was nothing in the way of cover, so everyone was either facedown on the floor, or plastered flat against the walls, retreating by odd and even counts through stroboscopic light, blasts of heat, and earsplitting explosions.

Backed around the first jag in the maze, they had a moment to catch their breath, while a horizontal hail of fire flew past them down the central corridor. In response to a tap on the shoulder from the radioman, Wolff raised the faceshield of his helmet. They had reestablished traffic with the Hovertank command.

"We must be outside the field already," Wolff said.

"Negative, sir. Command reports the barrier is softening. The Ghost Squadron's hammering it to death."

"Edwards, huh? Guess we shouldn't be choosy."

Quist smiled. "No, sir. The rest of his team—"

"We got troubles, Colonel," the team's point interrupted breathlessly, motioning up the corridor. "I'm picking up movement. They're boxing us in."

Wolff shifted his gaze between the storm off to their left and the corridor ahead. "But how . . . They would've had to pass the tanks—"

"Incoming!" someone yelled, and the corridor ceiling took two oblique hits.

Wolff and his team tried to meld with the floor as fire and explosive debris rained down all around them. The ceiling sustained two follow-up hits before he could even lift his head. Then he heard Quist say, "It's coming down!" just when everything began to crumble . . .

"It's no use," Rick announced in the dark, sitting straight up in bed.

Lisa stirred beside him and reached out a hand to find the light pad. He was already out of bed by the time the ceiling spots came on, hands on hips, pacing. Lisa said nothing, deciding to wait until he had walked off some of his frustration. She was exhausted and in no mood for a midnight support session, let alone an argument. Even so, she had managed only an hour of half sleep herself, expecting this very scene.

Rick had been impossible since the Tiresians' capture, and his behavior seemed to be having a kind of contagious effect on everyone around him. Suddenly there was an atmosphere of hopelessness, a sense that the situation had become untenable. Lives had been lost, the spacefold generators had been damaged, the very Masters they had come so far to meet were on their way to Earth . . . For Lisa the events of the past few days had given rise to a peculiar mix of thoughts and feelings; it was not unlike a time ten years ago, when the crew of the SDF-1 had been thrust overnight into a whirlwind of terror. But she refused to permit herself to relive those moments of dread and anticipation, and was determined to steer clear of behavioral ruts. And much to her surprise, she found that she had discovered the strength to meet all the fear and challenges head on, some inner reserve that not only allowed her to *maintain*, but to conquer and forge ahead. She wanted to believe that Rick had made the same discovery, but it was almost as if he had willingly surrendered to the past, and was actually desirous of that retro-gravitation. This from the man who had been so take-charge these past six years, who had devoted himself to the SDF-3's construction and its crucial mission.

"Rick, you've got to get some rest," she said at last. "This isn't doing either of us any good."

It seemed to be the only conversation they could have anymore, and she knew exactly what he was about to say.

"You just don't understand, do you? I *need* to be doing more than just standing around waiting for things to happen. I have to get back where I belong—even if that means resigning my command."

She met Rick's gaze and held it until he turned away. "You're right. Maybe I don't understand you anymore. I mean, I understand your *frustrations*, but you're going to have to tell me why you need to risk your life out there. Haven't you proved yourself a hundred times over, Rick?" Lisa threw up her hands.

"It's my duty to be with my team."

"It's your duty to *command*," she said, raising her voice. "It's not your duty to get yourself killed!"

Rick had an answer ready for delivery when all at once Lisa's com tone sounded. She leaned over, hit the switch, and said, "Admiral Hayes."

It was the bridge: scanners had picked up two Invid troop carriers closing fast on the fortress.

Rick saw Lisa blanch; agitated, she pushed her hair back from her face. He was about to go over to her when his own intercom erupted.

"Tell General Reinhardt to meet me in the Room," Rick said, responding to the brief message. He switched off, and rushed to the wardrobe, pulling out one of his old flight suits.

"I'm on my way," he heard Lisa say into the com.

She watched him suit up in silence; there were tears in her eyes when he bent over to kiss her good-bye.

"I have to do it," he told her.

Lisa turned away from him. "Expect me to do the same."

CHAPTER FOURTEEN

We have a desperate new mission: to mine enough of Fantoma's mysterious ore to rebuild the fortress's damaged spacefold generators, and journey to the other side of the galaxy to save our beleaguered world from destruction at the hands of the Robotech Masters. If this mission sounds suspiciously like the old mission, it's because it is the old mission, played backwards. I am growing weary of the ironies; I am growing weary of the whole thing.

The collected Journals of Admiral Rick Hunter

THE CLAM-SHAPED INVID TROOP CARRIERS REMANIFESTED IN Fantoma's brightside space, using the giant's rings for ECM cover and yawning more than a thousand Pincer Ships into the void, while the Earthforces' superdimensional fortress raised its energy shields and swung itself from stationary orbit. As the fortress's secondary batteries traversed and ranged in, teams of Alpha and first-generation Veritech fighters streamed from the launch bays. Inside the mile-long ship, men and women answered the call of klaxons and alert sirens, racing to battle stations and readying themselves in dozens of command posts and gun turrets. Scanners linked to the Tactical Information Center's big boards swept and probed; computers tied in to those same systems assessed, analyzed, executed, and distributed a steady flow of data; techs and processors bent to their assigned tasks, requesting updates and entering commands, hands and fingers a blur as they flew across keyboards, decks, and consoles.

On the enemy's side, things were much less complicated: pilots listened and obeyed, hurling themselves against the Humans' war machine with a passionless intensity, a blind obedience, a violent frenzy . . .

"Are you sure you want to go through with this?" Max Sterling asked Rick over the tac net. Rick's image was on the VT's right

130

commo screen. Miriya was on the left one. There was still time to turn back.

"Positive, Skull Leader," Rick responded. "And I don't want either of you babysitting me."

"Now, why would we want to do that?" Miriya said.

Rick made a face. "Well, that's what everybody else is trying to do."

Max made light of his friend's plight, but at the same time was fully aware of the concern he felt. He had no worries about Rick's combat skills—he had kept his hand in all these years. But Rick seemed to have forgotten that out here stray thoughts were as dangerous as annihilation discs. *Nothing extraneous in mind or body,* Max was tempted to remind him. Any pilot, no matter how good he or she might be, had to keep those words in mind; it was as much a warning as it was a code. Mechamorphosis was a serious matter even under optimum conditions; but in space combat it meant the difference between life and death.

Max took a long look at the cockpit displays; the Invid crabships were just coming into range. The field was so packed the enemy registered as a white blur on his radar screen. Signatures and targeting information came up on one of the peripherals.

"Block party of bandits," Max said evenly, "nine o'clock clear around to three. ETAs on closure are coming in . . ."

"Roger, Skull Leader," Rick radioed back. "Talk about your target-rich environment. They're going to be all over us."

Max could hear a certain excitement, an *enthusiasm,* in Rick's tone.

"We've got a job to do," he advised. "Let's just take them as they come. Nothing fancy. Go for target lock."

Rick acknowledged. "Ready to engage."

Max tightened his hand on the HOTAS. He had visuals on the lead ships now, pincers gleaming in starlight.

An instant later the cold blackness of space was holed by a thousand lights. Death dropped its starting flag and the slaughter recommenced.

Jonathan Wolff had yet to see a finish line for the hellish race his team was running in Tiresia's cruel underground. Four had died instantly in the corridor's collapse, and two more had been pinned under the superheated debris; the rest of the team was huddled on top of each other at the junction, throwing everything they had around the corner. But there was something to be thankful for: the cave-in had only partially sealed off their escape route.

Moreover, while the drones were continuing their slow advance, whatever had hit them from behind was gone.

"I'm not picking up any movement, sir," the pointman was shouting above the clamor of the weapons.

Wolff wiped bits of cooled metal from his bodysuit and regarded the mass that had almost buried him. It was the same smooth, ceramiclike material that made up Tiresia's surface streets and many of the city's buildings. Some ferrocrete analogue, he guessed.

A corpsman was seeing to the wounded.

Wolff motioned to Quist and asked in hand signals if they still had contact with the tanks.

The radioman nodded.

"Advise them of our situation and tell them we need support," Wolff said into Quist's ear. "I want to see a fire team down here in ten minutes. And I don't care if they have to blast their way in with the tanks."

Quist crouched down along the wall and began to repeat it word for word. Wolff moved to the medic's side. The wounded soldier was a young woman on temporary duty from one of Grant's units. She couldn't have been older than eighteen, and she was torn up pretty badly. *Powers,* Wolff recalled.

He reached down to brush a strand of damp hair from her face; she returned a weak but stoic smile. Wolff gritted his teeth and stood up, infuriated. He spoke Minmei's name in a whisper and hurried to the junction, his handgun drawn.

Deeper in the maze, Edwards had had his first glimpse of the enemy; but he hadn't stopped to puzzle out or catalog just what it was he had killed. His team was simply firing its way through corridor after corridor, stepping over the bodies and smoking shells their weapons leveled. Hellcats, Scrim, Crann—it made no difference to Edwards; he was closing the access stairway to the nave of the Royal Hall, and that was all that mattered.

Colonel Adam's splinter group had rejoined the main team after throwing some red-hot rear fire Wolff's way. If they hadn't been entirely successful in burying the Pack alive, Adam's team had at least seen to it that Wolff was no longer in the running for the grand prize, the Invid brain.

Edwards, at point with a gun in each hand, was the first to see the jagged trench Obsim's enforcers had opened in the floor of the Hall. He had no notion of its purpose, but he guessed that the narrow band of overhead light was coming from a room close to the nave, perhaps even adjacent to it. He waved the team to a halt and spent a moment contemplating his options. Surely the brain was aware of their presence, unless the Ghost's bombing runs had given it too much else to think about. Even so, Edwards decided, the enemy was down to the dregs of its force. The things he killed in the corridors were easy prey, and if the Tiresian's word could be trusted, that was all the more reason to assume the brain was preoccupied.

He asked himself whether the brain would expect him to come up through the breach. It would be a difficult and hazardous ascent. But then, why would they have trenched the Hall's floor if they knew about the stairway? He forced any decision from his mind and fell back, allowing his instincts free rein.

And something told him to push on.

Five minutes later the team was creeping up the steep stairway Cabell had described, and Edwards's hand had found the panel stud that would trigger the door. He gave the team the go sign and slammed the switch with the heel of his fist. They poured up and out of the tunnels wailing like banshees, rolling and tearing across the nave's hard floor, lobbing concussion grenades and loosing bursts of death.

Two rows of Invid soldiers who were waiting for them to come through the nave's front entrance were caught by surprise and chopped down in seconds. But two Shock Troopers stepped out of nowhere and began dumping annihilation discs into the hole, frying a quarter of the team before the rest could bring the ships down with a barrage of scanner shots. One of the ships cracked open like an egg, spilling a thick green wash across the floor; the other came apart in an explosion that decapitated the lieutenant.

The nave was filled with fire, smoke, and pandemonium now, but Edwards moved through it like a cat, closing on the brain's towering bubble chamber while the team mopped up. Two seven-foot-tall sentries came at him, spewing bolts of orange flame from their forearm cannons, but he managed to throw himself clear. At the same time he heard the simultaneous discharge of two rocket launchers, and covered himself as the projectiles found their mark.

Edwards was on his feet and back on track before the explosions subsided. Out of the corner of his eye he caught sight of an unarmed robed figure making a mad dash for the brain. The alien started babbling away and waving its arms in a panicked fashion, as if to plead with Edwards to cease fire. Edwards held up his hand and the nave grew eerily silent, save for Obsim's rantings and the crackle of fires.

"What's it saying?" Major Benson asked.

Edwards told them all to keep quiet. "Go ahead, alien, make your pitch."

A rush of sounds left Obsim's mouth, but it was the brain that spoke. In English.

"Invaders, listen to me: you must not destroy the brain. The brain lives and is a power unto itself. Your purpose and desires are understood, and the brain can see to your needs."

Again Edwards had to tell everyone to cut the chatter. The tall Invid continued to mouth sounds from its snaillike head, which was bobbing up and down at the end of a long, thick neck.

"Behold," the brain translated, as the communicator sphere began to glow. "Your people are at this very moment battling our troops near the rings of Tirol's motherworld."

The communicator showed them a scene of fierce fighting, Pincer Ships and Veritechs locked in mortal combat.

Obsim made a high-pitched sound and swung around to face Edwards, hands tucked in his sleeves. "The brain can put an end to it."

Edwards stared at the alien, then leveled his weapons at the bubble chamber. "Showtime."

From the command chair's elevated position on the SDF-3 bridge, Lisa had a clear view of the battle's distant light show, countless strobelike explosions erupting across an expanse of local space like so many short-lived novas. The Veritech teams were successful at keeping most of the Invid ships away from the fortress, and those few that had broken through were taken out with the in-close weapons systems. But the silent flares, the laser-array bolts, and annihilation discs detailed only half the story; for the rest one would have to turn to the tac net and its cacophony of commands and requests, its warnings and imprecations and prayers, its cries and deathscreams.

Lisa had promised to keep it all at arm's length, to maintain a strategic distance, much as she was doing with the fortress. Resolute, she voiced her commands in a clipped, almost severe tone, and when she watched those lights, it was with a deliberate effort to force their meaning from her thoughts.

An update from one of the duty stations brought her swiveling around now to face the threat board: the two motherships had changed course. Lisa called for position and range.

"Approach vectors on-screen, sir," said an enlisted rating tech. "They're coming straight at us."

"The Skull team requests permission to engage."

Lisa whirled around. "Negative! They're to pull back at once."

She turned again to study a heads-up monitor and ordered a course correction. Reinhardt's voice was booming through the squawkboxes, his bearded face on one of the screens. He asked for a second correction, a subtle maneuver to reposition the main gun.

"Coming around to zero-zero-niner, sir. Standing by . . ."

"Picking up strong EV readings. We're being scanned and targeted."

"Get me Lang," Lisa ordered.

Lang addressed her from a peripheral screen; he had anticipated her question. "We've shunted power from the shields to the main gun, but we're still well protected." At the same time, she heard Reinhardt say, "Prepare to fire on my command."

"Has the Skull pulled out?"

"Uh, checking . . ."

"Quickly!" she barked.

"Affirmative," the tech stammered. "They're clear."

"On my mark—" Reinhardt started to say.

Suddenly two brilliant flashes flowered into life in front of the ship, throwing blinding light through the viewport. Caught in the grip of the explosions, the fortress was shaken forcefully enough to toss techs from their stations and send them clear across the bridge.

Lisa's neck felt as though it had snapped. She put one hand to the back of her head, and asked if everyone was all right. Sirens somewhere off in the ship had changed tone; the fortress had sustained damage.

"What happened?" Lisa said as reports poured in.

"No trace of the ships, sir."

"God, it's like something *vaporized* them . . ."

Lisa watched in awe as the light show began to wink out.

"What's going on out there—has the enemy disengaged?"

The threat-board tech scratched his head. "No, sir; er, yes, sir. That is, the VT teams report all enemy ships inactive. They're dead in space."

The tech on the SDF-3 bridge wasn't the only one scratching his head. In a corridor fifty feet beneath Tiresia's Royal Hall, Jonathan Wolff was doing the same thing.

"They just stopped firing," one of the Pack was saying.

Certainly no one was about to argue with that or be anything less than overjoyed, but the question remained: *why?*

Wolff poked his head around the corner of the corridor like some of the others were doing, and saw half-a-dozen bipedal Inorganics stopped not ten yards from the junction. And not simply stopped, but shut down—frozen. Presently, everyone who could stand was out in the middle of the central corridor gaping at the silent drones; it was first time any of them had had a chance to inspect the things up close, and they found themselves relieved enough to comment on their remarkable design. Wolff, however, put a quick end to it.

The requested fire team had arrived without incident from the other side of the collapse. Wolff sent the wounded back, along with most of the original squad—it was looking better for Powers—and pushed on toward the Royal Hall. The field command post had yet to hear word one from Edwards's team.

They remained cautious and alert as they regained the ground they had surrendered. Wolff led them past the computer room and on into a confusing warren of tunnels and ducts. Along the way they passed dozens of Inorganics in the same state of suspended animation. But at last they came to the trench Edwards had seen earlier, and instinctively Wolff knew they were close to reaching the center.

"It's blue smoke and mirrors," Edwards sneered as the image in the communicator sphere de-rezzed. He had seen the explosions that wiped out the two troop carriers, but remained unconvinced. "You could be running home movies for all I know."

Obsim made a puzzled gesture and turned to the brain.

"You have a suspicious mind, Invader." The synthesized voice had a raspy sound to it now, as though fatigued.

"That's right, Mister Wizard, and I'm also the one holding a gun to your head." Edwards half turned to one of his men. "I want immediate confirmation on what we just saw. See if you can raise anyone."

The radioman moved off and Edwards continued. "But if you *are* on the level, I've got to say I'm impressed. The brain is certainly far too valuable to destroy—but then again, it's far too dangerous to remain operative."

Obsim showed Edwards his palms, then fumbled to open a concealed access panel in the bubble chamber's hourglass-shaped base.

"The brain can be deactivated. It can be yours to command."

Interested, Edwards stepped forward, brandishing the weapon.

"Go ahead, alien."

Obsim pulled two dermatrode leads from the panel and placed them flat against the center of his head; his fingers meanwhile tapped a command sequence into the panel's ten-key touchpad. At the same time, the brain seemed to compress as it settled toward the bottom of the chamber. After a moment Obsim reversed the process, causing an effervescent rush inside the tank as the brain revived.

"Again," said Edwards, and Obsim repeated it. Then it was Edwards's turn to try, while Colonel Adams held a gun to Obsim's snout. Edwards got it right on the first take; the brain was asleep.

Edwards shut the panel and stood up, grinning at the alien. "You've been a most gracious host." Without taking his eyes off Obsim, he yelled, "Do we have that confirmation, soldier?"

"Affirmative," came the reply.

"Waste him," Edwards said to Adams.

The burst blew out the Invid scientist's brain; the body collapsed in a heap, Obsim's once-white robes drenched in green.

"Wargasm." Adams laughed.

Edwards regarded each of his men individually; the gaze from his single eye said much more than any verbal warning could.

Just then, Human voices could be heard on the staircase. Edwards and his men swung around, weapons armed, only to find Jonathan Wolff crawling cautiously from the hole.

Wolff took a look around the room, as his team followed him out. There were two devastated Shock Trooper ships and twenty or more Invid corpses. Wolff had seen the charred remains of what looked like four men on the steps. Now he focused his attention on the bubble chamber.

"This the thing the Tiresians were talking about, sir?"

"That's it, Colonel," Edwards said.

Wolff glanced down at Obsim, then at Edwards. He had questions for the general, questions about what had gone on in the corridors and what had gone on here, but he sensed it wasn't the right time—not with Edwards's team looking as though they weren't full yet. Ultimately, he said, "Too bad I didn't arrive sooner, sir."

"You're lucky you didn't," Adams told him with a sly smile. "It was a real horror show."

"Yeah," Wolff mused, watching Edwards's men trade looks, "I can imagine."

Edwards broke the subsequent silence by ordering his radioman to make contact with the ship.

Edwards was jubilant. "Tell them the mission was a complete success."

Without warning, he slapped Wolff on the back.

"Smile, Colonel—you're a hero!"

CHAPTER
FIFTEEN

It was without question a mind-boost for [Edwards], comparable to the one Dr. Emil Lang had received while reconning the SDF-1. And in the same way Lang became almost instantly conversant with Zor's science, Robotechnology, Edwards became conversant with the lusts and drives of the Invid Regent. This, however, was not engrammation, but amplification. Edwards and the Regent were analogues of one another: scarred, vengeful, and dangerous beings.

Constance Wildman, *When Evil Had Its Day:*
A Biography of T. R. Edwards

THE BATTLE WAS OVER AND AN UNEASY CALM PREVAILED; NO one aboard the SDF-3 was sure how long the lull would last, but if the Robotech War had taught them anything, it was that they should make the most of tranquil interludes.

None dared call it peace.

One by one the inert Invid ships were destroyed, after it was determined that the pilots were all dead. Dr. Lang and Cabell speculated that the living computer, in addition to vaporizing the troop carriers and shutting down the Inorganics, had issued some sort of blanket suicide directive. Many among the RDF found this difficult to accept, but the explanation was strengthened by Cabell's recounting of equally puzzling and barbarous acts the Invid had carried out. On the moon's surface, a building-to-building search was under way, and most of Tiresia's humanoid population had already been freed. The hundreds of drones that littered Tiresia's subterranean passageways remained lifeless; one day soon that labyrinth would be sealed up, along with the Royal Hall and the sleeping brain itself. But that would not be before Cabell had had a chance to show Lang around, or before the Pollinators had been rescued and removed.

There was something of a mutual-admiration society in the works between Lang and the bearded Tiresian scientist. And while it was true that the Expeditionary mission had "liberated" Tirol, it was questionable whether that could have been achieved without Cabell and Rem's intelligence. More to the point, Cabell's importance in the work that lay ahead for the mission's robotech teams was beyond dispute. Lang had taken every opportunity to press him for details of the mining operation, and was eagerly awaiting the RDF's clearance for a recon landing on Fantoma. Earth's survival depended on their being able to mine enough ore to rebuild the SDF-3's damaged engines, and to fold home before the Masters arrived.

During the course of the discussions, Lang learned something of Tirol's gradual swing toward militarism in the years following Zor's great discoveries. Cabell spoke of a short-lived but wonderful time when *exploration* had been his people's main concern. Indeed, the Zentraedi themselves were originally created to serve those ends as miners, not as the galactic warriors they would eventually become. The defoliation of Optera, the Invid homeworld, had been their first directive under the reconfigured imperative. There followed a succession of conquests and police actions, and, ultimately, warfare against the very creatures whose world they had destroyed.

Then they had traveled halfway across the galaxy to die . . .

As Lang listened he began to feel a kind of sympathy for the Invid; it was obvious there were mysteries here even Cabell had yet to penetrate. But what also gripped Lang was a sudden existential dread, rooted in the fact that war was not something humankind had invented, but was pervasive throughout the known universe. It brought to mind the rumors he had been hearing, to the effect that General Edwards was already pressing for the construction of an entire *fleet* of warships. According to his camp, the return mission had to recognize a new priority: the idea of peaceful, preventative negotiations was no longer viable—not when war against the Masters was now viewed as a certainty.

Oddly enough, Cabell took no issue with Edwards's demands. It was not so much that he wished to see the Masters of his race obliterated—although he himself would have gladly put to death the cloned body politic they had created—it was his unassailable fear of the Invid.

"Of course I applaud this victory and the freeing of my people," Cabell told him. "But you must believe me when I tell you, Doctor, that the greatest threat to your planet is the Invid. Put aside your sympathy—I know, I saw it in your face. They are not the race they once were; they are homeless now, and *driven*. They will stop at nothing to regain their precious Flowers, and if that matrix exists—they will find it."

Lang wore a sardonic look. "Perhaps it would be better to do nothing—except pray that the Masters find the matrix and leave."

"I fear they will not leave, Doctor. They have all they need with them, and your world will be nothing but a new battleground."

"So what choice do we have?"

"Defeat them here, Doctor. Exterminate them before you face the Masters."

Lang was aghast. "You're talking about genocide, Cabell."

Cabell shook his head sadly. "No, I am talking about *survival*. Besides," the old man thought to add, "your race seems to have a penchant for that sort of thing."

Rick was among the dozens of VT pilots who had ended up in sick bay. There was no tally of the dead and wounded yet, but the hospital was already overcrowded and shuttles were still bringing up men and women from the moon's surface.

When Lisa first received word of his injuries she thought she might faint; but she was relieved now, knowing that his condition had improved from guarded to good, and that he had been moved out of ICU and into a private room. But she wasn't exactly rushing to his side, and couldn't help but feel somehow vindicated for her earlier remarks. At the same time, she recalled the last visit she had paid Rick in sick bay. It was shortly before the SDF-1 had left Earth for a second time—ordered off by Russo's council—and Khyron's Botoru had been waging a savage attack against the fortress. Rick was badly wounded during a missile barrage Lisa herself had ordered. She remembered how frightened and helpless she had felt that cool Pacific morning, seeing him in the throes of shock and delirium, his head turbaned in gauze and bandages . . . It was a painful memory even now, eight years later, but she was determined not to let it soften the anger that had crept in to replace her initial dismay—an easy enough challenge when she found him sitting up in bed and grinning, well-attended by the nursing staff.

"Here you go, hero," she said, placing a small gift on the sheet, "I brought you something."

Rick unwrapped the package and glanced at the audio disc it contained—a self-help guide that had been a best-seller on Earth and was enjoying an enormous popularity on the fortress. He showed Lisa a confused look. "*The Hand That's Dealt You* . . . What's this supposed to mean?"

Lisa sat on the edge of the bed. "I think it's something you should hear."

Rick put the disc aside and stared at her a moment. "You're still angry."

"I want to know what you intend to do, Rick."

He looked away, down at his bandaged arm. "I'm going to meet with the Council tomorrow."

Lisa couldn't believe what she was hearing, but managed to keep her voice even and controlled. "You're making a big mistake, Rick. Can I talk you out of it?"

He reached for her hand and met her gaze. "No, babe. I know where I belong. I just want you to respect my decision."

She let go of his hand and stood up. "It's not a matter of respect, Rick. Can't you understand that you've picked the worst possible moment to resign? Who else has your experience? This ship is as much yours as anyone's, and Lang is going to need you to supervise the recon—"

"I don't want to hear it."

Lisa huffed at him. "Edwards will be taking over. Doesn't *that* mean anything to you?" Lisa paced away from the bed and whirled around. "You haven't heard the latest, have you?"

"And I don't want to. I'm a pilot."

"You're a disappointment," she said as she left the room.

On another level of the fortress, Jean Grant was crying in her husband's arms; Vince, in his usual fashion, was trying to be strong about it, but there were tears in his eyes. They had just shuttled up from the GMU, their first time offworld in days, and fatigue and intensity finally had had a chance to catch up with them. Perhaps in a last-ditch effort to escape this moment, Jean had tried to run off to sick bay to assist the med teams, but Vince had restrained her. Max and Miriya were present in the couple's spacious cabin.

Max handed them both a drink. "Medicine for melancholy," he said, forcing a smile.

Max, too, wore his share of bandages under his uniform; there had been more than the usual complement of close calls, at least one of which could be traced to his protective attitude toward Rick. Max had suffered some minor burns because of it, but Rick had nearly gotten himself killed. That he saved Rick's life was all that mattered—a secret only he and Miriya shared.

Jean thanked him for the drink and wiped her cheeks with the palms of her hands. "What are we going to do?" she put to all of them.

"We're going to pitch in and make it happen," Vince said, knocking back the drink in one gulp. "It can't take forever to get the generators back in shape."

Max and Miriya traded looks. "Five years," she said.

Jean gasped. "Miriya, no!"

"That's just Lang's first estimate," Max added hurriedly, trying to be helpful. "And I'm sure he's playing it well on the safe side."

"But *five years*, Max ... The kids ..."

Vince put a massive arm round his wife's trembling shoulders and quieted her. "They're both better off where they are."

"With war on the way?" Jean's face flushed with anger. "Don't patronize me, any of you!" Distraught, she sighed and apologized.

Miriya said, "Even if it takes five years we'll reach Earth ahead of the Masters. They abandoned Tirol ten years ago, and Cabell's guess is that it will take them another ten."

"Estimates," Jean said. "Is that how we'll explain it to Bowie and Dana—that we guessed wrong in thinking the Masters would be here?"

No one had an answer for her.

"So *this* is all that remains of Tirol's children."

Arms akimbo, Breetai drew himself up to his full Micronized height and made a disappointed sound. All around him Tiresia's humanoid citizenry—the weak and aged fringe who had taken to Tirol's wastes during the Great Transition—were being cared for by med-staff personnel from the GMU, which had been moved from its LZ to an area near the center of the ruined city. Elsewhere, Destroids and Hovertanks patrolled the streets, continuing their search-and-sweep and cordoning off restricted areas, including the Royal Hall's vast circular plaza.

Exedore, who had shuttled down to the surface with members of Lang's Robotech team, heard the anger and frustration in Breetai's words. And he knew that Breetai spoke for all the Zentraedi under his command.

"You would no doubt have preferred a face-to-face encounter with the Masters, Commander."

"I won't deny it." He looked down at his companion. "I feel ... what is the word, Exedore?"

"*Cheated*, my lord."

Breetai inclined his head knowingly. "Yes. Although ..."

Exedore raised an eyebrow.

". . . on some level, we failed."

To recapture Zor's ship and return the matrix, Exedore completed. It was the Imperative reasserting its hold, the Masters' cruel imprint. He was tempted to point out that the matrix would only have made it as far as Dolza's hands in any case. But what was the use of contradicting Breetai? Besides, Exedore had more pressing concerns on his mind.

"Commander," he said at last, "have you arrived at a decision yet?"

Breetai grunted. "You have become quite the diplomat, Exedore." He turned to regard Fantoma's sinister crescent in the skies behind him, thinking, *Zarkopolis, where my real past lies buried.* To be returned there after so much space and time . . .

"We will comply with Lang's request."

Exedore smiled. *An even older imperative.* "It was meant to be," he said, eyes fixed on the living remnants of the Masters' fallen empire.

T. R. Edwards studied his reflection, leaning in toward the mirror in his quarters, fingertips playing across the raised and jagged devastation of his face. The scars could easily have been erased by microsurgical techniques, but a *cosmetic* solution was the last thing Edwards desired. In their raw ugliness, they were a constant reminder of the deep-seated injuries spread through the rest of his body and soul—areas no laser scalpel could reach or transform.

He was feverish, and had been so since the incidents in the Royal Hall; it was almost as if his brief contact with the Invid brain had stirred something within him. Beneath the fever's physical haze his thinking was lightning-quick and inspired; his goal was clear, and the path to it well-marked. He realized now that he had been guilty of a kind of reductionist approach to both purpose and destiny. He had convinced himself that Earth was the star—a Ptolemaic sin—when actually the planet was little more than a supporting player in a much grander drama. But he was finally beginning to understand that *there were worlds for the taking!*

He rationalized his failures, however, blaming fate for having kept him Earthbound while the SDF-1 had spent two years of cosmic journeying.

Let Zand and Moran and Leonard play their little games on Earth. Edwards laughed to himself. *And let the Masters arrive to* soften *things up.* In the meantime he would construct the fleet to conquer all of them! It was going to require a good deal of manipulation to wrest the Council from Hunter and Lang's control, but he suddenly felt more than up to the task. Perhaps if Hunter could be fooled into setting off on some secondary mission . . .

Edwards savored the thought. Lang would be preoccupied with overseeing the mining project, Reinhardt was no problem, and the

Zentraedi would be offworld. That still left Max Sterling and that troublemaker Wolff, but how difficult could it be to undermine them?

Edwards struck a gleeful, triumphant pose in front of the mirror. "No more demolished man," he said to his reflection. "Let the games begin."

A week went by, then another, and still there was no sign of the Invid. The high command began to wonder if the battle for Tirol hadn't been won after all. With the Masters gone and no trace of the Flowers of Life, the Invid had little use for the world; so perhaps they had simply disregarded it. Cabell spoke of other planets the Invid were thought to occupy—worlds that had been seeded by Zor. Surely those constituted more than enough to satisfy them; and moreover, what quarrel could they possibly have with Earth at this stage of the game?

With all this in mind, a gradual transfer of personnel, stores, and equipment to the surface of Tirol had commenced. Refortified, Tiresia would serve as the RDF's tactical and logistical headquarters. The SDF-3, with a substantially reduced crew and half the VT squadrons, was to remain in stationary orbit, protecting both the moon and the soon-to-be-operative mining colony on Fantoma.

Hope and optimism began to find their way back into the mission once everyone accepted the conditions of the extended stay, and it was only a matter of time before a certain celebratory air took hold. Terrans and Tiresians worked side-by-side clearing away the horrors of the recent past, and the city seemed to rejuvenate. Both sides had known death and suffering at the same alien hands, so there was already a bond of sorts. The Council, hoping to enlarge on this and at the same time take advantage of Earth's New Year's Day, finally scheduled a holiday.

A rousing set from Minmei and Janice accompanied by their newly-formed backup band kicked things off. The superstar of the SDF-1 performed with an enthusiasm she hadn't demonstrated in years, and dug into everyone's collective past to blow the dust off songs like "We Can Win" and "Stagefright," classics for most of the crowd, nostalgia for some. After the set she danced the night away with heroes and rear-echelon execs, but spent most of that time in the embrace of Jonathan Wolff. No one was surprised when the two of them disappeared together halfway through the festivities.

Nor was Dr. Lang surprised to see that his AI creation had zeroed in on Rem, whom Lang, despite Cabell's claims to the contrary, seemed desperate to accept as Zor incarnate. He had been meaning to urge Janice to move in just that direction—for who knew what secrets Rem and Cabell might be hiding?—but Lang's personal encoding of the android had made that unnecessary: Janice was as attracted to Zor's likeness as Lang was. Cabell, unaware of Janice's laboratory origins, seemed positively delighted by the fact that she and Rem had coupled off; round midnight he was even out on the dance floor executing a Tiresian clogging step that looked to some like an old Geppetto jig straight out of *Pinocchio*.

Elsewhere in the crowd, Jack Baker and Karen Penn were talking; when Vince Grant had rescinded the order that had kept them both confined to quarters, Karen had reversed her own decision never to speak to Jack again.

"Come on, Karen—just one dance," Jack was saying, tailing her as she threaded her way across the floor. "One dance is gonna kill ya?"

Karen stopped short and whirled on him; he brought his hands up expecting a spin kick, and she began to laugh. "I'm talking to you, Jack—isn't that enough?"

"Well, no, dammit, it's *not* enough." Karen was back in motion again. Jack ignored a bit of razzing from friends and set out after her.

"All right," she said, finally. "But just *one*." She held up a finger.

"My choice?"

"Anything you want. Let's just get it over with."

He waited until the band played a long, slow number.

"You gotta admit," he said, holding her, "it was a good ride while it lasted."

She held him at arm's length for a moment, then smiled.

"The best . . ."

Not everyone was dancing, however. Or smiling. Years later, in fact, some would say that the "New Year's" celebration showed just how factionalized the Expeditionary mission had become in less than a month out of Earthspace. At the center sat Lang, Exedore, and the Council, joined now by Tirol's unofficial representative, Cabell; while the fringe played host to two discreet groups, Edwards's surly Ghost Riders, and Breetai's Zentraedi, on what would be one of their last nights as Micronized warriors. And separate from any of these groups were certain RDF teams, the Skull Squadron, the Wolff Pack, Grant's GMU contingent.

Rick Hunter, recovered from his wounds, seemed to occupy a middle ground he and Lisa had staked out for themselves. They had been trying hard to make some sense of their dilemma, slowly, sometimes painfully. But at least they were lovers again, back on the honeymoon trail, and confident that things would work themselves out. The Council had yet to rule on Rick's request, and for the time being the topic was shelved.

"Home, sweet home," Rick was telling Lisa. He put his arm around her and motioned with his chin to Tirol's star-studded sky. "We'll have to draw up a new set of constellations."

Lisa rested her head on his shoulder.

"Which way's Earth?"

Lisa pointed. "There—our entire local group."

Rick was silent a moment. "Whaddaya say we dance, Mrs. Hunter?"

"Thought you'd never ask."

They walked hand-in-hand toward the center of the floor, and were just into their first step when the music came to an abrupt stop. Murmurs swept through the crowd and everyone turned to the stage. Dr. Lang was at a mike stand, apologizing for the interruption.

"Listen to me, everyone," he was saying. "We have just received a dispatch from the SDF-3. An unidentified ship has just entered the Valivarre system. It is decelerating and on a probable course for Tirol. General Reinhardt has put the fortress on high alert, and suggests that we do the same. Skull and Ghost Squadrons are ordered to report to the shuttle-launch facilities at once. CD personnel are to report to their unit commanders immediately. Admiral Hayes and Admiral Hunter—"

"Lisa, come on," Rick shouted, tugging at her arm.

She resisted, hoping she would wake from this, so they could continue their dance—

"Come on!" Rick was repeating . . .

The war had come between them again!

DARK
POWERS

THIS ONE'S FOR THE MEN OF THE "BIG E,"
THE AIRCRAFT CARRIER USS *ENTERPRISE*,
WITH THANKS FOR THE KIND WORDS.

CHAPTER ONE

> *All I have learned of the Shapings of the Protoculture tell me that it does not work randomly; that there is a grand design or scheme. I feel that we have been brought here, kept here, for some reason.*
>
> *Yet, what purpose can there be in SDF-3's being stranded here on Tirol for perhaps as long as five years? And during that time will the Robotech Masters be pursuing their search for Earth?*
>
> *Since tempers are short, I do not mention the Shaping; I'm a little too long in the tooth, I fear, for hand-to-hand confrontations with homesick, frightened, and frustrated REF fighters.*
>
> Dr. Emil Lang, personal journal of the SDF-3 mission

ON CAPTURED TIROL, AFTER A FIERCE BATTLE, THE HUmans and their Zentraedi allies—the Robotech Expeditionary Force—licked their wounds, then decided it was time to mark the occasion of their triumph. It was, as nearly as they could calculate, New Year's Eve.

But far out near the edge of Tirol's system, a newcomer appeared—a massive spacegoing battleship, closing in on the wartorn, planet-sized moon.

Our first victory celebration, young Susan Graham exulted. *What a wonderful party!* She was just shy of sixteen, and to her it was the most romantic evening in human history.

She was struggling to load a bulky cassette into her sound-vid recorder while scurrying around to get a better angle at Admirals Rick Hunter and Lisa Hayes Hunter. They had just stood up, in full-dress uniforms, clasping white-gloved hands, apparently about to dance. There had been rumors that the relationship between the two senior officers of the Robotech Expeditionary Force was on shaky ground, but for the moment at least, they seemed altogether in love.

149

Sue let out a short romantic sigh and envied Lisa Hunter. Then her thoughts returned to the cassette which she was bapping with the heel of her hand. A lowly student-trainee, Sue had to make do with whatever equipment she could find at the G-5 public-information shop, or Psy-ops, Morale or wherever.

At last the cassette was in place, and she began to move toward her quarry.

In Tiresia, the moon's shattered capital city, the Royal Hall was aglow. The improvised lighting and decorations reemphasized the vast, almost endless size of the place.

The lush ballroom music remained slow—something from Strauss, Karen Penn thought; something even Jack Baker could handle. As she had expected, he asked her to waltz a second time.

And he wasn't too bad at it. The speed and reflexes that made him such a good Veritech pilot—*almost as good as I am,* she thought—made him a passable dancer. Still, she maintained her aloof air, gliding flawlessly, making him seem clumsy by comparison; otherwise, that maddening brashness of his would surface again at any second.

They were about the same height, five ten or so, he redheaded and freckled and frenetic, she honey-blond and smooth-skinned and model-gorgeous—and long since tired of panting male attention. Jack had turned eighteen two months ago; Karen would celebrate her majority in three more weeks.

They had been like oil and water, cats and dogs, Unseducible Object and Irrepressible Force, ever since they had met. But they had also been battle comrades, and now they swayed as the music swelled, and somehow their friendly antagonism was put aside, at least for the moment.

The deepspace dreadnought was a bewildering, almost slapdash length of components: different technologies, different philosophies of design, even different stages of scientific awareness, showed in the contrasts among its various modules. From it, scores of disparate weapons bristled and many kinds of sensors probed.

With Tirol before it, the motley battlewagon went on combat alert.

On the outer rim of the ballroom, members of General Edwards's Ghost Squadron and Colonel Wolff's Wolff Pack traded hostile looks, but refrained from any overt clashes; Admiral

Lisa Hunter's warnings, and her promises of retribution, had been very specific on that point.

Edwards was there, a haughty, splendidly military figure, his sardonic handsomeness marred by the half cowl that covered the right half of his head.

Per Lisa's confidential order, Vince Grant and his Ground Mobile Unit people were keeping an eye on the rivals, ready to break up any scuffles. So far things seemed to be peaceful—nothing more than a bit of glowering and boasting.

Hanging in orbit over the war-torn ruin of Tirol, Superdimensional Fortress Three registered the rapid approach of the unidentified battleship.

SDF-3 had been tardy in detecting the newcomer; the Earth warship's systems had been damaged in the ferocious engagement that had destroyed her spacefold apparatus, and some systems were still functioning far short of peak efficiency.

But she had spotted the possible adversary now. According to procedure, SDF-3 went to battle stations, and communications personnel rushed to open downlinks with the contingent on Tirol's surface.

Perhaps the strangest pair at the celebration was Janice Em, the lovely and enigmatic singer, and Rem, assistant to the Tiresian scientist Cabell.

Janice was Dr. Lang's creation, an android, an artificial person, though she was unaware of it.

Lang shook his head and reminded himself that the Shapings of the Protoculture were not to be defied. He was really quite happy that the two were drawn together.

He turned to Cabell, the ancient lone survivor of the scientists of Tirol.

What were once the gorgeous cityscape of Tiresia and magnificent gardens surrounding the Royal Hall, were now only blasted wasteland.

Above was a jade-green crescent of Fantoma, the massive planet that Tirol circled. Its alien beauty hid the ugliness that Lynn-Minmei knew to be there in the light of Valivarre, the system's primary. The green Fantoma-light cast a spell with magic all its own. How could the scene of so much death and suffering be so unspeakably beautiful?

She shivered a bit, and Colonel Jonathan Wolff slipped his arm around her. Minmei could feel from the way he had moved closer that he wanted to kiss her; she wasn't sure whether she felt the same or not.

He was the debonair, tigerishly brave, good-looking Alpha Wolf of the Wolff Pack—and had rescued her from certain death, melodramatic as it might sound to others. Still, there was a danger in love; she had learned that not once but several times now.

Wolff could see what was running through Minmei's thoughts. He feasted his eyes on her, hungered for her. The Big, Bad Wolff, indeed—an expression he had never liked.

Only this time, the Big Bad was bewitched, and helpless. She was the blue-eyed, black-haired gamine whose voice and guileless charm had been the key to Human victory in the Robotech War. She was the child-woman who, unknowingly, had tormented him with fantasies he could not exorcize by day, and with erotic fever-dreams by night.

She hadn't moved from the circle of his arm; she looked at him, eyes as wide as those of a startled doe. Wolff leaned closer, lips parting.

I love her so much, Rick thought, as he and Lisa went to join the dancing. His wife's waist was supple under his gloved hand; her eyes danced with fondness. He felt himself breaking into a languorous smile, and she beamed at him.

I can't live without her, he knew. *All these problems between us—we'll find some way to deal with them. Because otherwise life's not worth living.*

The music had just begun when it stopped again, raggedly, as Dr. Lang quieted people from the mike stand. The ship's orchestra's conductor stood to one side, looking peeved but apprehensive.

Everyone there had already served in war. Something inside them anticipated the words. "Unidentified ship . . . course for Tirol . . . Skull and Ghost squadrons . . . Admiral Hayes and Admiral Hunter . . ."

The war's come between us again.

Rick started off in a dash, but stopped before he had gone three steps, realizing his wife was no longer with him. Fortunately, in all the confusion, only one person noticed.

He looked back and saw Lisa waiting there, head erect, watching him. He realized he had reacted with a fighter jock's reflexes, the headlong run of a hot scramble.

It was the argument they had been having for days, for weeks now—tersely, in quick exchanges, by day; wearily, taxing to the limit their patience with one another, by night. Rick was a pilot, and had come to the conclusion that he couldn't be—*shouldn't be*—anything else. Lisa insisted that his job now was to command, to oversee fight-group ops. He was to do the job he had been chosen to do, because nobody else could do it.

Rick saw nothing but confidence in his wife's eyes as she looked at him, her chin held high—that, and a proud set to her features.

Sue Graham, wielding her aud-vid recorder, had caught the whole thing, the momentary lapse in protocol, in confidence—in love. Now, she rewound the tape a bit, so that the sight of Rick Hunter dashing off from his wife would be obliterated, and began recording over it.

Just as people were turning to the Admirals Hunter, Rick stepped closer to Lisa. In that time, conversation and noise died away, and the Royal Hall itself, weighted by its eons of history and haunting events, seemed to be listening, evaluating. Rick's high dress boots clacked on an alien floor that shone like a black mirror.

He offered her his arm, formal and meticulously correct, inclining his head to her. "Madam?"

She did a shallow military curtsy, supple in her dress-uniform skirt, and laid her hand on his forearm. The whole room was listening and watching; Rick and Lisa had reminded everyone what the REF was, and what was expected of it.

"Orders, Admiral?" Rick asked his wife crisply, loudly, in his role as second-ranking officer present. By speaking those words, he officially ended the ball and put everyone on notice that they were on duty.

Lisa, suddenly their rock, gazed about at them. She didn't have to raise her voice very much to be heard. "You all know what to do, ladies, gentlemen.

"We will treat this as a red alert. SDF-3 will stand to General Quarters. GMU and other ground units report to combat stations; all designated personnel will return to the dimensional fortress."

There was already movement, as people strode or hurried to their duties. But no one was running; Lisa had given them back their center.

"Fire-control and combat-operations officers will insure that no provocative or hostile acts are committed," she said in a sharp voice. "I will remind you that we are *still* on a *diplomatic mission*.

"Carry on."

Men and women were moving purposefully, the yawning hall quickly clearing. Lisa turned to an aide, a commo officer. "My respects to the Plenipotentiary Council, and would they be so gracious as to convene a meeting immediately upon my return to SDF-3."

The aide disappeared; Lisa turned to Rick. "If you please?"

Rick, his wife on his arm, turned toward the shuttle grounding area. REF personnel made way for them. Rick let Lisa set the pace: businesslike, but not frantic.

When the shuttle was arrowing up through Tirol's atmosphere for SDF-3 rendezvous, and the two were studying preliminary reports while staff officers ran analyses and more data poured in, Rick paused for a moment to look at his wife as she meditated over the most recent updates.

He covered her hand with his for a moment; squeezed it. "We owe each other a waltz, Lisa."

She gave him a quick, loving smile, squeezing his hand back. Then she turned to issue more orders to her staff.

To Rem, the Humans and their REF mission had been bewildering from the beginning, but never more so than now.

With this news of an unidentified warship, he and Cabell—who had been a father to him, really, and more than a father—were hastened toward the shuttle touchdown area, to await their turn to be lifted up to the SDF-3. Their preference in the matter wasn't asked; they were an important—perhaps crucial—military intelligence resource now, even though they were just as mystified as anybody else.

There was confused snatches of conversation and fragments of scenes as Rem guided Cabell along in the general milling.

There were the two young cadets Rem had come to know as Karen Penn and Jack Baker. They had been pressed into service as crowd controllers and expediters of the evacuation. Jack kept trying to catch Karen's eye and call some sort of jest or other; she just spared him the occasional withering glance and concentrated on her duties.

Rem couldn't blame her. What could be funny about a situation like this? Was Jack psychologically malfunctional?

Then there was the singer, Minmei, Janice Em's partner, possessed of a voice so moving that it defied logic, and a face and form of unsettling appeal. The one they called Colonel Wolff seemed to be trying to usher her along, seemed to be proprietary toward her, but she wasn't having any of it. In fact, it appeared that she was about to burst into that startling and alarming human physiological aberration called tears.

The Ghost and Skull and GMU teams were cooperating like

mindlinked Triumvirates, though Rem had seen them ready to come to blows only a short time before.

He looked about for Janice Em, Minmei's partner and harmony and, in some measure, alter ego, but couldn't see her. She had been with Lang only moments before, but now Lang was gone, too. Rem tried to push troubling thoughts from his mind, such as the rumors that were rife about Lang and Janice. Lang was supposed to be like an uncle to her, though some said he was "much more."

But *what*? Rem barely understood the concept "uncle," and had no idea what "much more" might mean. Yet his cheeks flushed, and he felt a puzzling rage when he thought of Jan having some nebulous relationship to Lang that would make the old Human scientist more important to her than, than . . .

Then all at once Rem and Cabell were being rushed into a shuttle, and a sliding hatch cut off the haunted nighttime view of ruined Tiresia.

CHAPTER TWO

I never got tired of covering the Hunters, the admirals. To me, they were a perfect couple, the best the Earth could field.
But in another sense, the enemy had fielded his worst.

Susan Graham, narration from documentary *Protoculture's Privateers: SDF-3, Farrago, Sentinels, and the REF*

O N THE BRIDGE OF THE SUPERDIMENSIONAL FORTRESS Three, Lisa Hayes surveyed the preparations for battle and despaired, thinking the REF diplomatic mission might be doomed to find nothing but war.

Approximately twenty minutes had passed since the unidentified dreadnought was spotted, and it was nearly upon them. Yet it had not responded to any visual or electromagnetic signal. Peace was important to her, but so were the lives of her crew and the survival of her command. She was as edgy as any enlisted-rating gunner, but didn't have the luxury of simply hoping she could shoot first.

And, the SDF-3 was only partially combat-worthy; letting the enemy get to close range might mean ultimate disaster. Still, the REF mission *had* to mean something more than crossing the galaxy only to fight battle upon battle, had to mean more than war without end.

She went over every detail, to see if there wasn't one more preparation she could make. Lisa looked around the bridge. There was the same small bridge watch-gang setup that her mentor, Captain Gloval, had used, except that the three enlisted-rating techs were male, as were the watch officer and Lisa's exec, Commander Forsythe.

Rick and the other officers from the Tactical Information Center—the ship's cavernous command, communications, and control facility—kept up the flow of information, but none of it was very helpful. The Plenipotentiary Council, the civilian body in overall control of the Robotech Expeditionary Force, had convened just long enough to give Lisa operational control over the situation; they were satisfied that she wasn't trigger-happy, and that she was well aware of the dicey tactical dilemma.

Veritechs were scrambled, sent out to block the newcomer's way, and intercept and engage if necessary. Alphas, Betas, and Logans were deployed to their appointed places. Lisa's eye found the tactical display symbol for the Skull team for a moment, and she thought of Rick—trapped down there among the rows of consoles and techs' duty stations, monitors, and instruments. She knew he was longing to be out there with his beloved former outfit.

She supposed his heart was even more with them in this moment than it was with her. If so, that was something she could understand, could forgive, as long as he carried out his current assignment.

She thrust the thought aside; the Veritechs were coming within range of the unidentified dreadnought. Although the ship was as big as any Earth battlecruiser, it was still far smaller than the mammoth SDF-3. It maintained its worrisome silence.

According to the rule book, the next step should be a close flyby, performed by VTs—a warning to the intruder. If there was still no acknowledgment, it would be time for a shot across the battlewagon's bow.

She found herself about to order Ghost in for the flyby, avoiding the use of Skull, but stopped herself. Although Rick would want to be with his old outfit in the thick of things, he would just have to maintain his duties as a commander. Edwards was too rash—he might even enjoy goading the newcomers into a shooting incident. Max Sterling, who had taken over Skull, was a more reliable man and the best flier in the REF.

She opened her mouth to give the command to Skull, when one of the male enlisted-rating techs said, "The incoming ship is decelerating, Captain. Changing course for possible insertion to Tirol orbit. It's deactivating its weapons systems."

As soon as the tech relayed the information, a female voice from the Tactical Information Center came up. TIC commo instruments were intercepting radio transmissions from the newcomer.

When the transmissions were patched through to the bridge, Lisa found herself listening to a strange, voice-processed-sounding garble. But bit by bit, she began to recognize syllables.

"Zentraedi," Lisa's bridge officer, Mister Blake, said softly, but Lisa was already turning to have a comline opened to Dr. Lang's science/research division.

"Respond, please," the transmissions came, in that strange,

processed-sounding voice that might have been computer generated. "Alien vessel, please respond."

Alien? Lisa pondered as Lang came onscreen. He was flanked by Breetai, and Exedore. Once Humanity's greatest enemies, these two Zentraedi were now staunch allies.

"Can you speculate on what this means, Doctor?" Lisa asked. "Or Commander Breetai? Lord Exedore?"

It was Exedore who answered, his voice still holding something of the weird Zentraedi quaver, even though he had been Micronized to Human size.

His was the greatest mind of his race, and the storehouse of its accumulated—in some cases, fabricated—lore and history. "The language is Tiresian," he confirmed, "with loan-words from our own battle language and some elements of the Robotech Masters' speech. But it is being spoken by a non-Zentraedi, non-Tiresian.

"As for the ship, it fits no profile known to my data banks, although certain portions of it bear resemblances to the spacecraft of various spacefaring cultures."

"But this is no Zentraedi ship," boomed Breetai. "Of that I feel sure. Our race conquered thousands of worlds, contacted tens of thousands of species. The language of Tirol became the lingua franca of much of this part of the galaxy. This warcraft might come from anywhere in the entire region, or even beyond."

All of them heard the next transmission from the battleship. "We come in peace," that eerie voice said. "We come in friendship. Do not fire! We are desperately in need of your help!"

"Identify yourselves," a commo officer transmitted in her clear contralto. "Incoming vessel, who are you?"

"We are the Sentinels," the eldritch voice answered. "We are the Sentinels."

Down in the TIC, Rick Hunter had a sudden vision of black obelisks and dire events to the tune of *Also Spracht Zarathustra.*

Lisa looked at the bridge's main viewscreen.

Suddenly Edwards's face appeared in an inset at one corner of it. "It's some kind of trick! Admiral, you can't let them—"

"General, that ... will ... *do!*" Lisa thundered, and blanked him from the screen. A moment later she was talking to the Plenipotentiary Council.

"Ladies and gentlemen, I recommend that we allow the, er, alien ship to land under close escort by our VTs and with its weapons systems inert. We can track it with the SDF-3's main gun, and cover it with the GMU's as well, once it's down. If it turns out that they want to fight, let it be from a position of such tactical disadvantage."

That touched off a hectic, bitter debate in the council. Some members shared Edwards's attitude after the almost mindless hatred with which the SDF-3's arrival had been greeted by the Invid.

It was Lang who cut through the rancor with a single quiet plea, perhaps the most *Human* thing he had said since that Protoculture boost so long ago.

"My dear companions, we've traveled across the better part of the Milky Way galaxy with the express hope of hearing the word they've just used: friendship."

Permission to land was carried unanimously.

Exedore was less the frog-eyed, misshapen dwarf he had once been, thanks to Human biosurgery and cosmetic treatments. It seemed to make people more at ease in his presence, but other than that it meant little to him.

Now he pushed back his unruly mass of barn-red hair and squinted at the readouts as his own data banks interfaced with those of the SDF-3 mainframes, with input from the detectors tracking the newcomer battleship's descent. As had happened so often in the past, he could feel great Breetai looming nearby.

Exedore, Breetai, and many of the star players of the REF were in the Tactical Information Center. Techs, intel, and ops officers were scurrying around the compartment, which was two hundred feet on a side and half as high, crammed with screens and instrumentation. A main screen fifty feet square dominated the place.

Exedore was matching disparate parts of the newcomer's hull features with profiles in Zentraedi files. "You see? That portion toward the stern, starboard—it's Praxian! A-and the section there just forward of midship's starboard: is that not a Perytonian silhouette, I ask you?"

Nobody there was about to argue with him, nobody understood what it meant—and neither did Exedore. "It's as if these Sentinels slapped together a variety of space vessels and united them with a central structure—you see?—to form, oh, I don't know—a sort of aggregate. Certainly, it's not a design well suited to atmospheric entry."

Exedore was correct. The assemblage ship, asymmetrical and unbalanced in gravity and atmosphere, was already being battered as it fought its way down toward Tirol's surface.

But by some miracle the lumbering vessel held together. Rick Hunter found himself rooting for the Sentinels, whoever they were. He felt emotions he hadn't felt in years—buried exaltation from his days in his father's air circus.

"Our analyses of their power systems don't make any sense,"

a female tech officer reported to the bridge. "Some indications are consistent with Protoculture, but other readings are totally incompatible. We're even picking up systemry that appears to be—well, like something from the steam age, Captain."

"Thank you, Colonel," Lisa said, and the woman's image disappeared from the bridge's main screen.

She turned to Exedore and Breetai. "Gentlemen—*friends*—can you tell me what we've encountered?"

Breetai drew a breath, expanding his massive chest, then crossed his tree limb arms across it. "It is galling to us, Lisa, and so we were slow to bring it up, but many of the memories of the Zentraedi are false—constructs of the Robotech Masters, implanted when they—"

For once she saw Breetai's head, as huge and indomitable as a buffalo's, hang in dejection. Lisa could feel immense grief and loss coming from him. "They deceived us; made a mockery of our loyalty, our valor, our sacrifices . . ."

Exedore hastened to fill the ensuing silence. "We know less of this local star group than we do of far-distant ones; the Zentraedi were expanding the Masters' empire—the outer marches, as your ancient Romans might put it. But you must understand, Mrs. Hunter—um, Captain!—that we *cannot trust our own memories* in matters like these."

Breetai's chin had come up again. "Still, we'll tell you what we know. Praxis, Peryton, Karbarra, and the other planets whose technology you see mingled there—they were all valued parts of the Masters' empire. Planets of the local star group, easily reached, they were allowed to keep a large measure of their self-determination so long as they subordinated themselves to the Robotech Masters' ambitions. They survived, in their fashion, in the eye of the storm."

"So—they would be the last to fall to the Invid," Lisa said slowly.

Exedore nodded. "The last, except for Tirol. And worlds upon which the Invid Regis and Regent might wish to vent their anger, or as much of it as they can mount, now that both sides have been so reduced in numbers."

It was true that the Invid were victorious in the long war against the Masters, but in many cases what they ruled was an empire of ash. Planets, even suns, had died. What was left in that region of the galaxy seemed scarcely worth taking.

Rick's face appeared on the main screen. "Landing party standing by, Cap'n." He saluted his wife. He showed nothing but an unerring precision, aware that his demeanor and expression would be studied on a thousand other screens throughout the SDF-3. Behind him were the two heavily armed landing craft that would fly down with the expedition's envoys to greet the Sentinels. Max's Skulls were forming up to fly escort and cover. The GMU had already churned into position, its titanic cannon trained on the grounded space-battleship.

Lisa returned Rick's salute. They cut their hands away from their brows smartly, just like the manual said. She wondered if anyone who was witnessing the exchange could tell how *happy* he was, now that he was once more venturing into danger. She wondered if he knew it himself.

The Sentinels' ship had chosen a big patch of ground that would serve as its landing pad. VTs and ground units came in to cover; fearsome armored vehicles clanked and wheeled on their tracks. The descent of the landing craft kicked up clouds of sand and dust that settled quickly.

The protocol had been argued a bit, but nobody on the council wanted to be the one to go up and knock on the Sentinels' door. So it was Lisa and Rick, flanked by Breetai and Exedore and Lang, who approached the ship unarmed. The group walked under Fantoma's light and the glare of a hundred of the two-legged Tiresian Ambler spotlights, to what appeared to be the main hatch of the Sentinels' starship.

But when the main hatch of the ship rolled open, there were none of the dramatics Lisa had unconsciously braced herself for. Instead, a robed figure stood there, at the top of a ramp extended like an impudent tongue from the side of the Sentinels' ship.

Actually, the figure *floated* there; the hem of its robe billowed gently an inch or two above the ramp.

Lang had been elected to speak for the REF. He coughed a bit in the swirling dust, one foot on the ramp where it met the sand. "If you come in friendship, I offer you my hand, on behalf of all of us, in friendship."

The being looking down on him was virtually smooth-faced, like some blank mask. "I cannot offer mine," it said in the same voice they had heard over the commo.

Other figures, larger, loomed up behind it. Still more crowded at the sides, lower and surreptitiously slinky. Outgassing from the Sentinels' ship's atmosphere put a sudden mist in the air of Tirol, and it got even harder to see.

Then Rick heard Lisa's scream, and he cried out her name. All at once he was grappling hand-to-hand with the devil.

CHAPTER THREE

I suppose we shouldn't have been surprised. We had already discovered, back during the Robotech War, that wherever the basic chemical building blocks of life coexisted, they linked preferentially to form the same subunits that defined the essential biogenetic structures found on Earth. In other words, the ordering of the DNA code wasn't a quirk of nature.

The formation and linking of amino acids and nucleotides was all but inevitable. The messenger RNA codon-anticodon linkages seemed to operate on a coding intrinsic to the molecules themselves. We knew that life throughout the universe would be very similar, and that some force appeared to dictate that it be so.

But that didn't keep the sight of the Sentinels from knocking most of us right off our pins.

Lisa Hayes, *Recollections*

T HE DEVIL WHO WAS FENDING RICK OFF WASN'T QUITE THE ONE from Old Testament scare stories. At least he seemed to lack the power of fire and brimstone, and was trying to reason in accented Tiresian rather than condemning Rick to the Lower Depths and Agony Everlasting.

"Release me! Unhand me!"

All Rick could see was a grinning, slightly demonic face from which horns grew. Then Rick felt himself pulled away with such strength that he thought the massive Vince Grant or even Breetai himself had laid hands on him.

To Rick's astonishment it was Lang, carefully but forcefully preventing a diplomatic catastrophe.

The Protoculture, working through him? the young admiral wondered.

The air was clearing and a riot had been averted. The Humans' jaws dropped in wonder as the Sentinels presented themselves.

"I am Veidt, of Haydon IV," the robed one—the one who had

refused Lisa's hand—said. "And as I was about to say, I cannot offer you my hand, for I have none, nor have I arms, as you understand the concept. Yet, I welcome your words of friendship, and reaffirm mine." Veidt floated down the ramp toward them and inclined his head solemnly.

Lisa, finding no words, returned the gesture.

The envoys from the Sentinels adjourned with those of the REF to a big, round table, set out at the council's decree, under the jade glow of crescent Fantoma in the long Tiresian night. The area was lit by banks of illuminator grids, and by the odd-looking, two-legged Tiresian searchlights.

Human servitors brought trays of food and drink, and some of the Sentinels showed no reluctance about helping themselves, though others declined, having different nutritive requirements.

Great Breetai, his oversized chair creaking ominously beneath him, noticed figures pressed against viewports and observation domes in the thrown-together battleship. At his suggestion, a wide assortment of provisions was placed in the airlocks; the Sentinel envoys were loud in their thanks, and mentioned, almost as a matter unworthy of discussion, that they had been on near-starvation rations.

The beings who looked like male and female bears walking around on broad, elephantine feet—and wearing harnesses that supported cases and pouches and hand weapons of some sort—were Karbarrans.

Veidt and his mate Sarna were from Haydon IV, a revelation that made Cabell and Rem exchange significant glances that Lang and the others didn't have time to question them about. All of a sudden, Micronized Zentraedi seemed about as Human as most in-laws, Jack Baker reflected, looking on from the sidelines.

The couple who looked like they were made of living crystal were from a world called Spheris. And the big, supremely proud and athletic women in the daring, barbaric gladiatorial outfits, Gnea and Bela, came from the planet Praxis.

Karen Penn, watching from her vantage point on the roof of a commo van, stared in fascination at a foxlike pair, known as "Garudans." They had feet whose tripartite structure reminded her of a hat-rack's base, and their mouths and snouts were hidden by complex breathing apparatus. Garudans liked to thrash their long, luxuriant tails when they talked, and on-the-spot adaptations had to be done on their chairs to accommodate them.

Cabell and Exedore had helped Lang and a scratch task force from G-2 Intel and G-5 Community Affairs prepare translation programs for interpreter computers, but in general the envoys managed with broken Tiresian. Most of the REF spoke a Zentraedi-modified version of the language, and virtually everyone in the SDF-3 had had some exposure to it, while all the Sentinels spoke it—as Breetai had said, a lingua franca.

One of the first things to become clear was that the Sentinels weren't an army, or a governmental body—they were fugitives.

"Fugitives from the Invid tyranny," Veidt said in his whispery, processed-sounding voice. The voice came from no source Lisa could detect; Veidt and Sarna did not have mouths, but they could be heard and they were being recorded.

"Haydon IV, Karbarra, Peryton, Garuda, Praxis, Spheris—our homes are worlds under the Invid heel, to one degree or another. The ship in which we arrived was to be our prison, a sort of—zoo? No, what's the word?—trophy case! Yes, and the hundreds and hundreds of us aboard, its artifacts—all for the pleasure of the Invid Regent."

"And what happened?" inquired Justine Huxley, former United Earth Government Superior Court Judge, now a council member. Her tone was neutral, from years of habit. "What changed your circumstances?"

Lang noted that Burak of Peryton—the devil-horned one—the only Sentinel with neither mate nor companion, had looked fretful throughout the getting-acquainted proceedings. Now he slammed a six-fingered hand—equipped with a second opposable thumb where the edge of a human's hand would be—on the table and raised a whistling, furious voice.

"What do the details matter? We overcame our captors, and took the ship! And for every minute we delay here, every minute we wait, sentient beings suffer and die under the Regent's savagery! Our instruments have shown us your battles; you should recognize by now that the Regent will never offer you peace, or even a truce!

"Here you sit with your dimensional fortress all but disabled. You don't dare wait for the Regent to bring the battle to you, do you deny it? Very well! Help *us* bring it to *him*! Join us, for our sake and your own survival!"

The wicked points of Burak's horns seemed to be vibrating. He glared at them with pupilless, irisless eyes from beneath heavily boned brows. "Help us for the sake of those who are in slavery and anguish, and dying, even at this moment!"

Something was plainly tearing at Burak's guts, and Rick was afraid the Perytonian was going to come across the round table at somebody. But Lron, the big male of the two bearish Karbarrans, laid a weighty hand on Burak's shoulder, and he quieted.

Nearly Breetai's height, but far heavier, Lron looked around with what he perhaps meant as an amiable smile. On him, though, it was rather scary, at least as far as Rick was concerned—with those ferocious teeth, so long and white and keen.

Lron had lowered his heavy goggles, leaving them to hang loosely at his throat. He said in his gruff, moist, somehow mournful growl, "What Burak has said, we've all made a solemn pledge to carry out. No matter what the cost, we will fight until we win or the very last one among us is dead. Maybe you, in this REF, don't understand, but you would, I think, if you spent weeks or months in cages—animals, exhibits for the Invid's pleasure."

Lron's mate, Crysta, uttered a deep, gurgling snarl, a noise like the draining of some underground lake system. Like her husband/mate, she had horns suggesting diminutive mushrooms sprouting from her forehead.

Crysta added, "We buried at space many more of us than survived; such was the care the Invid meted out to us. You may ask why we survivors made a *pact*, to call ourselves the Sentinels—a Zentraedi term, and we hope you comprehend it.

"Sentinels. The Watchmen. The sentries who say, 'This place, I protect! *Protect with my life!* Meddle here, and you start a war only one of us can survive!' "

Crysta was in full roar now. The Humans could smell her fur and muskiness. Lisa was pale, mesmerized, wondering if anything the universe could create was more awesome than an angry she-bear.

Crysta lapsed into her own language, and computers supplied the translation. "The Regent and his Invid have had their way! And now here is a war only one side can survive!"

Crysta deliberately drew her paw-hand toward her over the gleaming Tiresian wood of the round table, her nonretractile claws digging in. Corkscrew shavings of wood curled up between her fingers; lacquered on one side, naked and unfinished on the other.

When the squeal of the tortured wood had died away, Baldan, the living gemstone from the planet Spheris, spoke to fill the silence. "Will you help us? We need supplies, weapons, and allies."

"What is your plan?" Justine Huxley asked. She maintained that neutral voice, but Rick could see compassion on her face.

"First, to liberate Karbarra. There, we can reactivate the weapons mills and arm ourselves completely. Next, open the prison camps of Praxis, where thousands upon thousands of warriors wish only to exact revenge for what has been done to them."

"Then we liberate Peryton!" Burak said, pounding his strange fist.

Baldan ignored him, and Rick saw that the Sentinels weren't all of a single mind. "Eventually, after Garuda and Spheris are freed, we'll have certain knowledge we require to free Haydon IV—and then we'll be ready for the campaign to liberate Peryton. In the course of this war, we will battle the Invid, of course—perhaps we will even defeat them.

"But if not, our united planets will hunt down the Regent, and force him to surrender or die."

While the Plenipotentiary Council withdrew to discuss the Sentinels' request, Lisa, Rick, and a few others were offered a tour of the peculiar spacecraft.

Poor Lang seemed torn in two, as his determination to sway the council fought against his passionate desire to examine the ship. As it turned out, though, there was something much more immediate to worry about.

"Confirmed enemy spacecraft approaching on definite attack vector, I say again, definite attack vector," a loudspeaker announced. Sirens and warning whoopers were sounding. Humans and Zentraedi looked to the Sentinels suspiciously.

"It must be the Invid Pursuer," Burak grated.

"But we destroyed the Pursuer!" Baldan cried. "Our instruments confirmed it!"

"Then they were in error," Burak shot back. "We destroyed a decoy, perhaps."

"What's this all about?" Rick demanded. "What's a Pursuer?" Lisa was busy on a commo patch, making certain that the SDF-3 was at battle stations.

Exedore explained, "The Pursuer is a weapon the Invid used in the days when their empire was vast and powerful; I am surprised that there are any left."

"Perhaps this is the last," Lron grunted. "When we rebelled and took the ship, we destroyed its escort vessel, but not before it loosed its Pursuer at us. For two days we dodged and fought the Pursuer, and thought we'd obliterated it, but now it has found us once more."

Edwards had come up, his skullpiece throwing back Fantoma's glow and the glare of the Ambler searchlights. "Well, it's not going to trouble anybody much longer; not when my Ghost Riders are through with it."

"No!" Exedore barked. He turned to Lisa. "Admiral, mere Veritechs haven't the firepower to deal with a Pursuer. This is a weapon even the Zentraedi feared! Your GMU cannon, even the SDF-3's primary weapon—none of these have sufficient power to penetrate its shields! It is relentless, and once it finds its target . . ."

He gazed up at the Sentinel ship. "It will detonate with enough force to rupture Tirol's crust."

"Yes," Baldan the glittering Spherian said sadly. "Since its seeking mechanism is locked onto our ship, there is only one answer: we shall lead it away, into deepspace once more, and try to deal with it there."

"Is that any way for allies to talk?" Judge Huxley frowned, coming over to them from where the council had abruptly adjourned. She smiled at the surprise on their faces. "The Sentinels and the REF are now officially *involved*. The vote was five to four."

"Madam," Exedore got out, unable to express himself, knowing hers had been the swing vote. In a wave of emotion, he took her hand, pressing his lips to it, as he had seen Humans do. When he realized what he was doing, Exedore nearly swooned.

"If the SDF-3's main gun and the GMU's and the VT ordnance isn't enough to zap this Pursuer," Rick was saying, "what about throwing everything at it at once? We can lead it into the crossfire with the Sentinels' ship."

There was no time to try to come up with a better plan; the Pursuer was only minutes away. Once again, Lisa found herself in overall control; she was on the SDF-3 patch-in right away, ordering the dimensional fortress to leave orbit and swing low for the ambush.

There was no time to process orbital ballistics and computer data; she calculated variables and unknowns and, with a guess and a prayer, set the moment when the trap would be sprung. It was not far off.

"Somebody'll have to go along with our new *friends*," Edwards said with a sharkish grin. Plainly, he meant to be that one; to make early inroads with these creatures. Privately, he saw it as a possible means toward his own ends.

But Rick Hunter said, "Forget it, General. You look after the TIC and your Ghost Team." He turned to Lisa. "Admiral, I'm the logical one to go."

He had her there; Rick knew how the SDF-3's nerve centers operated, how the strikes would be coordinated and carried out, the proper command procedure for orchestrating the whole business from the Sentinels' end . . .

And he looks so happy at the chance to risk his life, Lisa thought. She almost hated him at that moment, but she was a flag-rank officer with more important things to do.

"Carry on," she said, her jaw muscles jumping. Rick saluted, turned, and dashed up the ramp along with the Sentinels.

CHAPTER
FOUR

> *With the death of Zor, the grand Tiresian design to sow the Flower of Life among the stars came to a stop. In fact, in most cases it was reversed. The Flower couldn't be made to prosper where it didn't wish to, and couldn't be coerced. The shrinking, embattled Tiresian empire was forced to divert its resources to its fight for survival.*
>
> *The Invid/Robotech Masters conflict that had promised to engulf the galaxy collapsed. The fighting on that side of the Milky Way shrank to the few remaining Haydon's Worlds, where a handful of Flower-viable spots still remained.*
>
> *There was a pattern at work, but none of the combatants had eyes with which to see it.*
>
> Jan Morris, *Solar Seeds, Galactic Guardians*

ONE OF THE PRIME SELECTIVE CRITERIA FOR REF PERSONnel had been a capacity to function in crisis and under severe stress. As hasty preparations were made to bushwack the Pursuer, the REF showed its mettle.

Not only did arrangements have to be made to have the SDF-3 and the GMU in precisely the right place at precisely the right time, but a makeshift commo/data link to the Sentinels' ship had to be established. In addition, large numbers of Humans and Zentraedi had to be redeployed, Protoculture weapons fire missions had to be laid on, and VTs had to be hot-scrambled and correctly positioned.

Lisa, being shuttled to the GMU with the council because there was no time to rejoin her ship, was even too busy to think about how things might never be the same again between her and Rick.

Entering the Sentinels' ship, Rick was assailed by strange sights and even stranger smells.

He had little time to look around as he pounded along behind Lron and Burak and the rest, but from what he could see, the ves-

sel was anything but sophisticated. The air was thick with a sol-
vent smell. Welds and power routing and systemry interfaces,
even accounting for the fact that it was alien, all seemed so *makeshift*.

Lron had howled orders back at the ramp, and now the ship
tremored as its engines came up. Rick fought down a flood of
doubt; maybe this wasn't as good as being in the cockpit of an
Alpha, but it sure beat vegetating down in the SDF-3's Tactical
Information Center!

Still, this alien scow was a strange piece of machinery; there
were safety valves venting steam, bundles of cable looping overhead in different directions, mazes of ducting and conduit everywhere he looked, and even—

He skidded to a stop as Lron and the rest made a sharp right
turn at a junction of passageways. Rick found himself staring into
what appeared to be a Karbarran version of perdition.

Or at least something close enough to pass. Rick saw dozens of
Karbarrans shoveling tremendous scoops of some kind of fuel into
furnaces that seemed to be burning in colors of the spectrum Rick
had never seen before. Whatever the fuel was, it was piled high
in bunkers nearby; the Karbarrans might have been stokers in a
nineteenth-century ironclad, allowing for their thick goggles and
long, gleaming teeth.

Rick stood transfixed, breathing the stench of singed fur.

Suddenly, Lron's enormous paw closed around his arm, and he
was yanked off toward the bridge. The trip showed him more of
the same mismatched machinery. He recalled Lron saying that the
Sentinels' ship had been put together as a sort of aggregate trophy
for the Regent, but this was carrying things rather far.

Then he was shoved into a cramped elevator thick with the
odor of machine lubricants and metal filings. Whatever the occupancy limit was, the group exceeded it, and Rick found himself
pressed up against Bela, the taller—six foot eight or so, he
estimated—and brawnier of the two amazons from Praxis.

Her body showed the definition of a bodybuilder's; the pleasant
scent of some kind of skin oil or balm emanated from her. While
most of her definitely looked Human, Bela's eyes resembled those
of an eagle.

He was acutely aware that her skimpy ceremonial fighting costume left a lot of skin exposed, and that a good deal of it, along
with metallic bosses and leather-set gems, was pressed up against
his uniform. To the primary mission of dealing with the Pursuer
a most important secondary one was added: making sure Lisa
never found out about the elevator ride.

Bela smiled at him, showing white, even teeth and deep-dish dimples. "Welcome aboard the—" Here she used a word that his translator chip rendered as *Farrago*.

"Thanks for throwing in with us, Admiral," Bela added. "You're as brave as any woman I ever met."

"Um. Thanks . . ." was all Rick managed to say before the lift door spiraled open and the group charged out onto the bridge. The bridge was a blister of transparent material, a few hundred feet through its long axis, fifty across, set high up and forward on the bizarre megastructure of the *Farrago*.

In the few seconds he had to look around, Rick noticed the same design contrasts he had seen on the rest of the ship. Then he spotted the command station of the *Farrago*.

"Why am I not surprised?" Rick asked himself aloud, walking toward it slowly, almost unwillingly.

"Gorgeous, isn't it?" Lron grunted heartily. "It's Karbarran, of course."

Of course. Who else but the hulking bears could spin a wooden ship's wheel ten feet in diameter? The wheel was made of polished purple wood, set with fittings of white brass. It looked like a giant carved spider with extra legs that had suffered rigor mortis and had an enormous hoop affixed to all its ankles.

"Sentinels' flagship, do you copy?" Lisa's voice was saying over the commo. The Praxians and Karbarrans and Gerudans and others who had been manning the communications consoles made way for Rick as he walked over, in a daze, to respond.

The mike resembled an old-fashioned gramophone horn. A beautifully luminous Spherian woman showed him how to throw the beer-tap lever so that he could transmit. "This is the *Farrago*, reading you five-by-five, Admiral. When does the party start?"

That drew a low chuckle from Gnea, Bela's younger sidekick— who looked like a giant sixteen-year-old—and an amused rumble from Lron. Lisa answered, "We're ready when you are. Lift off, meet the Pursuer at altitude one hundred thousand or so, and bring him back here in a pass from magnetic east to west, altitude three thousand feet, is that clear? We've accessed old Zentraedi battle tapes; maintain a distance of at least ten thousand feet from your attacker at all times! Do you roger, *Farrago*?"

Rick repeated the instructions word for word, then it seemed like there was nothing to say. The Sentinel ship rumbled and quaked, then it was airborne, blasting away into the sky, and still he couldn't decide what it was he wanted to say to his wife. "We still owe each other that waltz, Lisa," he finally blurted.

There was a silent hesitation at the other end of the link, then the brief throb of her laughter. "You rat! Watch your tail."

The Pursuer was the last of its kind.

Deployed now for a kill in atmosphere, it resembled an umbrella blown inside out by the wind, its fabric stripped away. It plunged toward its prey only to find that its prey was rising to meet it.

It hadn't been an easy hunt; the Pursuer had been created to home in on the Protoculture systemry of an enemy and eliminate the target, but the bizarre ship it had been stalking fit no known profile. Sometimes *Farrago* was a target; sometimes it simply wasn't.

And so the silent duel had been waged across the light-years, the Pursuer stymied again and again, frustrated by the lifethings in the ship it hunted. But now the kill was near; soon the Pursuer would know the detonation/orgasm/death for which its guiding AI sentience longed.

But now its prey seemed to be coming directly toward it, and that felt wrong. But then the Sentinels' ship did a shuddering wing-over, and plunged back toward the low-hanging pall of Tirol's atmosphere. The Pursuer plunged after, ardently.

"They track Protoculture, y'see," Lron was bellowing above the noise of reentry, holding Rick down with one hand and spinning the cyclopean wheel with the other—and a little help from Crysta. "That's how we could keep the Pursuer at bay for so long: we don't *run* on Protoculture!"

The atmosphere was giving *Farrago* a radical case of the shakes; crewbeings smaller than the Karbarrans were being jostled around just like Rick. The bridge was bedlam. "W-what *do* you run on?" Rick managed to ask.

The word Lron snarled in his guttural basso wasn't one Rick had heard in Zentraedi before, and he managed to query the thin, chip-size translating package clipped to his dress uniform lapel.

"Peat!" it rendered. Rick tapped the transmitter a few times to make sure it was not malfunctioning. He was about to ask for another translation when the bridge screens were filled with the horror of the Pursuer plunging down at them. The *Farrago* turned over and dove back toward Tirol's surface.

Rick was feeding course information through to the TIC, and trying not to calculate his own chances. The Sentinels' ship had risen high into the light of Valivarre and Fantoma, but it was falling back quickly. One good thing Rick noted was that the Sentinels' vessel, like the SDF-3, had artificial gravity, and so he wasn't likely to get sick before the Pursuer vaporized him.

Suddenly the Pursuer appeared again, looking like an enormous squid about to swallow a minnow. Rick shook off his sense of unreality and slugged Lron in the arm to get his attention. "How come it can track us now?"

Lron made *wuff*ing sounds of amusement. "We set up a Protoculture homing device in the center of the ship, see?"

Rick saw; it was a beacon on the computer-driven schematics off to one side. "Listen, Lron: I've been doing some thinking, and—"

He was interrupted as an especially heavy blow from the Tiresian atmosphere nearly sent him sprawling; Lron had caught him. Amazons and crystal people and foxlike Gerudans were struggling out of the heap they had ended up in.

"—and if this Pursuer of yours had the kind of warhead you're talking about, we're gonna end up fried right along with it when the SDF-3 and the GMU start blazing!"

Lron's muscles stood out against his pelt as he wrestled the wheel around, while holding Rick in place with his free hand. "Do you think we're *stupid*?"

"No-no-no," Rick responded weakly, as Lron spun the gargantuan wheel and the ship took up its approach.

The Pursuer had its target at last: a bright, strobing Protoculture marker at the center of *Farrago*. It plunged down. It knew its opponent's performance profile from computer analysis and hard experience, knew that the lumbering Sentinel vessel couldn't possibly pull out of its dive or avoid the final destruction of Pursuer's detonation.

The guidance AI's death was near; it cut in auxiliaries, eager for that moment.

Rick clung to the wooden wheel, looking back through the bridge's clear blister to where the Pursuer was already a discernible speck in the cosmos.

Lron virtually *handed* Rick over to Crysta. "You're right!" Standing at the wheel, the bear-being pressed the titanic circle against its stem, deepening the dive. "It's almost time to go! Well? Tell your mate and your people! That thing will be in their laps in another minute!"

Rick struggled to be heard over the winds that bucked and jostled the ship. "What're you talking about? It's following *us*!"

Lron made a sawing sound that Rick took as laughter. "No time to explain! Hold on!"

Rick didn't have to, because Crysta scooped him up. The smell of her fur was actually rather pleasant, rather relaxing.

Rick, seeing parts of *Farrago* fly in separate directions, suppressed a certain sadness that he and the REF hadn't been able to do much to help the Invid's victims. It was just bad luck; he waited to die.

Then he saw that the bridge was *ascending*.

Lisa saw it, too, from her place in the GMU: the *Farrago* was an amalgamation of the prizes of war, and now the components had broken away.

A module like a streamlined, art-deco grasshopper arced away in one direction; a thing like a glittering bat deployed wings and banked in another. Diverse segments headed toward every point of the compass.

Suddenly, the only thing remaining where the Sentinels' ship had been was a blinking transceiver package attached to a rocketing, remote-guided paravane. It lined itself up and then glided right down into the cross hairs of SDF-3's main gun and the GMU's monster cannon, while ordnance from the VTs closed in.

The creatures so used to sleeping through the long night of Tirol in its transit behind Fantoma were stirred by the light. Something as bright and hot as a sun burned above, interrupting their hibernation.

But then the glare died, and the darkness took charge of the moonscape. The things that lived in Tiresian soil and water went back to their sleep, even though long, low-register sound waves shook them.

In the barely flightworthy framework of what had been the *Farrago*, which was attached to the big Karbarran vessel that was its largest single component, Bela wiped away the crimson seeping from the bloody nose Rick Hunter had gotten when he lost his footing.

She dabbed at it with the snow-white headband she had worn under her metal war helm. Rick looked through the blister, down at Tirol and the expanding ball of gas that had been the Pursuer, and the far-off spacecraft that had been parts of the Sentinels' battlewagon.

"When we saw through intercepted messages how soundly you

Humans and your Zentraedi friends whipped the Invid on Tirol," she was telling him, "we thought you'd make good allies. But now we know for sure it's nice to meet you, friend."

She had his right hand in a kind of clasping grip, but a moment later she had his hand open, examining it, while Rick tried to make the compartment stop spinning.

"Not much callus," Bela observed. "How do you keep your sword from rubbing your skin raw?"

Rick shook his head, little neuron-firings making stars seem to orbit before his eyes, trying to figure out how to answer her.

Just then, there was an angry growl from Lron, who was overseeing the rejoining of the sundered parts of the Sentinels' ship. From what Rick could make out, it had something to do with a master junction that was located down near those impossible peat furnaces.

"Battle's over, so Crysta and Lron will be demoralized for a while," Bela said, releasing Rick's hand. "They're really quite dour, much of the time. Like all Karbarrans: morbid, always preoccupied with Fate and all of that . . ."

She snatched his hand back for a second, taking a longer look at his palm. "I don't think you're in for a very long or serene life, by the way, Admiral."

"No surprise there," he muttered, taking his hand back and frowning at it. Then he looked to Bela again. "Listen, this ship, you Sentinels—it's all so fantastic! How did you put together a fighting alliance like this? How did you assemble such a starship?"

They were on their feet once more and the other envoys had gathered round, except for Lron, who was still at the helm. "We *didn't*," Burak said. "The *Invid* did, by imprisoning us together."

When Rick asked, "But how'd you turn the tables?" everyone looked to Veidt. A moment or two elapsed while Veidt considered the question.

"I think you'd better come with us," Veidt said. "It will be more to the point to show you . . . certain things . . . than to talk about them."

A few minutes later, Rick stood at the barred cage that had once housed the ship's menagerie—Karbarrans in this case, if he was any judge of scent. But what lay moaning and clanking its shackles was nothing like any Karbarran, or any other Sentinel.

He spoke into a commo-patch mike the Sentinels had somehow crafted for him in their careless, make-do fashion. The microphone looked like some kind of jet-black motion-picture trophy, while the outlandish earphones were so big that he had to sort of drape them over his shoulders. The whole time, he was looking at the thing before him—the Sentinels' prisoner.

"Lisa, don't bother asking me to describe what they've got here, please. Just get a couple of security platoons over to me on the double. And interpreters, recording equipment, a couple yards of anchor chain, some portable sensors—oh, babe, send the whole toyshop over here!"

He could hear a certain iciness in her voice. "Understood. Keep me posted, if you'll be so kind, Admiral."

One part of him berated itself for having hurt her feelings so; but most of Rick Hunter was simply staring, aghast, at what crouched in the cell.

CHAPTER
FIVE

It was almost as if I had called up something from the unformed, the ultimate Potential, into existence. The appearance of the Sentinels was the answer to my every requirement, in the wake of the vast power I had secretly wrested from the Invid, power I was as yet unable to exercise.

There are a few individuals in the timestream of this universe who have been granted the gift of sheer Will, to mold events according to their desire. I am one of them.

Or perhaps, in a way, I am all of them.

General T. R. Edwards, personal journal

"NOT A MERE SCIENTIST," THE INVID CORRECTED sharply, with a rattling of manacles that made some of the guards put their hands to their pistol butts. "*I* am *Tesla*, Master Scientist to the Invid Regent! Now, release me, you pitiful lower life-forms!"

Tesla turned his huge wrists, testing the strength of the forged-alloy shackles the Sentinels had put on him. His grainy green skin rasped against the metal. He stretched the three thick fingers of both hands and flexed the opposable thumbs. "Release me, I say! Or you will feel the vengeance of the Invid!"

Tesla was a creature about ten feet tall, with a thick, reasonably humanoid torso and limbs. But his head was a slender extension resembling a snail's snout, with two huge black liquid eyes set on either side. At the tip of the snout were two sensor antennae like glistening slugs that glowed whenever he spoke.

Rick found himself looking at those eyes, much as he tried to avoid it, while Lang and the others made their recordings and measurements. The eyes were as unemotional and unrevealing as a shark's, but they were set forward in the sluglike head. And conventional Darwinian reasoning said that the main purpose for such placement was *pursuit*—the Invid were predators.

176

Just like Humans.

Rick had yielded the floor to the astounded sci/tech squads from SDF-3 who had come in answer to his call, to evaluate Tesla and try to gain some kind of understanding of the bizarre turn the whole mission had taken.

Rick had a towel around his shoulders, wiping his forehead from time to time; he suddenly realized that Veidt was hovering near.

Wasn't he on the other side of the compartment a second ago? Oh, well. "Ah, Lord Veidt—"

" 'Veidt' will suffice," the being corrected.

"Okay, okay, 'Veidt,' then: I guess we need to know first things first. You Sentinels aren't so much in a shooting war with the Invid as trying to put together an uprising, right?"

Veidt hesitated, and Rick threw the towel to the deck. Some of his blood was drying on it, scarlet going to rust-red. "Let's save fine distinctions for later! Am I right or am I wrong?"

"You are right," Veidt said as he and Rick and the Sentinels watched the Human sci/tech teams push and shove each other to get closer to Tesla. "Once, the Invid and the Zentraedi savaged this entire part of the galaxy, fighting their war. With the collapse of that struggle, contact with all the outlying stellar systems has been lost.

"Now, the war has boiled down to the few habitable planets in this close stellar group: Tirol, Optera, Haydon IV, Garuda, and the rest. The ability—and perhaps the will—to venture out into the horrible aftermath of the great Invid-Zentraedi wars has been lost, Admiral.

"But, as I have said, you're right. The worlds unlucky enough to be here in the 'close stars'—accessible with non-Protoculture superluminal drives—are still under the Invid heel. Yet, time and history and the Shapings of the Protoculture have their own rhythm, Admiral. And while the . . . *slavery!* . . . we've suffered, the cruelty and mistreatment, may not be high on your Earthly agenda, the war to free the Near Planets is the thing that unites the Sentinels in a blood oath."

Veidt was quivering like a tuning fork; Rick had thought him robotic and cold, but he now saw passion in his face. "We were in cages. Do you know what that's like, young Admiral? To be caged like an animal?

"Of course you don't! The Sentinels will accept you as allies, and enlist others who are willing to fight, but I'll tell you something, Admiral Hunter: none among us will ever feel quite the same bond with anyone who wasn't caged with us—trust them to fight, as we intend to, *until we win or until we die!*"

Rick thought for a moment about Earth history. Of monstrous freight trains and mass gas chambers. He picked the towel up off the deck, folding it carefully. "Fair enough." He looked to Veidt. "But we're going to help you. And if you want to know why, just look through our ship's history files."

Veidt nodded as if he already had. "We have all agreed to recrew this ship, if possible, and set course for Karbarra. Without delay."

"What? Wait a second!" There would have to be meetings, resolutions from the council, personnel allocations, resource diversion, interdivision liaison, staff meetings, marital counseling, maintenance checks . . .

"What d'ya *mean,* 'without delay'?"

"I mean that within twenty-four of your hours, we intend to depart," Veidt answered in a reasonable tone. "Would ten days be better? Or ten months? You may multiply the beings who will die under Invid tyranny by the *minute!*"

"All right; you've made your point," Rick grunted in a sound like something Lron would make. "I guess it's doable." He was staring over at the people who seemed to be prepared to climb *into* the cage with Tesla to get good shots of him.

So that's the enemy. Or at least one form of him. "He was your, zookeeper, right?" Rick asked Veidt.

"I think the words coincide," Veidt allowed. "Though I suppose Tesla had much more *unhappy* plans for us. Why?"

"How'd you beat him?" Rick pressed. "How'd you take the ship?"

"Ah. Well. Sarna and I were chained by the neck—no arms, of course—and fed by Invid functionaries, from beyond a line they'd drawn on the deck. But after some time we came up with a way to eradicate *their* line, and draw one of our own, a line much closer to us. The rest was even simpler than fooling the Invid."

So all this apparent limblessness didn't mean that Veidt and his kind couldn't knock some Invid out of commission, although they had perhaps used a method that had nothing to do with savate or tae kwon do. Rick filed the information in his memory, and was about to get on to matters at hand, when he heard a mighty roaring.

The Invid Master Scientist, Tesla, wasn't happy with Sentinel protocol. Praxian amazons harried him with electrified prods; Karbarran deck apes jostled him in rude fashion—preparing him for interrogation. Not a single Sentinel showed any excessive brutality, but not a single one showed the least kindness, either.

In that moment, long before his conversations with the Plenipotentiary Council or his consultations with his wife, Rick Hunter understood that the Sentinels would do just what they had pledged one another: win or die.

And he knew that he would go with them, even though it might mean the death of his marriage. But the courage he admired in the Sentinels wasn't very much different from the courage he adored in Lisa.

The Sentinels were adamant about their departure schedule, despite the council's demand for time to mull it over. Then Miriya Sterling came up with a little salesmanship. She considered the problem with a soldier's insight, and whispered a suggestion into the ear of her husband, Max Sterling, Skull Leader. Max passed it on to Lisa.

Lisa Hayes Hunter still didn't know exactly what to feel about the Sentinels' appearance. Aside from the new crisis it had thrust upon the SDF-3, there was the striking change in Rick. But when she found herself hoping the council would vote *not* to extend aid to the revolutionaries, Lisa reminded herself of the lives being crushed and extinguished by the Invid.

So, she took Miriya's advice, and gave the Sentinel leaders a quick tour of some of the superdimensional fortress's armories in an aircar. The Karbarrans, in particular, showed their delight at the ranked mecha, howling and pounding the aircar's railing until they threatened to damage it. The pilot guided them slowly past Hovertanks and Logans, and second-generation Destroids along with armored ground vehicles and self-propelled artillery.

The women of Praxis, in particular, were loud in their praise of such wonderful war machines. Lisa felt fascinated and a little threatened by their bigger-than-life, bloodthirsty beauty. She looked to her husband from time to time; he seemed lost in thought. But she could tell, could almost hear, what he was thinking, and it made her feel empty inside.

"Amazing," Lang kept mumbling, skimming the preliminary reports from the sci/tech people and the intel teams that had gone aboard the Sentinels' flagship.

Justine Huxley, next to him at the council table, made an exasperated sound and leaned over to whisper into his ear. "Emil, please! This is crucial!"

He wanted to object, to tell her how much more fascinating his

data was than more of the endless wrangling and political maneuvering the Sentinels' appearance had generated. But she was right;
even the council sensed the urgency of the situation, and was
moving with unaccustomed speed.

Still, there was a wealth of information the Sentinels had given
the expedition teams! Take the drive of that incredible Karbarran
vessel, for example. Hunter hadn't been hallucinating: it was powered by furnaces that consumed a substance analogous to peat or
lignite. But the stuff seemed to be some sort of distant forerunner
of the Flower of Life itself—an Ur-Flower! And then there was
the half myth, half religion that surrounded the ancient being or
entity known as Haydon . . .

He realized someone was addressing him. "Eh? What was that,
Mr. Chairman?"

Senator Longchamps controlled his temper and began again. "I
asked if, in your opinion, it would be feasible for the SDF-3 to accompany the Sentinels and lend her firepower in support of their
mission."

Lang threw down his papers. "The entire idea is asinine, my
dear sir! The damage we suffered is far from repaired, and it will
be two years, at the very least, before our primary drive is repaired!

"But more to the point, the SDF-3 *must* remain here to insure
that the mining of monopole ore goes on uninterrupted. Without
Fantoma's ore, we have no way home. So you see, what the Sentinels proposed is the wisest course—the only sensible one open
to us, in my opinion. We must detach what military forces we can
to aid them in their cause and at the same time divert the Invid."

"I concur," Exedore said, and Justine Huxley nodded.

"You tell 'em," T. R. Edwards smirked from one side, having
finished his testimony a short time before.

Edwards's sudden willingness to see SDF forces seconded to
the Sentinels—his almost *eager* advocacy of the plan—perplexed
and worried Exedore and some of the others. It wasn't like the
man to feel compassion for non-Humans; in fact, his hatred of
Zentraedi was well known, and his hostility toward Rem and
Cabell was already evident.

But, Edwards saw the opportunity presented by the Sentinels'
arrival as something of a miracle. The incredible secret to which
he had been exposed during the first assault on Tirol had expanded his horizons until they spanned the galaxy.

With a little shrewd maneuvering, he could get rid of most or
all of those who stood in his path to power. They would be out

of the way for as long as the Sentinels' war lasted, and perhaps forever, given the vagaries of combat.

"We estimate that we can assign mixed forces totaling some thousand or so to the Sentinels' cause, along with mecha, equipment, and so forth, and still leave ourselves sufficient resources to defend the SDF-3, Tirol, and the mining operations on Fantoma," a G-3 operations staff officer was telling the council. "The Sentinels will need experienced senior commanders to help them plan strategy and arm, organize, and train the troops they mean to recruit as they go along."

He sat down; Justine Huxley spoke. "It comes down to this, ladies and gentlemen: shall we let these people fight for their freedom unaided? And shall we simply wait here, with the SDF-3 barely mobile, for the Invid to bring the battle to us?"

There wasn't much arguing after that; the motion was carried seven to three, with two abstentions. A G-1 personnel officer explained that records were being reviewed by computers, to pick the most appropriate people for the contingent to be assigned to the Sentinels.

"Along with the obvious criteria of combat performance and so forth," he went on, "will be such things as adaptability and mental/emotional profile—especially the capacity to work with non-Human life-forms."

Edwards hid his smile. His own aversion to aliens was well known; there was little likelihood that he would be selected.

The meeting broke up quickly, with people hurrying off on assignments, burdened by a tremendous workload and a ridiculously close deadline. Only Edwards, shadowed by his aide, Major Benson, seemed to feel no urgency. But on his way out of the Royal Hall, he spied Colonel Wolff.

Wolff was trying to start a conversation with Lynn-Minmei, who in turn was doing her best to listen for news of what had happened at the meeting.

Edwards frowned at his rival. He murmured to himself, "Yes, Colonel. I think 'The Sentinels Need You!' "

Adams, his aide, heard, and said in a low voice, "But sir, what if Wolff doesn't volunteer?"

Edwards turned to the man, one arched brow going up, the other hidden behind his mirror-bright half mask. "Major, everyone in the SDF-3 is *already* a volunteer."

CHAPTER SIX

One of the Karbarran scientists was named Obu, and I posed to him some questions about the amazing Ur-Flower-powered starship they had arrived in. I asked him why the ursinoids had to actually handle the stuff for the process to work.

His answer, even with help from a translating chip, was, "The Sekiton's [ ] likes our [ ] and then fondly yields up the conversion that permits the [ ] to take place and delights in energy being bestowed."

Fortunately, scientists don't live or die according to their ability to figure things out; they just want to try.

Exedore, *SDF-3 and Me*

TWENTY-FOUR HOURS WERE NOT ENOUGH, BUT THE SENTINELS would only push back their departure time on an hour-by-hour basis.

Preparations for the Sentinels' campaign had people working around the clock. The first lists of personnel assigned to the Sentinels appeared only two hours after the end of the council meeting.

Anyone on the list had the option of applying for a deferment; fewer then twenty percent did so.

Lang was one of those who *knew* his name wouldn't appear on the list. Despite his vast curiosity about the things that lay ahead for the liberators, he knew he could not go along.

At his request, Janice Em interrupted her labors as a computer operator and gofer for the Council Advisory Staff, and joined him in his office. He was alone, sipping tea, when she got there. She refused the offer of some orange mandarin, but accepted a chair.

Janice felt an undercurrent—not fear, but a reaction to Lang that she could never pin down. She knew he had been her friend for a long time, and that she trusted him implicitly. Still, she always felt things crowding on the edge of her consciousness, things she couldn't name, when he looked at her like this. After a little small talk Lang put down his cup and saucer and leaned very close to her. Janice wanted to move away, or tell Dr. Lang to, but found that she couldn't speak, and somehow hated the unfairness of it . . .

"Janice," he said evenly. "Retinal scan."

The part of her that was the conscious Janice Em slipped away, even as her eyes took on an inner glow that grew quite bright for a moment, then faded.

When it was gone, her eyes and face had lost all animation, and her skin its color and tautness. "ID confirmed, Dr. Lang. Your request."

Lang blinked a bit from the dazzle of her ID scan. "Janice, I have arranged for you to be selected to accompany the Sentinels' mission. You will accept the assignment."

"Yes, Doctor."

"Bring back all relevant data, with particular attention to Protoculture, the Flower of Life, Zor, the Invid Regis and Regent, and the nature and activities of the Robotech Masters."

"Of course, sir."

Lang rubbed his eyes. What else? "Oh yes: I am also *extremely* interested in matters pertaining to the life-form, being, or mythical figure known as 'Haydon.' Gather all pertinent data."

"I will, Dr. Lang."

"Good. Now hold still a moment . . ."

Lang reached behind her neck to remove the dermal plug concealed by her thick fall of pale lavender hair. He inserted a jack into the access port there, and began a high-speed transferral of information.

Janice was the most sophisticated android ever created, the crowning achievement of decades of work. She was programmed with a wealth of skills and abilities, but she was going forth now as part of a military expedition. Lang was giving her as much combat programming as he could, and he regretted that he would be forced to break up the formidable weapon of Janice and Minmei, and the tremendous effect of their harmonies.

But it couldn't be helped; Minmei simply wouldn't be permitted to go along on the liberation campaign, and Lang *had* to have an absolutely trustworthy agent on the scene.

He had detached the jack and replaced the dermal plug when there was a knock at his door. With a word, he transformed the android back into a woman. He was stroking her hair back into place when the door opened.

Apparently, it wasn't a Praxian custom to wait for permission to enter a private chamber. Bela stood there, with a large Terran book in her sinewy right hand. She was looking strangely at Lang and Janice, as Janice blinked and resumed coherent thought. Bela was wearing a two-handed short sword with a well-worn grip, and a basket-hilted knife with a foot-long blade.

"Is this some sexual rite?" she asked, her hawk eyes moving from one to the other, with no sign of embarrassment. "Should I leave?"

"No, no, er," Lang hastened to hand Janice a packet of notes he had prepared. "Miss Em was simply picking up some receipted documents for the Council Advisory Staff."

Janice seemed a little dazed, but recovered in moments. "Yes. I'll hand-deliver them and bring back your receipt, Doctor."

"That would be fine, my dear."

Bela's gull-wing brows furrowed, and when Janice had left, she scrutinized Lang with a certain distant attention.

Lang considered her: a magnificent specimen, wasp-waisted, full-hipped and high-breasted, dressed, if that was what one would call it, in an ensemble of leather and metal that left her more naked than clothed.

So far, Rick Hunter had kept the Praxians separated from the SDF-3's self-appointed Romeos, but Lang assumed that some very interesting, and perhaps robust, social dynamics would come into play somewhere down the line on the Sentinel mission. Of course, Lang assured himself, he was above all that sort of thing. However, he couldn't help but admire Bela's amazing length of leg, her incredible abdominal definition . . .

He shook himself just a bit, blinking, just as Janice Em had only moments before. "How may I help you, er, Bela?"

She put her book down on one of his lab tables, handling it reverently. "I found this in one of your lore-houses. You know this creature?"

She had opened the mythology textbook to a series of photos and lithos of Pegasus, and similar winged horses. Bela tapped one photoplate with a spatulate fingernail that wasn't altogether clean. "You recognize this?"

Lang nodded. "But this is a . . . a creature that never truly existed. It's only a fairy tale."

Bela was nodding impatiently. "Yes, yes, that's been explained to me! But we Praxians have such creatures in our legendry, too. Or at least, near enough. They are icons of tremendous power, and their appearance signifies a time when every Praxian must do her utmost, a time of decision, and ultimate sacrifice."

Bela carefully closed the book, then looked at Lang. She wasn't sure what to think of this fey Earther, with his eyes that were all pupil, and the reek of Protoculture Shaping steaming off him. The image of the winged horse had taken hold of her, though.

"You and your teams have the power to shape new mecha. I've seen your SDF-3 production machines work wonders. Can they make me such a mecha, such a *winged* mecha? On Praxis, this creature would be worth a thousand rousing speeches, a million brave words!"

Lang pretended to be considering the proposal, but deep inside he had already been swayed. The Tokyo Center's teams had studied Robotech adaptations to quadruped models in great detail, and surely the equine data was in the SDF-3's memory banks. But winged horses weren't the optimal mecha for going up against Invid terror weapons and Enforcer skirmish ships. Especially skysteeds ridden by wild women brandishing swords and lances.

However, if a Robotech Pegasus would have the kind of motivational impact Bela was claiming, it would be well worth the effort. Besides, the idea intrigued him, and he was pretty sure there were still some horse behavioral engrams lying around somewhere in the memory banks.

"Very well. Come back in, oh, say, forty-eight hours, and I'll have it ready for you."

Her eyes went very wide, but Bela had been told that Lang promised nothing that he couldn't deliver. She set her winged-owl helm down on the book, clapped her right hand to the sword on her left hip, and took Lang's right hand with her left, holding it to her heart.

"By the Eternal She and the Glory of Haydon, your enemies are mine, your debts are mine, your praise is mine to sing, and my life is yours."

Lang, so used to hearing false words from the council, and from most of the ship's aspiring politicians, heard the unaccustomed bell tone of truth then. It was like some half-forgotten song.

He was trying to get hold of himself, trying to pull his hand away from its sublime resting place without seeming to. He mumbled something about having to hold onto her helm for a day or two for the installation of control receptors.

The mind-boost of his long-ago exposure to raw Protoculture hadn't changed him from a man *that* much, and he was feeling certain inhibitions start to drop away.

Then Bela had let go of him. Lang's automatic, ironclad control reasserted itself—but for a moment he didn't know whether to be happy about that, or sad.

* * *

In one of the largest compartments of the SDF-3, a much-repaired and refurbished monolith of Zentraedi technology glowed and sent out deep, almost subsonic tones.

Exedore looked up at it worriedly. The Protoculture sizing chamber was perhaps the last that could still function, certainly the only one the Expeditionary Force had. Constructed for the Zentraedi fleet back when the miracles of Zor were commonplace, it was, like the Protoculture matrices, one of the few pieces of technology that combined Human-Zentraedi efforts could not duplicate.

Exedore held his breath. Monitoring indicators were already reading in the danger zone, but it was too late to stop the transformation now.

Returning Micronized Zentraedi to full, giant size, so that they could mine the monopole ore of Fantoma, had been a tricky business. The sizing chamber had already been pressed far beyond its rated limits. Without exception, the Zentraedi on the SDF-3 mission had volunteered—practically demanded—to be part of the mining operation. All were badly needed down on the giant world—all except one.

The rest had gone before, naturally; it was a commander's prerogative and honor to take on the greatest risk. And so Exedore, the one Zentraedi who must remain Micronized, waited and worried while the giant among giants underwent the trial of the sizing chamber.

Readings were all at maximum and some were beyond, yet the sizing chamber somehow held together. Then the semicylindrical door opened in an outrushing cloud of icy gas and billowing Protoculture brimstone.

Great Breetai stepped forth.

He was naked, of course, but turned to accept the clothing and skullpiece an aide brought to him. Exedore tried not to stare at the destroyed portion of the right side of his lord's face.

Sixty feet tall, Breetai squared his gargantuan shoulders and breathed so deeply that it seemed to lower the pressure of the compartment. He glanced around him as he fitted on the skullpiece. "So, Exedore! It worked!" He stretched, and his titanic muscles creaked like mill wheels; his joints cracked like cannon shots; the muscles of his back rose and spread like some bird of prey spreading its wings.

Breetai threw his head back and let forth a laugh that made the bulkheads quake. "Now we go back to where it all began, eh? Back to Fantoma! And Zarkopolis!"

Exedore nodded measuredly. "*You* do, my lord."

Breetai nodded, suddenly solemn. "But don't fear, my friend: when there's no more need for you on the SDF-3, you'll rejoin us at your true size!"

Exedore's first impulse was to shake his head and tell his friend and master the truth. The sizing chamber had *given up the ghost*, as the Humans would say. *That's all she wrote!* Why did human soldiers use that wording? Exedore had never investigated the matter. What's that other phrase? *"The last hurrah!"*

Hurrah?

But Breetai was in high spirits, and no amount of agonizing could change what Exedore read from his instruments. The sizing chamber would never work again.

The Zentraedi miners, Breetai, and Exedore would remain as they were forever.

Exedore, looking away from his lord to the huge panorama of Fantoma hanging there in the sky, hid his despair. He would never stand by his lord's shoulder again; he was forever Micronized, an insect by Zentraedi standards.

Exedore braced himself, smiled up at his lord, as brave as any samurai. "One or two things to attend to, my lord." He grinned. "And then, I shall be my true size."

Rick had just left the bridge and was signing off on an intel update when someone passing by in the other direction pressed a packet into the forearm-load of stuff Rick was holding, saying only, "Unit patches, sir."

It took him a few minutes before he could turn his attention to what he was holding. From the square red courier packet, he pulled a dozen insignia, holding them fanned out like a bridge hand.

They were all the same: rampant eagles face-to-face, with the legend SENTINELS at the bottom, and a crowned medieval jousting helmet at the top. The main part was a skull alongside a tip-uppermost sword that had a viper twined around it.

It didn't look at all like anything the Military Heraldry Institute would come up with. It looked more like the logo of some old time rock band. "Hey, who the hell approved . . ."

But he realized he was talking to himself; the companionway was empty. Everyone had gone off on their errands, and the mysterious patch deliverer was long gone.

Rick considered the patch again, giving particular attention to the skull. And the serpent.

What does all this mean?

Behind him, a hatch opened as a marine announced, "The admiral is off the bridge." Then there was the swift securing of the gas-tight hatch; Rick Hunter and Lisa Hayes Hunter were standing there looking at each other in the unflattering light of companionway glowtubes.

Lisa looked tired, looked *old*, it occurred to Rick—the same way he had looked after leading Skull Team in sustained combat.

"May I see?" she asked after a moment. He couldn't figure out what she meant for a second, until he realized that he was clutching the Sentinels' insignia. "I think they're sorta unofficial," he said, fumbling a bit, shifting burdens, then extending one toward her.

How do these things get decided? he wondered. Apparently the lower orders—the enlisted ranks, and perhaps a few NCOs—had made up their minds. So, the Military Heraldry Institute would have something quirky to fit into its grand scheme—provided anybody got back to Earth alive to tell about it.

Rick looked more closely at one of the patches, admiring the stitching—trying to avoid Lisa's eyes. Somebody had reprogrammed the automated garment manufacturing equipment in fine detail. The skull was a leering, bleached thing with sketchy ridge-lines, the sword sort of shiny in silver-white thread, the snake convincingly constrictor-looking, the eagles strikingly noble and angry.

Not bad. So, at least somebody had a little esprit de corps. Somebody way down in the ranks, maybe somebody who had befriended Lron or Veidt or the others.

And now this is our emblem, take it or leave it. He put down his various bundles and held the patch up against the breast of his uniform's torso harness, over his heart, where the duty patch went.

"Not bad," Lisa echoed his thought, reminding Rick she was there. She looked him in the eye, not so tired now that she was alone with him, and they shared a slow smile together. Rick suddenly remembered why they were in love.

Then she held the Sentinels' insignia over her own SDF-3 duty patch, studying his reaction. "How does it look?"

He drew a quick breath and then turned away from her for a split second, gathering himself and making sure he had heard correctly. His heart pounded; he had thought he was about to lose her. But she was telling him, in her own way, that she was coming along on *Farrago*.

What words were appropriate? None . . .

They took one another's hand and went to the Captain's quarters. There were not too many hours left until the Sentinels' flagship must leave.

They had some packing to do, but that could wait a while.

CHAPTER
SEVEN

By order of the plenipotentiary council and in accordance with applicable military regulations, the following personnel are assigned detached duty with the XT force designated "the sentinels":

Baker, Jack R., Ensign
Grant, Vincent G., Lieutenant Commander
Grant, Jean W., Lieutenant Commander (Med)
Hunter, Lisa Hayes, Admiral
Hunter, Richard B., Rear Admiral
Penn, Karen L., Ensign
Sterling, Maximilian A., Commander
Sterling, Miriya P., Lieutenant Commander
Wolff, Jonathan B., Colonel

(Excerpted from seconding orders, mission "Sentinels,"
UEG starship SDF-3.)

"**Y**OU CAN HANDLE IT," LISA ASSURED COMMANDER—
now Captain—Forsythe. She concentrated on tossing a few last possessions into a ditty bag. Her quarters—hers and Rick's—were so stark and cold now, stripped of decor and furnishings, ready for Captain Raul Forsythe, the new occupant.

Forsythe ran his hand over a forehead rubbed smooth of hair by decades of military-cap sweatbands. "I *know* I can handle it, Lisa; I'm just not so sure I can do it as well jumping in flat-footed like this. You know how many people alive have *ever* commanded a superdimensional fortress? Only one: you."

"Then, it's time there were two." She stopped, having come across something under the blotter on Rick's desk. It was a laminated snapshot of Lisa as a teenager, looking adorable, with a kitten perched precariously on her head. She had given it to him in a moment when she had thought it was all over between them; she felt a tremendous burst of love for him, discovering that he had kept it so close to him all this time.

Admiral Lisa Hayes drew a breath to keep from sniffling. "Um, Captain—*sir*, remember what you taught me at the academy? The first day, I think it was."

Forsythe allowed himself a chuckle. "That business about not 'consolidating knowledge or expertise in such fashion as to present a tactical disadvantage in event of death, disabling, or disappearance of senior personnel' *wasn't* supposed to apply to putting me in the hot seat, Admiral. Lisa."

Lisa ran her forefinger along the seam of her duffel bag, its microfield sealing up behind as if she had touched it with a magic wand. She hoisted the duffel, grunting a little, and Forsythe somehow restrained himself from the lèse-majesté of snatching luggage away from his admiral in macho assistance.

The bag landed next to Rick's: two remarkably small bundles of strictly personal possessions. Lisa looked back to Forsythe. "Captain, you've got more time in the service than I've got in *life*; we both know that. You'll do fine. If you have any questions, ask the bridge gang; enlisted ratings run that damn place anyway. Mr. Blake and I just let outsiders think otherwise." That notwithstanding, Blake was accompanying her on the *Farrago*.

Forsythe laughed a little, and then Lisa did, too. He remembered the terribly intense and *focused* cadet—daughter of another Admiral Hayes—who had come to the academy as a gawky, pale, set-jawed, frightened midshipman.

She put her hand on his shoulder. "It's time there were *two* SDF-qualified skippers." They saluted, then shook hands solemnly.

She leaned to him, kissed him on the cheek. Forsythe, eyes closed, inhaled the somehow exotic scent of her, and thought wistful thoughts that broke service regs, rationalizing it on the basis of the fact that she would be gone soon. No temptation or threat; just a memory.

Then Lisa was sniffling again, pulling one of those new-fangled totally-recyclable tissues from a dispenser, blowing her nose, and tossing it into the recycler. Forsythe busied himself with realigning the duffels by the quarters' hatch. The hatch slid open, and Rick Hunter was standing there.

"Admiral." Forsythe touched his cap's braided brim, and moved past, into the companionway, headed for the bridge. Time to take command.

Lucky dog! Forsythe thought of Rick Hunter as he went along.

Rick went to lock his hands around Lisa's waist, but she kept him at a distance for a moment. "My giving up this ship, dead in space as she is, useless for now as she is, means even more than your giving up Skull. You acknowledge, Skull Leader?"

He had been taken by surprise, but now he nodded. "I do, Lisa. But the Sentinels need me more than the SDF-3 does, and they need you more, too, and you *know* that."

She inclined her head, perhaps a little unwillingly. "And it works out so well, for you. No more situation rooms, Rick; no more sidelines. We're about to enter that Ur-Flower furnace that Lang keeps talking about. You'll be right out there on the edge, and so will Max and Miriya and the others."

Only, would that be enough? Or would he find out there was nothing short of flying combat that would satisfy him? She pretended to adjust her duffel's straps. Somehow, that puerile Minmei song, "My Boyfriend's a Pilot," started playing in her head and it took an act of will to exorcise it. Lisa closed a last side-pocket seam, and hoisted her bag up onto her shoulder. "Ready?"

Rick had been about to offer help, but knew her well enough to know she didn't want any. He wrestled his own bag onto his shoulder and wondered what he and his wife looked like: the willowy, overachieving-service-brat success story, new captain of the *Farrago*; and the shorter, maybe-muddled-looking guy at her side who suddenly found himself honcho of combat-operations coordination for the Sentinels.

"I love you," he said all at once. Not much of an apology, really, or a rationalization, but the only guidewire there was to his life.

Her duffel shouldered, she nudged his hip with hers. Lisa had to dip a bit to do it. "Mutual. You know that! But we *have* to understand each other."

She dumped the bag and put both hands on his shoulders, as Rick let his own duffel fall. "I know you were unhappy here. But I know, too, that if the war turns out that way, I'll be listening to your voice, out there in the Danger Zone, and I won't be able to do a single thing about it but hope and pray."

She could barely keep the resentment out of her voice. "You and I are married; we're mates for life," she said, taking him into her embrace and feeling his arms close behind her, the strong fingers locking with a kind of determination.

Suddenly the resentment was gone; whether it would reappear or not, she didn't know. Lisa brushed back the thick black hair over his ear. "Husband and wife," she whispered. She could see a tear fall from his cheek to her uniform's breast. Her own were streaming, too.

"It's a rifle!" Karen Penn hollered, having had about enough.

"A goddamn projectile weapon, but it's *not* a rifle!" Jack Baker screamed back at her, blood vessels standing out in his neck. He was wrestling the huge Karbarran musket around, about to shake it at her if he could get it off the deck.

Karen was pleased to see that she had gotten a rise out of him. Being stuck down in what was apparently the lowermost hold of the Sentinels' ship, inspecting alien weapons and recording evaluations for the G-2 staff, would ordinarily have been fascinating, but she was down there with J. Baker, the World's Most Obnoxious Ensign.

Now he tried to hold up the Karbarran firearm, its ornate, jewel-set buttplate still planted on the deck. All hand-polished wood and burnished metal fittings, it looked like some primitive work of art. Its wide leather sling was thick with embroidery, and its muzzle was decked with a rainbow of parrot-bright feathers.

Jack indicated the big, globular fixture just forward of the trigger guard. "Penn, we both agree that there's a lot of air in here, right? Under pressure, because the Karbarrans jack it in with this forestock lever, right? And it shoots bullets pneumatically, with the velocity of a primitive rifle, *right*?

She cringed involuntarily as he shrieked the last word. "So!" he concluded, "It ... is ... a ... *gun*!"

Karen made a fist, her knuckles protruding, wishing she could punch him. She answered through clenched teeth, "Not by the G-2 guidelines, which specify propellant-ignition or energy. Now, d'you want to turn in a faulty report, or are we gonna list these pump-up blunderbusses properly?"

Perhaps, she thought, there was some sort of berserk sadist in the assignments office, and that was how she had been thrown in with Baker yet again. That would explain everything, but easy explanations were so often suspect ...

Jack grumbled something she took as acquiescence, and they went back to work. They inventoried the strange-looking weapons of those Praxians—weirdly-conformed *naginata*, which looked like long halberds with a curved blade at one end and a spike at the other, and short, one-handed crossbows with their grips protected by boiled, shaped leather, and the rest. Swords, shields— the peculiar crystalline Spherian gadgets that looked like frozen lightning bolts—what were two ensigns to make of those, or of a

Gerudan grapnel-shaped thing that didn't seem to come with instructions?

Jack made terse notes in the aud-vid recorder, wondering at the same time how a girl who was such a sweet armful at a dance could be such an awful pain in the neck on duty. He prided himself on keeping an open mind, but really, he was right and she was wrong, just about always, and some streak of perversion in Cadet Penn seemed to make it impossible for her to admit that.

Karen, for her part, was thinking of the Praxians and their maleless society. Dynamite! Where could she sign up?

Jack was inspecting a two-handed longsword that the Praxians used in fighting from chariots, a razor-sharp whip of steel. Suddenly, he lowered it and turned to her. "Look, Penn, I'm not trying to make life tough on you, y'know. It's just that I take my job very seriously."

She was weighing some kind of bulky slug pistol in one hand. "So do I, Baker."

Jack suddenly felt very confused. Her honey-blond hair smelled wonderful, and the strange, slightly sloe eyes that were fixed on him were exotically beautiful, as mysterious as any XT's. And now that he noticed it, her upper lip was longer and fuller than her lower, giving Karen a, well, kind of *sexy* look, really . . .

Except—why did she have to be so damn competitive? Why couldn't she just come right out and admire him, yield to his judgment, the way the girls back home used to do? "Okay," he answered her, wondering what in the world he meant. "Okay, then."

He held the aud-vid rig out toward her. "Let's do this right, agreed? You record, and I'll dictate notes and observations."

She put her fists on her hips. "Why don't *you* record, and *I'll* dictate notes and observations?"

He felt his lips pulling back to reveal his teeth. "For one thing, because I was the Academy First in military history, and I think I could bring a little extra insight to evaluation of XT weaponry."

"Oh, well, pardon me for consuming valuable oxygen! But it so happens *I* won a New Rhodes scholarship for a *thesis* in comparative military history, Mister!" Jack let go an exasperated growl and took a half step toward her; Karen raised a precisely folded fist, middle knuckle cocked forward. "And I have a first *dan* in *Uichi-ryu* karate. Want proof?"

He tried to calm down, then lost it. "You just offered the wrong thing to the wrong guy on the wrong day, *meathead!*" He began tearing at the fastenings of his torso harness. "I'll mail your dog tags to your daddy!"

"That does it!" she shrilled at him, kicking things out of the way for some fighting room. "Where d'you want your corpse shipped, *moron?*"

He couldn't think of a comeback, and so roared like Lron, fighting to get his tunic off. Karen was quartering the air with whistling hand cuts, taking practice snap kicks that reached higher than her head.

There was a sudden sound from the cargo hold's outsized hatch, the deliberate, diplomatic clearing of a throat.

"Admiral Hunter." Jack tried to figure out whether he should button back up first, salute, or get busy thinking up the least preposterous alibi he could, even while Karen was bracing to attention and stuttering, "T-T-Tensh-*hut!*"

"As you were," Rick said, wandering in and gazing curiously at the racked Sentinels' weapons, to give the two cadets a moment to pull themselves together. He sort of regretted intervening; it might have been educational to sit at ringside for a few rounds.

Now, who do they remind me of? Rick Hunter asked himself. A young hot-dogger VT ace and a pale, intense SDF-1 first officer, maybe? He suddenly felt old, but it wasn't such a bad feeling, in view of what youth had yet to go through. "Pardon the interruption, Ensigns, but G-1 just cut the orders, and as I was coming aboard anyway to settle in, I thought you'd want to know."

They were both a little rocky from the adrenaline of the would-be-brawl, and from the surprise of his appearance. It took them several moments to realize that he had promotion orders in one hand and lieutenant jg bars in the other.

Rick took a secret pleasure in their shock. "Can't have ensigns assigned to the Sentinels; it muddles the chain of command. Congratulations, Lieutenant; congratulations, Lieutenant."

They shook his hand warily, as if afraid it were going to come off, and gazed down at the badges of rank he had put in their palms.

"Yes; well, carry on," Rick bade them when he saw that they were going to be flummoxed for a while. He returned their salutes crisply, and resolved not to listen at the hatch to find out what was going to happen next, even though he wanted to.

"Well? Let's do it," Jack Baker said. Tradition dictated a certain ceremony. Karen nodded.

They silently removed the ensign pips from each other's epaulets, and fastened the jg bars there. Then they braced at attention and saluted each other, and then shook hands slowly, all without a word.

"Congratulations, Lieutenant," Karen echoed Rick.

"Same to you, Lieutenant," Jack told her emphatically.

CHAPTER EIGHT

> *I felt that my place lay with the Sentinels—with observing and recording a unique event in Human history. But I was a little schizo about it, because I could feel that there were things shaping up at REF-Tirol that the Folks Back Home would need to know about, too. Heroes to be sung and villains to be fingered.*
>
> *But one of the first things you learn when they hand you an aud/vid recording rig is that you can't be every place at the same time.*
>
> *Or even two places.*
>
> Sue Graham, narration from a documentary *Protoculture's Privateers: SDF-3, Farrago, Ark Angel Sentinels, and the REF.*

JEAN GRANT PAUSED AS SHE WAS ABOUT TO SECURE THE MED-center diagnostic robot for transferral to the Sentinels' ship. As she had done intermittently through the morning, she glanced through the viewport at Tirol, and looming Fantoma.

"It sure isn't home," she muttered again, "but at least we know the dangers here."

She felt her husband's massive arm go round her shoulders. He brushed his lips against her cheek. She reflected again on the oddness of it—how a man so big and incredibly strong could be so gentle.

"But we're not needed here," he pointed out. "Lang will be years repairing the SDF-3, and in the meantime there are people suffering and dying."

And so the Ground Mobile Unit was being attached, figuratively and literally, as a new module of the *Farrago*, secured to the starship's underside. And Skull Team, now augmented to near-squadron size with Beta and Logan VTs, was now the main component of its assigned air group.

She clutched his hand. At least there was comfort in the fact that, with the GMU suddenly reallocated to the Sentinels' mission,

Vince would be near her; she didn't know if she could have endured being parted from him as she had been before.

Jean took a determined breath to keep back tears, having made up her mind that there was no point to doing any more crying. Vince patted her shoulder. "I know, darling, I know. I miss Bowie, too. But I'm glad he's safe on Earth, he and Dana both. Rolf will take good care of them."

She sighed, leaning her head against his broad chest, wondering what their son was doing at that moment, on the other side of the galaxy.

On Fantoma, the first dropships began disgorging the mining equipment that the Zentraedi would use to wrest monopole ore from the heavy-g world.

Breetai stepped out onto the surface in his pressurized armor, stretching his arms and feeling his muscles work. Nearby, heavily shielded and powered mining vehicles were being off-loaded. They looked like high-tech dinosaurs, octopi, centipedes.

Breetai looked around him at the bleak planetscape, a scoured and blasted vista of grays and browns and black, with a typically high-g scarcity of prominent features; planets like Fantoma quickly pulled down mountains and hills.

It looked like a haunted world. And it *was* haunted, in fact: haunted by memories the Zentraedi had accumulated over generations as miners, only to have those memories wiped away by the Robotech Masters and replaced with false ones, implanted glories of the warrior race the Masters needed for their plan to conquer the universe.

Battlepods came off the dropships, too, to stand guard and serve as security for the operation. Breetai let his subordinates take care of the details, and paced here and there, looking around him.

Lang and the other Earth savants had expressed surprise that the Zentraedi had been conceived as colossal laborers for the Fantoman mining operation. "If anything, it would seem to me, very *small* organisms would be more appropriate," one Human had ventured.

But that was because they still didn't understand the exact nature of the sizing chamber, and how it altered Zentraedi physiology to meet the challenges of a gravity more than three times that of Terra.

Breetai stretched again, feeling energized and exultant, rather than tired, by Fantoma's pull.

It was the oddest thing, but—*memories* seemed to be coming

back to Breetai. The first dropship landing had been centered on an open-pit area, and it seemed to Breetai that he recognized the landscape around him. Something drew him up a slope—twenty degrees, he estimated; a steep climb—until he reached the summit.

There was a bench there, a mere trestle of stone slabs, but how had he *known* he would find it at just that spot? Conversations from his past, or perhaps hallucinations, drifted in and out of his thoughts. He suddenly felt an impotent fury at having been deprived of his own past—at being unable to trust his own memory.

In that moment, an image of himself and Exedore came to him, sitting on the bench side by side, and Exedore saying something that Breetai was having trouble following.

I remember! The words were a thunderous rumbling in his chest.

"No; of course we won't remember this life, my friend," Exedore was saying, "but the Robotech Masters plan momentous things for us. We will become much like a force of nature—something that will sweep the galaxy—the universe—in glory and triumph!"

Breetai saw himself stop and ponder that; he was only a miner—though he was, aside from Dolza, the biggest and strongest Zentraedi ever created, the most durable and formidable of them all—and had difficulty understanding the interstellar *jihad* that Exedore was painting in words.

Now he recalled the peculiar stirrings in him when he had heard Exedore's exhortation. The thought of a life of battle and triumph had made him feel exalted. And he had had a preternaturally long lifetime of it, just as Exedore foresaw.

But where could these recollections be coming from? Surely the Masters had expunged all true memories. Breetai shook his head within the huge helmet, mystified and troubled.

"Lord Breetai?" He turned in surprise, both at the fact that someone was standing there, and at the realization that it was a Zentraedi *female*. "The construction gang is about to begin work on permanent housing," she said, "but they'd like you to make final approval of the site."

She was wearing Quadrono powered armor that had been retrofitted for labor and mining duty, he could see. One of Miriya Parino's spitfires, no doubt; Breetai had heard that the Quadronos had never quite forgiven their leader for undergoing Micronization, marrying Max Sterling, and having his child. Many of them had deserted to follow the mad Khyron and his, his *lover*, Azonia, but some had remained loyal to Breetai, and a few of those had survived the final battle against Dolza and the Malcontent Uprisings and the battle with the Inorganics.

Breetai looked at her uneasily. The Zentraedi had always been rigidly segregated by sex, and most of them found the thought of fraternization disquieting to the point where it had been known to make them physically ill. But the unusual circumstances here in the primitive Fantoman start-up effort had made it impossible to preserve the old ways altogether.

Breetai forced himself to look her over. Not easy to tell much about her in the bulky powered armor except that she was tall for a female, well over fifty feet. Through her tinted facebowl, he could see that she had prominent cheekbones and slightly oblique eyes, looking rather like what Lang or Hunter would call Slavic, and her purple hair was cropped masculinely short. But there was something else about her face . . .

He realized, stunned, that she was wearing cosmetics. The thought passed through him. *Great suns! Where did she get them? Surely a female of our race uses as much in one application as an Earth woman uses in a month!*

She had accentuated the fullness of her mouth, the length of her glittering lashes, the line of her long-arched brows. Breetai stared at her, openmouthed, as she saluted and began to about-face.

"Wait!" he said on sudden impulse. "What's your name?"

She turned back to him. "I am Kazianna Hesh, formerly of the Quadronos, my lord." She gave a slight smile, thumping the plastron of her armor with a gauntleted fist. "And now a Quadrono again, it seems. Some of our battle suits have been in storage all this time, and the hour is come when they're needed again."

"So it is." Breetai inspected Kazianna Hesh, not sure why he was doing so. It was one thing to interact with human females like Lisa Hayes, knowing there was no possibility of . . . of *relations* with them, at least not as far as he was concerned. It was quite another, and very unsettling, to have the smiling, rather alluring-looking Quadrono staring at him so boldly.

"And, if I may say so, sir, what with all the perils that Fantoma harbors, it is good to be serving in a danger zone under the command of my Lord Breetai once more."

She saluted again, precisely, but still with that odd half smile. Breetai responded, and Kazianna did a careful high-g march back down the little hillock. Breetai watched her go, studying her walk, wondering whether it was something about her armor—a malfunction, perhaps?—that put that nonregulation sway in her gait.

* * *

"I don't care what your platoon leader told you," General T. R. Edwards roared into the face of the cleanup-detail sergeant. "I'm telling you to stack those things in the catacombs for further study by my evaluation teams! And make goddamn sure you don't damage any!"

The sergeant chose the better part of valor, saluting Edwards, then shrugging to his men and reorganizing them. They had been using their powered equipment to move the inert forms of the Invid Inorganic fighting mecha up out of the catacombs so that the demolition crews could dispose of them for good.

The biped Inorganics, and the massive Inorganic feline automata called Hellcats, were immobilized once the huge brain controlling them was deactivated. But it still made the REF uneasy to have thousands of them lying all over Tiresia, as though they might wake up at any moment. Orders had come down to move them to an appropriate site and blow them all to smithereens.

Lang and Cabell and the other big IQs had taken a few of the things for study, but didn't seem otherwise inclined to countermand the council's orders. Be that as it might, all the lower ranks knew you didn't rub General Edwards the wrong way without risking some real grief. The heavy machinery began lugging the inert enemy mecha for careful storage in the catacombs under the Royal Hall.

Edwards took an aide, Major Benson, aside. "Get some of the Ghost Riders and keep an eye on things. Make sure the Invid mecha are all kept intact, understood?"

"Yes, sir." Benson recalled the bizarre events of the original capture of the Royal Hall: how Edwards had arranged to be first to break into the Invid command center deep beneath it.

Benson could only guess at what his general's plans were, but the aide made every attempt not to seem surprised or curious. Hitching your wagon to Edwards's star offered the chance of vast rewards somewhere down the line, but stars had a way of flaring up and destroying the things around them. Discretion was the indispensible tool for survival in Ghost Squadron.

"Wise-man, I'm told you wish to see me," Bela said, entering Lang's lab. She seemed cheerful with the prospect of having her heart's desire fulfilled, but she stopped dead, glaring, when she saw Cabell and Rem standing by Lang's side.

Gnea had been following close behind her warlord, and now collided with her back. The smaller, younger amazon had the same lithe grace as Bela, but she was more prone to show wide-eyed wonder at the things around her, and lacked that hair-trigger temper that was already gaining Bela fame in the REF.

Gnea's eyes were a gold-flecked green, her long, straight hair a sun-bleached white. Her helm was crested with a long-necked reptilian image that had a head like a horned lizard. Her battle costume was of a different design from Bela's, but had that same look of erotic glamour to it. Gnea wore sword and knife on her harness like Bela, but where the taller woman carried a crossbow, Gnea bore a Praxian *naginata* and a shield with a spiked boss in its center.

"What are *they* doing here?" Bela indicated Rem and Cabell with an angry gesture of her chin, fingering her bow as if she were ready to fire. Gnea seemed about to bring her halberd's curved blade into the ready position, glaring beneath feathery black brows.

"They have been helping me with my research," Lang answered, surprised. "They are allies of the REF now, just as you are."

"We Sentinels do not trust these spawn of the Robotech Masters," Bela spat, "any more than we do the Zentraedi who brought suffering like the Invid did!"

Gnea, eyes narrowed at Rem, added, "And you, you who so resemble Zor—we have reason to hate *Zor*, too, for the ruin his meddling brought down upon us."

"But he is not Zor," Cabell told her, stroking his long white beard with one mandarin-nailed hand. "Nor am I a Robotech Master. Think of us, please, as two Tiresians who wish to help free all planets from the Invid."

Bela hissed at him in scorn and anger. Lang intervened. "Without their help, I couldn't have finished *this* for you in time."

He gestured, and a powered partition folded aside accordian style. Bela gasped, and Gnea cried aloud, seeing what waited there.

No one would ever mistake it for a live horse, even though it tossed its head, snorting, and dug its hoof at the deck in imitation of a real animal's movements. The two wings that sprouted from its back were articulated, and changed shape and position, but were more like something from an airplane or ornithopter than any bird.

Its leg structure widened somewhat down toward the hock, so that it seemed Lang's wonder horse was wearing bell-bottoms from which its shining hooves poked. The thing was a glittering silver with jet-black trim. Its noble mane and forelock and tail of hair-fine wire tossed and glittered as it stamped, waiting.

"She is magnificent," Bela breathed, forgetting her anger. "Superb." She went toward the mecha with one hand extended; the thing appeared to sniff at her. "Magical."

She appeared ready to vault astride, but Rem called out,

"Wait!" As she whirled on him he held out her helm, showing her that the interior padding had been changed.

"Control receptors," Rem explained. "This is still a Robotech mecha, after all, and in order to control it, you'll need to do a certain amount of mental imaging—visualizing what you want it to do." She took the helm from him, settling it onto her head.

Bela held her hand out to the horse again. "I shall call you 'Halidarre,' girl—after the free sky-spirit of our great heroine."

"Halidarre I shall be," the horse-mecha answered, in a synthesized voice that sounded much like Bela's. Both women drew breath in surprise.

"There are other things you will learn about Halidarre," Cabell said, "as time passes. Things like this . . ."

He touched a control, and Halidarre's wings straightened, their area shrinking somewhat. From a niche in the mecha's back, a cylindrical reconnaissance module rose into the air, using the wings and its own lifting field. Cabell touched another control, and the module returned to its niche.

"Halidarre flies, too, just as promised," Lang put in. "But more by her antigrav apparatus and impellers than by using her wings; the aerodynamics of a *live* flying horse are quite impossible, of course."

"He is also compatible with some of the other REF mecha, like the Cyclone combat cycles—" Rem was adding, but Bela cut him off with a gesture and leapt astride the Robotech Pegasus.

"Halidarre, attached to a mere machine? Don't be absurd!" she snorted. "Gnea, come!" Gnea obediently took her hand and swung up behind, one arm around Bela's waist.

"Thanks for this gift, Dr. Lang; I salute you and pledge my fealty to you."

Her expression hardened. "But as for you, Zor-clone, and you, servant to the Robotech Masters, do not try my patience, and stay well clear of the women of Praxis!"

By way of underlining her warning, she turned and aligned her arm at the wooden leg of a lab table. She clenched her fist and made a sudden downward curling gesture with it, keeping the rest of her arm steady. A thin, gleaming object shot from the slightly bulky feature built into her forearm sheath.

The three men turned to spy it quivering in the wood: a slim, hiltless throwing dagger—fired by some sort of spring-loaded device in the sheath, Lang supposed.

Bela looked to Rem and Cabell again. "Be warned," she said.

CHAPTER NINE

How I was torn when I saw that she wasn't going! Surely, the Sentinels are venturing forth on a mission far more likely to bring enlightenment than is the mere mining of Fantoma and rebuilding the SDF-3!

Just as certainly, along with the contemptible bloodshed that is war, there will be access to stupendous new horizons of knowledge and awareness. Perhaps keys to the Ultimate Truths that grow from the First Light, the birth pangs of the Universe!

Enough; Minmei will stay behind and that's only to be expected. Though the synergistic harmonies with Janice Em (and what of her? So many mysteries!) will be sundered, Lynn-Minmei seems to sense that the place for her and for her voice and her role in the Shapings—as Lang and Zand would have it—is here, with the REF.

And so it is my place too; I am content. She'll be here, away from Hunter, away from Wolff—here, near me. What feelings this stirs, I don't find myself able to put into words yet. I will allow myself some irony in this matter, and sign myself, when these writings turn to Minmei . . .

REF Service #666-60-937

FROM AN ENLISTED LOUNGE OF SDF-3, THERE WAS A GREAT view of the Sentinels' flagship and the small escort flotilla from the dimensional fortress, preparing to get under weigh.

Drives flared in the night of Valivarre's umbra; the strange, orange-red fans of propulsive energy from *Farrago* stood out like a half-dozen immense, slitted search lights—like no drives the REF had ever seen before, dwarfing those around the dreadnought. The Ur-Flower "peat" furnaces beamed incredible power out into space.

Off duty, Minmei sat at the lounge's piano by a big span of viewport, not even realizing that she was picking absently at the keys. The Agitprop and Psych/Morale people had wanted her to sing a final farewell concert with Janice. Something to work everybody up into a liberationist fervor and prepare them for whatever lay ahead—either the back-breaking labor of putting SDF-3 in working order or the life-on-the-line campaign to dislodge the fearsome Invid hordes from the planets they had enslaved. The REF was already exhausted from the round-the-clock working shifts to get the Sentinels' mission ready.

But Minmei didn't feel like singing with Janice again. She refused to sing with the woman who had, in her opinion, betrayed her. For that matter, Minmei didn't feel like singing for the war effort. The whole Superstar-savior-voice-of-humanity act was behind her, couldn't they understand that? She was just another lowly recruit, and that was the way she wanted it.

"The voice that won the Robotech War," they had called her. But what had it ever brought her but a few glimmers of the spotlight, then pain and bitterness and loneliness? She considered the things she had been forced to endure in the wake of her triumphs, and decided that one more such victory would be her undoing.

The escort flotilla had fallen in around the Sentinels' flagship now, ready to guard it until it went superluminal. Then *Farrago* and the mismatched aliens and Earthers aboard would be on their own.

Minmei realized that she was hitting familiar keys, one at a time and very slowly. The tempo was different now, mournful, like some old torch song from one of the great blues singers.

She sang the words softly, letting her suffering come through, savoring the lyrics but filling them with irony.

> *Life is only what we choose to make it*
> *Let us take it*
> *Let us be free*

Minmei chorded it unhurriedly, downbeat, so that the song sounded like it was time for the bartenders to be putting chairs upside down on the tables for closing. She felt her shoulders sag under a weight she simply wasn't strong enough to bear anymore.

There was a lamenting in each word. The famous voice caressed, rasped resentfully, then caressed again.

> *We can find the glory we all dream of*
> *And with our love,*
> *We can win . . .*

But there was a strength in the melancholy, a strength the blues had owned from the beginning, something stronger than all the up-tempo marches put together.

The strength of survival—of going through the worst and coming out the other side saddened and chastened but alive and prepared to stay with the life that had done such unspeakable things to you, because there *was* no other life ...

Her head was bent over the keyboard now, long raven wings of hair shrouding her face. Perhaps a few, nearby, would hear, but she didn't care. She looked again, briefly, to where the Sentinels' engines lit the night, and the conventional drives of its REF escorts grew brighter in anticipation of departure.

Minmei watched them as her fingers found unhurried chords that seemed predestined.

If we must fight or face defeat,
We must stand tall and not retreat

Unseen by anyone but their owner, hands manipulated the lounge sound system control panel: turning down the gain; adjusting the very fine room directionals; punching a ship's-intercom code that only certain selected commo personnel were supposed to know. Adjusting this; amplifying that—and it was all very practiced, very expert.

Minmei's song, low and intimate, was playing through the lounge softly, as if it were something a loud sound would shatter, amplified so discreetly that Minmei herself didn't realize the sound system was on.

It was channeled into the ship's commo, and Lang's head raised from his lab researchers; Exedore's eyes took on a faraway look; Captain Forsythe and the bridge gang stopped what they were doing and listened; many in SDF-3 fought the tide of emotion as *the voice* swept through them. Breetai, confronting bleak Fantoma, heard it through a commo patch-in over which he had just wished Rick and Lisa Hunter good fortune.

Rem and Cabell wondered if any perfection of the Muse Triumvirate of the Robotech Masters could surpass the aching beauty of this song; they doubted it. Exedore heard it and thought, *This power she has—it's astonishing. No; it's humbling.*

Thousands of people froze, hearing Minmei, knowing her and her song, but never having heard either sound like this.

It's love's battle we must win ...

The line rose and lingered; losing in personal battle was the epitome of the blues. Minmei was pure and high and luminous with pain at one moment, breathy with a return to the call of life the next. More in touch with her music than the gamine superstar version of herself had ever been.

We will win
We must win . . .

Minmei twisted the last note around with the wail of a suffering animal, then let it down gently with some chords that said *it's all right; life goes on. Lived through everything else. Not gonna die from this.*

She wavered a little on the piano bench, a bit dazed by the understated power of what she had just released—something that hadn't been there, in her, before. She was unaware that so many others had heard it, unaware that the lounge was now utterly quiet.

The Sentinels' drive flared bright; the starship moved away, its escorts guarding the vessel, as Minmei thought of it, only so far as the end of the proverbial garden path, and then letting it set out into the long night alone.

"Nothing to report to me? Nothing to report? Is that all you can say?"

The Invid Regent stalked through his vast halls in the Invid Home Hive on Optera, and his closest aides, knowing his moods, trailed him dutifully but warily. He was capable of becoming violent without warning—feeding an unfortunate bystander to one of his huge, gem-collared Hellcats, or having them devolved in one of the Genesis Pits or simply lashing out with a physical blow.

And an enraged blow from the Regent was something few might hope to survive. Some twenty feet high, he was the tallest of his race, among whom an average height was some six or eight feet. His advisers, though, like Tesla, stood twice average height.

Unlike the underlings following him, the Regent was draped with an organic cape that grew around the back of his neck and resembled a manta ray, lined from front to back with tuberclelike sensors that resembled eyeballs. He often spread the strange structure like a cobra's mantle in times of fury, and the mantle was stirring restlessly, even now.

"No word from the reinforcements I sent to retake Tirol? No message on the whereabouts of Tesla? No answer from the Regis? Perhaps my servants need *motivation*."

He stopped to turn to them.

"Your troops have barely had time to reach Karbarra, to pick up forces from the garrison there for the attack on Tirol, much less reach Tirol itself," one of the lackeys managed to get out, trembling.

"A-and perhaps Tesla has paused to gather more varieties of the Fruit of the Flower of Life," another one ventured. "He has great hopes that a preparation made from them will be of vast advantage to you, Mighty One!"

"And it may be that your communications have simply not reached the Regis yet," the third pointed out. "She has always responded to Your Magnificence's messages in the past."

Yes. Usually with mockery and defiance. Repelled by his de-evolutionary experiments, just as he was provoked by her insistence on maintaining a form that was Tiresoid—that was so like the females of the race of the hated Zor—the Regis had abandoned him, followed by half their species, like the dividing of some unimaginable insect colony.

And with his resources of troops and vessels and Flower essence so limited in the wake of the vast Invid–Robotech Master war, he could scarcely afford to begin a civil conflict against his own mate and half his race. At least, not yet.

The Regent was in no mood to listen to his underlings' rationalization, in no mood to be reminded of logistical limits, or of Tesla's semimystical theories about the Fruit of the Flower of Life. He stood now near the center of the Home Hive, a stupendous network of domes and connecting conduits that stretched far and wide across Optera like an incandescent spiderweb. But, with its energy reduced now and its population so depleted, it seemed to mock the power that had once been his.

The feeler-sensors on his snout glowered angrily with the words, "Yes: *motivation*."

He seized the adviser nearest him, not really caring which one it was, and flung him across the chamber. The underling sprawled and lay quaking. "Kill him," the Regent told the other two.

They didn't hesitate for a moment. Snatching weapons from a pair of armored-trooper sentries, they turned the guns on their former colleague and opened fire. Streams of annihilation disks flew, flaring bright when they struck, enveloping the fallen Invid in a brief inferno. The stench of the charred body wafted through the Hive.

The Regent debated whether he should order the remaining two to shoot each other, or, perhaps more interestingly, themselves. But that would waste more time, since new lackeys would have to be trained from scratch.

His bloodlust had been sated a little. He contented himself with telling them, "Go now and do as I've commanded. And bring me no more news of failure."

Senep, the commander in charge of the Invid mission to send fresh troops to Tirol, was aware of the Regent's state of mind. He was at pains to do his duty well, but *quickly.*

Reports from Tirol were somewhat sketchy—word that Zentraedi and some apparently unknown Tiresoid race had attacked the planet in concert. Senep's hastily assembled task force, manned by troops borrowed from Karbarra's ample garrison, now moved out for deepspace, still preparing itself for the rather protracted voyage to its objective.

Senep was relieved that his plan to commandeer resources from Karbarra had been approved. To gather units in dribs and drabs from various other worlds, and from the forces patrolling the outer marches of the Invid's shrunken empire, would have cost him time that he could ill afford to waste.

But Senep had been able to make two telling arguments in favor of his idea. One was that Karbarra had more than sufficient Invid strength to perform its task, even with its garrison thus reduced. The second, and more important, was that the Karbarrans were most unlikely to become intractable or demonstrate any resistance or defiance.

No, the Karbarrans had a very *good* reason to obey their overlords' every whim without objection.

The Invid commander was still getting his ships into proper formation when a communications tech turned to him, its snout-sensors agleam with emotion as it spoke.

"Commander! Alien starship approaching from deepspace! It just went subluminal and appears to be on course for Karbarra!"

For Karbarra, and Senep's task force. "Identify."

"Impossible, sir. It does not match anything in our data banks."

Senep puzzled for a moment over the long-range sensor image of the Sentinels' ship. "I'm not going to ask questions. Battle stations. All units prepare to attack."

CHAPTER TEN

> *It is a critical point that each new form of enemy in the Wars was a new problem in the use and application of Earth mecha. What would work against a Battlepod was suicide against Invid Inorganics; the vulnerable points, weaponry, and performance profiles were completely different.*
>
> *The Human fighters were lucky they had all those curious and experimenting monkeys in their ancestry; the REF in particular was a climate wherein only quick learners survived.*
>
> Selig Kahler, *The Tirolian Campaign*

THE VOYAGE FROM TIROL TO KARBARRA HAD BEEN FILLED with a schedule even more exhausting than the preparations for the Sentinels' departure. Rick, like all the others aboard, had been forced to take what little sleep he could get in catnaps.

They had had to familiarize the non-Human Sentinels with Robotech weapons, of course—as much as was feasible while under way. Some of them, like Burak and Kami, were more than willing to learn, while others—the Karbarran ursinoids and the Praxian amazons in particular—seemed unwilling to trust any small arms but their own. This, though the Karbarrans appeared inclined to try out mecha and Bela and Gnea could barely wait to ride that completely crazy winged horse of Lang's into battle.

Rick and his staff had racked their brains coming up with ways to try to integrate the wildly varied forces in battle and make everybody understand what they were supposed to do. Rick had moments of agonizing doubt that it had been accomplished, wondering if he was heading into one of the worst debacles in military history.

Then there had been the various misunderstandings and frictions to mediate. The Sentinels' resentment of Cabell and Rem; run-ins between the Humans and non-Humans as cultural difference led to clashes (well, the Hovertanker *did* have that fractured jaw coming to him for calling the Praxian woman a "brawny wench," even if it was meant jokingly); the constant insistence of Burak and the other Perytonians that their planet be given higher priority in the campaign—it was all beginning to give Rick migraines.

And there was the bewildering job of understanding the alien Sentinels themselves. As the ship drew closer and closer to Karbarra, Lron and Crysta and their people became more and more withdrawn and morose. Veidt was puzzled by it, too.

Normally, as Rick understood it, the gloomy Karbarrans—preoccupied with the tragedy of fate and the ultimate futility of things—made Earth's teutonic types look giddy by comparison; but the prospect of battle was one of the few things that made the big ursinoids cheerful. That wasn't true now, though, and none of them would explain why.

Rick tried to put it from his mind, along with things like this business about Haydon. Apparently, Haydon was some sort of extraordinarily important historical figure or deity or *something*, but beliefs and convictions varied among the Sentinels and led to sharp disputes. And so part of their pact had been to avoid all mention of Haydon. Lang was desperate for more information concerning the matter, but the Sentinels had clammed up about it.

Those were Rick's lesser problems. Bigger ones included trying to make things more efficient and organized, and constantly being stymied by explanations he couldn't quite grasp.

One of his first ideas had been to automate the feeding of the Ur-Flower peat—Sekiton, it was called—into the furnaces, freeing up the stoker gangs for other work. Lron and Crysta had given him a long explanation, which he didn't comprehend in the least.

They seemed to be saying that the Sekiton had to be *physically touched and handled by Karbarrans to be of any use*. If relegated to robotic handling, its affinity for Karbarran life-forms thus frustrated, Sekiton would have its feelings hurt or sulk or whatever, and refuse to yield up its energy properly.

It *had* to be a translation problem, Rick decided. Didn't it?

He just hoped that he had understood the Karbarrans' intelligence assessments properly. When they had left their homeworld, the Invid were maintaining a relatively small occupation force, and it sounded like something the Sentinels could cope with. Rick's plan was to use the production facilities on Karbarra—famous for their adaptability and output—to begin assembly lines to turn out mecha and ships with which to arm native recruits, increasing the Sentinels' strength perhaps tenfold.

Lron and his folk were disinclined to comment much about the idea, and apparently held the conviction that fate would bring what it would bring. That gave Rick reservations about the plan, and so he convinced the other Sentinel leaders to scout out the situation carefully before beginning any offensive.

To that end, the starship resumed sublight speed drive far out from the planet itself. Lisa, in her capacity as captain, gave the command to carry out the maneuver.

She had left behind the more formal REF uniform with its tail-coat and skirt. Now she wore the tight-fitting unisex bodysuit that seemed more appropriate for the Sentinels' rough-and-ready style, the group's insignia high on the left breast of her yokelike torso harness, just as it was on all the other Humans. The starship made its transition.

And found itself, all in an instant, practically in the lap of Senep's task force.

Lisa turned and yelled for battle stations.

As for Crysta and Lron, they had taken advantage of the preoccupation of most of the ship's company with the return to sublight speed to find their way to the hold in which Tesla was being kept.

The Praxians who were on guard were only too glad to let the Karbarrans relieve them long enough for the amazons to go get something to eat. Besides, it lay well within Lron's authority to conduct an interrogation.

When they were alone with him, the ursinoids went over to where the Invid scientist sat, shackled, behind bars. "You begged us to spare you," Crysta said in a growl. "You said you would be of use. Well, now you can be. Tell us what you know of the prison, and of its ... its captives. How are they guarded? How may they be freed?"

Tesla had been watching her almost indifferently, Crysta thought, though it was difficult to tell any Invid mood by appearance. But when the scientist spoke, it was with an almost saintly kindness.

"Ah, Madam Crysta! If only I knew these things, I could tell them to you, and atone at least in some small part for the crimes I've committed against your race back when my will was enslaved by the Regent! But I know nothing of such military arrangements, you see."

His chains rattled as he struggled to his feet. "However, another idea occurs to me. Release me, that I may go down to the surface of Karbarra and negotiate for you at once. The Invid commander, without the Regent there to contradict, will listen to me."

Lron showed his teeth. "I told you asking this slime-thing was useless," he told his wife. And to Tesla, he added, "Now we try a different approach. Let us see how much you can remember with one of those antennae twisted off your snout!"

Tesla shrank back, even though he was the larger of the two. "Keep your distance! Your leadership circle said I was not to be tampered with. Have your forgotten so soon?"

"But the others aren't here now," Lron pointed out, putting one hand on the lock. "And I am."

Crysta, worried that this possible key to the Karbarran dilemma might not survive her mate's vigorous questioning, was just saying, "Lron, perhaps he's telling the truth—" Just then the alarms went off, exotic ululations and crystal gongs and warhorns and the various other calls to arms of the assorted Sentinel races.

Lron made sure the cage was secure, then he and Crysta pounded off for the bridge. As they rounded a corner in the passageway, they were unaware that they were being watched from the shadows.

Burak stayed back until the two were out of sight, then stared thoughtfully at the door to the compartment holding Tesla's cage. At last, the sounding of the alarms drew him slowly, unwillingly, off toward his battle station. Then he began to run, to run as if something were chasing him.

"They haven't fired on us out of hand; that's a piece of luck we didn't have coming," Lisa conceded. "Rick, I suggest we *not* scramble the VTs, at least not yet."

Rick met her gaze for a moment, then nodded.

There were far fewer of the enemy than the SDF-3 had confronted over Tirol. Four of the rust-colored Invid troopships, shaped like gigantic clams, were deploying around a much more modest version of the Invid command ship the Humans had glimpsed—the one Cabell had pronounced to be the royal flagship of the Regent himself. If the troop carriers were clams, this thing was an ominous starfish.

The Sentinel leadership was piling onto the bridge now, reacting or not according to the fashion of their species. "They've got the drop on us," Rick said softly.

Lisa shook her head. "I don't think so, or they would've opened up right away; the Invid are the shoot-first type." *But I don't understand.*

Aboard Senep's flagship, the task-force command finally got some results from the vessel's Living Computer. It seemed that most of the components of the unidentified craft matched with space vehicles from many Invid-controlled worlds, and the central structure to which they had been joined fit the profile of an outlandish craft that the scientist Tesla had had under construction.

Senep's antennae shone with anger. That blithering idiot! But—if it was Tesla, why hadn't he identified himself? Perhaps something was wrong.

Senep queried the Living Computer about the offensive capabilities of the newcomer. Of the weapons that could be identified from memory banks, none could match the range or power of the flagship.

It certainly didn't resemble anything the new foe—the Human-Zentraedi alliance—would conceivably field. And no ship of a subject race posed much threat to an Invid command ship.

"We'll close with it, then," Senep decided, "within range of our main guns, but out of Tesla's. Then we'll send our mecha to investigate."

Lisa refused to answer the enemy's query signals, of course; none of the Sentinels could imitate an Invid, and there wasn't even time to get Tesla up to the bridge, much less coerce him.

"But why are they approaching?" Veidt's eerie voice came.

Lron growled, "They know what our weapons can do; they know their flagship has us outgunned."

There were only seconds to act; Lisa turned to one of the gramophone mikes. "Patch me through to Commander Grant."

"Way to go," Rick whispered to his gutsy wife, realizing what she had in mind.

"I'm beginning to get unfamiliar Protoculture readings from that craft, Commander," the ship's Living Brain relayed.

"Launch mecha," Senep said, having taken up his position of advantage. "And at the first sign of resistance, open fire—"

It was as if he spoke into the ear of a listening deity. At that moment a tremendous bolt sprang from a peculiar design feature on the underside of the lone ship. It struck Senep's vessel almost dead-center, a star-hot stiletto of energy that pierced the command ship's shields and hull, stabbed it to its heart, and lit the vessels around it with its dying eruption.

But Senep had given a last order, and as the ball of superheated gas that had been the command ship expanded like a balloon, the troopships swung open like oysters about to yield pearls.

Invid mecha began boiling forth from them: bizarre, armored crab-shapes of assorted types riding powerful thrusters, diving for the Sentinels.

"Launch fighters!" Rick yelled. He could feel the ship shake as the Alphas and Betas of Skull Team roared from their launch tubes in the Ground Mobile Unit, and from the improvised bays in the rest of *Farrago* as well. "Vince, see if you can take out some of those other troop carriers!"

But before the command was out of Rick's mouth, the Sentinels' ship shuddered from a second firing of the GMU's monster cannon. Fastened to the underbelly of the ship as it was, the GMU wasn't in the best position for accurate volleys; but Vince's gunners and targetting equipment were unsurpassed. A second novabeam went through a troop carrier like a leatherpunch through a bug. Less than half its mecha launched, the enemy craft vanished in outlashing starfire.

"Commence firing! All batteries, commence firing!" Lisa was saying loudly but calmly into a mike. In all the mismatched portions of the ship, turrets and launchers opened up. The GMU's secondary weapons began putting out the heaviest possible volume of fire. So did the non-transformable Destroid mecha that Vince Grant had moved into the ground unit's larger airlocks, using them as gun emplacements—just as Henry Gloval had on SDF-1 during the desperate battle with Khyron out in Earth's Pacific Ocean, so long ago.

In rushed the Invid Pincer Ships, the massive Enforcers and comparatively small Scouts, firing as they came, enraged though they had no individual emotions, with the single-minded fury of a swarm of hornets.

Out to meet them came the second-generation Alphas, sleekly lethal despite their deepspace augmentation pods; the burlier Betas, with their brute firepower and thrust; and the new Logans, with their rowboat-shaped noses, the latest word in Veritechs.

Leading Skull Team were Max and Miriya Sterling, as cool and alert as ever. To them, as to the rest of the veteran Skulls, heavier Invid numbers just meant there were that many more opportunities to make kills. The dying began at once. Skull Team's tactical net crackled with terse, grim exchanges, the pilots automatically maintaining an even strain, upholding the generations-old Yeager tradition of Cool In The Saddle.

"Y'got one on your six, Skull Niner."

"Roger on that, Skull Two. Kin ya scratch my back?"

"That's affirm. Scissor right, and I'll swat 'im for you."

The Beta that was Skull Nine drew the pursuing Invid Pincer Ship into Skull Two's line of fire. Brief, flaring bursts of free-electron laser cannonfire skeeted the bogey out of existence.

"Skull Leader," Lisa's voice came, "enemy element of six

mecha has broken through your screen and is attacking the flagship."

"Skull Two, Skull Seven, go *transact* 'em," Max delegated, still concentrating on the Pincer that was trying to get into Miriya's six—the tail position, from which it could make the kill.

Two and Seven, leading their wingmates, headed off on a rescue at least as dangerous as the dogfighting; the Sentinels' AA fire was not as well coordinated as the REF fliers would have liked, and there was a very good chance the Skull two-ship elements would be flamed by friendly fire if the people on the bridge weren't completely on top of things.

On the other hand, that was what made combat more interesting to Max and his gang. They were the ultimate Robotech aces, living out on the edge where the juices flowed and death waved at you from every passing mecha.

"Skull One, Skull One, go to Battloid and hold 'em; we'll be right there," somebody was saying. Miriya pulled off an amazing maneuver, flipping her Alpha like a flapjack while the pursuing Pincer shot past her, its annihilation disks missing. Max's wife was suddenly in the six position.

Predator that she was, the onetime battle queen of the Quadronos lost no time in chopping away at the Pincer with short, highly controlled bursts of pumped-laser blasts. It trailed flame, debris, and outrushing gases for a moment, then became a drifting, brilliant cloudfront.

Max and Miriya came as one to a new vector, to engage three oncoming armored-trooper skirmish ships.

CHAPTER ELEVEN

In my android state, I lack the appropriate Human referents to explain sufficiently what is transpiring here. I can only give factual synopses. But there is a Human phrase, employed in description of sporting events, that occurs to me, Dr. Lang: "playing over his-or-her head," which refers to achievement—due to psychological, emotional, and other factors that resist analyses—in excess of what one might logically expect under given circumstances.

Given that parameter, I think I can safely say that the Sentinels are playing over their heads. But the game has yet to reach its final score.

Janice Em (in android state) in a report to Dr. Emil Lang

RICK WAS TRYING TO FOLLOW THE BATTLE BOTH BY eyeball—through the huge inverted bowl of the bridge canopy—and via the Sentinels' still-unfamiliar tracking displays and tactical-readout screens. At the same time, he was doing his best to coordinate the Human and non-Human elements of the Sentinels, and make sure foe, not friend, was the target of *Farrago*'s gun turrets and missile tubes.

But always, in the background, there was that small voice prodding and eating at him. He wanted so much to be out there in a VT, doing the only thing he had ever really done well in his life—piloting. To be left out of the rat race and yet be so close, so intimately involved in it, was such heartbreaking torture that it seemed the universe must be against him—that Creation was malign, after all.

He was also keeping a nervous eye on that huge Sekiton-powered junction that held the ship together and made *Farrago* a functioning whole; if it failed, the Sentinels would be history.

The pair of two-ship Skull elements dispatched by Max tackled the flight of six armored Shock Troopers that had penetrated the Sentinels' defensive sphere. Far less maneuverable than the Pin-

215

cers, the Shock Troopers mounted heavier firepower and had been no doubt sent in as kamikazes.

But the VTs were there first, two Alphas and a scratch element made up of a Beta and a Logan. The Alphas went to Guardian mode, in that process unique to Robotechnology that Lang had dubbed mechamorphosis.

The Beta reconfigured like some ultratech origami, thinning and extending as components flowed until it was in Battloid mode, a gleaming Herculean-looking Robotech body.

The Logan went to Battloid, too, mechamorphosing in response to its pilot's imaging. Where Alphas looked more Humaniform in Battloid, the Logan's boatlike radome made it seem like the upper half of a Robotech torso had been lifted away and some Egyptian icon-mask, the Spirit of the Twin-Thrustered Rocketcraft, had been lowered into its place.

But all the VTs were swinging and angling to confront the Invid. The Battloids clutched the repositioned cannon that had been integral weapons systems to the Beta and Logan but were now handheld infantry weapons, with barrels as wide as water mains, for the Robotech knights.

The attackers came in, and crewbeings on the bridge ducked involuntarily, as the darkness lit with crisscrossed beams of pure destruction and streams of annihilation disks.

The Shock Troopers looked like bipedal battleships, their clawed forearms bulging like ladybug carapaces. Their single sensor-eye clusters betrayed no emotion, and the twin cannon mounting at either shoulder made them appear invincible. But then the Battloids were there, and the mecha darted in and out of one another's line of fire; the enormous energy discharges lit the bridge crew below.

The hulking Logan stood in the teeth of withering fire from a Shock Trooper, the gun duel a simple question of who could get a telling hit first. In the meantime, a second Trooper was looping around for a pass from six o'clock, and nothing Rick could do in the bridge could get him a clear connection to that doomed pilot. Just about the time the oncoming Trooper broke up into fragments before the monstrous outpouring of the Beta-Battloid's gun, torso missile-rack covers flew back and a host of Swordfish air-to-airs corkscrewed at the Invid.

The armored Shock Trooper disappeared in a cloud of detonating warheads. The Beta changed its attitude of flight with a complex firing of its many steering thrusters, and opened up again with its handheld artillery in support of the Logan.

* * *

On the bridge, Lisa looked at Rick. No one could fault the job he was doing; despite the disadvantages of the Sentinels' slapdash organization and communications systems, he was keeping things sorted out—was, perhaps, an even more pivotal part of the battle than she. And yet she could see, in the moment's glance she could spare her husband, that he couldn't cope with the frustration of his job much longer; that he was actually *in pain* because he wasn't out there in the rat race.

Another concussion shook the flagship and a beam leapt out from the muzzle of the GMU's main gun. It was set for wider dispersal this time, since the clamshell troopships weren't a worthwhile target anymore. The stupendous cannonshot took out a few of the enemy mecha, like killing several flies with a howitzer. But this was no artillery duel; the mecha would decide the day.

The Alphas sent by Max Sterling mopped up the enemy machines that the Battloids hadn't stopped. The very last armored Shock Trooper tried a headfirst dive at the very bridge canopy, and most of the beings there dove for the deck, useless as that was, by sheer reflex.

The Beta got in its way, backpack thrusters flaring so hard that the wash of flame blew across the adamantine bridge canopy. Some systems overloaded and areas of the shields failed. There were explosions, sending flame and shrapnel flying, and everybody's ears popped as the ship began to lose atmosphere.

There were only a few Sentinels on their feet. Lron, at the wheel, held his place and let forth a challenging rumble. From where she stood, hands at the small of her back, Lisa looked every inch the captain—near the helm. She saw Rick still at his place; he turned, with a frantic look on his face, a look that was haunted and bereft—yet it held so much fear, wildness . . .

But at that moment, he saw that Lisa was all right, and he burst into a grin and gave her the thumbs-up, then turned back to his coordinating duties. Lisa understood that the panic in his eyes was that she might have been hurt, or killed. It had been a sudden vacancy—an immobility, really. True fear, and Lisa recognized it because she had seen it before, and felt it herself. *Terror* that he had lost her; it had debilitated him for a moment.

She thrust the thought aside. A few hundred yards above the long blister of the bridge, the damaged Logan had actually *bulldogged* an incoming armored Shock Trooper, interposing itself and going hand-to-hand with one of the enemy's most feared mecha.

The bridge crew couldn't hear the creaking of metal, the hiss of compromised seals, the parting of welds and seams. They watched the silent wrestling match as the bigger, stronger Beta rushed in to lend support. But the Beta was too far away.

The armored Shock Trooper grappled the Logan around into a certain mecha-infighting position, spread-eagling it, and bent it backward across one knee. There were the puffs of escaping atmosphere and the electrical arcing of destroyed systemry.

The Beta blindsided the Shock Trooper, rebounding to hit thrusters again and lock with it in mortal combat. Despite everything the Shock Trooper could do, the Beta Battloid forced its arms back and back—and worked a wholly Human wrestling hold, freeing one arm to grip the monolithic turret-head, seize, strain, apply torque with everything it had.

Rick was ordering the Beta clear; the flagship had been maneuvered so that the GMU's cannon had been brought to bear. But the Beta wouldn't relinquish its death grip on its foe. The Shock Troopers' pincers scraped deep furrows in the Beta's armor; its oval forearms levered in moves conceived to let it break free.

To no avail. The Beta bent the Shock Trooper's arm up around behind it, and Rick understood in that moment that where matters of Robotechnology stood even, a deciding factor emerged. That factor had to do with things that were *the exact opposite* of mechanical processes. Emotion and belief, a passion for victory that was fueled by hatred of the outrages the Invid had perpetrated; in place of the unquestioned instructions the Invid got from their Hive, the Beta was animated by a reasoned mind's drive to win.

The Beta got its free elbow under the Shock Trooper's chin and pressed up and back, and back. All this, while VTs and enemy mecha swirled and fought, while the kill scores climbed, while *Farrago*'s gun emplacements hammered.

There was a slight outventing, then seals gave and atmosphere rushed from the Invid, along with what appeared to be a green liquid that became weightless beads and globules and vapor as soon as it hit vacuum. The Invid came apart with explosive separations of its joints. The Beta braced one bulky foot against the dead carcass of it, and pushed free.

The Beta sailed like some lumpy puppet toward the dead Logan. "No life readings," somebody relayed the readout to Lisa; the Logan was so mangled that it came as no surprise.

Rick looked up from his apparently primitive but surprisingly sophisticated scopes. His features were closed of expression; self-contained. "Those are the Valdezes."

Everyone knew them, brother and sister VT hotdoggers, top-of-the-roster aces. Henry had flown the Logan; his sister had just avenged his death in the mighty Beta.

The repeated attacks of the Invid had only turned the battle into a turkey shoot; what the REF mecha didn't bag, the Sentinels' guns had managed to find. Lisa heard from her commo analysts that the instant destruction of the task force's command ship had kept word from going out to Optera, *or even Karbarra*, of the presence of the Sentinels. Something groundside might have detected the weapons discharges in space, but the Invid garrison must have been at a loss as to what they meant. Karbarra had a thick planetary ring, and the Invid below might think that was the cause of the commo breakdown. It didn't make much difference to the Sentinels now; Human and XT alike, they had gone to war—and in this Robotech era that meant something they were all used to: win or die.

The energy salvos and counter-salvos sent narrow beams of blindingly bright light and streams of angry red-orange annihilation disks skewing through the blackness. The mecha whirled and pounced like craft maneuvering in atmosphere, though that was prodigiously wasteful of power; such were the peculiarities of Robotech, the pilots' Earth-honed flying instincts channeled to action by the thinking caps.

It was the thickest of the rat race, the centerpoint of the fighter pilot's life, the Heart of Unreason—the terrible venue of the dogfight.

Barrages of missiles *whooshed* and energy blasts of such power were exchanged that they seemed almost *material*. Holed and damaged machines tumbled and spun, leaking atmosphere and flame, and dying. The Invid fought with the unanimity of the group mind, but it became manifest that the REF, too, had learned to wage war with total concentration. Neither side lacked for ferocity.

But the tide turned in the Sentinels' favor; in a mass Robotech rat race like that, the shift didn't take long to make itself apparent.

Max and Miriya flew through it like gods, dealing death when they saw an opponent and, by their intervention, granting life to beset VT fliers. Max felt like he had an extra edge, with Rick behind on the bridge.

Once Max's boss as Skull Leader, Rick had been away from combat flying too long to be jumping into a VT seat, no matter *how* restless he might feel. Max had already saved Rick's life once, at considerable risk to his own, since Rick had begun chafing at the restrictions of flag-rank life.

Max had to endure no such distractions now; with the enormously augmented power the pods and other enhancements of their Alphas gave them, Max and Miriya, wingmates and soulmates, flew where they willed. Mighty Enforcers and evasive Pincers were their prey, like prey for tigers. The Invid quarry stalked the VTs, too, with fire that could kill them, but that only made the hunt more worthwhile.

Computer and sensor constructs of the battle in various tactical-analysis thinkpools showed a moving nimbus of death and destruction—Max and Miriya Sterling, in an almost superhuman performance of cunning and aero-combat excellence.

The tide turned quickly and surely against the survivors of the late Senep's task force. In seconds, the scale had dipped unmistakably; the Invid were trying to disengage, to run for troop carriers that weren't there anymore, as the volcanic cannonshots of Vince Grant's GMU found their mark again and again.

The Invid's turning tail tripped some essential instinct of pursuit in the VTs, and they rushed in, crowding one another, for the kill. A whole field of retreating Invid mecha were suddenly in a shooting gallery like nothing seen in any Robotech scrap so far. Some turned to fight, others ran and dodged; the Skull fliers went after them all, merciless because they had seen what the Invid did to captive worlds, and hungry for kills. Wolves flying at the fold were no more voracious.

Screened from Karbarra by its planetary ring and by the jamming efforts of the ECM techs, the Sentinels had managed to win their first battle with a sort of unintended stealth. But the first of their main events waited below.

The last of the killing was still going on, the mopping-up of the Invid mecha being carried out by the men and women of the Skull squadron, but that was already a fait accompli. Rick Hunter wanted to stay where he was until the last of the VTs was back, safe, or at least accounted for. But he knew he couldn't; the strike at Karbarra must be launched *now*, within the hour, because the Sentinels' presence might already have been discovered.

Rick had a sudden vision of Henry Gloval, and knew what had been trying to bow the old man's shoulders as he stood there on the deck of SDF-1 in the old days. Rick thought of Lisa with a vast burst of love, and wondered whether any of the Sentinels would be alive in a few hours.

"We hit them now; take them by surprise, and the whole of Karbarra is ours!" Kami, the foxlike Garudan, said from behind his breathing mask.

The rest of the Sentinels agreed with that and Rick Hunter slammed the flat of his hand down on the U-shaped table, making everybody, even the stolid Lron and Crysta, start a little.

"I lost eight good people in the fight just now, and eight mecha *we couldn't afford to lose*; I won't lose more if I can help it! The quicker we jump the planetary garrison, the fewer our losses and the quicker we win major mecha-producing facilities."

Lron suddenly reared up, there beneath the bridge dome where a trestle table had been set out atop empty Karbarran beer barrels. "And I say we, we . . ."

He seemed to be drifting in thought, and many of the Sentinels looked at one another, especially the Humans. But nobody appeared to have an explanation. Still, the deaths of REF-assigned fighter pilots were Rick's direct responsibility, so he found himself pressing his own view.

"We *must* exploit our current tactical advantage to the fullest, to minimize our losses, by attacking at once! Intel-computers and sensors and the G-3 ops staff have already pinpointed the primary and secondary Invid targets on Karbarra. Our VTs are being refueled and rearmed at this moment; we can strike in something under an hour. Fellow Sentinels, let's free Karbarra."

Lisa was looking at Rick in a new light. Granted, he hated his desk job, but he had shouldered the responsibility that had been given him and was undergoing that torment, that near-schizophrenia, that any decent commanding officer knew in combat: the need to carry out the mission weighed against the lives of his or her command. She wouldn't have wished it on him, but she saw now that he had come into his full growth, as Captain Gloval had always put it.

Rick, for his part, looked over at his wife and saw that she understood the forces vying to rip him apart—understood, too, more vividly than he ever had, the forces that had pressed Lisa so agonizingly when she was SDF-1's first officer, and later SDF-3's captain.

Rick has something of a revelation. *I'd rather be in a cockpit, responsible for one VT and my own life, because it's* easier! *Let this cup pass . . .*

But it didn't. Nonetheless, Rick saw that Lisa fully understood, and that gave him a strength that surprised him. He also felt a measure of shame; how often had *she* been in this kind of dilemma, when he couldn't see beyond his own Skull Leader problems?

Every time he thought he had run out of reasons to love her, a new one appeared.

Except it didn't help him with his Karbarran problem. Lron, till now, the Papa-bear stalwart, swung a fist the size of a Thanksgiving turkey, and took a considerable portion off the lip of the table nearest him.

"No!"

CHAPTER TWELVE

Here's where you get back
Some of your own;
Here's where we visit
Part of the horror upon its author

From an Augury chant of the Karbarrans

NOBODY WAS ABOUT TO TELL LRON HE COULDN'T HAVE HIS say, or to try to stifle Crysta, who had risen up next to her mate.

Their goggles were pushed down around their thick, furry necks; The armor and accoutrements they wore only made them seem that much more like captive and dangerous wild animals.

"We cannot attack yet," Lron roared, and Lisa began to consider the tactical problems of having half-ton ursinoids turning mean on the bridge. Stun guns might not even faze them, given the thick pelts and subcutaneous fat. It was either shoot to kill, or listen. And given how much Humans still had to learn about their allies, she followed the example of Veidt and the other Sentinels, and listened.

Rick saw her decision clearly by the lines of her face; he backed off, too, and for one moment they shared a brief, small smile—but it was something that warmed them both out of all proportion to the moment.

"We cannot attack," Lron was grunt-howling, "because the [here he made an ursine noise that didn't translate into the lingua franca the Sentinels used] is not correct! You are outsiders, and blind to the ways of Karbarra, and yet I tell you: if you go against the [that same word again], then there is nothing but total disaster awaiting you."

It took considerable time to sort out, during which Rick fidgeted. Long-horned Burak and the crystal-bright Baldan spoke in defense of Lron's past accomplishments. Rick felt like pulling a fistful of hair out of his head.

But it seemed that Karbarrans had a certain sense of fate, and Rick got the impression that it was depressingly downbeat and debilitating. And the fate of the bears was that there be no all-out attack on Karbarra at this time. What Lron and Crysta wanted was a very small recon group, a handful, to go down and scout things out.

"That's crazy!" Rick yelled. "We *know* where the Inorganics and the rest of our targets are! Let's *paste* 'em, then go in and save the Karbarrans! My *god*, is there anybody here who doesn't understand what we're talking about? The Invid aren't going to spare your people, no matter what concessions you make! There'll be another demand, and another!"

Crysta came out of her big chair with a growl, showing her snow-white peglike canines. Rick stood his ground—arguably the bravest thing he had ever done; Lisa's hand was clawing for a pistol that wasn't at her belt.

"The Shapings of the Protoculture do not dictate . . . that," Crysta said slowly, as if in a dream. She lowered her head as though she had come at bay. "Do not necessarily say that."

Rick shook his head, unable to understand what it was they were getting at. "What's wrong with you? We hit 'em high, then hit 'em low, and Karbarra's *yours* again! Your planet's *yours* again!"

Lron spun on him, one paw raised high, its claws standing out from the splayed hand, looming over Rick. There was almost a debate in the slow orbiting of it, and Rick Hunter knew death hovered close.

"We . . . won't . . . hit . . . them . . . at . . . *all*, yet!" Lron bellowed, at such volume that the others winced.

Lisa Hayes Hunter was the first one to raise her head again and look Lron in the eye. Rick tried to pull her back down, and wished he had thought to bring a firearm. Something in the elephant-gun category.

Lisa looked Lron in the eye. She said, "In case you've forgotten, we didn't come here to be frightened away. Now, do we attack with your help, or without it?"

Lisa had put herself on the other side of the argument without qualification. And Rick was bracing himself to fight, because he was pretty sure the bears were going to charge his wife in a second or so.

But instead, Lron and Crystal subsided, making gnawing sounds but not objecting. Lisa went on. "It's clear that we have the Invid at a disadvantage, since it is highly probable that the ground forces aren't aware that their task force has been wiped out. Computer projections and G-3 evaluations are unanimous: we have a window of advantage at this moment and it won't last long. On the behalf of the Human Sentinels, I say that we should take our shot."

Other Sentinels pounded the table and cried their support. Rick looked at his wife and felt a powerful pulse of love mixed with a certain envy; but when he thought about it, the envy was separated out into equal parts of desire and admiration. Both of those were good for a love affair, better yet for a marriage.

But the Karbarrans were up, like grizzlies on their back haunches, to rebut. "You do not understand the——"

For that, they made a sound incomprehensible to the Sentinels, something the translation computers had to labor at, at last rendering up a marked and qualified interpretation: "the Shaping of Things."

Rick looked to his left, to Kami, the foxlike Gerudan who sat there in his breathing mask that was fed from the tank on his back. "What in the world are they talking about?"

Kami made an exasperated sound that somehow penetrated the mask. Rick leaned his way. "I don't know what to think. Crysta and Lron aren't behaving as they did when we formed our alliance," Kami said.

"We could *sock* into that garrison before they knew what'd hit them, then mop up the remains," Rick pointed out.

Kami nodded. "But something seems to be holding the Karbarrans back," he pointed out.

"Are you gonna let that hold *you* back?"

Kami regarded him with a long look. "I would give some benefit of the doubt to you or the Praxians or any of the others. There are many things we don't understand about one anothers' species, and so we must proceed with caution. Am I wrong-thinking?"

Rick didn't quite know what to say. "What we must do is make a reconnaissance of the situation below," Lron announced. "Crysta and I and a half dozen of our people—"

"No." Lisa was shaking her head. She wasn't sure what the ursinoids were being so secretive about, but she was wholly opposed to letting them go off on their own. She wanted very much to trust them—had come, in fact, to like Crysta and Lron—but couldn't shake the feeling that they were concealing something.

Everyone had something to say, of course. The Sentinels' alliance was put to its first real test, and for some moments it seemed that the need that bound them together wouldn't hold. Unexpectedly, Cabell was one of those who put things back on track. "Have you all forgotten the horrors the Invid inflicted on my planet? We must work together—compromise! The life and death of whole worlds are at stake!"

In the end, it was agreed that recon would be carried out by living beings rather than by remotes or drones. Veidt, acting as chairman, finally decreed that the unit would be composed of Lron, Kami, Rick, Gnea, and Bela, along with Jack Baker and Karen Penn. Those last names surprised Rick, but then he supposed Veidt had come to know the two lieutenants.

Lisa wanted to object, wanted to be included, but knew that Veidt's selection was right; her place was on the bridge of the starship, especially now. But one last name was added to the roster: at both Cabell's request and his own, Rem was included.

For the insertion, they would take a Karbarran shuttlecraft; with its Sekiton drive, it was much less likely to be detected by the Invid Protoculture instruments. This was no job for a VT or a Hovertank, as even Rick had to concede.

The recon party moved through the ship's armory, gathering handguns and rifles, along with rocket launchers and grenades. Meanwhile, human techs were checking out the assorted survival gear the team would need. Rick noticed that while the women from Praxis had no objection to buckling gunbelts around their waists or slinging Wolverine assault rifles over their shoulders— indeed, they seemed to understand firearms quite well—they still insisted on bringing sword, crossbow, and Gnea's *naginata*-like halberd.

He shrugged; to each his own. Besides, silent weapons might come in quite handy. Lron seemed set on bringing his pneumatic musket, too, and his huge, cleaverlike knife, but Kami was apparently more than happy to carry Human weapons with their greater firepower.

The equipment and the shuttle were checked while sensors and intel staff people and computers debated over optimal landing sites. There was still no sign that the Invid garrison below had any inkling of the Sentinels' presence in the planetary ring; at least the recon group had that advantage.

Rick had found time to snatch a few hours' sleep before the final briefing was to commence. He had hoped for a moment or two alone with Lisa, but she had been preoccupied with preparations—and with trying to figure out contingency plans for dealing with whatever the scouting mission might run across.

Now, though, she entered their quarters as he settled his web gear and ran yet another check of his equipment. Medpack, spare ammo, emergency ration concentrates, inertial tracker—

"Happy, Rick?"

"Lisa, we can't have this same argument again! Veidt picked me; I didn't even volunteer."

"You didn't have to. You've made your preferences known."

"I took an oath to serve in a military outfit, not sit on the sidelines!"

"Well, you got your wish, hmm?" But she couldn't stay mad at him, not with his departure so near. "Oh, just make sure you come back safe and sound, get me?"

He took her in his arms. "Quit worrying; I'm not looking for any medals. Rick 'Cautious' Hunter, that's me."

They kissed, then she pushed him away. "And no flirting with those Praxian lady wrestlers, or we're going to be short one admiral around here."

"No, ma'am. Yes, ma'am."

At the shuttle lock, Jack Baker was making final adjustments on his thinking cap. While the team wasn't bringing any large transformable mecha, there were still a couple of Cyclone combat cycles and Hoverbikes. Besides, Jack didn't favor climbing into anything fast-moving, or, for that matter, being in a combat zone without all the protection he could get. He wished Lang's researchers had given the Sentinels some prototypes of the bodyarmor they were working on, full armor that was supposed to integrate with the Cyclones somehow.

Anyway, the helmet would be necessary for communications, with its built-in commo gear. Apparently Gnea and Bela were going to stick with their showy Praxian helms as reengineered by Lang; sometimes, Jack found their blending of the old and new rather illogical.

"Well, well, so they're sending the scrub team along to see how *real* soldiers get the job done, hmm?"

Karen Penn had a way of making even a combat suit look good. She was shrugging into her web gear, resettling her burdens, giving Jack a mocking smile.

"*Somebody's* got to be there to chafe your wrist after you faint, Penn." They were about to get into another row when Jack became aware of a sound that made him turn with his mouth hanging open.

They're not serious!

It was Bela, mounted on the Robotsteed, Halidarre, with Gnea riding pillion behind. Halidarre's hooves rang against the deckplates. It took him a few seconds to get out any sound.

"What d'you think you're doing? This is a recon mission, not a carnival!"

The towering Bela's brows knit ominously as she glared down at him. "Halidarre is my steed; with her, we'll cover more ground and be able to rest assured that triumph in battle shall inevitably be ours!" Bela slapped the sword on her thigh, but Jack noticed that she carried a Wolverine assault rifle in a saddle scabbard too, and had a heavy energy pistol in a shoulder holster.

Gnea was carrying her halberd and her shield, although she was adorned with grenades and firearms. Jack could see now that the inner rim of the shield was lined with a row of throwing knives held in place by clips, convenient to her hand. Gnea slid to the deck, then Bela did, taking Halidarre's bridle and leading her toward the shuttle's open freight hatch.

The Karbarran spacers and the others standing around were too stunned to interfere, and in a moment the amazons were easing the mecha horse into place in the cargo area. Totally unskittish, Halidarre looked like she went through this kind of thing every day.

"The admiral's not going to like this," Jack muttered.

Karen shrugged. "Oh, well, at least she didn't decide to bring along that four-winged miniature gunship that she—"

Just then Bela turned and uttered a piercing whistle, adding, "Hagane. To me!"

Jack and Karen, like the rest of the ship's complement, had learned to duck when Bela gave that whistle. Something small and fast, moving and darting like a hummingbird, came blurring through the air on a whirring of multiple wings, buzzing the two lieutenants just for the fun of it. Jack felt like taking a swipe at Hagane, but decided it wasn't worth the risk of having a finger nipped off by a beak as keen as a pair of tin snips.

Hagane was what Bela called a malthi, as much a royal bird to the Praxians as the falcon was to the pharaohs. It settled on the heavy sheath on her forearm now, a creature no bigger than a sparrow-hawk, ruffling its double set of wings and gazing around suspiciously. Her eyes bulged strangely, savage and unreadable, and Hagane let out the *birring* hunting sound that seemed to go right through one's eardrums.

"*God*, I hate when she does that," Jack frowned. "Horses and birds! Why don't we take along some clowns and a tightrope walker while we're at it?"

"You don't approve of the TO&E, Lieutenant?"

Jack spun. "Oh, Admiral! The Table of Organization and

Equipment's just fine with me, sir! I, uh—that is, I was just surprised, that's all."

Rick was, too, but decided not to let it show. Actually, he was curious about how useful the Robotech horse and the Praxian hunting bird would be. Certainly, they wouldn't exactly be inconspicuous if Bela insisted on tearing all over the sky—but on the other hand, they were nothing that the Invid would connect with an expedition from Tirol.

He sighed, not looking forward to getting Bela to see reason and use her pets with restraint. Maybe Lisa was right, and this outing wasn't such a great idea after all.

But it was too late for that. Lron showed up, and Rem, and Kami. They boarded the shuttle and belted in, as Lisa began her careful approach swing through the planetary ring.

CHAPTER
THIRTEEN

The pivotal point, unanswered as yet, is what success the Regent felt he was achieving in his "devolution," and how he chose his course. That he still felt an unshakable desire—perhaps love, perhaps obsession—for the Regis is obvious.

But this doesn't jibe with "de-evolution" as Humans would picture it; surely his self-remolding should have taken him away from such feelings. Did he refuse to give up those feelings, or was de-evolution something completely different from what we might surmise?

Lemuel Thicka, *Temple of Flames: A History of the Invid Regent*

ONCE AGAIN, CRYSTA STOOD BEFORE TESLA'S CAGE. "I ask you yet again, Invid: what can you tell me of the situation on Karbarra?"

Tesla spread his hands with infinite sadness. "Only what you yourself know. Yet, I say to you once more: release me and let me go down to your planet and do my best on behalf of peace and the opening of new dialogues."

Crysta made an impatient sound. "If I discover that you're lying, I'll throw you out an airlock." She turned to go.

"Wait," he blurted. "Why haven't you told the others of—this matter?" As a scientist, he had discovered interesting things about the ursinoids' belief system. He had expected Lron and Crysta would have explained their quandary to the Sentinels long ago; though it was perhaps some slight advantage to him that they hadn't, he found it puzzling.

Crysta made an irritated sound. "You understand nothing, Invid! The knowledge that comes from our Seeing is fragile. Revealing it can change the Seeing and the Shaping to something else, something even worse. If you hadn't already known about—about our dilemma, I would never have mentioned it."

Tesla nodded to himself. So. It might be that there was hope for him yet, if he could manipulate things. Certainly, he hadn't much

else going for him. He, above all, had reason to hope that the
Karbarrans' vision of the future came out well; otherwise, Tesla
would be among the first to feel their wrath, and he knew how
terrible their vengeance could be.

The entry was more of a free-fall, really, Lron's piloting veering
between the suicidally reckless and the professionally competent.
He peeled part of the ablative layer off the shuttle but got them
down without registering, as far as they could tell, on any Invid
instruments.

Jack Baker found himself pressed into his seat, eyeballs in, slipping into and out of a red-out. He just hoped Lron had a greater
tolerance of g-forces, because this felt like it might be an embar-
rassing moment to have the pilot take a snooze.

Karbarra was a barren, windswept place, pockmarked and
wormholed as a result of their generations of intensive mining.
Lron pulled out of his bone-jarring entry and gave the ship some
thrust, leveling off at virtual landing altitude, searching. He
quickly had his bearings, and closed in on the landing site he had
selected.

All the Sentinels were alert, manning weapons stations and
ready to open fire. But the spot selected by Lron, an abandoned
operation where a major vein of iron ore had given out, was deserted. The Sentinels had been counting on decreased surveillance
and patrolling, what with the Invid occupation forces presumably
cut to minimal strength. It seemed they had won the bet—so far—
but that still left an awful lot of enemy.

Lron set the shuttle down gently through a huge gaping hole in
an enormous cracked dome at the center of the processing area. It
was a location already noted by the Karbarran resistance, he explained. It was as safe a base of operations as the team was likely
to find, at least for now.

Rick began getting things organized even before they unbelted.
Bela was anxious to get Halidarre up for a look around and to feel
the freedom of the sky; it took some strong talk to make her see
that a ground sweep and sensor scan of the immediate area would
be necessary first, to make sure the Sentinels weren't spotted by
somebody before they could do the spotting themselves.

Karen Penn felt some foreboding, seeing the young admiral
standing up to the imposing amazon and calmly telling her it was
about time she started learning to take orders. Her hand went to
her sword again. "Orders? You dare tell me I lack discipline? And
who are you to give *me* orders?"

His mouth had become a flat line. "I'm one of the people you

Sentinels came to for help, remember? I'm part of the force that's giving you a fighting chance at winning back your planet. Now, when our joint council makes a decision, we stick by it; that was the bargain. And the decision in this case was for a recon mission with me in command and Lron in second place. So let's see if you can take orders as well as you give them."

Bela suddenly grinned, throwing her head back. "I keep forgetting that you males can be just as hard-nosed as a woman! All right, Admiral, we'll do it your way—but, mind: when I'm put in charge of an operation, I'll expect the same from you."

"Fair enough." Privately, Rick decided that he didn't want anything to do with an operation run by the impulsive warrior-woman.

His every footfall in the vast, echoing halls of the Invid Home Hive seemed to be mocking the Regent.

There was still no word of the task force he had sent to Tirol, no answer from the Regis. It was all too troubling for him to even take pleasure in punishing subordinates. He paced along now with his elite bodyguard marching a discreet distance behind, their armored steps resounding.

And he cursed again the tactical misfortunes that had made it necessary to abandon the Living Computer, the newest and by far the best of the giant Invid vat-grown brains, under the Royal Hall. It was inactive, and could fall prey to harm, could atrophy—could even be damaged by the upstart mongrel species who had somehow routed his legions.

He had been obliged to recall more troops from the outer marches of his crumbling realm to insure that nearby worlds under his dominion remained that way. The Regent rasped angrily at the thought that perhaps his task force had met with some reversal. At the worst possible time!

And then there was the thought that chilled him as much as any. What if the Robotech Masters should return to wage bloody war, and catch him in this disorganized state? He rumbled with displeasure, kicking out at a pillar that resembled a neural axon.

He cursed his mate again, for taking half his race from him. What could she need them for? She wasn't even engaged in conquest! Wasn't even pretending to help him maintain sway over the realm. It wasn't fair; this was all *her* fault.

Something had to be done.

The Regent paused, turned, started off in another direction. When he got to the vast egg chamber, he was pleased to find that nothing was amiss, and the Special Children of the Regis were all there, unmoving and unaware in their gelatinous suspension. Row by row, rank on rank.

"Special Children." Typical of her, she hadn't even deigned to tell him what the phrase *meant*. The Regis had merely made it clear that these were to be some ultimate manifestation of the Invid genetic heritage, and that theirs would be some higher destiny.

"Indeed?" the Regent snorted to himself. When the empire was crumbling and the enemies of the Invid might be at the very Home Hive soon? What higher destiny could such Special Children have than to defend their Regent and conquer, conquer for the glory of the Invid?

Yet—he must proceed carefully. He wasn't even sure what he was dealing with. It wouldn't do to unleash some new and even worse danger—perhaps a generation of Invid who would know no loyalty to him, or even be infected with aspirations of their *own*.

No, best to go cautiously. In the interim, he could reassign his forces, maintain the status quo for the time being. He had already managed to scrape up some frontier troops and dispatch them to reinforce the depleted Karbarran garrison. Perhaps he could even use the Special Children as a bargaining chip—get the Regis to trade him the loyal fighters he required in return for these quiescent eggs.

And Tesla! With his mystical talk about the Fruit of the Flower and his promises to bring a menagerie of defeated enemies for the Regent's entertainment! What of him?

Seething, the Regent went off to dispatch another message to Haydon IV and demand immediate word of Tesla, on pain of horrible punishment to those all along the line who might fail to provide it.

"I simply have a feeling she'll listen to you," Vince Grant told his wife. "You just have that way with people, darling."

She put down the medical report she had been filling out, preliminary evaluations of the vast array of salves, preparations, pills, and powders from every Sentinel's homeworld; she was trying to understand them and the physiologies of the patients she would be expected to minister to.

"Vince, why don't *you* talk to Crysta. I mean, you're more her size."

That got a grudging chuckle out of him. "I don't think this has anything to do with size. I'm just a jumped-up engineer who got a commission 'cause he knows what makes the GMU tick. But you understand people, and Crysta's just big furry people. Besides, you're a mother."

Jean looked him over. "What's that got to do with it?"

"I'm not sure. I was showing her around the GMU and, you know, there's that picture of Bowie on my desk. When I explained about him, it made her clam up, and she cut the tour short."

Jean felt a mixture of curiosity and professional obligation now; he had seen her get interested in a case, just like this, so many times before. "We really don't know much about the Karabarran children, do we? Oh, the reproductive cycle's right there in the data banks, nothing unusual—especially when you compare them to those Spherians! But I mean, what's happening to them right this second?"

"That occurred to me, too," Vince said soberly.

She rose and kissed her husband, standing on tiptoe to do it. "You're pretty smart for a jumped-up engineer, y'know that?"

He gave her a half smile. "Smart enough to come to you when I run into a *real* problem."

The sensors and detectors indicated that they had made their landing without being spotted. Sweeps by Rick, Jack, and Karen on hovercycles, and, inevitably, a surveillance flight by Bela and Gnea on their flying horse, just confirmed the fact.

Then it was Rem who got stubborn, as Rick assigned him, along with Gnea, to guard the shuttle and man the commo-relay equipment, so that the recon team would be sure of getting a direct link to *Farrago* if and when it was needed.

"This whole mission is pointless if we can't report back what we find here," Rick fumed at him. "Now, I don't want any more arguments from anybody!"

Rem subsided, and the team began loading up with weapons and gear. Lron casually weighted himself down with twice as much paraphernalia as any of the others and didn't seem to feel the burden a bit. Something was making him most untalkative, though.

As it was, Rick was more concerned with trying to get the right mix of equipment and weapons distributed among his team. Lron had revealed that the network of natural caverns and abandoned mines constituted a virtual underground roadway, and that the unit could make most of the distance to its objective that way.

That meant spare handheld spots, night-sight gear, and so forth. Rick let Bela keep her Wolverine rifle, but assigned Kami to a much more powerful but short-range Owens Mark IX mob gun, in case of close fighting down below. Rick took a Wolverine for himself. Karen was assigned an elaborately scoped sniper rifle, her marksmanship scores being the best of any of them.

Lron lugged the magazine-fed rocket launcher and an assortment of ammunition; Jack was given a solid-projectile submachine gun that fired explosive pellets. Rick made sure they were all wearing "bat-ears," in case there was any subsurface fighting. The bat-ears amplified soft sounds, left normal ones unchanged, but dampened loud ones—so the scouts wouldn't be deafened in an underground firefight.

Bela didn't put up the expected argument about leaving Halidarre behind; even she could see how impractical it would be to drag the horse through the tight spots the team could expect to hit down below. She put aside most of her Praxian weapons, taking only her long knife.

Lron led the way to a mine elevator that smelled of must and stale air. He fiddled with a power connection that looked dead, and made the elevator's motor hum with readiness. The group boarded, turning on helmet lights. Rem and Gnea watched them descend into the darkness.

Veidt, Cabell, and the others were mystified by what they saw—or, rather, didn't see. Long-range readings on the surface of Karbarra indicated that there had been little or no battle damage on the planet below. Their main city, Tracialle, was still shining and whole under its crystalline dome.

"This isn't logical," Veidt said. "The Karbarrans are fierce haters of the Invid, and we assumed the fighting had been furious."

But instruments definitely indicated heavy Invid military activity below, although there was no sign of combat. With some few exceptions, the industrial and technical infrastructure seemed to be intact and functioning to a modest degree, the buildings still standing for the most part, the social systems operating normally.

"Perhaps this is all some ruse?" Sarna wondered, turning to her husband. "Can it be that Karbarrans went through all this to lure us into a trap?—but no. Surely they could have diverted the ship here on one pretext or another as soon as we staged our mutiny?"

"And it makes no sense for them to have risked their lives against the Pursuer, or again in combat against the task force we surprised," Cabell pointed out. "Then there's this business of the reconnaissance. Some piece of the puzzle is still missing."

They were interrupted by the ship's mismatched alarms again, and Lisa's voice came over a PA speaker that resembled a cornucopia.

"Battle stations, battle stations! An enemy force has left hyperspace for approach to Karbarra. They have detected us and are maneuvering for attack. Skull Squadron and Wolff Pack, prepare for launch. All weapons stations prepare to fire on my command!"

For Jonathan Wolff, it was a relief to be called to the cockpit of his Hovertank. He had been driving his Wolff Pack all through the voyage, trying to wrench his mind away from the thoughts that tormented him, with preparation and drill, maintenance checks, and intense briefing and training sessions.

It hadn't helped. There was still the guilt that he had left his wife and son far behind so that he could share in the REF glory, and now it would be years before he saw them again.

But an even worse guilt, grinding his conscience raw and then grating at the bloody wound, was the undeniable image of Minmei, Minmei. The sound of her voice, the aroma of her hair, the face and eyes, her coltish charm. The recollection of how it had felt to put his arms around her in the garden at the New Year's Eve party on Tiresia. Her kiss, which had made him as light-headed as some school kid.

The ship was shuddering at the launching of the Skull VTs. Wolff snapped rapid commands, and his own Hovertanks went to Battloid mode, sealed for combat in vacuum, following him in a dash for the designated cargo lock. The Destroids assigned to the GMU would be going to their firing positions, Wolff knew, and the Ground Mobile Unit itself would be warming up its weapons.

But there would be no question of an ambush this time; today both sides were forewarned. Wolff had felt disappointed at not being included in the recon team, but that had proved premature. Now, the Wolff Pack looked like it was going to get all the action it could handle.

And as for Hunter and the rest, trapped below? Wolff felt briefly sorry for them, then got his mind back on running his little corner of the war.

CHAPTER FOURTEEN

Of course I heard all those cracks about "aliens," and to her great credit, my wife let them pass, knowing what it was like for people fighting a war.

I'd hoped the Human race had learned, in meeting the Sentinels, to be a little less indiscriminately prejudiced. But few aside from the Skulls were.

Miriya overlooked all that, and fought like a tiger on behalf of the Human race and the Sentinels. And you're telling me that's alien? Then so am I.

Max Sterling, from *Wingmates: The Story of Max and Miriya Sterling*
by *Theresa Duvall*

"**F**ORM UP ON ME, SKULL TEAM, AND STICK WITH YOUR wingmates," Max Sterling recited automatically, his attention devoted to the tactical displays in his Alpha cockpit. He knew his wife, comrade and wingmate, would keep an eye on the team for him.

Max found a moment in which to be concerned for Rick. At least Rick wasn't out here trying to fly combat in a VT; he was a good flyer, a natural, and once he had ranked only behind Max in proficiency. But Rick was years out of practice, and that had been obvious the last time he had gone into space combat with Skull. If Rick and his gang just kept their heads down, they would be all right—perhaps a lot better than the Sentinels' main force was going to be, unless Skull got on the stick and took care of business.

Luckily, this new enemy contingent wasn't as numerous as the task force the Sentinels had handled when they arrived: two saucer troopships, and no command vessel at all. On the other hand, the Sentinels weren't going to get in any surprise Sunday punches today. Even now, the clamlike troop carriers yawned open and

Pincer ships poured forth, interspersed with some Shock Troopers and even a few of the fearsome, armored Shock Troopers.

The Veritechs leapt to meet them in a mass duel. It was a mad, swirling combat wherein friend and foe were so intermingled that it was often dangerous to risk a shot. But those Invid who got through found that the Sentinels' flagship was throwing out an almost impenetrable net of fire, augmented by Wolff's tanks and the GMU's firepower.

Novas lit the night as mecha erupted in fireballs; tremendous streams of destructive energy were hosed this way and that, and clouds of missiles flew. Jamming and counterjamming made guidance systems erratic and put both sides in almost as much danger from their own ordnance as from their opponents'.

A small group of Pincers, led by an Armored Officer mecha, got to the upper hull of the Sentinels' ship after suffering heavy casualties. But as they were about to attack the craft at close range—and get aboard to wreak havoc if possible—they were met by Wolff and a squad of his Battloids. Most of the fighting was too close even for hand weapons, and the conflict came down to REF alloy fist against metallic Invid claw—mecha feet and elbows and knees came into play.

A Pack member wrenched off a Pincer's arm and flung it away; the Pincer's power systems overloaded and blew it apart from within. The enemy Armored Officer unit and two Pincers seized a Battloid from behind and began pulling it to pieces.

But the Invid were outnumbered, being beaten or kicked or torn to bits. Just then more Hovertanks showed up, in Gladiator mode: stumpy, two-legged walking artillery pieces the size of a house. Their tremendously powerful blasts nailed the last of the interlopers; then all the tanks went to Gladiator to repulse any further attempts to land on the starship.

The GMU's massive main gun had sent out its inferno shots again and again, but all the enemy mecha had dispersed, the clamships unimportant for the moment. Vince Grant ceased fire and diverted power to the secondary gun emplacements, to conserve energy for the battle.

An Invid suicide attack got through the Sentinels' net of AA fire toward the stern, and Vince dispatched Destroid war machines across the outer deck to join a pair of Hovertanks in trying to maintain cover back there. He had his exec doublecheck with Jean to make sure the sick bay would be ready for casualties, and got back an answer that rattled him.

"Sick bay standing by, sir, but Lieutenant Commander Grant

isn't there and hasn't reported in yet. Her whereabouts are unknown at this time."

Far below, on Karbarra, the Invid noted the military action being fought high above.

In accordance with standing orders, certain specialized units were mobilized and moved out en masse, weapons primed. Karbarrans in the street, frozen with dread and hollow-eyed with fear, watched them go. But the big ursinoids could only stand rooted to the spot, and pray.

Even with the inertial trackers, it was tough to figure out where Lron was leading them.

Lron, however, didn't seem to have any doubts. Down abandoned mineshafts, along connections that had been made to drain underground watercourses, and through cavern systems, they made their way, the spotlights stabbing through the utter blackness. Rick had had them moving combat-style at first, wary of attack despite Lron's reassurance that the Invid were unaware of this underground travel system. But infantry tactics slowed the recon party down considerably, especially since the alien Sentinels were unfamiliar with REF procedures.

So in time Rick settled on modified procedures, with Lron on point and Jack and Karen taking turns on rear guard, the rest of the group together or spread out somewhat as circumstances dictated. The team moved faster than combat-zone precautions would ordinarily have dictated.

At one point they passed through a mined-out, shored-up space where an ore seam had been, a place not quite four feet high, though it was fifty yards wide and went on for over two miles. It was backbreaking travel, especially hard on Lron. Their shuffling progress raised a fine dust that had them all black-faced in no time.

Kami, with his Garudan breathing mask, was relatively comfortable, and after a while the REF members closed their flight helmets. Lron improvised a face mask from strips of fabric.

At another point, though, the group rode two ore cars that they powered with energy cells Lron had brought. It was a welcome relief, even with the weight of a planet hanging overhead, and they made good time along the railway.

Lron and Crysta had explained that the apparently limitless tunnel system had grown up over the years before the coming of the Invid and the Robotech Masters, when Karbarra, center of industry and trade, had had its assorted rivals and enemies. War production under the planet was seldom slowed down as a result of attack from space, but nowadays much of the system had fallen into disuse and disrepair.

Sometime later, after a short break to eat and rest, Lron led them into a cavern system of unutterable phosphorescent beauty, and they paced along the brink of an underground lake in which strange, blind, parasollike, glowing things could be seen to swim and drift. The cavern ceiling was like a dome mosaic with jewels of every conceivable color. There were plants that looked like coral formations made out of tiny crystalline needles.

During the journey, the scouts maintained contact with Rem and Gnea, taking turns raising the shuttle guards at thirty-minute intervals for a commo check. Slightly more than eleven hours after they had started out, Rick formed them up into as good a security perimeter as he could achieve in the confines of the cave, and took Lron aside.

"All right; you said we'd reach the first checkpoint two hours ago, but I don't see it around here yet. And don't give me any more of this 'it's just ahead' stuff, I'm warning you." Every muscle ached, and sheer fatigue was making him edgy and paranoid, fearing a trap or a terrible screwup that the big XT was afraid to admit.

Lron rumbled, "If we'd moved as quickly as Karbarrans are used to, we *would* have been there long since, Admiral. But never mind; a hundred paces or so—*my* paces!—along that way over there will bring us to the beginning of our ascent. If you can keep up with me for another hour—two at the most, if we go slowly—we will sleep tonight in a cave overlooking one of the Invid outposts in the Hardargh Rift.

"And in the meantime, do you realize what we've passed under? Inorganics; flying Scout patrols; prowling packs of those murderous Hellcats; formations of Enforcers in their skirmish ships; Terror Weapons drifting along on their surveillance routes; and more! Save your breath on this final climb, little Human; you'll need it to do some gasping when you realize how far we've come."

Now it was Rick's turn to grunt. *Talk's cheap; let's see you prove it!* But he kept the remark to himself, trying to avoid more friction. Instead, he turned and whistled; then, with voice and hand signals, formed up his tiny command to move out again.

They had barely reached the beginning of the long ascent when Rem contacted them with word of the new battle.

When things go wrong around here, they really do it in rows, Lisa thought, but there wasn't much time for regret. Reports coming in to the bridge indicated that the Skulls had repulsed the enemy attack, inflicting extremely heavy losses; the few Invid survivors were limping for Karbarra, their saucer troopships having been blown to particles by the GMU's big gun.

There had been losses in all Sentinel combat elements and the ship had suffered damage. Skull had lost two Betas, an Alpha, and a Logan, and several other VTs were badly damaged. Rick's group was standing pat in a relatively safe position, apparently, but a pickup was impossible, and it looked like the whole recon would be a failure. Lisa refused to think about what would happen if the Invid garrison's heightened state of alert on Karbarra meant that the shuttle was permanently pinned down in its present location.

And perhaps most shocking of all, Jean Grant had been absent from her post in time of combat. Lisa still didn't have all the details, but it involved Crysta and the Invid scientist, Tesla. Whatever it was, it had old Cabell about ready to throw a fit.

"Report," Lisa snapped. Subordinates reassured her that things were being seen to. Damage-control parties were already at work, casualties being attended to by various Sentinel healers and the medical staff. Skull was refueling and rearming in case of another hot scramble, but that didn't seem likely for the moment; apparently the Karbarran garrison had been stripped of its spacecraft, or else didn't care to launch a counterstrike quite yet.

Not after the way we've bloodied their snouts twice running, she thought with a small glimmer of satisfaction. Lisa issued orders that the flagship be held in orbit, and added, "I'll be down in medical."

Her first thoughts upon entering the big compartment where Jean Grant's medical labs abutted the hole set aside for Cabell's equipment and research was, *This must be a violation of the Geneva accords!*

Even though the Zentraedi had shown no impulse to obey the Rules of War, and the Robotech Masters and the Invid were no better, the Human race had made it a point of honor not to sink into unnecessary cruelty. And that was most definitely what this appeared to be.

How else could you explain Tesla's being suspended inside an enormous glass beaker of greenish fluid, only the end of his snout sticking up into the air, and all sorts of electrodes and sensor pads connected to various parts of him, particularly his head?

"Admiral, please do not jump to conclusions," Cabell hastened. "The Invid isn't being hurt, and what we're finding out here may change the course of the war." Veidt and Sarna, looking on, nodded agreement.

Tesla objected loudly, "Not hurt? They torment me with their probings! They strip me of my dignity and take the vilest liberties with my person! They seek to slay me through sheer fright, so that they may dissect me. Save me!"

He thrashed a little in the cylinder. Jean Grant looked up from reading her instruments and rapped, "Be still. Or do you want me to hand you over to the Karbarrans? I bet *they* could get some information out of you, if I told them you've been holding out on them all this time!"

The thought of that made Tesla suddenly quiet down and float, trembling. Jean turned to Lisa. "I'm coming up with a sort of lie detector for Invid. At least I think I am. About all I can tell so far is that he's got high concentrations of Protoculture-active substances in various parts of his body, especially his skull. And their composition and signature varies quite profoundly. It's like some weird variation on a lymphatic system—and hormones, endocrines—but bizarre alien analogues, of course."

Lisa put aside the list of questions *she'd* like to put to Tesla. "But why are you doing this *now*, Doctor?"

Jean gestured to a corner, where Crysta slumped against a bulkhead. "I finally got Crysta to tell me why the Karbarrans have been acting so strangely. Lisa, the Invid have their children in a concentration camp. At the first wrong move from the populace down below, or in the event a defeat of the garrison becomes imminent, the Invid will kill every cub on the planet."

Lisa spun on Crysta. *"Why didn't you tell us before?"*

Crysta was actually wringing her pawlike hands. "The Invid had been an occupation force, had made us work for them, but they'd never forced us to fight for them, never made actual slaves of us. They knew we could not stand for that.

"But we didn't understand how truly evil they were. They'd been preparing their plan for a long time; in a single afternoon, they swooped down to take up thousands of our young, and that immobilized us. You don't know how precious our cubs are to us, now that our population has dwindled so!

"And so we were helpless, as the Hellcats and the Inorganics rooted out most of the rest of our children—only some few managed to remain in hiding. My people held a great Convocation, chanting and seeking a Unified glimpse of the Shaping . . ."

Lisa had been briefed on it, a sort of religious ceremony that could go on for days, as the Karbarrans sought contact with the Infinite. "The Shaping was that we must not defy the Invid, but that *neither could we tell any outsider of our plight*! That part of the Shaping was very clear."

No wonder the Karbarrans had been against the Sentinels' simply leaping into the attack with both feet and a roundhouse swing! Their children were hostage, and the big ursinoids had to simply let the crisis carry them along, with nothing but a forlorn hope that circumstances would change—or that they could *be* changed.

"That's why Lron wanted the recon party," Lisa suddenly saw. "That way, you wouldn't have *told* us; we'd've seen for *ourselves*."

Crysta nodded miserably. "But now I have transgressed."

Jean disagreed. "No, you didn't. I had a pretty fair idea what was wrong—it was Vince who gave me a clue—and I wormed the rest out of you, Crysta. But don't worry; the Sentinels didn't come all this way just to let a generation of children die."

She turned back to Tesla. "Okay now, Slimy: Cabell and Veidt are going to ask you one or two questions. If my instruments say you're lying, I'm gonna zap a coupla thousand volts through that bath you're in, get me?"

She turned the knob, and a nearby generator hummed louder. Tesla thrashed a bit. "I—I hear and will comply."

Veidt stepped closer to the vat. "There must be a Living Computer controlling the Inorganics below—coordinating and animating them. That much we know. But is it like the Great Brain that was sent on the expedition to Tirol, or is it one of the lesser sort?"

Tesla bobbed for a moment, studying Jean Grant's hand on the control. She looked straight back at him. "It is one of the first, one of the most primitive and smallest," Tesla said, "placed there when one of the earliest Inorganic garrison was assigned to duty on Karbarra."

Jean looked at her instruments and turned up the control knob, so that a hum filled the compartment. Tesla churned the green fluid around him and cried, "Stop, *aii*! I am slain!"

Jean turned off the apparatus. "Looks like he's telling the truth." To Tesla she added, "Oh, shut up! That was just some low-frequency sound and a volt or two."

Veidt told Lisa, "That being the case, my wife and I have a plan that may serve ideally."

Lisa was giving instructions at once. "Get the rest of the leadership together for a briefing, ASAP. And have the intel people get all the information they can from the Karbarrans aboard ship; now that the cat's out of the bag, they ought to be willing to talk. And *somebody get that recon party on the horn and tell them what we're up against!*"

* * *

In the abandoned mining camp, Rem frowned as he listened to the word from the Sentinels' flagship. "But how can—I don't understand why—"

"You're not required to understand, soldier," a commo officer barked at him. "Just relay the message, word for word, exactly as I gave it to you. At once, do you understand?"

"I understand," Rem replied sullenly. "Ground-relay base, out."

He broke contact, grousing to himself about the high-handed tone these Human military types took with each other and everyone around them. As Cabell's pupil and companion and sometimes protector, he wasn't used to being treated like a lesser intellect or an unimportant cog.

He was switching over to the recon party's freq when he realized he felt a stirring of air, and it came to him that Gnea hadn't spoken or made a sound in some minutes. The shuttle hatch was open.

Stay buttoned up, had been Admiral Hunter's order, *and no wandering around!* Confinement and inactivity had chafed on the free-spirited amazon more than it had on Rem, who had been forced to sit out most of the terrible Invid onslaught on Tirol in a bunker.

He went to the hatch and peered around, then let out a yell. Overhead, Gnea guided Halidarre through slow banks and turns, getting used to guiding her. "Is she not beautiful?" Gnea called down, plainly pleased with herself.

"Come down!" Rem shouted. "You know our orders! We're to stay hidden, and not attract attention!"

She sniffed, "Mere males do not give orders to the warriors of Praxis! Besides, I'm *tired* of sitting in that machine-reeking ship. And who is there to see us, so far from any settlement or outpost? Go back in, if you're afraid."

Rem had a mind to close the hatch and leave her outside, too. And there was the urgent need to relay the awful, bewildering message about the Karbarran children. But he knew that Hunter had experience with war, and that extreme caution was always advisable when one was dealing with the Invid.

He took a few steps further into the open, craning his neck to look up at her. "If you're through with your little games, you can act like a soldier, and—"

He was stopped by a voice-processed growl, a feline hunting cry as uttered by a terrifying machine. A Hellcat had come around the shuttle's bow, moving to cut him off from the hatch. A second appeared at the stern, and let out a scream of pure catlike anger.

CHAPTER FIFTEEN

Consider the sentient "Tiresiod" brain—Praxian, Terran, Karbarran or what have you. Roughly one hundred billion-plus neurons. The potential number of connections these neurons can make with one another, according to some calculations, exceeds the total number of atoms in the Universe.

One sets mere machinery against such a creation only at some risk of unlooked-for results.

Cabell, *A Pedagogue Abroad: Notes on the Sentinels' Campaign*

BELA SAW THE HELLCATS, TOO. REM WONDERED WHY THEIR presence hadn't registered on the much-touted sensors of the winged horse. Perhaps Gnea's flying lessons had distracted it.

The Hellcats, their slitted eyes glowing like coals, stalked closer. They were a form of four-legged Inorganic mecha, so jet black that they shone with blue highlights, and much bigger than the biggest saber-tooth that ever lived. The Hellcats were armed with razor-sharp claws, sword-edged shoulder horns and tail, and gleaming fangs.

Rem had kept an Owens Mark IX mob gun nearby in case of trouble, but not near enough; the short, heavy two-handed weapon and its shoulder-strap-equipped power pack were lying near the inner side of the hatch beyond reach as the two Inorganics moved toward him.

That left only the pistols he and Gnea were wearing—and from what Rem had seen on Tirol, it took more stopping power than the heavy handguns had to put down a 'Cat. Rem backed up slowly, step by step, the Hellcats padding after; they were gaining a little each second but savoring the moment, not quite ready to pounce.

Then he recalled the saddle scabbard Bela had mounted on Halidarre, with its Wolverine rifle. "Gnea, do you have—"

Somehow, his voice triggered the Robotech beasts, and they

both slunk forward, segmented tails lashing, preparing to spring. Rem tugged at his pistol, doubting he had time to get a single shot off, doubting that Gnea could take accurate aim from a banking winged horse even if she *did* have the Wolverine.

The Hellcats sprang just as something brushed past him and he felt himself struck from above and behind. Or at least, that was what he thought. The next thing he knew, he was being hoisted aloft, held against Halidarre's saddle, by the Robohorse's lifting fields and beating wings, and by Gnea's firm grip on his torso harness.

The lead 'Cat almost got him, its wicked claws sliding along Halidarre's flank but leaving no mark. The horse banked, eluding the second 'Cat's aim, and gained altitude. A sizzling bolt from Gnea's pistol missed both felines.

"Your jostling spoiled my aim!" she scolded Rem, as he kicked and grabbed wildly for purchase. Then, between her hauling and his struggling, she had him up and draped over the saddle bow, belly-down.

Rem thought the horse's power of flight would save them from the surface-bound Hellcats, but he could see he was wrong. One was already leaping up a small hill of discarded equipment and stacked crates with astonishing speed, giving chase. His field of vision was severely limited by Halidarre's neck, body, and wing, and by Gnea; he couldn't see where the second 'Cat had gotten to.

He called a warning to Gnea, but she had already seen it. Halidarre changed course abruptly. With its fantastic quickness and strength, and in the confines of the dome, the Invid mecha came close to nailing them. Halidarre almost bucked Rem into the air, filling with her wings and cutting in her impeller fields. Gnea herself only kept her seat by a determined gripping with her long, strong legs.

But the Hellcat missed, landing on a lower ledge of the heap and turning to surge up its side again for another try, missing its footing twice in the shifting debris. Gnea turned the winged horse for the opening in the dome, to reach temporary safety.

"No!" Rem yelled. "I left the shuttle hatch open! We can't let them get inside!" It was very likely their only hope of escape, now that the flagship was engaged in battle, and probably the only way of linking up with the recon team again in time to get them offworld.

To his horror, as he looked down dizzily, he saw the second 'Cat's tail disappear through the hatch.

Rem spied the Wolverine rifle in its scabbard and somehow managed to get it out without dropping it. But by that time Gnea had banked around a mountain of decrepit machinery off at the far side of the dome, and he had no clear shot. She picked a spot that looked stable and landed, high above the floor of the dome.

He slid down off the saddle and Gnea leapt down after. Off in the distance they could hear growling and the shifting of junk that meant the first Hellcat was still stalking them.

"There's no time to waste," Rem decided. "I have to go after the one that got into the ship. Can you handle this one?"

She pulled her own sidearm from its shoulder holster and took his from his belt as well, balancing them in hands bigger than his. "It seems I must, doesn't it? And so I will, somehow."

Halidarre snorted and reared a bit, wings deploying and beating a little faster, half lifting her into the air. A sudden thought occurred to Rem. "We'll have to split up and take on both Hellcats at once. Gnea, how good is your control over the horse? How fine is your touch?"

She smiled grimly. "Try me, Tiresian!"

A few moments later, the feline mecha bounded up among the peaks and sinkholes of discarded industrial rubble and came around the corner to behold Bela standing, waiting, with both pistols leveled. There was no sign of the male Tiresiod, but the sound of jumping and occasional slipping told it that he was in all probability making his way down toward his ship.

The Inorganic ignored the sound of Rem's frantic escape; its huntmate would take care of him. And, more to the point, once a Hellcat had zeroed in on a particular quarry, it pursued that quarry to the exclusion of all else.

The limitations of the early-model Living Computer in Karbarra's capital meant that the central brain could spare no attention for the 'Cat's report of the encounter, what with the outbreak of battle above the planet and the immediate need to prepare for defense. The Hellcats would simply return with slain enemies, to show what they had found and eliminated.

Surprise wasn't a mental trait of any great importance to the Invid mecha; when it saw that the tactical situation had changed only slightly, it simply began an even more straightforward attack, dodging Gnea's inexpert shots by jumping behind a mound of debris. Then it began working its way in her direction. There was no sign of the winged-quadruped mecha, but the 'Cat kept eyes and ears and other sensors alert for possible air attack.

It watched from concealment as Gnea crouched in the inadequate shelter of a smelting processor, and the Hellcat began gathering itself for the final rush, choosing a route around a convenient bit of broken machinery.

The 'Cat rushed, and knew that it would have her before she could so much as bring the handguns around, much less get off a volume of fire sufficient to stop or damage it. But just as it skittered around the debris to cover the final few yards, the debris came alive.

Armor-hard, scalpel-sharp rear hooves lashed out with the power of twin battering rams, scoring on the Hellcat's jaw and side; the Invid machine was thrown off-balance, leaking power from damaged systemry in its shattered jaw and crushed "rib cage." It went tottering off the ledge of the junk mountain with a yowl.

Gnea rushed to the brink, imaging a call to Halidarre. The winged horse disengaged itself from the splayed pose it had taken, pretending to be part of the ruined jumble of a millwork multirobot—the debris the 'Cat had seen. Halidarre was wingless now.

Gnea looked down to where the Hellcat lay squirming and partially broken, but took no chances; she held out the pistols side by side, pouring down bolt after bolt until it stopped moving, and internal disruptions sent flames shooting from its seams. It gave a last great howl and lay inert, smoking and molten.

Gnea was up on Halidarre's back at once; surely the second Hellcat was warned, and Rem had gone after it alone.

The second 'Cat was indeed aware, and waiting. It had no fear, but it did have cunning and a total commitment to slay the enemy and carry out its mission; since the 'Cat's destruction would prohibit that, such destruction and defeat were to be avoided.

Now it crouched within the shuttle, making low sounds to itself. It had scanned and recorded the nature and construction of the ship for later analysis by the Living Computer on Karbarra, then began demolishing the shuttle, only to be given pause by the death sounds of its huntmate.

Its first impulse was to go out and meet its enemies, then it decided to do as much damage as it could in the ship—perhaps drawing *them* to *it*, the better to avoid its enemies' ambush. It swiped at another bank of intrumentation; shattered pieces and shredded console housing fell to the deck. The 'Cat watched the hatch avidly, certain that it could defeat either of the Tiresiods or the bulky winged-quadruped mecha in the limited space of the shuttle, before they could make any effective moves.

But what came zipping through the hatch was neither the Tiresiods nor their odd machine; it was something small and fast, darting about the cabin at great speed, spoiling the Hellcat's savage calculations and provoking it to launch itself for the kill before it had really planned to.

The Invid mecha landed on the far side of the main cabin, snapping the copilot's chair off its mount. The flying thing made an audacious dive, smacking the 'Cat rudely on the head, then zooming for the hatch again. The furious Hellcat catapulted after it, and out the hatch.

Rem, kneeling against the outer hull by the hatch and sweating profusely, saw the flying remote-reconnaissance module that fit in the niche on Halidarre's back come flashing out of the shuttle. He braced himself, feeling his hands slick with perspiration on the Wolverine rifle.

The Hellcat came through the hatch like a dark comet. Its powerful pseudo-muscles gathered and it launched itself into the air, but the quick-moving remote module had changed course with the agility of a dragonfly, and eluded it. When the 'Cat came down, Rem was ready, holding down the Wolverine's trigger and spraying a steady stream of white-hot devastation at it.

The 'Cat reacted with amazing dexterity, almost somersaulting out of the line of fire. Rem stood his ground and he slewed the beam back and forth in an effort to get a sustained hit. He was unaware of Gnea's ululating war cry as she guided Halidarre down from the junk hills, heedless of the peril to herself, rushing to help even though it might mean a fatal fall . . . even though she knew she was too far away.

Rem held the trigger down still, in spite of what his Human instructors had cautioned. The explosion of an overloaded power pack was preferable to being rent and savaged by a Hellcat.

Then the 'Cat seemed to stagger, howling, as he had it in his sights for a second and more, washing the Wolverine's raving blast across it. But a moment later, the Wolverine's beam quit, its systemry burned out. The assault rifle was so hot that he dropped it rather than have the flesh scorched from his palms.

The 'Cat, mortally wounded, lurched and limped toward him, still agile enough in its dying moments that Rem saw that he could never outrun it. One eye was cold and dead; the other was all the brighter with hatred. It cut him off from the hatch he would surely have headed for.

He scuttled backward and sprawled. The Inorganic was about to throw itself upon him when it wavered, its systemry fluxing. At that moment something swooped into view, flying erratically. The remote module from Halidarre could barely stay aloft, bearing as it did a burden it wasn't designed for. Like a butterfly delivering a key chain, it did a snap roll and slipped the strap it had managed to catch with its wing, dumping its cargo into Rem's lap.

The 'Cat shook off its momentary malaise and looked back at its prey. Rem activated the power pack and fumbled at the thick olive-drab cable that connected it to the blunt, heavy Owens gun, opening fire. The Owens was built for just the kind of sustained close-range annihilation that had burned out the Wolverine; the Hellcat threw up a terrible screech and seemed to collapse in on itself.

Rem didn't take his finger off the trigger until the 'Cat looked like a lava runoff. Gnea was standing by; the module had already returned to its place in Halidarre's back, and Halidarre was stretching her wings once again, making a sound-processed whinney.

Gnea offered her hand to help Rem to his feet. He pushed the Owens and its power pack aside wearily and accepted. Gnea, who had followed Bela's lead in showing hostility to Rem, now thumped him on the shoulder.

"We'll make a woman of you yet," she told him with vast approval.

Rem was happy for a split second, until he remembered that the second Hellcat had been in the shuttle. With a cry, he leapt past her for the hatch.

The scene within made him slump against the hatchframe. From what he could discern from the damage the huge 'Cat mecha had done, the shuttle could lift off again, and the uplink to the Sentinels' flagship might still work. But the recon-relay rig was in fragments, and the scouting party was out of touch, maybe for good.

CHAPTER SIXTEEN

Here's a peculiar thing: I wasn't the only one at the Academy with something to prove or disprove; I never asked, but it seems to me now that there were a lot of 'em like me, pushing the envelopes of their own lives the way the test pilots were pushing the envelopes with their aerospacecraft.

My father's Doctor Penn, naturally, and everybody calls him the leading brain on Earth after Emil Lang. I like my father, but I think he has the conviction that because I didn't accept that New Rhodes scholarship, and went into the Academy instead, I'm some sort of intellectual failure. Since I'm enjoined to tell you about all the things that pertain, I'll say that my father still holds the death of my mother, in childbirth, against me—unconsciously, of course.

I forgive him—he's a brilliant man. But I don't want him running my life. I have my own agenda.

From REF-selection diagnostic session, cadet-graduate Penn, Karen

RICK'S GROUP KNEW THAT SOMETHING WAS WRONG ALMOST at once; when one of their thirty-minute-interval commo checks failed to draw any response after repeated efforts, Rick called a halt to consider what to do.

The equipment the team was carrying couldn't punch a signal through to the Sentinels' flagship, certainly not without giving the group's position away. Only the more sophisticated system aboard the shuttle could do that, and Rem and Gnea weren't answering.

There wasn't much dissention; the recon party had become closer through shared hardship, and Rick's position as leader had solidified. "We can't stop so close to our objective," he told them. "Maybe Rem will reestablish contact. But even if he doesn't, reaching our objective and carrying out our scouting mission before we turn back won't cost us that much more time."

Nobody seemed inclined to object, least of all Lron. But it was Bela who came up with an interim solution. She approached Rick with what he now thought of as "that goddamn canard-winged pest"—her malthi—resting with its many claws dug into her fore-arm sheath. "Hagane can serve as our messenger," she said.

Rick and the others looked at the woman and the little hawk. "You mean she can find her way to Rem?" Rick asked slowly. "What if she gets lost?"

Bela gave him an indignant look. "Hagane does not *get* lost." She was already taking banding and writing materials from a fancy tooled pouch at her belt, nodding. "Any route she has passed over, she can retrace, even one underground."

Bela looked to Lron. "And *much* faster than any Karbarran. If the shuttle is gone or the others are dead, my Hagane will simply return without a message."

And it seemed unlikely the creature would have any trouble with the winged things the team had spotted in the caves; Hagane's few exploratory flights had shown that the cave's inhabitants were only too eager to stay clear of the diamond-clawed, knife-beaked whirlwind that was Bela's pet.

Rick's head was swimming, but he made a few decisions then and there. "We'll send Hagane on her flight from the observation point, so that she'll know her route all the way back to us and—and won't, uh, have to track us." He had a vision of the avian thing whizzing through the caves, and tried to figure out how fast Hagane could make the trip. Hell; it would be a quick commute.

Bela nodded at Rick's wisdom, and he returned the courtesy. They pressed on and, as Lron had promised, soon found themselves looking out over a huge expanse of weather-tormented Karbarran landscape. The cave's irregular opening might have been any one of hundreds honeycombing the wind-and sand-scoured landscape of cliffs, but it was the only one that connected directly to the Karbarrans' secret underground maze. Natural phosphorescence gave the place a dim blue-green glow, so that they didn't need their vision devices to see one another. They shed the bat-ears, too.

The Praxian had settled down to work. "Now, the message must be short, so what will it say? Bear in mind, Gnea can send an answer back to me here, but that reply must be concise, too."

The message Bela laboriously wrote, her tongue in one corner of her mouth, was in cramped glyphics, the whole-concept code symbols of the Praxians, using a pen with a point as narrow as a syringe. She tucked the tissue-fine bit of paper into a tiny metal capsule and bound it to Hagane's leg. Hagane sat still, though her menacing beak opened in objection to this liberty, even taken by her beloved mistress.

Bela kissed the lambent-eyed Hagane's feathers and Hagane

nuzzled her. The amazon released the creature from her hands. Hagane dove down the cave, retracing her route. "How long will it take, do you think?" Kami asked, voice muffled by his mask.

Bela considered. "To get there and back? Perhaps there will have to be consultation with the flagship. Let us say, two hours."

"Then, we'll get what rest we can," Rick decided. Everybody was bushed, and the call to move fast and hard again might be no further away than Hagane's return. He saw no reason to set up double guards, or anything more than short lookout watches, so that everybody could get some rest. There wasn't likely to be anything to observe or analyze for military intelligence purposes under the Karbarran night sky in the next few hours. The guard on watch would also make periodic commo calls in an effort to reestablish contact with the shuttle.

Karen Penn volunteered for the first half-hour shift. No one objected. Lron, who felt no need of blanket or bedroll, curled up by the mouth of the cave, and looked off into the night. The rest of them took swigs of water or went off into a private alcove to attend to personal business, and then composed themselves for sleep.

Karen Penn, muscles still cramped from the grueling traverse of the Karbarran underground, moved to a rock surface off to one side and silently began a t'ai chi routine, moving with precision and a flowing grace that wasn't occidental. Jack, curled in his mummy bag with only one eye showing, followed her every move but said nothing.

"What is that you do?" asked Bela suddenly, her voice unexpectedly soft, while the others began nodding off.

Karen spoke softly, too, without stopping. "This is an exercise/combat system that was devised long ago on my world. It gives a person focus and intimate awareness of the body and of nature."

She stopped and assumed another pose. "We have more vigorous, forceful systems as well." She went through a brief *kata* at full speed, snapping punches and kicks, demonstrating rotary blocks and stiff-fingered blows with much less grace but as precisely as a machine.

When Karen was done, Bela regarded her for a moment, then said, "These are beautiful and effective-looking fighting forms, and you seem adept. You are not so foolish as I thought, Karen Penn." She began pulling her campaign cloak, the only cover she appeared to need, around her.

Karen blinked. "Foolish?" *Listen, honey, as big as you are, I'll*—

"Foolish for placing such importance on a mere male," Bela

said, and closed her predatory eyes, turning away to sleep. Karen stared at Bela, thinking about what she had said. Luckily for Jack, he covered his face completely before Karen glanced his way, immersed in confused thought and crosswired impulses.

The fourth watch was Kami's; Rick woke him, then retired to his own ultralight but warm and comfortable mummy bag. He was asleep in seconds.

Kami went off into a small cul-de-sac so as not to disturb anyone and tried another commo call to Rem and Gnea, without success. Putting the apparatus aside, he realized he was feeling a certain oddness in his perceptions, a lack of depth and a flatness of feature. It occurred to him that he had lowered the flow from his inhalant tank, to economize during sleep.

The tank wasn't his sole source of air, of course; such a supply would have been too bulky to carry. Instead, his mask frugally mixed his homeworld's atmosphere with that of the local surroundings at any give time.

He increased the flow, and in moments felt the Higher Reality come into sharp focus again, with its enhanced perceptions and expanded awareness. The winds rustling the sands whispered their secrets to him, and the stars overhead twinkled messages from the moment of their birth. Ghostly—but unfortunately, minor—Sendings made themselves known in the form of images or disembodied voices. But still he couldn't perceive the greater Truths of this war.

Lron, his snore surprisingly soft, had rolled away from his watching place at the cave's mouth. Kami stepped to the very edge to gaze out into the night. A glow lit the horizon, and he knew that somewhere over there was the great domed capital city, Tracialle, the single major population center of Karbarra.

Kami and his people diplomatically refrained from ridiculing the Karbarrans and their days-long chanting rituals and dramatic, sometimes painful rites and grandiose reenactments, all performed in the name of some Foresight the ursinoids claimed to achieve. The Higher World was nothing one could contact that way; the Karbarrans were simply indulging themselves in mass delusions.

The Higher World spoke to the Garudans through their every sense, thanks to their strange ecosystem, and showed them routes and possibilities. Thus, they were allowed to listen in on the constant monologue put forth by *every single extant thing*, by dint of its very existence, and—sometimes—to comprehend what was being said.

Kami saw a vision and didn't hesitate. Noiselessly gathering his equipment, he scampered down the narrow ledge leading from the cave mouth to the foot of the cliff.

It was as his vision had shown him. Kami raced lightfooted across the sands toward the glow on the horizon. He followed the lay of the land, as sure in his skills as any wild animal.

Yet, somehow his vision hadn't shown him a swift flight of Enforcer skirmish ships that, flying high above, picked him up on infrared heat detectors. Nor had it shown him the troll-like Inorganic Scrim and Odeon mecha that appeared without warning in the darkness and surrounded him.

Kami turned to run, but they were everywhere, as big as any Battloid, reaching for him with their multiple appendages—metallic claws and segmented tentacles and waldolike Robotech hands. He groped for the Owens gun, but it was ripped from his back.

There was no time to use his commo link with the rest of the scouting party; he tore his breathing mask away to howl a single mournful, echoing cry into the desert night.

The cry woke Lron at once, and Bela leapt up, throwing back her cloak. The Humans were a little slower, but not much.

They didn't dare show a light, but donned their night-sight equipment. Between Lron's sense of smell and Bela's eye for tracks, the two reconstructed what had happened.

"Another Garudan follows his mirages to a bad end," *wuffed* Lron.

"He came here to help your people, just like the rest of us," Jack sneered back, "so quit mocking 'im." Bela nodded in agreement, and Karen, standing to one side, studied Jack anew.

"As you *were*, Lieutenant!" Rick snapped.

The question was, what to do now? As many as three of the original eight on his team might be dead, and the remainder—himself included—were quite possibly stranded in the midst of an aroused Invid stronghold. All of a sudden, the Tactical Information Center back in SDF-3 didn't seem like such a bad tour of duty.

Rick was prepared to believe that Kami was in the hands of the biped Inorganic grotesques of the Invid. But was he supposed to lead his remaining scouts out for a desperate rescue mission, like the Fellowship of the Ring off on their marathon jog across the plains of Rohan?

Damn it, this operation was in a very tight spot, and he couldn't sacrifice more people for the sake of a vanished team member who was possibly hallucinating and quite probably dead.

"We'll stay put right here and give Hagane a chance to get back," he went on. "Everybody make ready to leave on a moment's notice. Baker, Penn: warm up some rations over in the cul-de-sac, where the Invid won't pick up the heat readings. And try another commo call to the shuttle while you're at it.

"Bela, stand watch at the cave mouth. Are your night-sight goggles working? Good. Lron, come here and help me orient my map readouts on the local topo features."

The rest of them got busy, and suddenly they were a unit again. They were so intent on their tasks that Hagane's sudden, screeching return came as a shock that made them raise weapons' muzzles, wide-eyed.

This time, Bela's pet wore a capsule on each leg. As she read through the delicate papers, Bela frowned. In a few terse Zentraedi lingua franca phrases, she told the rest of them what she read. Rem and Gnea had resumed contact with the Sentinels' ship, and the shuttle was spaceworthy, but the special commo rig for reaching the scouting team was permanently out of commission.

Then Bela went on to reveal the secret of the children of Karbarra. As she did, Lron's shoulders slumped more and more, until they began heaving, outlined against the growing light of day. It took the rest of them a moment to realize that the poor old fellow, as strong as an oak, was weeping.

In the end, he told them the same story Jean Grant and the rest had heard up above. They also had hope, because Lisa and the other leaders had put a plan together. Bela's brows knit as she puzzled over the symbols. When she caught on, she threw her head back and roared, and smote Lron on the back.

Jack Baker cussed under his breath, and Karen's features drew taut with resolve. Rick stood up from the rock he had been sitting on. "It looks like we get the desert tour after all. Bela, do you think the Invid will be able to sweat any information out of Kami?"

She was caressing Hagane's Alpha-sleek head. "If you think that, you don't know Kami. They could dismember him, and he would regard it as a learning experience granted him by the Universe."

Rick nodded. He did some calculating and realized that there was no time to retrace the whole journey from the shuttle's landing place.

"Send Hagane back to the shuttle to let them know that we acknowledge the plan and will stand ready at our present position. Mention Kami's capture, too." He wanted to send some special word to Lisa, but that would take unfair advantage of his rank. He rubbed the bridge of his nose between thumb and forefinger.

As Bela bent to her task, mumbling something about being regarded as a "lowly scribe, instead of a war leader," Rick turned to Jack and Karen.

"Double-check all gear, especially the weapons. Lron, check the route Kami took down the cliff. Do it carefully, to make sure there are no tracks to lead the Invid back to us."

"The toughest duty of all, now, eh, sir?" Karen said.

Rick nodded ruefully. "Yeah: waiting."

They say the dying part's not so bad; but then, we haven't got much firsthand testimony.

CHAPTER SEVENTEEN

> *This book won't tell you how to cheat, because when you fail to deal with reality, you only cheat yourself. What I mean to do is turn you into a shrewd player who wins whenever possible.*
>
> Kermit Busganglion, *The Hand You're Dealt*

TESLA ALMOST FELT LIKE HIS OLD SELF AGAIN, BATHED AND ARrayed in fine raiments—robes far above the station of most mere Scientists, more appropriate, in fact, to the Regent himself—and ushered along by numerous attendants.

But the attendants were wary Sentinels armed with an alarming variety of weapons, and he was still a captive. A large hold had been converted into a commo studio, and techs were warming up equipment for contact with the Invid-occupied Karbarran capital.

Ah, if only this illusion were the truth! thought Tesla.

Before him some of his worst enemies stood chained, disheveled and bedraggled-looking, thanks to makeup and wardrobe. Learna, Kami's mate, was there, and Crysta, her paw-hands restless in their confinement. Between them stood Lisa Hayes Hunter, who wasn't about to be left out of this grand swipe at the vaunted Invid group intellect.

Glimmering Baldan, forward Burak, and one of Bela's lieutenants, a Junoesque brunette, were fastened in place, too—all looking like they had been dragged in the mud and given a taste of the energy lash. At either end of the slave coffle, like living bookends, were the Haydonites, Veidt and Sarna, hovering some few inches off the deck-plates. Their robes were torn and faces smudged, and their necks were encircled by riveted collars, since they had no wrists to cuff.

Janice Em watched from the sidelines, ostensibly a guard but more of a media adviser—and more of an observer than anyone there knew. Sue Graham, the young camerawoman, was produc-

tion coordinator for the project. She had signed on the Sentinels'
mission because it offered her more freedom to do her job her
own way.

"You know that this can never work." Tesla tried, one last time,
to get them to understand. "We Invid are a perceptive and wary
race, our intellect boundless! Are we to be fooled by this naive bit
of play-acting?"

"We'll worry about that," Lisa said to him. "Just do as we've
told you. Oh, and by the way . . ."

She motioned, and two Spherians came forward with a gorgeous jeweled collar, a kind of regal gorget. They fastened it
around Tesla's thick neck, and it clicked shut with a strange finality. He could see that it had been fashioned from some of the
dragon's-hoard of gemstones, collected from many planets, that he
had planned to take back to the Regent, before the Sentinels
staged their inconvenient and patently unfair uprising.

Still, he thought, admiring himself in the reflective metal of a
nearby power panel, it looked quite striking on him. Something he
would one day gloat over, when he had his revenge.

"Thirty seconds," Sue Graham called out.

The ersatz slaves moved to their place in the background. Out
of vid-pickup range, guards on either side trained their weapons
on Tesla. As the time counted down, Lisa stepped forward a bit,
her chains ringing, a sardonic look on her face. "And, Tesla? One
more thing: you'd better play your part exactly right."

"Is that a threat, female?"

"It's a fact," Lisa told him evenly. "That collar's locked on you
now, and it's got fourteen ounces of shaped Tango-Seven explosive charges built into it. If you *disappoint us,* I'll blow your head
off in front of all your friends down there."

"Surely, in this lower-lifeform gender business, the females are
the worst of a bad lot!" Tesla nearly wept. But then a tech was si-
lencing them. A moment later, the image of an Invid officer
unit—the heavy cannon mounted on its shoulders making it look
like Robotech Siamese triplets—peered out of the screen at them.

It seemed to recoil a bit in a gesture of surprise. "Tesla!" it said
in a strange, single-sideband sound of a mecha drone.

"Yes, of course it's me!" Tesla broke in. The lights around him
felt disturbingly hot, and he wondered if they might set off the explosives around his tender throat. The Sentinels couldn't be *that*
deranged, could they? On the other hand . . .

"Let me speak to the Living Computer!" Tesla burst out. "I arrived just in the nick of time to drive our enemies from this star
system, but I have important news!"

The officer appeared to hesitate, but Tesla screamed, "Do as you are ordered!"

Used to obeying, it complied. In another moment, a Living Computer appeared before Tesla on the screen. It was far smaller then the one captured on Tirol, and seemed to have less peripheral equipment and fewer convolutions.

We're inside their system! Lisa exulted, trying to look defeated and numbed from beatings. *Here goes.*

Tesla began his spiel again: how he had returned to Karbarra in time to repulse the Sentinel raid, and how he needed landing clearance, to repair damage and hold urgent consultation with the Living Computer.

What the Computer didn't see, what Tesla himself barely felt (and dared not register), were lines of mental energy reaching out from Veidt and Sarna. The Haydonites—bracketing Tesla from either side in a kind of mental crossfire—meshed their wills and thoughts with his, guiding and reinforcing, sending a steady current of emphasis and believability along the link Tesla had established with the Invid brain.

Invisible to all, Veidt and Sarna manipulated Tesla and, through him, the brain, though their powers were very weak here, so far from Haydon IV. But it didn't take a vast, brute effort of mental force to accomplish what the Sentinels needed; it only took a slight touch here, a psychic stroke there, to create a conducive atmosphere. It only took a convincing patina of truth.

The Living Computer went so far as to call off its red alert—even more than the Sentinels were hoping for—and granted immediate landing clearance.

"And, incidentally," it added. "The Inorganics have captured an alien, a Gerudan, out in the wastes. He's being brought here now. I shall begin the torture slowly, so that you may enjoy the finale."

"No, no, er . . ." Tesla didn't know exactly what to say, but knew his captors wouldn't take kindly to having one of their number subjected to Invid inquisition.

There was no time to consult with the Sentinels, so the scientist improvised. "I wish to examine him whilst he is still intact. Therefore, have him imprisoned with the other hostages for now."

"Very good, Tesla," the brain responded. "When do you expect to make planetfall?"

"Um, my vessel has suffered damage in the heroic fight to drive away those insurrectionists, and so I will make one decelerating orbit before making my landing."

"As you wish." When the brain signed off, Tesla's knees buckled. He moaned weakly, begging for his captors to remove the resplendent collar. Lisa turned and shouted orders for the bridge. The helmswoman, a Karbarran nearly Lron's size, brought the enormous wooden wheel over. The *Farrago* left orbit, to edge out of the planetary ring for a Karbarran approach.

Down in the bays and holds and hangar decks, the mecha came to full alert, systems at high pitch. Logans, Alphas, Betas, Hovertanks; drum-armed Spartans with their giant, cylindrical missile launchers; long-barreled MAC IIs that were walking hydras of cannon tubes; quadmuzzle Raider X self-contained artillery batteries; and ground-shaking Excalibers bristling with a half-dozen diverse heavy-weapons systems—the Godzillas of the second-generation Destroids.

Scuttlebutt about the Karbarran children and the concentration camp had filtered its way through all ranks in no time, though nobody had made any official announcements.

So, they think they're gonna gun down a buncha kids, huh?

The mecha formed up and waited, their crews avid for the word to go.

"That's it," Rem said. "That's as much as I can get working. *Farrago* says turn-to, and that means there's no time left."

Gnea nodded, taking a place behind him in the communications officer's chair since there had been no time to repair the copilot's. She took one last look in the aft hold, to make sure that Halidarre was well secured. Then she said, "Prepared."

Rem smiled, punching up the ridiculous mission the shuttle would have to fly. Admiral Hunter's book said he should let the computers do the flying, but the computers had been used as a scratching pole by a very *big* polecat. Besides, Rem had invented new computer designs and he didn't trust them as much as people who knew less about them.

The shuttle's engines shrilled, coming up to power.

"Not long now," Rem told Gnea.

The *Farrago* began its long approach orbit on a course chosen by the Sentinels because it led through the least-well-monitored portions of the enemy detection skynet.

This time, Tesla's face filled the communication screen. His would-be slaves couldn't be exhibited because they were all otherwise involved in getting *Farrago* and its fighting forces ready to hit Karbarra like a sledgehammer.

"Er, Karbarra Control," Tesla said delicately. He still wore that dismaying, priceless bib; moreover, there were unsmiling Sentinels surrounding him, just out of camera range, with an appalling collection of energy devices and even cruder things—pointed, glittering implements with unpleasant implications.

"Some of these pesky ablative surfaces and hull features on the captive ships I've incorporated into mine have begun to break up under the stress of entry. Inferior technology, you know. I'm sure they'll burn up upon hitting the deeper atmosphere, but you might, um, alert your sensor techs not to pay any attention to the little cloud of objects coming down with me."

The Haydonites' spell was still in effect. "Of course," said the Living Computer, "of course. Your landing area is at coordinates 12–53–58 relative; we will roll back a segment of the Tracialle city dome to permit your entrance."

Tesla tried to sound enthusiastic and grateful, especially since one of those horrid, overmuscled Praxian harridans stood ready to stick a halberd into his side if he made a mistake.

"Oh! How very kind! I will speak to the Regent of your cooperation and efficiency."

"Thank you, Tesla." The brain signed off.

"We've got a tentative location on that concentration camp," Vince relayed up to Lisa, "but it's still not dead certain. It's obvious that they're not in the camp Lron mentioned, because that's been torn down. But we're ninety percent sure we've got the new one spotted."

"We'll go in with a wide deployment of the attack forces," she decided. "I want everything we've got in the air."

"All set," he answered.

"Then, begin launch operations."

The composite ship began seeding the sky with air-combat elements. The VTs and the Logans went first; then the Skulls dropped and deployed, beginning a slow approach toward Tracialle, skimming the ground. Max and Miriya got the Skulls in proper array. Down almost at the surface, Jonathan Wolff's tankers made their drop and took up least-conspicuous routes, minimizing the chances of being spotted and riding low on their surface-effect cushions.

Farther along, the flagship moving even slower, Lisa ordered the dropping of the scouting force. Fighters on Tiresian airbikes, one-passenger Garudan flitters and Perytonian skycars, and even Veidt and Sarna in their bubble-topped Haydonite flier—shaped like a Robotech ice-cream cone—dispersed. They took up an immediate search formation, preparing to move closer to the city in order to pinpoint the location of the Karbarran children.

* * *

Rick and the others heard the roar, were ready for it. With a wash of sand and superheated air, the shuttle set down at the foot of the cliffs. The star Yirrbisst was just rising, bringing daylight to Karbarra's barren landscape.

Rick and the others dashed aboard while the ship was still hovering, the engines barely lowering in pitch. "Move it! Move it!" Rick was yelling, even before they reached their seats.

Rem complied, the shuttle leaping away only a yard or two above the flat desert. Rick had started for the copilot's seat, to take over, when he saw with some shock that it wasn't there. Rem had neglected to mention that particular piece of damage. Rick knew Rem was a pretty fair pilot; he would just have to trust the youngster to handle the mission, because there was no time to land and change places. Rick buckled into an acceleration seat and hung on.

Rem cut the shuttle in the direction of the concentration camp as Lron had spotted it on the map. They saw no Invid patrols; Rem said that Invid occupation forces had pulled back most of their mecha in anticipation of Tesla's arrival, to render military honors.

Rick checked the screens and could see, far to the west, the approach of the *Farrago*. The Skulls and the Wolff Pack could reach the objective faster than the shuttle; Rick just hoped they hurried.

"Patch me through to Captain Hunter," he told Gnea, who was sitting at the commo officer's station, but she shook her head.

"Can't, sir. We had some system burnout when we applied power to lift off. No commo with the flagship at all."

We're on our own, Rick realized. What else was new? He hoped the timetable didn't change, because if it did, he was living his last few moments then and there.

"No!" Tesla wailed. "I refuse! Put me back in irons; torture me! I will not go down that gangway to be roasted like an insect!"

Lisa Hunter showed him a control unit. "If you do as I tell you, you'll be all right; if you don't, your head's going bye-bye, snail-face."

She tried to sound as ruthless as she could, but she doubted she could actually do it in cold blood. It was against REF rules of war, and went against what she believed in. On the other hand, she was counting on Tesla to evaluate things in terms of what *he* would do if the situation were reversed.

* * *

A minute or so later the *Farrago* drifted at a near-hover through the opening in the Tracialle city dome. It settled down on an acres-wide landing area near the heart of the capital, amid the blunt, functional buildings typical of Karbarran architecture.

The city stood on a mesa surrounded by chasms thousands of feet deep; the glassy hemisphere over it and the upper portion of the city itself rested on an immense cylinder reinforced by hydraulic shock absorbers something like a cross between an insect's leg and a flying buttress. It reminded her of a titanic mushroom sprouting limbs.

The ship's forward ramp opened and Tesla stepped out. Arrayed below him in rank upon rank were the biped Inorganics— Scrim and Crann and Odeon. Few Hellcats were present; they were difficult to control among dense populations. Other troops were keeping crowds of curious but silent Karbarrans back beyond the far periphery of the landing site.

"Hail, Tesla!" cried the local commander, in his eerie, artificial voice. "And welcome to the Regent's loyal and contented dominion of Karbarra!" That brought an angry rumbling from the crowd, but no outbursts.

Tesla, trembling a little, replied over the loudspeaker, "A-and hail to the stalwart Invid garrison! To add to our glory, I bring you captives lately taken in my . . . my momentous clash with the Sentinels!"

At that, cargo ramps extended from the various independent modules that made up the flagship, including the GMU. The Destroids marched down them, mostly single file or at most two abreast, due to their size.

"Prisoners of war!" Tesla was haranguing. "New slaves to fight for the honor and increase of our Regent!"

The garrison commander hesitated, surprised, conversing with the Living Computer for a moment before saying, "Well done. To serve the Regent is the only reason for living."

The first of the Destroids had reached the landing-zone surface, and began forming up in single ranks. Still more emerged from the flagship. "But, perhaps these examples will suffice for now," the commander added.

"They are all completely under my sway," Tesla vouched, voice cracking a bit, as he edged toward the hatch.

"That may be," the commander replied, "but such creatures are lower life-forms, wild animals, unpredictable." He turned to his Inorganics. "Deactivate those mecha and remove their occupants from them!"

As the first ranks of Inorganics moved at once to obey, Tesla turned and dove headlong through the hatch. Lisa, watching from the bridge, thought, *Dammit!* She had hoped all the Destroids could emerge and get to more advantageous positions before the crunch came.

"Fire at will!" she yelled.

CHAPTER
EIGHTEEN

*The 'Gaia' model was by then so thoroughly entombed, we had to
blow the dust off it and study up in a hurry once we met the Garudans.
The theory of a planetary ecology as, in essence, a single interactive
metaorganism? Too absurd to accept, right?*

You wouldn't last long in the Great Beyond, Citizen.

Jack Baker, *Upwardly Mobile*

LIVING WELL ISN'T THE BEST REVENGE. GENERAL T.R.
Edwards thought, lounging in his luxurious chair. Revenge *is the
best revenge!*

But better yet to have both: comfort, and the blood of an enemy
flowing.

And surely the blood of his enemies was flowing even now.
Despite the spottiness of interstellar communications, the *Farrago*
had gotten through a message that the Sentinels had suffered casualties in one battle and were now launching themselves against
an Invid stronghold in another. There were those on the Plenipotentiary Council who had talked vaguely of sending reinforcements, but Edwards had managed to nip that one right away.

Now he gazed out over Tiresia with vast satisfaction. For the
most part, the city had been cleared of rubble, its unsalvagable debris and structures removed, and was quickly being rebuilt. Not
much of a miracle, really, given Robotechnology. And REF Base
Tirol was well on its way to completion; in fact, Edwards was
looking down from his office on the top floor of the headquarters
building.

It stood like the lower half of some early ICBM missile, a
vaned cylinder at the center of great ribbon loops of elevated
roadway. There had been some nonsense about putting the council
up here, but with pressure tactics and backstage maneuvering,
Edwards had gotten his way. That was becoming more and more
the case.

Edwards wasn't altogether satisfied that some resources were being diverted into urban renewal, rather than into building the fleet of starships he meant to commandeer for his own designs, but some things couldn't be helped. At least it was making the Tiresians more tractable and grateful, and they, too, would have their uses, not far down the line.

Of course, Lang, and the sprawling research complex he was setting up with Exedore, were necessary inconveniences. He had to be kept pacified and working on the SDF-3 and the fleet above all.

A buzz from his aide announced that Lynn-Minmei was waiting to see General Edwards. He acknowledged, then flicked the control in his chair's arm, spinning back to look across a gleaming, polished desk as big as a landing field.

Lynn-Minmei? Now what in—

It was a bit of a shock when she stepped through the door in a cadet uniform, halted before his desk, and saluted smartly. He still didn't think of her as military. "Cadet Lynn, requesting permission to speak to the general, sir."

He returned the salute slowly. "Permission granted. Stand at ease."

She only relaxed a little. "General, I know something about people, and while everybody's been working like dogs to accomplish our mission here, time's been passing and, well . . ."

"I haven't got all day, Cadet," Edwards grated. "Spit it out!"

He was pleased to see he had made her flinch. "People need something to keep them going," she burst out. "I *know*! I saw it in SDF-1! They're sort of coming up with what recreation they can now, of course, but that's very makeshift and haphazard.

"What we need is an organized program of entertainment, and some kind of center where people could go to unwind, no matter what shift they're working or who they are. So they could forget their troubles and have their spirits lifted. A place where they could remember—remember why we all came here in the first place."

She said that last softly, she who hadn't been invited on the REF mission in the first place.

Edward's own voice took on a softness, a dangerous tone from him. "Let me be clear on this. Knowing your past, do I assume you're suggesting we open up a *cabaret*?"

"No, a service club!" she corrected. "People need their morale kept up, sir!"

"And you're just the one to organize it, hmm?"

She couldn't meet his gaze for a moment. She knew that all her arguments were true, but Edwards had seen right through her. When she had sung that last good-bye aboard the super-dimensional fortress when the *Farrago* left, she had sworn she wouldn't sing in public again.

But bit by bit, her resolve had crumbled. She missed it too much. She missed the good things her songs did for people, the happiness they brought. But she had to admit that she missed the spotlight, too, the applause and adulation and attention. They were in her blood. She *needed* them.

The REF's situation was so much like Macross's in the old SDF-1 that it was as if her life were a Möbius strip. And so she found herself following old forms, feeling old longings and dreaming dreams she had told herself to bury.

"I'm more knowledgeable about show business than anybody else we've got, sir," she pressed on. "I'll do it on my off-duty time! But I was hoping you'd speak to the council, General."

It all sounded like something out of one of those twentieth-century films for which he had such utter contempt. *Hey, I've got it, we'll put on the show in the barn! Yeah, you can make the costumes! Swell; they can build the sets!*

He almost ridiculed her out loud, would have enjoyed it, but at the last second held back. There *was* something about her presence, her gamine appeal and wide-eyed winsomeness. Where other men might have felt attracted to her, and suddenly protective toward her, Edwards began to feel possessive.

He knew she had been courted by hundreds of love-struck admirers, worshipped by thousands, perhaps millions, of fans. And none had had her, none had really touched her, save only two. One of those, Lynn Kyle, her distant cousin, was long since missing and presumed dead back on Earth.

Edwards also knew that Minmei had once been Hunter's passion. He was aware, too, through his spies, that that fool Wolff had a hopeless crush on her.

Minmei wasn't sure what reactions or thoughts she was seeing cross Edwards's face; the gleaming half cowl and scintillating lens-eye made it difficult to tell.

Edwards steepled his hands before him and tilted his chair back. "This idea may have some merit, Cadet. We'll discuss it further over dinner."

In Edwards's mind, she was already his, body and soul.

Kami realized blearily that he was being borne along to the clanking of mecha. Reviving a little, he saw to his horror that he was in the grip of a Crann Inorganic.

The memory of being jumped, mixed with his Vision, began to sort out as he struggled like a wild thing to no effect. The dreadful recollections of being caged by Tesla made him look about for a way to take his own life. The Inorganic's armor and grotesque design screamed mindless hatefulness; the sky was screeching a death song at him.

But he was held fast and couldn't squirm free. That changed in a few moments, though, as he was dropped without ceremony. He landed in a heap on hard, gritty soil, dazed, the Vision almost clouding over into unconsciousness. He could hear the Invid marching away, and could make no sense of it.

Something prodded him. Kami rolled over with a sharp yip of alarm, to find himself looking up at a ring of furry faces. "What are you?" one of them said. "Are you an Invid, then?"

One of the others made an exasperated sound and jabbed the first with an elbow. "Stupid! How could he be an Invid?"

"Well, he's no Karbarran!" the first shot back, and they seemed about to scuffle.

"I'm a Garudan," Kami said tiredly. "Don't they teach you whelps anything in school?"

He could see he had found the Karbarran children, even if he had arrived in somewhat ignominious fashion.

They started to babble, and a few of them worked up the courage to actually give him a hand getting to his feet. The Karbarran children were roly-poly versions of their elders, some of them nearly as tall as Kami himself; but unlike their parents, the cubs wore no goggles. Their eyes were round, dark, and moist.

He groaned, trying to bring things into focus. One of the cubs tried to touch his mask and he gave the paw a little slap; it was withdrawn. Kami couldn't understand why the Invid had taken his weapons and gear and yet left him his mask and tank. Perhaps they knew that they wouldn't have a sane prisoner for very long—or a live one—if they took the breather from him.

There were some hundred or so miniature Karbarrans around him, and many, many more walking around an extensive barracks area. From the size of the place, he was prepared to believe that just about every cub of the planet's reduced population was there. Most of them seemed listless though, not caring that something was going on.

Kami squinted a bit in the early light of Yirrbisst, glancing around to orient himself to the landmarks he had seen on the map and get his bearings. It wasn't long after sunrise; the raiders would be here soon and he must prepare the cubs as best he could. But the three-in-a-row spike crags weren't there; the broken butte was nowhere in view, the foothills covered with scrub growth couldn't be seen.

His blood suddenly went cold. *The Invid have moved them! This isn't the place on the map!*

"Where are we?" he asked the first cub who had spoken to him, a tubby little male with streaked highlights in his pelt.

"The old Sekiton works," the cub said. "They moved us here from the prison compound near the city so they could guard us easier." The young Karbarran pointed vaguely toward the rising greenish primary, Karbarra's star. "You can barely even see Tracialle from the tallest tower here."

The raid on the old prison had provided for searching possible alternative sites near the city, but not this far out. Kami looked off the way the cub had pointed, feeling waves of defeat flow over him.

"Sir? Sir?" the little one was saying. "Who are you?"

He shook off his despair as he would have shaken off water, fur ruffling and standing out, tail fluffing. He held out his hand to them for silence.

Somehow the valve of his breather had been turned down. He increased the flow a bit, looking at the sky, inhaling.

Lron had been unfair, and wrong, in accusing the Garudans of using hallucinogens. The fact was that the Garudans' mental processes were symbiotically linked with an astounding range of microorganisms and a wide variety of complex trace molecules found in their planet's ecosystem.

Their brain activity was a result of interaction with these factors in their environment. It reacted to and was influenced by those stimuli on a subcellular and even atomic level, in ways that left Human molecular psychologists shaking their heads and talking to themselves.

Garudan life was a partnership with their world; their neurological systems were a vital part of the reproductive cycle of the microscopic life-forms that were indispensible to the Gerudans' perception and very ability to think.

Kami inhaled and thought. Certain perceptions began to shift and intensify. The sky sang a dirge and the windblown sand took on strange shapes. Then he realized something was chanting, in a register so low he could barely hear it. He knelt and put his ear to the ground; the cubs looked at one another dubiously.

Kami listened to the dull thrumming.

Sekiton. Sekiton. Sekiton.

Of course. He spun to the cub who had spoken to him. "My name is Kami. Who are you?"

The cub drew himself up proudly. "I'm Dardo, son of Lron and Crysta, leaders among our people. The children needed a leader, too, and so I got them organized. My parents—"

So apparently this was the action committee, the ones who hadn't succumbed to hopelessness.

"I know them. Listen, all of you! We haven't much time. There's still Sekiton around here, is there not?"

"Over in the warehouse." Dardo pointed to a low bunker. "There's not much use for it now that the Invid stopped us from spacefaring."

But between the prisoners and the Sekiton was an imprisoning Invid energy wall, a ghostly curtain of angry red power a hundred feet high, generated by pylons spaced every hundred yards around the prison compound. Kami knew that it meant a searing burn and unconsciousness to get too close to one, and immolation to try to pass through.

"So Sekiton's not much good to us anymore," Dardo said. "Worse luck, because there's still plenty of it around here everywhere."

He scuffed the sand aside with his foot, digging down a depth of several inches. Pushing aside thicker, grittier soil, Dardo dug stubby fingers in and came up with a fistful of darkish Sekiton mixed with sand. "See?"

"Yes; I've seen the stuff, thank you," Kami said offhandedly. Yirrbisst was getting higher, and there wasn't much time left. With the first air strikes or the attack of the Destroids, the order would go out for the killing to begin at the concentration camp.

Dardo shrugged, formed the clot into a dirtball, and heaved it. The dirtball went up in a blaze as it hit the energy wall. Another cub took some and heaved it for an even bigger fireworks effect. From the gouges here and there around the compound, Kami could see that they had done it quite often to pass the time.

Sekiton. Sekiton. Sekiton. The ground thumped it into his feet like the vibration of some huge pile driver, but the message was lost on him. Kami picked up a clot of the stuff, too, made a ball of it, and heaved it disgustedly at the wall.

The dirtball passed through unharmed, to land and break up several yards beyond.

"It—it didn't burn up," Dardo blinked.

"That's because . . . *it wasn't handled by a Karbarran!*" Kami fairly howled through his breather. He didn't understand any better than anyone else what the weird Karbarran affinity for Sekiton was, but he had seen for himself that the stuff was stubbornly in-

ert if a Karbarran didn't come in actual physical contact with it at
some point.

"Quick, get sticks or boards from the buildings, or anything
else you can dig with, and start uncovering more, but *don't touch
it directly*! And fetch me water, lots of water!"

A short time later the cubs stood in a crowded circle shielding
him from view, although the Invid had shown little interest in
keeping the prisoners under close surveillance, trusting their
energy wall. Kami packed the thick mud onto himself. It was grat-
ifyingly adhesive.

"I'm going to need a weapon. Did anyone see what the Inorganics did with my equipment?"

One of the taller cubs, a female with a dark tinge to her fur,
pointed at the blockhouse. "I saw them set some things down over
there just before they brought you here."

Kami was slapping mud onto himself frantically, trying to be
thorough, because any missed spot would probably get him fried,
but trying to be quick, too, because time had just about run out.
"All right! *If* I get my gun, and *if* I can blow out one of these pylons, all of you run as fast as you can for the Sekiton storage
bunker! If the rest come along, fine, but don't wait for them, because I'm going to need you over there! Do you understand?"

They said they did. He was about as covered as he would ever
be, except for his eyes. He had layered over his breather mask,
and would have to get by on pure Garudan air from his tank.

"But—what are we going to do then, sir?" Dardo inquired.

"Send a message," Kami told him. He made his way stiffly and
cautiously toward the energy wall, until he could feel the heat of
it on his exposed eyes. He made a last application to the bottoms
of his feet from the armload of mud he carried and slapped more
over his eyes until they were covered. He took a deep breath and
stepped in the direction in which, he hoped, the wall waited and
glowed.

And promptly lost his footing, falling.

He expected to be burned to ash, but he was still alive after he
thumped to the ground. But he had lost his bearings completely
and didn't dare remove the blinding mud.

Hoping for the best, Kami rolled and rolled in what he thought
was the right direction.

CHAPTER
NINETEEN

I'm runnin' away an' joinin' th' Robotechs! Then *you'll be sorry!*

Popular threat among Earth children during the period of preparation
for the SDF-3 Mission

AT LISA'S COMMAND, THE DESTROIDS OPENED UP WITH ALL
weapons. The first terrible barrage of pumped lasers, particle
beams, and missiles struck the nearest organics at virtual point-
blank range, like a tidal wave rolling over a shore.

Inorganics went up like roman candles or simply vanished from
sight. The Destroids trained their weapons on the next target and
the next, exploiting the element of surprise for all it was worth,
because the odds were still badly against them. Those on the
ramps were firing, too, and marching down, heavy-footed, to join
their fellows.

The assorted weapons of the *Farrago* opened up, showering
down fire like burning hail, careful to keep their aim in close to the
ship where the Invid were, to avoid hitting the Karbarran crowds.

Invid were blown to smithereens, or holed through by star-hot
lances of energy. They were confused and indecisive for those
first few seconds, and in that time dozens of them were wiped
out. Lisa watched a monitor, as a Crann under the flagship's bow
was hit dead center by a laser cannon round, like a white-hot nee-
dle going through a beetle. The Crann's characteristic snout tenta-
cle, or flagellum, or whatever it was, was still snapping like an
angry whip as the thing flew apart in all directions.

The Inorganic bipeds seemed to be the last word in the
strangely perverse Invid design preferences, misshapen and
wrongly articulated to Earthly eyes. The low-hanging arms and
malformed bodies—stick-thin here, bloated there—made them appear as if the Invid had set out to make them as repulsive as possible.

Not that the Sentinels needed that added incentive to fight; *Farrago* and all her personnel were committed now and the only way out was victory. Inorganics flew into the air like burning, bursting marionettes, or were blown back into the ones behind them, to explode.

But the Invid were firing back now, their annihilation disks and beams ranging in among the Destroids. With the last of the Destroids down on the landing surface, the big Earth mecha stood shoulder to shoulder and put out a stupendous volume of fire, a walking barrage that reaped rank after rank of the troops who had been drawn up for Tesla's review.

But with each enemy down, another moved up to take its place, firing dispassionately. And Enforcer skirmish ships darted in overhead now, to fire on the flagship. Many of the upper hull batteries had to turn from ground support to AA fire. Lisa was just glad the task force drawn from Karbarra had taken away its Pincers and Scouts and Shock Troopers; that left a lot fewer flying mecha to contend with, a critical point in this battle plan.

The biped Inorganics were doing their best to contain the Destroids' advance, as the Earth machines began a slow march, traversing their fire here and there, pounding away at the enemy in an inferno of skewing cannon beams and boiling missile trails.

A cluster of Scrim made a stand, and concentrated their fire. A Spartan, busy emptying its racks at another target, was riddled; it lurched and then flew apart in flame.

The Karbarrans had all fled for their lives, ducking into the first shelter they could find. The Destroids suffered another loss, a Raidar X, and a skirmish flier got a shot through a weak point in the upper hull shields, disabling a powered twin-Gatling gun mount on the Gerudan module of the ship.

Nonetheless, the Destroids had driven the Inorganics back from the landing area. Damage reports were pouring in, but the ship was still spaceworthy. But, it was a sure bet that the Invid were moving up more reinforcements. Lisa gave the order for the Destroids to move out and secure the area—dig in and hold. Then she gave Vince Grant the go-ahead, and the GMU began to uncouple from the *Farrago*.

The enormous Ground Mobile Unit rolled out on its eight balloon tires, tires some hundred feet or so in diameter. Once out from under the flagship, it could add its own upperhull missile and gun batteries to the antiaircraft defenses.

Lisa wasn't too worried about the skirmish ships; there were fewer of them than there had been a while ago, and she was sure the Sentinels could handle the rest. Nor did the Invid seem to have any supercannon—anything in the GMU's class, anything big enough to take out the flagship with a single round—in Tracialle.

No, this would be a battle of ground mecha, Destroid and Inorganic. It was already beginning to the east, where a quartet of Odeons had arrived to try to dislodge some MAC IIs, and they were slugging it out almost toe-to-toe, the hastily-abandoned buildings collapsing around them. But the MACs' multiple barrels, firing beams and solids both, were beginning to tell.

There were requests for reinforcements from another sector, and reports that the Invid were bringing up more troops and even some Hellcats from a third.

Lisa did her best to look calm. *Max, Miriya—Rick! Hurry!*

In the sanctum of the Living Computer, the Invid brain seethed with something very much like wrath. Far above it, the sounds of battle sent vibrations through the entire colossal concrete-and-glass mushroom that was the capital city.

"The Karbarrans have somehow betrayed us!" it said. "Give the order! Slay the children; exterminate them all!"

The Hovercycles and airbikes and the rest had checked out all nearby outposts and seen nothing; the VTs and Hovertanks closed their pincer movement and swept in from every point of the compass, converging on the objective.

The mecha swept down with half of each unit in Battloid form, the better to sweep through the compound, while the rest supported them in Guardian or Gladiator mode, or flew cover in Veritech.

Battloids needed no special forced-entry tools; they simply ripped the buildings open and peered inside, being careful because they didn't want to hurt the hostages. They ran from building to building, pulling doors off or prying up roofs, calling in amplified voices.

It didn't take long for the report to be relayed back to the appalled Max Sterling. "Results negative, sir. They're not here. We hit the wrong place!"

"Come onto course 115," Lron roared to Rem.

"But—the locator says—"

"Do it!" Lron shook the bulkhead with his anger. "I see a Sekiton fire over there, where the old processing plant is. The Invid don't build infernos like that, and the Karbarrans have little cause to, but the Gerudans love signal bonfires. Do it, I tell you!"

"Take 'er in, Rem," Rick said. "All of you, get set."

"Sensors are picking up a lot of heavy Protoculture activity over in the direction of the city, Admiral," Jack told Rick. "Looks like the party started without us."

"Rem, *floor it!*"

Rem wasn't sure exactly what Rick meant, but he made a screaming approach, handling the shuttle with quiet skill. In seconds, they were retroing in over the camp, looking down on a scene that made them all gasp.

An eerie blaze had been started in a processing pit, flaring in the indescribable colors of Sekiton, being fed by a chain of what looked like Karbarrans. But Inorganic bipeds were headed that way, and still more were approaching from the far distance along with the sinewy forms of Hellcats moving at top speed.

Most of the Crann, Scrims, and Odeon, though, were ranging around an area marked off by what the Sentinels had come to recognize as energy-wall pylons. But the energy wall was gone. Apparently the enemy mecha were intent on keeping the rest of the prisoners from escaping, and hadn't been given the command to execute them—yet. The bipeds were firing short bursts into the ground, driving the vast majority of Karbarran children back toward the barracks area.

One tiny figure, crouched behind a building, jumped out to let a Scrim have it with a fierce wash of brilliant blast. The Invid was rocked and its fellows halted. Their counterfire smashed and consumed the corner of the building, but by then the sniper had fallen back. Only he had no place else to hide; he had his back to the flames.

"Hard-nosed little runt, that Kami," Jack said admiringly.

"Karen . . ." Rick called to her. She was seated at the main fire-control station.

"I've got 'im, sir," she said with vast composure. With one shot from the shuttle's pumped-laser tube, Karen took out the Scrim Kami had hit, and traversed the stream of brilliant energy to the next, bisecting it.

As the shuttle zoomed past, the third Scrim turned to fire at it, but Rem's evasive piloting frustrated it. Kami took the opportunity to duck past it and around the building, headed for the blockhouse. He would have cheered at the shuttle's arrival, but he didn't have time and couldn't spare the breath.

Kami hadn't had to shoot up the pylons of the energy wall because he had discovered a power-system junction, over by the blockhouse where he had found his Owens gun and power pack.

Shutting down the barrier was simply a matter of wrestling down a Karbarran-scale knife switch.

But now the Inorganics were closing in on the masses of cubs who hadn't or couldn't make a break when Dardo and his pals did. Kami had to do something fast, or the slaughter would begin in seconds. He knelt in the shelter of the blockhouse doorway, calculated his timing carefully, got his shoulders under the massive porcelain handle of the knife switch, and heaved it back up again to close the circuit.

The energy wall sprang back into existence, a red curtain of death—and there were two Odeons standing in its field. Both appeared to writhe in agony. An instant later, they vanished in twin flares of blinding discharge.

Kami saw that he had been in time; the rest of the Inorganics were outside their own wall, cut off from the hostages. That might not last more than a few seconds, but every second was infinitely important now.

He gathered up his gun and turned, racing back to the fire pit.

"Are you sure we can't raise Max and Wolff?" Rick asked without turning to Jack; Rick was busy assuming control of the missile racks, retracting their covers and adjusting his targeting scope.

Jack frowned at his commo board. "Negative, sir. Maybe if we got up high enough and tried one of the helmet radios in an outer hatch—"

"No time!" Rick cut him off, and he was right. Even as he spoke, a Hellcat leapt into view and covered the ground between itself and Kami with frighteningly long leaps. But Rem had already snapped the shuttle through a turn and was beginning another run.

The guy's a natural, Rick concluded—how else to explain Rem's facility with a Karbarran vessel? He might be a scholar's apprentice, but he had great reflexes and coordination.

Rick got the Hellcat in his sights even while Karen was zeroing in on another Inorganic, an Odeon that had been circling toward the children by the fire pit. Karen hit her mark with a sustained beam; it stood its ground and shot back with everything it had.

They felt the shuttle jar from a partial hit and Rem started assessing the damage, wondering if he could keep the vessel in the air. Karen's long burst cut the Odeon in two at the waist and it fell apart in a cluster of secondary explosions. Rick's first two missiles missed the Hellcat completely, their warheads fountaining flame and dirt and rock to either side of it.

But even though the shuttle's flight was becoming more and more erratic, Lron—who had taken over the stern gun pods—got a stream of autocannon rounds into the 'Cat. Its hindquarters began dragging, crippled, and Kami was increasing his lead on it.

Rick thought it was unlikely that the shuttle could get high enough to attempt contact with the Skulls even if it could break away from the battle when he heard a hatch open. He turned and saw Bela disappearing into the aft hold.

"Hey! Get back here!" But she was gone, though the hatch stood open. Rick didn't know what she was up to, but he wasn't sure the amazons really knew how advanced technology worked. "Baker, make sure she doesn't wreck us!"

He looked at Gnea, who had looked up from her weapons position. "You stay at your post!" He didn't need two of these over-developed Valkyries wandering around in the middle of a fight. Gnea looked as if she might give him some lip, then went back to manning the upper-hull ball-turret mount via remote.

Jack lurched aft, grateful that the shuttle wasn't doing—couldn't do—any sudden maneuvering that would mash him against the hull. When he got through the hatch he found Bela crouching by the emergency ejection hatch. Apparently, she had fired the escape capsule that was there and, when the outer hatch reclosed, had somehow gotten Halidarre to sort of crouch with legs folded and wings pulled in.

She looked up at him. "It's the only way to get a signal through," she said, tapping the mike Lang had installed on her battle helm. "And I could use a gunner, Jack Baker."

No time to go ask permission. *Personal initiative, Baker!* he told himself. But the thought of the Inorganics closing in on the defenseless cubs made it even easier to decide.

"How d'you stay on one a' these things?" He said it as he jumped to a rack of weapons, unclipped a magazine-fed rocket launcher—about all the extra weight he could safely handle, he figured—and staggered over to her while the shuttle jarred.

"Mount behind me," she said, "and fasten yourself in with the belt there." He did, finding a retractable safety belt built into the rear of the cantle. Bela was already secured with the saddle's belt. Jack managed to both hang onto the launcher and close his flight helmet. Activating his commo unit, he heard Rick ranting.

"—the hell are you two doing back there? Get up here, that's an order!"

"Sorry, Rick Hunter," Bela said calmly. "But I'll give your regards to Max Sterling. By the way, Baker here is braver than he looks."

Or maybe dumber, Jack thought.

She punched a button on the inner hull and pulled her hand back quickly. The ejection-port cover rolled shut and there was a feeling like being shot from a cannon. Jack glimpsed the ground, spinning up at him.

CHAPTER
TWENTY

FILE #28364-4758
BAKER, JACK R.
  Subject was orphaned of all close family members during the Robotech War, his last relatives having been killed during Khyron's final onslaught.
  This young man has erected defenses against close emotional ties, although, bafflingly, he manifests none of the hostility or self-destructiveness that traditional theory would predict. He demonstrates far-above-average intelligence, dexterity, and, in cases where it is not threatening to him, compassion—particularly toward individuals who have been victimized.
  He simply seems to have turned off his pain by not investing anyone with the considerable affection of which he seems capable.
  While there is no valid justification for denying this youth Academy entrance, particularly in light of his scores, it should be remembered by military authorities that this client shows a certain hostility toward discipline and may be unsuited to military service.

  Caseworker 594382, Global Care Authority

"**I**'M SORRY, LISA; THEY'RE JUST NOT HERE. WE'RE WIDENing the search pattern," Max Sterling said, sounding a little helpless. He had a child himself, back on Earth.

The Skulls and Wolff Pack and all the scouts were unable to locate the Karbarran children, and more and more Invid reinforcements were arriving at the capital city. Three more mecha had been lost: a Spartan, a Raidar, and, tellingly, an Excaliber that had virtually disappeared under a mass of flailing Scrim and Crann and Hellcats.

The Destroids were holding their own in some places. But in others they were pushed back inexorably, in furious, point-blank, sometimes hand-to-hand exchanges, by Invid who didn't seem to care how heavy their losses were. The GMU had deployed to a point on the other side of the landing site, bringing all but its heaviest weapon to bear; but given the nature of the street-fighting, neither it nor *Farrago* could give much fire support without the risk of hitting friendlies or civilians.

Lisa had hoped the general populace might pitch in, if only to create diversions. But the Karbarrans were staying out of it, no doubt hoping against logic that their children might still be spared.

A report came in that the perimeter to the south was collapsing; the Invid had somehow brought down an entire row of high rises on the MAC IIs and Spartans there, literally pinning them down, and had waded in to dismember them.

Lisa was reluctantly coming to the conclusion that the mission was a failure. She looked out from the bridge at the flaming city, and prepared to give the Destroids and the GMU the command to fall back in orderly fashion to the ship to withdraw from the city.

If we can just get through that dome, she reminded herself.

The order was on her lips when a strange sound came over the command net. It was a kind of—of singing. Three notes like a hunting bird's scream made into music. Then a voice said, "This is Bela, of Praxis! We've found the children! Home in on my beacon! Sentinels, *come join the fight!*"

Jack Baker struggled to steady the launcher over Bela's shoulder, the skirmish ship in and out of his sights, as Halidarre banked and evaded and the Enforcer peppered shots at the wonder horse and its riders.

Jack fired, but the rocket went wide as the skirmish ship rolled and got ready for another pass. "Can't you hold this nag still?"

"Yes, Jack Baker," Bela said, almost laughing. "Still enough so that slug cannot miss. Would you like that?"

She would be just crazy enough to do it, too. Her wild laughter in battle, her bravado and amazing skill at handling Halidarre—they were a little tough to top. What do you say to a woman who rides through the air on a winged Robosteed, firing a pistol with one hand and waving a *sword*, for god's sake, with the other?

I'll tell you what old Jack Baker says, he thought angrily. "Yeah!" he said, before he could think about it twice. "Yeah, hold still for a second, if it's all the same to you. Looks like the only way I'm ever gonna hit anything today."

So she did. Halidarre hovered on her impeller fields, wings beating at half speed to steady her, as Jack wrestled the launcher around. He hadn't hit anything yet; three rockets were gone and only two remained in the magazine.

The Enforcer was on a new attack run, firing at long range.

Bela was as good as her word, holding Halidarre in a dead hover, laughing that wild laugh again, brandishing her sword. Jack lined up his shot with the tube resting on Bela's shoulder and let both rockets go. "Let's get outta here!"

Halidarre rose abruptly just as a line of annihilation disks shrilled through the spot where she had been a moment before. The Enforcer, intent on its aim, tried to bank away from the rockets a bit too late. It blew apart and began raining down in tiny, burning scraps.

Bela gave a howl like a Hellcat. "That's my lad!" Then she spied something and put Halidarre into a dive that nearly sent Jack's breakfast up into his throat.

The Invid had shut down the energy wall again. They were closing in ominously on the barracks where most of the Karbarran cubs had taken refuge. The bipeds began firing at long range, setting the buildings ablaze to drive the prey out for more convenient extermination.

Jack threw the launcher away and got his pistol out. He and Bela dove straight at the Invid, firing and hitting, but having no effect.

Over by the fire pit, Kami backed up, Dardo and the others behind him, as Hellcats closed in all around them. The Owens gun was dead, out of power; Kami yanked its cable free of the backpack, threw the backpack aside, and held the gun as a club.

The recon party's shuttle had last been seen losing altitude, plummeting away to the east. Kami hoped dully that they had survived the crash. In any case, there was no hope of evacuation now.

The 'Cats' eyes seemed as bright as lasers; for some reason of their own, they spread out and began herding Kami and the helpless children toward the fire they had built—a pit eighty feet across, now carpeted with burning Sekiton. Kami, exhausted and still half caked with mud, could feel it singeing the fur on his tail. The cubs had thinned out in a ring one or two deep, all the way around the fire. Hellcats hemmed them in at every turn, forcing them back into the inferno.

His heightened senses shrieked torment and nightmare at him— agony was like a fog all around him, and gruesome death like electricity shooting up into him from the very ground under his feet.

"I'd rather die fighting than roasting!" With that, Kami raised the club wearily and began to totter straight at the 'Cat confronting him, preferring a quick death from claws to a slow one from flame . . .

Suddenly the 'Cat was bashed aside as something immense and heavy hit it like a multiton lineman. It took Kami a moment to realize that it was a Veritech, an armored Alpha in Battloid mode—white with red markings.

Battloid and Hellcat tumbled and fought, the feline's claws ripping at its foe, but the Battloid's big armored fists pounding and pounding at the 'Cat like huge pistons, staving in its sides, shattering one of its eyes.

The other 'Cats turned to throw themselves into the fight, but were prevented when Battloids began dropping from the sky on them, back thrusters blaring—Betas and Logans mixed in with the Alphas. Kami skipped back out of the way as the red Alpha and the 'Cat it had jumped tumbled and tore and beat at one another.

The Skulls had arrived.

In Guardian and VT configuration, they swooped at the Inorganics over in the barracks area, driving them back or blowing them sky-high. Even the Hellcats who broke and fled found that their speed wasn't enough to save them; a second attack wave, diving from high altitude, overtook the things and chopped them down with missiles and cannonfire.

More Invid bipeds, rallying from outposts and patrols, headed for the camp by way of a canyon to the west, forming up to steamroll into the rescuers. The first problem with that plan was that the Wolff Pack was there, and met them head-on.

It was no open-country tank battle; it was a murderous set-to in a limited space, both sides throwing themselves into it without restraint, like a knife fight in a commomphone booth. Tank and Gladiator mode didn't offer enough agility, so the Wolff Pack went to Battloid and grappled, fired, kicked, and punched. The Invid met them with claws, tentacles, chelae, and feet, annihilation disks and explosive globes. The valley was a slaughterhouse, but the heavier and more numerous Hovertanks began pushing back the tide inch by inch.

Kami watched as the Hellcat rolled to the upper position, determined to bite the Alpha's throat out or rip its head off with those enormous fangs.

But the Alpha got one forearm under the 'Cat's jaw, slowly levering it away. Then the Battloid had both hands on the feline's throat, squeezing with Robotech strength. The 'Cat screamed and went wild, tail thrashing, but it couldn't free itself. Alloy groaned and squeaked as it gave way, crushed. The light in the 'Cat's remaining eye slowly dimmed.

Then all at once it was dark, and the thing's body went limp and lifeless. The Alpha rose to its feet, lifting the Hellcat up, then threw it to the ground with an impact that made Karbarra quake under Kami's feet. The Invid mecha was a shapeless mass of smoking scrap.

The Skulls had turned things around in minutes. The ground was littered with the remains of Invid mecha, and no enemy was standing. But there were VTs down, too, and their fellows were attending to them.

The functioning Veritechs deployed repair servos that snaked forth on metal tentacles to fix what damage they could. Many of the disabled mecha were beyond such help, though, and would require the facilities of a full Robotech engineering bay.

But some of the damaged Skulls would never rise again, and their pilots had paid the final price. The living descended from their ships for the wrenching and ghastly duty of gathering up the remains. In several cases there was simply nothing left.

The red Alpha turned and walked over through the drifting smoke of battle to look down at Kami. A female voice said over an external speaker, "Sorry we cut it so fine, my friend." It was Miriya Sterling.

Kami could still smell his own singed fur. "It could have been much worse—by several seconds." She laughed. Then he thought of something. "The shuttle! It disappeared over that way!"

Miriya paused for a moment—perhaps informing Max of the situation—then blasted away through the air on her back thrusters, quickly mechamorphosing to true Veritech mode, and heading like a missile in the direction Kami had indicated.

At the landing site, each second seemed like an hour on the rack to Lisa. The Destroids had redoubled their efforts to hold out and, in a few places, had even retaken a little ground. But the Invid were pressing hard again.

Suddenly there was a crackling noise over the command net, and Max spoke, sounding choked up. "We got the kids, Lisa. They're all okay. Do you roger? I say again, all hostages are safe."

Max was starting to talk about arrangements to get the cubs to safety, but Lisa cut him off. "Max, things are deteriorating here. Leave a security force and then get back here with every VT you can spare. Repeat, I need you here ASAP with every mecha you can—"

"Cap'n! Look!" A Spherian tech was pointing through the vast blister that roofed the bridge.

"What—" she said, ignoring Max's efforts to get her to finish her sentence.

All through the city, doors and windows and access panels were opening up on roofs and other vantage points, and intense fire was pouring forth, mostly Invid-style annihilation disks and beams. From what she could see and what she began hearing over the tac net, Lisa concluded that all the fire was directed at the Invid. It was as if the whole city had been turned into one giant shooting gallery. Caught from behind or above and sometimes even from below, the Invid army was being wiped out before her eyes.

She told Max, "Wait one, Skull Leader!" Then she got Crysta, who was with Jean Grant in the GMU, on the ship's internal net. "Crysta, what's happening?"

"I—I knew my people were secreting weapons against this time," Crysta answered. "But Lron and I—we had no idea!"

It's not wise to make an enemy of your armorer, it occurred to Lisa. "Crysta, when did they start—how long have the Karbarrans been preparing for this?"

"Since the hour they took our children," Crysta answered.

Lisa watched the weapons fire incandesce as the Karbarrans had their revenge.

"Baker!"

Karen Penn went straight for him as he sat there nonchalantly on the rump of a defunct Hellcat, looking off into the distance as if he didn't have a care in the world.

That stunt he pulled! Deserting his post in time of battle! Karen just wanted a little piece of him before Admiral Hunter went to work on him.

Of course, part of her anger was the ignominy of being carried back to the compound in the shuttle by three Battloids, like some kind of broken-down commuter craft. That wasn't the heart of it though, and she couldn't have explained just *why* she was so furious.

To top if off, he was sitting there with a stupid grin on his face, *whistling*! "Baker, say your prayers, because I'm gonna—"

He turned to her with a beatific look on his face. "Hi, Karen. Have a seat and enjoy the show; you'll never see another one like it."

She was clenching her teeth, but decided to see what he meant before the fight commenced. "Huh—Oh!"

Down the hill a bit, the Karbarran children were being coaxed out of hiding by Dardo and his buddies. Battloids had put out most of the fires, and then stood back; the cubs had good reason to be wary of giant mecha.

But Dardo and the rest had the hostages coming out now, in droves. Most of the freed cubs were looking around blankly, but some of them were already beginning to caper and skip, jumping for joy.

Without thinking about it, Karen sat down next to Jack to watch. The cubs rushed around in the sunlight, romping and giving in to elation over their rescue. "I'd rather see this than get a duffel bag full of medals," Jack said soberly.

Karen looked at him for a second, then back at the cubs. "You have your moments, Baker, y'know that?"

"*Et tu*, Penn."

A little while passed. They saw Lron arrive, wading through the cubs, to lift up his son and fling him aloft. The cubs got braver where the mecha were concerned, and some of them were playing ring-around-a-rosy about the foot of Max Sterling's Battloid.

"What was that you were whistling?" Karen asked suddenly, without looking at him. "I sort of recognized it."

Still watching the cubs, he began again, a half smile touching his lips. After a few notes, Karen found herself laughing and shaking her head at him in exasperation.

It was "The Teddy Bears' Picnic."

CHAPTER
TWENTY-ONE

A tragedy worthy of the Greeks, to be sure, or Shakespeare. A Universal Force or righteous Deity had forged a ring of iron, the Sentinels' leadership. And yet somehow a flaw had been tempered in.

One is tempted to paraphrase, "Look upon these frailties, ye mighty, and be humbled."

Ann London, *Ring of Iron: The Sentinels in Conflict*

IN THE AFTERMATH OF THE SENTINELS' FIRST TRUE CONQUEST—while the Karbarrans were still exacting their fearsome revenge and the cubs had yet to be calmed down for transport back to their parents—there were details that slipped through the cracks. Trying to bring order out of the chaos, and make sure they had really *won* the day—that there were no Invid backup divisions waiting in the wings—was keeping almost everybody busy beyond any reasonable demand.

And so no one noticed when Burak of Peryton rather than the regular duty officer showed up at the head of the security squad that was supposed to take Tesla back to his cell.

Burak was certainly on the roster as being able to commandeer a security detachment; he was within his rights as a principal signatory of the Sentinels to take custody of Tesla. But he had chosen this time because he didn't want to be interrupted, didn't want to be overheard, while he spoke to the enemy. Once Tesla was back in irons, the aurok-horned young male of Peryton dismissed the mixed unit of Praxians and Spherians, and stood regarding the captive.

Tesla had turned away, but it came to him that Burak was still there. "Well? Can't you leave a helpless victim of war to his misery? I've given you what you wanted." An Invid stronghold was in flames, dashed under an invader's foot, and he, Tesla, had been instrumental in that. "Go away! Or, kill me. I no longer care

286

which." He fingered the gorgeous collar with its hidden explosives.

"I want to save Peryton," Burak got out at last. "And if you don't help me, I *will* kill you."

Tesla saw that he meant it; a young Perytonian, scarcely more than a boy, he was as headstrong as any from the planet where there was still an annual ceremony in the rubbing off of the velvet from the males' horns and where fights over females still frequently led to death.

So, here was Burak, determined to short-circuit the Sentinels' judicious timetable because he suspected, not without reason, that it wouldn't address Peryton's crisis in time. "How do I save Peryton, Invid?"

Tesla saw that Burak had somehow gotten the detonator switch for the collar around his neck. But for once, Tesla wasn't afraid—no, not at all. Standing there in his grand robes with the shimmering gems draped from his neck, he saw that the key to Burak was that *Burak was vulnerable: Burak needed knowledge.*

A certain *kind* of knowledge, but that didn't matter. That kind of craving put any seeker at a disadvantage if the teacher was unprincipled enough. And conniving was Tesla's speciality, even before he availed himself of the Sentinels' hospitalities.

Tesla came up close to the bars, so close that Burak backed away a step, one hand holding the detonator and the other a little firearm that seemed to be made of white ceramic and hammered brass.

But as he neared the front of his cage, Tesla settled down. He folded his tree-bough legs and sat in a meditative pose, the level of his gaze still higher than Burak's. Tesla's thoughts were like drowning rats, seeking any avenue of escape, marshaling in vaguest terms things that Burak might want to hear.

"The answers lie more within you than within me," Tesla intoned. "My powers tell me that your hour comes near. You have been chosen by Destiny to free your people from the curse under which they live second to second, constantly. This source of such pain to you has made it your Destiny. You have been aware of this for some time now."

Tesla could barely keep himself from dissolving in laughter. What blather! What transparent ego-stroking! Surely, the very Regent, end-all of egotism, would have struck Tesla down for saying such things.

But Burak was an untried youth whose planet was near disaster, and to him it was something of a miracle that he hadn't been swallowed up by it already.

He sat down, cross-legged like Tesla but safely out of the Invid's reach, on the other side of the bars. "Teach me what I need to know, and I'll free you."

Tesla had already anticipated that, and knew that he had to up the ante. Besides, the robes and the gemstones and the turn of events had him thinking along new pathways now.

He tried to think up something suitably muddled and nebulous, something appropriate for a hazy Sentinel mind. "Free? All beings are free. It is only distorted awareness that imprisons them."

Tesla was beginning to enjoy this. "But there are specific things, things like the process for reversing the damage that has been done to Peryton, and freeing all your people from their terrible curse."

Tesla leaned toward the bars with what he calculated to be the correct fervor. "And *these things are not so difficult!* I shall help you accomplish them. And you will deliver up your people."

Tesla assumed what he hoped looked like a prayerful attitude. "I don't ask you to free me. Nor even to trust me. I only ask you, Burak, to *listen* to me."

Burak stayed back out of range, but he leaned closer.

Rick Hunter had been thinking about taking some disciplinary action against Jack Baker until he found him gathered with most of the rest of the scouting party, sitting there on the rump of the dead Hellcat overlooking the Teddy Bears' Picnic.

Lron was still down among the cubs, and transports were on the way to lift the Karbarran youngsters out now that Lisa and the others in Tracialle had gotten the dome open and the last of the Inorganics were dead.

Rick moved toward them, just in time to hear Bela avow, "He's got the guts of a Praxian! Jack Baker's just like a daughter to me!"

She didn't seem to understand why several people were guffawing and Jack was turning pinker than usual. *Maybe he's been punished enough,* Rick thought; it was a line that would pursue Baker for the rest of his military career. Sackcloth and ashes could be no worse.

Bela spit in her palm and held it out. Jack spit on his and clasped with her, arm-wrestling style, then winced a bit when she inadvertently crunched his fingers together.

Kami was there, too, and cubs kept running up to him with every sort of minor update on what was going on, or simply to hold onto a tuft of his fur. He had freed them, and his pelt was a lot more familiar to them than all the armor and uniforms they saw around them. Several had found their way up into his lap, even though Karbarran cubs were big for a Garudan to hold.

Rick forgot all about his official duty and just stood to one side, watching. If he went over to join them, things would change. The issue of rank would appear.

So he leaned against the corner of the bunker and watched. Gnea put a well muscled arm around Rem and gave him a buss on the cheek, yelling something about Hellcats. Halidarre, like something from the *Arabian Nights*, reared a bit every now and then, beating her wings slowly.

He left them to their moment and went off to get a lift back to the capital. He just didn't feel like it was a win yet; he had to hear it from Lisa, see it on her face.

Things about love you hadn't quite anticipated: lesson 207, he thought wryly.

Lightning like this would shake any Human's faith in God, Breetai thought as a passing observation, while one of the rolling, rainless storms of Fantoma lit the sky, exciting the chancy tectonics of the planet and resounding against the hard sides of the mining machines and armored workers.

Here in the thicker medium of the unbreathable Fantoman atmosphere, great Breetai gazed down on a place out of memory. *Zarkopolis!*

The history of a people, a *race,* all stemming from the first awakenings there; the things that had been blanked from neuron altogether but somehow, stubbornly, remained in marrow and soul—the past was washing in on him and he could no more sort it out than pick a handful from a wave.

With the mining operation safely established, Breetai had flown back for a look at Zarkopolis, the city where the Zentraedi had begun. *A haunted world,* he thought yet again, for the latest of times past counting.

Breetai took a step forward, to go down and look at the Zentraedi past. The officers who accompanied him made that same step, like shadows.

"Stay back," he bade them. "You may return to the camp; I wish to be alone." They hesitated, then obeyed.

There were only two Zentraedi from those days still alive, the ultimate survivors, and Exedore was now a happily diminutive little *Human.* The thought was unkind, but he couldn't help it; only Breetai was left.

With his vast strides, it didn't take him long to make his way down into the deserted city. He saw the high, fluted spires that had been erected by his people in defiance of the terrible gravity, not to announce their greatness so much as to affirm the Zentraedi ability to endure, to overcome, through sheer stubbornness and backbreaking hard work. How different a legacy from what the Robotech Masters had given them!

As a memory-wiped warrior for the Masters, he had always felt contempt for the scurrying, insect-colony industriousness of subject races—of workers. But now he looked upon Zarkopolis, remembering the pain and striving in each chisel mark, each laboriously-raised slab.

And memories began returning to him, recollections of what his people had been at the outset: builders and strivers, who had more in common with the Micronians of Earth, and Macross, and SDF-1, than the Robotech Masters had dared let the Zentraedi know.

It is no wonder to me, now, that we were moved so deeply by Minmei's songs, he thought. *At last, at last, I understand!*

With that there came a measure of peace within him.

Now he plodded down—the soil falling *so* fast, and abrading his boots with its weight—toward the stand of cream-colored bunkers and low domes and hunkering complexes that had been the center of all Zentraedi life so long ago.

He stopped. Why return to the source of so much pain and regret and resentment? But—he couldn't hold himself back, despite his iron will.

He had to go down yet again into the weathered, haunted precincts of the Zentraedi workers, and the multitude of voices that spoke to him across the ages. He didn't know why, knew only that he must stand there again, in the center of it all.

"My lord?"

He turned more slowly than he would have under lesser gravity; sudden moves could injure even the mightiest Zentraedi here. Kazianna Hesh was catching up with him, moving with unwise haste in her modified Quadrono suit.

She was again wearing those *cosmetics* the Human females favored. It confused him, seeing her features behind the tinted facebowl of her helmet. He said, "What do you want here? You should be at your work."

She was a little out of breath. Kazianna panted, looking at him earnestly. "My work is done and I am off shift, my lord. I—I had hoped that you would tell me why Zarkopolis obsesses you so, and show me the city where once the Zentraedi dwelt."

He looked down at her and wondered how old she was. In the heyday of the Robotech Masters' empire, the life expectancy of a clone warrior was less than three years, and it was virtually certain that she was one of the hordes brought forth to fill the empty spots in the ranks.

But—whence this curiosity? This disturbing *presence* that she seemed to have? Breetai turned to look out upon Zarkopolis and suddenly understood that these characteristics were things manifest in *all* Zentraedi, in times past. That they should surface again now was, it could be argued, a very good sign.

"Very well; I shall." He started off again and she fell in with him. Breetai led the way down into the city, pointing this way and that, telling her the things that had come buzzing back into his head with the return to Fantoma and, all of a sudden, not hiding in the gaps in his memory.

"In that hall we met to thrash out problems, all of us; it took a very long time to cut the stone columns perfectly, so that they would support the weight of the roof, and even longer to assemble the roof."

A little further on, "Here, the clones were grown, coming forth when they were ready for work, descending those steps over there to adulthood." Steps he had never walked until recently; Breetai antedated the city, had helped raise it.

And so they went. Breetai was pleased, for reasons he couldn't name, to have someone with whom to share his memories. At last they came to a nondescript little house in a tract of them. It was only slightly more prestigious than the mass barracks in which most Zentraedi had lived.

Breetai pressed a button with an armored finger; the airlock swung open. Kazianna could see that it had been refitted to function again after a span of centuries. She had no doubt that Breetai had done it. Lightning was breaking again, and the odd, emphatic thunder of three-g Fantoma was sounding as the outer hatch slid shut.

Inside, the place was unprepossessing, the quarters of a worker/engineer. He had cleaned up the mess, but there were still a few models left, still a few mounted sketches, from the days when a different Breetai had dreamed larger dreams than all the Robotech Masters' fantasies of galactic conquest—dreams of building.

Breetai saw Kazianna looking around, and realized how spartan the furnishings were. In the age since he had lived in that place, he had learned to deceive, but he spoke the simple truth now. "I was the biggest and the strongest of the miners, the first of them," he said. "Only our leader, Dolza, was bigger than I; only he and Exedore were older.

"But—I had few friends—no life, really, except in my work. It seemed to me that they all thought me—"

He stopped, astonished, as she cracked the seal on her helmet and threw it back. Of course, her suit's instruments would have told her there was breathable atmosphere in the tiny quarters—atmosphere he had put there. Only he hadn't seen her check her instruments, and suspected she had done it on what the Humans called "instinct."

"They all thought you *what*," Kazianna Hesh encouraged him, walking around, glancing at his sketches, opening the other seams in her armor. "Thought you too stoic, thought you too formidable, great Breetai? Treated you so that you felt easier when you were either working or alone?"

She had always been deferential toward him, but now she sounded somehow teasing. She had made her circuit of the tiny living room and stopped now to flick the control that broke the seal on his own helmet. "They didn't see what was there inside?"

She unsealed his helmet and lifted it off, having to rise on her tiptoes to do it even though she was tall. The reinforced floor groaned beneath them. Breetai was too astonished to speak, and the wall was behind his shoulders so he couldn't retreat.

"Couldn't see the real Breetai?" she went on. "Well, my lord, I can." She pulled his head down to her, like some *Human*, and he found himself being thoroughly kissed. How had she learned about things like this, forbidden to the Zentraedi?

Many of his race had spent time Micronized to Human size. Maybe that had affected her somehow, or she had seen or heard something.

But he had little time to wonder about that. A kiss; the sight of such an act had almost debilitated him once, when Rick Hunter and Lisa Hayes performed it on a Zentraedi meeting table. He was awkward at first, self-conscious, but Kazianna didn't appear to mind and in fact didn't seem to know a great deal more about it than he.

When the kiss ended, he would have caught her up in his arms for more, but she held him off and began alternately popping the seals on his suit and her own.

It suddenly came to him what she had in mind. "You . . . this is proscribed."

"By whom? By Robotech Masters who have fled beyond the stars? By laws that were never really ours?"

Breetai thought about that, and considered his hunger for her, too. The bed was refurbished; he had slept there once or twice on his off-duty hours, waiting for the past to filter into his mind once again.

Breetai put his arms around Kazianna and kissed her carefully, very happy about it but aware that he had a great deal to learn. Then he took her gauntleted hand and led her to his sleeping chamber. Since he had built the house back in the early days of the Tiresian Overlords who were to become the Robotech Masters, no one else had ever been in that room.

CHAPTER
TWENTY-TWO

In spite of her resistance, he presses her. His great evil is attracted to her illuminating goodness, like some primal circling of forces.

Does he sense that he only continues to live on my sufferance? I believe so; something in him is too animalistic to miss the emanations. But he has only a little time to mend his ways.

Otherwise, I shall kill Edwards in the next day or so.

REF
#666-60-937

"**A** LITTLE TO THE RIGHT. NO, NO! *MY* RIGHT!"

The enlisted men hanging the REF SERVICE CLUB sign were certain that it was centered and even, but not surprised that Minmei wasn't satisfied. The club had been her obsession ever since the council had given her the go-ahead. Her headache and her firstborn, all wrapped up in one.

Minmei tried to be patient and remind herself that the techs had volunteered their own time to help. But the sign was just about the last thing to take care of; the club would open that night. And she had been through a lot to see her dream come true. But soon—in hours—she would be standing under the spotlights again, singing out to the dim sea of faces, making contact with fellow Human beings in the only way that had ever been possible for her, really . . .

Speaking of ongoing problems—General Edwards's military limo pulled up right behind her, almost tickling her bottom with one of the flags mounted on its front fenders.

Edwards, in a rear seat bigger than some living quarters, lowered his window with the touch of a button. "How's our nightingale's cage coming along?"

She wished he would stop talking like that, but Minmei knew she was walking a fine line again. Offending him would no doubt make him withdraw his support from the project, and that might very well be the end of things.

On the other hand, she didn't know how much longer she could keep him at bay. Since that very first interview he had kept her on the defensive, and Minmei was running out of excuses—why she couldn't have dinner with him, give a private recital for him, attend a diplomatic function on his arm, or take any one of a dozen other first steps on a path that ended at his bedside.

"Top drawer, sir, as you can see. The doors open at 2000 hours SDF time." She saw a flicker of frown cross the exposed half of his face; she still wasn't using his first name.

Edwards pressed another button and the door lifted out of the way, brushing against her. Minmei started for the club entrance as if she had something to do, but he caught up with her in moments. The volunteer techs watched the two enter the club, looked at one another, then began fixing the sign into place.

Edwards took her elbow as if to assist her through the doorway, but in reality he was simply grabbing her—was just barely restraining himself from shaking her. He swept a hand at the club's main lounge—the stage and tables and chairs.

"Are you going to keep pretending *this* is going to make you happy? When it didn't before, when applause from audiences all over *Earth* didn't?"

He dropped her arm in disgust, the visible part of his face flushed. "You're a fool, Minmei. This club of yours—it was a minor gift from me, haven't you figured that out yet?"

The cold metal of his half cowl contrasted with red anger on the rest of his face. "But before long I'll give you things that *will* satisfy you, things that only the greatest power and glory can command!"

He almost told her about the Living Computer, and what use he meant to make of it. Minmei had come to fill his waking thoughts and his dreams. Somehow evading his advances, somehow immune to the charisma and power he had plied so often before, she had only made him want her more. Especially since she had once been Hunter's!

I will not be thwarted in this, he vowed. But in some way that he was at a loss to explain, the upper hand had slipped to Minmei. Edwards had roused himself wrathfully, not to be frustrated by this waifish little spellbinder; and in the all-out effort to make her love him, he had somehow made her the embodiment of all his desires and dreams. He saw that now, but it was too late to change things.

Be that as it might, some iron core of self-preservation and caution kept him from confessing his plots to her. Instead he leaned close, with a look on the exposed half of his face that made her cringe.

"Is it that ass Wolff? Is *that* who you think's going to come home like a white knight and give you some sort of happily-ever-after? If so, you hear me well, Lynn-Minmei: Wolff isn't fit to stand in my *shadow*!

"*I'm* the one who'll give you what you want and fulfill you at last! *I'm* the one who'll stop the aching in your heart!"

He vaguely knew that he was raving, dimly understood that whatever sorcery it was that Minmei had cast over all the others had been cast over him, too. Only, he was T. R. Edwards, and he was not about to meet some lovelorn fate.

He grabbed her arms, and Minmei felt such power in the grip that she knew it was useless to fight. He pressed his mouth to hers; she didn't resist but she didn't cooperate. He might as well have been kissing a corpse. He thrust her from him, and she landed on the floor with a small cry.

"Go on, then, Minmei! Pine for him, while *he's* thinking about the wife and child he left back on Earth! Do you really suppose you're anything but a hardship-tour convenience for Wolff?"

Then he was kneeling by her, lips drawn back from his teeth as if he might devour her. She put the back of her hand to her mouth and shrank away from him, but couldn't take her eyes off him.

"Perhaps I can't give you some doglike devotion, or whatever it is that you think love is, Minmei. But power and immortality and passion—those are what drive me, and you and I *will* share them."

She thought dizzily that he was going to grab her again, or—or something else, something she couldn't put a name to. Instead, as if he were teetering on the brink of an abyss, Edwards pulled himself back, rose, and stared down at her with all emotion closed from his face.

"And you no longer have any choice in the matter," he told her. Then he turned on his heel and strode from the club.

He had barely gotten out the door when his driver came rushing up to him. "Sir, a code 'Pyramid' signal from the Royal Hall."

Edwards didn't break stride. "Get me there. Now."

In the catacombs under the Royal Hall, past room after room of inert Inorganics stacked like cordwood, Edwards hurried to the chamber where the deactivated Living Computer drifted at the bottom of its tank.

On a nearby communications screen, Edwards saw an image. The Regent, of course; he had seen photos and sketches from the intel summaries, had taken a good look at Tesla, and could extrapolate from there.

The Regent, for his part, glared down at the half-masked Human and drew conclusions of his own. The Living Computer hadn't been destroyed, nor had the Inorganics. Yet this couldn't be the leader of the Human expedition; there was a furtiveness about the way in which the Regent's communications signal had been received.

Ah, good! A schemer! Luck was with him again at last.

Bad luck had certainly had its run. The Regent had only received a few spotty reports of the Sentinels' onslaught before his commo links went dead. He had grown bored with inflicting horrible fates on advisers and, more to the point, it didn't accomplish much but diminish the available pool and make those around him very nervous.

Then came his master stroke: pretend to sue for peace! He cursed himself for not having thought of it before. Freeze the battle lines now. Call for negotiations and draw them out, and stall as long as possible while he rebuilt his armies and prepared to launch a sneak attack.

But instead of the REF council, he found himself staring at this half-flesh, half-metal face—the Human they called General Edwards. "Call back the forces that have launched this unprovoked sneak attack on my realm," the Regent blustered, "or I shall utterly and completely wipe them out of existence!"

"Can I rely on you to be thorough?" Edwards asked.

The Regent realized the game he was playing wasn't the one he had counted on. "Is there some semantic problem, or do I understand you to mean that you do not care that the pitiful Sentinels will be crushed like vermin?"

Edwards smirked. "You and your boys haven't been doing so well, huh? Mmm, here's something you might want to keep in mind, next time."

Edwards turned and grabbed a memory disk holding the full G-2/G-3 analyses of the *Farrago*, including its one glaring Achilles' heel.

The Regent could scarcely believe what he was seeing, and personally looked at an indicator there at the Home Hive to make sure all this critical information was being recorded. The key to destroying the Sentinels.

"Haven't you got anything for me?" Edwards asked disingenuously, with a nod toward the somnolent Living Computer.

The Regent was still recovering from his phenomenal success.

"Hmm. Yes, yes, I do, provided that your information is accurate. I think that you and I must talk, General Edwards."

"By all means. But let's do it here on Tirol, eh?" Edwards's tone didn't brook much debate.

The Regent thought about that. "Indeed we will, friend General, indeed we will. Let me make arrangements and get back to you on the matter."

Edwards made an ironic salute with a forefinger. "Don't take too long; there's a lot to do."

"As soon as I've attended to the Sentinels," the Regent agreed.

"If they beat your boys at Karbarra, they'll be headed for Praxis next."

"Ah. Thank you. I look forward to communing with a, um, kindred spirit."

Edwards inclined his head in a courtly fashion, then blanked the screen. When he straightened, he saw Ghost techs looking at him in some shock.

"Wipe those looks off your faces!" Edwards jerked a head at the screen, and by implication at the Regent. "When the time comes, I'll handle him, too."

With a new lease on life, the Regent swaggered through the soaring halls of the House Hive issuing orders and dictating memos. He had had his doubts about the Earther's veracity, but a battery of Living Computers verified what Edwards had told him, and the Regent was ready to gamble.

Even with the strategic data Edwards had given him, it might not be easy to destroy the *Farrago*.

Then there was the matter of this visit to Tirol. It was beyond the realm of possibility that the Regent would place himself in danger, and yet this gullible Edwards creature seemed to assume it would be normal. Perhaps there was some way to—The Regent stopped so suddenly that a hapless adviser plowed into him.

The Regent flung the adviser aside in a carelessly non-lethal way, and began talking excitedly to his attendant Scientists. "Are my wife's Genesis Pits here on Optera still functional? Well, find out! And if they're not, make them ready for a project of monumental proportions! Divert workers and technicians and Scientists from other projects; bring them here by starship if need be!

"Oh, what a joke on the cursed Humans!" the Regent hooted. *So, the Regis thinks I lost my sense of humor when I decided to devolve, eh?*

Burak sealed the hatch and slipped into place, seated before Tesla's cage. There were a few Karbarrans on guard outside in the passageway, but they had been joined by friends for a kind of victory feast, and nobody was being very . . . very "strac," as the humans called it.

Tesla said nothing, only sat looking like an immense Buddha. Burak reached inside his robes, eyes averted, his horns dipping.

He came up with three luminous perfect spheres, as green as a breaking wave, as green as molten bottle glass. Seeing them, Tesla almost broke his guru pose and reached, but knew that he would only receive a shock charge from the bars of his cage for his troubles.

"The Fruit of the Flower of Life, as grown on Karbarra," Burak said.

"So." Tesla sat, looking down at the three.

There was legend among the Invid, and among many other cultures as well, about consuming the Fruit of the Flower. The implication was that the consumption of Fruit from all the worlds Especially Touched by Haydon—all the worlds, it happened, from which the Sentinels came—would bring forth some larger, more magnificent manifestation of the one who consumed it.

Tesla had spent a lifetime steeped in this occultish lore; he was convinced that there was a scientific basis to it. "Give those to me," he said, "and give me Fruit from the rest of Haydon's Worlds, the other worlds of the Sentinels."

"I don't trust you," Burak said.

"I don't expect you to," Tesla shot back. "Why do you think peace is so difficult to achieve?"

Burak slammed his fist on the deck. "Stop talking around it! Can you take the curse off Peryton or not?"

Tesla saw a bulge in the waist rope of Burak's robes and knew a pistol was there, knew what his fate would be if he couldn't sway Burak right here and now.

"I can. But you're going to have to help me. Trust me. And I'll help you win back your family, Burak, and your planet, and everything you've lost. Because you're the one fated to be Peryton's messiah."

Burak sat trembling for a long time, looking at the deck. Then he dipped his head once, horns swaying, nodding in agreement.

CHAPTER
TWENTY-THREE

*Why did Jonathan leave me? How come Lisa's bouquet came right
into my hands after the wedding and yet everything's gone wrong?
It all started off so beautifully.*

The diary of Lynn-Minmei

THE KARBARRANS THREW THEMSELVES INTO THE EFFORT TO
get the Sentinels ready for the next step in their war with the same
energy the ursinoids had shown in destroying the Invid garrison.

Unfortunately, a good deal of the capital's industrial area had
been razed. There were shops capable of repairing most of the
damaged VTs and tanks, and spaceship yards where *Farrago* could be put back in full battle-worthiness, but no new
mecha could be built anytime soon.

Some Sentinels argued that it would be better to wait, to build
new war machines and perhaps even construct more ships, but
Rick and Lisa, among others, argued that lives would probably be
lost on Praxis in the meantime, and the decision to continue on to
the amazon homeworld became unanimous—except for Burak's
stubborn abstention.

The vote was one of the few things Rick and Lisa *did* agree on.
Though the mecha were being repaired, there were gaps in the
ranks of the Human fighters, casualties who had left unmanned
machines behind. The two were silent on the subject until that
night, in their private quarters, when he admitted, "I'm going back
on combat duty with the Skulls, Lisa. They need me. And we still
won't be able to get every VT manned."

She rolled over and looked at him for a long moment. "I wish
there was something I could say that would stop you. But there
isn't, is there?"

He shook his head. She lay back down and they both stared at
the ceiling for a time. "You're just so damned cavalier with a life

that's important to *me*," she said at last, and he could hear the tears in her voice. "It hurts, Rick."

He reached over to take her hand, but she moved it away. She wanted to lie there and see if she could think of some way that she could change things so that she wouldn't be hurt ever again.

Jonathan Wolff returned to his quarters after twenty-one straight hours of meetings, briefings, consultation, training, and planning sessions. He had forgotten what a bed felt like.

But as he lay down, his eye caught something—a small locket lying on his night table. That type of locket was popular among REF personnel; many carried such a keepsake. He picked it up and activated it; the little heart-shaped face opened like a triptych.

A tiny hologram of Minmei hung in the empty air. "I hope this makes you feel near to me, Jonathan, because I feel very near to you, and I always will. Come back to me safe and soon, darling. I'll be waiting for you, however long it takes."

"It's very kind of you to act as our guide," Cabell said, as the Karbarran skywain sailed through the afternoon sunlight.

"Oh, we love going out to the monument," Crysta gushed, and at the controls, Lron nodded agreement. Off to one side, Rem and Dardo paused in the pattycakelike game Lron's son was trying to teach. "And how old is the monument?" Rem asked.

"Centuries, ages," Lron rambled. "No one's exactly sure. History says it was erected right after Haydon visited Karbarra, and that was long, long ago."

The skywain began its descent, alighting on the top of one of the higher mountains overlooking the city. Rem asked again if Cabell would be warm enough; the old sage reassured him.

Lron and Crysta led the way, up to an open pavilion carved from the living rock of the mountaintop. There, in the middle of an acres-wide floor, stood a statue that reared up and up—a colossus a thousand feet high.

It was of Haydon. It had been carved by Karbarrans, and time and weather had eroded it, but the figure appeared to be a human-oid male, wearing flowing robes and poised with an air of nobility and wisdom.

"It was Haydon who taught our ancestors the secrets of Sekiton," Crysta said. "Just as he breathed life into the crystals of Spheris and created Baldan's people, and decreed that the Praxians' should be an all-female planet."

"And Haydon taught the Garudans how to think," Dardo said,

reciting his school lessons. "And some people even say he gave the Flower of Life to the Invid!"

Cabell already knew all that, of course, but he tried to look impressed by Dardo's erudition—Crysta and Lron were so proud of the cub, after all.

Rem stood staring up at the stone face now worn to anonymity. Haydon, certainly one of the galaxies' great enigmas, fascinated him just as Haydon fascinated so many others. Where had the bringer-of-miracles come from? What had prompted him to spend a Golden Age in this sector of space, traveling among local worlds and working his magic?

Rem had always vowed that if he got to travel among the stars, he would do his best to find out. And now that time had come. Rem stared up at the smooth visage, wishing it could speak to him. He swore to himself at that moment that before his travels were done, he would know what face belonged on the monument.

"Red alert," whispered one Ghost Squadron yeoman to another. "Stay out of the Old Man's way!"

The second yeoman nodded and did his best to look busy as Edwards marched from his office with a murderous look on his face.

The Sentinels had won a smashing victory on Karbarra! Edwards tried to suppress his fury, but wasn't having much luck. To make matters worse, when he had called Minmei, she wasn't at the club. Nobody seemed to know *where* she was.

This, after he had been there at a ringside table every night to hear her sing, had wined and dined her, had made sure the council listened to her and that her service club was a success. Yet each time he was sure he was making her forget Wolff, she was sure to bring the halfwit's name up.

Edwards stopped in midstride. He suddenly knew just where she would be.

Sure enough, he found her there, looking at the posted casualty reports along with many others, searching the alphabetized lists of KIAs and WIAs. The names would go on the REF broadcast screens momentarily, but there were a lot of people who couldn't bear to wait. There was quite a press, and those at the back were calling out names for those in the front to check.

Just as the general came up behind her, Minmei turned with a thousand-watt smile on her face. "Oh, General! He's not on it! Jonathan's not on the lists, so he's all right!"

Edwards forced a smile. Yes, Wolff had survived Karbarra, but the Sentinels would be headed for Praxis soon, and the Regent was aware of it.

"Yes; he's a lucky man." He showed her what he had brought for her.

"Oh, they're beautiful!" Minmei took the bouquet and held it to her face, inhaling the sweet, exotic alien scents. She was delighted, and pleased with the good news about Jonathan; even though he could be cold, almost cruel at times, Edwards had been such a help, had been there whenever she needed someone to listen to her or reassure her . . .

Without pausing to reconsider, Minmei put her free arm around his neck and kissed him once, quickly, on the lips. Then she was racing off for a rehearsal.

Edwards watched her go, thinking of the day when he would comfort her in her grief over the death of Jonathan Wolff.

When Edwards got back to his HQ he was in visibly better spirits, but not for long. Adams entered, looking grim, and cued up a recording. "The internal-security people monitored this with the bug we put on Lang's private commo rig," Edwards's aide told him. "It went out earlier today, before Tirol Base lost contact with Karbarra."

Lang was saying, "General Hunter, I'm not opposed to the building of more starships per se; SDF-3 will not be ready for a return voyage to Earth for a prolonged period, and we might very well need this armada that General Edwards keeps pushing for.

"But I must tell you in confidence that I have my doubts about Edwards's motives."

Rick's face, on the other half of the split screen, looked drawn and tired. "Just what are you saying, Doctor?"

"That Edwards may very well be furthering his own ends. I think a coup attempt is a quite plausible danger at such time as this armada is ready."

Rick considered that. "If the other Sentinels' worlds can be liberated as quickly as Karbarra, we'll be back long before the armada is finished, Doctor. And we'll have plenty of Sentinel allies to help us make sure Edwards is checkmated. But after what we've seen—I'm more convinced than ever that the Invid have to be rooted out of these planets they're occupying."

Lang nodded. "I agree, Admiral, but I wanted you to be aware of the gravity of the situation here."

Adams stopped the recording. "What are we going to do, sir?"

Edwards leaned back. "For the time being, nothing. We need Lang to build that fleet and get SDF-3 fully operational. And once the Sentinels show up at Praxis . . ."

He allowed himself a thin smile. "Once they're out of the way, the REF belongs to me completely."

When he returned to Tracialle, Rem was surprised to find Janice Em waiting for him.

They hadn't spent much time together in the rush of the Karbarran campaign. Now, she took his hand and said, "I thought we were friends, Rem. Have I done something to offend you?"

His brows knit. It was sometimes hard to understand what Humans were getting at. "Of course not! What makes you say that?"

She showed a slight pout. "I was beginning to think a gal's got to be a butch weightlifter to get any attention from you."

He realized she was talking about Gnea. "Hmm? Gnea and I are friends, of course—we went through a lot on that scouting mission." He *had* been spending considerable time talking to the young amazon, learning about her life and her world.

Jan had both his hands in hers now. "If you want me to step aside, just come out and say so!"

He shook his head in confusion. "What? No, no I—"

Janice was suddenly in his arms with a happy laugh. "Oh, I'm so glad! You—you've become kind of important to me, you know."

It felt very good to have her embracing him, brushing her lips against his cheek, his neck, his lips. Very unsettling, but simply wonderful. "Let's go somewhere and be alone," she said.

He yielded as she drew him away. "And you can tell me all about this expedition you took to the Haydon monument," Janice added. "What did Lron and Crysta have to say about this Haydon, anyway? And Cabell; what was *his* reaction?"

Why was she nattering away about *Haydon*, of all things, when she was back with Rem at last? But Janice felt something puzzling, something that made her curious about the subject, and about Cabell and the Sentinels' plans too. And there was something about Rem that excited her and made her want to be with him and know everything about him.

Maybe that's what love is, she shrugged to herself.

On Praxis, the Regis flung her hands high, throwing her head back crying, "Hear me, O my Children!"

Wherever they were, whatever they were doing, her half of her species paused to listen to her.

Just as no subject of her husband's could eavesdrop on her mental link, so none of the Regis's children bore any further allegiance to him.

She looked more Human than a Haydonite, though she was fully as tall as her mate—some twenty feet. And yet there was something ethereal about her, an alienness that showed in her cobalt eyes. Slender and hairless, she wore a full-length robe and curious, tasseled five-fingered gloves. Four emerald-green sensor scarabs, like beautiful brooches or oriental masks, decorated her robe's collar and neck closure.

"Hear me!" she cried again. "My investigations here tell me that the answer I seek is to be found on Haydon IV! There at last I will learn where the Robotech Masters have gone, and what has happened to the last Protoculture matrix, the treasure that we must have in order to carry out my Great Work!"

And an age of deprivation and conflict would be brought to a close. Still shielded in her thoughts, like a hot cinder, was that night so long ago in the Flower gardens of the paradise that had been Optera.

There she had surrendered at last to the emotional enticements and seductive intellect and form of Zor—had surrendered herself to him and surrendered the secrets of the Flower as well.

And was discovered in the act by the Regent, who flung himself off on the descending spiral of devolution. But soon, all those torturous memories and misdeeds would be behind her, and her Children.

"Therefore, prepare yourselves, my Children! Gather and make ready, for we abandon this planet at once, for Haydon IV!"

In the Genesis Pits abandoned on Optera by his wife, the Regent peered into a cloning vat. Work on his project had not been without its problems; his biogenetic workers were less adept than the Regis's, and had been forced to start from scratch after the first abortive attempt.

But now things were going well. The workers had used the most perfect egg available, an unquickened one from the clutch that had spawned the Regent, feeling it was the ultimate perfection of Invid plasm.

The Regent gazed into the vat as into an aquarium. What floated there was no ordinary Invid clone, though. It had a cobra hood like his own, a row of eyelike turbercle sensors that mimicked his.

It was a new Regent, a false one.

"I am pleased," he said. "Make certain that it's ready by the time I've crushed the Sentinels."

* * *

Karen found Jack in one of the training areas the Sentinels had set up near their temporary groundside billeting area. She had been looking forward to teasing him about being compulsive in his training, but the look on her face changed when she saw he wasn't alone.

Bela was with him on the firing range, showing him how to use the Praxian crossbow. He was getting the hang of it, and put a quarrel within a foot or so of a bull's-eye at twenty paces.

"Ah, Karen Penn," Bela smiled. "You once asked me about our weapons; now you see they're so easy that even a male can use them. Jack here is making fine progress; would you care to try?" Bela clapped Jack on the shoulder in comradely fashion and gave him a sisterly hug. She towered over him, a full head taller.

Karen made no effort to keep the frosty tone out of her voice. "No, thank you. Lieutenant Baker, I'm just here to let you know that your request has been approved; you've been reassigned to Hovertank duty in the Wolff Pack."

"Hey, that's great!" He had studied Jonathan Wolff's style, and decided he wanted to serve under the man. "Did you get what you wanted?"

She looked at his grin and felt like belting him. He didn't even understand that she was sore at him. "Yes. I'm going over to Commander Grant's GMU staff as of tomorrow morning."

"Congratulations! Let's go celebrate. Bela, want to join us?"

But Karen was shaking her head. "No. I'm sure you two have lots of—exercising to do. And I wouldn't want to intrude."

As he watched her walk off, Jack said, bewildered, "Did I say something wrong, Bela? I don't think I understand what just happened."

Bela shrugged and recocked the crossbow with one swift, powerful pull on its forestock grip. "Personally, I often find it difficult to comprehend your species at *all*."

At last, after weeks of frantic preparation, training, reequipping and rearming and reorganizing, the *Farrago* was ready to lift off.

The original plan for a Karbarran starship and fighting force to accompany the Sentinels had had to be abandoned; the Invid had disabled all Karbarran ships, and the new ones on the drawing boards wouldn't be ready for months yet.

"The new production lines for VTs and other mecha will be fully operational in another six weeks," the senior Karbarran administrators had assured the Sentinels. "When you've freed the women of Praxis, we will be ready to help them become an army."

The word was that the Invid garrison on Praxis was much smaller than that on Karbarra, and the Sentinels were hoping for a brief campaign. The Karbarrans cheered as the Sentinels lifted off and passed through the open wedge of the dome. Lisa looked down on the planet and thought that in spite of the pain and losses the war had cost so far, the sight of a liberated planet and a free people made it worthwhile.

Still, she breathed a prayer that the worst was behind them.

CHAPTER TWENTY-FOUR

> *In a way, the very things I've counseled the others against are what the Sentinels' mission is all about: hurling one's self into the midst of the Shapings and taking the risk that their design will not turn to one of utter tragedy.*
>
> *And yet, in the Sentinels there is that added dimension that most of the species on Farrago are from Haydon's Worlds. I pray, for them, that it brings out the most benign manifestations of the Workings of the Protoculture.*
>
> Dr. Emil Lang, *The New Testament*

THIS TIME, *FARRAGO* WENT IN READY FOR TROUBLE, FINGER ON trigger. The ship emerged from superluminal drive even further from Praxis than it had from Karbarra, since Lisa wanted to get a handle on the situation before any shooting started.

Encountering no immediate opposition—in fact, no sign that the Invid had detected the ship's arrival at all—Lisa moved fast to consolidate what she hoped was the advantage of total surprise. VTs launched to fly cover and screen any enemy attack; the strike forces readied for their go signal. The flagship bore in toward the planet and still there was no sign of a response.

"Nothing in the air, zero activity on the ground, no commo, no power sources—nothing," a tech officer reported from the GMU. "Captain Hunter, if they're playing dead, they're doing an amazing job. It looks to me like there might be nobody home."

"Oldest trick in the book," Lisa heard Jonathan Wolff murmur over the command net. But what if Wolff was wrong? She had learned to expect the unexpected from this war, and surely an uncontested landing would be the most unexpected thing of all.

She warily brought the flagship in close, but not too close, staying beyond the orbit of the outermost of Praxis's two small moons. The next move wasn't hard to figure out, but it brought her a personal pang of regret.

"Skull Leader, we're going to need recon; pick your elements and tell 'em to watch their tailerons down there."

"Roger," Max Sterling answered.

It had come as a bit of a surprise to Lisa that Rick, in returning to combat duty with his old unit, hadn't attempted to step into the command slot. But the Skulls, like the oldtime Israelis and Swiss before them, didn't let mere rank or seniority determine who flew lead.

That was decided by who had the most experience with the particular mecha, knew the current situation and tactics best, had the superior performance record, and so forth. And right now, Rick Hunter, admiral or not, was far from the top of the roster. So, he had swallowed his pride and taken his place as wingman to a young lieutenant commander who had been in high school when Rick Hunter was Skull Leader.

Still, there was no question that Rick would be going down on the flyby; with the ranks of the Skulls thinned as they were, and Max preferring to use veterans on an iffy mission like this, it was only to be expected.

At Max's command, several Alphas—Rick's among them—broke formation and mated their tail sections to the rear of the same number of the powerful Betas, forming aggregate ships with tremendously increased range and firepower. The problem was that maneuverability was decreased and mechamorphosis capability was nonexistent.

The Alpha-Beta conjoinings swept out for a pass at Praxis. The rest of the Alphas, Betas, and Logans fell back to guard *Farrago* under Miriya; Max had led the overflight, of course.

The mission elapsed-time counters ticked off tense minutes. But there was nothing to report, beyond the stillness on the planet and the static of the commo channels.

The Skulls were very low on fuel by the time they finished the low orbit, and *Farrago* moved in to retrieve them. Lisa gave the word that the second recon group go in, this time lower, and had the shuttle stand by with its landing party.

In due course, Battloids trod the deserted streets and countryside of Praxis. A contingent of Wolff's Hovertanks, with Jack Baker among them, was checking one of the largest cities on Praxis—a large coastal town, really—block by block, house by house, for use as a base of operations. Technical teams from the shuttle swore that there was nothing on or under the planet's surface higher up the evolutionary ladder than native wildlife. There were plenty of indications of Invid occupation, but the fortifications and temporary Hives were abandoned.

There was no sign of the women of Praxis.

"But—why would they leave with the Invid? What use would that be?" Gnea was close to tears.

Bela patted her shoulder. "I don't know, warrior, but we're going to find out. And woe to the Invid if we don't find our sisters well and whole."

Lisa had those same fears for the Praxians, and other problems besides. Without the firing of a single shot, the Sentinels' war had been brought to a shuddering halt. The Praxians weren't likely to budge until they had some idea what had happened to their people, but at the same time, each hour used up by delay gave the enemy a chance to regroup and redeploy.

She couldn't afford to spend much time there if it would be to no advantage.

It was at such times that Lisa wished dearly that the *Farrago*'s bridge was small, like the SDFs'. She longed to sit in the command chair she had installed, as Henry Gloval was wont to do on *his* bridge, perhaps with a uniform cap visor pulled down over her eyes, and try to mull her way out of her current fix.

But she didn't have that luxury, and every hour was a precious resource she couldn't replace. The senior Sentinel leaders, Baldan and Veidt and the rest, wanted to confer about what to do next— even though Bela and most of the other Praxians refused to even leave the surface of their planet and return to the flagship.

Lisa exercised her authority as captain and, at this stage of things, de facto overall commander. She got Vince Grant on the horn.

If the Praxians won't come to Mohammed . . . she thought.

"We're going to make one low pass with the flagship and drop the GMU; GMU will begin an intense study of the situation on Praxis and attempt to reach some logical conclusion while I convene a full meeting of the principal Sentinels. Give me a shopping list, Vince; what will you need?"

Most of what he needed was already aboard the Ground Mobile Unit; the rest of it quickly was transferred. It was also becoming obvious that there were no hostile forces or booby traps on Praxis; for that reason she began to fear for the flagship's safety. Lisa ordered that a minimal force of VTs and Hovertanks be assigned to ground duty, but that most surface security would be the job of a small detachment from the remaining Destroids. All but a few of the Skulls would be pulled back to protect *Farrago*.

She had a sudden thought as she was about to conclude the call, and said, "Vince, there's one more thing that might come in handy. Tell Jean to make sure she's got her Invid lie detector; I'm going to have Tesla transferred to the GMU."

The architecture of the Praxians seemed like a cross between classical Japanese and Dark Ages Nordic. They used mostly woods and rough-cut stone, and somehow there was the impression that they were used to structures catching fire or crashing down in a quake, and had come to accept it—didn't feel they had to build for posterity.

They also tended to fortify places, even though the last of their generations-long feud-wars—epic bloodbaths of tremendous strife and cruelty and valorous deeds—ended centuries before. But the fortifications were at lower levels, and the higher stories of the amazons' structures could be opened to the air, with mosaic walls or panels of inlaid wood that moved aside or could be lifted.

The local castle at the GMU landing site was the summer palace of the planet's elected ruler. Bela showed some hesitation, in the spacious throne room; then, as senior warrior of her people, she took her place by the foot of the throne. She did not sit down, however.

Other Sentinels had gathered there among the huge ancestral images and holy statuary. This high up, one could see the green, restless bay filling the vista to one side and gray mountains with blue-white caps of snow to the other.

According to Praxian custom, all the war mecha had been stilled, shut down, so that peace and quiet would reign. Even the GMU was powered down, its Protoculture engines inert.

Jack Baker, there as an observer and Wolff's aide, watched Bela falter as she called the meeting to order. *She's really just a kind of ranger, a backwoods cop*, he thought, *thrust into the spotlight by events*. For once, he figured, events had picked the right person.

Bela's confidence grew quickly, especially with Gnea and the other Praxian women there to back her up. Halidarre was standing to one side, stamping just a bit and snorting from time to time, acting more and more like a real animal with each day she served Bela.

Bela threw the first pitch without a windup. "I'm not as good at coming around sideways to things as are the diplomats," she allowed. "I know a lot of you want to go on to the next front in this war. In some ways I don't blame you, because there are no enemies to fight here. But the women of Praxis aren't about to leave until we've tried our best to find out what happened to our people.

"If you can't wait for us, we wish you well. But something's happened on our planet that we have to puzzle out before we're ready to make our next move." She said it in a way that brooked no contradiction.

That left everybody silent and thoughtful, including the senior Sentinels. Karen grudgingly reflected that the Southern Cross Advanced Leadership Program could have learned a thing or two from Bela.

But it was Burak who stepped out of the crowd, out onto the richly polished red hardwood floor of the throne room. "My heart goes out to my sisters from Praxis," he said. "But the question is, *Do theirs go out to the rest of us?* It's time to make rational decisions.

"We sought mecha on Karbarra but came away from there with a grievous net loss. We sought new recruits on Praxis but find an untenanted world. When will the leaders of this campaign see the obvious? There are no fighters on Haydon, no war machines on Garuda! Peryton, *Peryton* is the key here! Let us bypass this and other worlds that cannot advance our cause, and free Peryton from its curse! Then we'll have *legions*!"

Rick, listening, wasn't sure what had changed in Burak, but something was giving him a new and more penetrating gaze, a ringing note to his voice, a larger-than-life aspect to his gestures. It was as if Burak had come into a sense of personal destiny. Rick had seen that sort of thing before, and the memories didn't make him feel comfortable.

Veidt somehow made a sound like a clearing of a throat, even though he had no mouth with which to speak. "Burak, I've already told you in private why I think it is essential to let Peryton wait until our forces have grown—why I think it is suicide for the Sentinels to try to address themselves to your planet now. The difficulties involved are—"

Burak interrupted, slashing the air with his horns. "I've heard that too often, and too easily, from you! And I say this to the Sentinels: you care so little for Peryton? So be it! The *Farrago* comes apart even more easily than she went together! And the module that is my ship is mine to do with as I please; that was our compact.

"So then, bid me farewell; for today, this very hour, Burak of Peryton leaves, to pursue his own quest and bring salvation to his world, whether you are with me and my people or not!"

There were mutterings, and a dozen voices were raised to try to mollify him, but Burak was having none of it. The few other Perytonians there, stone-faced, fell in behind him and trooped toward the exit.

Lisa jumped as her wrist communicator beeped piercingly for her attention. All over the throne room it was the same, distress calls reaching Sentinels in a variety of ways.

"*Farrago* under attack by large Invid force," was all most of them heard. Then the transmissions stopped.

It was his hour, the beginning of a new age; the Regent resolved to decree a new calendar with that sublime moment as its starting point.

He had stripped outposts and far-flung garrisons, put together a force even greater than the one he had assembled to send against his enemies on Optera.

And this time fortune was with him. His fleet emerged from superluminal at just the correct angle of attack, in good formation and proper deployment. Scouts and Pincers rocketed off, this time under competent veteran commanders, to join combat with the enemy mecha trying to protect their flagship.

And the flagship! How long he had hungered for *that* morsel! A Living Computer in the Regent's command ship matched it up with the specifications Edwards had given him, and with exquisite precision the Invid sensors penetrated down into it until they found the junction and the components Edwards specified—the ones Lron had explained to the REF and Lang when the Sentinels first appeared.

Lacking the grand slam of the GMU's cannon, the *Farrago* turned to its lesser weapons, gamely firing and firing, weapons crews staying at their stations even though things seemed hopeless. Most of them had been in Invid cages, and had no intention of being there again, whatever the price of freedom—even if it was death.

But luck wasn't with them this time. The Regent's techs and scientists had prepared a super cannonbolt in accordance with the things Edwards had revealed to them; they fired it now.

It struck to the heart of *Farrago*, sending a pulse throughout the ship's structure. In another moment the flagship was *coming apart*. The forces that unified it had become forces sundering it.

The Regent watched, one fist under his chin, wondering if there was some lesson here. Then he roused himself to bellow at his communications drones. "Haven't you contacted the Regis yet? *Well?*"

Ah, what a sweet victory this would be! To wipe out the approaching enemy in the nick of time, to humble the Sentinels and destroy them forever here, where his mate could see it all—and be won back by him by this proof of his strength at war and military brilliance! A true, savage, devolved stroke of greatness.

Farrago was ripping itself to pieces; shields were down, power systems were failing, communications were all but nonexistent. Always a patchwork ship, she was being driven apart by the Regent's single bolt.

A string of explosions opened a power conduit all along a main passageway, like something being stitched by a monster sewing machine, inflicting awful casualties among the crewbeings trapped there. The last of the explosions sent shrapnel and fire into Mr. Blake, Lisa's trusted bridge officer.

He had almost made it; the Spherian module was before him, the last that was intact. There was no one aboard the Spherian; at least, no one alive. Concussion, blast, fumes, and flying debris had downed them all.

Blake barely dragged himself inside; he was losing consciousness and had lost a tremendous amount of blood. Yet he somehow held himself up with one hand on a commo box and reached through the hatch, feeling for the emergency release.

He had to strip off the safety seal, ripping fingernails loose in the process but scarcely feeling the pain. Tiredly, he took the little quartz lever there and pulled it down. A crystal tone began to sound in the empty Spherian ship as its hatch closed and the strange repelling forces generated by the Regent's volley began to separate it from *Farrago*.

But another internal explosion blew out that whole part of the passageway and penetrated the Spherian hull, killing Blake instantly and damaging the Spherian ship. It would never make its programmed rescue run; it broke in half, the drive section tumbling off on a vector of its own, the rest consumed, along with Blake's body, by another huge detonation from *Farrago*.

The VTs, taken by surprise and surrounded by a horde of Invid mecha, closed ranks and tried to defend themselves as best they could. A few elements tried to break through and run for Praxis, but the Regent's forces were deployed to stop them. The Skulls re-formed and got ready for a fight to the death. There were some garbled transmissions from the Invid, something about surrender, but the fighter jocks had all heard the tales from the Sentinels who had been prisoners, and decided they weren't interested.

Outnumbered five to one, and at times ten to one, they flew from second to second, and died at full throttle. A few joined Alpha to Beta and catapulted themselves into the enemy midst; others got into tight flight elements and rat-raced, skeeting enemies until their own number was up.

They were the best Earth had to offer, people who had contended with cramped living conditions, low pay, and a long separation from home to serve a cause greater than themselves. And no one was there to thank them as they died in the gun turrets, the flight decks, the cockpits. But they hadn't signed on for thanks, and hadn't expected them.

Farrago came apart, its outlashing throwing portions and scraps of it toward unreachable stars. The teeming Invid swarmed in to slay the last of the VTs and strafe the flagship's remains.

"Still no contact with the Regis?" the Regent howled, shaking a gargantuan fist. "Has she no idea what I've accomplished?"

A drone technician looked stricken, realized that he might die in the next few seconds. "Oh, All-Powerful One! The Regis is no longer on Praxis! The readings we receive indicate that she may be on her way to Haydon IV with her half of our race, but—there are no Protoculture readings on Praxis, no power sources, no movement—nothing!"

The Regent screamed aloud, but it would have been too much of an inconvenience to leap from his throne and smite the technician. Instead, he tried to wipe the taste of disappointment from his mind.

"A waste, a waste! Did you record every bit of my victory, so that she may see it? Then, make ready to depart!"

"To Praxis, my lord?" an Enforcer asked.

The Regent cuffed the Enforcer aside, and the Enforcer's armor buckled against the deck with the impact of it. "No, of course not to Praxis! Back to Optera! I'll find that female and *make* her see the truth, *make* her appreciate me!"

He felt acceleration around him even as he issued more orders. "Send a small observation force to Praxis in case any of my enemies return; this place is of no use to me now. Have them set up a transmitter to warn me if there's trouble here again. And then back to the Home Hive!"

There was his alter ego to groom, and set on its pathway. Enough of these meddling Humans; he would send in his simulagent double to do away with the Tirol base, then consolidate the near stars at his leisure. And when he held all the cards, he would bring the Regis to heel.

A sudden thought struck him. If he could produce a copy of himself, why not a copy of the Regis? Yes! One who would be dutiful and compliant and a proper wife? Meek and obedient and

... *receptive* to him. The very image of that made him feel rather paternal and husbandly at the same time.

But no; he snarled at the realization that the Regis was gone, and she had taken all detailed biogenetic models of herself with her. Even more to the point, possessing a mere image of her wouldn't be the same as possessing *her*, of bending his mate to his will; he would always be aware, on some level, that the real thing was out there in the universe somewhere.

"Why are we dawdling?" he bellowed. The command ship blurred forward to superluminal speed.

CHAPTER
TWENTY-FIVE

We should protect the Seed,
or we could all fade away
Flower of Life
Flower of Life

Song of the Tiresian Muses*

DAMN HER!

T. R. Edwards tried to tell himself that he didn't care anymore. Wasn't his staying away from the ringside table tonight proof enough of that? The storied Lynn-Minmei enchantment had no power over him, and now the world knew it. Oh yes, the world knew it ...

He hadn't meant to have more than that one jigger of Tirol-made bourbon with Adams and the others, but it had gone a little beyond that, and while he wasn't unsteady on his feet, it was time to go home. The planning of a coup d'état took a sharp mind and unrelenting work. To bed, then.

Except—the door to his quarters was slightly ajar.

He silently drew the pistol that was with him day and night, entering without a sound. He could have called security, but tonight he was in the mood to kill someone.

He edged in, peering around a corner—and froze.

"Come on; sit down quick, before it gets cold." Minmei blew out a long match as the candles on the improvised dinner table filled the room with a warm glow.

She threw the dead match into the fireplace, looking as awkward as a teenager. "This is just home cooking." It was almost a whisper. "The guys at the club got me the ingredients, but I'm a good chef, T. R.; from way back. Worked in my folks' restaurant."

She swallowed and watched him. Edwards felt like doing something violent; the idea of having feelings this strong for anyone was anathema to him.

"Do you really love me?" Minmei asked him all at once. "I have no way of making you, but *please* don't lie to me! Can you love me—"

She was cut off by the beep of the special commo apparatus in his study. Without saying a word, he unlocked it by retinal scan, went into it, and locked the door, making the room a secure, soundproofed facility.

He was glad he was sitting down when he keyed the call. It was a patch-through from the loyal Ghost Team techs manning the Invid equipment beneath the Royal Hall. The Regent stared out at him. "You take your time about answering a transmission."

Edwards found his voice. "My apologies. Had I known I would have—made arrangements." Not "been waiting"; he had to keep a certain parity here.

The Regent made an annoyed gesture. "There are other arrangements you *don't* have to make; the Sentinels are destroyed, one and all."

Edwards felt the color rise in his face, and the grip of his hands as he made triumphant fists, but he gave no other sign as a silent victory cry rang through him. "And now it is time you and I met face to face," the Regent continued.

Edwards's eyes narrowed. "Surely, you don't expect me to, to—"

"Come to Optera? No; you wouldn't, would you? But *noblesse oblige*, and all that; *I* will come to *you*, this one time. Do us all a favor, Human, and see that you make it worth my while."

The Regent broke the connection and Edwards sat there, his head swimming. *My rivals are dead. The would-be Overlord of the Galaxy wants to cut a deal with me.*

Edwards instantly began trying to figure out ways to gull, use, and betray the Regent.

Minmei looked up as Edwards came back into the candlelit dining room. "Good news, I hope?"

"No news at all." He had his hands on his silvery headpiece, straining a bit. "But . . . where were we? You said please don't lie to you; you said please tell you if I can love you."

He drew the half cowl off his face, letting her see him there in the soft light.

Once, the face had been handsome; but now there were raised white scars in a violent, puckered crisscross, a slash from his hairline to the bridge of his nose and from there a reverse angle to the heel of his jawbone. The eye was scarred shut, with only a little prosthetic fitting showing now. A half-devastated face that gave him a doomed look.

" 'Do you really love me?' " he quoted her own words to her. " 'I have no way of making you, but *please* don't lie to me!' "

Where did the act end and truth begin? If she rebuffed him at this moment, Edwards resolved to launch his coup now, taking her as his first hostage and the one he would never let go.

She reached out tentatively, touching the ravaged side of his face. He had never endured that touch from anyone. He returned the touch but otherwise sat like a granite statue. Then she was around the table, in his lap, kissing him.

"*Farrago* destroyed," Vince Grant said. "But it doesn't look like the Invid are coming after us; something's happening."

The rest of the Sentinels stood around him, repressing their questions; they had already learned that it was bedlam when they all talked at once.

They were gathered in a deactivated GMU; the Praxian requirement that all mecha power down during the meeting in the castle had been an unexpected godsend.

Is this where our luck turns? Gnea wondered.

The Invid fleet above suddenly let forth a myriad of minor sensor "paints", then accelerated for superluminal.

The small observation force of Pincers and Scouts and armored Shock Troopers swept down confidently to take up their places. They quartered the globe that was Praxis. They isolated the important civic-commercial centers, and came in for landings.

The VTs rose up to meet them, having received the word that the Regent was gone. Wolff's Hovertanks fired as Gladiators, or flew on back thrusters as Battloids, dragging the enemy from the air. Again there was that total environment of warfare, so insane—and yet so emphatic that it seemed to the fighters that it was the only time they were truly alive.

"Skull Ten, you got a bogey; scissor right!"

"Skull Six, Skull Six, scissoring; get 'im off my back, Max!"

And the GMU cannon fired, its first round hitting the Invid command ship. There would be no distress call to the Regent.

The Invid threw themselves into the engagements with utter ferocity. But they were met by young Earth soldiers who were angry about Karbarra and confused and scared about Praxis: in a certain sense, the Invid had made their enemies too scared to give in and too scared to lose.

Neither side could withdraw, and so the fighting went on. One by one, the VTs fell, despite their high kill ratio. The mecha hunted one another across Praxis, the VTs using up ordnance and fuel. Both Rick and Max were forced to land when their mecha began to lose power; Miriya had been forced to eject earlier, her VT too shot up to stay in the air.

When the Invid were also forced to take to the ground, the Destroids and the Wolff Pack moved in, with other Sentinels on Hovercycles and in flitters, and riding whatever else they could get into the air. The Invid still had the advantage of numbers, but the Hovertanks and REF irregulars were comparatively fresh. In a half-dozen separate, desperate actions, the Invid were surrounded and annihilated, but at terrible cost.

In the aftermath, the principal Sentinels gathered—stunned and bloodied by what they had abruptly endured—and realized what had happened to them.

The two or three surviving VTs had landed, spent, no longer capable of lifting off Praxis. Only a handful of Hovertanks and Destroids had survived the no-quarter fighting.

Hundreds were dead, in addition to the thousands who had perished with *Farrago*. The GMU was their only resource; they had no way of communicating with Tirol, or any other potential source of rescue.

Bela came by to help a weary Jack to his feet as he sat near the GMU; he had barely escaped his burning Hovertank, and it looked like he was plain old leg infantry again, at least for the foreseeable future.

He was filthy and tired. He had just come in from two sleepless days and nights of recon patrol, trying to make sure there were no Invid left and to find something, *anything*, that would help the Sentinels get out of their dead-end dilemma. And he and his squad had come back empty-handed.

Bela was leading Halidarre, one of the few operating mecha left. "Admiral Hunter wants to see you, old son," she said. He groaned wearily as she pulled him up, and shouldered his Wolverine.

"Where are you headed?" he asked. She and the Robohorse were laden with gear and weapons, and so was Gnea, who was hurrying up to meet her.

"To scout the planet for Hunter, and for myself. Jack, they can't all be gone." Bela turned and put her hands on his shoulders, Halidarre's rein drooping from her grasp. Her face, with its hypnotic raptor eyes, held him, its lines pulled into fierce but frightened lines. *"They can't all be gone!"*

He reached up and thumped her shoulder with his fist. "We'll *find* 'em, sis. You'll see."

She gave him a hug, kissed his cheek, and rumpled his hair. It felt a little like an affectionate mugging. Gnea hugged him too, and then both Valkyries were on their winged horse. Halidarre reared and gave a whinny so realistic that Jack wondered if something wasn't going a little strange with its engrams.

Then Halidarre was away, into the sky, and Hagane, the malthi, went zipping and zooming after like a hummingbird. The rallying cries of the Praxians drifted back, sounding sad now, all alone in the emptiness.

In the GMU, Karen, with Jan Em's surprisingly capable help, was bending over readouts to tabulate what resources were left: there were very few.

Admiral Hunter was starting to look pretty grizzled. "I want you to take a team out and check on a possible Invid base for me," Rick told Jack Baker.

"Sure thing, sir," Jack answered. "But I think we should go belowdecks and apply a welding torch to that Tesla first, and get a little more intel information out of him."

Then he realized Lisa was about to brief those assembled. Jack nodded understanding to Rick's hand signal, and took a seat to listen.

Another recon, Jack thought. *Wish I had a flying horse.*

"All right, there's no getting round it. We're—we're *stuck* here," Lisa was telling Vince and the Sterlings and the principal Sentinels.

We might be here for the rest of our lives, it occurred to Jack. He found himself stealing another look at Karen, but she was busy.

"But *that's just for the moment,*" Lisa went on forcefully. They all seconded her, from varying places on the emotional spectrum: anger, growing misgivings, stoic determination, or, in Burak's case, a kind of starry-eyed disregard of reality.

We'd better *get out of here,* Jack Baker thought. *'Cause I'm not so sure how long we can last all thrown in together like this.*

Lisa outlined new strategies, new possible solutions. After the group had broken up, she drew Rick aside. "I'm afraid I'm not very good at dog-and-pony shows."

"You did fine."

They left the GMU, headed for their quarters at the palace. At least there was no shortage of living space, or food; a vacated Praxis provided plenty of those.

Halfway there, Lisa stopped and began pounding her fist on a stone wall. "We've got to get things moving again, before the Sentinels fall apart and everybody settles down to become subsistence farmers, or hunters. The Invid aren't going to leave us alone forever; you *know* that."

He put his arm around her waist and they went their way again. "Everybody's gonna realize that, Lisa, once they get a chance to think. Believe me."

"Rick, they *must*!"

She drew an uneven breath. "Listen, tell me: what were you thinking about when you were standing back there with Baker, during the briefing? You had a peculiar look on your face."

He clicked his tongue. "Unworthy, maybe, but I was thinking that at least we're together, and . . ."

She didn't let the hesitation go on long. "And what?"

"And if one of us had had to go with *Farrago*, I'd rather it would have been me. Because I couldn't have faced this or anything else without you."

Lights were coming on with the dusk, in the GMU and the palace.

DEATH
DANCE

FOR BEN WILSON,
WHO HAS HIS OWN ROLE
TO PLAY IN THE FUTURE.

CHAPTER ONE

It was as if the Expeditionary mission was fated to strike a truce with someone, and the Regent just happened to be the only enemy in residence. In another five years the Robotech Masters would arrive in Earthspace, followed three years later by the Regis and her half of the Invid horde; but in 2026 (Earth-relative) this was still speculation, and for a few brief days there was talk of peace, trust, and other impossibilities.

Ahmed Rashona, *That Pass in the Night: The SDF-3 and the Mission to Tirol*

A FLEET OF INVID WARSHIPS EMERGED FROM THEIR TRANS-temporal journey through hyperspace into the cool radiance of Fantoma's primary, like so many shells left revealed on a black sand beach by a receding tide. The mollusklike carriers positioned themselves a respectful distance from the moon they had captured then lost; only the fleet's mullet-shaped flagship continued its approach, menacing in its sealed silence.

At the edge of the ringed giant's shadow, Tirol's guardian, the SDF-3, swung round to face off with the Regent's vessel, the crimson lobes of its main gun brilliantly outlined in starlight.

Aboard the Earth fortress, in the ship's Tactical Information Center, Major General T.R. Edwards watched as a transport shuttle emerged from the tip of one of the flagship's armored tentacles. Edwards trusted that the Regent was aboard the small craft, accompanied certainly by a retinue of guards and scientists. The presence of the Invid fleet made it clear that any acts of aggression or duplicity would spell mutual annihilation for Invid and Humans alike.

Admiral Forsythe, who commanded the SDF-3's bridge in the wake of Lisa Hayes's departure with the Sentinels, was now in constant communication with the Invid flagship. It was the Regent who had taken the initiative in suggesting this extraordinary visit, but Forsythe had insisted that the fortress remain at high alert status at least until the Regent was aboard. Disillusioned by decades of war and betrayal, and hardened by the grim realities of recent reversals, it was the Human race that had grown wary of summits, distrustful of those who would sue for peace.

Scanners and camera remotes monitored the approach of the Regent's shuttlecraft and relayed relevant data to screens in the fortress's cavernous Tactical Center, where techs and staff officers were keeping a close watch on the situation. Edwards moved to the railing of the command balcony for an overview of the room's enormous horizontal situation screen. Studying the positions of the Invid troop carriers in relation to the SDF-3, it occurred to him how easy it would be to fire at them right now, perhaps take half of them out along with the Regent himself before the Invid retaliated. And even then there was a good chance the fortress would survive the return fire, which was bound to be confused. Numerous though they might be, the Invid seemed to lack any real knowledge of strategy. Edwards was convinced that their successful strike against the SDF-3 almost six months ago had been the result of surprise and old-fashioned blind luck. More to the point, he felt that he had an intuitive understanding of this enemy—a second sense birthed during his brief exposure to the brainlike device his own Ghost Squadron had captured on Tirol.

Edwards reminded himself of the several good reasons for exercising restraint. Apart from the fact that the actual size of the Invid fleet remained unknown, there was this Regis being to wonder about; her whereabouts and motivations had yet to be determined. Besides, he sensed that the Regent had something more than peace negotiations in mind. In any case, the data Edwards had furnished the Invid regarding the Sentinels' ship had already linked the two of them in a separate peace. But Edwards was willing to play out the charade—even if it amounted to nothing more than an opportunity to appraise his potential partner.

He dismissed his musings abruptly and returned to the balcony console, where he received an update on the shuttlecraft's ETA in the fortress docking bay. Then, giving a final moment of attention to the room's numerous screens and displays, he hurried out, adjusting his alloy faceplate as one would a hat, and tugging his dress blues into shape.

The docking bay had been transformed into a kind of parade grounds for the occasion, with everyone present as decked out as they had been at the Hunters' wedding extravaganza. There had been no advance notice of what, if any, protocols were to be observed, but a brass band was on hand nonetheless. The impression the Plenipotentiary Council wished to convey was that of a highly-organized group, strong and decisive, but warlike only as a last resort. The twelve members of the council had a viewstand all to themselves at the edge of a broad magenta circle, concentric to the shuttle's touchdown zone. A majority of the council had ruled against the show of force Edwards had pushed for, but as a concession, he had been allowed to crowd the bay with rank after rank of spit-shined mecha—Battloids, Logans, Hovertanks, Excalibers, Spartans, and the like.

The shuttle docked while Edwards was making his way to a preassigned place near the council's raised platform; since he had been the council's spokesperson in arranging the talks, it had been decided that he represent them now in the introductory proceedings. Edwards had of course both seen and fought against the enemy's troops, and he had met face-to-face with the scientists Obsim and Tesla; but neither of these examples had prepared him for his first sight of the Invid Regent, nor had the Royal Hall's communicator sphere given him any sense of the XT's size. Like the lesser beings of the Invid race, the Regent was something of an evolutionary pastiche—a greenish slug-headed bipedal creature whose ontogeny and native habitat was impossible to imagine— but he stood a good twenty feet high and was crowned by an organic cowl or hood, adorned, so it seemed, with a median ridge of eyeball-like tubercles. Dr. Lang had talked about *self-generated transformations and reshapings* that had little to do with evolution as it had come to be accepted (and *expected*!) on Earth. But all the Protoculture pataphysics in the galaxy couldn't keep Edwards from gaping.

A dozen armed and armored troopers preceded the Regent down the shuttle ramp (a ribbed saucer similar in design to the troop carriers), and split into two ranks, genuflecting on either side of what would be the Regent's carpeted path toward the council platform. Recovered, Edwards stepped forward to greet the alien in Tiresian, then repeated the words in English. The Invid threw back the folds of his cerulean robes, revealing four-fingered hands, and glared down at him.

"I learned your language—*yesterday*," the Regent announced in a voice that carried its own echo. "I find your concepts most . . . amusing."

Edwards looked up into the Regent's black eyes and offered a grin. "And rest assured we'll do our best to keep you amused, Your Highness." He was pleased to see the alien's bulbous snout sensors begin to pulsate.

Edwards's one-eyed gaze held the Regent's own for an instant,

and that was all he needed to realize that something was wrong—
that this being was *not* the one he had spoken to via the communications sphere. But he kept this to himself, falling aside theatrically
to usher the Regent forward to the council platform.

The Plenipotentiary members introduced themselves one by
one, and after further formalities the Regent and his retinue were
directed to the amphitheater that had been designated for the talks.
The Regent's size had necessitated a specific route, along which
Edwards had made certain to place as many varieties of mecha as
he could muster. Each hold the summit principals passed through
found combat-ready Veritechs and Alphas; each corridor turn, another squad of RDF troops or a contingent of towering Destroids.
While aboard, the Regent's every word and step would be monitored by the extensive security system Edwards had made operational as part of his Code Pyramid project—a system that had also
managed to find its way into the council's public and private
chambers, and into many of the fortress's Robotechnological labs
and inner sanctums.

There was a smorgasbord of food and drink awaiting everyone
in the amphitheater's antechambers; the Regent nourished himself
on applelike fruits his servants brought forth. Edwards noticed
that Lang was doing his best to attach himself to the Invid leader,
but the Regent seemed unimpressed, refusing to discuss any of the
topics the Earth scientist broached. In fact, only Minmei succeeded in getting a rise out of the Regent. Edwards noted that the
Invid could barely take his eyes off the singer after she had completed her songs, and he retained a slightly spellbound look long
after the introductory addresses had commenced.

Terms for a truce were slated for follow-up discussions, so civilians and members of the press were permitted to enter the amphitheater itself. Edwards saw to it that Minmei was seated beside
him in the front row, where the Regent could get a good look at
the two of them.

The alien's initial remarks put to rest any doubts that may have
lingered in Edwards's mind concerning the ongoing impersona-
tion. The Regent spoke of misunderstandings on both sides, of a
desire to bring peace and order to a section of the galaxy that had
known nonstop warfare for centuries. He claimed to understand
now just what had prompted the Human forces to undertake their
desperate journey, and he sympathized with their present plight,
hinting that it might be possible to accelerate the timetable for the
Human's return trip to their homeworld—providing, of course,
that certain terms could be agreed upon.

"It's a pity there has been so much loss of life," the Invid continued in the same imperious tone, "both in Tirolspace and during the so-called 'liberation' of Karbarra. But while we may have no cause for further quarrel with your forces here, it must be understood that no leniency could be expected for those of your number who chose to join the Sentinels. And despite what you may have been told by the Tiresians, those worlds—Praxis, Garuda, and the rest—belong to me. The reasons for this are complex and at present irrelevant to the nature of these negotiations, but again we wish to stress that the Sentinels' cause was a misguided one from the start. It was inevitable that they fail sooner or later."

A charged silence fell over the auditorium, and Edwards had to restrain himself from laughing. The Sentinels had not been heard from for four months now. Official word had it that the *Farrago* was maintaining radio silence for strategic reasons. Then, recently, there had been open speculation that the ship had been badly damaged during the battle for Praxis. But Edwards knew better. He felt Minmei's trembling grasp on his upper arm. Colonel Adams, also seated in the front row, leaned forward to throw him a knowing look.

"We have only recently lost contact with the *Farrago*," Professor Lang was saying. "But I'm certain that once communications are re-established and an accord of some sort is enacted, Admiral Hunter and the others will abide by its terms and return to Tirol."

The Invid crossed his massive arms. "Yes, I'm sure they would have honored it, Dr. Lang. But I'm afraid it's too late. Four months ago the Sentinels' ship was destroyed—with all hands aboard."

A collective gasp rose from the crowd, and Edwards heard Minmei begin to sob. "Rick . . . Jonathan," she said, struggling to her feet, only to collapse across Edwards's lap.

Someone nearby screamed. Lang and the rest of the council were standing, their words swallowed up in the noise of dozens of separate conversations. News personnel and members of the general staff were rushing from the room. Edwards snapped an order to his aide to summon a doctor. Adams, meanwhile, was shoving onlookers aside.

Edwards held Minmei protectively. Once again he sought out the Invid's lustrous eyes; and in that glance a pact was affirmed.

But on Praxis the dead walked—those Sentinels who had escaped the destruction of the *Farrago*, and, unknown to them, a deadly host of archaic creatures returned to life in the bowels of the planet's abandoned Genesis Pits . . .

"Take a look for yourself," Vince Grant suggested, stepping

back from the scanner's monitor screen. Rick Hunter and Jonathan Wolff leaned in to regard the image centered there: an intact drive module that had been blown clear of the ship and had fallen into low orbit around Praxis. Vince was reasonably certain the module's Protoculture-peat engines were undamaged.

"And there's no way to call it down?" Rick asked. "A hundred miles or so and an Alpha could reach the thing." Normally, one could fly a Veritech to the moon and back, but not one of the Sentinels' all-but-depleted Alphas was capable of attaining escape velocity.

Vince shook his head, his brown face grim. "We barely have enough power to keep the nets alive."

"Then it might as well be a million miles away," Wolff thought to add.

Vince switched off the screen and the three men sat down to steaming mugs of tea one of the Praxians had brewed up from some indigenous grass. After four months it had come down to this: the GMU's stores were nearly empty and foraging had become one of the group's primary activities. And in all those months they had yet to come up with an explanation for the disappearance of the planet's native population. What was left of the central city and all the surrounding villages were deserted. But whether what Bela called "the Praxian Sisterhood" had *chosen* to leave had not been ascertained.

Puzzling, too, were the tectonic anomalies and quakes that were continuing to plague the planet, as often as three times a day now. The quakes had convinced the Sentinels' Praxian contingent that Arla-Non—Bela's "mother" and the leader of the Sisterhood—had struck a deal with the Invid to move the planet's population to some other world. Rick wasn't sure if he bought the explanation, but it certainly served a therapeutic need if nothing else.

"Look," Rick said, breaking the silence, "they're probably already searching for us. Lang's not about to write us off. And even if the mining operation is *close* to on schedule, they'll have at least one ship readied with the capability for a local jump. We just have to hope the Invid have lost interest in this place."

The horde's absence these months bordered on the conspicuous; and with the quakes and deserted villages, Cabell had speculated that it was possible the Invid knew something the Sentinels didn't.

Rick's optimism in the face of all this had Vince smiling to himself. *Rick would always be a commander whether he liked it or not.* "It's not Lang we're worried about," he said, speaking for himself and Wolff.

Rick caught his meaning. "Edwards has to answer to the council." There was an edge to his voice he didn't mean to put there. Lang had warned Rick about Edwards during one of the last links the *Farrago* had had with Base Tirol, and it was difficult to keep the memory of that brief deep-space commo from surfacing.

"Don't underestimate the man's ambitions, Rick," Wolff cautioned. "I'm sure they're going to come looking, but I'm willing to bet that Edwards will have the council eating out of his hand by then. Maybe one of us should have—"

"I don't want to go over old ground," Rick cut him off. "The only thing that interests me right now is a way to reach that drive module."

Grant and Wolff exchanged looks and studied their cups of tea. Rick was right, of course: there was no use dwelling on the choices they had made, individually and collectively. Wolff liked to think that at least Vince had Jean by his side and the precious GMU under his feet. But Rick had all but resigned his commission, and Wolff himself had left his heart behind.

A rumbling sound broke the silence, causing the mugs to skitter across the tabletop. The tremor built in intensity, rattling the command center's consoles and screens, then subsided, rolling away beneath them like contained thunder.

No one spoke for a moment. Wolff wore a wary look as he loosened his grip on the edge of the table and sat back to exhale a whistle. "Course, Praxis could do us in long before the Invid or Edwards."

"Pleasant thought," Vince told him.

Rick gave them both an angry look. "We're going to get to that module if we have to pole-vault there."

Tactical concerns (and personal preference) had kept Vince Grant and Rick somewhat anchored to the GMU (which had been moved inland from its original seaside landing zone); but the rest of the substantially reduced Robotech contingent, along with the XT Sentinels, had opted for Praxis's wooded valleys, the planet's often glorious skies, and rolling hills. Max and Miriya's Skull Squadron had spent most of the past months reconning remote areas, hoping to come upon some trace of the vanished Sisterhood; but they had only succeeded in further depleting already critical reserves of Protoculture fuel. Consequently, the Wolff Pack stuck close to base, Hovertanks shut down. Bela and Gnea and the other Praxians had voluntarily detailed themselves to serve the group's logistical needs, and were assisted in this by the bearlike Karbarrans and vulpine Garudans. Cabell had all but isolated himself, disappearing for long walks from which he would return with samples of native rock or flora. Still a bit uncomfortable with the Humans and not yet fully accepted by the XTs, the Tiresian was often found in the company of Rem, Baldan, Teal, and the limbless Haydonites, Veidt and Sarna. Janice, too, had become an unofficial member of Cabell's eldritch clique, much to Rick and Lisa's puzzlement.

Presently, Cabell and Janice were off together on a long walk; they were on a forested slope about fifteen miles from the mobile base when the tremor that had shaken the GMU struck. The minor quake did little more than knock them off balance and loosen some gravel and shale from nearby heights; but it was the morning's second shakeup and it brought a severe look to Cabell's face.

Janice had thought to take hold of the old man's arm and utter a short panicked sound as the ground began to tremble. It was a performance worthy of Minmei's best, although Janice could hardly appreciate it as such—any more than she could fully understand just what had compelled her to seek out Rem and Cabell's company in the first place. That this should somehow *please* Dr. Lang was a thought as baffling to her as it was discomforting.

"There, there, child," Cabell was saying, patting her hand. "It will be over in a moment."

They recommenced their climb when the tremor passed. Janice disengaged herself and urged Cabell to go on with what they had been discussing.

"Ah, yes," he said, running a hand over his bald pate, "the trees."

Janice listened like a student eager for *A*'s.

"As you can see, they're nothing like the scrub growth we found on Karbarra—far healthier, much closer to the unmutated form." He motioned with his hand and went up on tiptoes to touch the spherical "canopy" of a healthy-looking specimen. The tendrils that encased the solid-looking sphere and rigid near-translucent trunk seemed to pulse with life. Gingerly, Cabell plucked one of the verdigris-colored applelike fruits, burnished it against his robe, and began to turn it about in his wrinkled hand.

"Even the fruit they bear is different in color and texture—although still a far cry from the true Opteran species. Nevertheless, it may tell us something." He took off his rucksack and placed the sample inside. "Look for the ripest ones," he instructed Janice, as she added a second fruit to the pack.

Cabell was straightening up when a sudden movement further

up the slope caught his eye. Janice heard him start, and turned to
follow his narrowed gaze.

"What was it?"

Cabell stroked his beard. "I thought I saw someone up ahead."

"A Praxian?" Janice asked, craning her neck and sharpening
her vision.

"No," he said, shaking his head. "I would swear it was *Burak*!"

Later, a stone's throw from the grounded GMU, inside the
wooden structure that had been designated both quarters and cell,
Tesla wolfed down the fruits Burak had picked from the sinister
orchard Zor's Flower of Life seedings had spawned on Praxis.

"Yes, yes, different, ummm," the Invid was saying in a voice
tinged with rapture.

The young Perytonian tried to avert his eyes, but in the end
couldn't help himself from watching Tesla as he ingested fruit after fruit. Moist sucking noises filled the cell.

"And you think they may have seen you?" Tesla asked him.

"It is possible—Cabell, in any case."

Tesla scoffed, still munching and handling the fruits as if they
were wealth itself. "Cabell is too old to recognize the nose on his
own face. Besides, they know I can't subsist on what you call
food."

Burak said nothing. It was true enough: the Invid's food stock
had been destroyed with the *Farrago*, and the Sentinels had
agreed to place Burak in charge of securing alternative nutrient
plants. But Cabell, who was anything but a doddering old man,
and perhaps fearing the very transformations Tesla was beginning
to undergo, had suggested that the Invid's fruit and Flower intake
be regulated—this in spite of the fact that Tesla had to some extent ingratiated himself with the group since their victory on
Karbarra. Each evening, Cabell and Jean Grant would look in on
Tesla. Burak had been asked to furnish them with a daily log of
the amounts gathered and ingested; and the devilish-looking
Perytonian was complying—inasmuch as he would file a report.
But the report was hardly a reflection of the actual amounts Tesla
consumed. Fortunately, though, the Invid's transformations had
been limited to brief periods following meals, when neither Cabell
nor Jean were present.

"More," Tesla said now, holding out his hands.

Burak regarded the Invid's newly-acquired fifth digit and pulled
the basket out of reach. "I think you've had enough for today."
Burak had heard it said that extraordinary powers could be gained
from ingesting the fruits of Haydon's Worlds, but he had never

understood that to mean physical transfiguration, and the Invid's recent changes were beginning to fill him with fear.

Tesla's eyes glowed red as he came to his feet, taller by inches than he had stood on Karbarra. "You *dare* to say this to me after all we've been through? You, who sought me out before fate landed us in this despicable situation? And what of your home-world and the curse you were so feverish to see ended—have you given up hope? Would you renounce your destiny?"

Burak took a hesitant step toward the door, the basket clasped to him. "You're changing!" he said, pointing to Tesla's hands. "They're going to notice it, and what then? They'll cut back on the amounts, put someone else in charge of you. Then what becomes of your promises—what becomes of Peryton?"

Tesla continued to glare at him a moment more, transmogrifying even as Burak watched. The Invid's skull rippled and expanded, as though being forced to conform to some novel interior design. Gradually, however, Tesla reassumed his natural state and collapsed back into his seat, spent, subdued, and apologetic.

"You're right, Burak. We must take care to keep our partnership a carefully-guarded secret." His black, ophidian eyes fixed on Burak. "And have no fear for your tortured world. When the time comes for me to assume my rightful place in these events, I shall reward you for these efforts."

"That's all that I ask," Burak told him.

The two XTs fell silent as a gentle tremor shook the building.

Tesla stared at the floor. "I sense something about this planet," he announced, his sensor organs twitching as his snout came up. "And I think I am beginning to see just what the Regis was doing here."

CHAPTER TWO

> *Unfortunately, there are no detailed descriptions of the Genesis Pits,*
> *other than Rand's colorful but highly personalized and impressionistic*
> *accounts (specious, as some would add), and the notes Colonel Adams*
> *hastily scribbled to himself while on Optera. And despite a plethora of*
> *theories and explanations, the sad truth is that the mechanism of the*
> *Pits remains a complete mystery—except to say that they were devices*
> *utilized by the Regis for purposes of creative evolution. Praxis appar-*
> *ently played host to the largest of these, and Lang, to name one, has*
> *speculated that the Pits not only gave rise to extinct creatures, but suc-*
> *ceeded in regressing the entire planet to a formative stage of destruc-*
> *tive vulcanism.*
>
> Zeus Bellow, *The Road to Reflex Point*

I F BURAK AND TESLA HAD BECOME THE SENTINELS' SILENT PART-
nership, then Jack Baker and Karen Penn were certainly the
group's inseparable pair. But that, each liked to believe, was
merely a result of duty assignments. And even four months on
Praxis hadn't provided them with enough time to work through
the competitive trifles that fueled their relationship. They were not
only marooned, but marooned together; and Praxis had become
the proverbial town that just wasn't big enough for the two of
them. Bela, Praxis's wasp-waisted local sheriff, was only one
of the contributing factors; but Karen nevertheless took every opportunity to keep Jack as far from Bela as she could, often en-
couraging the Hovercycle recons that had become something of
Jack's stock-in-trade.

A joyride disguised as a scouting mission had brought Jack and
Karen to a series of caves two hours out from the GMU. Lron and
Kami had ridden with them. Four months had given the Sentinels
plenty of time to grieve for those who had gone down with the
Farrago; but Karen often wondered just how long it was going to
take for her to grow accustomed to her XT comrades. She wasn't

a bit xenophobic—a fact that had won her a place with the Sentinels to begin with—and in actuality it wasn't so much the strangeness of Lron or Kami that overwhelmed her, but the *similarities*. If only Karbarrans didn't so resemble Kodiak bears, she would tell herself. And if only Kami didn't look like upright versions of the foxes she used to see near the cabin her father had once owned . . . She had much less trouble with Baldan and Teal, with their bodies of living crystal. Or Tesla, for that matter—now *there* was an alien you could *believe* in!

But wolves and bears and snail-headed things . . . Karen was in the midst of wishing that Bela had had a more alien form—even a more *rotund* form—when without warning, Jack hissed: "Cut it out!"

The four Sentinels were well into the central cave now, inside a huge vaulted corridor that was as hot as blazes and reeking of sulphur. Curiosity had drawn them in; but Jack, never one to do things halfway, had insisted they go "just a little further," and here they were a good half a click along. There were primitive sketches on the walls of the caverns they had passed through— depictions of hideous spiderlike creatures Jack claimed were "symbols"—and Karen was in no mood for fun house games or laugh-in-the-dark surprises.

"Huh?" she said, gulping and finding her voice.

"I said cut it out."

"I know what you said, Jack . . ."

She threw him an angry look in the darkness, wondering suddenly if she had actually *voiced* some of her private musings about Bela. Then all at once something hit her on the top of the head. XTs or not, she decided, someone was trying to be funny. Karen whirled around, hoping to catch Kami in the act, but he was way off to her left inspecting a chunk of rock near the cave wall. Lron, too, seemed to be preoccupied with other things. So, wiping sweat from her face, she turned back to Jack, and said, "Not funny."

"What?"

She put a hand up to shield her eyes from his miner's light. "Throwing things. I'm not real thrilled about being in here to start with."

"I didn't throw anything," he started to say, when Lron's gurgling snarl interrupted him.

"Who hit me?" the Karbarran growled.

Jack felt a tap on his shoulder, swung to it, then instinctively looked up. His light illuminated what looked like an assemblage of globular-shaped deposits on the cave's ceiling. Suddenly he saw one of the things move, and realized that it was some sort of free-floating, translucent sphere. Kami switched on the light strapped above his muzzlemask and shined it on another portion of the ceiling; here were more spheres, ranging from baseball size to almost four feet in diameter, all bobbing against the rock like helium balloons.

"What the . . . ?" Jack said, moving his head around, the beam finding more and more globes. "Jeez, the place is crawling with them."

"Jack!" Kami shouted, training his light on something further along the corridor. Everyone turned in time to see a medium-sized globe emerge like a bubble from a conelike projection in the cave floor. Jack rushed ahead, watching the milky thing ascend, and soon found himself perched on the rim of a large shaft, roughly circular and belching up a lot of heat and noxious fumes. Kami, Lron, and Karen joined him a moment later, just as another globe was beginning to make its way up and out.

"What a stink," Karen commented.

Warily, Jack reached out to touch the basketball-sized orb. It was hot, but not dangerously so; what surprised him was the thing's misleading solidity.

"Jack, don't," Karen warned him when he tried to capture it.

But as was so often the case with Jack, the warning came too late: no sooner had he taken hold of the sphere than it shot toward the ceiling, lifting Jack off the floor. Arms extended over his head, he rode it up for fifteen feet before letting go and landing on the other side of the cavern in a neat tuck-and-roll that blew out the miner's light.

"Yeah!" he whooped, as Kami helped him to his feet. It wasn't unlike the spill he had taken six months ago in Tiresia, but this time he had landed among friends.

Karen hauled off and whacked him in the arm. "Jack, can't you just—"

"That thing took off like a rocket! Almost pulled my arms out of the sockets."

"Yeah, we noticed, Jack," Karen said, miffed.

They were all staring at the ceiling now.

Jack watched the spheres bob against one another. "Almost seems like they're looking for a way out of here, doesn't it?"

"Yeah, just like we are," Karen and Lron said at the same time.

In the commo chamber of his hivelike domain on Optera, the Invid Regent received a transmission from the simulagent who was representing him on Tirol. It seemed that the so-called *Humans* now occupying the Robotech Masters' ravaged and forlorn moon had put on quite a show—with the kind of pomp and circumstance the Regent strived to imitate. He was almost sorry he hadn't gone there himself. What with most of his remaining fleet anchored in Fantomaspace, was there really anything to fear? he asked himself. Still, the fact remained that there were too many unanswered questions. What, after all, did the would-be commander of the Human forces—this Major General Edwards—want? He had been so quick to come to the Regent's aid in that matter of the Sentinels' ship . . . But it bothered the Regent that the Human had yet to ask for anything in return. Did he simply wish to capitalize on the Sentinels' defeat to move himself higher in the chain of command, or were these machinations part of some larger scheme?

In a certain sense the answer was unimportant, the Regent decided at last—providing he could make use of that factionalism that divided the Human forces.

He regarded the image in the communications sphere, catching a look in his double's eyes that troubled him. "Is there news of Tesla?"

"There is," the simulagent said. "It appears that Tesla was aboard the *Farrago* when our forces destroyed it."

Tesla, dead, the Regent thought. It touched him in a way he would never have believed possible. But perhaps it was not true, perhaps there were survivors of that battle? He had yet to hear from the follow-up forces who had been sent in to resecure the planet. "Who seems to be in charge?" he asked after a moment.

"As you surmised," the simulagent continued, "there are signs of an ongoing power struggle, principally between Edwards and a certain Dr. Lang—a scientist who did his best to charm me during the introductory sessions."

"Is Lang the weaker one, then?"

"No . . . no, this is not my belief. The scientist in fact seems to have the backing of the Humans' council—an assembly that functions as a kind of governing body."

The Regent found the idea odd—as he had the puzzling gerontocracy the Robotech Masters had favored. He couldn't understand how *twelve* minds could agree on anything, when he and his queen—merely *two* minds—had quarreled over every decision.

"Then, you must work on Edwards," the Regent said. "Promise your continued support to his petty struggle if it comes down to that. Tell him we'll join forces. But just make certain you learn the whereabouts of their homeworld and how they came to possess Protoculture. It may be that they know more than we do about Zor's matrix or the Masters' destination."

"Am I to make no demands of Edwards in return for our support, Your Highness? It hardly seems a wise move."

The Regent stared at the sphere's image in disbelief. Was this some evil mirror he was looking into now? "Just what would you have me demand?" he said, seething under the restraint he kept in his voice.

"The brain, to begin with. Along with their promise to keep out of the sectors we still control."

The Regent made a dismissive motion toward the sphere. "These things are obvious, servant. What else is on your mind?"

"Minmei," the simulagent said without explanation.

The Regent made an irritated sound and scowled. "What's a Minmei?"

"The Human female that sang for my benefit."

The Regent caught himself from staggering back from the sphere. He had only the vaguest understanding of this thing called singing, but the implication was clear enough: the simulagent was flawed in the same way that the Regis was. She had allowed herself to be seduced by Zor, and now this pathetic creature the Regent had sent to Tirol was falling victim to the same perverse urge! *Was there no end to these injustices!*

"Hear me, grub," the Regent growled, hood puffed up like a poisonous sac. "My reach is long enough to end your life where you stand. Do my bidding, or feel the power of my wrath."

The simulagent genuflected for the remote eye of the sphere. "My lord."

"Now and always," the Regent said, shutting down the device.

Rick had spent the better part of the Praxian day inside the GMU, brainstorming with Vince and Wolff about possible ways to contact the orbiting Spherisian drive module. Onboard computers had calculated the period of the module's eccentric course, and gone on to project just how much Sekiton fuel the thing contained, how far the module could be expected to fold, and just when its newly-attained orbit around Praxis might decay. But there were still no solutions to the big questions of how to reach the module or bring it down.

Rick left the base just before sunset, as had become his habit this past month, and joined the core group in their makeshift camp on the outskirts of the Praxian inland city. He wasn't fond of the scene, which reminded him more of a recreational campground than the billet it was supposed to be. Things were not just lax, but *loose*, as though everyone but him had grown to accept the situation. There was a logic to it, of course; it made no sense to walk around tied up in knots. But just the same, Rick had no patience with complacency, and he silently hoped that an idea would come to them one night while sitting around these campfires comparing cultural notes. So he stood in line with the rest of them now, Human and XT alike, and helped himself to the Praxian gruel the mess staff was cooking up to supplement the reconstituted meals and nutrient pills taken from the base's dwindling stores. Moreover, these sessions were the only waking hours he got to spend with Lisa—the *new* Lisa, that was, the liberated Lisa.

Where Gnea and Bela were still unforgiving of Miriya Sterling's Zentraedi past, they had embraced Lisa as though she were a long-lost member of the Sisterhood. At first Rick was not entirely unhappy about it, but all at once Lisa seemed a different person than the one who had argued so strongly against his joining the Sentinels to begin with. And while it was true that what was good for Lisa was good for the group, Rick couldn't help but feel a bit, well, *jealous* of the partnership Gnea and Lisa had formed. The Praxian seemed to draw this sort of reaction everywhere she stepped. Rick knew that Karen was having troubles with her, and he guessed that even Bela must be harboring some ambivalent feelings about her friend's sudden preoccupation with Lisa.

With Gnea it was martial skills that mattered most; but beyond speed and strength, Lisa had discovered something else: an independence and self-assertiveness that was taking some getting used to.

Rick had these thoughts in mind when she came over to sit beside him in the firelight, still flushed and exhilarated from her latest weapons training session. She talked about the *feel* of the halberd in her hands, the power of the *naginata*; she was practically poetic in describing Gnea's crossbow and two-handed shortsword. Rick took it all in, forcing a smile and offering all he could in the way of appropriate nods and utterances; but behind the smile his mind was doing backflips. *What next?* he asked himself. Would he come out here one evening to find her parading around in some skimpy fighting costume, like Bela's bossed and D-ringed body harness? Would she suddenly take to buccaneer boots, some totem-crested helm, long-bladed dirks and throwing knives? Rick shuddered at the thought, grateful for the fact that that damned Robosteed, Halidarre, was temporarily grounded. Unfortunately, however, the Praxian's lambent-eyed malthi, Hagane, was not, and the winged pest nearly parted Rick's hair as it came darting in just now to settle itself on Bela's bulky forearm sheath.

Rick muttered a curse and looked over at his wife. "Glad to hear how well it's going," he told her. "And I'm sure all this'll come in handy at the next Tirol decathlon."

She looked at him askance and took a forkful of food from his plate. "Something bothering you, Rick?"

"No, no, I mean, it's good to see you keeping busy, Lisa."

"Is that what you think I'm doing—'keeping busy'?"

Rick inclined his head, eyes narrowed. "It's what we're all doing, isn't it? What am I supposed to do: spit in my palm and pledge my fealty to someone? 'For the Eternal She and the glory of Haydon!' " Rick mimicked.

"Rick—"

"No, really. Maybe we should all be practicing swordplay and crossbow technique, leaps and high jumps. Then maybe one of us'll be able to reach that module instead of wasting away down here."

Almost everyone in the circle caught an earful of Rick's words, and the usual evening's chatter abruptly ceased. The fires crackled, and four Hovercycles could be heard approaching the perimeter. Lisa and Rick seemed to be locked in an eye-to-eye contest when Jack, Karen, Kami, and Lron entered the camp. Jack took a long look around, oblivious to the uncomfortable silence his swaggering entrance had dispersed, and announced cheerfully: "Wait'll you hear what we found."

"They've agreed to help us," Veidt said later on, hovering into the cavern where Rick and some of the other Sentinels were puzzling over the hideous cave paintings Karen had pointed out. "If 'agreed' is the proper word."

Karen noted that there were fewer globes than there had been that afternoon; several had apparently found their way out, as evidenced by the fact that one or two had been found bobbing against the ceiling close to the mouth of the cave.

"Then they are life-forms?" Rick said.

"Oh, most assuredly."

Rick heard Bela snort behind him. After Jack had told them of the find, the Praxian women claimed to have heard tales of these orb creatures from Arla-Non, chief of the Sisterhood. But the things were believed to be extinct, just as the beasts depicted on the cave wall were—or so Rick and the others hoped.

They had all tried to convince Rick that the orbs could wait until the morning, but he had insisted Jack lead them back to the caves immediately. Now, not quite four hours since Jack's return to the base, Rick and half a dozen or so of the core group were standing in the floodlit head of the cave, listening to the results of Veidt's telepathic probe.

"I register no sense of how they came to arrive here," the

mouthless Haydonite was mind-speaking, motioning to the cavern. "I only know that their destiny lies somewhere in space. This condition of . . . *levity* is but a transitional stage in their life-cycle. They are sentient, in what might be termed a primitive, or instinctual, fashion. But the important thing is that they seem to understand our need for their assistance—their *support*, if I may be permitted to play with your language some. In fact, Sarna and I detect a certain desperateness to their own flight—as if they are not merely obeying a behavioral directive, but are, in quite a real sense, escaping."

No one felt a need to state the obvious: Praxis was a tectonic nightmare from which they all wished to awaken. The heat and stench of the cave only reinforced that fact. And if the cave was indeed a volcanic vent of some sort, it was no wonder the globes were anxious to leave.

Cabell, his face and glabrous pate beaded with sweat, was watching one of the smaller creatures now, as it bobbed its way toward the entrance. He couldn't help but be reminded of Tiresia's antigrav spheres, and he began to question if there wasn't some mysterious connection here.

Rick was watching the same sphere; but he was wondering just how many it might take to lift an Alpha to the edge of the Praxian envelope. "Do they understand what we're asking of them?—the specifics, I mean."

Veidt hovered over to a position directly beneath a cluster of the creatures.

"The mecha should lift off on its own power," Sarna answered for him. "After that, Veidt and I will be able to herd the orbs into place."

Excited, Rick punched the palm of his hand. He swung around to Jack and Karen. "Contact the GMU. Tell Vince to round up the Skull and the Wolff Pack. We've got to work fast and assemble a crew for the module."

"Will we be heading back to base?" Karen thought to ask.

Rick shook his head. "Give Vince our position. Tell him what we've learned." He glanced up at the globes, rivulets of sweat running down into his eyes. "I want the base to come to us."

While members of the Sentinels hurried to break down the camp and ready the GMU for motion, Burak was breaking the news to Tesla. The Invid made him repeat it several times until satisfied he had all the details straight.

He had felt certain all along that he wasn't fated to end his days on Praxis, and now Burak had brought word that Hunter and the others had discovered a way to reach the orbiting drive module. With precious little time to spare, Tesla thought as he and Burak packed away the few belongings the Invid kept in his cell.

Ever since his earlier ingestion of the mutated fruits, his mind had been reeling, locked in a kind of revelatory state, where answers came to him full-blown, like short-lived explosions of light. He had been asking himself why the Regis had come to Praxis in the first place; it was a question that had been plaguing him on and off for months now.

It was before the mutiny aboard the *Farrago* that they had encountered one another, when Tesla had landed on Praxis to choose specimens for the Regent's zoo. The Regis had given him a vague explanation then, and it didn't occur to him until much later on to question her responses. With the continual quakes to spur him on, however, and the aid of the fruits, the answer became obvious: she had come here to conduct further Genesis Pit experiments—part of her grand scheme to transmute the Invid race into something Tesla himself could not yet begin to imagine. Optera had been the site of the first Pits, where Tesla and most of the other evolved Invid were birthed. But the Regis's experiment there had almost doomed the planet; it had, in fact, touched off the initial search for secondary worlds she might employ. Abandoning Optera and the Regent, she had finally come to Praxis to hollow out new Pits deep in the planetary core. And of course that was why she had left the place—because her experiment was following the same course it had taken on Optera.

Left. But for *where*? Tesla asked himself . . .

He put a hand on Burak's shoulder as they were about to leave the room. "You say they will be choosing a crew to pilot the first Alpha up to the module?"

Burak felt the strength of the Invid's grip, and tried to shake it off, but could not. "Are we going to die here, Tesla?" he asked in a faltering voice. "Peryton, my people—"

"Quiet, you fool!" Tesla stepped through the doorway, glancing around to assure himself that no one was within earshot, then swinging back around to Burak. "We won't die here—not if we're part of that crew, we won't."

Burak's face contorted. "But how—"

"You leave that to me. I just need to know one thing." Tesla sniffed at him. "Can you pilot that Spherisian module?"

"I suppose so," Burak said uncertainly.

Tesla stretched out his thick neck. "Then we're all set."

■■■■■■■■■■■■■■■■■■■■■■■■■■■

CHAPTER
THREE

In Admiral [Rick] Hunter's personal notes [recorded on Praxis], we learn of several discussions that took place between Cabell and Bela regarding the issue of child-bearing among the Praxians. (Hunter himself was nonplussed to hear Bela refer to Arla-Non as her "mother.") [Bela] even allowed Cabell to tour the whaashi—"birthing center," or creche—although refused to enter it herself. It was understood that certain members of the Sisterhood were preselected to receive female "offspring," who were then raised as "daughters of the Sun." The Praxians had little understanding of courtship, sexuality, or pregnancy; the "coupling rite" being a kind of catch-all mystery that was at the same time enticing and fearsome. Cabell, of course, was quick to see Haydon's hand at work.

A. Jow, *The Historical Haydon*

OF ALL THE WORLDS SHE HAD VISITED, THIS WAS THE SADdest, the Regis decided as she contemplated Haydon IV's cityscape from the uppermost tier of the Invid headquarters there. It was a small world, perfect in every respect, but with a heart as lifeless as the faceless beings who hovered across its surface and seemed to know one's every thought. The Regent liked to believe that he had conquered the place by cajoling his way into a position of absolute authority; but Haydon IV had seen many a would-be ruler come and go, while it itself remained unchanged, ungovernable, unreachable. It was one of the few open trading ports left since the Tirol-Optera war had spread like some contagion through the Quadrant; and as such Haydon IV enjoyed a semblance of peace. Still, the Regis sensed the presence of an incomprehensible evil here, far worse than the vulcanistic horrors her Genesis Pit experiments had unearthed on poor Praxis.

She had come to see for herself what the Invid scientists had found here, and now, as grateful as she was for the data they had supplied her, she could feel nothing but a kind of vague dread for

the future, for the very path she had embarked on. Haydon IV's
sophisticated scanners had picked up a trace of the Robotech Masters' course, and in effect pointed a way to Zor's ship with its ma-
trixed Flowers. But the Regis's private samplings of the planet's
vast store of metaphysical knowledge had revealed something of
potentially greater import—a suggestion that she had been as self-
deceived as the Regent had been. That her ostensibly *evolved*
nature—along with her continuing efforts to search out the physical form deemed most perfect to embody her intellect—was but
a carefully constructed delusion, self-generated and engineered to
keep her from the real truth. And yet it was a truth she refused to
contemplate, a mating she would not accept—one she was not at
any rate *prepared* to accept.

There would come a moment years hence when these truths
would dawn on her like the primordial fireball itself, and the Invid
Regis would willingly surrender the shackles of physicality and
ascend; but just now, she chose to keep Haydon IV's revelations
from her thoughts, and turn her attention to the Praxian woman
who had requested audience.

"This world is a paradise," the Regis said, turning from the
spire's incomparable view, but gesturing to it nevertheless. "I have
traveled the Quadrant over, and never have I known such an exquisite place."

Arla-Non flashed her a scornful look, and tossed back a luxuriant mane of sun-bleached hair. "Better a cave on Praxis than a
palace here," she sneered. "Every nerve in my body screams at
me to beware this place, this planet. Every breath of its wind car-
ries a lie."

She was tall and powerfully built, clothed in swaths of colorful
fabric and knee-high boots of soft hide. Looking at her, the Regis
couldn't help but be reminded of her own failed attempts to emulate that racial form, to please Zor . . .

"Is that fair?" the Invid Queen-Mother asked, an edge to her
voice as she approached the Praxian. "You knew nothing but
hardship, and now you have luxury beyond the dreams of most
beings."

"And you have Praxis," Arla-Non shot back.

The Regis made an impatient gesture. "You must learn to forget
Praxis, as *I* have Optera. Your world is doomed."

"So you continue to tell me. It is your way of decreeing that
Praxis had become nothing more than an Invid breeding ground."

"Praxis will breed nothing but asteroids!" the Regis seethed. "I
cannot change the past, Praxian. Make your peace with this world,
or live out your days in torment. I offer you no other choice."

Without a word, Arla-Non spun on her heel and headed for entrance to the spire's transport shaft; she stopped short of its triangular accessway. "I can choose to fight you to the last, Invid."

The Regis had her back turned, but the Praxian's words found their mark. She was beginning to understand why the Regent had never regarded persuasion as a viable option where force could be employed. The Regis made note of it, promising death for the next beings who attempted to thwart her.

Praxis, meanwhile, was beginning to come apart.

Forced by ground swells, fissures, and rock slides into taking the long way around, the GMU arrived at the caves precious hours behind its projected ETA. But with the region's numerous caves and shafts to vent the planet's internal pressure, the land here had been spared some of the tectonic turmoil afflicting other areas. Nevertheless, the air was filled with static charge, heat, and stench, and the cave that housed the orbs was fast becoming unworkable. The Skull had arrived hours earlier, and by the time Vince and Jean Grant, Janice, Rem, Wolff, Burak, and the others stepped from the mobile base, the rest of the core Sentinels were well into Rick's impromptu briefing. Several dozen orbs of varying size had already exited the cave, and were well on the way to their enigmatic deepspace destiny; but Veidt and Sarna had "persuaded" the stragglers to lag behind awhile longer. Kami and Learna had reported the emergence of yet more spheres from the cavern's internal chimney. Cabell speculated that it might be possible to widen the access some, and thereby increase the chances of additional creatures reaching the surface.

The plan called for the spheres to lift an Alpha with a crew of five clear through Praxis's suddenly albescent atmosphere. Once in space and under its own power, the mecha would complete the rendezvous with the drive module. When that was accomplished, the crew would drop the module into a lower orbit while the spheres continued to raise five-person crews. It was conceivable that the GMU would have to be abandoned, but at least the VTs and Hovertanks would survive. Although it sounded crazy the plan was straightforward enough; there remained, however, several variables to deal with. First, the Sentinels had no idea how many orbs might be required to lift a VT, or just how fast they would be able to raise it the requisite distance. An incorrect guess could leave the mecha hanging in space waiting for the module to complete another orbit, or, worse still, missing the thing altogether. Second, and equally problematic, the initial crew would have to be comprised of personnel capable of piloting the module into a lower orbit, and possibly—should the orbs for some reason withdraw their *support*—through a spacefold to Karbarra, or equidistant Fantoma. Third, someone was going to have to stay in touch with the orbs.

This last issue had been decided by the time the GMU contingent joined the others near the cave entrance. Sarna was going to be in charge of mustering and instructing the creatures in their task. Veidt had simply said, "Sarna will do it," and no one argued the point. Rick now had the module in mind.

Most of the XT aliens were out of the running for this slot, except Veidt—who was needed down below to mindlink with the spheres—and Lron. Rick had doubts that the burly Karbarran could successfully pilot the ship through a jump; and although the module was Spherisian in design, neither Teal nor Baldan were qualified to handle it. Vince was needed for the GMU. That left only Lisa, unless . . .

"Janice," Rick said suddenly, "can you handle it?"

Burak almost volunteered, but Tesla restrained him at the last moment, gesturing him silent while everyone's attention was focused on Minmei's former partner.

She nodded, without saying anything. If it came down to a fold for Tirol, Lang would be delighted to find her aboard. She sensed Lisa looking at her, and gave her a tight-lipped but understanding look.

"Lisa?" Rick said, figuring she would be safer with a crowd around him.

"I'm fine with your choice, Commander," she told him evenly. "But just who do you have in mind to pilot the Alpha?"

Rick looked around uncomfortably. "Well, I think I'm the most qual—"

Half-a-dozen voices interrupted him at once.

"It's too risky," Max said, speaking for all of them. "I'll go."

"Your place is with the Skull," Rick pointed out firmly, and everyone grumbled their agreement. Several of Max's squadron volunteered, including Miriya, but Rick rejected all of them for one reason or another. Then Jonathan Wolff stepped forward.

"I'm the logical choice," he said, addressing the circle. "With Vince and Max, we'll still have our air- and ground-based forces intact in the event of a follow-up attack. One less tanker isn't going to influence things one way or another."

Rick had to smile at Wolff's attempt at humility; but Wolff's reasoning was sound. "All right," he said at last, "you've got it."

Just then Tesla began to shoulder his way to the center of the circle. "Commander, I, too, would like to volunteer my services."

He turned to the Sentinels, some of whom were already ridiculing him.

"You've all seen how I can be *made* to cooperate. But now I wish nothing more than to demonstrate my *willingness* to cooperate. These four months have taught me a great deal about freedom and self-determination, and I would urge you all to begin to accept me as a member of your group, rather than a prisoner. Should the Regent's troops appear in Praxis-space, I will be there to foil them, much as I did in Tracialle."

Rick looked up at the Invid, remembering what Lisa had told him of the *Farrago*'s attack on the Karbarran city, and wondering whether Tesla was genuine or simply trying to save his own green skin. Rick asked him if he wasn't growing tired of his role—whether he had any reservations about betraying the Invid cause.

"It seems to be my lot in life," Tesla said in a theatrical manner. "Besides, I want this mission to succeed as much as the rest of you do."

Rick exhaled a short laugh. "We appreciate that, Tesla. But intentions aside, I think you might be too ... uh, *large* for the mecha."

"Too large!" Tesla said as though insulted. "Put me in the Beta's cargo section, then." He sucked in his breath, as if to narrow his bulk, and waited, making an effort to *will* the right words into the Human's mind.

"You think we can fit Burak and Tesla back there?" Rick asked Wolff hesitantly.

Wolff sized up the Invid and the horned Perytonian, who was looking a bit peaked. "Be a little tight, but I think we can manage them."

"Then let's hop to it," Rick said decisively.

Tesla and Burak lingered for a moment at the hub of the sudden activity. The Invid turned partway toward his accomplice and spoke in a hushed voice.

"Make certain you bring plenty of fruit aboard, my young friend. Destiny calls to us both."

On Tirol, too, things were off to a shaky start. During the first session of the truce negotiations, the Regent had thrown a kind of temper tantrum, which only Edwards recognized as being as false as the Invid himself. He had a perfect understanding of the imposter's aim, and so was hardly surprised to learn afterward that the XT had informed Dr. Lang and the council he would henceforth meet with Edwards only. The Regent had explained how difficult and *alien* it was for him to discuss terms with a *body* of representatives—especially when one of those twelve was a Zentraedi, with whom the Invid would never make peace. Once again Lang had tried to set himself up as ombudsman, and once again the Regent had rejected him out of hand. Edwards was the Human the Regent would talk to, and none other. Lang let the council know that he was against any one-to-one arrangements and insisted that his arguments be added to the record. But Edwards was delighted to hear that the council had overruled the scientist's objections and that Longchamps and the others were counting on him to see the talks through to their completion.

Just now the simulagent and the traitor were seated across from one another in Edwards's spacious quarters aboard the SDF-3. The two of them had already put on quite a show in the fortress amphitheater, but here they were safe from the prying eyes of the council and free to speak their minds. Edwards had decided to play it close to the bone, and congratulated the Invid on his performance.

"Why, whatever do you mean, General?" the false Regent said after a short silence.

There was just enough hesitation in the Invid's response to reassure Edwards that he was dealing with an imposter, but it benefited him to play along. "Your words for the council's scanners," Edwards told him. "All that talk about how there's more than enough room in the Quadrant for both our races."

"We are a reasonable people," the false Regent returned, sipping at the green grog he had brought with him.

"Yes, of course, you are. I'm encouraged by the very fact that you've come to Tirol. There are some who didn't believe you would."

"And you?"

"Oh, I think you're capable of almost anything, Your Highness."

The Invid set aside his goblet and looked across the desk at Edwards. "You speak boldly for one your size, Human. Are all those from your world so courageous?"

Edwards sat back in his chair and grinned. "To a man."

"And your weapons speak with equal power . . . But it intrigues me: how exactly did you come by your Protoculture systems?"

"We took them away from the Zentraedi," Edwards said, leaning forward on the desk. "They were annoying us."

The simulagent studied his four-fingered hands. "And you came here in search of their Masters?"

"We came here to finish the job, if you want the truth. Word had it that they were going to be showing up in our neighborhood, so we decided to take the fight to them instead. Save our planet the inconvenience of a backyard war."

"Yes, but you seemed to have missed them."

"We'll catch up." Edwards shrugged. "First we've got a little business here to take care of."

The Invid ignored the remark. "Just where is your 'neighborhood,' General?"

Edwards touched his faceplate. "A long way from Tirol."

"Yes, but where?"

"West of the Moon, east of the Sun."

"You trifle with me," the XT said menacingly.

Edwards shot to his feet and put both hands flat on the desk. "And you waste my time! What are you after?"

The Invid met his glare. "The return of the brain."

"In exchange for what?"

"Your lives," the Regent hissed.

Edwards laughed and walked away from the desk, only to whirl around and say, "You needed my help to eliminate a single Karbarran ship. And I know that your fleet is spread so thin you can hardly protect the worlds you've conquered. So what makes you think you can intimidate me now?"

The Regent, too, was on his feet, filling one half of the room. "I thought for a moment we were on the same side, General. But perhaps I was mistaken."

"You've already been more help to me than you know," Edwards told him. "But the brain stays until you've got something better to offer me than threats."

"Your egotism will be the death of you," the Regent said from the door.

Edwards smiled as the door slid shut. Everything he said had been calculated to draw out the real Regent; talk was useless until then. But he had faith that his gambit would pay off. Eventually the Regent would show himself—in person or as before in the sphere—and when that day came, there would be much to discuss.

Incredible as it seemed, the armored Alpha was actually being carried aloft by perhaps three dozen orbs of mixed size, clustered like grapes beneath the mecha's swept-back wings and Beta-elongated fuselage. Cheering seemed a bit premature, but that didn't stop any of the still-grounded Sentinels from sending up exclamations of encouragement.

The feat had required more orbs than anyone would have guessed—over a quarter of the number that remained in the cave, at last count—but Veidt, as promised, had been able to herd them under the hovering VT without much ado. Several of the creatures either didn't comprehend the Haydonite's telepathic instructions or thought better of them at the last moment and opted for solo flights into Praxis's cloudy and smoke-smudged skies. The others, however, rose quickly to the task, less like lighter-than-air balloons than anti-Galilean cannonballs. Cabell calculated that if the present rate of lift remained unchanged, the mecha would arrive at the Roche limit with ample time to rendezvous with the drive module. At that point, Sarna, copiloting the Alpha along with Jonathan Wolff, would bid the orbs what amounted to a "thanks and so long," and the VT would utilize its onboard computer and thrusters for guidance adjustments. Janice, Burak, and Tesla were squeezed together in the mecha's Beta hindquarters.

Rick threw a couple of enthusiastic shouts to the Alpha before rushing off to join Vince and some of the others, who were already in the GMU's command center monitoring the mecha's progress and supplying its telemetry systems with updates gleaned from the base's scanners and data mainframes.

Wolff was on the net when Rick entered the command center. "Everything checks out fine so far," he was telling Vince. "It's like an elevator ride to the stars." The net was relatively clear, except for occasional bursts of static.

"Ask him if Sarna anticipates any disengagement problems," Rick said to Vince.

"Uh, no problem," Wolff reported a moment later.

Rick leaned in to one of the console pickups. "And Janice?"

"Here, Rick. We're doing all right." Thumping noises could be heard in the background. "It's just a little close for comfort."

Rick made a mental note to tell Janice just how much he admired her. "Sit tight, Janice. You're almost there."

Wolff and Janice acknowledged and signed off. Rick found himself crossing his fingers, something he hadn't done in years. He laughed in a self-mocking way, optimistic but oddly disturbed at the same time.

Outside the base, members of the Skull Squadron and the Wolff Pack were beginning to prepare a second mecha for lift. This one was to include Lisa, Miriya, Cabell, Lron, and Crysta. The air was filled with lightning flashes and all-but-constant peals of thunder. Praxis trembled underfoot like the SDF-3 during fold maneuvers. Even Cabell refused to speculate on how much time the planet had, but to a few of the Sentinels each minute felt like something to be thankful for.

Kami and Learna had yet to emerge from the orb cavern deep

inside the region's now-floodlit central cave. The temperature had dropped considerably over the past half hour, and the air was breathable once more. Baldan and Teal had joined the Garudans to help keep count of the orbs, and with the first Alpha on its way, Jack, Karen, Rem, and Gnea appeared on the scene.

Everyone watched as two golf ball-sized spheres wafted up out of the shaft to join their brethren, who were grouped in various locations along the vaulted ceiling. A veritable parade of overhead orbs stretched from here all the way to the mouth of the cave. Jack directed his light down into the shaft and asked Karen and Gnea to do the same. He had discerned some sort of movement perhaps eight feet down the well; one of the larger creatures was struggling to fit through the constricted passageway. Each time the thing would back off, two or three smaller orbs would bubble up and out of the shaft. The Sentinels had discussed various ways to enlarge the opening, but Rick was leery of employing explosives or lasers for fear the orbs would misunderstand their intentions. Jack couldn't, however, see any harm in spelunking down for a closer look.

While Gnea and Rem went rushing back to the GMU for cord and anything they could find in the way of rigs and harnesses, Baldan and Teal were off in a corner of the cavern exploring a different route down. It had occurred to the male Spherisian—earlier, when he had melded his hand with the cave wall—that there were peculiar forces at work in the depths of Praxis, and Teal, her arms buried to the elbow in rock, was affirming that now.

"The mineral content is most unusual," she reported analytically. "Nothing like what we've experienced elsewhere on Praxis. It seems more a part of the planet's past than its present."

"I sensed the same thing," Baldan told her, gesturing to the cavern's outcroppings and formations. "These deposits have been exhumed from somewhere in the core, but in some unnatural fashion. They're not so much the result of the planet's vulcanism as they are the *cause* of it." Once again, Baldan pushed his arms deep into the wall. "Perhaps I can travel the Crystal Highways here as we do on Spheris, and communicate with the tortured substrata of this world."

"It's dangerous," Teal said, pulling one of Baldan's hands from the wall. "Praxis is destabilized. You might not be able to re-form . . ."

Baldan registered surprise at her concern for his well-being; it was unlike her. "Then keep hold of my hand," he said as he began to meld the rest of his crystalline being with the glistening rock that formed the cave wall. Teal could see a portion of the wall assume Baldan's features in bas-relief; he seemed to smile, then disappeared entirely.

"Good luck," she whispered, still grasping her friend's disembodied hand.

Elsewhere in the cavern, Rem, Gnea, and Karen heard Jack say, "There are thousands of globes down here! Enough to lift the whole damn base!" His voice rose from the shaft like that of an oracle. "They're huge ones! We've gotta give them a way out! Tell Hunter—"

Just then a violent tremor hit the cave, erasing Jack's words and eliciting a shower of rocks and dirt from the grotto's ceiling. The orbs began an excited dance when the tremor passed, hastening toward the entrance in what seemed an inverted ball-bearing stampede. Karen was leaning into the shaft yelling Jack's name.

"I'm okay," he yelled back at last. "Just took a spill off the rope. I'm on a ledge or something. Seems to be some kind of cavities down here . . . One of you better come down—and bring more light."

Teal had been knocked to her knees by the force of the quake, but she had managed to keep hold of Baldan's hand and forearm. She twisted around in time to see Kami and Learna picking themselves up off the floor. Then she saw Baldan's face manifest in the wall: he looked terrified.

"What? What is it, Baldan?"

His stone mouth formed the word *Invid*. "They've performed a horrible experiment here, brought back creatures from the planet's past—like these globes, but terrible ones also. You must hurry and warn the others. These creatures—"

"But you can't expect me to leave you here!" Teal was aghast.

"I'm trapped," he told her. "It's no use."

Teal tugged on his arm. "Don't—" Then she looked down and noticed a fissure in the wall that hadn't been there before the tremor.

"Baldan . . ."

"Hurry," he insisted.

Reluctantly, she let go of his arm. And as she turned to leave, she heard Karen scream from across the grotto.

"It's Jack and Rem!" a wide-eyed Karen was saying when Teal approached her. Kami, Learna, and Gnea were trying to calm her. "Something's taken hold of them!"

CHAPTER
FOUR

> [*The psychohistorian*] *Constance Wildman would have us believe that the Robotech Wars were nothing more than a series of incestuous struggles and Freudian-inspired rivalries—the Masters and their "children," the Zentraedi; the various intrigues that blossomed around "primal goddess" Lynn-Minmei; the Flower as grail, nutrient mother's milk . . . And she adduces the Regis-Tesla-Regent triangle to strengthen her case; for where else "do we find a more perfect archetypal representation of the rebellious son who wishes to kill the father and possess the mother?" To which one might be tempted to answer: in the relationship between Zor and Haydon.*
>
> Footnote in Reedy Kahhn's *Riders on the Storm: The Regent's Invid*

"**A**ND YOU ACTUALLY THREATENED EDWARDS?" THE Regent's voice screamed through the communicator. "You fool! You were supposed to entice him, not drive him further from my grasp."

In his quarters on the fleet flagship, the Invid simulagent gulped and found his voice. "I was only trying to get information out of him—as you yourself requested. But he wouldn't reveal anything about his homeworld. And worse still, he didn't seem to believe me when I spoke of the power of our empire."

The Regent made a sour expression. "Well, how could he, coming from the likes of you? Do you know nothing of subtlety? Have you forgotten all that the brain taught you about intelligence gathering? It's as though you've made up your mind to deal with the Humans in your own sloppy fashion, when your mission was to be my eyes and ears. *Not* my mouth!"

The simulagent winced, and turned to see if any of the soldiers were laughing behind his back. How could he begin to explain what he was going through—how the *feel* of power had worked its own magic on his mind, a magic that outweighed any concerns for diplomacy or "subtlety." But he kept these things tucked away from the being he was born to answer to, and instead thought to address the Regent as one might expect a servant to behave.

"I apologize, Your Highness. It's these Humans ... they confuse me."

"Yes," the Regent told him, softening his tone some, "I can understand that much. But I begin to wonder about this Edwards. It strikes me that perhaps he has seen through my ruse—no thanks to you."

The simulagent lowered his snout to the communicator remote. "Tell me how I can make amends. I am but your humble servant."

The Regent wagged a finger. "And it would profit you to keep that in mind." He showed the sphere the palms of his hands. "*Why* does everyone feel they can think for themselves? First my wife, now you ... Only Tesla served me well." He waved his hands in the air. "*Arg*, this whole affair is my fault anyway, sending a servant to do a conqueror's work." The Regent adjusted his robes. "I want you to return to Optera. There's nothing more you can do on Tirol, and if I permit you to stay any longer, it's likely you'll *undo* something."

"But, Your High—"

"Don't argue with me! We can do without the captured brain a while longer, and there are other ways to extract the information we want about the Masters, the Matrix, and the Humans' homeworld. Better to let the situation on Tirol deteriorate of its own accord. Then Edwards and I will talk." The Regent's eyes stared out from the sphere, gazing coldly at his simulagent. "You may have my looks"—he sighed—"but you certainly lack my talents."

Rick slammed his hand down on the console-mike stud and shouted Wolff's call sign into the pickup. One minute Jonathan had been reporting that all signals were go for disengagement, and the next thing anyone knew he was saying something about the Beta having separated from the VT. And now the GMU seemed to have lost contact with both components.

"Rising Star, come in," Rick urged. "Wolff! Respond. What's going on up there?" He swung around to Jean and Vince, who were busy at adjacent consoles. "Anything?"

Jean swiveled to face him. "Too much cloud cover for a visual on the Beta, but scanners show it on an accelerated course for the drive module. The Alpha's way off the mark. We should have some data soon."

"Was it the globes?"

"Can't tell, Rick," Vince said without turning around.

Just then Wolff's voice crackled into life through the room's speakers. "—actly sure what happened. Sarna was just passing along instructions to the orbs, then all of a sudden the Beta broke away. We're way off course. Can you give us a new heading?"

"Coming up," Rick answered him. "Do you have any traffic from Janice?"

"Negative, Rick. I can't even get a fix on the ship."

"She's closing on the module, Jonathan," Vince said. "Any guesses?"

"Not right now."

Rick was about to add something when the hatch hissed open. "We've got troubles, sir," a Skull pilot announced.

"We're aware of it," Rick said, more harshly than was necessary.

The captain took a puzzled look around. "No, sir, in the caves. We're under attack."

"Attack? From what?" Rick noticed for the first time that the woman was covered with dirt. Her face was smeared with some unidentifiable black fluid or grease.

"Uh," the pilot stammered, "you're going to have to decide for yourself, sir."

Rick and the pilot left the base at a run. Outside, Rick saw scores of orbs streaming from the mouth of the cave. Veidt and a handful of Praxians and mecha pilots were doing their best to calm the creatures, but Max and Miriya, along with half the Wolff Pack, were nowhere in sight.

"In here, sir!" the pilot was shouting, motioning to the cavernous entrance.

The floor of the cave was shaking, and Rick heard low rumbling sounds he initially attributed to tectonic tremors; then he realized that he was hearing explosions. These grew more concussive as he neared the grotto.

The place was in a state of near pandemonium, dozens of orbs bobbing along, underlit by intense flashes of explosive light that was pouring out from holes and shafts in the floor; strident voices raised above the clatter of weapon fire; and something else—a kind of shrill, clacking noise, as eerie as it was loud.

Rick glanced around, trying to make sense of things. Karen Penn was off in a corner, terrified, although Kami and Learna were by her side. Teal stood some distance from them, alone near what looked to be a limb of rock. Gnea and Bela were carrying coiled lengths of cord toward a shaft opening; close by were a couple of Perytonians and a few men from Wolff's team, donning gas masks and strapping on web-gear ammo packs.

Without warning someone thrust a Wolverine into his hands.

"Max!" Rick said, whirling around. "What's—"

"Cover up," Max cut him off. He tossed Rick a mask and trotted off toward the shaft, cradling an Owens Mark IX mob gun. "Jack and Rem are trapped down there," he called over his shoulder. "We've killed a bunch of them already, but they just keep coming!"

"Killed a bunch of what? Who keeps coming?"

At the opening, Max pulled down his respirator and hooked on to one of the cords that had been lowered into the shaft. "Ready?" he shouted above the din from down below. Breathless, Rick followed his lead, and the two of them took to the rigs.

A moment later, on the floor of an enormous sublevel room, Rick was certain they had overshot their mark and landed in hell. In the strobing light he could see they were standing on the rim of a massive well that seemed to drop straight down to the planet's molten core. Here, too, the ceiling was covered with orbs—most of them of greater size than any he had seen on the surface; but it was the creatures crawling up out of that well that had left him speechless. They might have been Hovertank-size spiders, except for their eyestalks, double-tiered segmented bodies, and front-facing mouths. And if they weren't the devil's own creation, Rick decided, then he didn't ever want to meet their maker. For no god could have loved so hideous and evil looking a beast.

It thrilled him to realize that the black stickiness coating the cavern's floor was blood from these things, but even that was not enough to wash the fear out of him. He remembered reading somewhere that there was an actual endogenous terror hormone certain creatures gave rise to in the human body; and indeed he seemed to *remember* them in some primal corner of his mind. But then he suddenly recalled where he had actually seen them: they were the creatures an ancient and unknown Praxian hand had depicted on the cave's walls!

Tesla was amazed by the Human female's strength. He had finally succeeded in dragging her backward into the Beta's cargo space and now had both of Janice's seemingly frail wrists firmly clasped in his own hands, but it had been a struggle all the way. Burak, meanwhile, had slid forward into the cockpit seat to handle the controls. The drive module was looming into view through the VT's canopy, right on schedule, and theirs for the taking.

"Welcome to our crew," Tesla was saying to the still-untamed female. "Glad to have you aboard." Jonathan Wolff's urgent voice could be heard over the open net.

Janice twisted around, almost breaking free of his hold, and glared at him. "Is this any way to treat a guest?"

"If I let you free, will you promise to behave?"

Janice gave her head a defiant toss. "Try me."

Tesla eased his grip, and the android everyone thought a woman lunged for Burak's neck. Tesla pinioned her arms and threw her roughly against the aft bulkhead; he was pleased to see some of the fight go out of her.

"Burak," Janice said weakly, one hand to her head. "What's your part in this? I can't believe you'd leave your friends to die back there."

Burak showed her his profile, velvety horns and heavily boned brows accented amber in the display lights. "It's the only way I can help free my planet," he offered. "You can't understand—"

"Enough of this," Tesla interrupted, taking stock of the wounds Janice's fingernails had opened on his arms. "Pay attention to what you're doing. And shut down the comm," he added, gesturing to the net switch.

The crystalline-shaped Spherisian module filled their view now, eclipsing the stars. Burak matched the Beta's course to the module's seemingly slow-motion end-over-end roll, and began to maneuver the mecha along the drive's scorched and much-abused hull. He utilized the onboard computer to communicate with the module's own, and within minutes the docking-bay hatch was opened; the Beta was home free.

When the bay had repressurized, the trio climbed from the Beta cockpit and eventually found their way to the bridge. Tesla carried Janice the entire way, bear-hugged to his huge chest like some sort of stuffed toy he couldn't live without. Burak lugged along the mutated fruits he had smuggled aboard the VT before liftoff.

The Invid was feeling omnipotent—not only because he had so easily outwitted the Sentinels, but because he would soon be on his way to Optera for the face-to-face encounter with the Regent he had so often envisioned these past periods. The fruits from Karbarra and Praxis had, so he believed, rendered him superior to the monarch he had once served as soldier and would-be son. And now it was time for the Regent to step aside and grant him his due position as leader of the Invid race. Tesla had come to understand that it took more than mere strength to lead; it took insight and vision, and these gifts were his in abundance.

But as they arrived at the drive's control room, some very real problems presented themselves, eroding Tesla's fantasies and summoning an anger from his depths.

"But you told me you could astrogate this ship!"

With a gesture of helplessness, Burak turned from the starmaps and spacefold charts he had called up on the Spherisian guidance monitors. "I thought I could, but now . . ."

Tesla stormed over to him and began to scan the screens, puzzling over the datascrolls. He pointed a thick finger at one of them. "Here. Here is Optera."

Burak's eyes opened wide. "Optera! But Tesla—Peryton, we're going to Peryton."

Tesla pushed him aside. "In due time," he said absently. "First there is something I must attend to."

Burak steeled himself. "Then attend to it without my help."

Tesla made a violent motion with his hands, but checked himself short of the Perytonian's neck, taking him instead by the shoulders, fraternally. "Of course, my dear. To Peryton, then." Tesla's hands urged Burak down into one of the acceleration seats. "Now, why don't we try to figure this out together, step by step. Let's just say for example's sake that we *did* want to fold for Opteraspace . . . Now, how would we do that, my friend . . . ?"

Janice took in the exchange from across the room. The two mutineers had all but forgotten about her, so it was easy enough to jack into the drive's systems while their attention was focused elsewhere. In a short time she had completed her bit of cybernetic magic. No matter what they fed into the ship's astrogational computers now, the module was locked on course for the Fantoma space system.

Janice smiled to herself, wondering how Tesla would take to surprises.

At first it was believed that Baker and Rem had been captured or eaten by the bristly eight-legged crawling nightmares delivered up from the Praxian netherworld; but subsequently the Sentinels found that their two teammates were simply being *detained*—the word someone from the Wolff Pack had used. Jack and Rem had been probed and manhandled, but apparently were safe. It seemed that the arachnids—Gnea and Bela had a name for them no one could pronounce—had no taste for meat. Moreover, the creatures weren't on a feeding frenzy at all—nor, for that matter, were they interested in counterattacking the beings who were busy lancing them with lasers and rockets. Like the orbs, these living anachronisms—unseen on Praxis for millennia—were attempting to flee the storms that burned at the planet's transformed core.

Rick was long past his initial fright, but the sour taste of fear remained in his mouth. It struck him as odd that while in his day he had fought fifty-foot giants and walking slugs, ridden into battle alongside humanoid clones, ursine warriors, and amazons on Robotsteeds, he could experience such utter terror at the sight of giant spiders. Maybe, he had decided, it was the very mindlessness of the creatures; after all, even the Invid weren't *monsters*, were they? The Praxian women had been equally frightened, and Rick tried to imagine what it might be like to go up against, say, *dinosaurs*.

But if the creatures hadn't actually added to the Sentinels' plight, they had done nothing to improve things. Countless orbs had exited the cave, and now there was a nasty bit of mopping up to do down below while the rest of the orbs were mustered for further lift assists. To make matters worse, there was still no word from the Beta, and one of the Spherisians had gone and gotten himself *stuck in a rock*!

Presently, Rick and some of the others were grouped around Teal and the hand that had once belonged to her friend. Baldan was merged with the wall—the way a Mesoamerican bas-relief could be said to be merged to a stela. His profile was frozen but plainly visible, and there was a crystalline mass protruding from the section of rock where his chest might have been. The crystal grew before the astonished eyes of the assembled group.

"No, you can't, Baldan—please stop this!" Teal was shouting to the wall. She swung around to Rick. "He is attempting to transfer his essence. But this has never been achieved on any world but Spheris." She looked back at the engorged growth. "And I don't want to raise it!"

Again the crystal enlarged. Teal put her hands to her head in a panicked gesture and pleaded with Baldan to stop. But ultimately her hands reached for the faceted thing and she began to tug at it.

"It's no use, Baldan," she cried. "It will die!"

Rick moved in to give her a hand, and with some effort the two of them managed to pull the crystal loose. The hollow *pop!* sent a shudder up Rick's back. Baldan's profile receded into the wall and vanished. Teal dropped the crystal from her trembling hands and regarded it.

"The child is lifeless . . . dead." She looked around at the others. "Baldan is lost to us."

Whimpering sounds found their way out from under Kami and Learna's breathing tubes. Rick took Teal by the shoulders. "What did he tell you?"

She stared at him blankly for a moment, then said, "The Invid. They must have been using Praxis for experiments of some sort. It was the chambers they hollowed out that gave birth to those creatures. And these same chambers have ushered in this world's demise."

"But what kind of experiments?" Rick demanded. "What were they trying to create?"

Teal shook her head.

Tight-lipped, Rick released her and motioned a radioman over to him. "Any word from the Beta?" he asked Vince when the GMU link was established.

"They've reached the module," Vince updated. "But we're not getting through to them."

Rick summarized what had gone down in the caverns. "I want to speak with Tesla as soon as they call in. He must know something about all this—these *pits*. Maybe there's a way to reverse it?"

"Unlikely," Vince responded. "But I'm sure Tesla will tell us what he knows. He's practically one of us now."

With a little help from the GMU's computers, the Alpha was back on course. Wolff and his Haydonite copilot were at a loss to explain the unexpected separation, but they assumed Janice had done so with some good purpose in mind, and that her radio silence was nothing more than a glitch in the system. It didn't occur to either of them that there was a conspiracy afoot.

Wolff continued in this hopeful vein, even after he had learned that the Beta had apparently made a successful docking with the drive module. That singed piece of orbiting space debris was above him now, and he was getting all he could from the Alpha to make up for lost time. It was only when his radio requests for docking coordinates were ignored that he began to suspect foul play. The hunch became full-fledged concern when he couldn't get the Alpha's onboard systems to interface with the module. Consequently, the docking-bay shields remained closed, and unless something could be done to open them, the Alpha was going to wind up dead in space.

Even if that meant going extravehicular.

Sarna took over the controls while Wolff suited up. Praxis turned below them like a cataracted eye. The telepath strapped in, bringing the Alpha as close as she could to the module's scarred hull; then Wolff blew the canopy. He floated up and out of the VT on a tether line, took hold of the side of the pinwheeling ship, and tried to center his attention on the alien external control panel. Sarna spoke to him through the helmet relays, avoiding the net in favor of frequencies of a cerebral sort. Wolff heard her thoughts as spoken words as he fumbled with Spherian switches designed for hands more sensitive than his own.

But a short while later the hatch was sliding open and pocketing itself in the crystalline hull. Sarna engaged the Alpha's attitude jets and began to maneuver the ship to safety.

The Beta was inside, empty; and fortunately, Wolff decided, there was no welcoming party there to greet them. Down on the hold floor now he armed himself with a rifle and two handguns; Sarna had perfect recall of the module's corridor and compartment layout, so she led the way. They were barely out of the docking area when the ship lurched.

"We're leaving orbit," Sarna told him.

Wolff felt the rumble of the module's drives ladder its way up his legs. Sarna hovered along the corridor at an increased pace, then abruptly right-angled herself into a large cabinspace and told Wolff to strap himself into one of the seats.

Wolff regarded the acceleration couch and threw her a questioning look.

"We're preparing to fold," she told him.

"They've *what*!"

"They folded," Vince Grant repeated. "The module's gone."

Rick leaned against one of the GMU command-center consoles to catch his breath. He had run all the way from the cave only to hear the bad news as soon as he came through the hatch.

"But, but, did they—"

"Not one word," Jean cut in. "The last message we had was from Wolff. He was sure something had happened to Janice."

"Tesla," Rick said, biting out the name.

Vince nodded. "That's my guess."

"But where's the Alpha now?" Rick added, looking back and forth between the two of them.

Jean pushed herself back from the console, her hands on the arms of the chair. "That's the weird part. The Alpha made it aboard."

Rick fell silent; it felt for a moment as though they were speaking to him in a foreign tongue. He shook his head, hoping everything would settle into some sort of order. "Maybe it wasn't Tesla. Maybe Janice knows something we don't . . ."

"Okay," Vince said.

"And maybe she managed to get word to Wolff, but he couldn't reach us . . ."

"Okay, again."

"And maybe they *had* to fold because they realized there was no way to get everyone offworld using the VTs . . ."

"Uh huh." Vince folded his arms. "So they take off for Karbarra or Tirol, figuring we'll be able to wait it out."

Rick left it unanswered. There was no need, anyway, now that the tremors had recommenced. A steady, thunderous roar filtered into the room; somewhere nearby, mountain ranges were beginning to crumble.

It was a short jump. Wolff could feel himself coming out of the fold's dizzying effects, and was on his feet even before Sarna had furnished him with an all-clear sign.

When the two of them burst onto the module's bridge, they found Tesla and Burak seated at the controls. Janice was off to one side, asleep, Wolff thought.

Tesla and Burak both swung around as they heard the hiss of the hatch. The Invid's snout dropped open when he saw Wolff standing there armed to the teeth, and he immediately fell backward against his coconspirator, hoping Wolff would read it as Burak attempting a capture.

The two XTs rolled across one of the console benches and down onto the floor. Taken completely off guard, Burak didn't know what had hit him. But Tesla was forcing himself into a subordinate position now, and ordering Burak to grab him by the neck.

"Fight, you idiot!" Tesla was whispering. "You've got to make them believe you had nothing to do with this!"

Burak finally got the message and threw his hands around the Invid's thick neck. The two of them butted heads and snarled and cursed at each other. Burak was working his thumbs up Tesla's snout by the time Wolff succeeded in pulling him away.

"Back off!" Wolff told him, brandishing one of the handguns. "Tesla, on your feet!"

Sarna hovered over to the com.

The Invid raised his hands, but remained on his knees, pleading with Wolff not to kill him, and confessing to his attempt to seize the ship.

"And if it wasn't for this horned fiend I'd have—"

"Cut the crap," Wolff said. He turned around to Burak, who was trying his best to look innocent, even heroic. "You threw in with this slug."

"I didn't!" Burak argued. "He put a spell on us!"

"A spell?" Wolff almost laughed. "You mean he *made* you do it?"

Burak pointed to Janice. "Ask her if you don't believe me."

Janice had reactivated herself. She looked at Wolff and said, "They were in it together—"

"Liar!" Burak yelled.

"—but they couldn't seem to agree on a destination. So I made the decision for them."

Tesla and Burak traded looks.

"Where are we?" Wolff said, as confused as anyone else.

"Fantoma," Janice said, and Tesla fainted.

■ ■ ■ ■ ■ ■ ■ ■ ■ ■ ■ ■ ■ ■ ■ ■ ■ ■ ■ ■

CHAPTER
FIVE

> *Betray (I looked it up): to deliver to an enemy by treachery or dis-*
> *loyalty; to be unfaithful in; to seduce and desert . . . Is this what I'm*
> *guilty of? Have I seduced and deserted him? Am I delivering Jonathan*
> *over to an enemy? Have I been unfaithful? As I repeat the word over*
> *and over to myself, it begins to lose all meaning; it becomes a mean-*
> *ingless sound, a bit of Tiresian or Praxian babble. But then I begin to*
> *think of it as a kind of war cry, a sound that echoes back and forth*
> *across the terrain of my life and these twenty years of bloodshed. If I*
> *am a betrayer, I am also the betrayed. I am the SDFs-1,2, and 3; I am*
> *all the councils and all the generals. I am the dead, the War itself.*

An excerpt from the journal of Lynn-Minmei

WITH RICK AND LISA AND ALL THE OTHER MEN AND women who had joined the Sentinels' cause missing and presumed dead, there were precious few people Dr. Lang could trust, let alone seek out for company or old-fashioned good counsel. Things had not been the same between Lang and Harry Penn since Karen left, and of the Plenipotentiary members, only Justine Huxley and Niles Obstat were still receptive. Edwards had influenced the rest to one degree or another, except of course for Exedore, who had become Lang's unofficial ally and close friend. Even Lynn-Minmei had been turned—by what, Lang wouldn't even try to imagine. Lang, however, was well accustomed to isolation; so even when it wasn't self-imposed he could get by. He had been managing to hold his own with the council, in spite of Edwards, and at the same time was overseeing both the mining operations on Fantoma and the repairs to the SDF-3. But the Regent's visit had introduced something new and threatening to the horizon: the possibility of a partnership between Edwards and the Invid. Lang had seen Protoculture shape stranger events these past twenty years, but none so potentially dangerous—to the Expeditionary mission, to Tirol, to the Earth itself.

Something within him refused to accept Hunter's death; he knew he wasn't standing alone here, but he had nevertheless been powerless thus far in persuading the council to launch a rescue ship—even now when there were several available with the capability for the required spacefold, some running on Sekiton, some on the recently mined monopole fuels. But it was the Regent's behavior at the introductory summit sessions that finally convinced him to take matters into his own hands. And it was that decision that brought him to Fantoma. He had allowed his godson and apprentice, Scott Bernard, to accompany him, but left Exedore behind on the fortress to safeguard their mutual interests while the Regent's fleet remained anchored in Fantomaspace. The crew of the newly christened prototype dreadnought he had commandeered was one that had been handpicked for the journey after a bit of chicanery by himself and General Reinhardt; they were a capable and loyal lot, commanded by Major John Carpenter, who was being considered as a candidate to head up the first return mission to Earth.

Lang's reasons for choosing Fantoma could be summed up in one word: *Breetai*. He was aware of the hostilities that had cropped up between Breetai and Edwards over the issue of the Regent's arrival, and he knew precisely where the Zentraedi's loyalties lay. And where Breetai went, so followed his hundred-strong cadre of sixty-foot biogenetically-engineered warriors—a force to be reckoned with no matter what the council's ultimate decisions might be.

No sooner did Lang step from the shuttle that had ferried his party to the surface of the ringed giant than Breetai insisted on escorting him through a tour of the mining complex. It was obvious that the Zentraedi was taking some pride in his accomplishments, so Lang didn't offer any resistance. But the opportunity to discuss the pressing issues that had brought him here didn't present itself until much later on, and by then Lang was nearly feverish. Breetai had led them to a massive Quonset-style structure that served as the colony's command and control center—the only such building in New Zarkopolis designed to accommodate both giants and Humans in relative comfort. There, Lang reviewed what had been said during the so-called truce talks, and what *reported* statements had been exchanged between Edwards and the Regent during the subsequent one-on-one sessions. Breetai said little, preferring instead to listen or grunt an occasional exclamation of anger or surprise. But when Lang finished—with an audible sigh—the Zentraedi collapsed his steepled fingers and leaned forward in his chair, gazing intently into the Humans' balcony area.

"One part of me wants to blame Admiral Hunter for allowing things to come to this," he told Lang. "But if anyone can appreciate the unpredictable nature of these things, I can." Lang didn't have to be reminded of the bizarre reversals the Zentraedi commander had witnessed and suffered through; and in this the scientist and warrior were brothers of a sort. "I suggest we take steps to secure our position against Edwards."

"Yes, but how?" Lang asked.

"Just as you have begun," Breetai said, motioning to where Carpenter and his exec were seated. "And you must arrange for additional mecha to be sent here . . ."

"Disguised as mining devices perhaps."

"Exactly. We have our own ship, our own mecha, but we must have our own weapons. New Zarkopolis could become our base of operation. And of course we possess something even more important than firepower . . ."

"The ore," Lang completed.

Breetai nodded. He had his mouth opened to say something more when a Human at the comm console interrupted him. "Report from the fortress," the tech announced, straining to hear the communiqué. "A ship has entered the system. Colonel Wolff and some of the Sentinels are said to be aboard."

"Thank God," Lang said, throwing his head back.

Breetai wore an enigmatic look. He touched his faceplate in an absent manner and rose from the chair to tower over the "Micronian" balcony.

"The Protoculture is at work again. We call out and it answers."

"Yes," Lang directed up to him. "And would that we could always predict its response."

Word of the drive module's approach spread to all stations and was relayed down to Tirol's surface. In her canteen in Tiresia, Minmei swooned upon receiving the news. She had returned to the surface only hours before, and now she tried to collect her thoughts before hastening back to the city's shuttle staging area.

At the same time in his quarters aboard the SDF-3, T. R. Edwards was in the midst of a session with the false Regent.

"It seems you were a bit premature in reporting the destruction of the *Farrago*," he said with a malevolent grin. Even the Invid's black, unreadable eyes failed to conceal a sense of shock; but the simulagent quickly rallied.

"And perhaps the data you supplied was in error," he countered angrily.

The Invid imposter had taken it upon himself to have one more go at winning Edwards over, despite the Regent's orders to the contrary. He had given careful thought to the Regent's harsh criticisms and was convinced that a follow-up discussion was in order. He now thought he had a clear understanding of the concept of sublety; but like Tesla he was not big on surprises, and the sudden appearance of the Spherisian module had completely undermined his efforts.

Edwards was waving a forefinger at him. "There, there, Your Highness, no call for insults, is there? Just when we were getting along so *famously*." Then Edwards's face grew serious, his one eye cold. "Besides, it's just a couple of our people and one of yours. There were bound to be survivors."

"One of mine?" the simulagent asked, alarmed.

"Tesla—isn't that his name? Or didn't you know he was aboard?"

The Invid curled one of his sensors. "You failed to mention that."

Edwards shrugged. "What's the difference? He's alive." *And so is Wolff*, Edwards thought. He glanced across the desk at the Invid, beginning to tire of the game. Would this Tesla be able to confirm his suspicions? he wondered, making a note to have the returnees monitored at all times. "Now, what was it you were saying before?"

The simulagent tore himself from concerns about the possible consequences of encountering Tesla. "I—I was about to make you an offer, I think."

Edwards waited for him to continue, then laughed. "Well, go ahead—let's lay our cards on the table."

The simulagent held up a hand. "Three planets—yours for the choosing. Free access to all the other worlds I control—a limited partnership—and last, my help in realizing your, *dreams*, shall we say."

Edwards felt his jaw. "In exchange for the brain . . ."

"And Tesla . . ."

"And Tesla."

"And one thing more."

Edwards's brow went up.

"I want Minmei."

Wolff and company stepped out of the module and onto the deck of the SDF-3 docking bay to the sound of cheers—a few, at any rate, from a section led on by Emil Lang, Lord Exedore, and several staff officers. And it was Lang who clasped Wolff's hand and wrist, as if he had never been so happy to see someone. Behind him, Janice was getting the same treatment; Sarna, Burak, and Tesla were all but ignored.

"What the hell's going on?" Wolff asked the scientist straightaway. "You've got half the Invid fleet out there!"

"There's much to discuss," Lang shouted as press and officers jostled one another to get close. "But tell me—the others—Rick and Lisa—"

"They're alive," Wolff returned, buffeted about by the crowd. "But they won't be much longer if we don't get a rescue ship to Praxis."

Lang frowned. "Well, we have to see about that."

"What do you mean, 'see about that'?" Wolff gestured back to the module. "We didn't have enough fuel to jump back, but Praxis—"

"Things have changed," Lang told him, just loud enough to be heard. "We have to talk."

Wolff felt something acidic wash through him. All the while he had been answering Lang's questions, his eyes had been darting around the hold, searching for some sign of Minmei. Now, after seeing a hundred Invid ships anchored in Fantomaspace, and with Lang's portentous whisperings in his ear, he found her, and the sight only served to double his dread. She was standing alongside Edwards, among that unresponsive group, offering him a weak and pathetic smile.

"Come, Colonel," Lang was saying, one hand at Wolff's elbow, "we must hurry."

Wolff pulled away and craned his neck to catch another sight of Minmei; but Edwards's contingent was already leaving the bay, and she was lost in the crowd.

"Listen, Lang, I need a minute," Wolff said, up on his toes now.

Lang turned around to track Wolff's gaze, then he took hold of him more firmly, more urgently. "The council is ready to hear you. Everything hinges on this."

"Look, I just wanted to—"

"I know. I understand," Lang added after a moment. "But things have changed, man. Aren't you listening to me? Think about your friends."

Wolff started to say something rash, but checked himself, slicking back his hair in a gesture of exhaustion. "I'm sorry, Lang." He turned and motioned Janice and Sarna forward, then pointed to Burak and Tesla. "I want these two placed in lockup." Peripherally, Wolff caught Lang's look. "I'll explain," he told him.

As everyone began to move off, Lang mentioned that the Regent had come to Tirol of his own volition; that he was in fact on the fortress at that very moment.

Wolff made a surprised sound—but not half the one Tesla uttered at overhearing the statement. Wolff was too wrapped up in Lang's subsequent remarks to hear it, however; but had he turned, he would have seen the look of near rapture on the Invid's suffused face.

The Plenipotentiary Council convened in extraordinary session to listen to Colonel Wolff's report and hear out his requests. Because both Janice and Sarna were "civilians" according to the council's guidelines, Wolff had to face the twelve alone. The session was held in the council's private chambers aboard the fortress, with the usual secretaries and officials in attendance. Representing the RDF were Generals Reinhardt and Edwards. Wolff had yet to learn about Edwards's relationship with Minmei, but he loathed the man nonetheless. Lang had instructed Wolff before the session convened to meet with him afterward in the scientist's quarters. "No matter what the outcome," Lang had said. And those words were repeating themselves now as Wolff stood before the council recapping the events of the past four months.

". . . But it appears that the Praxians abandoned their world for good reason," Wolff was concluding a short time later. "Praxis is unstable. Admiral Hunter—"

"I would caution Mr. Wolff from using any honorifics," one of the council members said. "The council no longer recognizes you as members of the Robotech Defense Force."

"Some of the council," Niles Obstat objected.

"*Most* of us."

Wolff scowled at the woman. "Then why aren't Janice and Sarna here, if we're all civilians?"

"Mr. Wolff," Senator Longchamps cut in, "we are just trying to set things straight for the record. You and the Hunters, Sterlings, and Grants are understood to be a part of the Expeditionary mission. The extraterrestrial Sentinels are another matter. And as for Ms. Em, she has never been affiliated with the RDF—or the mission, for that matter, if I'm not putting too fine a point on it."

Wolff fought down an explosive urge to tear the man's throat out. "I apologize to the council if I may seem *impatient*," he continued more calmly, "but the fact is that our *friends* are out there, marooned on a planet that for all I know is just a memory by now! All I'm asking you for is *one* ship with a skeleton crew."

"To do what, Mr. Wolff?" Thurgood Stinson asked. "To rescue

your friends, to be sure. But what then—continue on your campaign, or return to Tirol?"

Wolff tightened his lips. "I don't think I'm qualified to answer that, Senator."

"And we're not certain we can spare a ship just now, Mr. Wolff."

Justine Huxley broke the uncomfortable silence. "I think we're missing the point here." She motioned to Wolff. "*Friends*, is the term the colonel used. I ask you all to disregard for a moment the events of the past four months, and recall our first meeting with the Sentinels, especially the pledges that were exchanged then."

As the council members grumbled agreement in their individual fashions, Wolff caught Exedore and Lang sending hopeful looks in his direction.

Then Edwards got to his feet to address the twelve.

"I'd be the first to admit that the Sentinels are both our friends and allies," he began, "but there's an important issue here that's being neglected—the Invid. The Regent's position is very clear: any assistance we render will be considered a further act of war. And he makes no distinction between Humans and XTs in this matter."

Wolff's heart sank.

Edwards waited for the room to quiet. "I don't think it's necessary for me to remind the council of the presence of the Invid fleet. I'm not saying that if it came right down to mixing it up with them we couldn't come out on top, but the results of an engagement in any case would have disastrous effects on our long-range goal—to repair our ship and return to Earth. I'm sure General Reinhardt and Admiral Forsythe concur in this matter."

Reluctantly, Reinhardt inclined his head, averting Wolff's gaze. Edwards, however, was regarding Wolff.

"The timing couldn't be worse, Wolff. I'm sorry. Perhaps if we wait until the truce is signed—say, six months or so—"

"They don't have six months!" Wolff shouted. He looked to the council. "One ship! One goddamned—"

"The council will take these things into consideration and render its judgment in a few days, Mr. Wolff," the senator bit out, his face flushed.

"But—"

"In a few days, Wolff."

The senator's gavel went down.

"It is fate at work!" Tesla roared jubilantly. "Do you see, Burak—does it escape you how we came to be here, how we were *meant* to be here?"

Burak screwed up his devil's face and gestured to their surroundings. "Here? Meant to be here?"

Tesla made a dismissive motion. "In this ship at this particular time," he emphasized. "With the Regent close enough to touch." His hands flexed around an invisible throat.

The two conspirators were sequestered in the fortress's confinement area, opposite one another in separate laser-barred cells. Burak was sullen-faced, perched on the edge of an aluminum-framed bunk studying his hands, while across the corridor Tesla paced back and forth.

"We must find a way out of here," the Invid said, coming to a halt. "I must . . . *talk* to him, convince him—" He whirled to face Burak. "You don't think they would keep my presence from him a secret, do you?"

Burak shrugged.

"I cannot take the chance," he muttered, back in motion once more. "Burak, do you still wish to see your planet freed from its curse?"

"You know I do, Tesla. But how can I help you now? They've even taken your fruits from my care."

"Never mind the fruits." Tesla cautiously pushed his hand into the laser's field, and winced at the resultant burn. "Just do as I ask when the moment arrives. We have not come this far to be cheated out of our victory."

Betrayal of a different sort had Minmei in tears in Edwards's quarters. The general was lying on the bed, his back against the headboard, hands clasped behind his head. Minmei was well within reach in a chair by the bed, but otherwise remote. He had found her waiting for him upon his return from the council chambers, still ruffled from her impulsive flight to the fortress, her eyes red-rimmed and swollen. He didn't need to ask; so instead, he had fixed himself a drink, kicked off his boots, and settled himself on the bed while she cried.

"He's alive," Edwards said now, reaching for the drink. "Isn't that what counts?"

She lifted her face from her hands to stare at him. "That's the problem."

"Oh, you wish he was dead."

Minmei sobbed and shook her head. "You bastard," she told him.

Edwards laughed derisively and took a long pull from the glass, determined not to give in to her. "What do you want from me, Minmei?"

She wiped her eyes and glared at him. "Is it too much to expect some support?"

"You don't need my support. You're feeling guilty because Wolff was stupid enough to think you'd just sit around and pine for him. And I suppose I don't count anymore—I was just a shoulder to cry on."

"Stop it, T.R.—please." Minmei kneeled by the bed, resting her cheek on his thigh. "What am I going to say to him?"

Edwards made a harsh sound and pulled himself away from her sharply. He got up off the opposite side of the bed and walked to the center of the room, turning on her. "I don't have time for this kind of nonsense. Tell him whatever you want. Just quit whining about it."

He kept his back to her while he freshened his drink; but he could hear her slipping into her shoes and moving toward the door. "And tell him I said 'Hi,'" he managed before the door closed.

His hand was shaking as he downed the second drink; he was about to head for the shower when his com tone sounded. It was Major Benson.

"Some interesting conversation down in confinement," Edwards's adjutant reported. "Seems there's no love lost between Tesla and the Regent. He's pretty anxious to talk to his commander in chief, but it sounds to me like he's got murder on his mind."

Edwards's head went back in surprise. "An unexpected development."

"He's got some kind of deal going with that other alien. Can't make too much sense of it. Some payback after Tesla sets himself up as number one."

While Benson continued to fill in the scant details, Edwards concluded that an assassination might prove an advantageous event. He didn't believe the Invid fleet would go to guns over the death of an imposter—there was simply too much at stake—and by *allowing* the murder, Edwards would be sending a clear message to the real Regent. More than that, Edwards could lay the blame for a complete diplomatic breakdown on Wolff, and by extension, the rest of the Sentinels.

"Anything else from other quarters?" He heard Benson laugh shortly.

"You'll love this. I think Lang is going to offer Wolff the newest ship to come off the line. Of course Wolff would have to make it look like he pirated the thing ..."

Edwards mulled it over. A murder, the theft of a ship, an escape

. . . and the council's okay to hunt the assassins down—a chance
to finish the job the Invid had begun.

Edwards smiled down on the intercom. "I'll get back to you,"
he told Benson.

CHAPTER
SIX

Somewhere along the line, everyone seemed to lose sight of the fact that love had won the First Robotech War. Now it was down to ships and body counts; it was no longer a fight for survival but a war for supremacy, a savage game.

Selig Kahler, *The Tirolian Campaign*

Love is a battlefield.

Late twentieth-century song lyric

"IT'S BAD NEWS, COLONEL," DR. LANG TOLD WOLFF TWO hours after the council had adjourned.

They were in Lang's quarters now, along with Exedore, Janice, and the XT, Sarna. Wolff had spent the intervening time pacing the fortress's corridors like an expectant father. He had tried to locate Minmei, but no one seemed to know where she had disappeared to after leaving the docking bay with Edwards and his staff.

"The council is going to rule against you," Lang continued, passing drinks to everyone but Sarna. "Huxley and Obstat are on our side, possibly Stinson, and Reinhardt's vote counts for something, but we don't have enough to sway the rest."

Wolff scowled and sipped from his glass. "You know what's funny? In a crazy way I can see their point. You help us, and so long any hopes of a truce."

"You're correct, Colonel," Exedore affirmed. "The Sentinels were meant to be our ally, but instead they've become our liability. And as you yourself understand, Earth's safety remains the council's primary concern. A protracted war with the Invid will only diminish our chances of intercepting the Robotech Masters."

Wolff exchanged looks with Sarna and Janice; both women seemed curiously detached from the scene, almost as if they served some unknown, greater cause. "Look," he said, putting his

375

drink down in a gesture of finality, "now that we all understand
the diplomatic angles of this thing, *how in the hell are we going
to help them!*" He shot to his feet. "You think I can just sit around
here, knowing what they're going through? They're *stranded* out
there."

"Perhaps there is a way," Lang said after a brief silence. He
shook his head back and forth. "It could have disastrous consequences, Colonel, *disastrous.* And you'd have to prepare yourselves for hardships of an entirely new order . . ."

Prison, Wolff thought. *As an appeasement to the Regent after
the rescue.* Would Rick accept it, he wondered, or would they
choose to die on Praxis—outcasts? "A ship," Lang was saying
when Wolff looked up—*a ship!* He tried to follow the doctor's
nervous movements as he went on to explain.

"It's one of our prototypes—not large, and not especially well-
armed. But it's capable of local fold operations, Wolff, and there's
a skeleton crew standing by—volunteers, each one of them loyal
to the admirals."

Wolff's mouth dropped open; even Janice and Sarna were
stunned by the doctor's revelation. "But when could we get it?"
he asked.

Exedore turned to him. "First, Colonel, you'll be required to
steal it."

Just then the door tone to Lang's quarters sounded. Lang
looked around anxiously, then got up to answer it. A moment
later, he was showing Lynn-Minmei into everyone's midst.

"Janice," Minmei said, approaching her former partner.

Janice evaded Minmei's embrace, and nodded coolly.
"Lynn."

The singer began to look around the room. Lang cleared his
throat meaningfully. "I think we should give Minmei and the colonel some privacy," he said, already ushering Exedore, Janice, and
Sarna from the room.

When the door slid shut a moment later, it was Minmei who
eased out of Jonathan's embrace. "Lynn, what's wrong?" he said,
standing there with his arms open.

She fumbled with the hem of her jacket and forced a smile.
"Colonel, I can't tell you how hap—"

" 'Colonel'? Lynn, tell me what's going on. I saw you with
General Edwards this morning and now you're calling me colonel
after I haven't seen you in six months . . ." He tried to hug her
once more, but she deftly took his hand between hers and motioned him to the couch.

"Jonathan," she began hesitantly, "I know you're expecting us to take up where we left off, but things have changed."

"So I keep hearing."

Wolff was suddenly defensive, and she picked up on his tone. "You have to remember, we only had a few days together. And until yesterday I thought . . ."

"You thought I was dead."

Minmei nodded. "I didn't know what to do. I was practically crazy with grief and anger." She met his gaze and held it. "I hated you, Jonathan—hated you for leaving me, hated you for . . . so many things."

Wolff considered her words, then smiled in sudden realization. "And you found someone to fill in all those lonely hours."

Minmei's eyes flashed. "Why didn't you tell me you were married?"

Wolff tried to keep his face from registering surprise. "We're separated," he said. "Besides, it never came up. I was going to tell you. It's just that everything got fouled up."

" 'Blame it on the Invid,' " Minmei said, almost cracking a smile. The phrase had become something of a catch-all excuse in Tiresia. Wolff was blushing. "Listen," she told him, "I'm not angry anymore. I'm just . . . happy that all of you are alive. How are Rick and Lisa? And Max—"

"So when did you start seeing Edwards?"

Minmei stood up and stepped away from the couch, wringing her hands. "I told you: you weren't there for me, Jonathan. I needed someone to turn to."

"And you picked *Edwards*?" Wolff shook his head in amazement. "Don't you realize he's against everything we stand for? He's nothing but a self-serving, egotistical maniac."

"I won't have you talking about him like that!" Minmei said angrily. "He treated me with kindness and respect, and what's more, he's the only one interested in making peace with the Invid and putting a stop to all this madness. Not like you and the rest of those . . . *Sentinels*, tearing around space stirring things up, not giving a damn what goes on back here!"

Wolff was too numb to respond. Edwards, he thought, was like some kind of toxic spill, polluting everything he touched. Minmei had her arms folded across her chest, as though she were trying to hold herself together; her foot was tapping the floor. Wolff reached for his drink and drained the glass.

"Well, I guess there's nothing more to say, is there?"

Her lips were a thin line, trembling; then all at once she seemed to relax. "I want us to be friends, Jonathan. I've opened a kind of canteen in Tiresia, and I'd love you to see it. Will you promise to stop by?"

He regarded her as one would a memory, mulling over her performance, the scene the two of them had just played out. "Sure," he told her absently, "I'll stop by."

"There's a lot you'll be able to do here—all sorts of things. You'll see." Minmei seemed excited, like she had won a court case or something. She smiled at him from the doorway. "See you soon, okay?"

Wolff forced a smile and raised his empty glass to her. "To friendship," he offered.

She threw him a wink and stepped out.

Applause, Wolff said to himself.

While Wolff and Minmei were having their heart-to-heart and Exedore and Sarna were off somewhere discussing Haydon IV's curious history, Lang took his AI creation to his office and dumped Janice's memory into one of the lab's databanks. He scanned the android's recordings, briefly reviewing the events of the Karbarran and Praxian campaigns, but focusing in on Janice's monitorings and evaluations of the Sentinels' personnel. There was data about Veidt and Sarna, the beings from Haydon IV, that justified further analysis, and some anomalies concerning the Tiresian Rem; but for the moment Lang's main concerns were Burak and Tesla. He had found the Invid's bioreadings baffling, much different from those of the so-called scientists, and superior in some respects to the Regent himself! Moreover, the data provided suggested that Tesla was after nothing less than the Regent's throne. And apparently the Perytonian, Burak, had been assisting him in some unspecified way. Lang reminded himself to alert Wolff to these matters.

Minmei was gone by the time Lang and the others returned to the scientist's quarters, and Wolff seemed sullen, just as Lang had anticipated. There was a nearly empty brandy bottle on the low table in front of the couch.

"I want to talk about that ship, Lang," the colonel said without preamble. "When can we have it?—*steal* it, I mean."

"The sooner the better."

Wolff narrowed his eyes. "What's it going to mean to the summit?"

Lang let out his breath and traded looks with Exedore. If Wolff didn't want to mention Minmei, it was fine with him.

"We've already discussed possible scenarios with Reinhardt and Forsythe. It could set things back some, of course, but as long as we can make the Regent believe that you acted on your own, I don't think we'll be jeopardizing the truce."

Exedore concurred. "Furthermore, we think it best if you take Janice, Sarna, and Burak with you. There's no telling what the Regent might expect in the way of reprisals for our . . . *carelessness.*"

"We wouldn't have it any other way," Janice chimed in, seemingly unaware of the gaps in her recent past.

"What about Tesla?" Sarna thought to ask.

Lang stroked his chin. "We've been wondering about that. He could represent a welcome chip at our bargaining table. But as I understand it, that's been his primary function all along."

Wolff snorted. "I'm not saying we couldn't get along without him, but he has been useful to us."

"Not if the Regent begins to look upon him as a traitor," Exedore saw fit to point out.

Lang thought about the data he had screened, and Tesla's ambitions. "Take him," he decided at last. "I think he'll continue to serve you. In fact, from what Janice told me of the mutiny, our Tesla seems to have his sights set on leadership of the Invid. You might be able to encourage that some, Wolff."

Wolff slapped his hands on his thighs and stood up. "What are we waiting for? What about weapons and a shuttlecraft to reach the ship?"

"That's all been arranged," Exedore told him.

"What if Edwards decides to pursue us?"

"Somehow I don't think he will," Lang speculated. "But you will be hunted. You'll have to leave Praxis and remain incommunicado for a time."

Suddenly Wolff began to feel the immensity of it all. "Can you get Burak and Tesla out of lockup without arousing suspicion?"

"I think so," Lang answered him from the com.

Wolff heard him tell the guards in the confinement area to have the two XTs brought to the laboratory for testing. Then he saw Lang's face pale.

"What is it?"

"They've already been released," Lang said. "On Colonel Wolff's request."

Elsewhere in the fortress, Burak and Tesla were moving cautiously along an empty corridor space, closing on an area that had been designated for the Regent and his retinue. Only minutes before, they had overpowered their armed escorts; it had proved as simple a matter as it had been to inveigle information concerning the location of the Regent's guest quarters. Tesla was whispering self-congratulatory praises to himself now, while Burak remained in the larger being's shadow, fearful of discovery by Human personnel.

"What are you shivering about?" Tesla said, coming around, bold and aggravated. He motioned broadly to the corridor. "Fate has cleared a path for us."

Burak had to admit that that seemed to be the case. They had seen no one since leaving confinement; in fact, it was almost as if someone were running along ahead of them, sweeping the place clean. But what Tesla didn't realize was that Burak was as frightened of fate as he was anything else. It was fate that kept his planet locked in the recurring past; fate that had gotten him into this mess to begin with . . .

"I can feel his presence," Tesla announced, stopping short. Burak bumped into him and backed up a step. Tesla appeared to be growing larger as he approached his quarry. "Soon, my friend, soon."

It dawned on Burak that the Invid had more on his mind than talk, and he wanted no part of murder. He said as much to Tesla as they approached an intersection midway along the corridor. "I—I'll wait for you here—you know, s-stand guard."

Tesla looked down at him. "Fine. You do that," he sneered, and moved off into the perpendicular corridor.

A short distance from the intersection Tesla came upon the first line of Invid sentries. Recognizing the Regent's chief scientist, they immediately genuflected and offered their salute. Then four of the Regent's elite soldiers came forward to escort Tesla into the Regent's private chambers.

"Tesla!" the simulagent gasped, spilling a lapful of fruits to the floor as he stood up. "They've released you?" His snout went up in an approximation of a laugh. "I knew I could do it!"

Tesla regarded the gesture with indifference, too caught up in the moment to realize just who and what he was dealing with.

"I have things to discuss with you, sire," he said, taking a menacing step forward.

"Yes, I'm sure you do! Tesla, I'm delighted to see you."

"We'll see," Tesla told him. "But perhaps you should reserve judgment until you've heard me out."

The simulagent's elongated brow wrinkled. There was something in Tesla's tone . . . His black eyes began to dart around the room. *The guards*, he remembered, and made a move toward the door.

"Don't even think of it," Tesla said, stepping into his path. He thrust a powerful finger into the simulagent's chest and held his other hand up for inspection. "Five fingers, Regent. *Five!* There was a time when your wife alone had five fingers. Doesn't that tell you something about me?"

At Tesla's shove, the false Regent fell backward onto a table that somehow managed to support his bulk. "Tesla, you're mad! What are you trying to do?"

"Mad? Anything but mad, Your *Highness!* I have been ingesting the fruits of other worlds, while you've been playing silly war games with these Humans. And as a result I've had my inner eye opened to transcendent realities, while you've set your gaze on meaningless conquests. I have been *evolving*, while you have sunk to your neck back into the slime that gave us birth. The fruits were meant for you, but it is *Tesla* who has reaped their subtle benefits. You used to ridicule my delvings into such things, but regard me now: I *live*, Regent," Tesla intoned, raising his arms above his head, "and you will *die* unless you abdicate to me!"

The simulagent opened his mouth to cry for help, but nothing emerged.

"Kneel before me!" Tesla demanded, gesturing to the floor.

Paralyzed with fear, the simulagent gulped and found his voice. "Tesla, listen to me: you don't understand. I—"

"Kneel before me!"

"I—"

Tesla grabbed the false Regent by the cowl and dragged him to his knees. "I will rule in your place. I will lead our race from this moment on. Do you agree to it?"

"Tesla," the simulagent pleaded. "I can't agree—"

"Fool! Would you force me to kill you!" His hands were clasped around the simulagent's thick neck now.

"—"

"Abdicate!"

"—"

"Surrender to me!"

"—"

The simulagent's four-fingered hands tore desperately at Tesla's own, but could not counter the strength madness had lent them. Tesla's powerful thumbs found soft and vulnerable places as he continued to squeeze the life from his would-be foe. Black eyes bulged and a horrible death rattle began to emerge from the simulagent's ruptured throat. Then it was over.

He withdrew his hands and stepped back, as if waking from some somnambulistic experience. The Regent's body was sprawled on the floor below him, already drained of life's vernal colors. This being, who had been like a father to him ... And suddenly Tesla knew a gut-wrenching fear—a fear intense enough to engulf all the anger and hatred and maniacal urges he had given vent to only a moment before. He turned to the door, down in a fugitive's stoop, fluids running wild within him. He had been misguided! *He could not take the Regent's place!* The Regis would murder him for his betrayal. He would be devolved to the lowliest life-form, a mere troglodyte, exiled from his own kind. And what was he to do now? . . .

He remembered the Sentinels. Surely Wolff would be returning to Praxis, he thought. He would persuade Wolff and the others to take him along, remain with them until all this blew over. The Regis might rule for a time, but sooner or later he would assume his rightful place and rule by her side—the Sentinels would encourage him to do so!

Tesla gave a final look at the body. He began composing himself for the guards, then realized that no such charade was necessary. With the Regent dead, they were little more than mindless devices; it was possible they wouldn't even remember Tesla's visit.

With these things in mind, he opened the door.

Lang, Wolff, and the others had split up to search the fortress for Burak and Tesla, after agreeing on a time to rendezvous in the shuttle launch bay. With an all-Human crew aboard—save the Regent and his retinue—there wasn't much chance of the XTs escaping detection; but one never knew what to expect from Tesla. There was no time to investigate the release order that had freed them, either, but Lang promised to look into the matter later on.

It was Exedore who discovered Burak lurking in one of the corridors near the ship's designated Invid sector. It occurred to him that the fortress seemed unusually deserted, but he barely gave it a second thought. He was explaining the need for urgency to the Perytonian when Tesla showed up all in a rush, looking like he had just seen the face of the Creator.

"Where have you been?" Exedore said, toe-to-toe with the towering Invid.

Tesla began to stutter a response, then remembered himself and said, "I don't have to answer to some Zentraedi clone."

Exedore bristled at the comment, but decided against engaging in what would be a useless argument. Instead, he drew a handgun, informed the two of Wolff's departure plans, and hurried them along to the hold. Wolff, Janice, and Sarna were already there, anxious to get under way. The guards—some of whom were part of the plan—had already been dispatched, so it was safe for the moment for both Lang and Exedore to be on the scene.

"I guess this is good-bye for a while," Wolff was saying while Sarna and an armed Janice escorted Burak and Tesla aboard. "I don't know what to say, Lang."

"Just pray we're not too late," Lang said soberly. He offered Wolff his hand. "Godspeed, Colonel."

Wolff stepped back and saluted Lang and Exedore, gave one last look around the bay, and hastened up the ramp.

Lang said, "Have we done the right thing, Exedore?"

"We do what we can," the Zentraedi told him.

They didn't wait around to watch the launch.

"They're on their way, General," Colonel Adams reported to Edwards a short time later. "Your orders?"

"Your men are to give pursuit, but tell them to keep their enthusiasm in check. Just be sure it looks good, and make certain that the ship is allowed to fold. I don't want any slipups now."

"Roger, sir," Adams said, and signed off.

Edwards collapsed onto his bed, weary from the choreographing the plan had entailed. Freeing the aliens, supplying them with what they needed to know, keeping the corridors clear, instructing the guards in confinement and in the shuttle bay how to behave . . . It was more than most men could have handled. But then again, Edwards reminded himself, he was not *most men*.

And so far things had gone off without a wrinkle; the Invid imposter was surely dead, and Wolff was a criminal. The council could not help but see things his way from now on, and the threat of a stepped-up war with the Invid would result in the construction of the fleet he needed to carry out his more important plan: *the eventual conquest of Earth.*

CHAPTER
SEVEN

Miriya Parino Sterling's rescue of the Spherisian crystallite [sic] was an act of derring-do worthy to stand beside the infamous "costume change" that had earned her husband such plaudits during the early stages of the First Robotech War.

LeRoy La Paz, *The Sentinels*

"I WANT SOMEONE TO SWEEP THE CAVES," RICK SAID INTO his helmet pickup. "Then we're out of here!"

Bela volunteered. Rick looked around and spied her down below, waving to him from the area the GMU had occupied before Cabell's desperate plan had been set in motion. Rick chinned the helmut stud again and told Bela to make it quick. He saw her, Kami, and Learna scurry off toward the mouth of the cave and disappear inside. Rick called up a display on the helmet's faceshield; then, satisfied that he had sufficient oxygen remaining, he scrambled up the steep slope toward the relocated vehicle.

Praxis's atmosphere had grown superheated and unbreathable, forcing everyone but Veidt and Teal into helmets and environment suits. From the high ground above the caverns, where the GMU was maintaining its precariously angled position, Rick glanced back at the wrinkled terrain. Eruptions of volcanic light could be seen through the dense shroud that stretched from the hills all the way to the base of a distant escarpment. And out of this storm came two lone Veritechs, returned from a final reconnaissance flight. Rick tuned into the command freak, only to have his worst fears confirmed: there wasn't a safe region to be found anywhere on the planet.

The Alphas whooshed in overhead, reconfigured, and maneuvered into the open maw of the GMU's ordnance bay. The Hovertanks and the Skull's VTs were already aboard; only two mecha remained outside—the VTs Rick and Max would pilot up once Vince Grant gave the go signal.

Rick dug his toes into the ground and completed the climb, out of breath when he reached the rim of the chute the Sentinels had blown open in the roof of the cave. The front end of the GMU overhung the rim, elevated now by the hundreds of orbs that had streamed from the cave after the chute had been opened. It was Cabell's idea, and Veidt's peculiar talents, that made the plan workable.

As a last resort the Sentinels had decided to enlarge the diameter of the cave's internal passageways to accommodate the huge creatures stuck for want of an egress suited to their size. That way, Cabell reasoned, they could at least raise a few more Alphas before the planet blew itself to smithereens—providing of course that the orbs could be made to understand that the Sentinels weren't trying to destroy them, as they had those spiderlike monstrosities. And assuming for the time being that Wolff and Janice, or *someone*, would be coming to their rescue.

Rick couldn't recall just who had pointed out that some of the larger orbs were still going to face difficulties reaching the entrance; but it was Veidt who proposed boring an artificial chimney through the roof of the cave. Additionally, the Haydonite maintained, the Sentinels were wasting their time airlifting individual mecha, when the increased supply of globe-beings would allow them to raise the entire GMU—if the mobile base could be positioned in such a way that the orbs could get underneath. (Even with its one-hundred-foot tires, the thing was still too low to accommodate the largest of the orbs.) Vince, Rick, Lisa, and some of the others had determined that the GMU could sustain itself in orbit for a limited time, thanks to the modifications the landcrawler had undergone during its stint with the *Farrago*. It would mean a dangerously uncomfortable existence for as long as Praxis held together; but even weightlessness and privation were preferable to the death they were bound to suffer on the surface.

So after Veidt had relayed the details of the scheme to the orbs (who were in his words "thankful" and more than willing to reciprocate), and firepower had opened the chute, the GMU was repositioned at the rim of the opening to catch the creatures as they levitated from the cave.

As Rick regarded the all-but-floating vehicle now, he decided it was the most bizarre sight he had ever seen: the GMU looked as though it were sitting atop a mountain of unburstable bubbles. Veidt was hovering nearby directing the flow. And in spite of the scale and the incredible size of some of the orbs, the end result of the Sentinels' partnership with the creatures had rendered the GMU almost toy-like in appearance.

Rick continued to watch in amazement as more and more orbs attached themselves to the cluster. The GMU's massive wheels were fully off the ground now, and Rick was anticipating Vince Grant's words even before they issued through the helmet speakers.

"The ride's starting, Rick. You better get the Alphas up." Grant's tone was one of excited disbelief.

Rick turned in time to see Veidt give him a knowing nod, signaling that he had "heard" Grant's message. When the Haydonite began to move off in the direction of Max's Alpha, elevating some as he hovered along the rim of the chute, Rick chinned Bela's frequency.

"A moment more," the Praxian told him. "Teal is with us."

"What's she doing down there?" Rick asked, surprised. "Everyone was supposed to be aboard by now."

"You will hear it from her own mouth," Bela told him shortly.

Rick understood that it had something to do with Baldan's death, and thought better than to press for details. "All right," he said. "Tell Kami and Learna they'll be riding with Max and Veidt. You and Teal will go up with me."

Bela acknowledged, and Rick hurried off to the Guardian-mode Alpha, which was sitting at the edge of the GMU's bubble mountain like some diminutive bird-of-prey. He threw himself up into the cockpit and brought the mecha's engines to life. Beside him the mountain was lifting off, while Praxis continued to rumble its ominous farewells.

In Fantomaspace, meanwhile, the pirated shuttle carrying Wolff and company from the SDF-3 was closing fast on the anchored dreadnought Lang had been instrumental in procuring.

"They're warning us to come about and return to the fortress," Janice told Wolff from the command seat. "Scanners show two gunships on our tail."

Wolff leaned forward to study a monitor, straining against the chair's harness. Elsewhere in the small command cabin, Sarna and Burak were similarly strapped in. Too large for any two of the shuttle's acceleration couches, Tesla was in the cargo hold, shackled but free-floating.

"Any word from the cruiser?" Wolff asked in a determined voice.

"Negative. They're not even responding to the SDF-3 bridge."

"Good. Now if we can just get there in time . . ."

A blaring sound began to wail from the control station's exter nal speakers, and Janice swung to an adjacent console. "We're being targeted."

"Ignore it," Wolff snapped. "The first one will be a warning shot. With a little luck we'll be too close to the cruiser for them to risk a second."

"Steady . . ." Janice cautioned, and a split second later a bolt of angry light strobed into the cabinspace through the forward viewports. A second burst followed, singeing the shuttle's radome. Displays and monitors winked out, then revived.

Wolff showed the others a roguish grin. "Now we couldn't answer them if we wanted to."

"Cruiser's docking bay is opening. The bridge is patching into our guidance system. The SDF-3 thinks they're assisting in our capture."

"Let them take us in," Wolff ordered. He turned his head to take a final look at the SDF-3, suppressing a wish to see the fortress holed and derelict.

Janice straightened in her chair to obstruct his view. "The fortress is repeating the warning. Admiral Forsythe—"

"To hell with them," Wolff barked.

Four crewmembers were on hand to meet the shuttle in the docking bay. "We were attached to Major Carpenter's command," one of the young officers explained as Wolff stepped out. "Welcome aboard, sir."

Sarna hovered alongside Wolff; Janice was last out, keeping a watchful eye on Burak and Tesla.

Wolff accepted the proffered hands. "Carpenter, huh? Good man. Sorry he can't be with us."

"Dr. Lang has other plans for him, sir," an ensign supplied.

"So I understand," Wolff said. Then, as if remembering: "Listen, we've got to do something about those gun—"

"All taken care of, sir. We put a few shots across their bow and they showed their bellies."

Wolff returned a weak smile. "You know what that means, Captain—you're committed."

"We were all along. Now we can act on it."

"All right," Wolff said, nodding, his smile broadening. "Let's get under way."

As they left the bay, the ensign added, "Course is set for Praxis."

"What's our ETA?" Janice wanted to know.

"Two days relative." The captain saw their surprise. "We've made some improvements since you left."

"I guess you have," Wolff enthused. And he began to think

about those improvements as the captain hurried him to the bridge. Carpenter was one lucky soul, getting a shot at returning to Earth. Wolff never would have believed he could be envious of such an opportunity, but the events of the past thirty-six hours had punched a lot of holes in his former thinking. *Things have changed,* he seemed to hear both Lang and Minmei say; and indeed they had. He would be the next to return Earthside, he decided. One way or another. And for the first time in a year he thought about the family he had left behind, and the love he would try to reawaken.

The orbs had lifted the GMU to an altitude of almost twenty miles by the time Rick and Max brought their Alphas aboard. Below, hidden beneath a swirling, agitated pall of cloud cover, Praxis was fractured beyond recognition, the molten stuff of its core geysering to the surface and boiling away the planet's oceans and fragile atmosphere. Microclimates and cyclonic storms added to the fury, unleashing blinding blots of lightning and torrents of black rain, while volcanoes answered the skies with thunderous volleys of their own making. Praxis bellowed and roared like some tortured animal, rattling the GMU with its clamorous cries.

In the base's pressurized ordnance bay, Rick and the others began to wonder whether they would make it after all. Veidt had told them that the orbs could only remain clustered for a short time once they reached the outer edge of the planet's envelope; but with Praxis seemingly entering its final phase, the base would need to be hundreds of thousands of miles out—at least as far as the planet's primary satellite. The way Cabell saw it, the Sentinels had one recourse: to use the most fully fueled VTs and Logans to reach the far side of the moon. A preliminary count of the available mecha, however, had already pointed up the cruel truth half the Sentinels would have to face; and even so, what would the rest have accomplished outside of prolonging the inevitable? Were they to throw together a bivouac on the moon's frozen surface, or simply wander the wastes like some misguided flock until the mechas' power and life-support systems failed?

In another part of the bay, Gnea and Bela were asking Teal why she had gone back to the cave. Neither of the Praxians knew much about Spheris or the ways of its crystalline life-forms, but the women guessed that Teal would have been just as happy to have remained on Praxis with her dead comrade.

"But we've all endured losses and hardships," Bela was telling her, trying to be helpful. "Recall how Lron and Crysta suffered when the *Farrago* met its end, and how Gnea and I grieved for our Sisterhood. Now our very world . . ."

Lron, who was standing within earshot, made a kind of mournful growl. "Death is the way of the world," he muttered in the usual Karbarran fashion. "We do not mourn the loss of our friends; we are resigned to such things."

"I'm not mourning for Baldan," Teal said, looking up at him and Crysta. "I'm upset about the child."

"The dead child," Gnea started to say.

"It's not dead," Teal said harshly, standing up and walking away from them.

"It lives?" Bela said, catching up and spinning her around by the arm. "And you would knowingly abandon it?"

"Let her be, Bela," Lron cut in. "You know nothing of their ways."

"I know what it means to leave a being to die," she answered him. "Why, Teal?" she asked.

The Spherisian gazed at her coldly. "Because I will have to care for the infant. *That* is our way."

Teal snatched her arm away and Bela threw back her broad shoulders. "I will return for the child. *I* will raise it, if you won't."

Teal whirled on her, pointing a hand accusingly. "What do Praxians know of motherhood? I forbid you!"

Even Gnea had misgivings about the idea, and risked a step into Bela's path. "Think twice, Sister. Besides, it is too late—Halidarre rests and our Praxis is out of reach."

"I'll take you," a female voice rose up from the group of mecha pilots that had gathered round. Miriya Sterling eased her way through the group, until she was toe-to-toe with the amazon. "I'll take you," she repeated.

"A Praxian and a Zentraedi sharing the same small space?" Gnea scoffed. "Even such a mission of mercy—"

"No matter what you may think of me," the former Quadrono ace responded, "I know as much about the sanctity of life as any of you do. Give it a try, Bela—for the infant's sake." She thrust a helmet into Bela's hands.

Bela held on to the thing for a moment, then donned it, and raced with Miriya for one of the Skull's red VTs.

Rick didn't even consider trying to stop them—not that Bela or Miriya would have listened to him in any case. He had noticed a kind of latent xenophobia surfacing among the Sentinels— something stress had brought out—and reasoned that a rescue mission could provide just the rallying point everyone needed.

Bela and Miriya were suited up by the time Rick came over to wish them luck; and minutes later the bay had been cleared for the VT's launch. Miriya entered course headings as the mecha dropped down along the GMU's substantially reduced orb cluster and into the dark night of the planet's soul.

Once through the shroud, the two women witnessed for themselves the final, tormented moments of Praxis's tectonic death. Great, furious rivers of molten stuff coursed across the planet's surface now, burying forests and villages in liquid fire. Here and there, where the rivers were abruptly dammed by ground swells, were crater-sized lakes of lava, flailing white-hot tendrils into an equally hellish sky. Praxis seemed to be expanding while they watched, bursting its geological seams.

Miraculously, the region around the caves was practically unchanged, except for an expanding flow of lava that had sealed the entrance to the central cavern. The artificial chute, however, remained open and accessible.

"We'll have to go in through the top," Miriya shouted, struggling to keep the VT stabilized in the face of intense updrafts from the liquified valley floor.

Miriya imaged the VT over to Guardian mode and dropped the mecha into a controlled fall through the wide chimney the Sentinels had blasted through fifty feet of porous rock. With external temperatures registering in the red, there was no leaving the Veritech for a personal rescue; but years of experience in handling the mecha allowed Miriya to accomplish something even more extraordinary: foot thrusters holding the mecha motionless only inches above a pool of lava that had seeped in through the mouth of the cave, she utilized the radome to rake the throbbing crystal away from the wall where Teal had dropped it. Then, when the Spherisian infant was within reach, she took it gingerly into the VT's metal-shod hand, brought up the thrusters, and took the Guardian up the chimney, in a kind of stork reversal.

All the while, Bela was offering words of encouragement, and free of the chute now, she reached forward to give Miriya an affectionate squeeze on the shoulder.

Praxis did all it could to ground the tiny craft, hurling plumes of fire at its tail and chasing it to the edge of space with savage stabs of lightning; but there was no stopping Miriya, no way she would permit the planet to reclaim the child they had rescued from its unharnessed evil.

Once more through the pall, the VT reached the deceptive safety of the planet's stratosphere. Locked on to the GMU's frequency now, Miriya and Bela began to relax some; but as they approached the ten-wheeled battlewagon and its support cluster, they saw something that delivered them to the edge of panic: both the vehicle's launch doors were wide open, and local space was littered with VTs and Logans, even half-a-dozen reconfigured Hovertanks. Miriya and Bela thought for a moment that things had reached the hopeless level, and someone had given the abandon-ship order, a reckless last gasp for the moon . . .

Then they spotted the dreadnought, Wolff's bright spot in the galaxy—the Horizont-class rescue vehicle.

One day Rick and Lisa would compare the rescue of the Sentinels to the SDF-1's rescue of Macross from the Solar System's outer circle of frozen hell; there was the same sense of urgency, the same logistical problems and sacrifices—and chief among these would be the GMU itself. With the orbs beating a fast path for the safety of interstellar space, the Sentinels had no way to maneuver the base aboard, and there was no docking bay in the SDF-7 large enough to contain it even if they could. But just now, to everyone but Vince Grant, the GMU was of secondary concern. Distance was the crucial matter at hand—how much could be put between the cruiser and Praxis, and just how quickly.

They were close to a million miles out when the planet came apart, with enough force to obliterate the moon—the place Rick had recently seen as their possible salvation. Bela and Gnea were on the bridge to witness the brief fireball that flared where a world had once turned.

"We are homeless," Bela cried.

But from what Rick and the others were beginning to understand, the Praxians weren't the only ones. Again a comparison with the SDF-1 would present itself, the memory of a council's edict that forbade the fortress to remain "in" Earthspace, an edict that effectively betrayed the Robotech Defense Force. *And such betrayals,* Rick reminded himself, *had a cruel way of balancing out* . . .

Superluminal Reflex drives kept the fortress well ahead of Praxian debris, and during that brief run to the outer limits of the planetary system, Wolff related to his dazed comrades the sobering tale of his short stay aboard the SDF-3. Wolff knew nothing of the simulagent's assassination, and Tesla certainly wasn't talking; but even without that subplot, there was more than enough to leave the Humans dumbfounded.

As they continued to rehash the details, a curious understanding of the council's decision began to undermine their initial outrage. But that Wolff should have to steal a ship, and that the Sentinels would as a consequence be viewed as outlaws . . . these things were not so easily embraced. For the XT Sentinels, the revelations only meant that they had gained a second enemy instead of a much-needed ally. Among the group, however, there was the beginning of a renewed cohesiveness.

Rick thought he detected something unsettling in Wolff, but he dismissed it, speculating that he would probably have returned in even worse shape.

"Do we return to Tirol, or continue on as planned?" Rick asked everyone. "If we opt for going back, it could mean prison for most of us, death for some," he added, glancing over at Wolff. "On the other hand, it might give us a chance to explain ourselves to the council and keep Edwards from gaining any further influence."

"What do we care about your General Edwards?" Lron shouted, looking for support from the other XTs. "The Invid are our enemy. And if your forces decide to side with them against us, so be it."

Kami, Learna, Crysta, Bela, and Gnea voiced their support for Lron's position. Cabell, Rem, Janice, Sarna, and Veidt were curiously quiet.

Rick silenced them and directed the question to the RDF contingent. Lisa stood up to answer him.

"I understand the need for countering Edwards's influence," she said in a way that was aimed at Rick, "but we have to consider the broader picture. Our return could place the council in an awkward position with regard to further negotiations."

"We'll accomplish the same thing with continued acts of aggression directed against Invid-held planets," someone from the Wolff Pack pointed out. "What happens when Edwards comes gunning for us—do we fight our own forces?"

Vince Grant shot to his feet and turned on the pilot, even as Jean was trying to calm him down. "The council would never bow to the Regent's demands that we be hunted down! They'd break the truce before they'd do that—"

"Not if Edwards is running the council!"

"Waste 'em!" said a Skull pilot. "They were ready to let us die on Praxis! I say we're free agents!"

XTs and Humans cheered. Rick found himself thinking about pirates, and happened to notice Jack Baker slapping Lron on the back, while Karen raised her eyes in an imploring gesture.

"Put it to a vote," Max suggested.

Rick scanned the crowd and received nods of agreement from Lisa, Wolff, Miriya, Vince, and Cabell. "Will it be Garuda, then, or back to Tirol?" he asked loud enough to be heard above the tumult.

"*Garuda!*" came the overwhelming response.

"Then it's settled," he said, aware once more of how he had taken charge without being asked. And from across the room, Lisa's eyes burned into his own.

CHAPTER
EIGHT

I'm looking forward to Garuda in a way that has nothing to do with what I felt toward either Karbarra or Praxis. All things point to the possibility of our being able to regroup and restrengthen ourselves there, even if we will have to suit up for the visit. God knows Lisa and I need some uninterrupted time together. We spoke of dreams tonight, and made love like we haven't in far too long. It comes down to dreams in the end—holding fast to them no matter what else is thrown in your path. I want to get back to that place in my life, and Garuda sounds like it was made to order.

From the collected journals of Admiral Rick Hunter

ONCE AGAIN THE EXPEDITIONARY MISSION'S PLENIPOTENTIARY Council found itself in extraordinary session, the third time in as many days. Ex-colonel Jonathan Wolff and his small band of rebels had stolen a prototype warship and folded from the Valivarre system, after assassinating the Invid Regent. The ruler's body had been taken back to the fleet flagship by his retinue of scientists and soldiers, who were promising a swift and violent response to the Humans' treachery. Ships under General Edwards's command had chased the pirated cruiser, but stopped short of following it into hyperspace. It was believed, although hardly certain at this point, that Wolff was returning to Praxis; but the Sentinels' next destination was anyone's guess. And if their movements were open to question, their motives were positively baffling. Edwards was arguing this very point in the council chambers now, moving through the room like a trial lawyer, his speech angry and impassioned, his reasoning all but unassailable.

"Furthermore," he said, a forefinger raised, "it's my belief that Wolff's story was a ruse. The Sentinels sent Wolff here to kill the Regent. All his talk about the destruction of the *Farrago* and the rescue mission to Praxis was engineered as a diversion."

"That's arrant nonsense," Lang objected, getting to his feet and turning to face the rest of his group. "It was the Regent who first informed us of the destruction of the ship—"

"They *allowed* his troops to destroy the ship," Edwards cut in, but Thurgood Stinson quickly waved him silent.

"What's more," Lang said after settling his gaze on Edwards, "the Sentinels had no way of knowing the Regent's fleet was here."

Edwards laughed. "Need I point out that they could have been monitoring our transmissions, even while remaining incommunicado?"

"But to what *end*, General?" Lang asked. "Why would they knowingly sabotage the negotiations? Really, this makes no sense whatsoever, and I would caution the council to understand that General Edwards is offering us nothing more than an *interpretation* of the facts."

"The facts, Doctor, are that the Regent is dead and one of our ships has been stolen. What more do you require?"

Tight-lipped, Lang took his seat. Senator Longchamps cleared his throat meaningfully. "The council appreciates Dr. Lang's reminder, but I for one would like to hear the general's assessment of the Sentinels' motives."

Edwards sat in silence for a moment, then stood up and said, "They've become a private army. They've liberated Karbarra—Praxis, for all we know—and their plan is to continue in this vein until the entire local group is theirs to command. In the meantime, our efforts here will have been neatly undermined. The Invid will return in force and in the end it will be the Sentinels who will rescue us."

"This is too much," Justine Huxley interjected. "Admiral Hunter would never stoop to such measures."

"Then why did he resign his command?" Edwards threw back at her. "And why is it that the whole RDF apparat decided to follow his lead." Edwards enumerated on his fingers: "The Skull, the Wolff Pack, Vince and Jean Grant, even the Tiresian, Cabell. Hunter didn't like the idea of answering to the council's demands, and now he's out for himself."

Edwards returned to his chair, leaving the council members to argue among themselves. In the seat adjacent, General Reinhardt wore a look of complete disgust.

After a few minutes of deliberation, Longchamps announced, "The council is not yet fully convinced of the scenario you detail, General Edwards, nor of your interpretations of the Sentinels' 'master plan,' if you will."

Edwards scowled, waiting for the senator to continue.

"However, the fact remains that the actions of ex-Colonel Wolff, whatever their motivation, have placed us in a serious predicament. The council wishes to know if the Invid commanders have indicated to you any steps that can be taken to offset this injustice."

Edwards stood up, suppressing a self-satisfied grin. "Right now they seem willing to accept the facts just as we've presented them: Wolff acted on his own. But I must include this caveat: these are relatively low-echelon personnel we're dealing with, and I'm certain that once the Regis hears of this, we'll see renewed fighting—perhaps on a scale more reminiscent of the Robotech War than anything we've experienced here."

He waited for this to sink in before continuing. "As for what we can do, I would suggest that short of a preemptive strike against their forces right now, or the capture of the Sentinels, we devote all our efforts to the construction of a fleet of ships to rival their own."

Again, there were arguments and objections from various council members, but Longchamps silenced these with his gavel. "Would you be willing to oversee this project, General, if the council so votes?"

Edwards inclined his head slightly. "I would be honored, Senator. Of course, I would require the full cooperation of Dr. Lang's Robotech teams and control of the mining operations on Fantoma."

"Naturally," Longchamps said. "We will adjourn to consider our decision."

Edwards grinned in spite of himself. He shifted his gaze slightly to show Lang the cold hostility in his eye. Lang tried to return it, but could not.

The round had gone to Edwards.

In his hive complex on Optera, the Invid Regent sat alone with his two pet Hellcats, too stunned by the reports of his simulagent's murder to speak. He held his snaillike head in his hands, sunk deep into a sense of despair that was entirely new to him. Once before he had experienced such torment: when his wife had confessed to him her love for Zor. *Betrayal,* he thought, in the soft glow of the room's commo sphere.

"Your Highness, shall I give the order to attack?" a lieutenant repeated cautiously.

The Regent regarded the soldier's image in the sphere and sighed heavily. "No," he answered quietly. "Return the fleet to

Optera, and tell no one that I live. It may benefit me to remain hidden for a while longer."

"But, Your Highness, are the Humans to go unpunished? And what of Tesla?"

The Regent could feel the lieutenant's anger, and it was enough to refresh him momentarily. He had not been completely abandoned, then; *loyalty* still lived.

"For the moment do nothing more than let our intentions be known. Inform the Human high command that we hold them responsible for the ... Regent's death, and that terms for a cease-fire will not be discussed until the Sentinels have been brought to justice."

"My liege," the lieutenant returned with a note of reluctance. He offered salute and shut down the link.

The Regent placed a hand on the horned shoulder of one of the Inorganics, on its haunches beside his chair. "My pet," he said aloud, "will you, too, betray me someday?"

Tesla had murdered.

He found it almost inconceivable. Had the Sentinels put him up to it somehow, or, worse still, the Regis? They were known to have seen one another on Praxis ... Had she promised him something then, her favorite son? Certainly Tesla had undergone some sort of change, if he was to believe the words of the simulagent's guards. Perhaps he and the Regis had made a pact to rule in his place, and as a sign of good faith she had *evolved* him some. On Praxis? he wondered. Had she gone there to carry on with her dangerous Genesis Pit experiments? He would know soon enough, if her ships suddenly showed up in Opteraspace.

But in the meantime the Regent thought it best to allow the Humans to go on thinking that one of their own had assassinated the simulagent. If, as they maintained, the group had acted alone, it showed a definite carelessness on the council's part. But if this Edwards had permitted it to happen—even *engineered* it, as the Regent was inclined to believe—then the murder had more sinister implications. It was as if Edwards knew all along that the Regent had sent an imposter in his place, and the murder was the Human's way of responding to the substitution.

He made a note to treat Edwards differently the next time.

The simulagent hadn't been able to learn anything about the Masters' destination, or the location of the Humans' *Earth*; but it was possible that his death would have a positive side effect. Obviously the Humans were anxious to sue for peace, and although he couldn't grant them this just yet, that fact eased his concern about their presence in the Quadrant. And now it was likely that others besides Edwards would be willing to turn against the Sentinels.

The Regent called up a starmap in the sphere and leaned forward to study it. "Garuda," he decided after a moment, that's where they would be heading. A miserable world if there ever was one, a world that had its own way of dealing with intruders ... The Regent had recalled all of his warships from the planet to strengthen the fleet he had sent to Optera; but there was still a small garrison of soldiers and scientists there tending the orchards and farms and supervising the transport of the nutrient. Sufficiently forewarned, they just might be able to succeed where larger forces had failed.

The Regent rubbed his hands together in a gesture of renewed excitement. He grunted to the beasts that flanked his chair. *Perhaps it wasn't so bad being dead after all.*

When news of the Plenipotentiary Council's decision was released, the Expeditionary mission found itself more divided than ever. Everyone on Base Tirol and aboard the SDF-3 now felt compelled to take a stand. The council, by majority if not by unanimous decision, had effectively branded former admirals Hunter and Hayes, along with the rest of the Human and XT Sentinels, outlaws. In due time a ship would be detailed for their capture, but presently they were to receive no help from RDF personnel, and anyone found aiding or abetting the Sentinels' cause would be subject to prosecution to the full extent of the law. Moreover, General Edwards was being placed in full command of the RDF; he would be overseeing both the mining op and construction projects, and his staff would be supervising all aspects of civil defense, including minor police actions.

Lang, Exedore, Huxley, Obstat, Reinhardt and a few others had become a cabal overnight, and Lang realized that it wouldn't be long before Edwards's Ghost Riders would be keeping watch on their every move—if in fact this wasn't already the case. There were enough unanswered questions about the Regent's assassination to convince Lang that Edwards had had a hand in the affair. He surmised, too, that Edwards was aware of the assistance Lang had rendered Wolff; but if he had any proof, he was probably saving it for the next occasion the two men went toe-to-toe. Lang could only hope that Wolff had reached Praxis in time to rescue the Sentinels, because in every other way, the plan had done more harm than good. However, by taking such a hard-line stance, the council had inadvertently weakened Edwards—perhaps not now, but in the long run, when those loyal to Hunter would step forward in a show of strength.

Lang was in his quarters, compiling a mental list of the men and women who could be counted on, when the door tone sounded and Lynn-Minmei begged entry. She was the last person Lang wanted to see, but as he thought about her a plan came to mind. He had persuaded her once into accepting Janice as her partner; now perhaps he could talk her into assuming the android's role as a spy.

"Dr. Lang, I hope I'm not disturbing you," she said, coming through the door. "I just had to talk to someone."

He could see she was frantic. "Don't be silly, my dear. Sit down. Can I fix you something?"

"No," she said absently. "No, thank you. I just need to know if it's true, Dr. Lang—what they're saying about Jonathan and Rick."

Lang sat down, even though Minmei remained standing. "What do you think, Minmei?"

She threw her hands up in a nervous gesture. "I don't know what to think! General Edwards says one thing, you say another . . ." She looked directly at him. "Most of my old friends won't even talk to me anymore. And the way Janice acted . . ."

He offered her an understanding nod. "Well, maybe you've just ended up on the wrong side somehow. And everyone's waiting for you to return."

She sat down, facing him. "That's what I want to know: am I on the wrong side? People are saying the most horrible things about General Edwards. But I know him, I know what kind of man he is."

"You may think you know him, Minmei, but I assure you, you don't. It's . . ." Lang fumbled for the words, "it's as though he has some sort of personal vendetta against Rick. I can't even begin to understand it. I only know that he has turned the council against your friends, and I know they'd be crushed to learn that you're not supporting them."

Minmei bit her lip. "And that's just what Jonathan's going to tell them, too."

Lang thought he detected a flash of anger behind the words; he started to reply, but she cut him off, the anger visible now.

"That snake! Who is he to be calling people names? He's a *liar!*"

"Minmei—"

"Mr. Charm," she said, getting up from the couch. "He should talk about *loyalty*. Ha! What does he know about anything?" She shot Lang a look. "What do any of you know?"

Lang was never good at dealing with theatrics; he knew this much about himself and kept still.

"Liars, murderers, *outlaws*," Minmei was saying. "Things were just too *peaceful* for them on Tirol. They needed to go find themselves a war."

"That's Edwards talking," Lang managed.

"This is *me* talking!" she screamed at him. "I hate you! I hate the whole bunch of you!"

She began to cry into her hands. Lang made a move toward her, but she was gone by the time he reached the door.

"Go ahead, say it," Rick said to Lisa. "I could feel you saying it clear across the hold. So let's clear the air."

She looked at him and frowned. "What are you talking about? Say what?"

They were in the small cabinspace that had been set aside as their quarters aboard the Horizont. The dreadnought was approaching Garuda from the far side of the planet's massive sun after a brief period in hyperspace.

"You wanna say 'I told you so,' " Rick continued. "Edwards is getting stronger and now we're in no position to stop him. If we had remained on Tirol, all this would never have happened, and we'd probably have a truce worked out and be a long way toward repairing the SDF-3." Rick snorted. "Anything I've left out?"

"I'm not saying a word, Rick," she told him. "You're doing such a fine job without me."

"All right, so you think I made a big mistake, and maybe a part of me agrees with you. But the truth is that I would have been going out of my skull back there, and at least now I feel we *are* accomplishing something—maybe not for ourselves exactly, but for Lron and Crysta and Kami and everyone. You can't argue with that."

Lisa shrugged. "Who's arguing?"

"And another thing." Rick put his hands to his hips. "You figure that just because I'm suddenly all gung ho and take-charge that I really *am* a commander after all. But I'll tell you something: the only reason I'm okay with the role is because there's no damned council telling me what to think. We've got a democracy here, not some red-tape portable government, and that suits me fine."

"Well, I—"

"So don't go thinking that I'm going to ask to be reinstated when all this blows over."

"Do you think it will, Rick?"

He heard the desperation in her tone and it took the wind right out of his sails. He leaned over, took her hand, and kissed it. "You bet," he said softly. "And we'll be back on course."

She reached out to stroke his arm. "I don't want us to grow apart, Rick, and I feel that happening sometimes."

He was tempted to say something about Lisa's involvement with Gnea and Bela, but held his tongue. "I won't let that happen."

She sighed fretfully. "We used to have so many dreams—remember?"

"Of course I remember," he said, trying to sound cheerful. "And we'll make every one of them come true." He squatted down to face her. "Look, let's just see what happens on Garuda. From what Kami says, the Invid never actually conquered the place. And from what Wolff told me, it sounds like they pulled all their troop carriers away. They've got a small garrison there, and that's it. Maybe there won't have to be much fighting. We'll get to have some PT."

She laughed lightly. "Now *there's* a dream if I ever heard one."

"You'll see," he said, bringing her up into his embrace.

In the cruiser's med room, Jean Grant was trying to figure out what to do with the now-smooth, football-sized crystal on the gurney—the Spherisian infant Miriya and Bela had brought up from Praxis. The two women were watching Jean's every move, while Teal sat quietly in a corner of the room. Jean gave the crystal a gentle turn; it felt cool to the touch and seemingly inanimate, but scans had indicated a high level of bioenergy, or at least an approximation thereof. *God knew the thing was growing fast enough!* Jean sensed Miriya and Bela's eyes on her and said, "Well, what do you expect me to do with this, this . . . *child*?" She turned sharply to Teal. "Teal, get over here! At least tell me what I'm supposed to do."

Wearily, Teal got to her feet and joined Jean at the gurney. She glanced down at the crystal and fixed her transparent eyes on the infant's saviors. "You saved him, Bela. *You* raise him."

"It's a him?" Jean asked, peering at the crystal as though she had missed something. "How do you know that?"

"Because it is Baldan's child. It is Baldan."

Miriya made a face. "Wait a minute, let's get this straight: is it Baldan, or is it Baldan's child?"

"It is both," Teal told her.

"Well, it sure doesn't look like Baldan," Jean pointed out. "Is it, er, *he* in a state of gestation inside the crystal? Or do we need to incubate him? Speak to me, girl!"

Teal turned away from the gurney. "I don't want to care for it!" When she faced them again, it was obvious she was, in some Spherisian fashion, *crying.* "Baldan was not my mate," she explained. "It was the Invid Tesla who chose us, it was he who brought us together."

Jean put a hand on Teal's shoulder. "But I don't understand, honey. What does all this have to do with caring for the child?"

"He must be *shaped*," Teal answered her. "And to do so I must enter into a rapport with Baldan—I must become his mate."

No one said anything for a moment. "And if we do nothing?" Bela asked.

"Baldan will die." Teal continued to cry, muttering to herself in her own tongue—*praying,* Jean ventured. Then suddenly she produced a kind of crystalline paring knife from the bodice of her garment.

"Teal, no!" Jean started to say, but before she could stop her, Teal had struck the infant with the edge of the blade, as one might bring a tool to bear on a piece of ore. A chip broke away from the crystal, revealing a dazzling facet. Teal struck again and again, each stroke sure of its mark, each rendering the inanimate thing gemlike and complete. Crying all the while, Teal took the infant in her hands and began to carve away more of its extraneous crust. Miriya, Bela, and Jean could hardly believe their eyes when a polished face slowly emerged, then a miniature torso of sorts.

It was Baldan.

If the Sentinels remained divided on any one issue, it was what was to be done with Tesla. While certain they would exercise more caution the next time the Invid volunteered for a mission, they had as yet no clear-cut policy toward him. Was he a prisoner, a hostage, perhaps an ally in some sense? After the meeting in which the Sentinels' direction had been put to a vote, Tesla and Burak had had a chance to answer the "charges" Wolff brought against them. They were accomplices, Wolff maintained, in the laconic and cynical fashion that had everyone aboard guessing. (That Minmei was the cause of Wolff's distress was no secret, but he kept to himself the fact that she had been seeing Edwards.)

Tesla didn't deny that he had tried to commandeer the module; his actions, however, had not been directed against the Sentinels. In fact, quite the contrary. "I am your comrade in this war of liberation," he told the Human and XT assembly. "I am as eager for peace as the rest of you, and my aim in taking over the ship was simply to speed to Optera to convince the Regent of the error of his ways."

Burak, though, was innocent to hear Tesla tell it, and had merely been overpowered, as Janice had. And much to Tesla's surprise, Janice backed up the story. But what Tesla didn't realize was that Janice had briefed the Sentinels beforehand on the stand she would take, suggesting that they allow Burak and Tesla their partnership, which she herself would monitor. There was more here than met the eye, she had explained; and the arrangement would have the added benefit of keeping the Perytonian out of everyone's way.

This was the voice of Lang's reprogramming, but no one recognized it as such, least of all Janice. Tesla, Lang had established, was worthy of study.

So in the end it was decided that things would remain much as they had been before the attempted mutiny: Tesla was neither prisoner nor ally, but more in the way of "ambassador." And Burak was to remain the Invid's aide/jailer/keeper.

The two XTs were in one of the ship's cargo holds now, a place well-suited to Tesla's size. Only a few morsels of fruit remained, but Tesla knew that more would be available to him on Garuda—a crop as different from the Praxian variety as those had been from the Karbarran. He still hadn't gotten over his case of the guilts, and was in fear of the moment the Sentinels learned of the Regent's assassination. With luck, though, that news could be months off. The beauty of it was that there was no one who could even tie him to the act—not as long as the Horizont remained incommunicado. Even that little Zentraedi, Exedore, would have no proof. "Circumstantial" was the Human word for such evidence. So in spite of his anxiety, his spirits had improved.

Burak's, however, had not. Although pleased (albeit baffled) that he had been absolved of any wrongdoing, he felt as though the Sentinels had simply dismissed him and Peryton's cause.

"You mustn't be so glum about it, my friend," Tesla told him, while he contemplated one of the tidbits. "Your world is as good as freed."

"What makes you so certain?" Burak asked, his face a true devil's mask now.

Tesla popped the fruit into his mouth. "Because ... I sense something wonderful is about to happen."

Burak regarded him with a frown.

"Truly," Tesla continued. "You must have faith if you are to assume your proper place in the world. There may be one or two dark spots in our future, but afterward . . ." Tesla offered an approximation of a smile.

"But what about *now*, Tesla? All these grand events you speak of—they are always one step ahead of us."

Tesla threw back his shoulders. "No, my young friend, you have it backward. It is *we* who are one step ahead. But change is in the air. Soon the reshapings will catch up with us. And then we can begin to transform the world."

CHAPTER
NINE

A footnote in Kahler's work (The Tirolian Compaign, Fantomadiscs, third issue, 2083, scr. 1099) refers those interested in Garudan psychism [sic] to a series of twentieth-century autobiographical novels written by a young anthropologist recording his attempts to enter into various states of altered reality through the guidance of a Yaqui Indian "man of power." And while La Paz is willing to concede that there is some justification for Kahler's recommendation, he points out that the Garudans required nothing in the way of extrinsic agents to attain "non-ordinary states." Unless, however, one views the planet's atmosphere in this regard. It is hoped that the much-awaited translations of Haydon's texts will shed light on this continuing controversy.

Taken from the "Imminent Immaterial" column of
Psychophysics Digest

GARUDA. KAMI AND LEARNA HAD TOLD THEM WHAT TO EXpect. A mostly cold and barren world of steppes and tundra, with vast frozen regions and glaciated mountain ranges. What little there was in the way of flora and fauna was principally confined to a narrow band of equatorial forestland of evergreen analogues. There were two seasons, wet and dry; Garuda was in the latter now, and that, Kami explained, would account for the differences in fur coloration the Sentinels would notice among members of his and Learna's tribe. The Garudans, who numbered in the thousands, were not, generally speaking, offworlders. Some, however, had volunteered for mining work on Rhestad-system moons after the arrival of the Zentraedi generations ago, and later on, the Masters' clones. But most Garudans feared the thought of having to leave the planet, and had little tolerance for the breathing harnesses life anywhere else would require. Their society was a simple one, organized along the lines of any hunter-gatherer group; however, they were anything but nomadic, and kept domesticated animals and raised some crops. Religion was of a decidedly individual variety, with each clan answering to a different totem, and each member his or her own shaman. Oddly enough, neither Kami nor Learna had the slightest knowledge of history in the sense that most of the Sentinels, including Burak and Lron, understood the term. Unlike the Karbarrans, or Praxians for that matter, the Garudans seemed to live entirely in the present. This is not to say that they were a complacent group—they were certainly devoted to securing a free future for their world—but at the same time, they could supply no answers to questions concerning their racial past.

This enigma had become something of a preoccupation with Cabell during the four months the Sentinels had remained grounded on Praxis. Cabell was different than the Masters in this regard. Those who had ousted the Tirolian regime after the Great Transition were more interested in expansion and conquest than in the accumulation of knowledge; to the Elders and their subordinate Triumvirates, knowledge of the past presented something of an impediment to change. They had their gaze fixed on the day after tomorrow, on issues of uncontested rule, ultimate power, and selective immortality.

The rest of the Sentinels, though, saw Garuda more in terms of its tangible challenges, and foremost among these was its very atmosphere: though Earthlike in composition, it was essentially toxic to all but the planet's indigenous life-forms. There were one or two exceptions to this, but only Veidt and Sarna among the Sentinels qualified. Surface scans verified the presence of dozens of varieties of airborne spores and microorganisms whose chemistry Jean Grant likened to certain laboratory-produced psychotropic drugs. According to Cabell—based on what he had gleaned from Zor's notes—the vulpine beings' mental processes were linked to the planet itself in a kind of submolecular partnership. Life-forms incapable of entering into this long-established microcosmic symbiosis were not, however, simply ignored or exempted; rather, they were sensed as potentially disturbing to the ecological balance and consequently *counterattacked* by those same microorganisms responsible for the Garudans' nonordinary psychic states.

It had therefore fallen upon the med group to outfit the landing party with transpirators and resp canisters. But if logistics was about to hamper the operation's effectiveness, the Sentinels could take some comfort in the fact that the Invid had also fallen prey to the planet's proprietary nature. In fact, their presence on Garuda was essentially restricted to the hemispherically shaped hives they had erected in those areas where Zor's Flower of Life seedlings had taken root. The crop was a mutant but bountiful one, and it was believed that Garuda provided largely defoliated Optera with much of its needed supply of nutrient. With Karbarra liberated, the Regent had lost his mecha factories; now the Sentinels meant to strike him at the gut level, destroying as many of Garuda's orchards and "farms" as they could.

Rick, Lisa, Cabell, Rem, Jack, Karen, Burak, Kami, Learna, Gnea, Lron, and Crysta made up the drop group, with members of the Skull and Wolff Pack escorting the shuttle down. The Horizont would remain in orbit to deal with Invid transport vessels, known to make frequent runs between Garuda and Optera. Wolff and Grant shared the fortress command. Janice would be keeping an eye on Tesla. Veidt and Sarna had elected to stay behind, and Bela was apparently determined to help Teal with the infant Baldan.

The landing party was certain that the Horizont's arrival in Garudaspace had not gone undetected by the Invid; the shuttle landing would probably be monitored as well. So rather than risk immediate engagement or present any of the hives with an easy target, they opted to put down in the relatively unpoliced tribal sectors, close to Kami and Learna's village. Unexpectedly, they found themselves encircled by battle-ready troops nevertheless—even before the shuttle's landing gear made contact with the surface.

Kami had neglected to mention that some of Garuda's protectors were Tirolian Bioroids.

Kami and Learna consequently made certain they were the first to deplane, figuring their mere appearance would defuse the situation. It did so—and more. Within minutes, half of Kami's tribe had emerged from the trees to surround the shuttle and celebrate the return of their friends. The air was suddenly charged with joyous sounds—excited barking to Rick's ears—and Kami and Learna were embraced, jostled, and hoisted up on countless shoulders. With elaborate ritual, the two returnees threw off their breathing gear and pranced about, engaging in impromptu dances, shamanic steps of power.

Rick radioed the Skull and Wolff contingents to put down along the perimeter of the shuttle's rough strip, checked the integrity of his environment suit and transpirator, and followed Lisa out of the pilots' cabin to take part in the merriment. An hour later, he and the rest of the landing party were in the village's wooden longhouse powwowing with the leaders of Kami's tribe. Severed heads of Hellcats, Scrim, and Odeon Inorganics dangled from the roof tie-beams.

Also present were a number of the Bioroid pilot clones—androgynous-looking shaggy-haired humanoids with pointed features and exotic eyes. One of the clones—these Tiresian lost boys—was explaining to Cabell in a nasal, almost synthesized voice how they had come to ally themselves with the Garudan cause. They wore no breathing gear, and were apparently immune to the spores.

"The Masters left us here to police this world. But when the Invid arrived, communication with Tirol and the clone-masters became impossible. Our Hoverships destroyed, all ties with Tirol cut, we began to understand the concept of freedom, the loneliness that springs from abandonment . . ."

"So you joined the Garudans in their fight," Cabell finished, astonished.

"We thirst for freedom, just as they do."

"Remarkable," the old man mused, his own voice distorted by the mask's filters. "Absolutely remarkable." He hadn't been so astounded since learning from Lang that Miriya Parino had borne a child; and the revelation gave him some hope that the Masters' clones were actually capable of revolt.

Rick took advantage of a momentary silence to motion to the trophy heads. "What's the situation here? Do the Invid run patrols through this sector?"

The tribal chief answered him. "Their Inorganics patrol, but only when they wish to intimidate us, or gather up laborers for the farms. They don't seem to regard us as a threat—even with the firepower our comrades supply," he added, indicating the clones, "but I assure you that all Garuda is ripe for rebellion."

"You mean, they're using your people on the farms?"

"Lately, yes. And in the labor camps near them."

Lron and Crystal grunted, alarming some of the Garudans present. They were keeping a wide circle around the ursine XTs, and a wider one yet around Burak, whose mask only added to an already demonic aspect.

Rick could see that the news came as a shock to Kami and Learna also.

"So much for surgical strikes from the ship," Max said.

Rick regarded the chief for a moment. He found that he was not yet accustomed to seeing Garudans without their breathers; omnivores they might be, but there was a ferocity to their muzzles he wasn't all that comfortable with. Outwardly, the chief resembled Kami, but there was a solemnness to his aspect that was absent in the younger Garudan.

"What about mecha?" Lisa wanted to know. "Scouts, Shock Troopers?"

"Only when their transport ships arrive," the chief told her. "They patrol near the farms to protect the nutrient shipment while it is being loaded. Rarely do they venture into tribal sectors."

Rick watched the chief gnaw at a hunk of meat one of the women had offered him. "Is there any regularity to the shipments?"

The chief exchanged a few sentences with Kami in the Garudan tongue. The Sentinel translated. "Approximately every three standard months. "This was changed every so often in an attempt to foil what was an extensive underground network at work on Garuda. But the Invid never managed to keep anything secret for very long.

"And when did the last shipment leave?"

"One month ago."

Rick grinned beneath his transpirator mask. "That means we're in the clear for the moment. Even if they've already communicated with their fleet, reinforcements could take weeks to get here."

"The closest farm is about one hundred miles from here," Learna said, without being asked. "Kami and I know that area well."

"An aerial recon," Max suggested.

"No," Rick said. "I don't think we should tip our hand just yet. We'll go in on Hovercycles first. Take a quick look around before we plan an assault. Just because mecha haven't been observed doesn't mean they're not in there."

"I agree," Rick heard Jack say behind him.

Karen nudged Jack with her elbow for butting in. "Sir?" she then said to Lisa, hoping Jack would learn by example.

"Go ahead, Karen."

"I was just wondering what exactly happened to the first Invid troops that landed here—before the hives were built, I mean."

Again, Kami and the chief exchanged a few words.

"They went mad," the Garudan leader said evenly. "Then they died."

The recon team—Rick, Lisa, Jack, Karen, Rem, and Kami as scout—left the village shortly before dawn, sticking close to the northern fringe of Garuda's preternaturally quiet forest. They had traveled seventy-five miles by the time Rhestad rose—a massive oblate field of crimson that did little to warm the land. The two villages they passed en route had already been informed of the mission. Worried about attracting any undue attention to themselves, Rick had requested that the Garudans simply go about their business; but there was obviously too much excitement in the air for that. For sometimes miles at a stretch, Rick would see them crouched along the paths the Hovercycs cut through the woods, silent and feral, vulpine eyes aglow in the eerie morning light.

At mile eighty-five the team encountered its first Inorganic patrol—a pack of Hellcats a dozen strong, roaming the forest like some fiendish pride of saber-tooths. Kami had spotted them and passed the word; the Hovercycles were shut down and concealed. It was understood by now that the Inorganics were more than marauders or Robopolice units; they functioned as the remote eyes and ears for the Invid living computers, which in turn directed the scientists or command troops. Engagement, therefore, even if it ended in victory, would have only served to alert the hive to the team's position; so they lay as still as they could, pressed close to the chilled ground until the pack had moved through.

Rick and Lisa were on their stomachs, side-by-side, environmental suits adjusted to mimic the colors and textures of the area's fernlike ground cover. Rick had his arm flung protectively across his wife's back, and was gazing at her through the helmet's bubble-shield. Her eyes returned the wrinkled look his own were trying to convey. It was the first time he and Lisa had been out together in a long while, and if this wasn't exactly anyone's idea of an ideal date or the "closeness" Lisa had in mind during their most recent heart-to-heart, at least they were together. And somehow—though Rick would have been at a loss to explain it—he felt more assured with Lisa beside him. At the same time her presence had a kind of calming effect, because no matter what they might have to face, he was freed from having to worry about where she was or what dangers she might have otherwise been facing alone. Here, he had some measure of control over her situation—*their* situation.

Moving more cautiously after Kami gave the all-clear sign, the team took another hour to cover the last fifteen miles. They had portions of the enormous hive in sight for five of those miles, but didn't get an unobstructed view of the thing until they were almost on top of it. It sat in the center of an ancient impact crater, in a veritable forest of Optera trees, a dome-shaped structure with a base almost ten miles around, composed entirely of what appeared to be organic facets or geodesics; in fact, the hive had the look of something *grown* rather than erected. Four mile-high cattaillike antenna towers were positioned at cardinal points around the hive's oddly "bubbled" base.

Through field glasses, Rick could discern Garudan slaves gathering mutated fruits from the trees. Huge containers of these were being conveyed to the hive itself by Invid soldiers in specially outfitted suits, often piloting Hovercarts of various design. Tracking the carts' movements ultimately enabled Rick to discover one of the hive's tunnellike transport corridors.

"What happens later on?" Rick whispered to Kami, who had stooped down to ask for the binoculars. "Are the workers taken into the hive?"

"No," he said, bringing his muzzle close to the helmet's audio pickups. "The labor camp lies about two miles from here." Kami pointed out the direction.

"Are you certain there are no Garudans inside the hive?"

Kami shook his head. "Not certain." The hives were the only places on the planet impervious to Garudan Sendings and out-of-body flights; but the Invids' continued presence onworld in general had confused things. The clouds and wind were full of sinister whisperings.

"Then we've gotta find out," Rick said, turning around to motion the others forward.

Jack remained behind as rear guard, while the rest of the team began to work their way over the low ridge that was the crater's rim and down into the basin itself. It was warmer here, Rick realized without having to check the suit's sensor displays; redolent, too, he imagined, as the Optera tree forests on Praxis had been. They were closing on the edge of the cultivation area now, and it was time for Kami to go it alone.

"Don't take any chances," Rick cautioned him. He checked his chronometer. "One hour. If you're not back by then, we're moving out."

"I'll get word back to you from the camp if anything happens." *The underground,* Rick reminded himself.

"Just see that it doesn't," Rem said.

Karen and Lisa wished Kami luck, and he started to move off.

Then all at once a small mountain was growing under their feet. Rick thought for a moment that this might be how the bulb-canopied Optera trees pushed themselves from the ground. Lisa and the others had been knocked off their feet, but he was still riding the rise up, arms outstretched like a high-wire walker. Elsewhere he could see two more humps beginning to form. Kami yelled something incomprehensible, just before Rick leaped and caught hold of a network of vinelike tendrils encasing the canopy-bulb of the nearest tree. He was dangling ten feet above the ground now, looking down on his teammates and wondering why they had their weapons drawn, when a triple-clawed Scout pincer suddenly slammed into the tree not a foot from his head. The bulb split open like an overripe melon, showering him with viscous green gop and what he took to be seeds.

Lisa and Karen, meanwhile, were firing charges at the crab-ship, trying to position themselves for a shot at the mecha's scanner, a pouting red mouth low down on the ventral surface of its armored head. But the Scouts who had joined the first were advancing, and the two women were forced to hurl themselves out from under a pair of cloven feet. One mecha was stomping the ground, trying to pulverize them, even while Rem and Kami were stinging its ladybug-shaped carapace with Wolverine fire.

Rick disentangled himself before the first Scout could strike again, dropping, tucking, and rolling out of harm's way, and somehow managing to come up with his weapon raised. He nailed his giant assailant in the knee joint and brought it down in an earsplitting crash; then put a second shot through its scanner, and ducked for cover as the thing blew up.

The force of the blast threw one of the other Scouts hard against the trees, where it stumbled and fell after ripping open half-a-dozen bulbs. Rem saw to it that the ship didn't get up, lancing it open from crotch to scanner. Rick had been left dazed and temporarily deaf from the explosion, but he came to in time to see the remaining mecha raising its left foot to smash Karen and Lisa, who had also been leveled by the blast. He ran up behind the Scout, as if preparing to clip it behind the knee, and emptied his handgun straight up into the underside of the ship's rear tapered head armor, eliciting a cascade of energy bolts and a muffled roar that decapitated the ship, spilling its Invid pilot to the ground. Kami and Karen holed the creature, even though it was probably already dead, and moved quickly to Lisa's side. Rick did likewise, suddenly terror-stricken. Her suit was torn open; she was bloodied and unconscious.

"We've got to get her back to the cycs!" Rick said, looking up at his teammates. But all he got in return was a look of resignation. Rick saw Kami and Karen toss their weapons aside. He whirled around, still in a crouch, in time to see more than a dozen Invid soldiers emerging from the orchard to surround their patch of green-stained ground.

"Throw your weapon down," one of the Praxian-size soldiers said in Tiresian, brandishing an evil-looking rifle/cannon and gazing down at Rick through an elongated helmet.

Rick did so, just as an officer came shouldering its way through the circle. It regarded Lisa a moment, then swung its snout toward Rick.

"The hive has been expecting you," it announced.

"Our Regent has said that he finds your race most curious, and now I understand why. You are a little more like worms than I'd imagined, and indeed there is the stench of death about you."

The interior of the hive was greenhouse-hot, but the scientist's voice was cold and analytical. Rick, Rem, Kami, and Karen had been marched at gunpoint through the same entrance Rick had spied from the crater rim. There, their helmets and transpirators had been removed. One of the soldiers had carried Lisa in over his shoulder. She was still unconscious, groaning every so often in her delirium. Rick was being kept from her side. Kami, already succumbing to the hive's artificial atmosphere, had been shackled and dumped in a corner.

"That smell is the stink of your own soldiers' blood," Rick snarled at the scientist, gesturing to his green-smeared suit.

"The cornered creature's final attack," the Invid said to his white-robed group of barefoot assistants, in Tiresian for Rick's benefit. "The being uses words as weapons."

"What do you want with us? Why didn't your soldiers kill us?"

The scientist's snout sensors twitched, as if he was sniffing the air. "Perhaps we shall. But there is some information we require first. It would save us much bother if you'd simply agree to answer our questions—it might even save your lives."

Rick snorted. "Dream on, slug."

"As I thought," the scientist directed over his shoulder. He studied Rick a moment, then began to move down the line, pausing in front of Kami. "You were one of the Garudans selected by Tesla for the Regent's zoo, were you not?"

Kami leaned in as if to whisper something and snapped at the Invid's face, missing it by inches. Just as suddenly, a soldier threw a stranglehold on Kami from behind; in his weakened state, the Garudan was easily subdued.

The scientist shrugged it off and continued his appraisal of the group, *leering*, Rick thought, at Karen, and puzzling for a moment over Rem. "Why, you're *Tiresian!*" he said at last, and whirled through an excited turn to face his group. "We have a marvelous opportunity here to accomplish something invaluable for the realm. For the record," he added, looking to Rick, "where are the Robotech Masters?"

Rick beetled his brows. "The Masters?"

"Yes. Where is the Protoculture matrix?"

Rick groaned. *The thing had become a thorn in the galaxy's side.* "I don't know what you're talking about."

"That is hardly the response we require to justify sparing your lives, Earther. Be reasonable; you have Protoculture-fueled ships, Protoculture-based weapons ... How did you come by these if not through contact with the Masters or the matrix? Unless, of course, the Flowers of Life grow on your homeworld ..."

Rick fought to keep his surprise from registering. *So that's what they're after*, he thought, and recalled something Roy Fokker had told him almost ten years ago about the warning Lang had inadvertently keyed in the SDF-1—Zor's warning about the Invid! *The Tirolian knew!—he knew the Invid would eventually go in search of the matrix!* Cabell's word to Lang rang in Rick's ears: *You must destroy the Invid here, destroy them while you still can!*

"I see something in your eyes, Human," the scientist was saying. "You know something."

Rick tightened his lips to a thin line.

"Then perhaps your dreams will tell us what we wish to know." The Invid waved a hand at the soldiers. "Take the Humans outside."

"You can't!" Kami bit out, his windpipe pinced in the soldier's grip. Others had stepped in to take hold of Rick, Karen, Rem, and Lisa. "They'll die!"

"Yes," the scientist said matter-of-factly, "they probably will."

CHAPTER
TEN

HE MALE HUMAN WAS DREAMING OF PURSUIT. HE WAS BEING chased by some sort of bird creature with an enormous wingspan, and—an Invid scientist had noted—a body shaped curiously like those of the raptorial birds depicted face-to-face on the Human's uniform insignia patch. The Human was running downhill, hopelessly out of control, with the bird pecking at his neck and back, flapping its great wings all the while. The backdrop for the dream was a world of ravaged landscapes, barren, cratered expanses of solidified volcanic flow. The Human was, and at the same time was not, both the pursued and pursuer. Crowds of other Humans seemed to be viewing the event from the sidelines, gesturing, pointing, applauding, laughing. One wore the face of the injured Human female who was presently being terrorized by dreams of her own—although she was sympathetic here, eager to help the running man, so it appeared.

"There's nothing of use to us in this one's thoughts," the head scientist said dismissively. Disappointed, he turned from the images in the instrumentality sphere and moved to the sphere his assistants had set up to monitor the dreams of the injured female.

Lisa, like Rick, Karen, and Rem, was strapped on her back to a kind of gurney, with her head positioned beneath a thick and heavy-looking ring-shaped device that resembled a scaled-down version of an MRI scanner. What the Invid scientists were calling dreams, however, were of the wide-eyed variety—altered states of consciousness, hellish ones by and large, normally kept locked away behind those proverbial doors of perception. Five minutes of exposure to Garuda's tainted atmosphere had been enough to elicit them. The scientists had no way of knowing whether this constituted what would amount to a lethal exposure—some Invid had lasted as long as half an hour without suffering irreversible effects. But these Humans were fragile things; physically strong for their size, it was true, but with limited tolerance for even the slightest of psychic assaults. They were inhabitants of the base realms, the sensate worlds at the lower end of the spectrum, as insubstantial as interstellar dust, and therefore highly expendable.

The leader of the white-robed group now activated the sphere attached to the device above Lisa's head, and here, too, the scientists encountered images of pursuit. Kami, muzzled and shackled in a corner of the hive's lab, was too deep into his own delirium to take note of their dismay.

"It seems to be something of a fixation with them," one of the assistants ventured.

The Human female was for all intents and purposes trapped on a spiral staircase that lacked any clear-cut terminus. Moreover, whatever it was that was pursuing her, hunting her, was so vague a thing as to be untranslatable by the sphere's Protoculture circuitry. There were momentary flashes of a feline creature, however, that brought to mind the Invid's own Hellcats. But the central concern of the dream and dreamer was the female's seemingly *reduced* size.

"Some reference to the Zentraedi, perhaps?"

The master scientist made a disgruntled sound. "Who can tell with these beings? Let us move on."

They grouped together in front of Karen's sphere next, arms folded and four-fingered hands tucked into the sleeves of their robes. The master among them had found himself strangely moved by this green-eyed, honey-haired Human; but unfortunately her dream-terrors proved to be as pedestrian and unrevealing as the previous ones. Her world was at least populated with a host of other beings, but they were there principally to insure that Karen was suitably horrified by the prospect of being buried alive.

The master expressed his distaste after a minute's viewing. "What a pitiful race . . . One wonders why they don't walk in fear of their own shadows. They've been more traumatized than Optera itself."

By now they had reached Rem—the Tiresian—and to their absolute astonishment, there in living color and as big as life in the center of the attendant sphere was *Optera*. This much could have been accounted for and dismissed, but next they found themselves viewing images of the Regis *in her pretransformed state*! And this was not the defoliated Optera of their ravenous present, but the edenic homeworld of their racial past—a verdant wonderland, with fields of Flowers basking in the warmth of the planet's twin suns, stretching as far as the eye could see across a landscape of arcadian beauty. Here was the lost harmony, the innocent splendor, the paradisiacal ease they could now access only in moments of collective trance, or at the mystical promptings of the Queen-Mother herself.

The scientists were reduced to silence, to tears of an ethereal sort.

"It's as if . . ."

"Say it," the master demanded.

". . . as if this one knew our world before the techno-voyager's arrival."

"These are *his* thoughts."

With what would translate as shame, the master scientist deactivated the sphere and led his group to a sphere significantly larger than the rest—their communications instrumentality, overshadowed by a relatively small specimen of bubble-chambered brain.

"We must inform the Regent of this at once."

"And say what?"

"That we have found *Zor*!"

It had taken Jack all the inner strength he could muster to keep from tearing down into that basin orchard with guns blazing . . . He had heard the explosion that dropped the first Scout ship, and had scrambled up to the top of the crater rim like a mountain goat on amphetamines. Weapon fire, follow-up blasts . . . by the time he got there, Rick and the others were surrounded by Invid soldiers—more than even he wanted to go up against. Lisa was down, Rick bending over her. Kami, Rem, *Karen*! He had located a safe vantage point and watched as his friends were led off to the hive; then a short time later they had reappeared at the dome's tunnellike entrance, this time stripped of their transpirators. For some reason he had felt compelled to time their exposure, sitting there powerless and near crazed while the chronometer display counted off the minutes, *five heart-stopping minutes*! He had run for the place where they had stashed the cycs, found his way back to the trails they had cut in predawn light, reentered the village ... all the while expecting Shock Troopers to emerge from the ground, Hellcats or Robo-automata to leap on him from the treetops. Pursued by nightmares ...

Jack was just now finishing his hurried and breathless recap, sitting cross-legged in the village longhouse and sucking nutrient through a tube while the chief and some of the Sentinels watched him.

"We've gotta spring them," he said at last, his thirst slaked. "Right away, before they're moved."

The chief spoke to a member of the tribe; the male Garudan nodded his head a few times and took off in a rush. "He has been instructed to pass the word," the chief explained. "We will be alerted if and when they are moved."

Learna was beside herself, her neck fur on end. She had tried time and time again to Send herself to the hive, but each of her attempts had ended in failure. "Kami will die inside the hive. He must be returned to Garuda's air."

"He wasn't brought out with the rest of them," Jack told her, then turned to Cabell. "How long is too long?"

The old man made as if to stroke his beard under the suit. "I can't answer you, Jack. Tirol sent the Zentraedi here, the clones ... I believe Rem and I are the first Tiresians to set foot on Garuda since Zor himself landed here."

"Can't you even estimate it?" Jack pressed him.

Cabell saw Jack's frustration and concern. "I don't imagine anything less than fifteen minutes would prove fatal." He was relieved to see Jack relax some.

"But why would they do that—why not just kill them, Wise One?" Gnea thought to ask.

The chief shrugged his powerful shoulders. "To torture them, perhaps to see if they could learn anything from their thoughts."

"All right," Max broke in, "suppose we wait till dusk. Your people will be heading back to the camps by then, right?"

Learna and the chief nodded, uncertain.

"We stage a diversionary raid on one of the other hives. Try to draw off as many of their mecha as we can. At the same time, a rescue team goes in."

"Agreed," Jack said, and some of the others joined him in voicing their support.

"I don't know," Cabell objected when everyone had quieted down. "It's risky. Those hives are much more complex than they appear."

"Well, of course it's risky," Jack argued, "but I don't see that we have any choice. What are we supposed to do—walk up and knock on the door? Uh, excuse me, but we were wondering if you might be willing to return our teammates—"

"There is an easier way to get them back."

Jack swung around to see who had interrupted him. When he saw it was Burak he fell silent, along with almost everyone else. The Perytonian had become something of an invisible being since the attempted mutiny, and to hear him suddenly speak, much less offer an opinion, was something of an event.

"You are forgetting our race in the hold," Burak said to the group's collective puzzlement.

"You mean 'ace in the hole,' " Jack corrected him.

"Whatever—"

"Tesla," Cabell exclaimed.

The devil from Peryton nodded.

"A hostage exchange?" Max asked.

Burak grinned beneath his mask. "Something like that."

On Optera, the Regent's servant reported only that five Sentinels had been captured on Garuda; he knew better than to steal the scientists' thunder. The Regent was relaxing in his sterile nutrient bath when the communiqué was received, having discovered that he could essentially guarantee messages merely by setting foot in the Olympic-size tub. Anxious for some news of Tesla, or information regarding the next destination of the Sentinels, he had spent the better part of a week in the bath, waiting. Now he practically ran to the throne room, sashing his robe as he approached the communicator sphere.

"Five Sentinels," he said out of breath. "Which ones?"

"A Garudan, three Humans, and . . . a Tiresian."

The Regent was pleased to learn that he had correctly anticipated the Sentinels' destination. He had passed the word to all his lieutenants that their troops be placed on alert. But it was captives he was after this time, not body courts, and no mention was to be made of his supposed assassination. With captives in hand, he hoped to learn whether or not Tesla had been acting alone, or in league with the rebels.

"A Tiresian you say."

"Yes, my liege. We have him here with us now."

The Regent peered at the terror-stricken face centered in the sphere's image, and brought his hand to his snout in a gesture of contemplation. "This one looks . . . familiar somehow."

"Well he should, Your Highness," the master scientist said as

Rem's image de-rezzed. "We subjected the three Humans and the Tiresian to Garuda's atmosphere in an effort to extract the data you requested."

"And?" the Regent replied anxiously. "Did you discover the location of the Humans' homeworld—this *Earth*?"

"No. However, we may have a clue as to the whereabouts of the matrix," the scientist was quick to add. "My lord, allow us to screen for your pleasure the results of the Tiresian's exposure."

The Regent scowled at the sphere. "Do not bore me with details," he cautioned.

"You will find this anything but boring," the scientist told him.

The Regent viewed the playback for a moment, then staggered backward, collapsing into his high-backed throne. He sat agape, a defeated husband watching tapes of his wife . . . the seduction, the transgression, the cruel aftermath, all captured in graphic detail. That face, that face . . .

"How?" the Regent finally managed. "How is this possible? He is dead." *Or is he?* the Regent suddenly asked himself. Could he have been duped all these years into thinking Zor dead, when in fact . . . *No*, he thought. Zor was dead. But what then was the origin of these images? A simulagent, perhaps, like the very one he had created to take his place at the summit—

"We know Zor is dead," the scientist was saying. "But somehow his memory lives on in this one—a clone, we suspect."

The Regent came bolt upright in the chair. "The matrix!"

"Precisely."

"He must be sent to Optera at once!"

The scientist inclined his head some. "Of course, my lord. But would it not be best to take advantage of Garuda's proximity to Haydon IV? May I remind Your Highness of the devices there that are far superior—"

"Yes, yes. See that it is arranged. I will leave immediately," the Regent added, already on his feet.

"There is one small detail, however . . ."

"What?"

"We have learned that the Regis is there."

"On Haydon IV?!"

"Yes, my lord. Should we wait until she leaves before transporting the clone?"

The Regent started to agree, but bit off his words. *Why not let her see the clone?* he asked himself. *Why not let her look once more upon Zor's face, into his very thoughts and recollections?* He laughed out loud. *To be there, to see her face when the clone was presented . . .*

"No, you are not to wait," the Regent said shortly. "In fact, you are simply to say that you have a *gift* for her—a gift from her *loving husband*!"

"I need to see Tesla at once," Burak told Janice as he stepped from the shuttle's ramp into the Horizont's docking bay. Gnea and Max had ridden up with him, but they were already rushing off to meet with Wolff and Vince Grant.

Janice thought she heard something akin to arrogance in the Perytonian's voice, but decided to leave it unchallenged. "Of course, Burak," she said, motioning for him to follow her.

They didn't speak for the duration of the long walk to the cargo hold that had become Tesla's quarters; but short of the closed hatch Burak stopped and said, "Alone." The Perytonian positioned himself between Janice and the hatch.

"Something I should know?" she risked.

"You should know that he doesn't like you very much," Burak whispered back menacingly, gesturing over one shoulder with his two-thumbed hand.

Janice laughed. "And we make such an adorable couple. Is it my looks or my personality?"

Burak contorted his demon face for her benefit.

"Keep doing that and your face is going to stay that way," she said, moving off.

Burak snorted and entered the hold, pulling smuggled Fruits from his uniform and casually tossing them to Tesla, who was seated on an enormous crate.

"What's this all about?" the Invid asked peevishly, as one of the mutant Fruits bounced off his snout.

"I have good news," Burak announced, assuming a proud stance and allowing Tesla to regard him a moment. "You claim to be more evolved than the Regent. That means the scientists would recognize your greatness, does it not?"

Tesla ducked his snout, looked around the hold like a felon, and motioned for Burak to keep his voice down. "Yes, certainly," he said. "But what does this have to do with anything?"

Burak studied one of the Fruits. "Suppose I could arrange for an audience with the scientists here?"

Tesla shot to his feet, horrified by the prospect. "You must—"

"Hunter and a few of the others were captured," Burak quickly explained, gazing up at the Invid. "I suggested that we exchange you for them. That way—"

"*You what?*"

"That way you'll be able to assert your right to the throne—just as you . . . wanted . . . What's wrong?"

Wearily, Tesla had reseated himself. "You fool," he muttered, shaking his hands. "You've just sealed my fate."

"B-but . . ."

"It's too soon, Burak, too soon. The Regis will send me to the pits." He glanced up. "The next time you see Tesla he'll be a maggot."

Burak made a distressed sound, seeing his own dreams for Peryton go up in smoke; and just then Janice, Vince Grant, Gnea, and Lron burst into the hold. The amazon Praxian had an armed blaster in her hands.

"Everybody ready?" Janice said brightly, looking back and forth between Burak and Tesla. Cautiously, Lron and Grant had moved in to shackle the Invid's wrists and place a prisoner bib around his neck.

"All right, Invid, let's go," Gnea said, brandishing the weapon.

Lron gave Tesla a light shove.

Tesla looked down and caught Janice's smile.

"Guess this is your lucky day," she told him.

Jonathan Wolff sat on the bridge of the cruiser with his feet up on one of the duty-station consoles. He was alone for a change, Grant and most of the crew having rushed off for the ordnance bay. Well within reach, on the floor beside the command chair, was a bottle of Southlands brandy. It was almost empty.

"To rescues," Wolff said now, toasting Garuda through the forward viewport and lifting the bottle to his lips. He gulped down half an inch and shuddered.

The Hunters had gone and gotten themselves captured, along with Karen, Rem, and that Garudan—Kami. And Max or somebody figured they could swap them for Tesla, only Wolff didn't put much stock in it. Of course he hadn't said that to them—oh no, mustn't burst anyone's bubble, chin up and all that ancient rot. But that was what he *felt*. The Invid would go back on their word, maybe the Sentinels would go back on theirs, somebody would betray somebody else . . . he didn't need to be there to see it all go down.

"So here's to betrayals," he said, and took another pull. "Minmei you . . . *meanie*."

Doubled over in laughter, Wolff swung his legs off the control panel. Yes, she was a *meanie* all right, telling him to take a walk, falling in love with his enemy. "*Earth's* enemy," Wolff emphasized. "Have to give the man his due." He drank again, staring blankly at the bottle when he lowered it, rocking back and forth.

Without warning, a tone sounded on the bridge and nearly sent him out of his skin. He reached out for the com stud and slammed his fist down, missing it, but getting it on the third try.

"Wolff," he said.

"A small craft," one of the new crewmen reported. "Not much bigger than an Alpha. Transport, maybe."

"Put it up," Wolff said, swinging to a monitor screen.

"No can do, sir. Too far for visuals."

"Is it within range?"

"Just barely."

"Armed?"

"Negative, sir. But it launched from the sector where the Hunters are being held."

Wolff contemplated the blip on the screen.

"Let it go," he said. "The way things stand, what difference is one small ship going to make?"

CHAPTER
ELEVEN

Unlike the Zentraedi, who had in a sense taught them everything they knew about warfare, the Invid were not above the idea of taking hostages. The reason for this can be traced back to the chaotic period following the defoliation of Optera by the Masters' newly created clone warriors. The Regent was convinced that Zor had stolen the Flowers of Life merely to offer them up in exchange for the Regis herself. Emulating the Tiresian then, the Regent had sent out his new army not to kill, but to capture Zor, in the hopes of holding him hostage for the return of the Flowers!

Bloom Nesterfig, *The Social Organization of the Invid*

"I JUST THINK WE SHOULD TALK THIS OVER FIRST, THAT'S all," Tesla told the assembled Sentinels, Bioroid pilots, and assorted members of Kami's tribe.

He could see that the Garudans weren't exactly thrilled to have an Invid in their midst—particularly the Invid who had supervised the Regent's specimen mission some time ago—and he was beginning to wonder whether he would even make it out of the village alive, let alone into one of the farm-hives. Still, he reasoned, if he could come up with a better plan than the hostage exchange the Sentinels seemed to be favoring at the moment, he might be able to save himself from either fate.

"After all," Tesla continued, undaunted, "it doesn't sound to me like you have this thing entirely worked out. The whens, the wheres, the hows ... And for all I know, the Regent may have given orders for me to be shot on sight."

This much was true, and as a result the group lapsed into an uneasy silence. They couldn't simply *call* the farm, nor could they just waltz in waving the proverbial white flag. But this was where Tesla was supposed to supply answers; and instead he was suddenly acting as though he couldn't bear to part company with his

424

captors. In private Janice had told everyone to expect as much, although she had been vague about the reasons.

"Then what the heck have we been keeping you around for all this time?" Jack shouted. "You're supposed to be our ace in the hole, not some hunk of dead weight."

"Jack, I'm hurt, I'm really hurt," Tesla returned, trying to put emotion behind the words.

The shuttle was back on the planet's surface now. Vince Grant was still aboard the Horizont; but almost everyone else with the exception of Teal had shuttled down. Jean's team was in the process of erecting an atmosphere-controlled geodesic medical module on the outskirts of the village to house Rick and the others once they were freed. Veidt and Sarna had affirmed that five or even fifteen minutes' exposure to Garuda's atmosphere wouldn't prove lethal; but at the same time the danger to Rick and the others was increasing with each moment they were kept from proper treatment. Just what constituted "proper" treatment had yet to be determined; and Veidt refused to speculate until the Humans were rescued and run through a battery of tests.

Burak was sorry he had opened his mouth, but there was nothing he could do to change things. Besides, Tesla was giving it his best shot and might yet convince the Sentinels to adopt a different course of action.

"Let's hear it, if you've got a better plan," Miriya Sterling was saying.

Tesla put his hands behind his back and paced back and forth, the crown of his head inches from the longhouse rafters. The breathing gear the med group had fashioned for the Invid was a jury-rigged affair of masks, tanks, and tubes, giving Tesla a decidedly elephantine appearance.

"How's this?" he asked at last, swinging around to face Jack, Cabell, the chief, and a few others. "Divert attention away from the farm by initiating a raid—"

"We're one step ahead of you, Tesla," Max said, interrupting. "Infiltrate a small party at the same time, and end up giving your troops more hostages."

"It doesn't have to end that way," Tesla argued. "Not if I'm with the commando team."

Jack grunted. "What do you know that Rick didn't know? We went in quiet as mice and they nailed us."

"It was the mecha—your Hovercycles—that gave you away. The farm's defenses can sense Protoculture activity. So even though you got past the Inorganics . . ."

Tesla left the sentence unfinished, pleased to see that the Sentinels were offering one another surprised glances.

"No wonder they got the jump on us," Jack remarked.

"What about weapons, Tesla?" Cabell thought to ask.

"Weapons, too," the Invid answered him.

Max looked around the longhouse. "Where does that leave us?"

"Swords, crossbows, spears," Gnea said proudly.

Cabell shook his head. "They're no use against Inorganics."

"Grenades, then," Learna chimed in. "Rocket launchers—"

"And these," said the chief, as two of his tribesmen dragged an odd-looking crate into the hut.

Inside were a dozen Karbarran firearms not unlike Lron's own small-bore. Each wooden and metal-fitted rifle had a large globular fixture forward of the trigger guard and forestock lever. "We received many such crates during the final days of the Masters' empire," the chief went on to explain as Lron hefted one of the weapons.

"Yes," Lron said, "Karbarra was exporting rebellion then." He glanced over at Tesla. "Until the Invid appeared."

Max, too, was studying the Invid. "All right, Tesla," he said, coming to his feet. "We'll play this one your way. But all deals are off at the first sign of any monkey business."

Tesla regarded Max and the others through his hastily fashioned mask. "Now, why would I want to do that when I've had enough trouble just trying to act *Human?*"

This time the team was principally XT—Lron and Crysta, Gnea and Bela, with Learna as guide. That Jack would accompany them had been taken for granted; and, after Tesla's plan had been given the okay, Janice signed on. The Praxians felt more comfortable with their one-handed crossbows, shields, and shortswords than anything else the Sentinels could offer in the way of weaponry, and Gnea wouldn't part company with her spearlike *naginata*. But the others carried Karbarran air rifles, satchels of command-detonated explosives, conventional fragmentation grenades, and rocket launchers. Shortly after Garuda's midnight, the eight-member team was inserted by Garudan flitters to within twenty miles of the crater, allowing them ample time to reach the farm-hive before sunrise.

At the same time, Wolff and the Sterlings met back at the shuttle to coordinate plans for their joint diversionary raid against two neighboring farms. It was decided that the Veritechs and Hovertanks would commence their strikes at sunrise, when the Garudan slaves would still be in the camps.

"We're going to concentrate our fire against the orchards, here and here," Max briefed his squadron later on, pointing to areas on the maps Learna had provided. The hives themselves—processing plants really—were almost certainly protected by energy shields like the one the Invid had thrown over Tiresia's Royal Hall during the battle for Tirol. But since the Sentinels' main objective was to draw out the enemy mecha, Max saw no reason why targeting the precious Optera tree plantations couldn't achieve the same result.

"Colonel Wolff's tankers will position themselves along this ridgeline and move in after you've completed your initial runs. Then you're to pulverize that hive. If we dump enough into that shield we might be able to punch through." Similar all-out bursts had worked against the Karbarran hives. Max scanned his small audience. "Any questions?" When all the headshaking was over he added, "All right then, let's saddle up."

Outside the shuttle, he caught sight of Miriya, who had been off briefing the Skull's Red contingent, and hurried over to her just as she was scampering up into the Alpha's cockpit. She had seemed preoccupied during the meeting with Wolff, and absent even now when he asked her if everything was all right.

"Yeah, fine," she said, offering him a weak smile beneath her transpirator.

"You don't look fine," he told her, touching her hair. "Maybe you should sit this one out." She laughed at the suggestion, more out of surprise, he suspected, than anything else. A former Quadrono sit out a fight?

"Max, I'm just a little tired." She donned the thinking cap, climbed the notch ladder, and settled herself in the cockpit seat. "Now wipe that concerned look off your face," she told him before lowering the canopy.

He forced a smile her way, readjusted his mask, and ran to his own mecha. In five minutes both squadron teams were up, tearing through Garuda's crimson predawn skies.

The farms they had chosen to hit were some fifty miles southwest of the crater farm, surrounded by extensive forests of Optera trees, which from Max's point of view resembled outsized melon patches; the hive itself was a freeze-frame shot of a hydrogen bomb's first-stage canopy.

He took hold of the stick and ordered the Skull to follow him in, loosing a dozen napalm torpedoes from the Alpha's undercarriage pylons at treetop-level. Angry plumes of liquid fire fountained above the ground fog behind him as the VT went ballistic; Max turned to look over his shoulder as the rest of the squadron dove in for their runs, each explosion spreading dollops of burning stuff from tree to tree. Skull One rolled over and went in again, incinerating a patch of forest west of the hive now, while Miriya's team gave the east quadrant hell. Then all at once there were Invid Shock Troopers in the air, rising out of the leaping flames and black smoke like a swarm of angry hornets.

"We've got company, Skull Leader," one of Max's wingmen reported. "Multiple signals at eight o'clock."

Max turned his attention from the ascending mecha and twisted around to his right: twenty or more Pincer Ships were approaching from the direction of the crater farm.

"Coming around to zero one zero," Max said into the tac net. "Help me engage, Blue Danube."

"On my way, Skull One. Rolling out . . ."

Max went for missile lock on the lead Pincer and thumbed off two heat-seekers; they found the ship as it climbed, quartering it and a second Pincer in the process. But the Invid were answering the challenge, and Max was forced to break high and right as streams of annihilation disks screamed into the pocket he had vacated. His wingmen split and boostered out in the nick of time, chased by clusters of Shock Troopers from the Invid's counteroffensive group.

Max imaged the Alpha over to Battloid mode at the top of his climb, targeting data scrolling across his display screens now, and the net a tangle of requests and mad shrieks. A hail of missiles tore from the VT's open shoulder racks and dropped into the midst of the Invid pursuit group, wiping out five of their number. Max went to guns with the remaining two, hands clenching the HOTAS, trapshooting the Invid with the Alpha's rifle/cannon as they streaked by him.

Elsewhere in the field, Miriya's team was holding its own against the mecha born in that inferno below. Half the trees were on fire now, thick smoke roiling in Garuda's dawn, while Humans and Invid exchanged salvos of death. Battloids and Troopers grappled gauntlet to claw.

"Guess we succeeded in getting their attention," Max said to no one in particular. He chinned Miriya's frequency and asked for an update; he repeated the request when she didn't respond, then reconfigured his ship and dropped down to have a look for himself.

Miriya had gone to Battloid and was executing her own version of a Fokker Feint when Max caught up with her. There were four Shock Troopers hovering around her mecha, pulling sting-and-runs. He smiled as he watched her ace one of them with the autocannon; but that look collapsed when he realized how slow she was to react to follow-up energy Frisbees delivered by the remainder of the group. Max was close enough now to throw himself into the fight; but the sight of her sloppiness had left him shaken, and he almost got himself dusted.

"Miriya, what's wrong?" he said when the last of the four had been dispatched. "Miriya!"

"I ... don't know, Max," she answered him after a moment. "Dizzy spell."

"I want you to return to base."

Miriya's face came up on Skull One's commo screen. "I'll be all right. It's better now."

"Forget it—"

"Max!" Wolff's voice suddenly boomed through the net. "We've got troubles! Inorganics—hundreds of them!"

Max looked away from Miriya's image and chinned the com freak. "Your Pack should be able to handle those things, Wolff," he said.

"It's not us they're after, Commander," Wolff said, just as gruffly. "The sons of bitches have turned them loose on the camp—they're attacking the Garudans!"

A short distance from the besieged orchard, Wolff's Hovertank team was well into the forests surrounding the second farm. From the ridgeline above the dome-shaped hive, where the Pack had been Guardian-configured, Wolff had been able to observe the Skull's fiery treetop passes. He had then given the order for his tankers to open fire. They hadn't lobbed five minutes' worth of projectiles into the forest when the first wave of Inorganics had appeared—Hellcats, galloping across Garuda's tundra and heading straight for the ridge. They were followed a minute later by ranks of the bipedal demonic-looking Robo-trolls known as Cranns and Odeons.

Wolff had hated the things ever since he went up against them on Tirol, and had been looking forward to engaging them—anything to get Minmei off his mind for a while, to keep his hand from reaching out for a bottle ... So he had ordered the Pack over to standard mode and led the charge down the rocky slope, only to find that the Inorganics had changed course. And it had only taken a moment to figure out the reason behind the tactic: the Invid were planning to use the Garudans as the Sentinels had the Invid's life-giving trees—for *diversion!* The XT labor force was strung out for more than a mile along a sparsely wooded hillside guarded by a company of armed and weapon-wielding Invid soldiers. It was then that Wolff had opened the net to Max.

The Skull fighters were overhead now; Wolff could see them through breaks in the trees' clustered, billiard-ball canopies. Shock Troopers and Pincer Ships were right on their tails.

Wolff's Hovertanks broke out of the forest a moment after Skull One Touched down; the Alpha was in Guardian mode, with the rifle/cannon gripped in one gauntlet, stammering its harsh greeting to the Hellcats. Dozens of Inorganics burst apart as armor-piercing rounds ripped into the pack, but five times that number made it through the VT's still-forming line, bounding over the mecha and continuing their mad rush for the Garudans. Aware of the situation now, the helpless slaves had broken ranks and were attempting to flee; most of them were cut down instantly by bursts from the soldiers' forearm guns, while others fell to the first wave of Inorganics, torn apart by Hellcats or roasted by bolts from the Cranns' orifice-dimpled weapons spheres.

Wolff ordered the Pack to spread out and form a second line; the Hovertanks reconfigured and began to fire at will, decimating much of the second sortie wave, but suddenly forced to deal with the Shock Troopers as well. Annihilation disks stormed into the tankers' midst, tearing up the land and overturning two of the mecha. Wolff could see that members of Max's blue team were going over to Battloid and repositioning themselves opposite the Pack to form the second leg of a V formation. Wolff called for a cannonade as the Inorganics rushed into the notch. Pounded with explosive rounds the tundra shook and bellowed; the ridge trapped the concussive sounds and hurled them back, as Inorganics and Shock Troopers alike were reduced to gobs of white-hot metal, geysers of fire in the already superheated air.

Miriya's Red team came in just then to add their deafening movement to the score. Pincer Ships and VTs went face-to-face, hammering away at one another, while missiles and projectiles corkscrewed through the firestorm and smoke.

Wolff told his B team to hold their ground; at the same time he and the other A tankers battled their way over scorched terrain and through flaming stands of trees toward the Garudans' march of death. Prevented from ascending the hillside by rows of Invid soldiers and vulnerable below to the Inorganics' unchecked advance, the vulpine XTs were being slaughtered. Wolff thought he could hear their wailing clear through the tank's canopy and the tac net's cacophony of calls. The Pack couldn't fire for fear of killing even more of them; so instead Wolff led the tankers on a flat-out collision course straight to where the Inorganics had become bunched up at the base of the hill. The tanks smashed their way into the thick of the slaughter, downswept deflection bows cutting Cranns and Odeons in half. Hellcats leaped on the hovering mecha, only to be blasted to smithereens by in-close guns, or crushed by hand when some of the Pack reconfigured to Battloid mode.

Meanwhile, at the edge of the forest Max's VT teams were getting the upper hand. Pincer and Shock Trooper ships were falling out of the sky like ducks on a bad day at the marsh. Miriya's Reds accounted for most of those kills; Wolff could just discern them overhead, flying circles around the enemy pilots. He caught sight of one VT in particular as it was completing some sort of aerial pirouette that had left three Pincers in ruin; he was thinking that it must have been Miriya's, until he saw the VT sustain a shot any cadet could have dodged. Wolff watched it plummet toward a ravaged area of woodland.

"That's the place they got jumped," Jack said, pointing out a damaged row of Optera trees at the bottom of the slope. The hulks of the three Scout ships had been removed, but there was evidence of the fires the explosions had touched off. "Then they were dragged into the hive." Jack handed binoculars up to Lron, once again indicating the direction. "You can just make out the entrance or whatever it is."

Tesla gave him the Invid word for the portal, mumbling something Jack found unintelligible.

"Like I said: whatever it is."

Careful not to disturb his transpirator, Lron took a look through the armored glasses and passed them along to Crysta. She was upping the intensity some, when Learna's trill-like signal reached them from somewhere in the trees. A moment later, the Garudan appeared at the base of the slope, motioning the team down. Gnea and Bela were crouched behind her, masked and vigilant, looking more than ever like barbaric gladiators lifted from some Roman arena. Jack tapped Janice on the shoulder and got everyone under way.

They had reached the crater well before dawn, without incident despite the presence of stepped-up Inorganic patrol teams. Not just Hellcats, but Cranns and Odeons—bizarre enough creatures by daylight, and positively frightening in the predawn ground fog. Even these hadn't deterred the free Garudans from putting in an appearance, though; only this time it was more than curiosity that motivated them: many had armed themselves with Karbarran air rifles, hoisting them in a display of support as the team passed.

Just before sunrise at the crater rim, Jack had seen flashes of explosive light in the southwestern skies, rolls of distant thunder—the Skull's bombing run against the neighboring farm. Shortly thereafter, scores of Shock Troopers had risen from the basin and flown toward the sound of the guns.

"Any activity?" Jack asked when he reached the base of the slope.

"Nothing so far," Learna told him. "We went as far as the hive."

Jack turned to Tesla. "What do you think?" he said angrily. He had no patience left for the Invid's malingering. Keeping Tesla concealed on the trail had led to more than a few hairy moments; and on the slope he behaved less like a sentient creature than an out-of-control boulder. But now the time had come for Tesla to earn his keep. "What's their routine?"

Tesla glanced at what could be seen of the hive through the trees. "Difficult to say, what with all the activity you've stirred up. Normally, the slaves would be arriving any minute now." Tesla looked up at one of the trees' vine-encrusted globe canopies. "Pity, too," he mused. "All this ripe fruit going to waste."

Jack brandished a long-bladed dirk as Tesla reached out to pluck a particularly succulent-looking piece. "You haven't earned it yet, Tesla. Besides, you don't really want to take off the mask, do you?"

Tesla thought it over. There was no reason he couldn't lift the mask for the time it would take to gobble down some fruit; but he decided not to bother arguing the point. So he simply left the fruit to rot instead of adding it to the samples he had already stuffed into the pockets of his robes.

"No, I suppose not," he said after a moment.

Jack ordered him to take the point; and in ten minutes the team arrived at the hive's entrance. It was faintly lit, a half-moon–shaped tunnel twenty-five-feet high and composed of what looked like solidified sea foam. There seemed to be a slight shimmering to the air inside, but this ceased when Tesla identified himself to the scanner. A voiceprint, Jack thought, but he couldn't be sure.

The tunnel was deadly hot, evil-smelling even through the masks' filters, and reminded Jack of fiber-optic vids he had seen of the human body's arterial system. It terminated in a rotunda, whose enormity and crepuscular illumination Jack found disorienting. Dozens of corridors emptied into the area, like detonator horns on an old-fashioned naval mine.

"We can dispense with these contraptions," Tesla was saying, pulling the transpirator from his snout. He took a deep breath and smiled at everyone. Jack could see that he was taking obvious delight in their amazement.

"This is our foyer," Tesla said, with an elaborate wave of his arm.

Jack checked the display on the biosensor Jean had strapped to his wrist. Satisfied, he slipped the filtration mask from his mouth, determined to keep a straight face. Still wary, he sniffed at the air, found it slightly dank but breathable, and gave the all-clear for the others to follow his example. "Which way?" he demanded, leading with his chin.

Tesla pointed to the circular shaft directly overhead. "There." With a theatrical gesture, he motioned the team to gather round him. No sooner had they done so than they found themselves imprisoned by some sort of tractor beam that was lifting them en masse toward the overhead shaft. Gnea brought the tip of her lance to the ribbed underside of Tesla's neck.

"No," he told her, up on tiptoes to ease the contact. "You have it all wrong. This is simply our . . . elevator system."

Jack, and Janice were down in a combat crouch, weapons drawn, searching the beam's translucent circumference for any sign of danger. Lron, Crysta, Bela, and Kami were similarly postured, Karbarran air rifles at high port, crossbows armed. Tesla continued to protest for the duration of the thirty-second ascent into the dome's upper reaches.

Slowly, the tractor field began to de-rezz.

Jack had relaxed some by the time the beam shut down; then all at once he saw four Invid sentries swinging around to face them, forearm cannons raised.

Max had seen Miriya's Alpha go down. He had his own VT in Battloid mode now, and was running it toward the crash site through a section of burning forest. Two of his team were dead; at least that many of Miriya's had died as well. He wasn't sure how Wolff was doing, but he had seen more than one Hovertank overturned by Shock Trooper anni disks. Max didn't even want to think about the Garudan slaves. And suddenly there was Miriya to worry about.

The mecha's scanners caught sight of something up ahead, and Max called for increased intensity, studying the biosensor data displays. A minute later he had visuals. It was Miriya's Red Alpha alright, in lopsided Guardian configuration, radome tipped to the ground—a wounded bird.

Then Max spotted the Hellcats—four of them, attacking the VT's canopy with a frenzy, battering it with downward blows of their armored heads. He could see that one Inorganic had managed to get a claw inside, and was waving it around, presumably hoping to slice Miriya to shreds. The four turned at the same moment to show Max their gleaming fangs and sword-edged shoulder horns; two hunt-mates leaped for the VT straightaway, but he already had the rifle/cannon locked on them. They came apart in midair like clay pigeons. Max holed a third where it stood glaring at him, and now the final 'Cat snatched its paw from the punctured canopy, reared up, and came at him. Max tried to sidestep the Battloid when the Hellcat jumped, but his timing was off; the Inorganic latched on to the mecha's ablative head shields and began to ram its snout against the permaplas visor. Reflexively, Max pressed himself back into the cockpit seat; he had a larger-than-life view of the crazed thing's snapping mouth and false gullet. The 'Cat was snarling, trying desperately to slice open the Battloid's belly with the churning motion of its razor-sharp hind claws. Max shut down the external pickups and armed the head lasers. The angle was almost too oblique, but the Hellcat's back was heaving in and out of the targeting brackets and Max thought he might have a chance. He raised the Battloid's left arm, gripped the 'Cat around the waist, and tugged it into the lasers' field. Then he triggered the in-close guns. The Inorganic brought its head up as the light beams seared into its backside; it took Max's follow-up pulse right through the eyes and dropped to the ground, lifeless.

Max stomped the thing twice. He imaged over to Guardian mode and pulled his mask tight as he popped the mecha's canopy. Miriya had yet to show herself. Scampering up along the Red's downswept wing, he peered into the shattered cockpit and began to fumble with the manual-release levers.

"Miriya!"

He called her name twice more before he succeeded in springing the ship's protective blister. She appeared unharmed, but unconscious. More troubling, however, was the fact that the Hellcat had ripped off her mask; she had been breathing Garuda's atmosphere for a dangerously long time.

■■■■■■■■■■■■■■■■■■■■■■

CHAPTER
TWELVE

Several commentators have felt compelled to point out that Jona-
than's Wolff's "slip" [sic: see Mizner's Rakes and Rogues; The True
Story of the SDF-3 Expeditionary Mission] was perhaps the pivotal
event of the Third Robotech War. The reasoning goes something like
this: If Wolff had fired on the Invid ship, Rem would never have
reached Haydon IV; and without Rem, the Regis would not have been
as likely to instruct her Sensor Nebulae to search the Galaxy's outer-
most arms for evidence of the matrix, and would not, therefore, have
found Earth until years after the Expeditionary mission returned. The
reader must decide for him or herself whether anything is to be gained
by such speculation; but I would point out that [Mizner's] reasoning
can be made to apply in both directions. It is as easy to blame Lynn-
Minmei as it is Jonathan Wolff.

Footnote in Zens Bellow's *The Road to Reflex Point*

AN INVID SHIP, A SMALL SHUTTLE, HAD DOCKED AT HAYDON
IV's spaceport facility. The Regis had been told that it was from
Garuda—and bearing gifts.

She was in her temporary headquarters high atop one of the
city's ultratech architectural wonders when news of the ship's arrival was delivered to her. *Out of reach*, she liked to think; dis-
tanced from the cold, unsettling presence of the planet's armless,
hovering creatures, the displaced and still discontent Praxian Sisterhood, her own discomforting discoveries ... And out of the
Regent's reach, his dark schemes and mad plans.

But if anything, Haydon IV had only compounded the misery
she had carried here from Optera and Praxis. She felt at the mercy
of a confused longing she could not define; a need to break free
of this horizonless condition.

She supposed that she should have been grateful that Haydon
IV's inhabitants hadn't in any way trifled with her or denied her
anything; but neither had they accepted her as the evolved being

435

she fancied herself to be. It was more accurate to say they had *tolerated* her presence—as if they were all privy to some grand arcane mystery she couldn't even discern, much less unravel. And furthermore she sensed that this had something to do with the world's equally mysterious founder/creator—Haydon. The databanks she had searched for answers to her own evolutionary puzzles gave some glimpse into his life, but hardly enough to form a complete portrait of the being. And she confessed to a certain trepidation at expanding her efforts along these lines. Already the very foundation of her own life's work had been shaken by what she had uncovered in Haydon's transphysical musings, and all at once she felt too unsure of herself and her ambitions to permit much more in the way of contradiction. There were hints, though, that she was not, as she had imagined, *in control of things*; that the theft of the Flowers, the Invid's quest, even Zor's misdeeds, were but part of a much grander design—one in which she, too, did little more than play out a role. And that role . . . that role demanded she accept that what she sought was not the Flowers of Life, but the stuff that had been conjured from them by Zor himself—the *Protoculture*!

As she saw it—as she wanted to see it—Protoculture was a malicious energy, a malignancy that did nothing but fuel the war machine of the Masters and her deluded ex-husband. To see it as more would be to admit she had been wrong after all, that the Regent's course was the truer one, the predestined one.

And suddenly he had sent her some sort of gift.

She was pacing the floor like a caged beast now, waiting for the unsolicited thing to be brought up to her. Finally, two of her husband's "scientists" were admitted to her quarters; she recognized one of them as a master she had herself evolved for the express purpose of overseeing Flower gathering on Garuda—another of the cursed worlds Zor had for some reason seen fit to cultivate.

"Your Grace," the scientist directed up to her, bowing. "The Regent regrets that he could not be here in person to bestow his gift."

The Regis made a scoffing sound. "If he had come in person, I wouldn't be here to receive him. Now, have the thing brought in and take your leave, *underling*."

"Of course, Your Worship," the scientist said, bowing once more. "Only it is not so much a 'thing' . . ."

"What then?" she asked him, arms akimbo.

"More in the way of a live presentation—but one that will surely prove most enlightening." The scientist shouted a few quick commands over his shoulder, and two Invid soldiers marched into the room. Sandwiched between them was a small Tiresioid male, narcotized, so it appeared.

Puzzled, the Regis reduced her stature some to get a better look at him. One of the soldiers tilted the Tiresioid's face up for her inspection.

It was Zor.

A tight scream worked its way up from the very depths of her being, and she came close to losing consciousness, falling back from the soldiers and their terrible trophy and crashing against a communicator sphere.

"A clone, Your Grace, a *clone!*" the scientist was shouting, aware of the Regis's distress. "We meant you no ill."

"How dare you!" she bellowed, frightfully enough to send both soldiers and scientists to their knees, and Rem facefirst to the floor.

"We subjected the clone to the Garudan atmosphere and discovered that his dreams spoke of things we were certain you would find—"

"Silence!" the Regis said, cutting off the scientist's rush of words. "I know what you *thought*," she added, more composed now. "And I know what the Regent meant by sending me this . . . clone. On your feet!"

Hesitantly, the four Invid did as instructed, leaving Rem where he lay. "Your Highness," the master scientist began on a sheepish note, "Haydon IV's devices will permit us to gaze even deeper into the clone's cellular memory. Perhaps some clue regarding the Masters or the missing Protoculture matrix . . ."

"Yes," she answered him, looking down at Rem as he groaned and rolled over. It took all her strength to keep from reaching out to touch him. Would he remember her? she wondered. Would the clone's cellular memory reveal what Zor had been thinking when he seduced her, when he returned to Optera for the seedlings, backed by an army of warrior giants? Would that same memory reveal the path the matrix had taken, the course she would follow? . . . "Conduct your experiments," she told the relieved group. "Show me the future of our race!"

Jonathan Wolff was beyond believing in miracles, but he was hard-pressed for a better word to describe the sight of several hundred Garudans charging onto the scene to rescue their enslaved brethren. They were cresting the hilltop now—armed with everything from war clubs and bolos and grapnel-shaped things to Karbarran air weapons and antimecha rockets—and dropping down on the Invid soldiers who were keeping the slaves hemmed in. A dozen or so Bioroids on Hoverplatforms were providing them with air support, employing their stem-mounted cannons to rain destruction on Hellcats and Cranns alike.

Countless defenseless Garudans had been killed in the Inorganics' genocidal attack, but that didn't stop the survivors from rallying once they realized that their world had committed itself to an all-or-nothing stand. They rushed the Invid lines, which were already strained to the breaking point, and fell upon the offworlders with a violence only blind fury could release. It took five, ten, often fifteen Garudans to bring down a single armored soldier, but one by one the enemy fell. Some were pummeled to death, others disintegrated by their own weapons, and still others were stripped of their masks and respirator tanks and left to run amok, crazed long before the spores could work their effect—crazed by the naked fear of that end.

Spurred on by this reversal, the Wolff Pack and Skull Squadron pulled out all the stops. Until this moment, concern for the well-being of Rick and their other captured comrades had to some extent weakened their resolve; and it took the Garudans' desperate charge to make them remember what the fight for liberation was all about. Reinspired, VT pilots and Hovertankers let loose their own shadow selves, and swept like avenging angels through ruptured sky and forests infernal. Shock Troopers, soldiers, Optera trees, the farms themselves—nothing was to be spared their wrath.

With total abandon, Wolff urged his mecha deeper and deeper into the madness, destroying, crippling, killing. For one instant he rejoiced at hearing Miriya Sterling's voice over the tac net—she was presently riding tandem in Max's Alpha/Beta fighter—but that was no more than a fleeting reminder of a past life. He considered himself one of the dead now, in no world's hell but his own. And from that hollow center came a murderous intent that knew no bounds. He could only hope that some of the Sentinels would live to see victory that day.

"Behind you!" Janice shouted.

But Jack had already seen them and was halfway through his turn, the rocket launcher atop his shoulder. Three Invid soldiers were advancing up the corridor, their forearm cannons booming. Jack triggered his shot and caught one of the XTs dead center. The explosion was enough to drop the other two, but only momentarily; they were back on their feet in an instant, resuming their advance while Jack reached for the grenades clipped to his web belt.

"We've got them!" he heard Lron, or possibly Crysta, growl.

The Karbarrans were positioned on either side of the corridor terminus, grenades in their outstretched mitts. "Now!" Lron said, and the two pivoted and released.

Jack flattened himself against the floor and covered his head; the roar and concussive heat washed over him and he rolled to one side, running through a quick check of everyone's position. Janice was behind him, kneeling over the quivering mass that was Tesla; Gnea and Bela were off to the right, along a section of curved, featureless wall just short of a second corridor terminus. Learna was opposite them, near the tubestand and sphere arrangement Tesla had called a communicator. The four Invid soldiers who had greeted them after the "elevator" ride were sprawled on the floor, dead; two with arrows sunk inches deep into their thick necks. Close by two more were dead or dying, dropped by high-speed projectiles from the Karbarrans' air rifles.

"Get him up!" Jack yelled, scrambling to his feet and motioning to Tesla. "Gnea, Bela, check that corridor!"

The Praxian women had crossbows and swords held low as they moved in; Crysta came up behind them with her rifles ready to mete out additional force. Tesla was up now and dusting off his robes.

"Barbarians," he said, looking around at the dead soldiers.

"Save it," Jack spat, giving him a nudge in the gut with the launcher.

Tesla looked down his snout at the Human. For small and primitive beings, he decided, they were possessed of an incredible ferocity at times. And while this in itself was not uncommon, it was completely at variance with the sympathetic, *caring* traits they were so fond of displaying.

Tesla, Jack, Janice, and Learna were nearing the communicator sphere when something suddenly charged the air—a resonant, bone-rattling hum that carried a peculiar odor with it.

"An alert," Tesla announced, fingers on the sphere's activation controls. "Seems you've succeeded in calling attention to yourselves."

"Anything?" Jack called out to Gnea. She shook her head, then offered him a perplexed shrug.

"Ahh, there's the reason they're leaving us alone . . ."

Jack turned around in time to see an image come to life in the heart of the sphere. It took a moment to make sense of the scene, and Learna was the first to gasp.

"Looks as though we've a rebellion on our hands," Tesla ventured.

The sphere showed a virtual army of Garudans pouring into the basin. Invid soldiers were butchering them from dug-in positions close to the base of the hive. The Optera tree forest was ablaze, giving the crater the look of a devil's cauldron.

"It's suicide!"

Janice put her arm around Learna's soft shoulders.

"Then let's make it count for something," Jack said in a determined voice. He nudged Tesla into motion again, and the Invid began to lead them along one of the corridors. Shortly they were standing before a shimmering portal similar to the one at the hive entrance. Once again, Tesla's hand or voice "unlocked" the portal, and the team found themselves in a kind of control center, filled with "furniture"—strangely contoured chairs and fairly conventional tables and countertops—wardrobe closets, instrumentality columns, communicator spheres of various size and design, and what looked to be Tiresian Robotech devices.

The team fanned out to search the space and Lron made an important discovery behind one of the long counters: two cowering white-robed Invid scientists.

The Karbarran pulled them up by their necks and shoved them toward the center of the room.

"Tesla!" one of them seethed, following up with what Jack imagined to be a few choice Invid epithets. Janice translated: "He called Tesla a traitor. Said it was true what they'd heard about him."

"Meaning what?" Jack asked.

"Why, my leading you here," Tesla said too quickly.

"Where is Kami?" Learna demanded.

Tesla put the question to them, then grunted when the scientists had replied. "They refuse to say."

Jack grabbed Crysta's rifle and held it to the head of one of the scientists. "Ask him again."

Tesla listened to the reply and shook his head.

"All right then—"

"Hold it a moment, Jack," Bela interrupted. "Perhaps they crave a lungful of Garuda's fresh air . . ."

Tesla told the two what the Sentinels had in store for them; even Jack could see their snout sensors blanch at the prospect. No one really needed the translation.

"They've changed their minds," Tesla announced with a snort of disapproval.

And with that the scientists began to lead the Sentinels on a circuitous tour through the dome, descending always, via tractor tubes and spiral drops where there should have been stairs, past conveyor systems and vat after vat of Fruits or pulverized stem and Flower, in and out of corridors and rooms, commo stations and rotundas, all recently vacated by soldiers and worker drones who had ceased their tasks to protect the farm. Within minutes of leaving the control center Jack felt completely lost; he had no idea where they were in relation to the hive entrance, and began to wonder whether the scientists were leading them into a trap. But his concern faded by the time they reached what he guessed to be the lowest, perhaps underground level; they had passed numerous places where ambushes could have been sprung, but not a single soldier had been seen. Then at last they reached the end of the line—or so it seemed until one of the scientists actually walked the group *right through a wall*. The chamber beyond was a kind of membranous sac, veined and pulsating like something one might find in an unhealthy lung, and there, heaped together in the center of the floor, were Rick, Lisa, Karen, and Kami.

Fearing the worst, Jack hung back while everyone else ran to them—everyone but Janice, who positioned herself near the sac's osmotic gate where she could keep an eye on Tesla. Learna immediately slipped a transpirator over Kami's muzzle and hugged him to herself for all it was worth. Kami stirred some after a moment, but the three Humans were another matter; sickly pale and disheveled, they languished in a deathlike stupor, whimpering every so often.

"... subjected them to the atmosphere, then performed some sort of mind-probe experiments," Janice could hear Tesla translating.

Janice saw the two scientists take a step back as Jack and the others swung around to them. She pretended to preoccupy herself studying the chamber's portal, furnishing Tesla with a bit of illusory breathing space. At the same time, she sharpened her eyes and ears in his direction.

"Don't worry about a thing," Tesla was telling his comrades in a low but reassuring tone. "Now that the Regent has been ... killed, Tesla will rule in his place. I will make peace with these beings and—"

"Tesla, what are you saying?" one of the Invid cut him off. "The Regent killed? We just spoke with him. In fact, it was he who told us to expect you."

"What?" You spoke ... But, but what you said, what you said about it being true—"

"Yes," the other scientist sneered. "That you had taken up the Sentinels' fight, and that we should beware your treachery!"

"No!" Tesla said too loudly. He caught himself and risked a glance at Janice, but she kept her eyes averted from him.

Jack, Gnea, and Lron were storming up to him when he swung back around. Lron took hold of each of the scientists by the fronts of their robes.

"Ask them what they did with Rem." Jack barked.

Tesla peered over at the rescued group, noticing for the first time the Tiresian was not among them. Absently, he put the question to the two he had hoped were to be his first subjects, still stunned by what they had told him. *The Regent alive? How could it be?*

"Well?" Jack shouted. "What's he saying?"

Tesla waited for the scientist to repeat it, nodding as he listened. "Rem is Tiresian. His dreams were less, shall we say, *commonplace*. So he was sent elsewhere for further tests."

"Where?" Janice asked, walking over to him.

Tesla listened for a moment. "To Haydon IV. In fact, the Regent himself is on his way—" Tesla's eyes went wide and the words caught in his throat.

"Go on . . ."

He swallowed and found his voice—raspy as it was, all at once. "The Regent is on his way to Haydon IV as we speak."

"Then that's where we're bound," Bela said evenly, her eyes narrowed to slits.

Tesla gulped, loud enough for everyone to hear.

"We've got to get them to Jean's med team," Learna announced, still holding on to her mate.

Bela lifted Lisa from the floor. "We have no time to lose."

Lron and Crysta moved in to take hold of Rick and Karen.

Max and Miriya received Cabell's good news/bad news update over the com net: Rick and the others had been rescued, but they were still under the effects of the planet's microbe-laden atmosphere and delirious with fever. Moreover, the mission had gone smoothly with no casualties among the team, but Rem was no longer on Garuda. Jack's team was out of the crater hive now and awaiting extraction; Jean claimed that Rick, Lisa, and Karen were too weak to endure the trip back to the med group's temporary hq by Hovercycle or Garudan flitter.

Max signed off and immediately raised two of his wingmen on the tac, ordering them to rendezvous with Skull One at the crater hive. Reconfiguring the mecha to Guardian mode, he imaged the Alpha into a vertical takeoff and set his course northeast for the basin. As the VT rose, Max had a full view of the forests and steppes the Skull and Wolff Pack had turned to wasteland. Not since the battle on Karbarra had he seen so much death, such extensive destruction. The dome-shaped hive was in ruins, collapsed and in flames; the Optera tree forests, along with patches of grass-land and evergreen, were burning out of control. The terrain was ravaged beyond belief—pockmarked, holed, cratered, littered with legless or pincerless Invid mecha, bits of Hovertank and Veritech, Bioroid and Inorganic. An entire hillside was covered base to summit with Hellcat husks and Invid and Garudan corpses. Hundreds, perhaps thousands had died. And from what Max was hearing over the net, the same scene had played at each and every Invid farm and installation throughout the planet's equatorial belt. But Garuda had freed itself from the offworlders' yoke.

Good news . . . bad news.

Max said as much to Miriya as the VT covered the fifty or so miles to the crater. She was still in the Beta module and apparently all right, in spite of her ordeal. Max was cautiously optimistic; he had yet to quiz her about how her fighter had been brought down in the first place.

The crater hive was for the most part intact, but Max didn't expect it to last much longer. Fires encroaching on it from all sides. Skull One dropped out of the smoke and clouds onto a battleground much like the one they had just left, dead and wounded strewn across the field, a palpable commingling of triumph and loss. Those Invid who had survived were seeing the Garudan's barbaric side; but Max didn't suppose he could fault Kami's people for the day's bloody aftermath, this requisite catharsis.

Masked again, Jack, Gnea, and Bela directed Max and his wingmen in, and got Rick and the others into the VTs as fast as they could. Lron, Crysta, and Janice were keeping Tesla and a few Invid scientists under guard inside the hive—protected from the Garudans' bloodlust for the time being. Kami, still weak but ambulatory now, was off somewhere sharing the bittersweet taste of victory with Learna and their fellow warriors. Mopping up, Max ventured, much as the Wolff Pack was doing in other quarters.

Max caught a brief glimpse of Rick as he was being lifted into the cargo space of Blue Danube's Beta module. The transpirator prevented Max from being able to see his friend's face, but Rick looked as though the Invid had robbed him of his bones.

The three VTs raced for Kami's village, where Jean's team took over and carried Rick and the others to the safety of the geodesic med dome. Max couldn't help but see it as a miniature version of the Invid hives they had just destroyed.

He and Miriya entered on Jack's heels, doffed their masks, and took in a lungful of the dome's artificial atmosphere.

"Sweet, isn't it?" Max said, trying to sound cheerful.

Miriya gave him a weak smile, but said nothing.

He was reaching for her hand when she suddenly stumbled and collapsed into his arms.

CHAPTER
THIRTEEN

Use your discretion, but try to have your men hold off until you're certain that at least half of them [ed. note: the Zentraedi] are inside—that includes Breetai and that kingsize bitch, Kazianna. Instruct the demo team to use more charges than they think necessary; I don't want any of them coming out alive. In fact, it might be worthwhile to sabotage as many of their environment suits as possible beforehand. Neither of us believe in accidents, Adams, but we're going to call it that no matter what.

A "Code Pyramid" communiqué from T. R. Edwards, as quoted in Wildman's *When Evil Had Its Day*

A TIGHT CLUSTER OF LIGHTS WAS DESCENDING OUT OF Fantoma's perpetually brooding skies. Breetai watched them for a moment, then turned away from the command center's blister viewport to face his lieutenant.

"They've arrived, my lord."

"So I see," Breetai said soberly. He glanced back over his shoulder, snapped the faceshield that sealed his pressurized armor closed, and moved to the hut's airlock. The lieutenant and two armed soldiers followed him out into Fantoma's night.

A constant debris-filled wind had been scouring the ringed giant's surface for the past three days, and Breetai instinctively raised an arm against it as he marched in lumbering high strides toward the landing zone's illumination grid. Nearly all of the Zentraedi cadre had turned out for the confrontation, and Breetai spied Kazianna Hesh among them. Nearby were a dozen or so Micronians in environment suits—some of Lang's Robotechs. Edwards's Ghost Riders were reconfiguring their Veritechs now, imaging over from Guardian to Battloid as they touched down.

"He apparently has more on his mind than a friendly chat," Breetai said to his lieutenant while the last of the squadron was snapping into upright mode. As murmurs of discontent reached

445

him over the tactical freq, Breetai instructed his first officer to pass the word along that he wouldn't tolerate any incidents; no matter what Edwards said or did, his troops were to keep silent.

Edwards stepped his Battloid off the grid and began to move across the field in Breetai's direction. The Zentraedi knew better than to regard this as some gesture of compromise. Four of the Ghosts flanked Edwards, with a kind of threatening casualness to the way they cradled their rifle/cannons. Breetai threw his lieutenant a knowing glance. The show of force came as no surprise; Dr. Lang had already given him an idea of what to expect.

"New Zarkopolis welcomes General Edwards," Breetai said with practiced elaborateness. "We're sorry we couldn't provide the general with better weather." He could hear a few Zentraedi snicker.

"Very thoughtful of you," Edwards returned over the mecha's external speakers, mimicking Breetai's tone of voice. "And I'm sorry I can't bring you better news."

The two men fell into an uneasy silence; the wind came up, howling and pinging gravel against Breetai's armored suit and the Battloid's alloy. The Zentraedi commander narrowed his eyes and grinned, picturing Edwards in the mecha's cockpit, nervous hands on the controls. When one of the VT's gauntlets came up, Breetai almost made a grab for it, but restrained himself at the last moment. Edwards caught the gesture, however.

"A bit nervous today, are we, Breetai?"

Breetai snorted. "This wind has put me in a foul humor."

Edwards inclined the ultratech knight's head. "Well then, maybe this won't seem like bad news after all." The mecha's hand held out an outsize audio device for Breetai's inspection. "You and your ... *crew* are relieved, Commander. New Zarkopolis is now under REF jurisdiction, and I'll be assuming personal control of this facility. Tomorrow's cargo run will be your last. You can hear it straight from the council, if you wish."

The Zentraedi began to grumble among themselves, and Edwards's sentries took a step forward. Breetai motioned his cadre silent with a downward wave of his massive hand. He accepted the playback device and regarded it for a moment. "No need for that. But I should warn you, General, that you're going to find the conditions here somewhat harsh. This is, after all, *Zentraedi* work."

Edwards's short laugh issued from the speakers. "We'll manage all right. Of course, you're all welcome to stay on—as *laborers*, you understand."

"I'll consider it, General."

"Good, Breetai, good," Edwards said, pleased with the outcome. "I like a man who can follow orders. Could be that you and I will see eye to eye yet."

Breetai nodded, tight-lipped. Peripherally, he noticed Kazianna stepping deliberately into his restricted field of view.

Edwards went on to inform him that within a week's time several hundred men and women would begin arriving from Tirol, along with the new mecha Lang's teams had designed. Until then, Edwards was leaving behind six of his troops to oversee the transfer of command. *Six or six hundred*, Breetai said to himself, *it wouldn't matter now.*

When Edwards and most of his squadron had lifted off, Breetai swung stiffly into the wind and made for the mining Colony's Quonset-style headquarters. On the way, he asked the lieutenant if his men had completed their task.

"Almost, my lord."

"And the fool's ore?"

"Loaded for tomorrow's delivery."

Breetai grunted. "See to it that the last of the monopole is placed aboard the ship. The delivery will go as scheduled, but the monopole remains our property."

The lieutenant raised an eyebrow. "About Edwards's soldiers, Commander . . ."

Breetai came to a halt short of the headquarters hatchway. "Invite them along to 'oversee' the delivery. Afterwards, we'll give them the option of joining us."

"And if they refuse?"

"I leave that up to you," Breetai said, stepping inside.

"Pregnant?" Max asked, as Rhestad's morning rays touched the med team's geodesic shelter.

Vince shrugged his huge shoulders. "That's what Jean says. And Cabell concurs."

"That's right, my boy," Cabell affirmed. "It is most remarkable, but true." The Tiresian was all smiles for a change, his concern for Rem momentarily eclipsed. "I thought her first pregnancy the exception that proved the rule. But this—this is nothing short of . . ."

"Remarkable," Max finished for him, shaking his head in disbelief. "Yeah, tell me about it."

Vince laughed. "What's with you? It takes two, if I'm not mistaken."

Max looked up into Vince's brown face. "Yeah, but . . . Vince, you don't understand. Remember, Miriya's . . . *different.*"

"She had Dana," Vince started to say.

"Yeah, and Dana's *different*."

"How is she different?" Cabell wanted to know.

Max and Vince traded looks, but left the question unanswered. "Can I see her?" Max said suddenly, getting up.

Vince laughed. "That's a good start."

Max started off for the small area of the med dome Jean's team had partitioned off.

"Remarkable," Cabell mused as he and Vince walked back to where Rick, Lisa, and Karen were undergoing treatment. The three had yet to emerge from semiconsciousness ...

"Any change?" Vince asked his wife a moment later. She was standing over Rick just now, looking almost as drawn and pale as her patient. Vince put his arm around her narrow waist.

"I'm worried, Vince. They should have come out of it by now. We've tried everything—antipsychotics, transfusions ..." She threw up her hands. "I don't know what to do."

"It is the *hin*," Veidt said, hovering over to them from the foot of Karen's bed. He had spent the last several hours absorbing everything Jean's medical library databanks had to offer. "Garudans live in the womb of the *hin*. It is what you might term 'an alternate reality.' The microorganisms here, the same which keep Kami's people in a constant state of *hin*, have caused your friends to become *unstuck* in what constitutes *Human* reality."

"Yes, and it's killing them, Veidt. It's not providing them with psychedelic trips or allies or personal power. It's draining the life from them while we sit here and ... and—"

"Come on, Jean," Vince said. "You're doing what you can."

Cabell tugged at his beard. "There is a treatment, of course." He turned to Veidt as Vince and Jean's eyes fixed on him.

"I will be succinct," the Haydonite began. "On my world there are devices capable of reversing the Garudan effect. 'Mental illness,' as some of your disks name it, is unknown to us; it is as archaic a thing as your own smallpox."

"Then what are we waiting for?" Jean said, looking up at Vince. "Our work here is finished, isn't it? Garuda's liberated."

Vince removed his hand from her waist to feel his jaw. "Yes, in a way."

"In a way? What's that supposed to mean?"

"We've learned that the Regent is on his way to Haydon IV," Cabell told her. "With what remains of his fleet, no doubt."

Jean compressed her lips. "More fighting, then."

"It's not even as *simple* as that," Vince added.

"Our world," Veidt said, "cannot be approached with the same tactics you employed to liberate Karbarra, Praxis, and Garuda. Haydon IV is in a certain sense beyond both conquest or liberation. And while it is true that the Invid have assumed control of our political structure, they have not in any way attempted to tamper with our lives. They *could not*. Haydon IV is an open world and will always remain so."

"Couldn't we sneak through or something? I mean, isn't there a back door we could use, some way of getting to those devices without confronting the Invid?"

Veidt stared at Jean and shook his head. "It is impossible."

Vince was pacing up and down, hands clasped behind his back, "We've gotta ask ourselves whether it's worth the risk."

"Whether Rick, Lisa, and Karen are worth the risk, you mean."

"And Rem," Cabell added.

Vince nodded.

"Look what you've already risked to save them," Veidt pointed out.

Everyone fell silent; then Vince said, "Gather the Sentinels. We've got a decision to make."

"I will not have him here! I will not!" the Regis railed to one of her servants. *Was there no escaping him?* she asked herself. *Even here on Haydon IV?*

"I'm afraid it's too late, Your Grace," the servant said, unmoved from its posture of genuflection. "The Regent's flagship has already left Optera to rendezvous here with the remnants of his fleet."

"How long do I have?" she asked, whirling on the sexless creature, the tassels of her long gloves whipping about.

"Less than one period, Your Grace."

She dismissed the servant; when it left the room, she clenched her fists and waved them in the air. "Must he stalk me?" she said aloud. "Must he continue to punish me?"

Abruptly, she turned around to regard Rem; the Zor-clone was asleep, perhaps unconscious after his sessions with the Regent's scientists from Garuda. They had cured him of the madness induced by that world's atmosphere, only to induce a more controlled state of hallucinatory dread. And then they had picked his brain. *Oh, how they had picked his brain.*

For the better part of five days now the Regis had had him much to herself; hers to toy with, hers to examine—his dreams and thoughts to dissect, his memories to relive ... United with him on some psychic plane, she had walked again through those fields they had walked on Optera. Old Optera, Optera before the fall. She had been able to view those times through his eyes now, and had found herself stirred. He had seen how much she wanted to emulate him, in every way; and she had seen how much he had desired her. Not her physical being, not the form destiny had wed her to, but her spiritual self—her *essence*. There was at one time a semblance of love there, and this discovery filled her with joy. But it was a rapture that could not survive the realities his war-hungry race had introduced into her garden; a rapture that could only endure on that etheric plane, where things cast beautiful but ultimately painful shadows . . .

Still she could hardly tear herself away from that realm, even though her self-indulgence might mean death for the clone. He was her plaything; much as she had been Zor's!

She understood, however, that Zor had somehow meant to redeem himself by sending the Protoculture matrix far from his Masters' reach. But much of this remained unclear, muddled by what she had accessed from Haydon IV's data systems. These grand designs again: Zor, the Masters, the Invid, all locked together in some immense, unfathomable framework.

Along with this mysterious blue-white world revealed by the clone's thoughts, this nexus of events, this pleroma . . .

She had yet to learn either the name of the planet or its continuum coordinates, but she now had a sense of where to begin her search. And sooner or later her sensor nebulae would locate it.

I will follow the nebulae, she decided all at once. *I will quit this Quadrant and place myself as far from his reach as that matrix was from the Masters' evil embrace.*

She found herself excited by the prospect, laughing as she overlooked Haydon IV's artificial land- and cityscapes. She could even leave some of her Children behind until the moment arrived—the moment when that blue-white world was discovered and made her own!

She increased her size, towering up to fill the room, knowing a determination she had thought lost with love itself. Regarding Rem, she said, "Now let the Regent have his way with you, clone. Let him peer into your memories of our time together, and let him suffer for what he missed!"

Miriya did not look as well as Max had imagined she might. Where was that rosy glow, that special something? Instead, she seemed wasted; baggy-eyed, bone-weary, even slightly jaundiced.

"It's just from my exposure to the atmosphere," Miriya told him as he carefully sat down on the edge of her cot. "But Jea says everything's fine, all systems go. So smooth your wrinkled brow, my darling, and kiss me before I do something violent."

Max forced a smile and leaned into her arms; they held each other for a moment. Max patted her back and straightened up. "I'm not sure I know what to feel," he confessed.

"I know, Max. I'm just as concerned as you are about Rick and Lisa."

"Good news, bad news . . ."

"That's life, Max. And now Dana's going to have a sister."

Max's brows went up. "Jean tell you that?"

"She didn't have to." Miriya caressed her belly. "I can sense it."

Again, Max tried to feel good about things, but the more he looked at his wife, the more anxious he became. He was about to take her hand, when someone rapped against the partition. Crysta, Gnea, and Teal asked if they could come in for a moment. The Spherisian was carrying the infant—a two-foot Baldan, although still faceted and speechless as yet.

"As soon as I heard the news I came down," Teal explained. "I wanted you to see the infant."

"Congratulations," Gnea said to Miriya uncertainly.

"Hey, what about the father?" Max asked good-naturedly.

The Praxian turned to him. "Why? Did you have something to do with Miriya's condition?"

Max started to respond, but thought better of it, shutting his mouth and blinking stupidly.

"When does he become smooth, like you?" Miriya was saying to Teal.

"It doesn't. It's not necessarily a he."

Miriya looked around uncomfortably. "But I thought that Baldan . . . that this . . ."

"It is of Baldan," Teal replied, regarding the infant analytically. "But the features and what I think you call 'the sex' are ultimately left to the Shaper."

"The Shaper? You?" Crysta said, surprised, one huge paw to her muzzle.

"Who else? The young Spherisian remains faceted until smoothed by its Shaper. Soon I will de-facet it."

"But you'll shape him, er, it in Baldan's image, won't you?"

"Why would I do that? I am bonded with the infant now. I could just as easily shape it in my own image."

"But this is all that remains of Baldan," Crysta argued. "Don't you want to recapture his essence? It would mean much to all of us."

Miriya and Gnea agreed. Max kept out of it.

"Among Spherisians I am considered most attractive," Teal told them proudly. "A young one could do far worse than be shaped as I am." She regarded Max and Miriya a moment. "You Earthers don't even have a choice in the matter."

"No argument there." Max laughed. "But maybe that's the beauty of it."

Gnea made a face, astonishment in her gold-flecked eyes. "So you *did* have something to do with it."

Max looked from Praxian, to Karbarran, to Spherisian, to his own Zentraedi wife, and wondered if he could possibly explain himself.

The Zentraedi's cargo transport—named the *Valivarre* for Fantoma's primary—was the largest of the ships constructed to serve the needs of the mining op. It was essentially an enormous shell, with vast featureless cabinspaces and cargo holds, and numerous launch and docking bays sized to accommodate ranks of surface mecha and outsize shuttles. Typical of the new breed SDFs—4 through 8—the *Valivarre* was only lightly armed and somewhat slow by galactic standards; but unlike those fortresses the ship was equipped with Protoculture/Reflex drives that enabled it to astrogate near-instantaneous folds throughout "local space."

The transport was in stationary orbit over Tirol just now, offloading the latest of Fantoma's riches to cargo shuttles, which were making runs both to the SDF-3 and to the moon's surface.

On the *Valivarre*'s bridge, Breetai was informed that one of the returning shuttles was bringing up two passengers. He arrived in the busy docking bay just as Dr. Lang and Exedore were descending the shuttle ramp.

Lang took a look around. Under the watchful gaze of four Ghost Squadron Battloids, a dozen Zentraedi were loading the last of the monopole ore into a second shuttle. There was more noise than Human ears were meant to withstand, so he donned a pair of silencer muffs, and went on the amplibox to communicate with Breetai.

"It appears that everything is in order, Commander," he said trying to sound businesslike. "But I have some matters to discuss with you regarding the transfer schedule. Is there somewhere we can talk?"

Breetai led them out of the hold and into a small cabin-space outfitted with a Micronian commo balcony.

"This area is secure," Breetai told them after he had dogged the hatch.

Lang got right to the point. "You'll never get away with this, Breetai. What do you take us for?"

The Zentraedi grinned. "The fool's ore . . . It wasn't my intention to trick you, Lang. Only Edwards's men. As far as they are concerned, we are off-loading the monopole."

"But, Commander," Exedore said, "what are you trying to accomplish? You're aware that Lang and I will have to report this."

"And I fully expect you to. I ask only that you delay your report for three hours."

"You're leaving!" Lang said, excited. "I knew it."

Breetai folded his arms across his chest and nodded. "That's right, Doctor. We're leaving. And we're taking the monopole with us."

Lang was shaking his head. "It's a mad scheme, Breetai. Edwards will hunt you down."

"Perhaps. But he'll think twice about firing on us while we have the ore aboard. Not when he learns that Fantoma's yield is exhausted. I'm relying on you to make this clear to him."

"Commander, may we enquire—"

"To search for Admiral Hunter, Exedore. I don't accept that the Sentinels have become outlaws any more than I believe the Invid Regent is dead. We know that enemy, Exedore; we engaged them throughout this sector. If he had been assassinated, his queen's troops would have already massed against Tirol and atomized it." Breetai leaned closer to the balcony railing to regard his Micronized friend. "We are free of all imperatives now, Exedore. The Zentraedi will follow none but their own. Will you join us?"

Exedore bowed his head. "Commander, you honor me. But I, too, have an inner imperative."

Breetai mulled it over, then nodded. "I understand, my friend."

Lang looked at the two Zentraedi, suddenly aware of the import the moment held. A surge of misgiving washed through him; a shaping charge he could barely sustain. His voice cracked when he spoke. "To Praxis, Breetai? Garuda? Spheris? The ship you seek is small enough as to be insignificant."

Breetai fixed his eye on Lang. "I don't believe that, Doctor. Nor do you."

Lang rasped, "Haydon IV." *She is there,* something told him.

Exedore stretched out a hand. "Doctor—"

"Don't ask me to explain." Was it Janice, he wondered, or some other *she*? It was a presence the Shaping had alerted him to, a power unlike anything he had experienced . . .

Breetai regarded him for a moment. "I will begin my search there."

Lang nodded, weakly, wondering whether he would ever see the Zentraedi again.

On Garuda, the Sentinels grouped together in the longhouse to discuss their options and priorities, which meant that it was back to transpirators for almost everyone involved. Vince, Max, and Jack were so certain of where they stood that they had already had Rick, Lisa, and Karen brought up to the SDF-7. Under Wolff's and Janice's supervision, Tesla and the two Invid scientists had also been moved to the ship, along with Miriya—who was still too weak to take part in the meeting—and Teal and the Spherisian infant.

Most of Garuda was celebrating—the grieving would come later—and the wild sounds of song and dance made it all the more difficult for the group to come to any agreement concerning the Haydon IV option. They did find themselves united, however, on the issue of Garuda. With the Optera tree orchards in ruins, it wasn't likely that the Invid were going to have much use for the planet—especially not when their initial campaign against Garuda's inherent defenses had ended in so many deaths. But just in case the Regent decided to think along the lines of reprisals—which, Cabell maintained, was highly unlikely given the disastrous defeats the Invid leader had been suffering in other quarters—the Sentinels were prepared to leave most of their forces onworld to complement the strength of the remaining Bioroid clones. The one Invid hive that had come through the battle reasonably intact would serve as their base. Vince and Veidt were in favor of this even though it would significantly reduce the Sentinels' firepower. Haydon IV, though, was not to be thought of in terms of a military campaign; they were undertaking the journey for the sake of Rick, Lisa, Karen, and Rem.

Once again, as someone pointed out.

But the Karbarrans and Praxians, in any case, chose to disregard Vince's statement. They likewise ignored Veidt and Sarna's claim that the planet had not been adversely affected by the Invid presence. Haydon IV had Invid; therefore, Haydon IV needed to be liberated.

Kami and Learna were reluctant to leave, reluctant to abandon the *hin* and to have to reattach themselves to life-support systems; but they agreed to see things through to their completion after Lron and Crysta reminded them of how they had left their son, Dardo, behind on Karbarra.

The Sentinels were back to the core group.

And they were also back to unknowns.

It was possible they might beat the Regent's fleet to Haydon IV; get in and out without incident. But it was just as likely that things would continue in the same unpredictable fashion they had grown accustomed to.

Ten Earth-standard hours later, the Horizont left orbit and jumped.

CHAPTER FOURTEEN

> *While it was true that Invid had been existing on the very same fruits and flowers that were rapidly turning Tesla into something not-quite or more-than Invid, it must be pointed out that the liquified plant-stuff which reached Optera was of a "pasteurized" variety, and was principally utilized as nutrient bath for the soldiers' battle mecha—Scouts, Shock Troopers, Pincer Ships, and such. By forcing himself to subsist on the pure (or the impure, in actuality), Tesla was receiving megadoses of the same stuff that years earlier had sent the Zentraedi Khyron clear over the edge of the Imperative, and into undreamed-of states of metanoia.*
>
> History of the Second Robotech War, volume XXXVI "Tirol"

"I DEMAND TO KNOW WHERE SHE IS!" THE REGENT BAWLED as he and his eleven-trooper elite stormed across one of Haydon IV's ice-blue plazas, the splendors of the city lost on them.

The planet's indigenous beings paid the Invid little mind, and went about their mysterious business, hovering in groups of two or three in and out of Glike's spirelike buildings, across graceful bridges, and through parks too perfect to believe. But visitors, guests, and merchants from other worlds stopped to gaze upon the one whose race had most recently changed the face of the Fourth Quadrant. A few Karbarrans even had to be restrained from running forward to mock the Regent with reminders of their recent victory. "Sentinels! Sentinels!" they chanted, and succeeded for a moment in bringing the Regent around to confront them. No one, however, dared make a violent move, for beneath those very same plazas and parks lurked surprises of a decidedly punishing nature. Haydon IV had rules for citizens and strangers alike, and it enforced them without bias.

The Invid squad commander whispered as much to the Regent, while the ursine Karbarrans continued to hurl insults and imprecations. And at the same moment one of the Regis's servants approached, offering a brief and unconvincing genuflection.

"Your Highness," the servant said, with a condescending tone.

The Regent raised a fist. "How dare she refuse to honor my arrival!"

"Perhaps, my lord," the Regent's own lieutenant suggested, "she trembles in terror at the mere thought of your blinding presence."

"Grovel on your own time," the Regent snarled. He fixed his wife's servant with a gimlet stare. "Where is my shameful wife? Explain this breach of protocol, worm, before I find a place for you in the Pits."

The servant lifted his head. "She is gone, Regent."

The Regent knew as much already, and bristled at the servant's impertinence. "I'm aware that she is gone—her flagship has left orbit. But I want to know *where*."

"She left no word, m'lord. Save to say that she is not expected to return."

"Which explains your laxity." The Regent raised himself to his full height, and looked down his snout on the Regis's creature. "Perhaps I will make an example of you, grub. Now, lead me to our chambers before I forget myself ... See that my pets are cared for," he said to his lieutenant as an afterthought, "and have the Sentinel prisoner brought before me."

Several other servants appeared to usher the Regent and his retinue to the same rooms his queen had occupied and abandoned, and along the way he could not help but take note of some of Haydon IV's wonders. The planet was unlike anything he had ever seen, and yet there was a sense of familiarity everywhere he looked. Here, a structure that was reminiscent of Tiresia; there, a patch of forest seemingly lifted from Garuda. Spherisian crystal palaces, Karbarran factories without the dirt or stench, Praxian arabesque carvings, totems, statues, pillars, and pedestals—even some things which could only have come from Optera itself: fields of Flowers and rows of Fruit-bearing trees, all sterile to be sure, but so faultless, so *exquisite* in appearance.

And yet nowhere a hint of instrumentality.

He understood, though, why the Regis would leave: there was no warmth to the world, no taste of life to its clear skies and reflective waters. No, she would not have been at home here, he told himself. It was a *real* world she required, one like the Optera of their past. He refused to believe that his arrival could have forced her hand—certainly not after the *gift* he had sent her. This, however, didn't stop him from complaining to his lieutenant once they had reached the tall spire's uppermost rooms and his throne had been positioned.

"Decamped!" he sneered, hands stroking the gem-collared necks of his Hellcat pets. "She expects me to win the war while she's off flitting around the cosmos preening her tubercles and hatching plots against me—"

"M'lord," a servant interrupted, bowing from the doorway. "We have the prisoner."

The Regent smiled as Rem was dragged in. A lieutenant "persuaded" the Tiresian to assume a groveling posture. But the Regent's smile began to fade as he studied Rem. *Great suns!* he thought. *He does wear the face of the seducer!*

Two scientists had entered on the heels of the Zor-clone, and the 'Cats were suddenly snarling, pacing, and sniffing the air. "What did she think of him?" the Regent asked, rising from his chair.

One of the scientists made a coughing sound. "Uh, she was . . . *amused*, Your Highness."

"Yes, I can well imagine. Did you record their sessions together?"

The two Invid traded quick glances. "We did, my lord."

He turned to gaze at Rem. "I wish to view the results of their reunion. I want to see her guilt, the sadness in her heart, before I grant her forgiveness."

"But, Regent—"

The Regent slammed a massive fist down on the throne's contoured seat. "Bring me the recordings—*now*!"

There was silence on the bridge of the Horizont while Wolff and Vince waited for the ship's identification library to display its assessment. Wolff folded his arms and leaned away from the console when the data appeared.

"Well?"

"Signatures confirmed," Wolff said flatly. "Invid troop carriers the Regent's flagship. We're too late."

"Are they scanning us?"

Wolff exhaled loudly and swung to a peripheral monitor. "Affirmative. But it's low-level, cursory. Could be we're an unknown quantity. God knows there are enough other ships docked out here."

Vince had to agree; he had never seen so many different types and classes of starship. Haydon IV was obviously all that Veidt and Sarna had been telling everyone.

"So what do we do, Captain—open a hailing frequency, tell them we're just in for liberty, a little R 'n' R?"

Vince frowned and put a hand on the ship's address-system stud . . .

"Haydon IV is an open world," Veidt was explaining in the briefing room ten minutes later. "I thought I had already made myself clear on this point. The planet has never been taken by force; its defenses are legendary. There are, in the central records, references to an attempted invasion some two thousand Earth-standard years ago. Several hundred vessels were destroyed in a matter of moments."

"But the Invid—" Jack started to say.

"The Invid did not engage Haydon IV's defenses," Sarna picked up. "Any who come in peace are free to stay and trade. The Invid came and insinuated themselves into positions of political authority; but they are quite tame here. We may land in safety, but we will surely be taken into custody."

"Then we can't go in under arms," Crysta said.

Jack grunted. "Maybe you don't have the courage to try, but I do."

Lron glared at him from across the table. "You dare impugn her courage? Perhaps you—"

"Stop this!" Jean interrupted. "Both of you."

"Exactly what are these 'defenses,' Veidt?" Vince wanted to know.

"I have never seen them. As I stated, they have not been put to the test in two thousand of your years."

"Come on," Jack said, looking around. "Then how do we know they're still functioning?"

"Do you hunger to challenge them?" Sarna asked.

Jack returned a sullen stare.

Jean shook her head and snorted. "So to utilize the medical facilities, we have to go in with our hands raised."

"Yes, straight into an Invid stronghold," Bela said.

"We are given no choice," Gnea added. "Our comrades will have to be surrendered. But who among us will escort them down?" The Praxian glanced around the table.

"I'll go," Wolff volunteered.

Jean caught her husband's eye. "I will, too."

"Wait a minute, wait a minute," Jack said, standing up. "I'm as concerned about Karen and Rick and Lisa as any of you. But just suppose the Invid deny the request for medical help. Then they've not only got Karen, they've got you and you and whoever else is crazy enough to volunteer." He shook his head. "Uh, uh. We need to find some way around this."

"The Invid cannot deny that which is promised by the planet to all," Veidt said, loud enough to cut through all the separate arguments Jack's objection had raised. Everyone heard the Haydonite's remark, but the bickering continued.

"All right, simmer down," Vince told the table. "Max has an idea."

"Two landing parties," the Skull ace began when everyone was quiet. He was exhausted, having spent every minute by Miriya's side. Her condition had deteriorated after the fold to Haydon IV, and it was Jean's thought to number her among the patients. "Some of us take the four of them down; the rest of you go in unannounced to keep an eye on us."

"It will not work, Commander," Veidt said; but Jack, Lron, Bella, and Gnea were already enthusiastic. Even Burak added his voice to the group as a show of support.

"The planet's defenses will detect you," Sarna tried to warn them. "We'll have to risk it," Vince answered her.

And the plan was put to a vote.

Jean and Wolff had already volunteered, and now Max and Vince and Cabell joined them. Veidt and Sarna would escort them. Jack, however, insisted that Karen's cause would be better served by his *doing* something more than crying by her bedside; so he opted for the second team. Burak, Kami and Learna, Bela, Gnea, Lron, and Crysta threw in with him. Janice was undecided until the last minute; then she allied herself with Jack's group—on one condition: that they take Tesla and the two Invid scientists along with them.

"He did help out back on Garuda," Jack was willing to concede. "But I still don't trust him."

"I don't either," Janice said. "I'd just like to see what would happen if Tesla and the Regent came snout-to-snout."

Only Wolff heard Burak's gasp; but he didn't think anything of it.

"Breetai and his Zentraedi are traitors and criminals," T. R. Edwards told the council, positioning himself where he was certain the cameras would close in on his polished skullplate and furious expression. "They've stolen the very thing we need to return to Earth, and thereby condemned our world to defeat at the hands of the Robotech Masters." He swung around and walked angrily back to his seat, facing the audience now. "Some of you are probably thinking that this is the Zentraedi's way of avenging themselves on the RDF. But I suspect they have an even darker purpose in mind. It's my belief that Breetai means to band together with the Sentinels and form a cartel to take control of the spaceways.

"And with the Invid Regent dead and our own forces stranded, there will be little to stop them from putting their plans in motion—unless we take quick and decisive action against them. For this reason, I'm asking for the council approval of my request for the four ships that comprise our new flotilla. The Zentraedi must be hunted down and destroyed!"

There were conflicting reactions from the crowd, all of which Senator Longchamps silenced with three determined gavel blows. "The council will not tolerate these continued outbursts," he warned the audience. "If this occurs again, I'm going to order the room cleared. Now," he said, turning to Edwards, "the council appreciates the generals's concern, but there are a few issues that need to be addressed." He consulted his notes, then said, "Mr. Obstat?"

"Isn't it true, General, that action of the sort you propose could quite possibly jeopardize the very ore we're so desperately in need of?"

Edwards stood up. "Do you propose to let them have it, then?" he asked evenly.

"We don't know why they took it in the first place," Justine Huxley argued. "I for one am not convinced that they mean to do as you suggest—band together with the Sentinels and embark on some sort of transgalactic campaign. Can't we simply continue to mine ore until the Zentraedi make their demands known to us?"

Dr. Lang spoke to that. "I'm afraid that Fantoma has yielded up the last of its monopole ores. Only trace quantities remain, and further mining is hardly justified at this stage."

"What about our reserves, Doctor, here and on Tirol," Harry Penn asked. "Don't we have enough to repair the fortress's fold systems?"

"Unfortunately not," Exedore asserted. "The . . . *stolen* ore represented more than three months of mining. It is crucial to our goals."

Edwards waited for the gasps and buzzing in the room to subside. "With the council's indulgence, I have reason to question Dr. Lang and Ambassador Exedore's assessment of the situation. It's no secret to the RDF that both of them have special interests in furthering the Sentinels' cause—"

Longchamps banged his gavel. "General, I must caution you to refrain from using this session to cast aspersions on any members of this council. Is that understood?"

The cameras tracked in to catch Edwards's stiff and silent nod.

In Edwards's chambers aboard the SDF-3, where she was watching the proceedings, Minmei got up to fix herself another drink. Lang's face was on-screen when she returned to the edge of the bed.

"That's true, Senator," the Robo-wiz was saying. "Exedore and I were the first to discover that the material off-loaded from the *Valivarre* was a type of 'fool's ore,' if you will. We immediately reported this to General Edwards—"

"*After* that ship had folded out of Tirolspace, Doctor," Edwards barked.

"General Edwards," Longchamps cut in, "weren't some of your own Ghost Squadron aboard the *Valivarre* supervising the transfer?"

Minmei saw Edwards's face drain of color; the cameras captured the fury in his single eye. "I'm certain that those brave men were killed, Senator."

The cameras cut to Lang. "Council members, I can personally attest to the presence of the general's men. And Exedore and I both found them very much alive."

Minmei sipped her drink, anticipating Edwards's comeback; he didn't surprise her.

"Yes, and exactly *what* motivated you and the ambassador to shuttle up to the *Valivarre*, Doctor?"

"We were merely going over the transfer schedule with Commander Breetai—"

Minmei touched the remote and the screen went blank. She drained her glass and thought, *A few more of these and I'll be too numb to care.* And numb was just what she was after. She had lost her friends, her faith, her voice, any sense of purpose she might have once called her own. Rick, Lisa, Janice, Dr. Lang, Jonathan . . . And lately she had even been thinking about Kyle. She wasn't sure why, but guessed that it had something to do with Edwards and the control he had begun to assert over her. She imagined she saw a curious pattern at work that coupled Rick and Lynn-Kyle, now Jonathan Wolff and Edwards—some slide into self-abuse when she came too close to genuine love and commitment. *Property*, she thought in disgust. That was how she was beginning to view herself. Her voice co-opted by the RDF, her dreams destroyed by war, her will at the mercy of men who wanted nothing more than to rule and posses her, body and mind.

Numb, *comfortably* numb, she told herself . . .

Thirty minutes later the door hissed open and Edwards strode into the room, grinning evilly. Minmei realized she had dozed off, and, startled now, she began to back herself onto the bed. Edwards leered at her, perhaps thinking she was toying with him, and came down on top of her, elbows supporting his upper body. She pressed her hands against his chest and said, "Please . . ."

"What's the matter with you?" he asked, face-to-face with her.

"I'm just . . . confused." She tried to roll out from under him, but his arms held her fast.

"Oh, no, you don't," he told her, bringing his mouth hard against hers—a kiss he liked to think passionate, but one she felt was simply rough. "The council gave their okay."

"W-what does that mean—that you're going to—"

"Precisely that," he said, rolling off her onto his back.

He gazed at the ceiling and laughed. "First the Zentraedi, then the Sentinels." He looked over at her.

Minmei was aghast, gaping at him; he had his right hand curled tightly around her left wrist.

"When this is over I want you to marry me."

Her right hand flew to her face. "What!"

"It'll be just like the Hunters' wedding," he said, as though thinking aloud. "Except it'll be you and me, and the destination won't be Tirol, but Earth." His grin was still intact.

"And the mission won't be for peace, but for *war*!" she screamed all at once, yanking her arm away.

Edwards sat straight up as she made a move for the door. "What are you talking about? Minmei!"

She was slightly drunk and clumsy even through her fear and shock; she bumped against a table, sending some tapes to the floor, crashed against the bulkhead, fumbling for the door release.

"Minmei!" he yelled again, more harshly than before.

He was angry now and she was panicked. She left the room and ran barefooted along the ship's corridor. She heard someone behind her as she entered the elevator and swung around; but it wasn't Edwards. It was a VT pilot, wearing his helmet, oddly enough, a tall and slender bearded man she thought she had seen before. He was regarding her bare feet and disheveled appearance. She forced a trembling, smile, pushing and patting her hair back in place.

"Troubles?" he said.

"Yes," she told him, surprising herself.

"Anything I can do?"

"I need to get back to Tiresia. Are any shuttles leaving soon?"

"I'll take you myself," he said after a moment.

It made her laugh. "What—in an Alpha? I don't know . . .

"I'll take you wherever you want to go."

She stared at him, wondering why she was ready to believe him. "How about Garuda or Haydon IV . . . uh, 666–60–937?" she asked, reading the pilot's REF service number from his helmet.

"Long trip," he told her. But he didn't laugh, didn't think she was putting him on.

The elevator doors opened. The pilot extended his hand and Minmei allowed herself to take hold of it.

"A simulagent, a simulagent," Tesla mumbled, stuffing the last of Garuda's Fruits into his mouth. "I've been tricked—*tricked!*"

The two scientists the Sentinels had captured from Garuda backed themselves toward what they hoped would be a safe corner of the dimensional fortress's hold, certain that Tesla's ingestion of the mutated Fruits from that *infected* world had driven him half mad. First there was all that nonsense about the Regent being dead, and now this talk of simulagents and assassination.

"Has he been doing this everywhere you've been?" one of the Invid asked Burak in the lingua franca.

"Only on Karbarra, Praxis, and Garuda so far," the Perytonian devil said in low tones, shrugging. "I suppose his killing the Regent was nothing but an imagining, then—"

"An imagining!" Tesla had heard Burak's whisper and swung around to the three of them, monstrous in his anger. He knows that I tried, he knows that I'm out to usurp his throne . . . And I shall have it, do you hear me?! Tesla will *rule!*"

"He's going to get us all sent to the Pits," one of the scientists groaned. "We won't be repatriated—we'll be *devolved!*"

Something, some force, suddenly brought Tesla to his feet. Tesla's skin was rippling, muscles and sinews contorting beneath the flesh as though his internal systems were rearranging themselves, reconfiguring. An aura of light was swirling around his head, throwing rainbow colors across the ceiling, bulkheads, and floor of the hold. His head was listed, neck stretched out, mouth agape in a kind of silent scream. Burak stood rooted to the floor, astonished as he watched the Invid begin to lose stature and bulk, while at the same time Tesla's neck, head, arms, hands, and feet reshaped themselves. The two scientists had buried their heads against one another, but Burak was too awed to summon the will even to look away. He saw then what the Fruits were after, the final form they tried to birth, and he could hardly believe his eyes, much less grasp what such a transformation meant. For the shape was a *humanoid* one—like that of Jack Baker or Gnea or Rem.

Tendrils of energy were whirling around Tesla, reaching out to Burak where he stood. They danced between his horns and sent a downward rush of paralyzing light through the top of his head. Tesla's eyes were fixed on his as something beyond language coursed between them. Burak stiffened, as a cold fire engulfed his heart. He bellowed, and Janice came rushing through the hatch.

She had been outside listening to their muffled exchange, and though baffled by the sudden silence, she had not wanted to risk tipping her hand. Burak's animallike wail had changed all that, but now she couldn't see what was happening. Something or someone was throwing blinding, colored light across the hold. She could make out Burak and the two shadowy shapes of the Invid scientists behind him, but Tesla was concealed by the dazzling prismatic intensity, seemingly at the center of it. She brought her hands to her face, trying to shield her eyes, and all at once the light was gone. Tesla was on the floor, flat on his back.

She rushed over to him; he was alive, but his breathing was labored. And something else: he looked different. His snout was shorter, his head more defined, his hands and feet more humanoid than reptilian. His skin was a pale green, waxy and smooth.

"What happened to him?" Janice asked, turning around to Burak.

The Perytonian stared at her. "I ... I ..."

Janice took him by the arms and shook him. "What happened?"

Burak cleared his head and gave her a blank look. He reached up to feel his horns, then regarded Tesla for a moment. "I think he ate too much."

The Regent sat slumped in his throne, feeling as though some great weight had been placed on his chest. It was a mistake for him to have viewed the recording of the Regis's nostalgic lovefest with the Zor-clone, a terrible mistake. Looking for guilt, for some sign of regret, he had found only love, genuine and unfulfilled. And he began to wonder if he hadn't been wrong in not following her lead when there was still time; when she had pleaded with him to allow himself to be evolved. But he had been stubborn about it, hurt, unforgiving, and now she was lost to him. He had seen, too, the Zor-clone's memories of a world far removed from Optera and Tirol's strife, linked somehow to the Protoculture matrix planet was anything more than Zor's fanciful imaginings? Besides, he had good reason to believe that the Regis had gone off in search of that very world, and he would know if and when she found it. No, what he needed was accurate data, data the clone had not yet surrendered up to Haydon IV's mind-probe devices. Perhaps, he thought, it would have to be *conjured* from the clone, the way Zor had conjured Protoculture from the Flowers of Life.

In the meantime, however, his empire was crumbling. Garuda had fallen to the Sentinels, depriving the Invid of the Fruits needed for the mecha nutrient baths. And Tesla was still unaccounted for—although at times the Regent thought he could actually *feel* the traitor's bloodlusts reaching out for him.

Much the way he felt at the moment. Even his pets seemed stricken by the same lassitude. He overcame his mood somewhat when a servant entered to announce that an important message had been received. But it was the lieutenant's words that brought the Regent back to life.

"The Sentinels! Here?"

"Yes, m'lord. They are requesting permission to land. Four of their number are in need of treatments apparently only Haydon IV can provide. They are seeking a truce by way of surrender."

The Regent shot to his feet. "This is a dream!"

"No, m'lord."

The Regent stood motionless for a moment, then laughed. "Here! Of course they would surrender here, where to fire first means certain death." He reached up to feel his swollen cowl. "However . . ."

The lieutenant waited until the Regent paced in front of his throne. "Yes, yes, it could work." He swung around. "Inform the Sentinels that we accept their terms. And bring the Zor-clone to my chambers. I will put it to him simply: the matrix for the lives of his comrades. What could be more just?"

"May the Great Shaper Haydon watch over you this day," Teal told the the shuttle group from the balcony in the Horizont's launch bay.

Vince, Cabell, Max, and the others saluted their friends as the hatch sealed itself. In a moment the shuttle's attitude jets flared, and the craft began to descend toward the green and silver crescent that was Haydon IV.

The second group numbered twelve, including the three Invid— one in each of the three armored Alpha Veritechs. Jack had a no-nonsense air about him as he strapped into the forward cockpit of his mecha. Bela was behind him; Gnea, Kami, and one of the scientists in the Beta module. Janice was piloting the second VT, with Burak in the copilot's seat, and Lron and Tesla in the Beta.

The third VT held Learna, Crysta, and the second scientist. Jack had taken one last look at Rick, Lisa, and Karen before they had been moved into the shuttle, and the sight of their slack, colorless faces was with him now as he engaged the Alpha's thrusters and maneuvered the ship out of the launch bay. The SDF-7's human and XT crew had been instructed to keep the fortress clear of the Invid fleet, but in close enough proximity to Haydon IV's surface to eliminate any threat of an enemy sneak attack.

Veidt and Sarna had done their best to convince the Sentinels to abandon their plans for an unannounced approach, but Jack and the rest were determined to give it a try. Besides, it wasn't like they were going in with weapons blazing. Their approach would be a gentle one, Jack had insisted; a simple landing in the forests west of the planet's principal city. Surely, three small mecha weren't going to touch off Haydon IV's legendary (and somewhat questionable) defenses.

It is merely *intent*, Veidt had tried to tell him.

Jack heard the words surfacing in his thoughts, and made an effort to push them from his mind. In a moment he would be able to discern details of the planet's surface topography. It was bound to be an extraordinary sight—an entire world reconfigured to conform to the demands of its inhabitants.

Jack found himself wondering about the guiding intelligence behind such a feat.

Then he began to notice that the forest they had chosen as landing zone, was, well, *moving*—sliding east to west across the variegated landscape like some sort of by-pass door. And something very bizarre was rising up at them from the space that forest had vacated . . . Swirling vortices of energy, radiant silken scarves riding Haydon IV's savage updrafts.

Jack sent a telepathic plea to the planet: We've come in peace. *We've come in peace!*

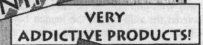

DEL REY ONLINE!

The Del Rey Internet Newsletter...

A monthly electronic publication, posted on the Internet, GEnie, CompuServe, BIX, various BBSs, and the Panix gopher (gopher.panix.com). It features hype-free descriptions of books that are new in the stores, a list of our upcoming books, special announcements, a signing/reading/convention-attendance schedule for Del Rey authors, "In Depth" essays in which professionals in the field (authors, artists, designers, sales people, etc.) talk about their jobs in science fiction, a question-and-answer section, behind-the-scenes looks at sf publishing, and more!

Online editorial presence: Many of the Del Rey editors are online, on the Internet, GEnie, CompuServe, America Online, and Delphi. There is a Del Rey topic on GEnie and a Del Rey folder on America Online.

Our official e-mail address for Del Rey Books is delrey@randomhouse.com

Internet information source!

A lot of Del Rey material is available to the Internet on a gopher server: all back issues and the current issue of the Del Rey Internet Newsletter, a description of the DRIN and summaries of all the issues' contents, sample chapters of upcoming or current books (readable or downloadable for free), submission requirements, mail-order information, and much more. We will be adding more items of all sorts (mostly new DRINs and sample chapters) regularly. The address of the gopher is gopher.panix.com

Why? We at Del Rey realize that the networks are the medium of the future. That's where you'll find us promoting our books, socializing with others in the sf field, and—most importantly—making contact and sharing information with sf readers.

For more information, e-mail delrey@randomhouse.com